1970

THE

Collected Tales
and Plays

OF

Nikolai Gogol

THE
Collected Tales
and Plays

OF

Nikolai Gogol

*Edited, with an introduction
and notes, by*

LEONARD J. KENT

❖❖❖❖❖❖

*The Constance Garnett translation has been
revised throughout by the editor*

THE MODERN LIBRARY

New York

For FRANCES,
and
JED, PAUL, MICHAEL, PHILIP,
our four sons

CONTENTS

PREFACE

This volume was born of a need. Almost forty years have elapsed since Constance Garnett's English translation of Gogol's works appeared in a six-volume edition. This is now out of print, is extremely difficult to find, and requires serious textual revision, updating, and editing. To be sure, limited selections of Gogol have recently appeared in various editions; indeed, the best translation of Gogol's only novel, *Dead Souls*, has been accomplished by B. G. Guerney, and appeared under the title *Chichikov's Journeys; or, Home Life in Old Russia*, in 1942; it has been reprinted in paperback as *Dead Souls*, minus Gogol's unfinished second volume of the novel. Further, there are varied (both in quality and scope), often overlapping selected collections of the tales available, sometimes in quite inferior and unscholarly translation, often with mediocre or very limited introductions, sometimes with none at all. Only one of Gogol's three genuine plays, *The Inspector General*, is readily and satisfactorily available. The fact remains that no single modern edition of all the tales and plays has been done, that there is no adequately annotated English text of Gogol available.

This volume aims at relative completeness. *Dead Souls* and a very poor, highly derivative poem Gogol had the good sense to publish under a pseudonym (and several slight and relatively unimportant lyrics and didactic dramatic exercises) are the only pieces of completed fiction excluded, Guerney's translation of the former being available, and the poem being of special interest only to Gogol scholars, who can find it in numerous Russian and Soviet texts or in the German edition of his collected works. Fragments have been excluded for much the same reason. Quite ample footnotes, keyed to the needs of the reader not intimately acquainted with Russia and things Russian, are provided, as well as a chart describing the various ranks in the Russian civil service of Gogol's day (a useful aid in understanding some of the later stories), a chronological list of his works, and a selected but quite full bibliography of books and essays concerned with Gogol. The introduction is of some length.

In general, Gogol remains the least known and appreciated of the great Russian writers of the nineteenth century. At best, the contemporary reader usually digests him in piecemeal fashion, commonly being introduced to only a single tale in an anthology (almost always *The Overcoat*). At worst, Hollywood makes the introduction as a grease-smeared Cossack and his mighty stallion gallop over the endless steppes of Argentina.

To ameliorate this unfortunate state of affairs, to make Nikolai Vasilievich Gogol available and readable and, hence, better known than he now is to the English-reading audience, is the hope and inspiration of the editor.

I would like to thank Norman Goldberg, Bartlett Giamatti, and Rhoda Spear for helping with the proofs, Richard Gustafson for discussing with me some of the problems inherent in such a work, and Miss Sheila Lois Meyers for her tireless typewriter.

The heaviest debt of gratitude I owe to two wholly remarkable people: to Nina Berberova, now at Princeton University, an author, poet, and critic, who sat at my side for so very many hours discussing the Gogol text with me, for her knowledge and insight and, as the work progressed, patience; and to my teacher, René Wellek, Sterling Professor of Comparative Literature at Yale University, for his suggestions and his encouragement, but most of all for the hours spent in his classes and in his company, during which time Russian literature became a love and this volume became a possibility.

L. J. K.

ABOUT THE TRANSLATION

The decision to use the Constance Garnett translation as the basic text was determined by one critical factor: eminent scholars of Russian literature with whom I consulted agreed with my point of view that, despite occasional errors and the often debilitating effects of Victorianism, her work remains a remarkably competent and wonderfully conscientious accomplishment. Too many more recent translators confuse sheer verve with scholarship. Some, in a misguided effort to be helpful, incorporate foreign material in the Gogol text to avoid the necessity of footnoting. Some either misread or consciously set out to improve the original. And some, incredibly enough, translate selectively, and sections of Gogol which they find either difficult or unpleasant or both simply disappear from the printed page.

The Garnett translation was carefully collated with the best Russian texts. Thousands of revisions, some very extensive, have been made, and one story, *The Portrait*, has been almost completely retranslated because Mrs. Garnett translated only the earlier version of the story. Many of the revisions are attempts to bring Gogol in English closer to the spirit of Gogol in Russian. The language has not been converted into the contemporary idiom because, as far as possible, the intention has been to preserve the tone of the original. To this end, Russian names are given in full, Cossacks have not yet learned to say "Hi," characters deal in kopeks and rubles, the syntactical structure has received most careful consideration, and so on.

Deciding between what is literal and what is understandable is difficult business indeed. I have tried to remain true to the letter and spirit of the original. Whenever direct translation was neither feasible nor possible, I have substituted equivalent expressions.

L.J.K.

INTRODUCTION

Almost all of Gogol's fiction is between the covers of this book; he wrote far less than any other major Russian and yet what he wrote is not of whole cloth. We have here the romantic, fantastic, Gothic, as well as the realistic and satiric; there is the sentimental, and yet there is the grotesque, too; we have here singular examples of Russian humor, but so too do we have extraordinary examples of Russian horror; we have writing that is brilliantly imaginative and highly original, but also that which is strongly derivative; there is the inimitable Gogol prose—coarse, dense, nervous, exuberant, hyperbolic, and there is another kind of prose—dignified and eloquent. Can we find a common denominator?

Ever since the publication of *The Overcoat* in 1842, Nikolai Vasilievich Gogol has generally been viewed from one of two extreme positions. Motivated more by subjectively created points of view (including those born of public and political pressures) than by objective analysis of textual, historical, and biographical evidence, many critics have approached Gogol with specific critical apparatus that is so strictured that it almost always precludes appreciation of diverse or inconsistent or contradictory or paradoxical elements within the works. By striving too hard to shove Gogol into a carefully labeled drawer—a convenient but hardly enlightened arrangement—these critics make simple that which is never so simple, even when dealing with a far less complex subject.

It was the very important Russian critic Vissarion Belinsky, an outspoken leader of the liberal wing, who created and championed one of the extreme points of view. Belinsky interpreted Gogol to serve his ends; he insisted that Gogol was a naturalist, a realist; life was in his works; he was a depictor of what was, a staunch benefactor of the much-abused "little man," the insulted and the injured; he was an apostle of progress (and this about an amazingly consistent archconservative who accepted even serfdom as a necessary and desirable condition of life). Belinsky fed Gogol's ravenous ego, and Gogol too much needed and enjoyed the accolades to correct the faulty premises on which Belinsky had based his arguments. Gogol awoke one morning to find himself a founder and inspirer of the Russian realistic movement. Even Dostoevsky (who certainly knew better, for his *Poor Folk*, so deeply indebted to Gogol's *The Overcoat*, is yet so imbued with genuine compassion for the downtrodden and the humiliated that it is an implicit criticism of the lack of sympathy Dostoevsky found in Gogol's treatment of the "little man") allegedly added to Gogol's stature as a realist by noting that "We all come from under Gogol's *Overcoat*." [1] If so, was it realism per se that Dostoevsky was referring to or, rather, the vistas that Gogol had helped open up, the subject matter with which he dealt that helped irreversibly broaden the horizon and scope of the literature which was to follow?

It remained for Dmitry Merezhkovsky, a leader of the Russian symbolist movement which flourished during the last years of the nineteenth and the first and second decades of the twentieth century, to break away from Belinsky's point of view. By the time of the emergence of the symbolist movement the pendulum of taste had swung to the opposite end of its arc. Gogol, the symbolists now proclaimed, cared nothing for "reality." He neither revealed nor exposed; he merely created fantasies, imaginative, distorted fantasies that had no relationship to reality; he projected himself, his own very marked neuroses; he was, they insisted, a creator and not a reflector. And it is not without irony that the Soviets, almost one hundred years after Belinsky's appraisal of Gogol, joined forces with the great liberal and pushed the pendulum back to its original position, and once more Gogol became "an apostle of enlightenment."

And what of Gogol's originality? Is he a phenomenon seemingly without roots and obligations? One might be led to such a conclusion after noticing that the question of his indebtedness to ante-

---

[1]Scholarly tradition has long insisted that Dostoevsky made this comment and we therefore include it; however, no one, to my knowledge, has ever been able to find this very famous line in any of Dostoevsky's writings. Melchior de Vogué is often thought to have attributed the statement to Dostoevsky, but he attributes it only to a Russian "very much involved in the literary history of the last forty years [1846-86]" (*Le Roman russe*, Paris, 1897, p. 96).

cedent literary history is usually ignored or mishandled, or paid such scant attention to that the implication of total originality is quite impossible to avoid. Or, as others insist, is he merely a reflection of the writers who had preceded him?

What of his influence? Is it true that among the great Russian writers only the young Dostoevsky learned from him, that Turgenev and Goncharov and Tolstoy, true realists, owe him nothing?

Nikolai Gogol contains multitudes. We cannot ignore historical and textual and, in Gogol's case especially, biographical data in trying to determine what he was, how he became what he was, how important he was, and the heritage he left behind.

There were at least five powerful literary influences operating in Russia at the time of Gogol's birth; these were assimilated and used to direct and shape the efforts of this most essentially original of all the great Russians: the sentimental novel, the fantastic (Gothic) novel, the historical novel, Ukrainian folklore, and the Russian literary tradition.

The sentimental novel, its obvious excesses aside (and who can forget Richardson's virtuous and nonvirtuous heroes, *les rakes*, his tightly corseted and forever-fainting heroines?), must be appreciated as much more than merely a framework for the expression of sentimentality which Meredith called "fiddling harmonics on the string of sensualism." It made profound contributions to the genres which were to supersede it.

Rousseauistic in origin and in philosophy, devised mainly to illustrate innocence and inherent human goodness, the sentimental novel had no choice (if its obvious didacticism was to be effective, if it was to depict positive characteristics) but to complement the goodness of its characters; and to accomplish this, stressful settings were created to show characters to have not merely, in Milton's terms, "blank virtue" (cloistered goodness), but "pure virtue" (experience-born goodness). The characters who peopled these books, therefore, were not at all unlike those we usually accept as being essentially naturalistic. The sentimental novel redefined the hero image. Social position and knowledgeability per se were no longer considered adequate or indispensable requisites. Virtue, moral fiber, became the essential criterion. The pathetic situation, in turn, to be artistically conveyed, demanded a setting that was immediately recognizable to the reader, hence realistic. Indeed, and this is not contradictory, much of sentimental literature was pervaded by a genuinely realistic tone, atmosphere, and framework. Its people, again despite their excess of sensibility, were identifiable human beings. The *Luftmensch* had settled to earth. Further, though it is generally agreed that "The great wave of the international romantic movement had spent its force in the fourth decade of the nineteenth century" (the exact decade during which both *The Overcoat* and *Dead Souls* saw life), we hold that it was this very movement that supplied the sentimental philosophy which enabled Gogol to use for major characters the insignificant, the iconoclast, the pariah, the lunatic, and the rogue (who owes much to the picaresque tradition, too). The earlier movement established the attitude that enabled the likes of Akaky Akakievich and Chichikov to serve as central characters. The new hero, the humbled, humiliated, insulted, injured, and his foils, the rogue, rascal, cheat, were born of a pathetic rather than an ethical attitude toward life. Not only was the seed that was to sprout into the naturalistic tree present in the sentimental novel, but, in the later genres, unmistakable vestiges of both Rousseauism and sentimentality remain. The influence of the sentimental novel was impossible to avoid in Gogol's Russia; indeed, Gogol often refers to such novels in his letters (he knew them in either Russian or German translations).

The sentimental novel, then, supplied Gogol with a general type of protagonist and the pathetic milieu and attitude within which he would function.

The fantastic school, essentially romantic to its shuddering core, supplied less clear but equally vital ingredients. Generally, "mood" best describes the contribution.

The relative neglect of this latter influence probably stems from a contemporary revaluation of its material. The works of Ann Radcliffe and even those of the much superior E. T. A. Hoffmann—enormously appreciated in Gogol's Russia—are now often considered crude and inept, somehow inferior art because tastes have changed. But in nineteenth-century Russia, Gothic writings were as popular as they were in Western Europe. The influence of Hoffmann was all-pervasive. The impact in Russia of this genre, perhaps out of all proportion to its inherent merit, was possible because of Russia's attachment to things Western, but was not a concomitant of general sophistication. The Russian public generally depended on foreign taste without having reached the level of foreign sophistication that would have enabled it to accept such material with more detachment, reserve, and critical insight. The public overreacted to it; it too avidly accepted this fresh import and established it, on the conscious level, as a standard to be imitated (and when Pushkin— with Hoffmann in mind—wrote *The Queen of Spades* the effect must have been staggering).

The popularity of the Gothic novel was such that it is impossible to avoid the conclusion that Gogol knew many of them at first hand, many more by reputation.

In brief, Gogol fell heir to the glorification of the supernatural. The symbolic dream had been born (or, rather, reborn) in Hoffmann. The irrational and incomprehensible world that lurks behind visible activity was lighted up. The spiritual and mystical became prominent. The dark corner became more important than the sun-drenched field. The shadows grew more central than the subjects that cast them. This view of life, focusing on the small, cramped, closed, struggling section of humanity, discovered man inextricably bound in a tightly constructed and airless room. Melancholia bathed the setting and its people, a melancholia intimately interwoven with sentimentality, yet expressing the "brooding" rather than the "aching" heart.

Certainly a great deal of Gogol's art may be viewed as a reaction against the sentimental and fantastic schools, but even this very reaction owed much to its precursors.

As for the historical novel, it had long been imported from the Western world, and novels of adventure were eagerly devoured. Walter Scott's romances were enormously popular; indeed, imitations were much in vogue years before Gogol wrote *Taras Bulba*. Even if we find it difficult to discover Scott reflected in *Bulba*, we must yet admit that the historical novel of the West was not only responsible, in great measure, for the inspiration and birth of *Bulba*, but, indeed, had for a long time been preparing an audience for its reception. *Bulba*, after all, essentially a highly romanticized recreation of the tone and quality of an historical period written in the epic tradition, had no direct Russian antecedents.

Ukrainian folklore and its tradition (for details of which Gogol incessantly pestered his mother) permeate the two volumes of *Evenings on a Farm near Dikanka*. With the exception of *Ivan Fiodorovich Shponka and His Aunt*, a highly realistic story with grotesque elements in it, *Evenings* consists of imaginative, escapist, fantastic, romantic stories which combine eloquent passages of descriptive narrative, realistic elements, coarseness, earthy humor, and gruesomeness. Much of the thematic material stems directly from the folklore tradition (that included the enormously popular puppet theater, of which Gogol was so fond that he included it in the setting of several of the stories). Gogol's early characters are drawn from this tradition (if inimitably shaped by him): sorcerers, demons, water spirits, and a peculiar kind of Russian devil who is at once earthy (e.g., he's not above trying to seduce a married woman —who is not above being seduced) and frightening (but defeatable); as well as superstition-motivated peasants almost always in pursuit of riotous and fleshy pleasures, intrepid and reckless Cossacks, boys with flashing eyes and pounding hearts, and the dark-browed beauties who dream of them. What Gogol drew from the Ukraine served him far beyond his earliest volumes. The coarseness, the densely textured prose, the search for the detail that strips away pretension, the sheer exuberance—all were qualities early learned and long retained.

There is the matter of Gogol's language. The tradition of restrictive pseudoclassical taste had been chipped away by many of Gogol's precursors (Karamzin, Krylov, and Zhukovsky, for example). The Russian tongue had been revivified, put to uses which were once imagined beyond its potential. Pushkin, more admired as a poet than as a writer of fiction, wrote prose that was measured and reserved. His success in disciplining Russian and making it highly functional was important to Gogol.

We have barely touched the list of influences (D. S. Mirsky, for example, has compiled his own list: "the numerous mixed traditions of comic writing from Molière to the vaudevillists of the twenties, [and] Sterne, chiefly through the medium of German romanticism," etc.), but perhaps we have made our point. The stage has been set. We focus on April 1, 1809,[2] the Ukrainian market town of Sorochintsy, where "our hero" is about to be born.

Nikolai Vasilievich Gogol was the third of twelve children born to Maria Ivanovna and Vasily Gogol and the first to survive infancy. His mother, eighteen years old at the time of his birth, also

---

[2] New Style. The Russians used the Julian calendar (Old Style) until 1917 and, in the nineteenth century, were twelve days behind the Gregorian calendar used in the West. Dates have been converted to correspond to Western practice.

contained multitudes: she was at once deeply pious and superstitious, a fervent believer in omens, premonitions, and dreams; she was incredibly naïve, and, to judge from her letters, was never more than semiliterate. It was not without difficulty that she distinguished between the actual and the fanciful, and she never quite reconciled her professed morality with a sense of ethics (she was, for example, eager for her son to supplement his income in the civil service by taking bribes! Wasn't everyone?). The extent of her sophistication can be garnered from material collected by her biographer, which includes, in her own words, the story of how the Queen of Heaven graciously appeared to her in a dream and indicated who her future husband would be. And much later, in an autobiographical sketch (which she knew would be read), there is a comment to the effect that she was so inordinately fond of her husband at the time of their marriage that she almost believed, though she could never quite decide, that she preferred him to her favorite old aunt.

Gogol's father, a small landowner, like his wife was one of those countless members of the petty gentry, but infinitely more worldly than she. An amateur playwright who even had one of his plays published, he was gregarious and apparently outgoing, but he was pathologically tainted. He suffered from two diseases: manic-depression and hypochondria; and worse, from a chronic Russian illness, lack of funds. We can well appreciate this comment by Janko Lavrin (a native Yugoslav with a penchant for British understatement): "The offspring of such a couple could hardly boast of overflowing vitality, energy, and health."

Nikolai Gogol, almost dead at birth, somehow survived. His mother lavished all she had on her sickly child. She smothered him with concern. His ego grew immense from such nourishment; the mother inculcated in him her own peculiarities, imbued him not only with her own mysticism, but, perhaps more important, with a totally unrealistic and debilitating sense of self-worth and self-esteem. And there was other "nourishment" too, which was to haunt him to his death: tales of the devil and of the eternal fires blazing in hell, the torment inflicted upon sinners which his mother, he wrote in a letter, "described so strikingly, in such a horrifying way." And from the same letter, recalling his childhood:

I felt nothing passionately; everything seemed created solely to gratify me. I loved only you, and I only loved you because Nature herself had inspired this feeling in me. I viewed everything with indifference. I attended church because I was ordered to go, or because I was carried there. . . . I crossed myself only because I saw others doing it.

In such a setting, with his own intrinsic nervousness serving as catalyst, early in life he began to withdraw from the threatening world of reality into the much more comfortable world of fantasy. He defended himself by becoming introverted, and he fed his ego with his vibrant imagination. But under such circumstances the personality is warped. Spontaneity is destroyed. And it is not difficult to understand complementary causes of his incipient psychosis when we cull from letters and reminiscences of his contemporaries descriptions of him as he attended school in Nyezhin, which he entered at twelve, during May 1821, and which he left not before the middle of 1828: his face "seemed to be transparent"; he had a persistent skin disease which caused him great discomfort; his shoulders were already stooped, and he was thin and short (with the unkindness common to young people, his schoolmates soon dubbed him "the mysterious dwarf"). He was nearsighted and, by his own admission, his nose was an enormous if not unfaithful beast. His Latin teacher described him as "always taciturn, as if there was something he was hiding in his soul; he had an indolent look and he walked with a shuffling motion." That he had an exceedingly difficult time of it at school is obvious. But he fought back. His wit was his only weapon, and he used it to destroy others. By shifting the focus of the coarse laughter he was able to succor himself. He was very capable of laughing, but only at the expense of others.

Reading the letters he wrote home from Nyezhin, one begins to appreciate his agony. Everywhere are to be seen the defensive forces that he mustered. He is overwhelmingly precious and melodramatic. The letters are a riot of pretentiousness. When he is involved with his favorite subject, "Me," he grows hyperbolic and delusional.

In two letters he wrote in October 1827, we can see the quality of his thought. The first is to one of his few friends; the second to his uncle:

I do not know if my plans will come true, whether I too will live in that heavenly spot [St. Petersburg] or whether the wheel of fate will heartlessly cast me with the crowds of the self-contented mob (what a horrible thought!) into the world of nonentities, consigning me to the dismal quarter of obscurity.

Cold sweat drenches my face at the thought that I may perish in dust without becoming famous for any extraordinary accomplishment. Living in this world would be terrible if I failed to make my being beneficial.

Gogol insisted that he had learned very little from that "stupid institution," but he had read. He knew something of Pushkin, and in letters to his mother he often requested literary magazines. Then, too, he had already begun work on a long poem inspired by Voss's *Luise*.

It is not surprising that Gogol was successful as an actor while at school (he had always been a good mimic, and he needed a place in the spotlight) and that, further, he was singularly effective in female parts.

Gogol's sexuality, or lack of it, has long been subjected to lively if not always enlightened debate. In letters to his father, there are several references to the fact that he had improved his state of morality while at Nyezhin, the implication being, of course, that while at home, perhaps on vacation, he had been sexually involved with one or more of the serf girls, but that he had since seen the light. We know of no other possible sexual experience he might have had throughout the course of his life, but even a not very close reading of his works strongly points to the sexual abnormality of their author.

Gogol's women are either highly idealized (there is a parade of alabaster-breasted heroines) or threatening or destructive: in *Ivan Shponka*, they appear in frightening numbers with goose faces; in *Taras Bulba*, it is the bloodless heroine who destroys Andrei; in *Viy*, the female is a fiendish ghoul; in *The Marriage*, the hero leaps from a window lest he be forced to give up his bachelorhood. In *The Nose*, there is obvious material available for a Freudian interpretation of a castration complex; in *Nevsky Prospekt*, we detect Gogol's deep revulsion toward the sensuous, and so on. Only Gogol's very coarse women contain the sparks of life.

It is possible that if Gogol did indeed have an affair on his father's estate, his sense of guilt caused him to overreact and destroyed his future capacity to love; but it seems more consistent, in the light of what we know of him and his situation, to believe that he created a sexual fantasy with which to torment his parents and titillate himself. He was able, using this fantasy, to create an opportunity to pat himself on the back for no longer doing what he had not done.

In an essay called *Woman,* Gogol's intrinsic make-up is manifest: "What is woman? The language of the Gods! She is poetry. . . ." One must give to love. Gogol had long been conditioned to receive.

Evidence of compulsive autoeroticism is consistent with our point of view. In the Russian edition of Gogol's collected works, there is a rarely discussed autobiographical piece in diary form, *Nights in a Villa.* In it, Gogol describes his friendship with a young man, Wielgorski, who died of consumption, in blatantly physical terms, something he could never accomplish when writing of or describing a woman. Probably not an overt homosexual, there is no reason to doubt his homosexual fantasies—which are wholly consistent with his literary fascination with corpses.

Late in 1828, at nineteen, this very complex human being left for St. Petersburg to make his mark. In letters home, he wrote of devoting himself to humanity, of "taking up jurisprudence." Perhaps he really went there to publish the long poem he had been working on even while at school. Most probably, Gogol left for St. Petersburg with little idea of what he was going to do there, knowing only that he had to do something.

St. Petersburg welcomed him coldly and cruelly—especially his nose—and this confused young man found himself in bed for days, his nose frostbitten and his eyes running from a severe cold. Wracked with depression, he wrote his mother that he was "sitting around and doing nothing . . . the [favorable] rumors spread about it [St. Petersburg] are nothing but lies. . . ." But something had to be done.

Whether he tried to get a job in the civil service at this time is moot. He wrote his mother that this was the case, but what Gogol wrote her sometimes bore no relationship to truth (he often fed her the pap on which she thrived). We know he did apply for a job in the theater, stammered his way through an excruciating interview, but his effeminate voice and a totally indifferent reading precluded success on the stage. The situation was desperate when he wrote his mother asking for information about the Ukraine, its traditions, and its dress ("to the last ribbon"). In cold St. Petersburg, stories of the warm and sunny Ukraine were very much appreciated, and

Gogol hoped that writing tales of the Ukraine would bring commercial success, or at least a respite from his poverty.

Maria Ivanovna answered. Information was supplied; money and the inevitable bits of tidy morality were furnished too. But even before this support arrived from home, Gogol had published (at expense he could ill afford) the poem he had brought with him from Nyezhin, *Hanz* [*sic*] *Küchelgarten*, under the pseudonym V. Alov. In the introduction to the poem, Gogol, in need of a heavy pat on the back, blew his own horn (even as Chartkov will later blow his in *The Portrait*):

> . . . we are proud to have been instrumental in acquainting the world with the creative work of a young man of talent. . . .

But Gogol had misjudged the world's eagerness to meet him. The reviews that appeared were fair: that is, they found nothing singular about it, and ridiculed its pretentiousness. Gogol was devastated, especially because it becomes increasingly clear that his intense desire to succeed, to serve as benefactor, to rise above the mass of mediocrity, grew from an ever-increasing conviction that the world was really no more than a haven for what he later called *poshlost,* that is, dullness and ugliness, triviality, pretentiousness, petty conceits; that he wanted to escape surrendering to a totally negative vision of humanity.

The poem is very long, without distinction, and derivative; Gogol burned all the copies he could get his hands on after its poor reception. Not translated into English, its primary interest lies in offering us an insight into the ambivalent forces within him, the contradiction between what was expected of him (what he feared he would yield to) and what he expected of himself. The hero (Hans-Gogol) is a restless romantic who leaves both home and sweetheart (and in letters to his mother Gogol had often mentioned some vague dream about sacrificing himself for humanity in some distant land) to travel the world and search for answers to the eternal enigmas of life, only to return to home and sweetheart and spend the rest of his days in comfort and joy, in *poshlost*. And this, in relative terms, was one of the choices open to Gogol: the civil service and a measure of respectability, some money and the creature comforts of a steaming samovar—a full belly and a dead soul. But Gogol himself was too disturbed and agitated to settle for this. He did what he had to do: he ran, but he could not enjoy running away. There was too much guilt (disappointing his mother, absconding with a sizable sum of her money) attached to preclude the need to rationalize. A proficient liar, he invented three excuses: it was God's will (and his mother saw everything in this light); he was in physical distress (not at all unusual); he had had a shattering love affair with an angel ("She was a divinity") who turned out to be more than slightly fallen (and some critics also believe this).

"Lacerated soul" and all, Gogol boarded a steamer, noting that he was going to America, where, theoretically, neurotic geniuses were more warmly welcomed, but the ship stopped in Lübeck, Germany, and so too did Gogol (though he did do some wandering through the Continent). He returned to St. Petersburg after several weeks, and surrendered to the civil service (taking a job that rivaled the triviality of Akaky's in *The Overcoat*); but in 1830, while he was still in the service, *St. John's Eve*, one of the stories to appear the following year in *Evenings on a Farm near Dikanka*, was published in a St. Petersburg magazine. It was the beginning of his literary career.

By the end of the same year, a number of his stories and articles saw print. He met Zhukovsky, a foremost romantic poet and translator, and Pletniov, poet, critic, and professor of Russian literature at the University of St. Petersburg. But money was still hard to come by, and though Pletniov got Gogol a teaching position in a school that catered to the daughters of noblemen, he had to take a job as a tutor as well (to a moron, to judge by the *Reminiscences* of Count Sollogub, whose relative was being tutored: ". . . and this is a cow, you know, cow, moo, moo . . ."). In 1831 things brightened considerably. He met the great Pushkin, whom he had long and sensitively admired, and somehow these two very different people became friends. That same year stories that Gogol had long been writing appeared in the first volume of *Dikanka*, and the next year the second volume of *Dikanka* appeared. Their success was immediate and profound. Nikolai Gogol found himself a famous man in a city that was no longer so cold and hostile.

Sandwiched between the eight stories which comprise these first two volumes is *Ivan Fiodorovich Shponka and His Aunt*. It is so different from the others, is so clearly an anticipation of the more mature works, that we need to discuss it separately, and at some length.

The other tales of these volumes, heavily saturated with folklore elements, are essentially romantic, escapist-motivated stories. Here there is already the curious Gogol mingling, e.g., the use of a preface which precedes each volume in which there appears the homely personal comment by a very earthy beekeeper, Rudy Panko, who, in quite matter-of-fact terms, guarantees the validity of the stories. These prefaces somehow add an aura of "factualness" even to the outlandish, somehow root even the most flagrantly romantic elements of the stories in the earth. The setting, the Ukraine about which Gogol waxes so eloquent, precludes a totally negative vision. If, for example, there is a devil who needs to be feared, he is at the same time to be ridiculed because he is a peculiarly Ukrainian devil, endowed with the same mentality as the very peasants he would outfox and destroy. Typically, many elements are combined in these seven stories. There is gaiety:

> She [Panko's grandfather's aunt] used to say that his father . . . had been taken prisoner by the Turks and suffered goodness knows what tortures, and that in some miraculous way he had escaped, disguised as a eunuch.

there is warmth and comfort:

> I remember as though it were today . . . my [Panko's] mother . . . on a long winter evening when frost crackled outside and sealed up the narrow window of our hut . . . would sit with her spindle pulling out a long thread with one hand, rocking the cradle with her foot, and singing a song which I can hear now.

there is coarseness:

> "What's lying there, Vlas?"
> "Why it looks like two men: one on top, the other under. Which of them is the devil I can't make out yet!"
> "Why, who is on top?"
> "A woman!"
> "Oh, well, then that's the devil!"
> . . . .
> "A woman straddling a man! I suppose she knows how to ride!"

the Gothic:

> A cross on one of the graves tottered and a withered corpse rose slowly up out of the earth. Its beard reached to its waist; the nails on its fingers were longer than the fingers themselves. It slowly raised its hands upwards. Its face was all twisted and distorted.

and the eloquent:

How intoxicating, how magnificent is a summer day in Little Russia [the Ukraine]! How luxuriously warm the hours when midday glitters in stillness and sultry heat and the blue fathomless ocean covering the plain like a dome seems to be slumbering, bathed in languor, clasping the fair earth and holding it close in its ethereal embrace!

There is indeed "the charm of wild flowers about them," a charm born of Gogol's extraordinary gift with language, its rich texture and exuberant expression. But *Shponka* is very different. The Ukrainian sun is less brilliant. Coarseness, the Gothic, gaiety, eloquence disappear. The romantic world disappears and is replaced by a world in which *poshlost* thrives (a "real" world which is not quite real because of the intensity of its reality). For the first time an element of sadness is introduced, and we sense the Gogolian *smekh skvoz sliozy* (laughter through tears). We laugh at the grotesqueness of Ivan Fiodorovich, but there are "tears" because he is a victim of a world perhaps no less ugly than our own.

Beginning with a middle-aged, not-too-bright bachelor (of course) placed in a realistic (identifiable) setting, in a realistic (recognizable) situation, Gogol begins the process of intensification that is so typical of almost all his later works: detail is heaped upon detail, minute observation upon minute observation, until the wholly mediocre and originally sympathy-provoking Shponka begins to lose our sympathy because he begins to lose his identity as a recognizable human being. We find ourselves roaring at the monster Gogol has created. He becomes what all Gogol's grotesque heroes become, *too* much: *too* naïve, *too* stupid, *too* complacent, *too* mediocre. He swims in a sea of *poshlost* and he finally drowns in trivia. Yet there is an aura of reality. Of what is it compounded?

Gogol's vocabulary, syntax, and verbal inventiveness drive many Russians to distraction, and even in English the amazingly full-bodied texture of his work is apparent. It is this very density that begins to supply an answer. The sheer collection and intensification of detail (e.g., the fact that a turnip is not merely large, but "more like a potato than a turnip") forces the reader to conclude that such a minutely detailed world must, in a sense, be real. After all, the author seems to know it so well, so intimately. But surely D. S. Mirsky is correct when he notes that Gogol's reality only *seems* real. It seems real because it is packed and stuffed and highly exaggerated reality. There are other factors accounting for this aura of reality.

His characters (and we exclude only the grossly romantic and Gothic) are, despite their excesses, identifiable and recognizable, too. His "little man," his coarse man, his rogue, his marvelous "vegetable man," his drunkard, his fool, his mediocrity—all are part of the real world, much more a part of it than the soulful romantic hero or the fiendish Gothic creation can ever be. And their motivation is real, their reaction to stimuli is real because it is predictable, and the code by which they govern themselves is also real. Despite all this, his characters are primarily caricatures. On occasion they are symbols of almost mythical dimension.

The frame of reference within which these characters move and function is very real indeed. *Poshlost* is real; so is corruption; so is injustice; so is selfishness. Gogol's intensive detailing accounts for its recognizability, and even his hyperbolic distortion of it cannot mask it. Need we be surprised to read of the bureaucrat who squirmed through a performance of *The Inspector General* or of the serf owner who was tortured by feelings of guilt (though such reactions are self-imposed)? Laugh as we will at Ivan Fiodorovich or Akaky Akakievich or the two old-world landowners or the two Ivans, the meanness of the world that reduced them to what they are is disturbing.

Stylistically, we understand how Gogol accomplished his grotesque. But what motivated him, what kind of personality can work in this genre with such unerring brilliance? We quote two of the many comments Gogol offered retrospectively:

> All is disorganized within me. I see, for example, that somebody has stumbled; my imagination immediately grasps the situation and begins to develop it into the shape of most terrible apparitions which torture me so much that I cannot sleep and am losing all my strength.

His deep-rooted neurosis explains not only the choice of subject, but explains its treatment, its density, its forcefulness, its microscopic vision.

> . . . in order to get rid of them [fits of melancholy] I invented the funniest things I could think of. I invented funny characters in the funniest situations imaginable.

It is easy to appreciate the cathartic function of his fiction. What is "funny" to a psychopathic personality may be viewed as grotesque by others. We may laugh when a fat man slips and lands in a puddle of water, but our normalcy insists we stop laughing when we realize that he may, after all, have hurt himself; but to laugh, as Gogol does, despite the fact that he may be in pain, or to laugh precisely because he is in pain, is something else again. It is the world of the grotesque.

Gogol accepted fame in a manner thoroughly consistent with his personality: he overreacted. He became a boor and something of a dandy (as grotesque a creature as he ever created), but because imaginary pain had become a necessary expiatory mechanism, he regaled his friends with stories of the incurable illnesses that ravaged him. In 1834, so few years after the publication of *Dikanka*, Gogol had influence enough to wangle a professorship of history from the University of St. Petersburg, no minor accomplishment considering the fact that his idea of the general subject was vague. It was a fiasco. Ivan Turgenev, soon to become the famous writer, was one of Gogol's students:

> We [the students] were all convinced . . . that he knew nothing of history. . . . At the final examination . . . he sat with a handkerchief wrapped around his head, feigning a toothache. There was an expression of extreme pain on his face, and he never opened his mouth. . . . I see . . . Gogol's lean figure, with a long nose and the two ends of his black handkerchief surging above his head like two ears.

Gogol soon left the school. During the next four years he devoted himself almost exclusively to writing, and the bulk of what he was to write throughout his life took shape during this period.

In 1835 the two volumes of *Mirgorod* were published, the first containing *Old-World Landowners* and *Taras Bulba* (which was to be thoroughly revised before its republication in a collected edition of his works in 1842), the second containing *Viy* and the altogether remarkable *The Tale of How Ivan Ivanovich Quarreled with Ivan Nikiforovich*. Of these, two stories, *Bulba* and *Viy*, belong to the earlier romantic Gogol tradition; the other two belong to the *Shponka* tradition, and stand as direct anticipations of Gogol's later works.

Taras Bulba, Gogol's longest tale, seems much less impressive now than it must have been to a contemporary reader. Without precedent in Russian literature, cast in the epic tradition, boisterous and romantic, peopled by nongrotesque characters who are led by a hero of classical strength and determination, rich in detailed scenes of battles and hand-to-hand combat, containing traditional comic elements—the sly Jew, for example—and a love affair, pervaded by the masculine odor of sweating men and their horses and their campfires and their strong drink, laced with eloquent passages and supported by some resemblance to historical fact, strongly anti-Polish (as were its readers on the date of its initial publication), it is not difficult to appreciate reasons for its popularity. But it now seems inferior to any of Gogol's nonromantic works. It suffers from a very poorly handled and totally unconvincing love affair. The Polish girl is, typically, less flesh than marble, and with the exception of Taras and his long-suffering wife, all the characters are highly contrived and artificial. Debilitating as these weaknesses are, there is a gusto about the work, a verve, that makes it at once vivid and exciting; and there is, on occasion, that peculiarly Gogolian touch:

> . . . but the majority [of the Poles] were the sort of people who look at the whole world and everything that happens in it and go on picking their noses.

and the deft realistic detail:

> . . . and at that moment [he] stumbled over something lying at his feet. It was the dead body of a woman, apparently a Jewess. She seemed to be young, though there was no trace of youth in her distorted and emaciated features. . . . Beside her lay a baby convulsively clutching her thin breast and pinching it with his fingers in unconscious anger at finding no milk.

Viy, which also belongs to the earlier Gogol tradition, to quote from Gogol's footnote, "is a colossal creation of the popular imagination." It is basically a horror story infused with humorous elements, the prosaic, and the realistic. That the story is at all successful bespeaks the singular ability of the author to mingle such diverse elements into something of a cohesive whole. At times the story seems to be melodramatic Poe that frightens less than it irritates. The realistic and comic descriptions of the seminary and its students are superior to the Gothic framework. But Viy and his ghoulish cohorts are so horrible that they cease being monsters; they are made of pasteboard.

As no discovery has ever been made of the alleged folklore source of this "colossal creation of the popular imagination," it is a fascinating document, and close examination of text reveals how many of Gogol's fears are here projected: demoniac woman, the threatened church (his soul), what the psychoanalyst would refer to as the imago (the unconscious infantile conception of parents).

Old-World Landowners and *The Tale of How Ivan Ivanovich Quarreled with Ivan Nikiforovich* are wonderfully successful stories which stem from the *Shponka* tradition and are representative of the mature Gogol, but they differ from each other, especially in tone.

Old-World Landowners is at once realistic and grotesque, but its grotesqueness is mitigated by the absence of overt hostility, by the presence of something idyllic. It concerns a symphony of digestion orchestrated by a couple who love and thoroughly enjoy their totally vegetable existence, their *poshlost*, their absolute Philistinism. Almost all of their lives is devoted to oral activity: they eat or they anticipate eating, or they prepare what is soon to be eaten. And during the small portion of each day when they are not so engaged, they warm their bellies on the stove. They are literature's most contented creatures, and Gogol cannot help but treat them with some measure of warmth and tolerance. If they are grotesque because they function on a totally animal level, they are yet sentimentally depicted because the "cage" in which they find themselves is both self-imposed and totally adequate to their needs. It is their complete lack of pretentiousness which dulls the barb of Gogol's pen, and at most, Gogol's outrage is cooled to diluted satire.

The Tale of How Ivan Ivanovich Quarreled with Ivan Nikiforovich is one of the most outrageously funny stories in print, but at its conclusion a very powerful element of depression, gloom, and hopelessness is introduced and alters the tone of all that preceded it, making it deeply ironic. Also told in a realistic manner, totally non-Gothic, it is an example of grotesque realism. The disastrous effects of *poshlost* are never clearer, and the story ends with the famous "*Skuchno na etom svete, gospoda!*" (It is a dreary world, gentlemen!)

The characterization, always Gogol's major strength, is superb. Gogol's art is never stronger, more sure, more controlled. A genius is at work, and his touch is everywhere ("Ivan Ivanovich's head is like a radish, tail downwards; Ivan Nikiforovich's head is like a radish, tail upwards."). Character is developed by focusing on mannerisms, on snuffboxes, on how often one shaves, on how one walks, eats, sleeps—and always with great precision. And what people we have here! The boy "who stood very tranquilly picking his nose" (and notice the effect of the Gogolian "very"), Agafya Fedoseevna who had *exactly* "three warts on her nose," the quite remarkable judge whose "upper lip served him instead of a snuffbox," and so on.

In 1835, under the title *Arabesques*, Gogol published what he himself called a "mishmash" of articles and stories. In the first part we find the first version of *The Portrait*, in the second part, *Nevsky Prospekt* and *Diary of a Madman*.

The Portrait is Gogol's least representative story, closer (but not very close) to *Viy* and *A Terrible Vengeance* than to anything else he ever wrote, especially in the earliest version. It is a German romance which happens to be written in Russian and, in its final version, suggests that Gogol is the author only because of the unmistakable didacticism infused in it. It is devoid of the grotesque and of Gogol's intense realism. It combines the Gothic, romantic, and didactic, and it is peopled with fleshless allegorical symbols: the hero (Vanity), the mother and daughter (*Poshlost*), the old man in the portrait (Devil), the professor (Reason), the artist who had painted the portrait (Sinner-Expiator). In its final version (1842) its didacticism offers us insight into Gogol's ever-increasing preoccupation with religion, morality, and the horrible wages of sin.

Nevsky Prospekt is essentially romantic, but it blends the tragic and the comic, and there are very full passages which are totally realistic. Nevsky Prospekt (the most important street in St. Petersburg) is described in great realistic detail. It comes alive, and the reader senses, alternately, its excitement and its early-morning sadness. One of the story's heroes, Piskariov, a disillusioned romantic who kills himself, almost certainly represents Gogol, and Piskariov's experience (except for his suicide for which Gogol substituted flight) closely parallels the mythical adventure about which Gogol once wrote his mother. Pirogov, the other hero, Piskariov's foil, is a realist. Disappointed if not disillusioned, the would-be lover goes not to kill himself but, rather, to a party (after calmly eating two creampuffs) where "he spent a very pleasant evening, and so distinguished himself in the mazurka that not only the ladies but even their partners were moved to admiration." Obviously, in Gogol's world, it is the romantic who fares poorly.

In *Diary of a Madman* another dreamer finds reality impossible and withdraws to the comfort of madness. The grotesque, the tragic, and the comic are mingled with eminent success. The tragic is born of the one lucid moment when the madman recognizes his desperate plight and would soar from his predicament, only to realize that flight is impossible. He utters the absurd (and considering the situation, grotesquely irrelevant) "And do you know that the Dey of Algiers has a boil under his nose?"

Gogol's sexual abnormality is again expressed with blatant clarity. The symbols might have been drawn from a Freudian primer. Here is part of an entry in the diary:

> Tomorrow . . . the earth will sit on the moon . . . I must confess that I experience a tremor at my heart when I reflect on the extreme softness and fragility of the moon. . . . there is such a fearful stench all over the world that one has to stop up one's nose. And that's how it is that the moon is such a soft globe that man cannot live on it and that nothing lives there but noses. And it is for that very reason that we can't see our noses, because they are all in the moon.

In a story written at about the same time, *The Nose*, once more a nose disappears, but this time it walks the streets of St. Petersburg in full dress and is not *in* the moon. Published in 1836, in the third issue of Pushkin's *The Contemporary*, *The Nose* is absolute nonsense, but, as Mirsky notes, "in it more than anywhere else Gogol displays his extraordinary magic power of making great comic art out of nothing."

There is wonderful satire here (the nose itself "is driving around town, calling itself a civil councilor"): the gray-headed clerk in the newspaper office who refuses to take an advertisement asking for information about the nose (because "the newspaper might lose its reputation"); the efficient policeman who finds the nose ("And the strange thing is that I myself took him for a gentleman at first, but fortunately I had my spectacles with me and I soon saw it was a nose"); the doctor (who "was a handsome man . . . magnificent pitch-black whiskers, a fresh and healthy wife, ate fresh apples in the morning, and kept his mouth extraordinarily clean, rinsing it out for nearly three-quarters of an hour every morning and cleaning his teeth with five different sorts of brushes").

The Nose is Gogol's final major effort in the realm of the fantastic (Akaky's corpse, in *The Overcoat*, is the only trace of it to appear again). Strongly reminiscent of Sterne (whose *Tristram Shandy* appeared in Russian during the first decade of the nineteenth century), it also owes part of its birth to a flood of literature and anecdotes concerned with noses. Gogol first called it *Son* (*Dream*), and some critics suggest that Gogol playfully reversed the letters of his title and arrived at *Nos* (*The Nose*). As ingenious as we admit this to be, it seems more likely that Gogol was probably dissatisfied with working *merely* on the dream level, and by transposing the dream to St. Petersburg reality, caused what was fantastic to become, in its realistic frame of reference, grotesque and satiric as well.

The Coach, published in the same issue of *The Contemporary*, is nothing more than an anecdote in which a pretentious humbug and liar is exposed. It is a story told quickly and with precision; there is a gaiety about it, life about it: the odor of vodka, leather, horses, cigar smoke, and strong men at cards.

The last of the Petersburg stories and the greatest and most influential is *The Overcoat*. Begun in 1839 (then called *The Official Who Stole Overcoats*), redrafted until 1841, it made its appearance in 1842, in the third volume of Gogol's collected works.

We have already noted its reception by liberals (and by persistent contemporary critics) as an example of "critical realism," and the spurious impression such an interpretation gives of its content and its author. Such interpretation refuses to recognize the grotesque nature of our hemorrhoidal hero (who so delights in his copying work that he even brings it home for amusement), and the grotesque quality of his existence which is so reminiscent of *Shponka*. Here we have again the grotesque-creating "*too* much": Akaky Akakievich is *too* content dealing in trivia; he has *too* much garbage resting on his hat, *too* many flies in his soup, tries to save money *too* carefully (by tiptoeing on the cobblestones to prevent wearing out his shoes); the tailor's toenail is *too* much like a turtle's shell and his shop stinks *too* much. Somehow, those who insist on seeing this as critical realism ignore the conclusion of the story when Akaky comes back to haunt St. Petersburg, and comes back not as a ghost but as a totally fantastic corpse. It is not easy to find in the text the compassion and humor with which Akaky is allegedly treated. At most there are only minor traces of social sympathy

But we must not overstate the case. If Gogol despised Akaky and what he represented, at the same time he may have felt sympathy for him because his grotesquely cruel, dreary, "real" world made him, at least in part, the monster that he is and, being more guilty than he, suffers the return of the corpse.

Gogol's last story, *The Overcoat*, strongly reflects his increasingly moralistic point of view. Akaky is subject to his derision not because of his dire poverty, not because he accepts his situation without struggling against it, but because there is in him a total absence of spiritual values, because he functions only on the level of an automaton. From Gogol's point of view, the overcoat is meaningless, as is the short-lived improvement in Akaky's social situation. It causes no spiritual change in Akaky; the inner man is still dead, only the surface has been altered, only trivialities are involved. The coat is the façade behind which Akaky hides his spiritual nakedness, and it is this, of course, that leads to his pitiless destruction.

The plot is slight, but the characters are remarkably vivid. Only in *The Tale of How Ivan Ivanovich Quarreled with Ivan Nikiforovich*, in *Dead Souls*, and in *The Inspector General* do we find creatures created with such consummate brilliance. Once met, Akaky Akakievich is unforgettable, as are the Person of Consequence, the tailor, his wife, the sneezing corpse; even the cockroaches, the stench, and the unbelievably shabby "dressing gown" come alive.

Gogol had long been interested in writing for the stage and, as early as 1832, only a year after the first volume of *Dikanka* brought him fame, he had already written two plays, *The Suitors* (later to become *The Marriage*, published in 1842) and *The Order of Vladimir of the Third Class* (whose theme—a frustrated official gone insane—reappears in *Diary of a Madman*). Of *The Order of Vladimir*, only four scenes survive, and these four have been translated by Mrs. Garnett: "A Lawsuit," "The Servant's Hall," "An Official's Morning," and "A Fragment."

The Inspector General (*Revizor*), the greatest of Gogol's three serious attempts at play-writing and the greatest comedy Russia has ever produced, begun during October 1835, was completed in only two months, performed for the first time on the first of May 1836, published the same year, and revised for the 1842 edition of Gogol's collected works.

Using the ancient literary device of mistaken identity for his plot,

Gogol peopled the play with as motley and vulgar a crew as he could create; even his hero, like all his heroes, functions on the same low plane. It is a delightful and outrageous caricature, although Gogol himself, already obsessed by religious mania, insisted that the arrival of the real Inspector General at the conclusion of the play is the call to the Last Judgment. It is a singular play in that it is devoid of love interest and functions beautifully without a single sympathetic character. It is one of the great ironies that this play written by a conservative who cared nothing for reform should be seen as a satire on social corruption. Like *The Overcoat*, it is very much concerned with the absence of moral fiber. It is the nakedness of the soul that is here mercilessly and hilariously exposed.

Densely textured, enormously imaginative, it contains incredibly funny dialogue. Gogol's feverish imagination found even the rich Russian language inadequate to his needs; he molded it, changed it, added to it. This makes much of the play almost completely untranslatable (for example, no dictionary can begin to meet the needs of Osip's long speech).

The characters, though nothing more than puppets, are vigorous and energetic puppets, recognizable as grotesque symbols of real counterparts. The hero is a fool (and a scoundrel), the mayor is a fool (and a crook), the mayor's wife is a fool (obsessed with delusions of grandeur), his daughter is a fool (too silly to be obsessed with anything)—fools, fools, fools, and how glorious it is to watch them function in Gogol's fool's paradise: a nonspiritual and godless world!

The Marriage, one of the remaining two genuine plays, is less great. It is less satiric, much more relaxed. It aims at being great fun and it is. It is very reminiscent of *Shponka* both because its hero is very much like Shponka, and because once more there is evidence of Gogol's castration complex. Contemplating marriage, Shponka is haunted by an endless array of imaginary wives, all with goose faces; Podkoliosin, about to be married, being less introspective than Shponka and a firm believer in direct action, does what any good Gogol character would do under the circumstances: he leaps from a window and makes his escape.

There is little action in the play and the characters dominate it. To complement them, Gogol reverts to an ancient (strongly antirealistic) tradition and makes rather full use of comic names. It is a device that made its first appearance in *Dikanka* and again appears very strongly in *Dead Souls*. There is Yaichnitsa (Omelet—who thinks of changing his name to Yaichnitsyn but hesitates because it sounds too much like *sobachiy syn*, "son of a bitch"), Pomoikin (Slop Pail), Perepreev (Overripe), Dyrka (Hole), and so forth.

It is a coarse play on a coarse theme played by coarse people, but Gogol accepts the situation without enmity, and what could have been biting satire is pleasant diversion.

The Gamblers, also published in 1842, is no more than a neatly constructed little play in which a cardsharp becomes himself the victim of cardsharps. It is inferior Gogol because it is devoid of Gogol's greatest gifts, comedy and exuberance. Eric Bentley's free translation of the play (*The Modern Theatre*, III, New York, 1957) is a valiant attempt to make it actable, but the play was stillborn.

There are three other completed dramatic pieces, all of them slight, all of them concerned with *The Inspector General*. *Homegoing from the Theater* (1836) is involved with fictional spectators who have just seen a performance of *The Inspector General* (an idea borrowed from Molière); *The Dénouement of the Inspector General* (1846); *Addition to The Dénouement of the Inspector General* (1847).

Gogol left for Lübeck, Germany, in a cold sweat, in June 1836. He was to remain away from Russia, excepting two eight-month visits, for twelve years. Various reasons are given for his departure, but it seems clear that he was bitterly disappointed by the staging of *The Inspector General* and in its misinterpretation. His vehemence can be clearly seen in a letter he wrote to a friend three months after leaving Russia:

> There are so many detestable faces in Russia that I couldn't stand looking at them. I still feel like spitting when I remember them.

With this taste in his mouth, Gogol wandered through Europe, often in ill health, running from himself. He found Rome an absolute delight, and he continued the work on *Dead Souls*, which he had begun in Paris and Vevey, but it came hard, so hard in fact that he asked a friend to get him a wig so that he could open the pores of his scalp because his inspiration was getting "clogged." The frail little genius almost completely toppled out of the real world. His hemorrhoids, it seems, "were spreading to [his] stomach!" In Paris, during September of 1838, he went through a new mental crisis, and by 1840 he was so overtly psychotic, so obsessed with the fear of death (which to Gogol always represented hell) that he often found it impossible to sleep alone in his room. He was tortured by imaginary illnesses and nearly drained of strength, but he managed, by the end of 1841, not only to complete *The Overcoat*, but to complete the first part of *Dead Souls*. Only sections of the second volume remain, for just before his death Gogol threw the manuscript of the second part into the fire, a masochistic ritual he engaged in at least three times during his life.

But there is no reason to treat the first part as anything less than a cohesive whole. Gogol had envisioned what Dante's *Divine Comedy* had accomplished: a three-part work involved with sin, expiation, and salvation. It is the first volume, the "sin" volume, that is brilliant; what remains of the second is not very good, primarily because Gogol's distorted vision could hardly portray positive virtues successfully, and it is not surprising that only the grotesque creation in the volume, Petukh, is well drawn. By the time of writing the second volume, Gogol was burning up with religious fever and consumed by a messianic complex. He believed that he was to serve, as Christ had served, to save the world.

Dead Souls, published in 1842, owes much to the picaresque tradition, to Sterne, and to Vasily Narezhny, an early-nineteenth-century Ukrainian novelist who worked in the genre. It was from him that Gogol borrowed for his story of the two Ivans.

Chichikov, another virtueless hero, is the personification of *poshlost*. Drab, vulgar, dishonest, Chichikov travels through Russia in quest of satisfying an outrageous scheme to buy dead souls (serfs) who are still registered (before a new census takes place) and therefore technically alive and of value. The title, however, serves another function. Gogol is very much occupied with the thought that the souls, literally, are dead too.

The greatness of the novel, typically, rests on its wonderful characters, those remarkably spirited caricatures that symbolize the vices of man. As always in the mature works, Gogol's pen is deft and the work is deeply grained and densely textured. Once more that famous everything-as-it-should-be world the Russians are so fond of is not really as it is supposed to be at all: flies are almost human; frock coats are alive; clocks are snakes; animals and furniture are reflections of their owners. Everywhere there is the distortion of reality.

The characters are masterpieces of comic creation: Sobakevich (*sobaka* means "dog") is a brute; Nozdrev ("nostril") is a braggart; Manilov (*manit* is "to lure") is nauseatingly sweet; Korobochka ("little box") is grossly stupid and a hoarder; Plyushkin (*pliushka* means "pancake," a coarse one, and Plyushkin suggests a soft, moist slap) is the most grotesque miser in literature.

The conclusion is eloquent. An exposed but hardly repentant Chichikov soars over the Russian roads, the *troika* becoming a symbol of all Russia: "Whither art thou soaring away, Russia?"

Pushkin is reported to have sighed a famous sigh upon reading it: "How gloomy is our Russia!" and Gogol is reported to have uttered a famous reply to Pushkin's famous sigh: "It is all nothing but caricature and mere fancy." We have tried to indicate that in Gogol there is no reason why the two points of view cannot be seen to live side by side.

In 1847 Gogol published his infamous *Selected Passages from a Correspondence with Friends*, a classic of reaction, a sermon on the wages of sin, in which Gogol and God stood hand in hand. Gogol played Christ and he offered heaven to the sinners if they would repent, but instead of gaining disciples he found himself mercilessly chastised by liberals *and* conservatives, who refused to recognize the "preacher of the knout, apostle of ignorance" as a messiah. The self-deluded Gogol was startled at the venom spit at him. It was the beginning of the end. The next five years, his last five, were the most excruciatingly painful of a life that had been full of pain. Thoughts of sin and suffering took full possession of him and, the flames of hell already licking at him, his creative power, already noticeably weak when he wrote the second part of *Dead Souls*, utterly deserted him.

In 1848, desperately ill and frightened, Gogol returned to Russia from a trip to the Holy Land. He grew increasingly frail, and in February 1852, he began a Lenten fast that he was never to break. Tortured by physicians who did not understand the nature of his disease, leeches sucking blood from his nostrils, totally exhausted, he wasted away.

On the morning of the fourth of March, not yet forty-three years old, Nikolai Vasilievich Gogol sacrificed himself for having failed to deliver God's message to the heathens of Russia, and literature lost a consummate artist.

Gogol's influence, in general, has been grossly exaggerated. Russian realism, we have pointed out, owes him a debt, but not one involving his "creation" of the first "little man," [3] his "creation" of the coarse and vulgar setting, or his "critical realism." Rather, the debt involves his apotheosis of the insignificant man and his dismal world, an apotheosis which helped lift taboos, which helped make such figures and such complementary settings subjects fit for competent and respectable literary treatment. In fact, as the Russian critic Vasily Rosanov pointed out, Russian literature following Gogol generally tapped a different vein, tended to move away from his work. A fresh reading of the mature Dostoevsky, of Turgenev, of Goncharov, of Tolstoy, seems to validate this point. Much that is basic to Gogol's art is absent in his followers.

We have noted some of Gogol's literary antecedents. We view him primarily as an intermediary who expresses ideas and uses techniques which existed in embryonic or relatively full-grown shape before his appearance in the world of letters, yet we do not deny that he is perhaps the most genuinely original of writers; indeed, it is his singular originality that precludes him from being an important literary influence. If there is a common denominator in Gogol, it consists of his verve, his exuberance, his linguistic intensity and skill, his great density and texture, his distorted vision of a world he felt destined for hell. All of these are the inimitable features of his art.

The best of Gogol can stand comparison with the best in literature. We need not tremble at putting him in the select company of Rabelais and Cervantes and Swift and Sterne and the others "who knew how to walk upside down in our valley of sorrows so as to make it a merry place." If Nikolai Vasilievich Gogol was hardly of this world at all, his works remain a brilliant and integral part of it.

LEONARD J. KENT

Quinnipiac College
Hamden, Connecticut
February, 1964

---

[3] The prototype of the "little man" in Russian literature seems to be the much-abused father in Pushkin's *The Postmaster,* completed in 1830 and published as one of the works of the "late Ivan Petrovich Belkin."

Nineteenth-Century Russian Civil, Military, and Court Ranks*

CIVIL RANKS	CORRESPONDING RANKS		
	ARMY	NAVY	COURT
1 Chancellor (of the Empire)	Commander in Chief	Admiral in Chief	. . . .
2 Actual Privy Councilor	General of Cavalry General of Infantry General of Artillery	Admiral	Chief Chamberlain Chief Marshal Chief Equerry Chief Huntsman Chief Steward Chief Cup-bearer Chief Master of 　Ceremonies** Chief Carver**
3 Privy Councilor	Lieutenant General	Vice Admiral	Marshal Equerry Huntsman Steward Chief Master of 　Ceremonies** Chief Carver**
4 Actual Councilor of State Attorney-general Master of Heraldry	Major General	Rear Admiral	Chamberlain (ranks 3, 4)
5 Councilor of State	. . . .	. . . .	Master of Ceremonies
6 Collegiate Councilor Military Councilor	Colonel	Captain (1st class)	Gentleman of the Bedchamber (ranks 5-8)
7 Court Councilor	Lieutenant Colonel	Captain (2nd class)	
8 Collegiate Assessor	Major (Captain or Cavalry Captain)	. . . .	
9 Titular Councilor	Staff Captain Staff Cavalry Captain	Lieutenant	. . . .
10 Collegiate Secretary	Lieutenant	Midshipman	. . . .
11 Naval Secretary	. . . .	. . . .	. . . .
12 County Secretary	2nd Lieutenant Cornet	. . . .	. . . .
13 Provincial Secretary Senate, Synod, and Cabinet Registrar	Ensign	. . . .	. . . .
14 Collegiate Registrar	. . . .	. . . .	. . . .

* According to Peter the Great's Table of Ranks, civilians held military titles which corresponded with the grade they had achieved in the civil service. Such titles were rarely used, except by those in the upper grades, the "generals."
** The titles of Chief Master of Ceremonies and Chief Carver could belong to persons of either the second or third class.

Tales

EVENINGS ON A FARM NEAR DIKANKA, I

Preface

"What oddity is this: *Evenings on a Farm near Dikanka?* What sort of *Evenings* have we here? And thrust into the world by a bee-keeper! God protect us! As though geese enough had not been plucked for pens and rags turned into paper! As though folks enough of all classes had not covered their fingers with inkstains! The whim must take a beekeeper to follow their example! Really, there is such a lot of paper nowadays that it takes time to think what to wrap in it."

I had a premonition of all this talk a month ago. In fact, for a villager like me to poke his nose out of his hole into the great world is —merciful heavens!—just like what happens if you go into the apartments of some fine gentleman: they all come around you and make you feel like a fool; it would not matter so much if it were only the important servants, but no, some wretched little snotnose loitering in the backyard pesters you too; and on all sides they begin prancing around you and asking: "Where are you going? Where? What for? Get out, peasant, out you go!" I can tell you . . . But what's the use of talking! I would rather go twice a year into Mirgorod, where the district court assessor and the reverend Father have not seen me for the last five years, than show myself in the great world; still, if you do it, whether you regret it or not, you must face the consequences.

At home, dear readers—no offense meant (you may be annoyed at a beekeeper like me addressing you so plainly, as though I were speaking to some old friend or crony)—at home in the village it has always been the peasants' habit, as soon as the work in the fields is over, to climb up on the stove[1] and rest there all winter, and we beekeepers put our bees away in a dark cellar. At the season when you see no cranes in the sky or pears on the trees, there is sure to be a light burning somewhere at the end of the village as soon as evening comes on, laughter and singing are heard in the distance, there is the twang of the balalaika and at times of the fiddle, talk and noise . . . Those are our *evening parties!* As you see, they are like your balls, though not altogether so, I must say. If you go to balls, it is to move your legs and yawn with your hand over your mouth; while with us the girls gather together in one hut, not for a ball, but with their spindle and carding comb. And at first one may say they do work; the spindles hum, there is a constant flow of song, and no one looks up from her work; but as soon as the young men burst into the hut with the fiddler, there is an uproar, fun begins, they start dancing, and I could not tell you all the pranks that are played.

But best of all is when they crowd together and begin guessing riddles or simply babble. Goodness, what stories they tell! What tales of old times they dig up! What frightening things they describe! But nowhere are such stories told as in the hut of the beekeeper Rudy[2] Panko. Why the villagers call me Rudy Panko, I really cannot say. My hair, I think, is more gray nowadays than red. But think what you like of it, it is our habit: when a nickname has once been given, it sticks to a man all his life. Good people get together at the beekeeper's on the eve of a holiday, sit down to the table—and then you only have to listen! And, I may say, the guests

---

[1] The stoves referred to throughout these stories were very large, two-level affairs made of brick. The top of each level was covered with clay or tile. Children and pets often napped on the lower level, and adults warmed themselves by sitting on it. The upper level—about one yard from the ceiling of the hut—was often utilized by all the members of a family, sometimes simultaneously, as they stretched out on it to enjoy its warmth. (ed.)

[2] "Red" in Ukrainian, i.e., "redhead." (ed.)

are by no means of the humbler sort, mere peasants; their visit would be an honor for someone of more consequence than a bee-keeper. For instance, do you know the sexton of the Dikanka church, Foma Grigorievich?[3] Ah, he has a head! What stories he can reel off! You will find two of them in this book. He never wears one of those coarse dressing gowns that you so often see on village sextons; no, if you go to see him, even on working days, he will always receive you in a gaberdine of fine cloth of the color of cold potato mash, for which he paid almost six rubles a yard at Poltava. As for his high boots, no one in the village has ever said that they smelled of tar; everyone knows that he rubs them with the very best fat, such as I believe many a peasant would be glad to put in his porridge. Nor would anyone ever say that he wipes his nose on the skirt of his gaberdine, as many men of his calling do; no, he takes from his bosom a clean, neatly folded white handkerchief embroidered on the hem with red cotton, and after putting it to its proper use, folds it up in twelve as his habit is, and puts it back in his bosom.

And one of the visitors . . . Well, he is such a fine young gentleman that you might any minute take him for an assessor or a high officer of the court.[4] Sometimes he will hold up his finger, and looking at the tip of it, begin telling a story—as choicely and cleverly as though it were printed in a book! Sometimes you listen and listen and begin to be puzzled. You can't make head or tail of it, not if you were to hang for it. Where did he pick up such words? Foma Grigorievich once told him a funny story satirizing this. He told him how a student who had been getting lessons from a deacon came back to his father such a Latin scholar that he had forgotten our language: he put *us* on the end of all the words; a spade was *spadus*, a female was *femalus*. It happened one day that he went with his father in the fields. The Latin scholar saw a rake and asked his father: "What do you call that, Father?" And, without looking at what he was doing, he stepped on the teeth of the rake. Before the father had time to answer, the handle flew up and hit the boy on

---

[3] Grigorievich is not Foma's surname. The second of the three names which Russians and Ukrainians possess is the patronymic (*otchestvo*). It is formed by adding *-ovich* or *-evich* (sometimes contracted into *-ich*) to the father's given name in the case of males, and *-ovna* or *-evna* in the case of females. The family name is used but rarely, usually on formal occasions or for official business. (ed.)

[4] A chart listing civil, military, and court ranks appears on p. xli. (ed.)

the head. "The damned rake!" he cried, putting his hand to his forehead and jumping half a yard into the air, "may the devil shove its father off a bridge, how it can hit!" So he remembered the name, you see, poor fellow!

Such a tale was not to the taste of our ingenious storyteller. He rose from his seat without speaking, stood in the middle of the room with his legs apart, craned his neck forward a little, thrust his hand into the back pocket of his pea-green coat, took out his round lacquered snuffbox, flicked his finger on the mug of some Mussulman[5] general, and, taking a good pinch of snuff powdered with wood ash and leaves of lovage, crooked his elbow, lifted it to his nose, and sniffed the whole pinch up with no help from his thumb—and still without a word. And it was only when he felt in another pocket and brought out a checked blue cotton handkerchief that he muttered the saying, I believe it was, "Cast not thy pearls before swine." "There's bound to be a quarrel," I thought, seeing that Foma Grigorievich's fingers were moving as though to make a fig. Fortunately my old woman chose that moment to set butter and hot rolls on the table. We all set to work upon them. Foma Grigorievich's hand, instead of forming the rude gesture, stretched out for a hot roll, and as always happened, they all began praising the skill of my wife.

We have another storyteller, but he (night is not the time to think of him!) has such a store of frightening tales that it makes the hair stand up on one's head. I have purposely omitted them; good people might be so scared that they would be afraid of the beekeeper, as though he were the devil, God forgive me. If, please God, I live to the New Year and bring out another volume, then I might frighten my readers with the ghosts and wonders that were seen in old days in our Christian country. Among them, maybe, you will find some tales told by the beekeeper himself to his grandchildren. If only people will read and listen, I have enough of them stored away for ten volumes, if only I am not too damned lazy to rack my brains for them.

But there, I have forgotten what is most important: when you come to see me, gentlemen, take the main road straight to Dikanka. I have put the name on my title page on purpose so that our village may be more easily found. You have heard enough about Dikanka,

---

[5] As used by Gogol, synonymous with "nonbeliever," "pagan," "infidel," etc. (ed.)

I have no doubt, and indeed there is a dwelling there finer than the beekeeper's hut. And I need say nothing about the park: I don't suppose you would find anything like it in your Petersburg. When you reach Dikanka, you need only ask any little boy in a dirty shirt minding geese: "Where does the beekeeper Rudy Panko live?" "There," he will say, pointing with his finger, and if you like, he will lead you to the village. But one thing I must ask you: not to walk here lost in thought, nor to be too clever, in fact, for our village roads are not as smooth as those in front of your mansions. The year before last Foma Grigorievich, driving from Dikanka, fell into a ditch, with his new chaise and bay mare and all, though he himself was driving and had on a pair of spectacles too.

But when you do arrive, we will give you melons such as you have never tasted in your life, I think; and you will find no better honey in any village, I will take my oath on that. Just imagine: when you bring in the comb, the scent in the room is something beyond comprehension; it is as clear as a tear or a costly crystal such as you see in earrings. And what pies my old woman will feed you on! What pies, if only you knew: simply sugar, perfect sugar! And the butter fairly melts on your lips when you begin to eat them. Really, when one comes to think of it, what can't these women do! Have you, friends, ever tasted pear kvass flavored with sloes, or raisin and plum vodka? Or rice soup with milk? Good heavens, what dainties there are in the world! As soon as you begin eating them, it is a treat and no mistake about it: too good for words! Last year . . . But how I am running on! Only come, make haste and come; and we will give you such good things that you will talk about them to everyone you meet.

RUDY PANKO
Beekeeper

THE FAIR
AT
SOROCHINTSY

I

I am weary of the hut,
Aie, take me from my home,
To where there's noise and bustle,
To where the girls are dancing gaily,
Where the boys are making merry!

From an old ballad

How intoxicating, how magnificent is a summer day in Little Russia! [1] How luxuriously warm the hours when midday glitters in stillness and sultry heat and the blue fathomless ocean covering the plain like a dome seems to be slumbering, bathed in languor, clasping the fair earth and holding it close in its ethereal embrace! Upon it, not a cloud; in the plain, not a sound. Everything might be dead; only above in the heavenly depths a lark is trilling, and from the airy heights the silvery notes drop down upon adoring earth, and from time to time the cry of a gull or the ringing note of a quail sounds in the steppe. The towering oaks stand, idle and apathetic, like aimless wayfarers, and the dazzling gleams of sunshine light up picturesque masses of leaves, casting onto others a shadow

---

[1] The name of the Ukraine before 1917. (ed.)

black as night, only flecked with gold when the wind blows. The insects of the air flit like sparks of emerald, topaz, and ruby about the gay vegetable gardens, topped by stately sunflowers. Gray haystacks and golden sheaves of wheat, like tents, stray over the plain. The broad branches of cherries, of plums, apples, and pears bent under their load of fruit, the sky with its pure mirror, the river in its green, proudly erect frame—how full of delight is the Little Russian summer!

Such was the splendor of a day in the hot August of eighteen hundred . . . eighteen hundred . . . yes, it will be about thirty years ago, when the road eight miles beyond the village of Sorochintsy bustled with people hurrying to the fair from all the farms, far and near. From early morning, wagons full of fish and salt had trailed in an endless chain along the road. Mountains of pots wrapped in hay moved along slowly, as though weary of being shut up in the dark; only here and there a brightly painted tureen or crock boastfully peeped out from behind the hurdle that held the high pile on the wagon, and attracted wishful glances from the devotees of such luxury. Many of the passers-by looked enviously at the tall potter, the owner of these treasures, who walked slowly behind his goods, carefully wrapping his proud crocks in the alien hay that would engulf them.

On one side of the road, apart from all the rest, a team of weary oxen dragged a wagon piled up with sacks, hemp, linen, and various household goods and followed by their owner, in a clean linen shirt and dirty linen trousers.[2] With a lazy hand he wiped from his swarthy face the streaming perspiration that even trickled from his long mustaches, powdered by the relentless barber who, uninvited, visits fair and foul alike and has for countless years forcibly sprinkled all mankind with dust. Beside him, tied to the wagon, walked a mare, whose meek air betrayed her advancing years.

Many of the passers-by, especially the young men, took off their caps as they met our peasant. But it was not his gray mustaches or his dignified step that led them to do so; one had but to raise one's eyes a little to discover the reason for this deference: on the wagon was sitting his pretty daughter, with a round face, black eyebrows[3] arching evenly above her clear brown eyes, carelessly

---

[2] *Sharovary*, very full trousers which are held below the knees by high boots. (ed.)

[3] A very common image in Gogol. Many Ukrainian women are blonde and

smiling rosy lips, and with red and blue ribbons twisted in the long braids which, with a bunch of wild flowers, crowned her charming head. Everything seemed to interest her; everything was new and wonderful . . . and her pretty eyes were racing all the time from one object to another. She might well be diverted! It was her first visit to a fair! A girl of eighteen for the first time at a fair! . . . But none of the passers-by knew what it had cost her to persuade her father to bring her, though he would have been ready enough but for her spiteful stepmother, who had learned to manage him as cleverly as he drove his old mare, now as a reward for long years of service being taken to be sold. The irrepressible woman . . . But we are forgetting that she, too, was sitting on the top of the load dressed in a smart green woolen pelisse, adorned with little tails to imitate ermine, though they were red in color, in a gorgeous *plakhta*[4] checked like a chessboard, and a flowered chintz cap that gave a particularly majestic air to her fat red face, the expression of which betrayed something so unpleasant and savage that everyone hastened in alarm to turn from her to the bright face of her daughter.

The river Psiol gradually came into our travelers' view; already in the distance they felt its cool freshness, the more welcome after the exhausting, wearisome heat. Through the dark and light green foliage of the birches and poplars, carelessly scattered over the plain, there were glimpses of the cold glitter of the water, and the lovely river unveiled her shining silvery bosom, over which the green tresses of the trees drooped luxuriantly. Willful as a beauty in those enchanting hours when her faithful mirror so jealously frames her brow full of pride and dazzling splendor, her lily shoulders, and her marble neck, shrouded by the dark waves of her hair, when with disdain she flings aside one ornament to replace it by another and there is no end to her whims—the river almost every year changes her course, picks out a new channel, and surrounds herself with new and varied scenes. Rows of watermills tossed up great waves with their heavy wheels and flung them violently down again, churning them into foam, scattering froth and making

---

have light-colored eyebrows, i.e., are "eyebrowless," hence black or dark eyebrows bespeak something striking, beautiful. (ed.)

[4] Ukrainian women wore a skirt made of two separate pieces of material, held together only by a girdle at the waist; the front breadth was the *zapaska*, and the back breadth the *plakhta*. (C.G.)

a great clatter. At that moment the wagon with the persons we have described reached the bridge, and the river lay before them in all her beauty and grandeur like a sheet of glass. Sky, green and dark blue forest, men, wagons of pots, watermills—all were standing or walking upside down, and not sinking into the lovely blue depths.

Our fair maiden mused, gazing at the glorious view, and even forgot to crack the sunflower seeds with which she had been busily engaged all the way, when all at once the words, "What a girl!" caught her ear. Looking around, she saw a group of young villagers standing on the bridge, of whom one, dressed rather more smartly than the others in a white jacket[5] and gray astrakhan cap, was jauntily looking at the passers-by with his arms akimbo. The girl could not but notice his sunburnt but pleasant face and fiery eyes, which seemed to look right through her, and she lowered her eyes at the thought that he might have uttered those words.

"A fine girl!" the young man in the white jacket went on, keeping his eyes fixed on her. "I'd give all I have to kiss her. And there's a devil sitting in front!"

There were peals of laughter all around; but the slow-moving peasant's gaily dressed wife was not pleased at such a greeting: her red cheeks blazed and a torrent of choice language fell like rain on the head of the unruly youth.

"I wish you'd choke, you worthless bum! May your father crack his head on a pot! May he slip down on the ice, the damned antichrist! May the devil singe his beard in the next world!"

"Isn't she swearing!" said the young man, staring at her as though puzzled at such a sharp volley of unexpected greetings. "And she can bring her tongue to utter words like that, the witch! She's a hundred if she's a day!"

"A hundred!" the elderly charmer interrupted. "You infidel! go and wash your face! You worthless rake! I've never seen your mother, but I know she's trash. And your father is trash, and your aunt is trash! A hundred, indeed! Why, the milk is scarcely dry on his . . ."

At that moment the wagon began to descend from the bridge and the last words could not be heard; but, without stopping to think, he picked up a handful of mud and threw it at her. The

---

[5] *Svitka,* a loose, long-sleeved jacket fastened by a girdle. (ed.)

throw achieved more than he could have hoped: the new chintz
cap was spattered all over, and the laughter of the rowdy pranksters
was louder than ever. The buxom charmer was boiling with rage;
but by this time the wagon was far away, and she wreaked her
vengeance on her innocent stepdaughter and her torpid husband,
who, long since accustomed to such onslaughts, preserved a determined silence and received the stormy language of his angry
spouse with indifference. In spite of all that, her tireless tongue
went on clacking until they reached the house of their old friend
and crony, the Cossack Tsibulya, on the outskirts of the village.
The meeting of the old friends, who had not seen each other for a
long time, put this unpleasant incident out of their minds for a
while, as our travelers talked of the fair and rested after their long
journey.

II

> Good heavens! what isn't there at that fair! Wheels, window-
> panes, tar, tobacco, straps, onions, all sorts of haberdashery . . . so
> that even if you had thirty rubles in your purse you could not buy
> everything at the fair.
>
> *From a Little Russian comedy*[6]

You have no doubt heard a rushing waterfall when everything is
quivering and filled with uproar, and a chaos of strange vague
sounds floats like a whirlwind around you. Are you not instantly
overcome by the same feelings in the turmoil of the village fair,
when all the people become one huge monster that moves its massive body through the square and the narrow streets, with shouting,
laughing, and clatter? Noise, swearing, bellowing, bleating, roaring—all blend into one jarring uproar. Oxen, sacks, hay, gypsies,
pots, peasant women, cakes, caps—everything is bright, gaudy,
discordant, flitting in groups, shifting to and fro before your eyes.
The different voices drown one another, and not a single word
can be caught, can be saved from the deluge; not one cry is distinct.
Only the clapping of hands after each bargain is heard on all sides.
A wagon breaks down, there is the clank of iron, the thud of
boards thrown onto the ground, and one's head is so dizzy one does
not know which way to turn.

---

[6] This epigraph and those which appear in VI, VII, and X are from comedies
by Gogol's father, an amateur playwright. (ed.)

The peasant whose acquaintance we have already made had been for some time elbowing his way through the crowd with his black-browed daughter; he went up to one wagonload, fingered another, inquired the prices; and meanwhile his thoughts kept revolving around his ten sacks of wheat and the old mare he had brought to sell. From his daughter's face it could be seen that she was not especially pleased to be wasting time by the wagons of flour and wheat. She longed to be where red ribbons, earrings, crosses made of copper and pewter, and coins were smartly displayed under linen awnings. But even where she was she found many objects worthy of notice: she was amused at the sight of a gypsy and a peasant, who clapped hands so that they both cried out with pain; of a drunken Jew kneeing a woman on the rump; of women hucksters quarreling with abusive words and gestures of contempt; of a Great Russian with one hand stroking his goat's beard, with another . . . But at that moment she felt someone pull her by the embroidered sleeve of her blouse. She looked around—and the bright-eyed young man in the white jacket stood before her. She started and her heart throbbed, as it had never done before at any joy or grief; it seemed strange and delightful, and she could not make out what had happened to her.

"Don't be frightened, dear heart, don't be frightened!" he said to her in a low voice, taking her hand. "I'll say nothing to hurt you!"

"Perhaps it is true that you will say nothing to hurt me," the girl thought to herself; "only it is strange . . . it might be the Evil One! One knows that it is not right . . . but I haven't the strength to take away my hand."

The peasant looked around and was about to say something to his daughter, but on the other side he heard the word "wheat." That magic word instantly made him join two dealers who were talking loudly, and riveted his attention upon them so that nothing could have distracted it. This is what the dealers were saying.

III

Do you see what a sort of a fellow he is?
Not many like him in the world.
Tosses off vodka like beer!

KOTLYAREVSKY,[7] *The Aeneid*

"So you think, neighbor, that our wheat won't sell well?" said a man, who looked like an artisan of some big village, in dirty tar-stained trousers of coarse homespun material, to another, with a big bump on his forehead, wearing a dark blue jacket patched in different parts.

"It's not a matter of thinking: I am ready to put a halter around my neck and hang from that tree like a sausage in the hut before Christmas, if we sell a single bushel."

"What nonsense are you talking, neighbor? No wheat has been brought except ours," answered the man in the homespun trousers.

"Yes, you may say what you like," thought the father of our beauty, who had not missed a single word of the dealer's conversation. "I have ten sacks here in reserve."

"Well, you see, it's like this: if there is any devilry mixed up in a thing, you will get no more profit from it than a hungry Muscovite," [8] the man with the bump on his forehead said significantly.

"What do you mean by devilry?" retorted the man in the homespun trousers.

"Did you hear what people are saying?" went on he of the bumpy forehead, giving him a sidelong look out of his gloomy eyes.

"Well?"

"Ah, you may say, well! The assessor, may he never wipe his lips again after the gentry's plum brandy, has set aside an evil spot for the fair, where you may burst before you get rid of a single grain. Do you see that old dilapidated barn which stands there, see, under the hill?" (At this point the inquisitive peasant went closer and was all attention.) "All manner of devilish tricks go on in that barn, and not a single fair has taken place in this spot without trouble. The

---

[7] Ivan Kotlyarevsky (1769-1838), an important Ukrainian writer, considered by many the founder of modern Ukrainian literature. These lines are from his comic version of Vergil's epic poem. (ed.)

[8] Inhabitant of Great Russia. Traditionally, Cossacks hated Great Russians, but the hatred was not necessarily reciprocal. (ed.)

district clerk passed it late last night and all of a sudden a pig's snout looked out from the window of the loft, and grunted so that it sent a shiver down his back. You may be sure that the *red jacket* will be seen again!"

"What's that about a red jacket?"

Our attentive listener's hair stood up on his head at these words. He looked around in alarm and saw that his daughter and the young man were calmly standing in each other's arms, murmuring soft nothings to each other and oblivious of every colored jacket in the world. This dispelled his terror and restored his equanimity.

"Aha-ha-ha, neighbor! You know how to hug a girl, it seems! I had been married three days before I learned to hug my late Khveska, and I owed that to a friend who was my best man: he gave me a hint."

The youth saw at once that his fair one's father was not very bright, and began making a plan for disposing him in his favor.

"I believe you don't know me, good friend, but I recognized you at once."

"Maybe you did."

"If you like I'll tell you your name and your surname and everything about you: your name is Solopy Cherevik."

"Yes, Solopy Cherevik."

"Well, have a good look: don't you know me?"

"No, I don't know you. No offense meant: I've seen so many faces of all sorts in my day, how the hell can one remember them all?"

"I am sorry you don't remember Golopupenko's son!"

"Why, is Okhrim your father?"

"Who else? Maybe he's the devil if he's not!"

At this the friends took off their caps and proceeded to kiss each other; our Golopupenko's son made up his mind, however, to attack his new acquaintance without loss of time.

"Well, Solopy, you see, your daughter and I have so taken to each other that we are ready to spend our lives together."

"Well, Paraska," said Cherevik, laughing and turning to his daughter; "maybe you really might, as they say . . . you and he . . . graze on the same grass! Come, shall we shake hands on it? And now, my new son-in-law, buy me a glass!"

And all three found themselves in the famous refreshment bar of the fair—a Jewess's booth, decorated with a huge assortment of jars, bottles, and flasks of every kind and description.

"Well, you are a smart fellow! I like you for that," said Cherevik, a little exhilarated, seeing how his intended son-in-law filled a pint mug and, without winking an eyelash, tossed it off at a gulp, flinging down the mug afterward and smashing it to bits. "What do you say, Paraska? Haven't I found you a fine husband? Look, look how he downs his drink!"

And laughing and staggering he went with her toward his wagon; while our young man made his way to the booths where fancy goods were displayed, where there were even dealers from Gadyach and Mirgorod, the two famous towns of the province of Poltava, to pick out the best wooden pipe in a smart copper setting, a flowered red kerchief and cap, for wedding presents to his father-in-law and everyone else who must have one.

IV

If it's a man, it doesn't matter,
But if there's a woman, you see
There is need to please her.

KOTLYAREVSKY

"Well, wife, I have found a husband for my daughter!"

"This is a moment to look for husbands, I must say! You are a fool—a fool! It must have been ordained at your birth that you should remain one! Whoever has seen, whoever has heard of such a thing as a decent man running after husbands at a time like this? You had much better be thinking how to get your wheat off your hands. A nice young man he must be, too! I'm certain he is the shabbiest scarecrow in the place!"

"Oh, he's not anything like that! You should see what a young man he is! His jacket alone is worth more than your pelisse and red boots. And how he downs his vodka! The devil confound me and you too if ever I have seen a fellow before toss off a pint without winking!"

"To be sure, if he is a drunkard and a vagabond he is a man after your own heart. I wouldn't mind betting it's the very same rascal who pestered us on the bridge. I am sorry I haven't come across him yet: I'd let him know."

"Well, Khivrya, what if it were the same: why is he a rascal?"

"Eh! Why is he a rascal? Ah, you birdbrain! Do you hear? Why is he a rascal? Where were your stupid eyes when we were driving past the mills? They might insult his wife here, right before his snuff-clogged nose, and he would not care a damn!"

"I see no harm in him, anyway: he is a fine fellow! Except that he plastered your mug with dung for an instant."

"Aha! I see you won't let me say a word! What's the meaning of it? It's not like you! You must have managed to get a drop before you have sold anything."

Here Cherevik himself realized that he had said too much and instantly put his hands over his head, doubtless expecting that his wrathful wife would promptly seize his hair in her wifely claws.

"Go to the devil! So much for our wedding!" he thought to himself, retreating before his wife's attack. "I shall have to refuse a good fellow for no rhyme or reason. Merciful God! Why didst Thou send such a plague on us poor sinners? With so many trashy things in the world, Thou must needs go and create wives!"

V

Droop not, plane tree,
Still art thou green.
Fret not, little Cossack,
Still art thou young.

Little Russian song

The fellow in the white jacket sitting by his wagon gazed absentmindedly at the crowd that moved noisily about him. The weary sun, after blazing through morning and noon, was tranquilly withdrawing from the earth, and the daylight was going out in a bright lovely glow. The tops of the white booths and tents stood out with dazzling brightness, suffused in a faint rosy tint of fiery light. The panes in the window frames piled up for sale glittered; the green goblets and bottles on the tables in the drinking booths flashed like fire; the heaps of melons and pumpkins looked as though they were cast in gold and dark copper. There was less talk, and the weary tongues of merchants, peasants, and gypsies moved more slowly and deliberately. Here and there lights began gleaming, and savory steam from cooking dumplings floated over the hushed streets.

"What are you grieving over, Grytsko?" a tall swarthy gypsy

cried, slapping our young friend on the shoulder. "Come, let me have your oxen for twenty rubles!"

"It's nothing but oxen and oxen with you. All that you gypsies care for is profit; cheating and deceiving honest folk!"

"Tfoo, the devil! You do seem to be in trouble! You are angered at having tied yourself up with a girl, maybe?"

"No, that's not my way: I keep my word; what I have once done stands forever. But it seems that old grumbler Cherevik has not a half pint of conscience: he gave his word, but he has taken it back. . . . Well, it is no good blaming him: he is a blockhead and that's the fact. It's all the doing of that old witch whom we jeered at on the bridge today! Ah, if I were the Czar or some great lord I would first hang all the fools who let themselves be saddled by women. . . ."

"Well, will you let the oxen go for twenty, if we make Cherevik give you Paraska?"

Grytsko stared at him in surprise. There was a look spiteful, malicious, ignoble, and at the same time haughty in the gypsy's swarthy face: any man looking at him would have recognized that there were great qualities in that strange soul, though their only reward on earth would be the gallows. The mouth, completely sunken between the nose and the pointed chin and forever curved in a mocking smile, the little eyes that gleamed like fire, and the lightning flashes of intrigue and enterprise forever flitting over his face—all this seemed in keeping with the strange costume he wore. The dark brown full coat which looked as though it would drop into dust at a touch; the long black hair that fell in tangled tresses on his shoulders; the shoes on his bare sunburnt feet, all seemed to be in character and part of him.

"I'll let you have them for fifteen, not twenty, if only you don't deceive me!" the young man answered, keeping his searching gaze fixed on the gypsy.

"Fifteen? Done! Mind you don't forget; fifteen! Here is a blue note[9] as a pledge!"

"But if you deceive me?"

"If I do, the pledge is yours!"

"Right! Well, let's shake hands on the bargain!"

"Let's!"

---

[9] Colloquial for five rubles. (ed.)

VI

What a misfortune! Roman is coming; here he is, he'll give me a drubbing in a minute; and you, too, master Khomo, will not get off without trouble.

From a Little Russian comedy

"This way, Afanasy Ivanovich! The fence is lower here, put your foot up and don't be afraid: my idiot has gone off for the night with his crony to the wagons to see that the Muscovites don't steal anything but ill-luck."

So Cherevik's menacing spouse fondly encouraged the priest's son, who was faintheartedly clinging to the fence. He soon climbed onto the top and stood there for some time in hesitation, like a long terrible phantom, looking where he could best jump and at last coming down with a crash among the rank weeds.

"How dreadful! I hope you have not hurt yourself? Please God, you've not broken your neck!" Khivrya faltered anxiously.

"Sh! It's all right, it's all right, dear Khavronya Nikiforovna," the priest's son brought out in a painful whisper, getting onto his feet, "except for being afflicted by the nettles, that serpentlike weed, to use the words of our late head priest."

"Let us go into the house; there is nobody there. I was beginning to think you were ill or asleep, Afanasy Ivanovich: you did not come and did not come. How are you? I hear that your honored father has had a run of good luck!"

"Nothing to speak of, Khavronya Nikiforovna: during the whole fast Father has received nothing but fifteen sacks of spring wheat, four sacks of millet, a hundred buns; and as for fowls they don't amount to fifty, and the eggs were mostly rotten. But the truly sweet offerings, so to say, can only come from you, Khavronya Nikiforovna!" the priest's son continued, with a tender glance at her as he edged nearer.

"Here is an offering for you, Afanasy Ivanovich!" she said, setting some bowls on the table and coyly fastening the buttons of her jacket as though they had not been undone on purpose, "curd doughnuts, wheaten dumplings, buns, and cakes!"

"I bet they have been made by the cleverest hands of any daughter of Eve!" said the priest's son, setting to work upon the cakes and with the other hand drawing the curd doughnuts toward him.

"Though indeed, Khavronya Nikiforovna, my heart thirsts for a gift from you sweeter than any buns or dumplings!"

"Well, I don't know what dainty you will ask for next, Afanasy Ivanovich!" answered the buxom beauty, pretending not to understand.

"Your love, of course, incomparable Khavronya Nikiforovna!" the priest's son whispered, holding a doughnut in one hand and encircling her ample waist with his arm.

"Goodness knows what you are thinking about, Afanasy Ivanovich!" said Khivrya, bashfully casting down her eyes. "Why, I wouldn't be surprised if you tried to kiss me next!"

"As for that, I must tell you," the young man went on. "When I was still at the seminary, I remember as though it were today . . ."

At that moment there was a sound of barking and a knock at the gate. Khivrya ran out quickly and came back looking pale.

"Afanasy Ivanovich, we are caught: there are a lot of people knocking, and I think I heard Tsibulya's voice . . ."

A dumpling stuck in the young man's throat. . . . His eyes almost popped out of his head, as though someone had just come from the other world to visit him.

"Climb up here!" cried the panic-stricken Khivrya, pointing to some boards that lay across the rafters just below the ceiling, loaded with all sorts of domestic odds and ends.

Danger gave our hero courage. Recovering a little, he clambered on the stove and from there climbed cautiously onto the boards, while Khivrya ran headlong to the gate, as the knocking was getting louder and more insistent.

VII

But here are miracles, gentlemen!

From a Little Russian comedy

A strange incident had taken place at the fair: there were rumors all over the place that the *red jacket* had been seen somewhere among the wares. The old woman who sold pretzels thought she saw the devil in the shape of a pig, bending over the wagons as though looking for something. The news soon flew to every corner of the now resting camp, and everyone would have thought it a crime to disbelieve it, in spite of the fact that the pretzel seller, whose stall was next to the drinking booth, had been staggering about all day and could not walk straight. To this was added the story—by now greatly exaggerated—of the wonder seen by the district clerk in the dilapidated barn; so toward night people were all huddling together; their peace of mind was destroyed, and everyone was too terrified to close an eye; while those who were not cast in a heroic mold, and had secured a night's lodging in a hut, made their way homeward. Among the latter were Cherevik with his daughter and his friend Tsibulya, and they, together with the friends who had offered to keep them company, were responsible for the loud knocking that had so alarmed Khivrya. Tsibulya was already a little exhilarated. This could be seen from his twice driving around the yard with his wagon before he could find the hut. His guests, too, were all rather merry, and they unceremoniously pushed into the hut before their host. Our Cherevik's wife sat as though on thorns, when they began rummaging in every corner of the hut.

"Well, gossip," cried Tsibulya as he entered, "you are still shaking with fever?"

"Yes, I am not well," answered Khivrya, looking uneasily toward the boards on the rafters.

"Come, wife, get the bottle out of the wagon!" said Tsibulya to his wife, who had come in with him, "we will empty it with these good folk, for the damned women have given us such a scare that one is ashamed to admit it. Yes, friends, there was really no sense in our coming here!" he went on, taking a pull out of an earthenware jug. "I don't mind betting a new cap that the women thought they would have a laugh at us. Why, if it were Satan—who's Satan? Spit on him! If he stood here before me this very minute, I'll be a son of a bitch if I wouldn't make a fig at him!"

"Why did you turn so pale, then?" cried one of the visitors, who was a head taller than any of the rest and tried on every occasion to display his valor.

"I? . . . Bless you! Are you dreaming?"

The visitors laughed; the boastful hero smiled complacently.

"As though he could turn pale now!" put in another; "his cheeks are as red as a poppy; he is not a Tsibulya[10] now, but a beet—or, rather, the *red jacket* itself that frightened us all so."

The bottle went the round of the table, and made the visitors

---

[10] "Onion." (ed.)

more exhilarated than ever. At this point Cherevik, greatly disturbed about the *red jacket*, which would not let his inquisitive mind rest, appealed to his friend:

"Come, friend, kindly tell me! I keep asking about this damned *jacket* and can get no answer from anyone!"

"Eh, friend, it's not a thing to talk about at night; however, to satisfy you and these good friends" (saying this he turned toward his guests) "who want, I see, to know about these strange doings as much as you do. Well, so be it. Listen!"

Here he scratched his shoulder, mopped his face with the skirt of his coat, leaned both arms on the table, and began:

"Once upon a time a devil was kicked out of hell, what for I cannot say . . ."

"How so, friend?" Cherevik interrupted. "How could it be that a devil was turned out of hell?"

"I can't help it, crony, if he was turned out, he was—as a peasant turns a dog out of his hut. Perhaps a whim came over him to do a good deed—and so they showed him the door. And the poor devil was so homesick, so homesick for hell that he was ready to hang himself. Well, what could he do about it? In his trouble he took to drink. He settled in the broken-down barn which you have seen at the bottom of the hill and which no good man will pass now without making the sign of the cross as a safeguard; and the devil became such a rake you would not find another like him among the fellows: he sat day and night in the tavern!"

At this point Cherevik interrupted again:

"Goodness knows what you are saying, friend! How could anyone let a devil into a tavern? Why, thank God, he has claws on his paws and horns on his head."

"Ah, that was just it—he had a cap and gloves on. Who could recognize him? Well, he kept it up till he had drunk away all he had with him. They gave him credit for a long time, but at last they would give no more. The devil had to pawn his red jacket for less than a third of its value to the Jew who sold vodka in those days at Sorochintsy. He pawned it and said to him: 'Mind now, Jew, I shall come to you for my jacket in a year's time; take care of it!' And he disappeared and no more was seen of him. The Jew examined the coat thoroughly: the cloth was better than anything you could get in Mirgorod, and the red of it glowed like fire, so that one could not take one's eyes off it! And it seemed to the Jew a long time to wait till the end of the year. He scratched his earlocks and got nearly five gold pieces for it from a gentleman who was passing by. The Jew forgot all about the date set. But all of a sudden one evening a man turns up: 'Come, Jew, hand me over my jacket!' At first the Jew did not know him, but afterward when he had had a good look at him, he pretended he had never seen him before. 'What jacket? I have no jacket. I know nothing about your jacket!' The other walked away; only, when the Jew locked himself up in his room and, after counting over the money in his chests, flung a sheet around his shoulders and began saying his prayers in Jewish fashion, all at once he heard a rustle . . . and there were pigs' snouts looking in at every window."

At that moment an indistinct sound not unlike the grunt of a pig was audible; everyone turned pale. Drops of sweat stood out on Tsibulya's face.

"What was it?" cried the panic-stricken Cherevik.

"Nothing," answered Tsibulya, trembling all over.

"Eh?" responded one of the guests.

"Did you speak?"

"No!"

"Who was it grunted?"

"God knows why we are so flustered! It's nothing!"

They all turned about fearfully and began rummaging in the corners. Khivrya was more dead than alive.

"Oh, you are a bunch of women!" she shouted. "You are not fit to be Cossacks and men! You ought to sit spinning yarn! Maybe someone misbehaved, God forgive him, or someone's bench creaked, and you are all in a fluster as though you were out of your heads!"

This put our heroes to shame and made them pull themselves together. Tsibulya took a pull at the jug and went on with his story.

"The Jew fainted from terror; but the pigs with legs as long as stilts climbed in at the windows and so revived him in an instant with a three-thonged whip, making him skip higher than this ceiling. The Jew fell at their feet and confessed everything. . . . Only the jacket could not be restored in a hurry. The gentleman had been robbed of it on the road by a gypsy who sold it to a peddler woman, and she brought it back again to the fair at Sorochintsy; but no one would buy anything from her after that. The woman wondered and wondered and at last saw what it was: there was no doubt the red jacket was at the bottom of it; it was not for nothing that she had felt stifled when she put it on. Without stopping to think she flung it in the fire—the devilish thing would not burn! . . . 'Ah, that's a gift from the devil!' she thought. The woman managed to thrust it into the wagon of a peasant who had come to the fair to sell his butter. The silly fellow was delighted; but no one would ask for his butter. 'Ah, it's an evil hand foisted that red jacket on me!' He took his ax and chopped it into bits; he looked at it—and each bit joined up to the next till it was whole again! Crossing himself, he went at it with the ax again; he flung the bits all over the place and went away. But ever since then, just at the time of the fair, the devil walks all over the market place with the face of a pig, grunting and collecting the pieces of his jacket. Now they say there is only the left sleeve missing. People have been shy of the place ever since, and it is ten years since the fair has been held on it. But in an evil hour the assessor . . ."

The rest of the sentence died away on the speaker's lips: there was a loud rattle at the window, the panes fell tinkling on the floor, and a frightening pig's snout peered in through the window, rolling its eyes as though asking, "What are you doing here, folks?"

VIII

His tail between his legs like a dog,
Like Cain, trembling all over;
The snuff dropped from his nose.

KOTLYAREVSKY, *The Aeneid*

Everyone in the room was numb with horror. Tsibulya sat petrified with his mouth open; his eyes were bulging as if he wanted to shoot with them; his outspread fingers were frozen in the air. The tall hero, in overwhelming terror, leaped up and struck his head against the rafter; the boards shifted, and with a thud and a crash the priest's son fell to the floor.

"Aie, aie, aie!" one of the party screamed desperately, flopping on the locker in alarm, and waving his arms and legs.

"Save me!" wailed another, hiding his head under a sheepskin.

Tsibulya, roused from his numbness by this second horror, crept shuddering under his wife's skirts. The valiant hero crawled into the oven in spite of the narrowness of the opening, and closed the oven door on himself. And Cherevik, clapping a basin on his head instead of a cap, dashed to the door as though he had been scalded, and ran through the streets like a lunatic, not knowing where he was going; only weariness caused him to slacken his pace. His heart was thumping like an oil press; streams of perspiration rolled down him. He was on the point of sinking to the ground in exhaustion when all at once he heard someone running after him. . . . His breath failed him.

"The devil! The devil!" came a shout behind him, and all he felt was something falling with a thud on the top of him. Then his senses deserted him and, like the dread inmate of a narrow coffin, he remained lying dumb and motionless in the middle of the road.

IX

In front, like anyone else;
Behind, I swear, like a devil!

From a folk tale

"Do you hear, Vlas?" one of the crowd asleep in the street said, sitting up; "someone spoke of the devil near us!"

"What is it to me?" the gypsy near him grumbled, stretching. "They may talk of all their kindred for all I care!"

"But he bawled, you know, as though he were being strangled!"

"A man will cry out anything in his sleep!"

"Say what you like, we must have a look. Strike a light!"

The other gypsy, grumbling to himself, rose to his feet, sent a shower of sparks flying like lightning flashes, blew the tinder with his lips, and with a *kaganets* in his hands—the usual Little Russian lamp consisting of a broken pot full of mutton fat—set off, lighting the way before him.

"Stop! There is something lying here! Show a light this way!"

Here they were joined by several others.

"What's lying there, Vlas?"

"Why, it looks like two men: one on top, the other under. Which of them is the devil I can't make out yet!"

"Why, who is on top?"

"A woman!"

"Oh, well, then that's the devil!"

A general shout of laughter roused almost the whole street.

"A woman straddling a man! I suppose she knows how to ride!" one of the bystanders exclaimed.

"Look, boys!" said another, picking up a broken piece of the basin of which only one half still remained on Cherevik's head, "what a cap this fine fellow put on!"

The growing noise and laughter brought our corpses to life, and Cherevik and his spouse, full of the panic they had known, gazed with bulging eyes in terror at the swarthy faces of the gypsies; in the dim and flickering light they looked like a wild horde of dark subterranean creatures, reeking of hell.

X

Fie upon you, away with you, image of the Devil!
From a Little Russian comedy

The freshness of morning breathed over the awakening folk of Sorochintsy. Clouds of smoke from all the chimneys floated to meet the rising sun. The fair began to hum with life. Sheep were bleating, horses neighing; the cackle of geese and peddler women sounded all over the encampment again—and terrible tales of the *red jacket*, which had roused such alarm in the mysterious hours of darkness, vanished with the return of morning.

Stretching and yawning, Cherevik lay drowsily under his friend Tsibulya's thatched barn among oxen and sacks of flour and wheat. And apparently he had no desire to part with his dreams, when all at once he heard a voice, familiar as his own stove, the blessed refuge of his lazy hours, or as the tavern kept by his cousin not ten paces from his own door.

"Get up, get up!" his tender wife squeaked in his ear, tugging at his arm with all her might.

Cherevik, instead of answering, blew out his cheeks and began waving his hands, as though beating a drum.

"Idiot!" she shouted, retreating out of reach of his arms, which almost struck her in the face.

Cherevik sat up, rubbed his eyes, and looked about him.

"The devil take me, my dear, if I didn't imagine that your face was a drum on which I was forced to beat an alarm, like a soldier, by those pig-faces that Tsibulya was telling us about. . . ."

"Stop talking nonsense! Go, make haste and take the mare to market! We are a laughingstock, upon my word: we've come to the fair and not sold a handful of hemp. . . ."

"Of course, wife," Cherevik agreed, "they will laugh at us now, to be sure."

"Go along, go along! They are laughing at you as it is!"

"You see, I haven't washed yet," Cherevik went on, yawning, scratching his back, and trying to gain time.

"What a moment to be fussy about cleanliness! When have you cared about that? Here's the towel, wipe your ugly face."

Here she snatched up something that lay crumpled up—and darted back in horror: it was the cuff of a red jacket!

"Go along and get to work," she repeated, recovering herself, on seeing that her husband was motionless with terror and his teeth were chattering.

"A fine sale there will be now!" he muttered to himself as he untied the mare and led her to the market place. "It was not for nothing that, while I was getting ready for this cursed fair, my heart was as heavy as though someone had put a dead cow on my back, and twice the oxen turned homeward of their own accord. And now that I come to think of it, I do believe it was Monday when we started. And so everything has gone wrong! [11] And the damned devil can never be satisfied: he might have worn his jacket without one sleeve—but no, he can't let honest folk rest in peace. Now if I were the devil—God forbid—do you suppose I'd go hanging around at night after a lot of damned rags?"

Here our Cherevik's meditations were interrupted by a thick harsh voice. Before him stood a tall gypsy.

"What have you for sale, good man?"

Cherevik was silent for a moment; he looked at the gypsy from head to foot and said with unruffled composure, neither stopping nor letting go the bridle:

"You can see for yourself what I am selling."

"Harness?" said the gypsy, looking at the bridle which the other had in his hand.

"Yes, harness, if a mare is the same thing as harness."

"But damn it, neighbor, one would think you had fed her on straw!"

"Straw?"

Here Cherevik would have pulled at the bridle to lead his mare

[11] Throughout Russia, Monday was traditionally considered a poor day on which to initiate anything—the result of an old superstition which died hard. (ed.)

forward and convict the shameless slanderer of his lie; but his hand slipped and struck his own chin. He looked—in it was a severed bridle, and tied to the bridle—oh horror! his hair stood up on his head—a piece of a red sleeve! . . . Spitting, crossing himself, and brandishing his arms, he ran away from the unexpected gift and, running faster than a boy, vanished in the crowd.

XI

For my own corn I have been beaten.

Proverb

"Catch him! catch him!" cried several young men at a narrow street corner, and Cherevik felt himself suddenly seized by strong hands.

"Tie him up! That's the fellow who stole an honest man's mare."

"Damn it! What are you tieing me up for?"

"Imagine his asking! Why did you want to steal a mare from a peasant at the fair, Cherevik?"

"You're out of your minds, fellows! Who has ever heard of a man stealing from himself?"

"That's an old trick! An old trick! Why were you running your hardest, as though the devil were on your heels?"

"Anyone would run when the devil's garment . . ."

"Aie, my good soul, try that on others! You'll catch it yet from the court assessor, to teach you to go scaring people with tales of the devil."

"Catch him! catch him!" came a shout from the other end of the street. "There he is, there is the runaway!"

And Cherevik beheld his friend Tsibulya in the most pitiful plight with his hands tied behind him, led along by several young men.

"Strange things are happening!" said one of them. "You should hear what this scoundrel says! You have only to look at his face to see he is a thief. When we began asking him why he was running like one possessed, he says he put his hand in his pocket and instead of his snuff pulled out a bit of the devil's jacket and it burst into a red flame—and he took to his heels!"

"Aha! why, these two are birds of a feather! We had better tie them together!"

XII

"In what am I to blame, good folks?
Why are you beating me?" said our poor wretch.
"Why are you falling upon me?
What for, what for?" he said, bursting into tears,
Streams of bitter tears, and clutching at his sides.

ARTEMOVSKY-GULAK,[12] *Master and Dog*

"Maybe you really have picked up something, friend?" Cherevik asked, as he lay bound beside Tsibulya in a thatched shanty.

"You too, friend! May my arms and legs wither if ever I stole anything in my life, except maybe buns and cream from my mother, and that only before I was ten years old."

"Why has this trouble come upon us? It's not so bad for you: you are charged, anyway, with stealing from somebody else; but what have I, unlucky wretch, done to deserve such a foul slander, as stealing my mare from myself? It seems it was written at our birth that we should have no luck!"

"Woe to us, forlorn and forsaken!"

At this point the two friends fell to weeping violently.

"What's the matter with you, Cherevik?" said Grytsko, entering at that moment. "Who tied you up like that?"

"Ah, Golopupenko, Golopupenko!" cried Cherevik, delighted. "Here, this is the fellow I was telling you about. Ah, he is a smart one! God strike me dead on the spot if he did not toss off a whole jug, almost as big as your head, and never turned a hair!"

"What made you ignore such a fine fellow, then, friend?"

"Here, you see," Cherevik went on, addressing Grytsko, "God has punished me, it seems, for having wronged you. Forgive me, good lad! I swear I'd be glad to do anything for you. . . . But what would you have me do? There's the devil in my old woman!"

"I am not one to hold a grudge, Cherevik! If you like, I'll set you free!"

Here he made a sign to the other fellows and the same ones who were guarding them ran to untie them.

"Then you must do your part, too: a wedding! And let us keep it up so that our legs ache with dancing for a year afterwards!"

"Good, good!" said Cherevik, striking his hands together. "I feel

---

[12] P. P. Artemovsky-Gulak (1790-1865), Ukrainian writer. *Master and Dog* is a short story in verse. (ed.)

as pleased as though the soldiers had carried off my old woman! Why give it another thought? Whether she likes it or not, the wedding shall be today—and that's all there is to it!"

"Mind now, Solopy: in an hour's time I will be with you; but now go home—there you will find purchasers for your mare and your wheat."

"What! has the mare been found?"

"Yes."

Cherevik was struck dumb with joy and stood still, gazing after Grytsko.

"Well, Grytsko, have we mishandled the job?" said the tall gypsy to the hurrying young man. "The oxen are mine now, aren't they?"

"Yours! yours!"

XIII

Fear not, fear not, little mother,
Put on your red boots
Trample your foes
Under foot
So that your ironshod
Heels may clang,
So that your foes
May be hushed and still.

A wedding song

Paraska mused, sitting alone in the hut with her pretty chin propped on her hand. Many dreams hovered about her little head. At times a faint smile stirred her crimson lips and some joyful feeling lifted her dark brows, while at times a cloud of pensiveness set them frowning above her clear brown eyes.

"But what if it does not come true as he said?" she whispered with an expression of doubt. "What if they don't let me marry him? If . . . No, no; that will not be! My stepmother does just as she likes; why mayn't I do as I like? I've plenty of obstinacy too. How handsome he is! How wonderfully his black eyes glow! How delightfully he says, 'Paraska darling!' How his white jacket suits him! But his belt ought to be a bit brighter! . . . I will weave him one when we settle in a new hut. I can't help being pleased when I think," she went on, taking from her bosom a little red-paper-framed mirror bought at the fair and gazing into it, "how I shall meet her one day somewhere and she may burst before I bow to her, nothing will induce me. No, stepmother, you've kicked me for the last time. The sand will rise up on the rocks and the oak bend down to the water like a willow before I bow down before you. But I was forgetting . . . let me try on a cap, even if it has to be my stepmother's, and see how it suits me to look like a wife?"

Then she got up, holding the mirror in her hand and bending her head down to it, walked in excitement about the room, as though in dread of falling, seeing below her, instead of the floor, the ceiling with the boards laid on the rafters from which the priest's son had so lately dropped, and the shelves set with pots.

"Why, I am like a child," she cried, "afraid to take a step!"

And she began tapping with her feet, growing bolder as she went on; at last she laid her left hand on her hip and went off into a dance, clinking with her metaled heels, holding the mirror before her, and singing her favorite song:

> Little green periwinkle,
>   Twine lower to me!
> And you, black-browed dear one,
>   Come nearer to me!
> Little green periwinkle,
>   Twine lower to me!
> And you, black-browed dear one,
>   Come nearer to me!

At that moment Cherevik peeped in at the door, and seeing his daughter dancing before the mirror, he stood still. For a long time he watched, laughing at the innocent prank of his daughter, who was apparently so absorbed that she noticed nothing; but when he heard the familiar notes of the song, his muscles began working: he stepped forward, his arms jauntily akimbo, and forgetting all he had to do, began dancing. A loud shout of laughter from his friend Tsibulya startled both of them.

"Here is a pretty thing! The dad and his daughter getting up a wedding on their own account! Make haste and come along: the bridegroom has arrived!"

At the last words Paraska flushed a deeper crimson than the ribbon which bound her head, and her lighthearted parent remembered his errand.

"Well, daughter, let us make haste! Khivrya is so pleased that I have sold the mare," he went on, looking timorously about him, "that she has run off to buy herself aprons and all sorts of rags, so we must get it all over before she is back."

Paraska had no sooner stepped over the threshold than she felt herself caught in the arms of the young man in the white jacket who with a crowd of people was waiting for her in the street.

"God bless you!" said Cherevik, joining their hands. "May their lives together cleave as the wreaths of flowers they weave." [13]

At this point a hubbub was heard in the crowd.

"I'd burst before I'd allow it!" screamed Cherevik's helpmate, who was being shoved back by the laughing crowd.

"Don't excite yourself, wife!" Cherevik said coolly, seeing that two sturdy gypsies held her hands, "what is done can't be undone: I don't like going back on a bargain!"

"No, no, that shall never be!" screamed Khivrya, but no one heeded her; several couples surrounded the happy pair and formed an impenetrable dancing wall around them.

A strange feeling, hard to put into words, would have overcome anyone watching how the whole crowd was transformed into a scene of unity and harmony, at one stroke of the bow of the fiddler, who had long twisted mustaches and wore a homespun jacket. Men whose sullen faces seemed to have known no gleam of a smile for years were tapping with their feet and wriggling their shoulders; everything was heaving, everything was dancing. But an even stranger and more disturbing feeling would have been stirred in the heart at the sight of old women, whose ancient faces breathed the indifference of the tomb, shoving their way between the young, laughing, living human beings. Caring for nothing, indifferent, long removed from the joy of childhood, wanting only drink, it was as if a puppeteer were tugging the strings that held his wooden puppets, making them do things that seemed human; yet they slowly wagged their drunken heads, dancing after the rejoicing crowd, not casting one glance at the young couple.

The sounds of laughter, song, and uproar grew fainter and fainter. The strains of the fiddle were lost in vague and feeble notes, and died away in the wind. In the distance there was still the sound of dancing feet, something like the faraway murmur of the sea, and soon all was stillness and emptiness again.

Is it not thus that joy, lovely and fleeting guest, flies from us? In

---

[13] The proverbial form of greeting to a newly wedded couple in Little Russia. (C.G.)

vain the last solitary note tries to express gaiety. In its own echo it hears melancholy and emptiness and listens to it, bewildered. Is it not thus that those who have been playful friends in free and stormy youth, one by one stray, lost, about the world and leave their old comrade lonely and forlorn at last? Sad is the lot of one left behind! Heavy and sorrowful is his heart and nothing can help him!

ST. JOHN'S EVE

A True Story Told by the Sexton

It was a special peculiarity of Foma Grigorievich's that he had a mortal aversion for repeating the same story. It sometimes happened that one persuaded him to tell a story over again, but then he would be bound to add something fresh, or would tell it so differently that you hardly knew it for the same. It happened that one of those people—it is hard for us, simple folk, to know what to call them, for scriveners they are not, but they are like the dealers at our fairs: they beg, they grab, they filch all sorts of things and bring out a little book, no thicker than a child's reader, every month or every week—well, one of these gentry got this story out of Foma Grigorievich, though he almost forgot all about it. And then that young gentleman in the pea-green coat of whom I have told you already and whose story, I believe, you have read arrives from Poltava, brings with him a little book, and opening it in the middle, shows it to us. Foma Grigorievich was just about to put

his spectacles astride his nose, but, recollecting that he had for-
gotten to mend them with thread and wax, he handed it to me.
As I know how to read after a fashion and do not wear spectacles,
I began reading it aloud. I had hardly read two pages when Foma
Grigorievich suddenly nudged my arm.

"Wait a minute: tell me first what it is you are reading."

I must admit I was a little taken aback by such a question.

"What I am reading, Foma Grigorievich? Your story, your own
words."

"Who told you it was my story?"

"What better proof do you want? It is printed here: 'Told by
the sexton of So-and-so.' "

"Hang the fellow who printed that! He's lying, the dog! Is that
how I told it? What is one to do when a man has a screw loose in
his head? Listen, I'll tell it to you now."

We moved up to the table and he began.

My grandfather (the kingdom of heaven be his! May he have
nothing but rolls made of fine wheat and poppy cakes with honey
to eat in the other world!) was a great hand at telling stories. Sometimes when he talked, one could sit listening all day without stirring. He was not like the gabblers nowadays who drive you to
pick up your cap and go out as soon as they begin spinning their
yarns in a voice which sounds as though they had had nothing
to eat for three days. I remember as though it were today—the
old lady, my mother, was living then—how, on a long winter
evening when frost crackled outside and sealed up the narrow
window of our hut, she would sit with her spindle pulling out
a long thread with one hand, rocking the cradle with her foot,
and singing a song which I can hear now. Sputtering and trembling as though it were afraid of something, the lamp lighted up
the hut. The spindle hummed while we children clustered together listening to Grandad, who was so old that he had hardly
climbed down from the stove for the last five years. But not even
his marvelous accounts of the old days, of the raids of the Cossacks,
and of the Poles, of the gallant deeds of Podkova, of Poltor-
Kozhukh and Sagaydachny,[1] interested us so much as stories of
strange things that had happened long ago; they always made our

---

[1] Famous Cossack headmen. (ed.)

hair stand on end and set us shuddering. Sometimes we were so terrified by them that in the evening you can't imagine how strange everything looked. Sometimes you would step out of the hut for something at night and think that some visitor from the other world had got into your bed. And, may I never live to tell this tale again, if I did not often mistake my coat rolled up as a pillow for the devil huddling there. But the main thing about Grandad's stories was that he never in his life told a lie and everything he told us had really happened.

One of his wonderful stories I am going to tell you now. I know there are lots of smart fellows who scribble in law courts and read even modern print, though if you put in their hands a simple prayer book they could not read a letter of it, and yet they are clever enough at grinning and mocking! Whatever you tell them they turn into ridicule. Such unbelief is spreading all over the world! Why—may God and the Holy Virgin look ill upon me!—you will hardly believe me: I dropped a word about witches one day, and there was a crazy fellow who didn't believe in witches! Here, thank God, I have lived all these long years and have met unbelievers who would tell a lie at confession as easily as I'd take a pinch of snuff, but even they made the sign of the cross in terror of witches. May they dream of—but I won't say what I would like them to dream of. . . . Better not speak of them.

How many years ago! over a hundred, my Grandad told us, no one would have known our village: it was a hamlet, the poorest of hamlets! A dozen huts or so, without plaster or proper roofs, stood up here and there in the middle of the fields. No fences, no real barns where cattle or carts could be housed. And it was only the rich who lived as well as that—you should have seen the likes of us poor ones: we used to dig a hole in the ground and that was our hut! You could only tell from the smoke that Christians were living there. You will ask, why did they live like that? It was not that they were poor, for in those days almost everyone was a Cossack and brought home plenty of good things from other lands, but more because it was no use to have a good hut. All sorts of folk were roaming about the country then: Crimeans, Poles, Lithuanians! And sometimes even fellow countrymen came in gangs and robbed us. All sorts of things used to happen.

In this village there often appeared a man, or rather the devil in human shape. Why he came and where he came from nobody knew.

He drank and made merry, and then vanished as though he had sunk into the water, and they heard no news of him. Then all at once he seemed to drop from the sky and was prowling about the streets of the village which was hardly more than a hundred paces from Dikanka, though there is no trace of it now. . . . He would join any stray Cossacks, and then there was laughter and singing, the money would fly, and vodka would flow like water. . . . Sometimes he'd set upon the girls, heap ribbons, earrings, necklaces on them, till they did not know what to do with them. To be sure, the girls did think twice before they took his presents: who knows, they might really come from the devil. My own grandfather's aunt, who used to keep a tavern on what is now the Oposhnyansky Road, where Basavriuk (that was the name of this devil of a fellow) often went for a drink, said she wouldn't take a present from him for all the riches in the world. And yet, how could they refuse? Everybody was terrified when he scowled with his shaggy eyebrows and looked from under them in a way that might make the stoutest take to his heels; and if a girl did accept, the very next night a friend of his from the marsh with horns on his head might pay her a visit and try to strangle her with the necklace around her neck, or bite her finger if she had a ring, or pull her hair if she had a ribbon in it. A plague take them, then, his fine presents! And the worst of it was, there was no getting rid of them: if you threw them into the water, the devilish necklace or ring would float on the top and come back straight into your hands.

In the village there was a church, and I think, if I remember right, it was St. Panteley's. The priest there in those days was Father Afanasy of blessed memory. Noticing that Basavriuk did not come to church even on Easter Sunday, he thought to reprimand him and threaten him with a church penance. But no such thing! It was he that caught it! "Look here, my good sir," Basavriuk bellowed in reply to him, "you mind your own business and don't meddle with other people's unless you want your billygoat's gullet choked with hot rice soup!" What was to be done with the cursed fellow? Father Afanasy merely declared that he should consider anyone who associated with Basavriuk a Catholic, an enemy of the Church of Christ and of the human race.

In the same village a Cossack called Korzh had a worker who was known as Petro the Kinless—perhaps because no one remembered his parents. It is true that the churchwarden used to say that they had died of the plague when he was a year old, but my grandfather's aunt would not hear of that and did her very utmost to provide him with relations, though poor Petro cared no more about them than we do about last year's snow. She used to say that his father was still in Zaporozhye, that he had been taken prisoner by the Turks and suffered goodness knows what tortures, and that in some miraculous way he had escaped, disguised as a eunuch. The black-browed girls and young women cared nothing about his relations. All they said was that if he put on a new coat, a red belt, a black astrakhan cap with a smart blue top to it, hung a Turkish sword at his side, and carried a whip in one hand and a handsome pipe in the other, he would outshine all the fellows of the place. But the pity was that poor Petro had only one gray jacket with more holes in it than gold pieces in a Jew's pocket. And that was not what mattered; what did matter was that old Korzh had a daughter, a beauty—such as I imagine you have never seen. My grandfather's aunt used to say—and women, you know, would rather kiss the devil, forgive the expression, than call any girl a beauty—that the girl's round cheeks were as fresh and bright as a poppy of the most delicate shade of pink when it glows, washed by God's dew, unfolds its leaves, and preens itself in the rising sun; that her brows, like black strings such as our girls buy nowadays to hang crosses or coins on from traveling Russian peddlers, were evenly arched and seemed to gaze into her clear eyes; that her little mouth, at which the young men stared greedily, looked as though it had been created to utter the notes of a nightingale; that her hair, black as a raven's wings and soft as young flax, fell in rich curls on her gold-embroidered jacket (in those days our girls did not tie their hair in braids and twine them with bright-colored ribbons). Ah, may God never grant me to sing "Alleluia" again in the choir, if I could not kiss her on the spot now in spite of the gray which is spreading all over the old stubble on my head, and of my old woman, always at hand like a sty when she is not wanted. Well, if a boy and a girl live near each other . . . you all know what is bound to happen. Before the sun had fully risen, the footprints of the little red boots could be seen on the spot where Pidorka had been talking to her Petro. But Korzh would never have had an inkling that anything was amiss if—clearly it was the devil's prompting—one day

Petro had not been so unwary as to imprint, as they say, a heartfelt kiss on Pidorka's rosy lips in the outer room without taking a good look around; and the same devil—may he dream of the Holy Cross, the son of a bitch!—prompted the old bastard to open the door of the hut. Korzh stood petrified, clutching at the door, with his mouth wide open. The accursed kiss seemed to overwhelm him completely. It seemed louder to him than the racket a pestle makes when smashed against the wall, a technique practiced in our day by the peasants who wanted to frighten away the devil though they had no gun with which to make noise.

Recovering himself, he took his grandfather's whip from the wall and was about to flick it on Petro's back, when all of a sudden Pidorka's six-year-old brother Ivas ran in and threw his arms around the old man's legs in terror, shouting: "Father, Father, don't beat Petro!"

What was to be done? The father's heart was not made of stone. Hanging the whip on the wall, he quietly led Petro out of the hut. "If you ever show yourself again in my hut, or even under the windows, then listen: you will lose your black mustaches, and your forelock,[2] too—it is long enough to go twice around your ear—will take leave of your head, or my name is not Terenty Korzh!"

Saying this, he dealt him a light blow on the back of the neck, and Petro, caught unawares, flew headlong. So that was what his kisses brought him!

Our cooing doves were overwhelmed with sadness; and then there was a rumor in the village that a new visitor was continually seen at Korzh's—a Pole, all in gold braid, with mustaches, a saber, spurs, and pockets jingling like the bell on the bag that our sexton Taras carries about the church with him every day. Well, we all know why people visit a father when he has a black-browed daughter! So one day Pidorka, bathed in tears, took her little brother Ivas in her arms: "Ivas my dear, Ivas my darling, run fast as an arrow from the bow, my golden little one, to Petro. Tell him everything: I would love his brown eyes, I would kiss his fair face, but my fate says no. More than one towel I have soaked with my bitter tears. I am sick and sad at heart. My own father is my foe: he is forcing me

---

[2] Cossacks shaved their heads, but left a long forelock which they twirled around an ear. (ed.)

to marry the detested Pole. Tell him that they are making ready the wedding, only there will be no music at our wedding, the deacons will chant instead of the pipe and the lute. I will not walk out to dance with my bridegroom: they will carry me. Dark, dark will be my dwelling, of maple wood, and instead of a chimney a cross will stand over it!"

Standing motionless, as though turned to stone, Petro heard Pidorka's words lisped by the innocent child.

"And I, poor luckless fool, was thinking of going to the Crimea or Turkey to win gold in war, and, when I had money, to come to you, my sweet. But it is not to be! An evil eye has looked upon us! I, too, will have a wedding, my dear little fish; but there will be no clergy at that wedding—a black raven will croak over me instead of a priest; the open plain will be my dwelling, the gray storm clouds will be my roof; an eagle will peck out my brown eyes; the rains will wash my Cossack bones and the whirlwind will dry them. But what am I saying? To whom, of whom am I complaining? It is God's will, apparently. If I must perish, then perish!" and he walked straight to the tavern.

My grandfather's aunt was rather surprised when she saw Petro at the tavern and at an hour when a good Christian is at prayer, and she stared at him open-eyed as though half awake when he asked for a mug of vodka, almost half a pailful. But in vain the poor fellow sought to drown his sorrow. The vodka stung his tongue like a nettle and seemed to him bitterer than wormwood. He flung the mug upon the ground.

"Stop grieving, Cossack!" something boomed out in a bass voice above him.

He turned around: it was Basavriuk! Ugh, what he looked like! Hair like bristles, eyes like a bullock's.

"I know what it is you lack: it's this!" and then with a fiendish laugh he jingled the leather pouch he carried at his belt.

Petro started.

"Aha! Look how it glitters!" yelled the other, pouring the gold pieces into his hand. "Aha! how it rings! And you know, only one thing is asked for a whole pile of such baubles."

"The devil!" cried Petro. "Very well, I am ready for anything!" They shook hands on it.

"So, Petro, you are just in time: tomorrow is St. John the Bap-

tist's Day. This is the only night in the year in which the fern blossoms.[3] Don't miss your chance! I will wait for you at midnight in
the Bear's Ravine."

I don't think the hens are as eager for the minute when the good-
wife brings their grain as Petro was for evening to come. He was
continually looking whether the shadows from the trees were longer,
whether the setting sun were not flushing red, and as the hours
went on he grew more impatient. Ah, how slowly they went! It
seemed as though God's day had lost its end somewhere. At last the
sun was gone. There was only a streak of red on one side of the sky.
And that, too, was fading. It turned colder. The light grew dimmer
and dimmer till it was quite dark. At last! With his heart almost
leaping out of his breast, he set off on his way and carefully went
down through the thick forest to a deep hollow which was known
as the Bear's Ravine. Basavriuk was there already. It was so dark
that you could not see your hand before your face. Hand in hand,
they made their way over a muddy bog, caught at by the thorns
that grew over it and stumbling almost at every step. At last they
reached a level place. Petro looked around—he had never chanced
to come there before. Here Basavriuk stopped.

"You see there are three hillocks before you? There will be all
sorts of flowers on them, but may the powers from above keep you
from picking one of them. But as soon as the fern blossoms, pick it
and do not look around, regardless of what you may think is behind
you."

Petro wanted to question him further . . . but behold, he was
gone. He went up to the three hillocks: where were the flowers?
He saw nothing. Rank weeds overshadowed everything and smothered all else with their dense growth. But there came a flash of
summer lightning in the sky, and he saw before him a whole bed of
flowers, all marvelous, all new to him; and there, too, were the simple fronds of fern. Petro was puzzled and he stood in confusion
with his arms akimbo.

"What is marvelous about this? One sees that green stuff a dozen
times a day—what is there strange in it? Didn't the devil mean to
make a fool of me?"

All at once a little flower began to turn red and to move as though

---

[3] Fern, of course, never blossoms. According to Ukrainian folklore, it blossoms
once a year, on St. John the Baptist's Day. Legend has it that the sight of
blossoming fern indicates a buried treasure beneath. (ed.)

it were alive. It really was a marvel! It moved and grew bigger and bigger and turned red like a burning coal. A little star suddenly flashed, something snapped—and the flower opened before his eyes, shedding light on the others about it like a flame.

"Now is the time!" thought Petro, and stretched out his hand. He saw that hundreds of shaggy hands were stretched from behind him toward it, and something seemed to be flitting to and fro behind his back. Shutting his eyes, he pulled at the stalk, and the flower was left in his hand. Everything was hushed. Basavriuk, looking blue as a corpse, appeared sitting on a stump. He did not stir a finger. His eyes were fastened on something which only he could see; his mouth was half open, and no answer came from it. Nothing stirred all around. Ugh, it was horrible! . . . But at last a whistle sounded, which turned Petro cold all over, and it seemed to him as though the grass were murmuring, and the flowers were talking among themselves with a voice as delicate and sweet as silver bells: the trees resounded with angry gusts. Basavriuk's face suddenly came to life, his eyes sparkled. "At last, you are back, old witch!" he growled through his teeth. "Look, Petro, a beauty will appear before you: do whatever she tells you, or you will be lost forever!"

Then with a gnarled stick he parted a thornbush and a little hut—on hen's legs,[4] as they say in fairy tales—stood before them. Basavriuk struck it with his fist and the wall tottered. A big black hound ran out to meet them, and changing into a cat, flew squealing at their eyes.

"Don't be angry, don't be angry, old devil!" said Basavriuk, spicing his words with an oath which would make a good man stop his ears. In an instant, where the cat had stood was an old hag wrinkled like a baked apple and bent double, her nose and chin meeting like the tongs of a nutcracker.

"A fine beauty!" thought Petro, and a shudder ran down his back.

The witch snatched the flower out of his hands, bent over it, and spent a long time muttering something and sprinkling it with water of some sort. Sparks flew out of her mouth, there were flecks of foam on her lips. "Throw it!" she said, giving him back the flower. Petro threw it and, marvelous to relate, the flower did not fall at

---

[4] Reference is to a becharmed dwelling in the woods inhabited by spirits and witches. Pushkin often refers to such places. (ed.)

once, but stayed for a long time like a ball of fire in the darkness, and floated in the air; at last it began slowly descending and fell so far away that it looked like a little star no bigger than a poppy seed. "Here!" the old woman wheezed in a hollow voice, and Basavriuk, giving him a spade, added: "Dig here, Petro; here you will see more gold than you or Korzh ever dreamed of."

Petro, spitting into his hands, took the spade, thrust at it with his foot, and threw out the earth, a second spadeful, a third, another . . . Something hard! . . . The spade clanked against something and would go no further. Then his eyes could distinguish clearly a small trunk. He tried to get hold of it, but the trunk seemed to sink deeper and deeper into the earth; and behind him he heard laughter that was like the hissing of snakes.

"No, you will never see the gold till you have shed human blood!" said the witch, and brought him a child about six years old covered with a white sheet, gesturing to him to cut off its head. Petro was struck dumb. A mere trifle! for no rhyme or reason to murder a human being, and an innocent child, too! Angrily he pulled the sheet off the child, and what did he see? Before him stood Ivas. The poor child crossed his arms and hung his head. . . . Like one possessed, Petro flew at the witch, knife in hand, and was just lifting his hand to strike . . .

"And what did you promise for the sake of the girl?" thundered Basavriuk, and his words smashed through Petro like a bullet. The witch stamped her foot; a blue flame shot out of the earth and shed light down into its center, so that it all looked as though made of crystal; and everything under the surface could be seen clearly. Gold pieces, precious stones in chests and in cauldrons were piled up in heaps under the very spot on which they were standing. His eyes glowed . . . his brain reeled . . . Frantic, he seized the knife and the blood of the innocent child spurted into his eyes. . . . Devilish laughter broke out all around him. Hideous monsters galloped in herds before him. Clutching the headless corpse in her hands, the witch drank the blood like a wolf. . . . His head was in a whirl! With a desperate effort he started running. Everything about him was lost in a red light. The trees all bathed in blood seemed to be burning and moaning. The blazing sky quivered. . . . Gleams of lightning like fire flashed before his eyes. At his last gasp he ran into his hut and fell on the ground like a sheaf of wheat. He sank into a deathlike sleep.

For two days and two nights he slept without waking. Waking on the third day, he stared for a long time into the corners of the hut. But he tried in vain to remember what had happened; his memory was like an old miser's pocket out of which you can't entice a copper. Stretching a little, he heard something clink at his feet. He looked: two sacks of gold. Only then he remembered, as though it were a dream, that he had been looking for a treasure, that he had been frightened and alone in the forest. . . . But at what price, how he had obtained it—that he could not recall.

Korzh saw the sacks and—was softened. Petro was this and Petro was that, and he could not say enough for him. "And wasn't I always fond of him, and wasn't he like my own son to me?" And the old fox carried on so sympathetically that Petro was moved to tears. Pidorka began telling him how Ivas had been stolen by some passing gypsies, but Petro could not even remember the child: that cursed devilry had so confounded him!

There was no reason for delay. They sent the Pole away after offering him a fig under his nose and began preparing the wedding. They baked wedding cakes, they hemmed towels and kerchiefs, rolled out a barrel of vodka, set the young people down at the table, cut the wedding loaf, played the lute, the pipe, the bandore, and the cymbals—and the merrymaking began. . . .

You can't compare weddings nowadays with what they used to be. My grandfather's aunt used to tell about them—it was a treat! How the girls in a smart headdress of yellow, blue, and pink ribbons, with gold braid tied over it, in fine smocks embroidered with red silk on every seam and adorned with little silver flowers, in morocco boots with high iron heels, danced around the room as gracefully as peacocks, swishing like a whirlwind. How the married women in a boat-shaped headdress, the whole top of which was made of gold brocade with a little slit at the back showing a peep of the gold cap below, with two little horns of the very finest black astrakhan, one in front and one behind, in blue coats of the very best silk with red borders, holding their arms with dignity akimbo, stepped out one by one and rhythmically danced the *gopak!* How the lads in high Cossack hats, in fine cloth jerkins with silver-embroidered belts, with a pipe in their teeth, danced attendance on them and cut all sorts of capers! Korzh himself, looking at the young couple, could not refrain from recalling his young days: with a bandore in his hand, smoking his pipe and singing, at the same time balancing a goblet on his head, the old man began dancing in a half-squatting position. What won't people think of when they are making merry? They would begin, for instance, putting on masks—my goodness, they looked like monsters! Ah, it was a very different thing from dressing up at weddings nowadays. What do they do now? Only rig themselves out like gypsies or Muscovites. Why, in the old days one would dress himself as a Jew and another as a devil; first they would kiss each other and then pull each other's forelocks. . . . My God! one laughed till one held one's sides. They would put on Turkish and Tartar garments, all glittering like fire. . . . And as soon as they began fooling and playing tricks . . . there were no limits to what they would do! An amusing incident happened to my grandfather's aunt who was at that wedding herself; she was wearing a full Tartar dress and, goblet in her hand, she was entertaining the company. The devil prompted someone to splash vodka over her from behind; another one, it seems, was just as clever: at the same moment he struck a light and set fire to her. . . . The flame flared up; the poor aunt, terrified, began flinging off all her clothes before everybody. . . . The din, the laughter, the hubbub that arose—it was like a fair. In fact, the old people had never remembered such a merry wedding.

Pidorka and Petro began to live like lady and lord. They had plenty of everything, it was all handsome . . . But good people shook their heads a little as they watched the way they lived. "No good comes from the devil," all said with one voice. "From whom had his wealth come, if not from the tempter of good Christians? Where could he have got such a pile of gold? Why had Basavriuk vanished on the very day that Petro had grown rich?"

You may say that people imagine things! But really, before a month was out, no one would have known Petro. What had happened to him, God only knows. He would sit still without stirring and not say a word to anyone; he was always brooding as if he wanted to remember something. When Pidorka did succeed in making him talk, he would seem to forget his troubles and keep up a conversation and even be merry, but if by chance his eye fell on the bags, "Stop, stop, I have forgotten," he would say, and again he would sink into thought and again try to remember something. Sometimes after he had been sitting still for a long time it seemed that in another moment he would recall it all . . . and then it would pass away again. He fancied he had been sitting in a tavern;

they brought him vodka; the vodka stung him; the vodka was repulsive; someone came up, slapped him on the shoulder; he . . . but after that everything seemed shrouded in a fog. The sweat dropped down his face and he sat down again, feeling helpless.

What did not Pidorka do! She consulted sorcerers, poured wax into water, and burned a bit of hemp[5]—nothing was of any use. So the summer passed. Many of the Cossacks had finished their mowing and harvesting; many of the more reckless ones had gone off fighting. Flocks of ducks were still plentiful on our marshes, but there was not a nettle wren to be seen. The steppes turned red. Stacks of wheat, like Cossacks' caps, were dotted about the field here and there. Wagons laden with bundles of twigs and logs were on the roads. The ground was firmer and in places it was frozen. Snow began falling and the twigs on the trees were decked in hoarfrost like rabbit fur. Already one bright frosty day the redbreasted bullfinch was strutting about like a smart Polish gentleman, looking for seeds in the heaps of snow, and the children were whipping wooden tops on the ice with huge sticks while their fathers lay quietly on the stove, coming out from time to time with a lighted pipe between their teeth to swear roundly at the good Orthodox frost, or to get a breath of air and thrash the grain stored in the outer room.

At last the snow began to melt and "the perch smashed the ice with its tail," but Petro was still the same, and as time went on he was gloomier still. He would sit in the middle of the hut, as though riveted to the spot, with the bags of gold at his feet. He shunned company, let his hair grow, began to look dreadful, and thought only about one thing: he kept trying to remember something and was troubled and angry that he could not. Often he would wildly get up from his seat, wave his arms, fix his eyes on something as though he wanted to catch it; his lips would move as though trying to utter some long-forgotten word—and then would remain motionless. . . . He was overcome by fury; he would gnaw and bite his hands like a madman, and tear out his hair in handfuls until he

---

[5] When anyone has had a fright and wants to know what has caused it, melted tin or wax is thrown into water and it will take the shape of whatever has caused the patient's terror; and after that the terror passes off. Hemp is burned for sickness or stomach complaint. A piece of hemp is lighted, and thrown into a mug which is turned wrong side up over a bowl of water placed on the patient's stomach. Then, after a spell is repeated, a spoonful of the water is given to the patient to drink. (N. Gogol)

would grow quiet again and seem to sink into forgetfulness; and then he would begin to remember again, and again there would be fury and torment. . . . It was, indeed, a heaven-sent infliction.

Pidorka's life was not worth living. At first she was afraid to remain alone in her hut, but afterward she grew used to her trouble, poor thing. But no one would have known her for the Pidorka of earlier days. No color, no smile; she was pining and wasting away, she was crying her bright eyes out. Once someone must have taken pity on her and advised her to go to the witch in the Bear's Ravine, who was reputed able to cure all the diseases in the world. She made up her mind to try this last resource; little by little, she persuaded the old hag to go home with her. It was after sunset, on St. John's Eve. Petro was lying on the bench lost in forgetfulness and did not notice the visitor come in. But little by little he began to sit up and look at her. All at once he trembled, as though he were on the scaffold; his hair stood on end . . . and he broke into a laugh that cut Pidorka to the heart with terror. "I remember, I remember!" he cried with a fearful joy, and, snatching up an ax, flung it with all his might at the old hag. The ax made a cut two inches deep in the oak door. The hag vanished and a child of about seven in a white shirt, with its head covered, was standing in the middle of the hut. . . . The veil flew off. "Ivas!" cried Pidorka and rushed up to him, but the ghost was covered from head to foot with blood and shed a red light all over the hut. . . . She ran into the outer room in terror, but, recovering herself, wanted to help her brother; in vain! the door had slammed behind her so that she could not open it. Neighbors ran up; they began knocking, broke open the door: not a living soul within! The whole hut was full of smoke, and in the middle where Petro had stood was a heap of ashes from which smoke was still rising. They rushed to the bags: they were full of broken potsherds instead of gold pieces. The Cossacks stood as though rooted to the spot with their mouths open and their eyes starting out of their heads, not daring to move an eyelash, such terror did this miracle cause in them.

What happened afterward I don't remember. Pidorka took a vow to go on a pilgrimage. She gathered together all the goods left her by her father, and a few days later she vanished from the village. No one could say where she had gone. Some old women were so obliging as to declare that she had followed Petro where he had gone; but a Cossack who came from Kiev said he had seen a nun in the convent there, wasted to a skeleton, who never ceased praying, and by every token the villagers recognized her as Pidorka; he told them that no one had ever heard her say a word; that she had come on foot and brought a frame for the icon of the Mother of God with such bright jewels in it that it dazzled everyone who looked at it.

But let me tell you, this was not the end of it all. The very day that the devil carried off Petro, Basavriuk turned up again: but everyone ran away from him. They knew now the kind of bird he was: no one but Satan himself disguised in human form in order to unearth buried treasure; and since unclean hands cannot touch the treasure he entices young men to help him. The same year everyone deserted their old huts and moved into a new village, but even there they had no peace from that cursed Basavriuk. My grandfather's aunt used to say that he was particularly angry with her for having given up her old tavern on the Oposhnyansky Road and did his utmost to get back at her. One day the elders of the village were gathered at her tavern and were conversing according to their rank, as the saying is, at the table, in the middle of which was stood a whole roast ram, and it would be a lie to call it a small one. They chatted of one thing and another; of wonders and strange happenings. And all at once they imagined—and of course it would be nothing if it were only one of them, but they all saw it at once—that the ram raised its head, its sly black eyes gleamed and came to life; it suddenly grew a black bristly mustache and meaningfully twitched it at the company. They all recognized at once in the ram's head the face of Basavriuk; my grandfather's aunt even thought that in another minute he would ask for vodka. . . . The worthy elders picked up their caps and hurried home. Another day, the churchwarden himself, who liked at times a quiet half-hour with the family goblet, had not drained it twice when he saw the goblet bow down to him. "The devil take you!" and he began crossing himself. . . . And at the same time a strange thing happened to his better half: she had only just mixed the dough in a huge tub when suddenly the tub jumped away. "Stop, stop!" But it wouldn't! Its arms akimbo, with dignity the tub danced all over the hut. . . . You may laugh; but it was no laughing matter to our forefathers. And in spite of Father Afanasy's going all over the village with holy water and driving the devil out of every street with the sprinkler, my grandfather's aunt complained for a long time that as soon as evening came on someone knocked on the roof and scratched on the wall.

But there! In this place where our village is located you would think everything was quiet nowadays; but you know it is not so long ago, within my father's memory—and indeed I remember it—that no good man would pass the ruined tavern which the unbaptized tribe[6] repaired long afterward at their own expense. Smoke poured out in clouds from the grimy chimney and, rising so high that one's cap dropped off if one looked at it, scattered hot embers all over the steppe, and the devil—no need to mention him, son of a bitch—used to sob so plaintively in his hole that the frightened birds rose up in flocks from the neighboring forest and scattered with wild cries over the sky.

---

[6] I.e., Jews. (ed.)

A MAY NIGHT
OR
THE DROWNED MAIDEN

The devil only knows what to make of it! If Christian folk begin any task, they fret and fret themselves like dogs after a hare, and all to no purpose; but as soon as the devil comes into it—in a jiffy— lo and behold, the thing's done!

I

GANNA [1]

A resounding song flowed like a river down the streets of the village. It was the hour when, weary from the cares and labors of the day, the boys and girls gather together in a ring in the glow of the clear evening to pour out their gaiety in strains never far removed from melancholy. And the brooding evening dreamily embraced the dark blue sky, making everything seem vague and distant. It was already dusk, yet still the singing did not cease. Levko, a young Cossack, the son of the village mayor,[2] slipped away from the singers with a bandore in his hands. He was wearing an astrakhan cap. The Cossack walked down the street strumming on the strings of

---

[1] Diminutive of Galina, as is Galya. (ed.)
[2] The village head, appointed by Cossack elders. (ed.)

his instrument and dancing to it. At last he stopped quietly before the door of a hut surrounded by low-growing cherry trees. Whose hut was it? Whose door was it? After a few moments of silence, he began playing and singing:

> The sun is low, the evening's near
> Come out to me, my little dear

"No, it seems my bright-eyed beauty is sound asleep," said the Cossack when he had finished the song, and he went nearer to the window. "Galya! Galya, are you asleep, or don't you want to come out to me? You are afraid, I suppose, that someone will see us, or perhaps you don't want to put your fair little face out into the cold? Don't be afraid: there is no one about, and the evening is warm. And if anyone should appear, I will cover you with my jacket, wrap my sash around you, or hide you in my arms—and no one will see us. And if there is a breath of cold, I'll press you warmer to my heart, I'll warm you with my kisses, I'll put my cap over your little white feet. My heart, my little fish, my necklace! Look out for a minute. At least put your little white hand out of the window. . . . No, you are not asleep, proud maiden!" he said more loudly, in the voice of one ashamed at having for a moment demeaned himself; "you are pleased to mock at me; farewell!"

At this point he turned away, thrust his cap rakishly to one side, and walked haughtily away from the window, softly strumming the strings of the bandore. At that moment the wooden handle turned: the door was flung open with a creak, and a girl in her seventeenth spring looked about her timidly, shrouded in the dusk, and, without leaving hold of the handle, stepped over the threshold. Her bright eyes shone with welcome like stars in the semidarkness; her red coral necklace gleamed, and even the modest blush that colored her cheeks could not escape the youth's eagle eye.

"How impatient you are!" she said to him in a low voice. "You are angry already! Why did you choose this time? Crowds of people are strolling up and down the street . . . I keep trembling . . ."

"Oh, do not tremble, my lovely willow! Cling closer to me!" said the boy, putting his arms around her, and casting aside his bandore, which hung on a long strap around his neck, he sat down with her at the door of the hut. "You know it pains me to pass an hour without seeing you."

"Do you know what I am thinking?" the girl broke in, pensively gazing at him. "Something seems to be whispering in my ear that from now on we shall not meet so often. People here are not good: the girls all look so envious, and the boys . . . I even notice that of late my mother has taken to watching me more strictly. I must admit, it was pleasanter for me with strangers."

A look of sadness passed over her face at these last words.

"Only two months at home and already you are weary of it! Perhaps you are tired of me, too?"

"Oh, I am not tired of you," she replied, laughing. "I love you, my black-browed Cossack! I love you because you have brown eyes, and when you look at me with them, it seems as if there is laughter in my heart; and it is gay and happy; because you twitch your black mustache so charmingly, because you walk along the streets singing and playing the bandore, and it's sweet to listen to you."

"Oh, my Galya!" he cried, kissing her and pressing her warmly to his heart.

"Stop! Enough, Levko! Tell me first, have you told your father?"

"Told him what?" he said, as though waking up from sleep. "That I want to marry and that you will be my wife? Yes, I have told him." But the words "I have told him" came despondently from his lips.

"Well?"

"What's one to do with him? He pretended to be deaf, the old rogue, as he always does; he wouldn't hear anything, and then began scolding me for strolling about all over the place, and playing pranks in the streets with the boys. But don't grieve, my Galya! I give you the word of a Cossack that I will get around him."

"Well, you have only to say the word, Levko, and you will have everything your own way. I know that from myself: sometimes I would like not to obey you, but you have only to say a word—and I can't help doing what you want. Look, look!" she went on, laying her head on his shoulder and turning her eyes upward to the warm Ukrainian sky that showed dark blue, unfathomable, through the leafy branches of the cherry trees that were before them. "Look, there; far away, the stars are twinkling, one, two, three, four, five . . . It's the angels of God, opening the windows of their bright dwellings in the sky and looking out at us, isn't it? Yes, Levko! They are looking at our earth, aren't they? If only people

had wings like birds, so they could fly there, high up, high up . . .
Oh, it's dreadful! Not one oak here reaches to the sky. But they
do say there is some tree in a distant land the top of which reaches
right to heaven and that God descends it on the night before Easter
when He comes down to the earth."

"No, Galya, God has a ladder reaching from heaven right down
to earth. The holy archangels put it up before Easter Sunday, and
as soon as God steps on the first rung of it, all the evil spirits fall
headlong and sink in heaps down to hell. And that is why at Easter
there isn't one evil spirit on earth."

"How softly the water murmurs, like a child lying in its cradle!"
Ganna went on, pointing to the pond in its gloomy setting of a
wood of maple trees and weeping willows, whose drooping boughs
dipped into it. Like a feeble old man, it held the dark distant sky
in its cold embrace, covering with its icy kisses the flashing stars,
which gleamed dimly in the warm ocean of the night air as though
they felt the approach of the brilliant sovereign of the night. An
old wooden house lay slumbering with closed shutters on the hill
by the grove of small trees; its roof was covered with moss and
weeds; leafy apple trees grew in all directions under the windows;
the wood, wrapping it in its shade, threw a peculiar gloom over
it; a thicket of nut trees lay at its foot and sloped down to the pond.

"I remember as though it were a dream," said Ganna, not taking
her eyes off him, "long, long ago when I was little and lived with
Mother, they used to tell some dreadful story about that house.
Levko, you must know it, tell it to me. . . ."

"Never mind about it, my darling! The women and silly folk tell
all sorts of stories. You will only upset yourself; you'll be frightened and won't sleep soundly."

"Tell me, tell me, dear black-browed lad!" she said, pressing her
face against his cheek and putting her arm around him. "No, I see
you don't love me; you have some other girl. I won't be frightened; I will sleep peacefully at night. Now I will not sleep if you
don't tell me. I'll be worried and thinking . . . Tell me,
Levko . . . !"

"It seems folk are right when they say that there is a devil of
curiosity in girls, egging them on. Well, listen, then. Long ago, my
little heart, there was a Cossack officer who used to live in that
house. He had a daughter, a fair maiden, white as snow, white as
your little face. His wife had long been dead; he took it into his

head to marry again. 'Will you care for me the same, Father, when you take another wife?' 'Yes, I shall, my daughter, I shall press you to my heart more warmly than ever! I shall, my daughter. I shall give you earrings and necklaces brighter than ever!'

"The father brought his young wife to her new home. The new wife was fair of face. All pink and white was the young wife; only she gave her stepdaughter such a terrible look that the girl uttered a shriek when she saw her, and the harsh stepmother did not say a word to her all day. Night came on. The father went with his young wife to his sleeping chamber, and the fair maiden shut herself up in her little room. She felt sad at heart and began to weep. She looked around, and a terrifying black cat was stealing up to her; there were sparks in its fur and its steely claws scratched on the floor. In terror she jumped on a bench; the cat followed her. She jumped on the oven step and the cat jumped after her, then suddenly leaped on her neck and was stifling her. Tearing herself away with a shriek, she flung it on the floor. Again the monstrous cat stole up. She was overcome with terror. Her father's sword was hanging on the wall. She snatched it up and brought it down with a crash on the floor; one paw with its steely claws flew off, and the squealing cat disappeared into a dark corner. All day the young wife did not come out of her room; on the third day she came out with her arm bandaged. The poor maiden guessed that her stepmother was a witch and that she had cut off her hand. On the fourth day the father bade his daughter fetch the water, sweep the house like a humble peasant girl, and not show herself in her father's rooms. It was a hard lot for the poor girl, but there was nothing she could do; she obeyed her father's will. On the fifth day the father turned his daughter, barefoot, out of the house and did not give her a bit of bread to take with her. Only then did the maiden begin sobbing, hiding her white face in her hands. 'You have sent your own daughter to perish, Father! The witch has ruined your sinful soul! God forgive you; and it seems it is not His will that I should live in this fair world. . . .' And over there, do you see . . . ?" At this point Levko turned to Ganna, pointing toward the house. "Look this way, there, on the very highest part of the bank! From that bank the maiden threw herself into the water. And from that hour she was seen no more. . . ."

"And the witch?" Ganna asked in a frightened voice, fastening her tearful eyes on him.

"The witch? The old women insist that ever since then all the maidens drowned in the pond have come out on moonlight nights into that garden to warm themselves, and the officer's daughter is leader among them. One night she saw her stepmother beside the pond; she pounced upon her and with a shriek dragged her into the water. But the witch saved herself even then: she changed under water into one of the drowned girls, and so escaped the scourge of green reeds with which the maidens meant to beat her. Trust a woman! They say, too, that the maiden assembles all the drowned girls every night and looks into the face of each, trying to discover the witch, but has not yet found her. And if she comes across any living man she makes him guess which it is: or else she threatens to drown him in the water. So, my Galya, that's how old people tell the story! . . . The present master wants to set up a distillery there and has sent a distiller here to see to it . . . But, I hear voices. It's our fellows coming back from singing. Good night, Galya! Sleep well and don't think about these old women's tales."

Saying this, he embraced her warmly, kissed her, and walked away.

"Good night, Levko," said Ganna, gazing dreamily at the dark wood.

At that moment a huge fiery moon began majestically rising from the earth. Half of it was still below the horizon, yet all the world was already flooded with its sublime light. The pond was covered with gleaming ripples. The shadow of the trees began to stand out clearly against the dark green grass.

"Good night, Ganna!" The words uttered behind her were accompanied by a kiss.

"You have come back," she said, looking around, but seeing a boy she did not know, she turned away.

"Good night, Ganna!" she heard again, and again she felt a kiss on her cheek.

"The Evil One has brought another!" she said angrily.

"Good night, dear Ganna!"

"That's the third one!"

"Good night, good night, good night, Ganna," and kisses were showered upon her from all sides.

"Why, there is a whole gang of them!" cried Ganna, tearing herself away from the crowd of boys, who fought with each other in trying to embrace her. "It is amazing that they are not sick of this eternal kissing! I swear that one won't be able to show oneself in the street soon!"

The door slammed upon these words and nothing more was heard but the iron bolt squeaking in its socket.

II

THE MAYOR

Do you know the Ukrainian night? Aie, you do not know the Ukrainian night! Look at it: the moon looks out from the center of the sky; the immense dome of heaven stretches further, more inconceivably immense than ever; it glows and breathes; the earth is all bathed in a silvery light; and the exquisite air is refreshing and warm and full of languor, and an ocean of fragrance is stirring. Heavenly night! Enchanting night! The woods stand motionless, mysterious, full of gloom, and cast huge shadows. Calm and still lie the ponds. The cold and darkness of their waters are walled in by the dark green gardens. The virginal thickets of wild cherry timidly stretch their roots into the cold of the water and from time to time murmur in their leaves, as though angry and indignant when the sweet rogue—the night wind—steals up suddenly and kisses them. All the countryside is sleeping. But overhead all is breathing; all is marvelous, triumphal. And the soul is full of the immensity and the marvel; and silvery visions rise up in harmonious multitudes from its depths. Divine night! Enchanting night! And suddenly it all springs into life: the woods, the ponds, and the stones. The glorious clamor of the Ukrainian nightingale bursts upon the night and one fancies the moon itself is listening in mid-heaven. . . . The hamlet on the upland sleeps as though spellbound. The groups of huts gleam whiter, fairer than ever in the moonlight; their low walls stand out more dazzlingly in the darkness. The singing has ceased. All is still. God-fearing people are asleep. Only here and there is a light in the narrow windows. Here and there before the doorway of a hut a family is still at supper.

"But that's not the way to dance the *gopak*. I feel that it won't be right somehow. What was that my crony was saying . . . ? Oh yes: hop, tra-la! hop, hop, hop!" So a middle-aged peasant, who had been drinking and was dancing down the street, talked to himself. "I swear, that's not the way to dance the *gopak*. Why should I tell a lie about it? I swear it's not right. Come: hop, tra-la! hop, tra-la! hop, hop, hop!"

"There's a man tipsy! And it's not as though it were a young man, but it's an old fool. It's enough to make the children laugh. Dancing in the street at night!" cried an elderly woman who passed by, carrying an armful of straw. "Go to your home! You ought to have been asleep long ago!"

"I am going," said the peasant, stopping. "I am going. I don't care about any mayor. He thinks (may the devil beat his father) that because he is the mayor, because he pours cold water over folks in the frost, he can turn up his nose at everyone! Mayor indeed! I am my own mayor. God strike me dead! Strike me dead, God! I am my own mayor. That's how it is and will remain," he went on, and going up to the first hut he reached and standing before the window, he passed his fingers over the windowpane and tried to find the door handle. "Wife, open! Look alive, I tell you, open! It's time the Cossack was asleep!"

"Where are you going, Kalenik? You are at somebody else's hut," some girls on their way home from the merry singing shouted from behind him, laughing. "Shall we show you where you live?"

"Show me the way, kind fair maidens!"

"Fair maidens! Do you hear," said one of them, "how polite Kalenik is? We must show him the way to his hut for that . . . but no, you dance on in front."

"Dance . . . ? Ah, you sneaky girls!" Kalenik drawled, laughing and shaking his finger at them, and he lurched forward because his legs were not steady enough to stand still. "Come, give me a kiss. I'll kiss you all, every one of you . . . !" And with staggering steps he fell to running after them. The girls shrieked and huddled together; then, growing bolder, ran over to the other side of the street, seeing that Kalenik was not very quick on his feet.

"There is your hut!" they shouted to him, pointing, as they walked away, to a hut, much larger than his own, which belonged to the mayor of the village. Kalenik obediently turned in that direction, beginning to curse the mayor again.

But who was this mayor who aroused such abuse and criticism? Oh, he was an important person in the village. While Kalenik is on his way we shall certainly have time to say something about this mayor. All the villagers took off their caps when they saw him, and the girls, even the youngest, wished him good day. Which of the young men would not have liked to be mayor? He was free to help himself to everyone's snuff, and the sturdy peasant would stand respectfully, cap in hand, all the time while the mayor fumbled with his fat, coarse fingers in the peasant's birchbark snuffbox. At the village council, although his power was limited to a few votes, he always took the upper hand and almost on his own authority sent whom he pleased to level and repair the roads or dig the ditches. He was austere, forbidding of aspect, and not fond of wasting words. Very long ago when the great Czarina Catherine, of blessed memory, was going to the Crimea, he had been chosen to act as a guide. For two whole days he had performed this duty, and had even been deemed worthy to sit on the box beside the Czarina's coachman. It was from that time that he had taken to bowing his head with a dignified and meditative air, to stroking his long, drooping mustaches, and to shooting hawklike glances from under his brows. And from that time, too, whatever subject was broached, the mayor always cleverly turned the conversation to the way in which he had guided the Czarina, and sat on the box of the Czarina's carriage. He liked at times to pretend to be deaf, especially when he heard something that he did not want to hear. He could not endure ostentation: he always wore a long coat of black homespun cloth, always with a colored woolen sash around his waist, and no one had ever seen him in any other costume, except on the occasion of the Czarina's visit to the Crimea, when he wore a dark blue Cossack coat. But hardly anyone in the village can remember that time; he still kept that one locked up in a chest. He was a widower, but he had living in the house with him his sister-in-law, who cooked the dinner and the supper, washed the benches, whitewashed the hut, wove him shirts, and looked after the house. They did say in the village that she was not his sister-in-law at all, but we have seen already that there were many who bore no good will to the mayor and were glad to circulate any scandal about him. Though, perhaps, what did lend credence to the story was the fact that the sister-in-law was displeased if he went out into a field that was full of girls reaping, or visited a Cossack who had a young daughter. The mayor had but one eye, but that eye was a shrewd villain and could see a pretty girl a long way off. He does not, however, fix it upon a bewitching face before he has taken a good look around to see whether his sister-in-law is watching him. But we have said almost all that we need about the mayor, while tipsy Kalenik was on his way there, still continuing to bestow on him the choicest epithets his slow and clumsy tongue could utter.

III

AN UNEXPECTED RIVAL

A Plot

"No, lads, no, I won't! What pranks you are up to! I wonder you are not sick of mischief. Goodness knows, people call us rogues frequently enough as is. You had better go to bed!" So said Levko to his rollicking companions who were persuading him to join in some new pranks. "Good night to you!" and with rapid steps Levko walked away from them down the street.

"Is my bright-eyed Ganna asleep?" he wondered, as he approached the hut with the cherry trees we've already described. Subdued voices could be heard in the stillness. Levko stood still. He could see the whiteness of a shirt through the trees. . . . "What does it mean?" he wondered, and stealing up a little nearer, hid behind a tree. The face of the girl who stood before him gleamed in the moonlight. . . . It was Ganna! But who was the tall man standing with his back toward him? In vain he gazed at him; the shadow covered him from head to foot. Only a little light fell upon him in front, but the slightest step forward would have exposed Levko to the unpleasant risk of being discovered. Quietly leaning against the tree, he resolved to remain where he was. The girl distinctly pronounced his name.

"Levko? Levko is still nursing," the tall man said huskily and in a low voice. "If I ever meet him here, I'll pull his forelock."

"I should like to know what scoundrel it is, boasting that he will pull me by my forelock!" murmured Levko softly, and he craned his neck, trying not to miss one word. But the intruder went on speaking so softly that he could not hear what was said.

"I am surprised that you are not ashamed!" said Ganna, when he had finished speaking. "You are lying, you are deceiving me; you don't love me; I shall never believe that you love me."

"I know," the tall man went on, "Levko has talked a lot of nonsense to you and has turned your head." (At this point the boy felt that the voice was not really unknown to him; it seemed as though he had heard it before.) "I'll show Levko what I am made of!" the voice went on in the same way. "He thinks I don't see all his malicious tricks. He shall find out, the young dog, what my fists are like!"

At those words, Levko could not restrain his rage. Taking three steps toward him, he swung his fist to give him a clout on the ear, which might have sent him flying for all his apparent strength; but at that instant the moonlight fell on his face, and Levko was stupefied to see standing before him—his father. An unconscious jerk of the head and a faint whistle were the only expression of his amazement. A rustle was heard. Ganna hurriedly flew into the hut, slamming the door after her.

"Good night, Ganna!" one of the boys cried at that moment, stealing up and putting his arm around the mayor, and skipped back with horror, meeting his stiff mustache.

"Good night, my beauty!" cried another; but this one was sent flying by a violent push from the mayor.

"Good night, good night, Ganna!" called several young men, hanging on his neck.

"Be off, you cursed hooligans!" cried the mayor, pushing them off and kicking them. "Ganna indeed! Go and be hanged like your fathers, you children from hell! They come around one like flies after honey! I'll teach you . . . !"

"The mayor, the mayor, it's the mayor!" shouted the young men and scattered in all directions.

"Aha, Father!" said Levko, recovering from his amazement and looking after the mayor as he walked away swearing. "So these are the tricks you are up to! A fine thing! And I have been brooding and wondering what was the meaning of his always pretending to be deaf when one begins speaking about it. Wait a moment, you old dog, I'll teach you to hang about under young girls' windows. I'll teach you to lure away other men's sweethearts! Hey, fellows! Come here, come here, this way!" he shouted, waving his hands to the boys who had gathered into a group again. "Come here! I advised you to go to bed, but now I have changed my mind and am ready to have fun with you."

"That's the way to talk!" said a stout, broad-shouldered fellow who was reckoned the merriest and most mischievous in the village. "It always makes me sick when we can't manage to have a decent bit of fun and play some prank. I always feel as though I had missed something, as though I had lost my cap or my pipe; not like a Cossack, in fact."

"What do you say to our giving the mayor a good going over?"

"The mayor?"

"Yes. What does he think he's doing? He rules us as though he were a Hetman.[3] He is not satisfied with treating us as though we were his serfs, but he has to go after our girls, too. I do believe there is not a nice-looking girl in the whole village that he has not tried to seduce."

"That's true, that's true!" they all shouted together.

"What's wrong with us, fellows? Aren't we the same sort as he is? Thank God, we are free Cossacks! [4] Let us show him that we are free Cossacks!"

"We'll show him," they shouted. "And if we give the devil to the mayor, we won't spare his clerk either!"

"We won't spare the clerk! And I have just made up a splendid song, it's the very thing for him. Come along, I will teach it to you," Levko went on, striking the strings of his bandore. "Dress up in anything at hand!"

"Come on, brave Cossacks!" said the sturdy rogue, striking his feet together and clapping his hands. "How glorious! What fun! When you join in the fun you feel as though you were celebrating bygone years. Your heart is light and free and your soul might be in paradise. Hey, fellows! Hey, now for some fun . . . !"

And the crowd moved noisily down the street, and God-fearing old women, awakened from their sleep by the shouts, pulled up their windows and crossed themselves with drowsy hands, saying: "Well, the boys are enjoying themselves now!"

IV

THE YOUNG MEN MAKE MERRY

Only one hut at the end of the village was still lighted up. It was the mayor's. He had finished his supper long ago, and would no doubt have been asleep by this time, but he had a visitor, the man

---

[3] Headman of the Cossacks appointed by the Poles. (ed.)

[4] In Czarist Russia the Cossacks were politically independent. They were not subjected to serfdom. (ed.)

who had been sent to set up a distillery by the landowner who had a small piece of land among the free Cossacks. The visitor, a short, fat little man with little eyes that were always laughing and seeming to express the pleasure he took in smoking, sat in the place of honor under the icons, continually spitting and catching with his fingers the tobacco ash that kept dropping out of his short pipe. Clouds of smoke were spreading rapidly over him and enveloping him in a gray-blue fog. It seemed as though a big chimney of some distillery, weary of sitting on its roof, had thought it would like a change, and was sitting decorously in the mayor's hut. Short thick mustaches stuck out below his nose; but they so indistinctly appeared and disappeared in the smoky atmosphere that they seemed like a mouse that the distiller, infringing the monopoly of the granary cat, had caught and held in his mouth. The mayor, being in his own house, was sitting in his shirt and linen trousers. His eagle eye was beginning little by little to close and grow dim like the setting sun. One of the village constables who made up the mayor's staff was smoking a pipe at the end of the table, and out of respect to his host still kept on his coat.

"Are you thinking of setting up your distillery soon?" the mayor asked, addressing the distiller and making the sign of the cross over his mouth as he yawned.

"With God's help, I bet you that by fall Mr. Mayor will be walking zigzag down the road, dragging his feet."

As he uttered these words, the distiller's eyes disappeared; where they had been were wrinkles stretched to his ears; his whole frame began to quiver with laughter, and for an instant his mirthful lips abandoned the pipe that belched forth clouds of smoke.

"Please God I may," said his host, twisting his face into something that looked like a smile. "Now, thank God, distilleries are doing better. But years ago, when I was guiding the Czarina by the Pereyaslav Road, Bezborodko, now deceased . . ."

"Well, old friend, that was a time! In those days there were only two distilleries all the way from Kremenchug to Romny. But now . . . have you heard what the damned Germans are going to do? They say that instead of burning wood in distilleries like all decent Christians, they are soon going to use some kind of devilish steam. . . ." As he said this the distiller looked thoughtfully at the table and at his hands lying on it. "How it is done with steam—I swear, I don't know!"

"What fools they are, those Germans, God forgive me!" said the mayor. "I'd give them hell, the bunch of bastards! Did anyone ever hear the like of boiling anything by steam? According to that, you couldn't take a spoonful of soup without boiling your lips like a young sucking pig."

"And you, friend," the sister-in-law, who was sitting on the bed with her feet tucked under her, interrupted, "are you going to stay with us all that time without your wife?"

"Why, what do I want with her? It would be different if she were something worth having."

"Isn't she good-looking?" asked the mayor, fixing his eye upon him.

"Good-looking, indeed! Old as the devil. Her face all wrinkles like an empty purse." And the stubby frame of the distiller shook with laughter again.

At that moment something began fumbling at the door; the door opened—and a peasant crossed the threshold without taking off his cap, and stood in the middle of the hut as though in hesitation, gaping and staring at the ceiling. This was our friend Kalenik.

"Here I am home at last," he said, sitting down on the bench near the door, and taking no notice of the company present. "God, how that damned devil lengthened the road! You go on and on, and no end to it! I feel as though someone had broken my legs. Woman, get the sheepskin to put down for me. I am not coming up beside you on the stove, that I am not, my legs ache! Get it, it's lying there under the icons; only mind you don't upset the pot with the snuff. Or no, don't touch it, don't touch it! Maybe you are drunk today . . . Let me get it myself."

Kalenik tried to get up, but an overpowering force riveted him to his seat.

"I like that," said the mayor. "Walks into another man's home and gives orders as though he were at his own place. Throw him out on his rear end!"

"Let him stay and rest, friend!" said the distiller, holding him back by the arm. "He is a useful man; if there were more folk like him, our distillery would do well. . . ."

It was not kindness, however, that dictated this remark. The distiller believed in omens of all sorts, and to turn a man out who had already sat down on the bench would have meant provoking misfortune.

"It seems as though age is creeping up on me . . ." muttered Kalenik, lying down on the bench. "It would be all right if I were drunk, but I am not drunk. No, indeed, I am not drunk. Why tell a lie about it? I am ready to tell the mayor himself so. What do I care for the mayor. May he choke, the son of a bitch! I spit on him. I wish a wagon would run over him, the one-eyed devil! Why does he drench people in the frost?"

"Aha, the pig has made its way into the hut, and is putting its feet on the table," said the mayor, wrathfully rising from his seat; but at that moment a heavy stone, smashing the window to fragments, fell at their feet. He stopped short. "If I knew," he said, picking up the stone, "if I knew what jailbird flung that stone, I'd teach him to throw stones! What devilry!" he went on, looking with angry eyes at the stone in his hand. "May he choke with this stone . . . !"

"Stop, stop, God preserve you, friend!" cried the distiller, turning pale. "God preserve you in this world and the next from blessing anyone with such abuse!"

"Here's a protector! Damn him!"

"Think nothing of it, friend! I suppose you don't know what happened to my late mother-in-law?"

"Your mother-in-law?"

"Yes, my mother-in-law. One evening, a little earlier than it is now, they sat down to supper: my mother-in-law and father-in-law and their hired man and their hired girl and their five children. My mother-in-law shook some dumplings out of a big cauldron into a bowl to cool them. They were all hungry after their work and did not want to wait for the dumplings to get cool. Picking them up on long wooden skewers, they began eating them. All at once a man appeared: where he came from no one can say; who he was, God only knows. He asks them to let him sit down to the table. Well, there is no refusing a hungry man food. They gave him a skewer, too. Only the visitor stowed away the dumplings like a cow eating hay. While the others had eaten one each, and were prodding after more with their skewers, the bowl was as clean as a gentleman's floor. My mother-in-law put out some more; she thought the visitor had had enough and would take less. Nothing of the sort: he began gulping them down faster than ever and emptied the second bowl. "And may you choke with the dumplings!" thought my hungry mother-in-law, when all of a sudden the man choked and fell on the floor. They rushed up to him, but the spirit had departed. He had choked."

"And serve him right, the damned glutton!" said the mayor.

"Quite so, but it didn't end with that: from that time on my mother-in-law had no peace. As soon as night came the dead man rose from the dead. He sat straddling the chimney, the cursed fellow, holding a dumpling in his teeth. In the daytime all was quiet and they didn't hear a sound from him, but as soon as it began to get dusk, look at the roof and there you would see him, straddling the chimney, the son of a bitch."

"And a dumpling in his teeth?"

"And a dumpling in his teeth."

"How marvelous, friend! I had heard something of the sort about your mother-in-law—"

The speaker stopped short. Under the window they heard an uproar and the sound of dancing feet. First there was the soft strumming of the bandore strings, then a voice joined in. The strings twanged more loudly, several voices joined in, and the singing rose up like a whirlwind.

> Boys, have you heard the news now!
> Mayors it seems are none too sound!
> Our one-eyed mayor's a barrelhead
> Whose staves have come unbound!
> Come, cooper, knock upon it hard,
> And bind with hoops of steel!
> Come hammer, cooper, on the head
> And hit with right good will!
> Our mayor is gray and has one eye;
> Old as sin, and what a blockhead!
> Full of whims and lewd fancies;
> Flatters the girls . . . the blockhead!
> You must try to ape the young ones!
> When you should be in your coffin,
> Flung in by the scruff and whiskers!
> By the forelock you're so proud of!

"A fine song, friend!" said the distiller, inclining his head a little to one side and turning toward his host, who was struck dumb with amazement at such insolence. "Fine! it's only a pity that they refer to the mayor in rather disrespectful terms. . . ."

And again he put his hands on the table with a sort of gleeful delight in his eyes, preparing himself to hear more, for from below came peals of laughter and shouts of "Again! again!" However, a penetrating eye could have seen at once that it was not astonishment that kept the mayor from moving. An old experienced cat will sometimes in the same way let an inexperienced mouse run around his tail while he is rapidly making a plan to cut off its way back to its hole. The mayor's solitary eye was still fixed on the window, and already his hand, after gesturing to the constable, was on the wooden door-handle, when all at once a shout rose from the street. . . . The distiller, curiosity being one of his characteristics, hurriedly filled his pipe and ran out into the street; but the rogues had already scattered in all directions.

"No, you won't get away from me!" cried the mayor, dragging a man in a black sheepskin, put on inside out, by the arm. The distiller, seizing the opportunity, ran to have a look at this disturber of the peace, but he staggered back in alarm at seeing a long beard and a horribly colored face. "No, you won't escape me!" shouted the mayor, still dragging his captive into the outer room. The prisoner offered no resistance but followed quietly, as though he were going to his own hut. "Karpo, open the storeroom!" said the mayor to the constable; "we'll put him in the dark storeroom. And then we will wake the clerk, get the constables together, catch all these hooligans, and today we will pass judgment on them all."

The constable clanked a small padlock in the outer room and opened the storeroom. At that instant his captive, taking advantage of the dark storeroom, wrenched himself out of his hands with a violent effort.

"Where are you off to?" cried the mayor, clutching him more tightly than ever by the collar.

"Let's go, it's me!" cried a thin shrill voice.

"That won't help you, that won't help you, my boy. You may squeal like a devil, as well as a woman, you won't fool me," and he shoved him into the dark storeroom, so that the poor prisoner uttered a moan as he fell on the floor, while, accompanied by the constable and followed by the distiller, puffing like a steamer, the mayor went off to the clerk's hut.

They walked along all three with their eyes on the ground, lost in meditation, when, turning into a dark lane, all of them at once uttered a shriek, from a violent bang on their foreheads, and a similar cry of pain echoed in response. The mayor, screwing up his eye, saw with surprise the clerk and two constables.

"I was coming to see you, worthy clerk!"

"And I was coming to your worship, honored mayor."

"Strange things have been happening, worthy clerk."

"Very strange things, honored mayor!"

"Why, what?"

"The boys have gone crazy! They are behaving disgracefully in the street, whole gangs of them. They describe your honor in language . . . I should be ashamed to repeat it. A drunken soldier couldn't bring his dirty tongue to utter such words." (All this the lanky clerk, in striped linen breeches and a vest the color of wine dregs, accompanied by craning his neck forward and dragging it back again to its former position.) "I had just dropped into a doze, when the cursed rogues roused me from my bed with their indecent songs and racket! I meant to take stern measures with them, but while I was putting on my breeches and vest they all ran away in different directions. The ringleader did not get away, though. He is singing now in the hut where we keep criminals. I was eager to find out what bird it was we'd caught, but his face is all sooty like the devils who forge nails for sinners."

"And how is he dressed, worthy clerk?"

"In a black sheepskin put on inside out, the bastard, honored mayor."

"Aren't you lying, clerk? What if that rascal is sitting now in my storeroom?"

"No, honored mayor! You yourself, not in anger be it said, are a little in error!"

"Give me a light! We will have a look at him!"

The light was brought, the door unlocked, and the mayor uttered a groan of amazement when he saw his sister-in-law facing him!

"Tell me, please," with these words she pounced upon him, "have you lost what little wits you ever had? Was there a grain of sense in your thick head, you one-eyed fool, when you pushed me into the dark storeroom? It was lucky I did not hit my head against the iron hook. Didn't I scream out to you that it was me? This damned bear seizes me in his iron paws and shoves me in! May the devils treat you the same in the other world . . . !"

The last words were uttered in the street, where she had gone for some purpose of her own.

"Yes, I see that it's you," said the mayor, recovering his wits.

"What do you say, worthy clerk? Isn't this a cunning rogue?"

"He is a cunning rogue, honored mayor."

"Isn't it high time that we gave all these rascals a good lesson and set them to work?"

"It's high time, high time, honored mayor!"

"They have taken it into their heads, the fools . . . What the devil? I thought I heard my sister-in-law scream in the street. . . . They have taken it into their heads, the fools, that they are as good as I am. They think I am one of them, a simple Cossack! . . ." The little cough that followed this, and the way he looked around from under his brows indicated that the mayor was about to speak of something important. "In the year eighteen . . . I never can remember these damned dates—Ledachy, who was then commissar, was given orders to pick out from the Cossacks the most intelligent of them all. Aie!" (that "Aie!" he pronounced with his finger in the air) "the most intelligent! to act as guide to the Czarina. At that time I . . ."

"Why tell us? We all know that, honored mayor! We all know how you won the royal favor. Admit now that I was right. You took a sin upon your soul when you said that you had caught that rogue in the black sheepskin."

"Well, as for that devil in the black sheepskin, we'll put him in chains and punish him severely as an example to others! Let him know what authority means! By whom is the mayor appointed if not by the Czar? Then we'll get hold of the other fellows: I have not forgotten how the confounded hooligans drove a herd of pigs into my vegetable garden that ate up all my cabbages and cucumbers; I have not forgotten how the sons of bitches refused to thrash my grain; I have not forgotten . . . But plague take them, I must find out who that rascal is wearing a sheepskin inside out."

"He's a wily bird, it seems!" said the distiller, whose cheeks during the whole of this conversation were continually being charged with smoke, like a siege cannon, and whose lips, abandoning the short pipe, were ejecting a perfect fountain of smoke. "It wouldn't be amiss, anyway, to keep the fellow for working in the distillery; or better still, hang him from the top of an oak tree like a church candlestick."

Such a witticism did not seem quite foolish to the distiller, and he at once decided, without waiting for the approval of the others, to reward himself with a husky laugh.

At that moment they drew near a small hut that had almost sunk into the earth. Our friends' curiosity grew keener: they all crowded around the door. The clerk took out a key and jingled it about the lock; but it was the key to his chest. Their impatience became acute. Thrusting his hand into his pocket he began fumbling for it, and swearing because he could not find it.

"Here!" he said at last, bending down and taking it from the depths of the roomy pocket with which his full striped trousers were provided.

At that word the hearts of all our heroes merged into one, and that one giant heart beat so violently that the sound of its uneven throb was not lost despite the creaking of the lock. The door was opened, and . . . the mayor turned white as a sheet, the distiller was aware of a cold chill, and the hair of his head seemed rising up toward heaven; horror was depicted on the face of the clerk; the constables were rooted to the spot, and were incapable of closing their mouths, which had fallen open simultaneously: before them stood the sister-in-law.

No less amazed than they, she, however, pulled herself together, and made a movement as though to approach them.

"Stop!" cried the mayor in a wild voice, and slammed the door in her face. "Gentlemen, it is Satan!" he went on. "A light! quick, a light! I won't spare the hut, though it is Crown property. Set fire to it, set fire to it, so that the devil's bones may not be left on earth!"

The sister-in-law screamed in terror, hearing this sinister decision through the door.

"What are you doing, friends!" said the distiller. "Your hair, thank God, is almost white, but you have not gained sense yet: a witch won't burn with ordinary fire! Only a light from a pipe can burn one of these creatures! Wait, I will manage it in a minute!"

Saying this, he scattered some burning ash out of his pipe on a wisp of straw, and began blowing on it. The poor sister-in-law was meanwhile overwhelmed with despair; she began loudly imploring and beseeching them.

"Stop, friends! Why take a sin upon us in vain? Perhaps it is not Satan!" said the clerk. "If it, whatever it may be that is sitting there, consents to make the sign of the cross, that's a sure token that it is not a devil."

The proposition was approved.

"Get thee behind me, Satan!" said the clerk, putting his lips to the keyhole. "If you don't stir from your place we will open the door."

The door was opened.

"Cross yourself!" said the mayor, looking behind him as though scouting for a safe place in case of retreat.

The sister-in-law crossed herself.

"The devil! it really is my sister-in-law! What evil spirit dragged you to this hole?"

And the sister-in-law, sobbing, told them that the boys had seized her in the street and, in spite of her resistance, had forced her in at the wide window of the hut and had nailed up the shutter. The clerk looked: the staples of the broad shutter had been pulled out, and it was only attached by a board at the top.

"All right, you one-eyed bastard!" she screamed, stepping up to the mayor, who staggered back and still scanned her with his solitary eye. "I know your plan. You would have been glad to do me in, to be free to run after the girls, to have no one see the gray-headed old grandad playing the fool. You think I don't know what you were saying this evening to Ganna? Oh, I know all about it. It's hard to deceive me, let alone for a blockhead like you. I am long-suffering, but when I do lose patience, you'll have something to put up with."

Saying this, she shook her fist at him and walked away quickly, leaving him completely stupefied.

"Well, Satan has certainly had a hand in it this time," he thought, scratching his head vigorously.

"We've caught him," cried the constables, coming in at that instant.

"Caught whom?" asked the mayor.

"The devil with his sheepskin inside out."

"Bring him here!" shouted the mayor, seizing the prisoner by the arm. "You are mad! this is the drunkard, Kalenik."

"What a strange thing! We had him in our hands, honored mayor!" answered the constables. "The confounded boys came around us in the lane, began dancing and capering, tugging at us, putting out their tongues and snatching him out of our hands . . . Damnation take it! . . . And how we hit on this crow instead of him, the devil only knows!"

"By my authority and that of all the members of the parish council, the command is given," said the mayor, "to catch that rascal this minute, and in the same way all whom you find in the street, and to bring them to me to be questioned!"

"Upon my word, honored mayor . . . !" cried some of them, bowing down to his feet. "You should have seen those ugly faces; we have been born and been christened but strike us dead if we have ever seen such horrid faces. Trouble may come of it, honored mayor. They may give a simple man such a fright that there isn't a woman in the place who would undertake to cure him of his panic."

"Panic, indeed! Why? Are you refusing to obey? I expect you are hand in glove with them! You are mutinying! What's this . . . ! What's the meaning of it . . . ? You are getting up a rebellion . . . ! You . . . you . . . I'll report it to the commissar. This minute, do you hear, this minute! Run, fly like a bird! I'll show you . . . you'll show me . . ."

They all ran off in different directions.

V

THE DROWNED MAIDEN

The instigator of all this turmoil, undisturbed by anything and untroubled by the search parties that were being sent in all directions, walked slowly toward the old house and the pond. I think that I need hardly say that it was Levko. His black sheepskin was unbuttoned; he held his cap in his hand; the sweat ran down his face in streams. The maple wood stood majestic and gloomily black, only sprinkled with delicate silver on the side facing the moon. A refreshing coolness from the motionless pond breathed on the tired wanderer and lured him to rest for a while on the bank. All was still. The only sound was the trilling of the nightingale in the deepest recesses of the wood. An overpowering drowsiness soon made his eyes close; his tired limbs were about to sink into sleep and forgetfulness; his head drooped. . . . "No, if I go on like this I'll fall asleep here!" he said, getting to his feet and rubbing his eyes.

He looked around and the night seemed even more brilliant. A strange enchanting radiance was mingled with the light of the moon. He had never seen anything like it before. A silvery mist had fallen over everything around him. The fragrance of the apple blossom and the night-scented flowers flooded the whole earth. He gazed in awe at the motionless water of the pond: the old manor house, reflected in the water, was distinct and looked serenely dignified. Instead of gloomy shutters there were bright glass windows and doors. There was a glitter of gilt through the clean panes. And then it seemed as though a window opened. Holding his breath, not stirring, nor taking his eyes from the pond, he seemed to pass into its depths and saw—first, a white elbow appeared in the window; then a charming little head, with sparkling eyes softly shining through her dark brown locks, peeped out and rested on the elbow, and he saw her slightly nod her head. She beckoned, she smiled . . . His heart suddenly began throbbing . . . The water quivered and the window was closed again. He moved slowly away from the pond and looked at the house; the gloomy shutters were open; the windowpanes gleamed in the moonlight. "See how little one can trust what people say," he thought to himself. "It's a new house; the paint is as fresh as though it had been painted today. Someone is living there." And in silence he went up closer to it, but all was quiet in the house. The glorious singing of the nightingales rang out loud and melodious, and when it seemed to die away, there was heard the rustle and churr of the grasshoppers, or the deep note of some marsh bird, striking his slippery beak on the broad mirror of the water. There was a sense of sweet stillness and space and freedom in Levko's heart. Tuning his bandore, he began playing it and singing:

> Oh, thou moon, my darling moon!
>   And thou, glowing clear sunrise!
> Oh, shine brightly o'er the hut
>   Where my lovely maiden lies!

The window slowly opened and the head whose reflection he had seen in the pond looked out, listening intently to the song. Her long eyelashes half hid her eyes. She was white all over, like a sheet, like the moonlight. How exquisite, how lovely! She laughed . . . ! Levko started.

"Sing me a song, young Cossack!" she said softly, bending her head on one side and veiling her eyes completely with her thick eyelashes.

"What song shall I sing you, my fair lady?"

Tears rolled slowly down her pale face. "Youth," she said, and there was something inexpressibly touching in her speech. "Youth, find me my stepmother! I will grudge you nothing. I will reward you. I will reward you richly, sumptuously. I have sleeves embroidered with silk, corals, necklaces. I will give you a girdle adorned with pearls. I have gold. Youth, find me my stepmother! She is a terrible witch. I had no peace in life because of her. She tormented me, she made me work like a simple peasant girl. Look at my face. With her foul spells she drew the roses from my cheeks. Look at my white neck: they will not wash off, they will not wash off, they never will be washed away, those dark blue marks left by her claws of steel! Look at my white feet: far have they trodden, not on carpets only, but on the hot sand, on the damp earth, on sharp thorns have they trodden! And at my eyes, look at my eyes: they have grown dim with weeping! Find her, youth, find me my stepmother . . . !"

Her voice, which had risen, sank into silence. Tears streamed down her pale face. The young man's heart was oppressed by a painful feeling of pity and sadness.

"I am ready to do anything for you, my fair lady!" he said with heartfelt emotion, "but how can I, where can I find her?"

"Look, look!" she said quickly, "she is here, she is on the bank, playing games among my maidens, bathing herself in the moonlight. She is sly and cunning, she has taken the form of a drowned maiden; but I know, I feel that she is here. I am oppressed, I am stifled by her. I cannot swim lightly and easily like a fish, because of her. I drown and sink to the bottom like a stone. Find her, youth!"

Levko looked toward the bank: in the delicate silvery mist there were maidens flitting, light as shadows, in smocks white as a meadow dotted with lilies-of-the-valley; gold necklaces, strings of beads, coins glittered on their necks; but they were pale; their bodies looked as though molded out of transparent clouds, and it seemed as though the moonlight shone through them. The maidens, singing and playing, drew nearer to him. He heard their voices.

"Let us play hawk and chickens," they murmured like river reeds kissed by the ethereal lips of the wind at the quiet hour of twilight.

"Who will be the hawk?"

They cast lots, and one of the girls stepped out of the group. Levko looked at her carefully. Her face, her dress, all was exactly like the rest. The only thing he noticed was that she did not enjoy playing her part. The group drew out in a chain; it raced rapidly away from the pursuit of the bird of prey.

"No, I don't want to be the hawk," said the maiden, weary and exhausted. "I am sorry to snatch the chickens from their poor mother."

"You are not the witch!" thought Levko.

"Who will be hawk?" The maidens made ready to cast lots again.

"I will be hawk!" One in the center of the group volunteered.

Levko began looking intently at her face. Boldly and swiftly she pursued the chain, and darted from side to side to capture her victim. At that point Levko noticed that her body was not so translucent as the others; something black could be seen in the inside. Suddenly there was shrieking; the hawk had pounced on one of the chain, seized her, and Levko thought that she put out her claws, and that there was a spiteful gleam of joy in her face.

"The witch!" he said suddenly, pointing his finger at her and turning toward the house.

The maiden at the window laughed, and the girls, shouting, led away the one who had played hawk.

"How am I to reward you, youth? I know you have no need of gold: you love Ganna, but your unreasonable father will not let you marry her. Now he will not hinder it: take this note and give it to him. . . ."

Her white hand was outstretched, her face seemed in a marvelous way full of light and radiance. . . . With his heart beating painfully, overwhelmed with excitement, he clutched the note, and . . . woke up.

VI

THE AWAKENING

"Can I have been asleep?" Levko wondered, getting up from the little hillock. "It was as vivid as though it were real . . . ! Strange, strange!" he said, looking about him. The moon standing right over his head showed that it was midnight; everywhere all was still, and a chill air rose from the pond; above him stood the old house with its shutters closed. The moss and high grass showed that it had been abandoned long ago. Then he opened his hand, which had been tightly closed all the time he had been asleep, and cried out with astonishment, feeling a note in it. "Oh, if I could only read!" he thought, turning it over and looking at it on all sides. At that moment he heard a noise behind him.

"Don't be afraid, seize him straight away! Why are you so scared? there are a dozen of us. I bet you anything it is a man and not a devil . . . !" That's what the mayor shouted to his companions, and Levko felt himself seized by several hands, some of which were trembling with fear.

"Throw off your dreadful mask, friend! Stop making fools of folk," said the mayor, seizing him by the collar; but he was astounded when he turned his eye upon him. "Levko! Son!" he cried, stepping back in amazement and dropping his hands. "It's you, you bastard! Aie, you child of hell! I was wondering who the rascal could be, what devil turned inside out was playing these tricks. And it seems it is all your doing—you half-cooked pudding sticking in your father's throat! You like to start fights in the street, compose songs . . . ! Ah, ah, Levko! What's the meaning of it? It seems your back is itching for the rod! Seize him!"

"Stop, Father! I was told to give you this letter," said Levko.

"This is not the time for letters, my boy! Tie him up."

"Stop, honored mayor," said the clerk, opening the note, "it is the commissar's handwriting."

"The commissar's," the constable repeated mechanically.

"The commissar's? Strange! It is more incomprehensible than ever!" Levko thought to himself.

"Read it, read it!" said the mayor. "What does the commissar write?"

"We shall hear what the commissar writes," said the distiller, holding his pipe in his teeth and striking a light.

The clerk cleared his throat and began reading:

"Instruction to the mayor, Yevtukh Makogonenko. The news has reached us that you, old fool, instead of collecting past arrears and setting the village in order, have become an ass and been behaving disgracefully . . ."

"I swear," the mayor interrupted, "I don't hear a word!"

The clerk began over again: "Instruction to the major, Yevtukh Makogonenko. The news has reached us that you, old foo . . ."

"Stop, stop! you needn't go on," cried the mayor. "Though I

can't hear it, I know that what matters isn't that. Read what comes later!"

"And therefore I command you to marry your son Levko Makogonenko to Ganna Petrychenkova, a Cossack maiden of your village, and also to mend the bridges on the high road, and do not without my authorization give the villagers' horses to the clerks, even if they have come straight from the government office. If on my coming I find my commands not carried out, I shall hold you alone responsible. Commissar, retired Lieutenant, Kozma Derkach-Drishpanovsky."

"Well!" said the mayor, gaping with wonder. "Do you hear that, do you hear? The mayor is responsible for it all, and so you must obey me unconditionally, or you will catch hell! . . . As for you," he went on, turning to Levko, "since it's the commissar's orders, though I can't understand how it came to his ears, I'll marry you: only first you shall have a taste of my whip! You know the one that hangs on the wall near the icons. I'll repair it tomorrow. . . . Where did you get that note . . . ?"

In spite of Levko's astonishment at this unexpected turn of events, he had the wit to prepare an answer and to conceal the true explanation of the way he had received the letter.

"I was in the town yesterday evening," he said, "and met the commissar getting out of his chaise. Learning that I came from this village, he gave me the letter and told me to give you the message, Father, and that on his way back he will come and dine with us."

"He told you that?"

"Yes."

"Do you hear," said the mayor with an air of dignity, turning to his companions, "the commissar is coming in person to the likes of us, that is to me, to dinner. Oh . . ." Here he held up his finger and lifted up his head as though he were listening to something. "The commissar, do you hear, the commissar is coming to dine with me! What do you think, worthy clerk, and you, friend? That's honor not to be sneezed at! Isn't it?"

"To the best of my recollection," chimed in the clerk, "no village mayor has ever yet entertained the commissar at dinner."

"There are mayors and mayors," said the mayor with a self-satisfied air. His mouth twisted and something in the nature of a husky laugh more like the rumbling of distant thunder came from his lips. "What do you think, worthy clerk? Shouldn't we for this distinguished visitor give orders that every hut should send at least a chicken and, well, some linen and anything else . . . eh?"

"We should, we should, honored mayor."

"And when is the wedding to be, Father?" asked Levko.

"Wedding? I'll teach you to talk about weddings . . . ! Oh well, for the sake of our distinguished visitor . . . tomorrow the priest shall marry you. Damn you! Let the commissar see what punctual discharge of duty means! Well, boys, now it is bedtime! Go home . . . ! What has happened today reminds me of the time when I . . ." At these words the mayor glanced from under his brows with his habitual air of importance and dignity.

"Now the mayor's going to tell us how he guided the Czarina," said Levko, and with rapid steps he made his way joyfully toward the familiar hut, surrounded by low-growing cherry trees. "God give you the kingdom of heaven, kind and lovely lady!" he thought to himself. "May you in the other world be smiling forever among the holy angels. I shall tell no one of the wonder that has happened this night; to you only, Galya, I will tell it. Only you will believe me and together we will pray for the peace of the soul of the luckless drowned maiden!"

Here he drew near the hut: the window was open, the moonlight shone through it upon Ganna as she lay asleep with her head upon her arm, a soft glow on her cheeks; her lips moved, faintly murmuring his name. "Sleep, my beauty, dream of all that is fairest in the world, though that will not be better than our awakening."

Making the sign of the cross over her he closed the window and gently moved away.

And in a few minutes all the village was asleep; only the moon floated, radiant and marvelous in the infinite spaces of the glorious Ukrainian sky. There was the same triumphal splendor on high, and the night, the divine night, glowed majestically. The earth was as lovely in the wonderful silvery light, but no one was enchanted by it; all were sunk in sleep. But from time to time the silence was broken for a moment by the bark of a dog, and for a long while drunken Kalenik was still staggering along the slumbering street looking for his hut.

THE LOST LETTER

A Tale Told by the Sexton
of N—— Church

So you want me to tell you another story about Grandad? Certainly, why not amuse you with some more . . . ? Ah, the old days, the old days! What joy, what gladness it brings to the heart when one hears of what was done in the world so long, long ago, that the year and the month are forgotten! And when some kinsman of one's own is mixed up in it, a grandfather or great-grandfather—then I'm done for: may I choke while praying to St. Varvara if I don't think that I'm doing it all myself, as though I had crept into my great-grandfather's soul, or my great-grand-father's soul were playing tricks in me. . . . But then, our girls and young women are to blame for plaguing me; if I only let them catch a glimpse of me, it's "Foma Grigorievich! Foma Grigorievich! Come now, some terrible tale! Come now, come now . . . !" Tara-ta-ta, ta-ta-ta and they keep on and on. . . . I don't grudge telling them a story, of course, but you should see what happens to them when they are in bed. Why, I know every one of them is trembling under the quilt as though she were in a fever and would be glad to creep under her sheepskin, head and all. If a rat scratches against a pot, or she herself touches the poker with her foot—it's "Lord preserve us!" and her heart's in her heels. But it's all over the next day; she'll pester me again to tell her a frightening story, and that's how it goes. Well, what am I to tell you? Nothing comes into my mind at the minute . . . oh yes, I'll tell you how the witches played "Fools" [1] with my grandfather. But I must beg you first, good friends, not to interrupt me or I will make a hash of it not fit to put to one's lips. My Grandad, I must tell you, was a leading Cossack in his day. He knew his ABC's and even how to abbreviate. On a saint's day, he would boom out the Acts of the Apostles in a voice that would make a priest's son of today feel small. Well, you know without my telling you that in those days if you collected all who could read and write from the whole of Baturin you wouldn't need your cap to contain them: there wouldn't be a handful altogether. So it's no wonder that everyone who met my Grandad offered him a bow, and a low one too.

One day our noble Hetman took it into his head to send a letter to the Czarina about something. The secretary of the regiment in those days—damn, I can't remember his name, the devil take him . . . Viskryak, no, that's not it, Motuzochka, that's not it, Goloput-'sek—no, not Goloputsek . . . all I know is that it was a peculiar name that began in an odd way—he sent for my Grandad and told him that the Hetman himself had named him as messenger to the Czarina. My Grandad never liked to waste time getting ready: he sewed the letter in his cap, led out his horse, kissed his wife and his two sucking pigs, as he used to call his sons, of whom one was my own father, and he made the dust fly behind him that day as though fifteen fellows had been playing a rough game in the middle of the street. The cock had not crowed for the fourth time next morning before Grandad had already reached Konotop. There used to be a fair there in those days: there were such crowds moving up and down the streets that it made one giddy to watch them. But as it was early the people were all stretched out on the ground asleep. Beside a cow would be lying a rakish boy with a nose as red as a bullfinch; a little further a peddler woman with flints, packets of bluing, buckshot, and pretzels was snoring where she sat; a gypsy lay under a cart, a dealer on a wagon of fish; while a Muscovite with a big beard, carrying belts and sleeves for sale, sprawled with his legs stuck out in the middle of the road. . . . In fact, there was rabble of all sorts, as there always is at fairs. My Grandad stopped

---

[1] *Durak*, a very popular card game. (ed.)

to have a good look around. Meanwhile, little by little, there began to be a stir in the booths: the Jewesses made a clatter with the bottles; smoke rolled up in rings here and there, and the smell of hot doughnuts floated all over the encampment. It came into my Grandad's mind that he had no steel and tinder nor tobacco with him, so he began sauntering about the fair. He had not gone twenty paces when he met a Dnieper Cossack.[2] Trousers red as fire, a full-skirted blue coat and bright-flowered girdle, a saber at his side, and a pipe with a fine brass chain right down to his heels—a regular Dnieper Cossack, that's all you can say! Ah, they were something! One would stand up, stretch himself, stroke his gallant mustaches, clink with his iron heels—and off he would go! And how he would go! And how he would go! His legs would whirl around like a spindle in a woman's hands: his fingers would pluck at all the strings of the bandore like a whirlwind, and then pressing it to his side he would begin dancing, burst into song—his whole soul rejoicing . . . ! Yes, the good old days are over; you don't see such Cossacks nowadays! No. So they met. One word leads to another, it doesn't take long to make friends. They fell to chatting and chatting, so that Grandad quite forgot about his journey. They had a drinking bout, as at a wedding before Lent. Only at last I suppose they got tired of smashing the pots and flinging money to the crowd, and indeed, one can't stay forever at a fair! So the new friends agreed not to part, but to travel on together. It was getting on toward evening when they rode out into the open country. The sun had set; here and there streaks of red glowed in the sky where the sun had been; the country was gay with different-colored fields like the checked petticoats our black-browed peasant wives wear on holidays.

Our Dnieper Cossack talked away like mad. Grandad and another jaunty fellow who had joined them began to think that there was a devil in him. Where did it all come from? Tales and stories of such marvels that sometimes Grandad held his sides and almost split his stomach with laughing. But the farther they went the darker it grew, and with it the gay talk grew more disconnected. At last our storyteller was completely silent and started at the slightest rustle.

"Aha, neighbor!" they said to him, "you have started nodding in

---

[2] *Zaporozhets*, a Cossack belonging to the military community settled at Zaporozhye (i.e., Beyond the Falls) on the Dnieper River. The community is fully described in *Taras Bulba*. (ed.)

earnest: you are wishing now that you were at home and on the stove!"

"It's no use keeping secrets from you," he said, suddenly turning around and fixing his eyes upon them. "Do you know that I sold my soul to the devil long ago?"

"As though that were something unheard of! Who hasn't had dealings with the devil in his day? That's why you must drain the cup of pleasure to the dregs, as the saying is."

"Ah, friends! I would, but this night the fatal hour has come! Brothers!" he said, clasping their hands, "do not give me up! Watch over me one night! Never will I forget your friendship!"

Why not help a man in such trouble? Grandad vowed straight off he'd sooner have the forelock cut off his own head than let the devil sniff his snout at a Christian soul.

Our Cossacks would perhaps have ridden on further, if the whole sky had not clouded over as though covered by a black blanket and if it had not turned as dark as under a sheepskin. But there was a light twinkling in the distance and the horses, feeling that a stall was near, quickened their pace, pricking up their ears and staring into the darkness. It seemed as though the light flew to meet them, and the Cossacks saw before them a tavern, leaning on one side like a peasant woman on her way home from a merry christening party. In those days taverns were not what they are now. There was nowhere for a good man to turn around or dance a *gopak*—indeed, he had nowhere to lie down, even if the drink had gone to his head and his wobbly legs began making circles all over the floor. The yard was all blocked up with dealers' wagons; under the sheds, in the mangers, in the barns, men were snoring like tomcats, one curled up and another sprawling. But one was busy. The tavern keeper, in front of his little pot-lamp, was making notches in a stick to mark the number of quarts and pints the dealers had drained.

Grandad, after ordering a third of a pailful for the three of them, went off to the barn. They lay down side by side. But before he had time to turn around he saw that his friends were already sleeping like the dead. Waking the third Cossack, the one who had joined them, Grandad reminded him of the promise given to their comrade. The man sat up, rubbed his eyes, and fell asleep again. There was nothing he could do; he had to watch alone. To drive away sleep in some way, he examined all the wagons, looked at the horses, lighted his pipe, came back, and sat down again beside his comrades. All was still; it seemed as though not a fly were moving. Then he imagined that something gray poked out its horns from a wagon close by. . . . Then his eyes began to close, so that he was obliged to rub them every minute with his fist and to keep them open with the rest of the vodka. But soon, when they were a little clearer, everything had vanished. At last a little later something strange showed itself again under the wagon. . . . Grandad opened his eyes as wide as he could, but the cursed sleepiness made everything misty before them; his hands felt numb, his head rolled back, and he fell into such a sound sleep that he lay as though dead. Grandad slept for hours, and he only sprang to his feet when the sun was baking his shaven head. After stretching twice and scratching his back, he noticed that there were no longer so many wagons standing there as in the evening. The dealers, it seemed, had trailed off before dawn. He looked for his companions—the Cossack was still asleep, but the Dnieper Cossack was gone. No one could tell him anything when he asked; only his coat was still lying in the same place. Grandad was frightened and didn't know what to think. He went to look for the horses—no sign of his or the Dnieper Cossack's! What could that mean? Supposing the Evil One had taken the Dnieper Cossack, who had taken the horses? Thinking it over, Grandad concluded that probably the devil had come on foot, and as it's a long journey to hell he had carried off his horse. He was terribly upset at not having kept his Cossack word.

"Well," he thought, "there is nothing to be done; I will go on foot. Maybe I shall come across some horse dealer on his way from the fair. I shall manage somehow to buy a horse." But when he reached for his cap, his cap was not there either. Grandad wrung his hands when he remembered that the day before he had changed caps for a time with the Dnieper Cossack. Who else could have carried it off if not the devil himself! Some Hetman's messenger! A nice job he'd made of taking the letter to the Czarina! At this point my Grandad fell to bestowing such names on the devil as I imagine must have set him sneezing more than once in hell. But cursing is not much use, and however often my Grandad scratched his head, he could not think of any plan. What was he to do? He turned to ask advice of others: he got together all the good folk who were in the tavern at the time, dealers and simple wayfarers, told them how it all happened and what a misfortune had befallen him. The dealers pondered for a long time. Leaning their chins on their whips, they shook their heads and said that they had never heard of such a marvel in Christendom as a devil carrying off a Hetman's letter. Others added that when the devil or a Muscovite stole anything, you whistle in the dark for it. Only the tavern keeper sat silent in the corner. Grandad went up to him, too. When a man says nothing, you may be sure he thinks a great deal. But the tavern keeper was sparing of his words, and if Grandad had not felt in his pocket for five silver coins, he might have gone on standing before him to no purpose.

"I will tell you how to find the letter," said the tavern keeper, leading him aside. His words lifted a weight from Grandad's heart. "I see from your eyes that you are a Cossack and not a woman. Listen now! Near the tavern you will find a turn on the right into the forest. As soon as it begins to grow dark you must be ready to start. There are gypsies living in the forest and they come out of their dens to forge iron on nights on which none but witches go abroad on their pokers. What their real trade is you had best not inquire. There will be much knocking in the forest, only don't you go where you hear the knocking; there'll be a little path facing you near a burnt tree: go by that little path, go on and on. . . . The thorns may scratch you, thick bushes may block the path, but you continue on and do not stop until you come to a little stream. There you will see whom you need. But don't forget to take in your pockets that for which pockets are made. . . . You understand, both devils and men prize that." Saying this, the tavern keeper went off to his corner and would not say another word.

My late Grandad was by no means a coward; if he met a wolf, he would grab him straightway by the tail; if he used his fist among the Cossacks, they would fall to the ground like pears. But a shudder ran down him when he stepped into the forest on such a dark night. Not one little star in the sky. Dark and dim as a wine cellar; there was no sound, except far, far overhead a cold wind playing in the treetops, and the trees swayed like the heads of drunken Cossacks while their leaves whispered a tipsy song. And there was such a cold blast that Grandad thought of his sheepskin, and all at once it was as though a hundred hammers began tapping in the forest with a noise that set his ears ringing. And the whole forest was lit up for a moment as though by summer lightning. At once Grandad caught sight of a little path winding between the bushes. And here was the burnt tree and here were the thorn bushes! So everything was as he had been told; no, the tavern keeper had not deceived him. It was not altogether pleasant tearing his way through the prickly bushes; he had never in his life known the damned thorns and twigs to scratch so badly. He almost cried out at every step. Little by little he came into an open place, and as far as he could see the trees seemed wider apart, and as he went on he came upon bigger trees than he had ever seen even on the other side of Poland. And behold, among the trees gleamed a little stream, dark as tempered steel. For a long time Grandad stopped on the bank, looking in all directions. On the other bank a light was twinkling; it seemed every minute on the point of going out, and then it was reflected again in the stream, trembling like a Pole in the hands of Cossacks. And here was the little bridge!

"Perhaps only the devil's chariot uses this bridge," he said. Grandad stepped out boldly, however, and before another man would have had time to get out his horn and take a pinch of snuff he was on the other side. Only now he saw that there were people sitting around a fire, and they had such charming pig-faces that at any other time God knows he would have given anything to escape making their acquaintance. But now he couldn't avoid it: he had to make friends with them. So Grandad tossed off a low bow, saying: "God help you, good people!"

No one nodded his head; they all sat in silence and kept dropping something into the fire. Seeing one place empty, Grandad, without making a fuss, sat down. The charming pig-faces said nothing, Grandad said nothing either. For a long time they sat in silence. Grandad was already beginning to be bored; he fumbled in his pocket, pulled out his pipe, looked around—not one of them glanced at him.

"Well, your honors, will you be so kind; as a matter of fact, in a manner of speaking . . ." (Grandad had knocked about the world a good bit and knew how to turn a phrase, and maybe even if he had been before the Czar he would not have been at a loss.)

"In a manner of speaking, not to forget myself nor to slight you —a pipe I have, but that with which to light it I lack." To this speech, too, there was not a word. But one of the pig-faces thrust a hot brand straight into Grandad's face, so that if he had not turned aside a little he might have parted with one eye forever. At last, seeing that time was being wasted, he made up his mind to tell his story whether the pig-faces would listen or not.

They pricked up their ears and stretched out their paws. Grandad guessed what that meant; he pulled out all the money he had with him and flung it to them as though to dogs. As soon as he had flung the money, everything was in a turmoil before him, the earth shook, and all at once—he never knew how to explain this part—he found himself almost in hell itself.

"Merciful heavens!" groaned Grandad when he had taken a good look around. What wonders were here! One ugly face after another, as the saying is. The witches were as many as the snowflakes that fall on occasion at Christmas. They were all dressed up and painted like fine ladies at a fair. And the whole bunch of them were dancing some sort of devil's jig as though they were drunk. What a dust they raised, God help us! Any Christian would have shuddered to see how high the devils skipped. In spite of his terror, my Grandad started laughing when he saw the devils, with their dogs' faces on their little German legs, wag their tails, twist, and turn about the witches, like our boys about the pretty girls, while the musicians beat on their cheeks with their fists as though they were tambourines and whistled with their noses as though they were horns. As soon as they saw Grandad, they pressed around him in a crowd. Pig-faces, dog-faces, goat-faces, bird-faces, and horse-faces—all craned forward, and here they were actually trying to kiss him. Grandad could not help spitting, he was so disgusted! At last they caught hold of him and made him sit down at a table, as long, maybe, as the road from Konotop to Baturin.[3]

"Well, this is not altogether so bad!" thought Grandad, seeing on the table pork, sausages, onion minced with cabbage, and many other dainties. "The damned scum doesn't keep the fasts, it seems."

My Grandad, I may as well tell you, was by no means averse to good fare on occasion. He ate with good appetite, the dear man, and so without wasting words he pulled toward him a bowl of sliced bacon fat and a smoked ham, took up a fork not much smaller than those with which a peasant pitches hay, picked out the most solid piece, laid it on a piece of bread, and—lo and behold!—put it in another mouth just close beside his very ear, and, indeed, there was the sound of another fellow's jaws chewing it and clacking with his teeth, so that all the table could hear. Grandad didn't mind; he picked up another piece, and this time it seemed as though

---

[3] I.e., eighteen miles. (ed.)

he had caught it with his lips, but again it did not go down his gullet. A third time he tried—again he missed it. Grandad flew into a rage; he forgot his fright and in whose claws he was, and ran up to the witches: "Do you mean to mock me, you pagan bitches? If you don't this very minute give me back my Cossack cap—may I be a Catholic if I don't twist your pig-snouts to the back of your heads!"

He had finished the last word when the monsters grinned and set up such a roar of laughter that it sent a chill to my Grandad's heart.

"Good!" shrieked one of the witches, whom Grandad took to be the leader among them because she was almost the greatest beauty of the lot; "we will give you back your cap, but not until you win it back from us in three games of 'Fools'!"

What was he to do? For a Cossack to sit down and play "Fools" with a lot of women! Grandad kept refusing and refusing, but in the end sat down. They brought the cards, a greasy pack such as we only see used by priests' wives to tell the girls their fortunes and what their husbands will be like.

"Listen!" barked the witch again: "if you win one game, the cap is yours; if you are left 'Fool' in every one of the three games, it's no use your fuming: you'll never see your cap nor maybe the world again!"

"Deal, deal, you old witch! What will be, will be."

Well, the cards were dealt. Grandad picked up his—he couldn't bear to look at them, they were such trash; they could have at least given him one trump just for the fun of it. Of the other suits the highest was a ten and he hadn't even a pair; while the witch kept giving him five at once. It was his fate to be left "Fool"! As soon as Grandad was left "Fool," the monsters began neighing, barking, and grunting on all sides: "Fool, fool, fool!"

"Shout till you burst, you bitches," cried Grandad putting his fingers in his ears.

"Well," he thought, "the witch didn't play fair; now I am going to deal myself." He dealt; he turned up the trump and looked at his cards; they were first-rate, he had trumps. And at first things could not have gone better; till the witch put down five cards with kings among them.

Grandad had nothing in his hand but trumps! In a flash he beat all the kings with trumps!

"Ha-ha! but that's not like a Cossack! What are you covering them with, neighbor?"

"What with? With trumps!"

"Maybe to your thinking they are trumps, but to our thinking they are not!"

Lo and behold! the cards were really of another suit! What devilry was this? A second time he was "Fool" and the devils started shrieking again: "Fool! fool!" so that the table rocked and the cards danced upon it.

Grandad flew into a passion; he dealt for the last time. Again he had a good hand. The witch put down five again; Grandad covered them and took from the pack a handful of trumps.

"Trump!" he shouted, flinging a card on the table so that it spun around like a basket; without saying a word she covered it with the eight of another suit.

"What are you beating my trump with, old devil?"

The witch lifted her card and under it was the six of another suit not trumps.

"What damned trickery!" said Grandad, and in his great anger he struck the table with his fist as hard as he could. Luckily the witch had a poor hand; this time, as luck would have it, Grandad had pairs. He began drawing cards out of the pack, but it was of no use; such trash came that Grandad let his hands fall. There was not one good card in the pack. So he just played anything—a six. The witch had to take it, and she could not cover it. "So there! What do you say to that? Aie, Aie! There is something wrong, I'll be damned!" Then on the sly under the table Grandad made the sign of the cross over the cards, and behold—he had in his hand the ace, king, and jack of trumps, and the card he had just played was not a six but the queen!

"Well, I've been the fool! King of trumps! Well, have you taken it? Aie, you bitches! Would you like the ace too? The ace! the jack . . . !"

Thunder boomed in hell; the witch went into convulsions, and all of a sudden the cap flew smack into Grandad's face.

"No, no, that's not enough!" shouted Grandad, plucking up his courage and putting on his cap. "If my gallant horse is not standing before me at once, may a thunderbolt strike me dead in this foul place if I do not make the sign of the holy cross over all of you!"

And he was just raising his hand to do it when the horse's bones rattled before him.

"Here is your horse!"

The poor man burst out crying like an infant as he looked at the bones. He grieved for his old comrade!

"Give me some sort of a horse," he said, "to get out of your den!" A devil cracked a whip—a highly spirited horse rose up under him and Grandad soared upward like a bird.

Terror came over him, however, when the horse, heeding neither shout nor rein, galloped over ditches and bogs. The places he went through were such that it made him shudder at the mere telling of it. He looked down and was more terrified than ever: an abyss, a fearful precipice! But that was nothing to the satanic beast; he leaped straight over it. Grandad tried to hold on; he could not. Over tree stumps, over hillocks he flew headlong into a ditch, and fell so hard on the ground at the bottom that it seemed he had breathed his last. Anyway, he could remember nothing of what happened to him then; and when he came to himself a little and looked about him, it was broad daylight; he caught glimpses of familiar places and found himself lying on the roof of his own hut.

Grandad crossed himself as he climbed down. What devils' tricks! Damn it all! What strange things befall a man! He looked at his hands: they were bathed in blood; he looked into a pail of water—and saw that his face was also bathed in blood. Washing himself thoroughly so that he would not scare the children, he went quietly into the hut—and what did he see! The children staggered back toward him and pointed in alarm, saying: "Look! Look! Mother's jumping like mad!" And indeed, his wife was sitting asleep before her loom, holding her spindle in her hands, and in her sleep was bouncing up and down on the bench. Grandad, taking her gently by the hand, woke her. "Good morning, wife! Are you quite well?" For a long while she gazed at him with bulging eyes, but at last recognized Grandad and told him that she had dreamed that the stove was riding around the hut shoveling out the pots and tubs with a spade . . . and devil knows what else.

"Well," said Grandad, "you have had it asleep, I have had it awake. I see I must have our hut blessed; but I cannot linger now."

Saying this Grandad rested a little, then got out his horse and did not stop by day or by night till he arrived and gave the letter to the Czarina herself. There Grandad beheld such wonderful things that for long after he used to tell the tale: how they brought him to the palace, and it was so high that if you were to set ten huts one on top of another they probably would still not be high enough; how he glanced into one room—nothing, into another—nothing, into a third—still nothing, into a fourth even—nothing, but in the fifth there she was sitting in her golden crown, in a new gray gown and red boots, eating golden dumplings; how she had bade them fill a whole cap with five-ruble notes for him; how . . . I can't remember it all! As for his rumpus with the devils, Grandad forgot even to think about it; and if it happened that someone reminded him of it, Grandad would say nothing, as though the matter did not concern him, and we had the greatest trouble persuading him to tell us how it had all happened. And apparently to punish him for not rushing out at once after that to have the hut blessed, every year just at that same time a strange thing happened to his wife— she would dance and nothing could stop her. No matter what anyone did, her legs would go their own way, and something forced her to dance.

EVENINGS ON A FARM NEAR DIKANKA, II

Preface

Here is a second part for you, and I had better say the last one! I did not want, I did not at all want to bring it out. One should not outstay one's welcome. I must tell you they are already beginning to laugh at me in the village. "The old fellow has become stupid," they say, "he is amusing himself with children's toys in his old age!" And, indeed, it is high time to rest. I expect you imagine, dear readers, that I am only pretending to be old. Pretend, indeed, when I have no teeth left in my mouth! Now, if anything soft comes my way I manage to chew it, but I can't tackle anything hard. So here is another book for you! Only don't scold me! It is not nice to scold at parting, especially when God only knows whether one will soon meet again. In this book you will find stories told by people you do not know at all, except, perhaps, Foma Grigorievich. That gentleman in the pea-green coat who talked in such refined language that many of the wits, even Muscovites, could not understand him, has not been here for a long time. He hasn't visited us since he quarreled with us all. I did not tell you about it, did I? It was a regular comedy. Last year, some time in the summer, I believe it was on my Saint's

Day, I had visitors to see me. . . . (I must tell you, dear readers, that my neighbors, God give them good health, do not forget the old man.) It is fifty years since I began keeping my name day; but just how old I am neither I nor my old woman could say. It must be somewhere about seventy. The priest at Dikanka, Father Kharlampy, knew when I was born, but I am sorry to say he has been dead these fifty years. So I had visitors to see me: Zakhar Kirilovich Chukhopupenko, Stepan Ivanovich Kurochka, Taras Ivanovich Smachnenky, the assessor Kharlampy Kirilovich Khlost; there was another one . . . I forget his name . . . Osip . . . Osip . . . I swear, everyone in Mirgorod knows him! Whenever he begins speaking he snaps his fingers and puts his arms akimbo. . . . Well, God help him! I shall think of it presently. The gentleman from Poltava whom you already know came too. Foma Grigorievich I do not count: he is one of us. Everybody talked (I must tell you that our conversation is never about trifles; I always like pleasant conversation, so as to combine pleasure and profit, as the saying is) —we discussed how to pickle apples. My old woman began saying that first you had to wash the apples thoroughly, then soak them in kvass, and then . . . "All that is no use whatever!" the gentleman from Poltava interrupted, thrusting his hand into his pea-green coat and pacing about the room majestically, "not the slightest use! First you must sprinkle them with tansy and then . . ." Well, I ask you, dear readers, did you ever hear of apples being sprinkled with tansy? It is true, people do use black-currant leaves, swineherb, trefoil; but to put in tansy . . . I have never heard of such a thing! And I imagine no one knows more about these things than my old woman. But there you are! I quietly drew him aside, as a good neighbor: "Come now, Makar Nazarovich, don't make people laugh! You are a man of some consequence; you have dined at the same table with the governor, as you told us yourself. Well, if you were to say anything like this there, you would set them all laughing at you!" And what do you imagine he said to that? Nothing! He spat on the floor, picked up his cap, and went out. He might have said goodbye to somebody, he might have given us a nod; all we heard was his chaise with a bell on it drive up to the gate; he got into it and drove off. And a good thing too! We don't want guests like that. I tell you what, dear readers, there is nothing in the world worse than these high-class people. Because his uncle was a commissar once, he turns up his nose at everyone. As though there were no rank in the world higher than a commissar! Thank God, there are people greater than commissars. No, I don't like these high-class people. Now Foma Grigorievich, for instance—he is not a high-class man, but just look at him: there is a serene dignity in his face. Even when he takes a pinch of ordinary snuff you can't help feeling respect for him. When he sings in the choir in the church there is no describing how touching it is. You feel as though you were melting . . . ! While that other . . . But there, God help the man. He thinks we cannot do without his tales. But here, you see, is a book of them without him.

I promised you, I remember, that in this book there should be my story too. And I did mean to put it in. But I found that for my story I should need three books of this size, at least. I did think of printing it separately, but I thought better of it. I know you: you would be laughing at the old man. No, I shall not! Goodbye. It will be a long time before we meet again, if we ever do. But then, it would not matter to you if I had never existed at all. One year will pass and then another—and none of you will remember or miss the old bee-keeper.

RUDY PANKO

CHRISTMAS EVE

The last day before Christmas had passed. A clear winter night had come; the stars peeped out; the moon rose majestically in the sky to light good people and all the world so that all might enjoy singing *kolyadki*[1] and praising the Lord. It was freezing harder than in the morning; but it was so still that the crunch of the snow under the boot could be heard half a mile away. Not one group of boys had appeared under the hut windows yet; only the moon peeped in at them stealthily as though calling to the girls who were dressing up in their best to make haste and run out on the crunching snow. At that moment the smoke rose in puffs from a hut chimney and passed like a cloud over the sky, and a witch on a broomstick rose up in the air with the smoke.

If the assessor of Sorochintsy, in his cap edged with lambskin and cut like a Turk's, in his dark blue overcoat lined with black

---

[1] Among us it is the custom to sing under the window on Christmas Eve carols that are called *kolyadki*. The mistress or master or whoever is left in the house always drops into the singer's bag some sausage or bread or a copper or whatever he has plenty of. It is said that once upon a time there was a blockhead called Kolyada who was taken to be a god and that these *kolyadki* came from that. Who knows? It is not for plain folk like us to give our opinion about it. Last year Father Osip was for forbidding them to sing *kolyadki* about the farms, saying that folk were honoring Satan by doing so, though to tell the truth there is not a word about Kolyada in the *kolyadki*. They often sing about the birth of Christ, and at the end wish good health to the master, the mistress, the children, and the entire household. (*The beekeeper's note*)

astrakhan, had driven by at that moment with his three hired horses and the fiendishly braided whip with which it is his habit to urge on his coachman, he would certainly have noticed her, for there is not a witch in the world who could elude the eyes of the Sorochintsy assessor. He can count on his fingers how many suckling pigs every peasant woman's sow has farrowed and how much linen is lying in her chest and just which of her clothes and household belongings her good man pawns on Sunday at the tavern. But the Sorochintsy assessor did not drive by, and, indeed, what business is it of his? He has his own district. Meanwhile, the witch rose so high in the air that she was only a little black patch gleaming aloft. But wherever that little patch appeared, there the stars one after another vanished. Soon the witch had gathered a whole sleeveful of them. Three or four were still shining. All at once from the opposite side another little patch appeared, grew larger, began to lengthen out, and was no longer a little patch. A shortsighted man would never have made out what it was, even if he had put the wheels of the commissar's chaise on his nose as spectacles. At first it looked like a regular German:[2] the narrow little face, continually twisting and turning and sniffing at everything, ended in a little round heel, like our pigs' snouts; the legs were so thin that if the mayor of Yareski had had legs like that, he would certainly have broken them in the first Cossack dance. But from behind he was for all the world a district attorney in uniform, for he had a tail as long and pointed as the uniform coattails are nowadays. It was only from the goat-beard under his chin, from the little horns sticking from his forehead, and from his being no whiter than a chimney sweep, that one could tell that he was not a German or a district attorney, but simply the devil, who had one last night left him to wander about the wide world and teach good folk to sin. On the morrow when the first bells rang for prayer, he would run with his tail between his legs straight off to his lair.

Meanwhile the devil stole silently up to the moon and stretched his hand out to seize it, but drew it back quickly as though he were scorched, sucked his fingers and danced about, then ran up from the other side and again skipped away and drew back his hand. But

---

[2] Among us everyone is called a German who comes from a foreign country; even if he is a Frenchman, a Hungarian, or a Swede—he is still a German. (N. Gogol)

in spite of all his failures the sly devil did not give up his tricks. Running up, he suddenly seized the moon with both hands; grimacing and blowing, he kept flinging it from one hand to the other, like a peasant who has picked up an ember for his pipe with bare fingers; at last, he hurriedly put it in his pocket and ran on as though nothing had happened.

No one in Dikanka noticed that the devil had stolen the moon. It is true the district clerk, crawling out of the tavern on all fours, saw the moon for no reason whatever dancing in the sky, and he swore that he had to the whole village; but people shook their heads and even made fun of him. But what motive led the devil to this illegal act? Why, this was how it was: he knew that the rich Cossack, Chub,[3] had been invited by the sexton to a supper of rice soup at which a kinsman of the sexton's, who had come from the bishop's choir, wore a dark blue coat and could take the very lowest bass note, the mayor, the Cossack Sverbiguz, and some others were to be present, and at which besides the Christmas soup there were to be spiced vodka, saffron vodka, and good things of all sorts. And meanwhile his daughter, the greatest beauty in the village, was left at home, and there was no doubt that the blacksmith, a very strong and fine young fellow, would pay her a visit, and him the devil hated more than Father Kondrat's sermons. In his spare time the blacksmith had taken up painting and was reckoned the finest artist in the whole countryside. Even the Cossack officer L——ko, who was still strong and hearty in those days, sent for him to Poltava expressly to paint a picket fence around his house. All the bowls from which the Cossacks of Dikanka gulped their borsht had been painted by the blacksmith. He was a God-fearing man and often painted icons of the saints: even now you may find his Luke the Evangelist in the church of T——. But the triumph of his art was a picture painted on the church wall in the chapel on the right. In it he depicted St. Peter on the Day of Judgment with the keys in his hand driving the Evil Spirit out of hell; the frightened devil was running in all directions, foreseeing his doom, while the sinners, who had been imprisoned before, were chasing him and striking him with whips, blocks of wood, and anything they could get hold of. While the artist was working at this picture and painting it on a

---

[3] "Forelock." (ed.)

big wooden board, the devil did all he could to hinder him; he gave him a nudge on the arm, unseen, blew some ashes from the forge in the smithy, and scattered them on the picture; but, in spite of it all, the work was finished, the picture was brought into the church and put on the wall of the side chapel, and from that day the devil had sworn to revenge himself on the blacksmith.

He had only one night left to wander upon earth; but he was looking for some means of venting his anger on the blacksmith that night. And that was why he made up his mind to steal the moon, reckoning that old Chub was lazy and slow to move, and the sexton's hut a good distance away: the road passed by cross paths beside the mills and the graveyard and went around a ravine. On a moonlight night spiced vodka and saffron vodka might have tempted Chub; but in such darkness it was doubtful whether anyone could drag him from the stove and bring him out of the cottage. And the blacksmith, who had for a long time been on bad terms with him, would on no account have ventured, strong as he was, to visit the daughter when the father was at home.

And so, as soon as the devil had hidden the moon in his pocket, it became so dark all over the world that not everyone could have found the way to the tavern, let alone to the sexton's. The witch shrieked when she suddenly found herself in darkness. Then the devil running up, all bows and smiles, put his arm around her, and began whispering in her ear the sort of thing that is usually whispered to all females. Things are oddly arranged in our world! All who live in it are always trying to outdo and imitate one another. In the old days the judge and the police captain were the only ones in Mirgorod who used to wear cloth overcoats lined with sheepskin in the winter, while all the minor officials wore plain sheepskin; but nowadays the assessor and the chamberlain have managed to get themselves new cloth overcoats lined with astrakhan. The year before last the treasury clerk and the district clerk bought dark blue duck at sixty kopeks a yard. The sexton has got himself cotton trousers for the summer and a striped vest of camel's hair. In fact everyone tries to be somebody! When will folks give up being vain! I am ready to bet that many would be surprised to see the devil carrying on in that way. What is most annoying is that, no doubt, he fancies himself a handsome fellow, though his figure is a shameful sight. With a face, as Foma Grigorievich used to say, the abomination of abominations, yet even he plays the dashing hero! But in the sky and under the sky it was growing so dark that there was no seeing what followed between them.

"So you have not been to see the sexton in his new hut, friend?" said the Cossack Chub, coming out at his door, to a tall lean peasant in a short sheepskin, whose stubby beard showed that for at least two weeks it had not been touched by the broken piece of scythe with which, for lack of a razor, peasants usually shave their beards. "There will be a fine drinking party there tonight!" Chub went on, grinning as he spoke. "If only we are not late!"

Hereupon Chub set straight the belt that closely girt his sheepskin, pulled his cap more firmly on his head, and gripped his whip, the terror and the enemy of tiresome dogs; but glancing upward, he stopped. "What the hell! Look! look, Panas . . . !"

"What?" articulated his friend, and he too turned his face upward.

"What, indeed! There is no moon!"

"What a nuisance! There really is no moon."

"That's just it, there isn't!" Chub said, with some annoyance at his friend's imperturbable indifference. "You don't care, I'll bet."

"Well, what can I do about it?"

"Some devil," Chub went on, wiping his mustaches with his sleeve, "has to go and meddle—may he never have a glass of vodka to drink in the mornings, the dog! I swear it's as though to mock us. . . . As I sat indoors I looked out of the window and the night was lovely! It was light, the snow was sparkling in the moonlight; you could see everything as though it were day. And here, before I'm out of the door, you can't see your hand before your face! May he break his teeth on a crust of buckwheat bread!"

Chub went on grumbling and swearing for a long while, and at the same time he was hesitant about what to decide. He had a desperate longing to gossip about all sorts of nonsense at the sexton's where no doubt the mayor was already sitting, as well as the bass choir singer, and Mikita, the tar dealer, who used to come once every two weeks on his way to Poltava, and who cracked such jokes that all the village worthies held their sides from laughing. Already in his mind's eye Chub saw the spiced vodka on the table. All this was enticing, it is true, but the darkness of the night recalled the charms of laziness so dear to every Cossack. How nice it would be now to lie on the stove with his legs tucked under him, quietly smoking his pipe and listening through a delicious drowsiness to the songs and carols of the lighthearted boys and girls who gathered in groups under the windows! He would undoubtedly have decided on the latter course had he been alone; but for the two together, it was not so dreary and terrible to go through the dark night; besides he did not care to seem sluggish and cowardly to others. When he had finished swearing he turned again to his friend.

"So there is no moon, friend?"

"No!"

"It's strange, really! Let me have a pinch of snuff! You have splendid snuff, friend! Where do you get it?"

"Splendid! What the hell do you mean by splendid?" answered the friend, shutting the birchbark snuffbox with patterns pricked out upon it. "It wouldn't make an old hen sneeze!"

"I remember," Chub still went on, "the innkeeper, Zuzulya, once brought me some snuff from Nyezhin. Ah, that was snuff! it was good snuff! So what is it to be? It's dark, you know!"

"So maybe we'll stay at home," his friend said, taking hold of the door handle.

If his friend had not said that, Chub would certainly have made up his mind to stay at home; but now something seemed egging him on to oppose it. "No, friend, let us go! It won't do; we must go!"

Even as he was saying it, he was angry with himself for having said it. He very much disliked going out on such a night, but it was a comfort to him that he was acting on his own decision and not following advice.

His friend looked around and scratched his shoulders with the handle of his whip, without the slightest sign of anger on his face, like a man to whom it is a matter of complete indifference whether he sits at home or goes out—and the two friends set off on their road.

Now let us see what Chub's daughter, the beauty, was doing all by herself. Before Oksana was seventeen, people were talking about nothing but her in almost the whole world, both on this side of Dikanka and on the other side of Dikanka. The young men were unanimous in declaring that there never had been and never would be a finer girl in the village. Oksana heard and knew all that was said about her and, like a beauty, was full of caprices. If, instead of a checked skirt and an apron, she had been dressed as a lady, she could never have kept a servant. The young men ran after her in crowds, but, losing patience, by degrees gave up on the obstinate beauty, and turned to others who were not so spoiled. Only the blacksmith was persistent and would not abandon his courtship, although he was treated not a bit better than the rest. When her father went out, Oksana spent a long while dressing herself in her best and preening before a little mirror in a pewter frame; she could not tear herself away from admiring herself.

"What put it into folks' heads to spread it abroad that I am pretty?" she said, as it were without thinking, simply to talk to herself about something. "Folks lie, I am not pretty at all!"

But the fresh animated face reflected in the mirror, its youthfulness, its sparkling black eyes and inexpressibly charming smile that stirred the soul, at once proved the contrary.

"Can my black eyebrows and my eyes," the beauty went on, still holding the mirror, "be so beautiful that there are none like them in the world? What is there pretty in that turned-up nose, and in those cheeks and those lips? Is my black hair pretty? Ough, my curls might frighten one in the evening, they twist and twine around my head like long snakes! I see now that I am not pretty at all!" And, moving the mirror a little further away, she cried out: "No, I am pretty! Ah, how pretty! Wonderful! What a joy I shall be to the man whose wife I become! How my husband will admire me! He'll be wild with joy. He will kiss me to death!"

"Wonderful girl!" whispered the blacksmith, coming in softly. "And hasn't she a little conceit! She's been standing looking in the mirror for an hour and can't tear herself away, and praising herself aloud, too!"

"Yes, boys, I am a match for you! Just look at me!" the pretty coquette went on: "how gracefully I step; my chemise is embroidered with red silk. And the ribbons on my head! You will never see richer braid! My father bought me all this so that the finest young man in the world may marry me." And, laughing, she turned around and saw the blacksmith. . . .

She uttered a shriek and stood still, coldly facing him.

The blacksmith's hands dropped helplessly to his sides.

It is hard to describe what the dark face of the lovely girl expressed. There was sternness in it, and through the sternness a sort of defiance of the embarrassed blacksmith, and at the same time a hardly perceptible flush of anger delicately suffused her face; and all this was so mingled and so indescribably pretty that to give her a million kisses was the best thing that could have been done at the moment.

"Why have you come here?" was how Oksana began. "Do you want me to shove you out of the door with a spade? You are all very clever at coming to see us. You sniff out in a minute when there are no fathers in the house. Oh, I know you! Well, is my chest ready?"

"It will be ready, my little heart, it will be ready after Christmas. If only you knew how I have worked at it; for two nights I didn't leave the smithy. But then, no priest's wife will have a chest like it. The iron I bound it with is better than what I put on the officer's chariot, when I worked at Poltava. And how it will be painted! You won't find one like it if you wander over the whole neighborhood with your little white feet! Red and blue flowers will be scattered over the whole ground. It will glow like fire. Don't be angry with me! Allow me at least to speak to you, to look at you!"

"Who's forbidding you? Speak and look!"

Then she sat down on the bench, glanced again in the mirror, and began arranging her hair. She looked at her neck, at her chemise embroidered in red silk, and a subtle feeling of complacency could be read on her lips and fresh cheeks, and was reflected in her eyes.

"Allow me to sit beside you," said the blacksmith.

"Sit down," said Oksana, with the same emotion still perceptible on her lips and in her gratified eyes.

"Wonderful, lovely Oksana, allow me to kiss you!" ventured the blacksmith, growing bolder, and he drew her toward him with the intention of snatching a kiss. But Oksana turned away her cheek, which had been very close to the blacksmith's lips, and pushed him away.

"What more do you want? When there's honey he must have a spoonful! Go away, your hands are harder than iron. And you smell of smoke. I believe you have smeared me all over with your soot."

Then she picked up the mirror and began preening again.

"She does not love me!" the blacksmith thought to himself, hanging his head. "It's all a game to her while I stand before her like a fool and cannot take my eyes off her. And I should like to stand before her always and never to take my eyes off her! Wonderful girl! What would I not give to know what is in her heart, and whom she loves. But no, she cares for nobody. She is admiring herself; she is tormenting poor me, while I am so sad that everything is darkness to me. I love her as no man in the world ever has loved or ever will."

"Is it true that your mother's a witch?" Oksana said, and she laughed. And the blacksmith felt that everything within him was laughing. That laugh echoed as if it were at once in his heart and in his softly tingling veins, and for all that, his soul was angry that he had not the right to kiss that sweetly laughing face.

"What care I for Mother? You are father and mother to me and all that is precious in the world. If the Czar summoned me and said: 'Smith Vakula, ask me for all that is best in my kingdom; I will give you anything. I will bid them make you a golden forge and you shall work with silver hammers.' 'I don't care,' I should say to the Czar, 'for precious stones or a golden forge nor for all your king-dom: give me rather my Oksana.' "

"You see, what a fellow you are! Only my father's no fool either. You'll see that, when he doesn't marry your mother!" Oksana said, smiling slyly. "But the girls are not here. . . . What's the mean-ing of it? We ought to have been singing long ago. I am getting tired of waiting."

"Let them stay away, my beauty!"

"I should hope not! I expect the boys will come with them. And then there will be dances. I can imagine what funny stories they will tell!"

"So you'll be merry with them?"

"Yes, merrier than with you. Ah! someone knocked; I expect it is the girls and the boys."

"What's the use of my staying longer?" the blacksmith said to himself. "She is jeering at me. I am no more to her than an old rusty horseshoe. But if that's so, anyway I won't let another man laugh at me. If only I see for certain that she likes someone better than me, I'll teach him to keep away . . ."

A knock at the door and a cry of "Open!" ringing out sharply in the frost interrupted his reflections.

"Stop, I'll open the door," said the blacksmith, and he went out, intending in his anger to break the ribs of anyone who might be there.

The frost grew sharper, and up above it turned so cold that the devil kept hopping from one hoof to the other and blowing into his fists, trying to warm his frozen hands. And indeed it is small wonder that he should be cold, being used day after day to knocking about in hell, where, as we all know, it is not so cold as it is with us in winter, and where, putting on his cap and standing before the hearth, like a real cook, he fries sinners with as much satisfaction as a peasant woman fries a sausage at Christmas.

The witch herself felt that it was cold, although she was warmly clad; and so, throwing her arms upward, she stood with one foot out, and putting herself into the attitude of a man flying along on skates, without moving a single muscle, she dropped through the air, as though on an icy slope, and straight into her chimney.

The devil started after her in the same way. But as the creature is nimbler than any dandy in stockings, there is no wonder that he reached the top of the chimney almost on the neck of his mistress, and both found themselves in a roomy oven among the pots.

The witch stealthily moved back the oven door to see whether her son, Vakula, had invited visitors to the hut; but seeing that there was no one, except the sacks that lay in the middle of the floor, she crept out of the oven, flung off her warm pelisse, rearranged her clothing, and no one could have told that she had been riding on a broom the minute before.

Vakula's mother was not more than forty years old. She was neither pretty nor ugly. Indeed, it is hard to be pretty at such an age. However, she was so clever at attracting even the resolute Cossacks (who, it may not be amiss to observe, do not care much about beauty) that the mayor and the sexton, Osip Nikiforovich (if his wife were not at home, of course), and the Cossack Korny Chub, and the Cossack Kasian Sverbiguz, were all lavishing attentions on her. And it must be said to her credit that she was very skillful in managing them: not one of them dreamed that he had a rival. If a God-fearing peasant or a gentleman (as the Cossacks call themselves) wearing a cape with a hood went to church on Sunday or, if the weather was bad, to the tavern, how could he fail to look in on Solokha, eat curd dumplings with sour cream, and gossip in the warm hut with its chatty and agreeable mistress? And the Cossack would purposely go a long way around before reaching the tavern, and would call that "looking in on his way." And when Solokha went to church on a holiday, dressed in a bright-checked *plakhta* with a cotton *zapaska*,[4] and above it a dark blue overskirt on the back of which gold flourishes were embroidered, and took up her stand close to the right side of the choir, the sexton would be sure to begin coughing and unconsciously screw up his eyes in her direction; the mayor would smooth his mustaches, begin twisting the curl behind his ear, and say to the man standing next to him: "Ah, a nice woman, a hell of a woman!" Solokha would bow to each one of them, and each one would think that she was bowing to him alone.

But anyone fond of meddling in other people's business would notice at once that Solokha was most gracious to the Cossack Chub. Chub was a widower. Eight stacks of wheat always stood before his hut. Two pairs of stalwart oxen poked their heads out of the barn with the thatched roof by the roadside and mooed every time they saw their crony, the cow, or their uncle, the fat bull, pass. A bearded billygoat used to clamber onto the roof, from which he would bleat in a harsh voice like the police captain's, taunting the turkeys when they came out into the yard, and turning his back when he saw his enemies, the boys, who used to jeer at his beard. In Chub's trunks there was plenty of linen and many caftans and old-fashioned overcoats with gold braid on them; his wife had been fond of fine clothes. In his vegetable patch, besides poppies, cabbages, and sunflowers, two beds were sown every year with tobacco. All this Solokha thought would not be improper to join to her own farm, and, already reckoning in what good condition it would be when it passed into her hands, she felt doubly well-disposed to old Chub. And to prevent her son Vakula from courting Chub's daughter[5] and succeeding in getting possession of it all himself (then he would very likely not let her interfere in anything), she had recourse to the common maneuver of all women of forty— that is, setting Chub against the blacksmith as often as she could. Possibly these sly tricks and subtleties were the reason that the old women were beginning here and there, particularly when they had drunk a drop too much at some merry gathering, to say that Solokha was certainly a witch, that the boy Kizyakolupenko had seen a tail on her back no bigger than a peasant woman's spindle;

---

[4] See p. 10, n. 4. (ed.)
[5] Had her son married Chub's daughter, she could not by the rules of the Russian Church have married Chub. (C.G.)

that, no longer ago than the Thursday before last, she had run across the road in the form of a black cat; that on one occasion a sow had run up to the priest's wife, had crowed like a cock, put Father Kondrat's cap on her head, and run away again. . . .

It happened that just when the old women were talking about this, a cowherd, Tymish Korostyavy, came up. He did not fail to tell them how in the summer, just before St. Peter's Fast, when he had lain down to sleep in the stable, putting some straw under his head, he saw with his own eyes a witch, with her hair down, in nothing but her chemise, begin milking the cows, and he could not stir he was so spellbound, and she had smeared his lips with something so nasty that he was spitting the whole day afterwards. But all that was somewhat doubtful, for the only one who can see a witch is the assessor of Sorochintsy. And so all the notable Cossacks waved their hands impatiently when they heard such tales. "They are lying, the bitches!" was their usual answer.

After she had crept out of the stove and rearranged herself, Solokha, like a good housewife, began tidying up and putting everything in its place; but she did not touch the sacks. "Vakula brought those in, let him take them out himself!" she thought. Meanwhile the devil, who had chanced to turn around just as he was flying into the chimney, had caught sight of Chub arm-in-arm with his neighbor already a long way from home. Instantly he flew out of the chimney, cut across their road, and began flinging up heaps of frozen snow in all directions. A blizzard sprang up. All was whiteness in the air. The snow zigzagged behind and in front and threatened to plaster up the eyes, the mouth, and the ears of the friends. And the devil flew back to the chimney again, certain that Chub would go back home with his neighbor, would find the blacksmith there and probably give him such a scolding that it would be a long time before he would be able to handle a brush and paint offensive caricatures.

As a matter of fact, as soon as the blizzard began and the wind blew straight in their faces, Chub expressed his regret, and pulling his hood further down on his head showered abuse on himself, the devil, and his friend. His annoyance was feigned, however. Chub was really glad of the snowstorm. They had still eight times as far to go as they had gone already before they would reach the sexton's. They turned around. The wind blew on the back of their heads, but they could see nothing through the whirling snow.

"Stop, friend! I think we are going wrong," said Chub, after walking on a little. "I do not see a single hut. Oh, what a snowstorm! You go a little that way and see whether you find the road, and meanwhile I'll look this way. It was the foul fiend put it into my head to go trudging out in such a storm! Don't forget to shout when you find the road. Oh, what a heap of snow Satan has driven into my eyes!"

The road was not to be seen, however. Chub's friend, turning off, wandered up and down in his high boots, and at last came straight upon the tavern. This lucky find so cheered him that he forgot everything and, shaking the snow off, walked straight in, not worrying himself in the least about the friend he had left on the road. Meanwhile Chub thought that he had found the road. Standing still, he started shouting at the top of his voice, but, seeing that his friend did not appear, he made up his mind to go on alone. After walking on a little he saw his own hut. Snowdrifts lay all about it and on the roof. Clapping his frozen hands together, he began knocking on the door and shouting peremptorily to his daughter to open it.

"What do you want here?" the blacksmith called grimly, as he came out.

Chub, recognizing the blacksmith's voice, stepped back a little. "Ah, no, it's not my hut," he said to himself. "The blacksmith doesn't come into my hut. Though, as I look it over, it is not the blacksmith's either. Whose place can it be? I know! I didn't recognize it! It's where lame Levchenko lives, who has lately married a young wife. His is the only hut that is like mine. I did think it was a little strange that I had reached home so soon. But Levchenko is at the sexton's now, I know that. Why is the blacksmith here . . . ? Ah, a-ha! he comes to see his young wife. So that's it! Good . . . ! Now I understand it all."

"Who are you and what are you hanging about at people's doors for?" said the blacksmith more grimly than before, coming closer to him.

"No, I am not going to tell him who I am," thought Chub. "I wouldn't be surprised if he gave me a good beating, the damned brute." And, disguising his voice, he answered: "It's me, good man! I have come for your pleasure, to sing carols under your windows."

"Go to hell with your carols!" Vakula shouted angrily. "Why are you standing there? Do you hear! Get out of here!"

Chub already had that prudent intention; but it annoyed him to be forced to obey the blacksmith's orders. It seemed as though some evil spirit nudged his arm and compelled him to say something contradictory. "Why are you screaming like that?" he said in the same voice. "I want to sing carols and that's all there is to it!"

"Aha! I see words aren't enough for you!" And with that Chub felt a very painful blow on his shoulder.

"So I see you are beginning to fight now!" he said, stepping back a little.

"Get away, get away!" shouted the blacksmith, giving Chub another shove.

"Well, you are the limit!" said Chub in a voice that betrayed pain, annoyance, and timidity. "You are fighting in earnest, I see, and hitting pretty hard, too."

"Get away, get away!" shouted the blacksmith, and slammed the door.

"Look, how he swaggered!" said Chub when he was left alone in the road. "Just try going near him! What a fellow! He's a somebody! Do you suppose I won't have the law on you? No, my dear boy, I am going straight to the commissar. I'll teach you! I don't care if you are a blacksmith and a painter. But I must look at my back and shoulders; I believe they are black and blue. The bastard must have hit hard. It's a pity that it is cold, and I don't want to take off my pelisse. You wait, you fiend of a blacksmith; may the devil give you a beating and your smithy, too; I'll make you dance! Ah, the damned rascal! But he is not at home, now. I expect Solokha is all alone. H'm . . . it's not far off, I might go! It's such weather now that no one will interrupt us. There's no saying what may happen. . . . Aie, how hard that damned blacksmith did hit!"

Here Chub, rubbing his back, started off in a different direction. The agreeable possibilities awaiting him in a tryst with Solokha eased the pain a little and made him insensible even to the frost, the crackling of which could be heard on all the roads in spite of the howling of the storm. At moments a look of mawkish sweetness came into his face, though the blizzard soaped his beard and mustaches with snow more briskly than any barber who tyrannically holds his victim by the nose. But if everything had not been hidden by the flying snow, Chub might have been seen long afterward stopping and rubbing his back as he said: "The damned blacksmith did hit hard!" and then going on his way again.

While the nimble dandy with the tail and goat-beard was flying out of the chimney and back again into the chimney, the pouch which hung on a shoulder-belt at his side, and in which he had put the stolen moon, chanced to catch in something in the stove and came open—and the moon took advantage of this accident to fly up through the chimney of Solokha's hut and to float smoothly through the sky. Everything was flooded with light. It was as though there had been no snowstorm. The snow sparkled, a broad silvery plain, studded with crystal stars. The frost seemed less cold. Groups of boys and girls appeared with sacks. Songs rang out, and under almost every hut window were crowds of carol singers.

How wonderful is the light of the moon! It is hard to put into words how pleasant it is on such a night to mingle in a group of singing, laughing girls and among boys ready for every jest and sport which the gaily smiling night can suggest. It is warm under the thick pelisse; the cheeks glow brighter than ever from the frost, and the devil himself prompts to mischief.

Groups of girls with sacks burst into Chub's hut and gathered around Oksana. The blacksmith was deafened by the shouts, the laughter, the stories. They fought with one another in telling the beauty some bit of news, in emptying their sacks and boasting of the little loaves, sausages, and curd dumplings of which they had already gathered a fair harvest from their singing. Oksana seemed to be highly pleased and delighted; she chatted first with one and then with another and laughed without ceasing.

With what envy and anger the blacksmith looked at this gaiety, and this time he cursed the carol singing, though he was passionately fond of it himself.

"Ah, Odarka!" said the lighthearted beauty, turning to one of the girls, "you have some new slippers. Ah, how pretty! And with gold on them! It's nice for you, Odarka, you have a man who will buy you anything, but I have no one to get me such splendid slippers."

"Don't grieve, my precious Oksana!" said the blacksmith. "I will get you slippers such as not many a lady wears."

"You!" said Oksana, with a quick and proud glance at him. "I should like to know where you'll get hold of slippers such as I could put on my feet. Perhaps you will bring me the very ones the Czarina[6] wears?"

"You see the sort she wants!" cried the crowd of girls, laughing.

"Yes!" the beauty went on proudly, "all of you be my witnesses: if the blacksmith Vakula brings me the very slippers the Czarina wears, here's my word on it: I'll marry him that very day."

The girls carried off the capricious beauty with them.

"Laugh away! Laugh away!" thought the blacksmith as he followed them out. "I laugh at myself! I wonder and can't think what I have done with my senses! She does not love me—well, let her go! As though there were no one in the world but Oksana. Thank God, there are lots of fine girls besides her in the village. And what is Oksana? She'll never make a good housewife; the only thing she is good at is dressing up. No, it's enough! It's time I gave up playing the fool!"

But at the very time when the blacksmith was making up his mind to be resolute, some evil spirit set floating before him the laughing image of Oksana saying mockingly, "Get me the Czarina's slippers, blacksmith, and I will marry you!" Everything within him was stirred and he could think of nothing but Oksana.

The crowds of carol singers, the boys in one party and the girls in another, hurried from one street to the next. But the blacksmith went on and saw nothing, and took no part in the merrymaking which he had once loved more than anything.

Meanwhile the devil was making love in earnest at Solokha's: he kissed her hand with the same airs and graces as the assessor does the priest's daughter's, put his hand on his heart, sighed, and said bluntly that, if she would not consent to gratify his passion and reward his devotion in the usual way, he was ready for anything: would fling himself in the water and let his soul go straight to hell. Solokha was not so cruel; besides, the devil, as we know, was alone with her. She was fond of seeing a crowd hanging about her and was rarely without company. That evening, however, she was expecting to spend alone, because all the noteworthy inhabitants of the village had been invited to keep Christmas Eve at the sexton's. But it turned out otherwise: the devil had only just urged his suit,

---

[6] Catherine II (1729-96); became empress in 1762, after her husband, Peter III, was dethroned by a conspiracy. (ed.)

when suddenly they heard a knock and the voice of the resolute mayor. Solokha ran to open the door, while the nimble devil crept into a sack that was lying on the floor.

The mayor, after shaking the snow off his cap and drinking a glass of vodka from Solokha's hand, told her that he had not gone to the sexton's because it had begun to snow, and seeing a light in her hut, had dropped in, meaning to spend the evening with her.

The mayor had hardly had time to say this when they heard a knock at the door and the voice of the sexton: "Hide me somewhere," whispered the mayor. "I don't want to meet him now."

Solokha thought for some time where to hide so bulky a visitor; at last she selected the biggest coalsack. She shot the coal out into a barrel, and the brave mayor, mustaches, head, pelisse, and all, crept into the sack.

The sexton walked in, clearing his throat and rubbing his hands, and told her that no one had come to his party and that he was heartily glad of this opportunity to enjoy a visit to her and was not afraid of the snowstorm. Then he went closer to her and, with a cough and a smirk, touched her plump bare arm with his long fingers and said with an air expressive both of slyness and satisfaction: "And what have you here, magnificent Solokha?" and saying this he stepped back a little.

"What do you mean? My arm, Osip Nikiforovich!" answered Solokha.

"H'm! your arm! He-he-he!" cried the sexton, highly delighted with his opening. And he paced up and down the room.

"And what have you here, incomparable Solokha . . . ?" he said with the same air, going up to her again, lightly touching her neck and skipping back again in the same way.

"As though you don't see, Osip Nikiforovich!" answered Solokha; "my neck and my necklace on my neck."

"H'm! A necklace on your neck! He-he-he!" and the sexton walked again up and down the room, rubbing his hands.

"And what have you here, incomparable Solokha . . . ?" There's no telling what the sexton (a carnal-minded man) might have touched next with his long fingers, when suddenly they heard a knock at the door and the voice of the Cossack Chub.

"Oh dear, someone who's not wanted!" cried the sexton in alarm. "What now if I am caught here, a person of my position . . . ! It will come to Father Kondrat's ears. . . ."

But the sexton's apprehensions were really of a different nature; he was more afraid that his doings might come to the knowledge of his better half, whose terrible hand had already turned his thick mane into a very scanty one. "For God's sake, virtuous Solokha!" he said, trembling all over, "your loving-kindness, as it says in the Gospel of St. Luke, chapter thirt . . . thirt . . . What a knocking, aie, what a knocking! Ough, hide me somewhere!"

Solokha turned the coal out of another sack, and the sexton, whose proportions were not too ample, crept into it and settled at the very bottom, so that another half-sack of coal might have been put in on top of him.

"Good evening, Solokha!" said Chub, as he came into the hut. "Maybe you didn't expect me, eh? You didn't, did you? Perhaps I am in the way . . . ?" Chub went on with a good-humored and significant expression on his face, which betrayed that his slow-moving mind was at work and preparing to utter some sarcastic and amusing jest.

"Maybe you had some entertaining companion here . . . ! Maybe you have someone in hiding already? Eh?" And enchanted by this observation of his, Chub laughed, inwardly triumphant at being the only man who enjoyed Solokha's favor. "Come, Solokha, let me have a drink of vodka now. I believe my throat's frozen stiff with this damned frost. God has sent us weather for Christmas Eve! How it has come on, do you hear, Solokha, how it has come on . . . ? Ah, my hands are stiff, I can't unbutton my sheepskin! How the storm has come on . . ."

"Open the door!" a voice rang out in the street, accompanied by a thump on the door.

"Someone is knocking," said Chub, standing still.

"Open!" the shout rang out louder still.

"It's the blacksmith!" cried Chub, grabbing his pelisse. "Solokha, put me where you like; for nothing in the world will I show myself to that damned brute. May he have a pimple as big as a pile of hay under each of his eyes, the bastard!"

Solokha, herself alarmed, flew about like one distraught and, forgetting what she was doing, gestured to Chub to creep into the very sack in which the sexton was already sitting. The poor sexton dared not betray his pain by a cough or a groan when the heavy Cossack sat down almost on his head and put a frozen boot on each side of his face.

The blacksmith walked in, not saying a word nor removing his cap, and almost fell down on the bench. It could be seen that he was in a very bad humor.

At the very moment when Solokha was shutting the door after him, someone knocked at the door again. This was the Cossack Sverbiguz. He could not be hidden in the sack, because no sack big enough could be found anywhere. He was fatter than the mayor and taller than Chub's neighbor Panas. And so Solokha led him into the garden to hear from him there all that he had to tell her.

The blacksmith looked absent-mindedly at the corners of his hut, listening from time to time to the voices of the carol singers floating far away through the village. At last his eyes rested on the sacks. "Why are those sacks lying there? They ought to have been cleared away long ago. This foolish love has made me stupid. To-morrow's Christmas and trash of all sorts is still lying about the hut. I'll carry them to the smithy!"

The blacksmith stooped down to the huge sacks, tied them up more tightly, and prepared to hoist them on his shoulders. But it was evident that his thoughts were straying, God knows where, or he would have heard how Chub gasped when the hair of his head was twisted in the string that tied the sack and the brave mayor began hiccuping quite distinctly.

"Can nothing drive that wretched Oksana out of my head?" the blacksmith was saying. "I don't want to think about her; but I keep thinking and thinking and, as luck will have it, of her and nothing else. How is it that thoughts creep into the mind against the will? The devil! The sacks seem to have grown heavier than they were! Something besides coal must have been put into them. I am a fool! I forget that now everything seems heavier to me. In the old days I could bend and unbend a copper coin or a horseshoe with one hand, and now I can't lift sacks of coal. I shall be blown over by the wind next . . . No!" he cried, pulling himself together after a pause, "I am not a weak woman! I won't let anyone make an ass of me! If there were ten such sacks, I would lift them all." And he briskly hoisted on his shoulders the sacks which two strong men could not have carried. "I'll take this one too," he went on, picking up the little one at the bottom of which the devil lay curled up. "I believe I put my tools in this one." Saying this he went out of the hut whistling the song: "I Can't Be Bothered with a Wife."

The singing, laughter, and shouts sounded louder and louder in the streets. The crowds of jostling people were reinforced by newcomers from neighboring villages. The boys were full of mischief and wild pranks. Often among the carols some gay song was heard which one of the young Cossacks had made up on the spot. All at once one of the crowd would sing out a New Year's song instead of a carol and bawl at the top of his voice:

> Kind one, good one
> Give us a dumpling,
> A heap of *kasha*[7]
> And a ring of sausage!

A roar of laughter rewarded the wag. Little windows were thrown up and the withered hand of an old woman (the old women, together with the sedate fathers, were the only people left indoors) was thrust out with a sausage or a piece of pie.

The boys and the girls fought with one another in holding out their sacks and catching their booty. In one place the boys, coming together from all sides, surrounded a group of girls. There was loud noise and clamor; one flung a snowball, another pulled away a sack full of all sorts of good things. In another place, the girls caught a boy, gave him a kick, and sent him flying headlong with his sack into the snow. It seemed as though they were ready to make merry the whole night through. And, as though by design, the night was so splendidly warm. And the light of the moon seemed brighter still from the glitter of the snow.

The blacksmith stood still with his sacks. He thought he heard among the crowd of girls the voice and shrill laugh of Oksana. Every vein in his body throbbed; flinging the sacks on the ground so that the sexton at the bottom groaned over the bruise he received, and the mayor gave a loud hiccup, he strolled with the little sack on his shoulders together with a group of boys after a crowd of girls, among whom he heard the voice of Oksana.

"Yes, it is she! She stands like a queen, her black eyes sparkling. A handsome boy is telling her something. It must be amusing, for she is laughing. But she is always laughing." As it were unconsciously, he could not say how, the blacksmith squeezed his way through the crowd and stood beside her.

---

[7] Groats. (ed.)

"Oh, Vakula, you here! Good evening!" said the beauty, with a smile which almost drove Vakula mad. "Well, have you sung many carols? Oh, but what a little sack! And have you got the slippers that the Czarina wears? Get me the slippers and I will marry you . . . !" And laughing, she ran off with the other girls.

The blacksmith stood as though rooted to the spot. "No, I cannot bear it; it's too much for me . . ." he said at last. "But, my God, why is she so fiendishly beautiful? Her eyes, her words and everything, well, they scorch me, they fairly scorch me. . . . No, I cannot control myself. It's time to put an end to it all. Damn my soul, I'll go and drown myself in the hole in the ice and it will all be over!"

Then with a resolute step he walked on, caught up with the group of girls, overtook Oksana, and said in a firm voice: "Farewell, Oksana! Find any lover you like, make a fool of whom you like; but me you will not see again in this world."

The beauty seemed amazed and would have said something, but with a wave of his hand the blacksmith ran away.

"Where are you off to, Vakula?" said the boys, seeing the blacksmith running.

"Goodbye, friends!" the blacksmith shouted in answer. "Please God we shall meet again in the other world, but we shall not walk together again in this. Farewell! Do not remember evil of me! Tell Father Kondrat to sing a requiem mass for my sinful soul. Sinner that I am, for the sake of worldly things I did not finish painting the candles for the icons of the Martyr and the Virgin Mary. All the goods which will be found in my chest are for the Church. Farewell!"

Saying this, the blacksmith started running again with the sack upon his back.

"He has gone crazy!" said the boys.

"A lost soul!" an old woman, who was passing, muttered devoutly. "I must go and tell them that the blacksmith has hanged himself!"

Meanwhile, after running through several streets, Vakula stopped to catch his breath. "Where am I running?" he thought, "as though everything were over already. I'll try one way more: I'll go to the

Dnieper Cossack Puzaty[8] Patsyuk; they say he knows all the devils and can do anything he likes. I'll go to him, for my soul is lost anyway!"

At that the devil, who had lain for a long while without moving, skipped for joy in the sack; but the blacksmith, thinking that he had somehow twitched the sack with his hand and caused the movement himself, gave the sack a punch with his big fist and, shaking it on his shoulders, set off to Puzaty Patsyuk.

This Puzaty Patsyuk certainly at one time had been a Dnieper Cossack; but no one knew whether he had been turned out of the camp or whether he had run away from Zaporozhye of his own accord.

For a long time, ten years or perhaps fifteen, he had been living in Dikanka. At first he had lived like a true Dnieper Cossack: he had done no work, slept three-quarters of the day, eaten as much as six hay cutters, and drunk almost a whole pailful at a time. He had somewhere to put it all, however, for though Patsyuk was not very tall he was fairly bulky horizontally. Moreover, the trousers he used to wear were so full that, however long a step he took, no trace of his leg was visible, and it seemed as though a wine distiller's machine were moving down the street. Perhaps it was this that gave rise to his nickname, Puzaty. Before many weeks had passed after his coming to the village, everyone had found out that he was a wizard. If anyone were ill, he called in Patsyuk at once: Patsyuk had only to whisper a few words and it was as though the ailment had been lifted off by his hand. If it happened that a hungry gentleman was choked by a fishbone, Patsyuk could punch him so skillfully on the back that the bone went the proper way without causing any harm to the gentleman's throat. Of late years he was rarely seen anywhere. The reason for that was perhaps laziness, though possibly also the fact that it was every year becoming increasingly difficult for him to pass through a doorway. People had of late been obliged to go to him if they had need of him.

Not without some timidity, the blacksmith opened the door and saw Patsyuk sitting Turkish-fashion on the floor before a little tub on which stood a bowl of dumplings. This bowl stood as though purposely planned on a level with his mouth. Without moving a sin-

---

[8] "Paunchy." (ed.)

gle finger, he bent his head a little toward the bowl and sipped the soup, from time to time catching the dumplings with his teeth.

"Well," thought Vakula to himself, "this fellow's even lazier than Chub: he does eat with a spoon, at least, while this fellow won't even lift his hand!"

Patsyuk must have been entirely engrossed in the dumplings, for he seemed to be quite unaware of the entrance of the blacksmith, who offered him a very low bow as soon as he stepped on the threshold.

"I have come to ask you a favor, Patsyuk!" said Vakula, bowing again.

Puzaty Patsyuk lifted his head and again began swallowing dumplings.

"They say that you—no offense meant . . ." the blacksmith said, taking heart, "I speak of this not by way of any insult to you— that you are a little akin to the devil."

When he had uttered these words, Vakula was alarmed, thinking that he had expressed himself too bluntly and had not sufficiently softened his language; and, expecting that Patsyuk would pick up the tub together with the bowl and fling them straight at his head, he turned aside a little and covered his face with his sleeve so that the hot dumpling soup might not spatter it. But Patsyuk looked up and again began swallowing the dumplings.

The blacksmith, reassured, made up his mind to go on. "I have come to you, Patsyuk. God give you everything, goods of all sorts in abundance and bread in proportion!" (The blacksmith would sometimes throw in a fashionable word: he had got into the way of it during his stay in Poltava when he was painting the fence for the officer.) "There is nothing but ruin before me, a sinner! Nothing in the world will help! What will be, will be. I have to ask help from the devil himself. Well, Patsyuk," the blacksmith said, trying to break Patsyuk's silence, "what am I to do?"

"If you need the devil, then go to the devil," answered Patsyuk, not lifting his eyes to him, but still chewing away at the dumplings.

"It is for that that I have come to you," answered the blacksmith, offering him another bow. "I suppose that nobody in the world but you knows the way to him!"

Patsyuk answered not a word, but ate up the remaining dumplings. "Do me a kindness, good man, do not refuse me!" persisted the blacksmith. "Whether it is pork or sausage or buckwheat flour or linen, say—millet or anything else in case of need . . . as is usual between good people . . . we will not grudge it. Tell me at least how, for instance, to get on the road to him."

"He need not go far who has the devil on his shoulders!" Patsyuk pronounced carelessly, without changing his position.

Vakula fastened his eyes upon him as though the interpretation of those words were written on his brow. "What does he mean?" his face asked dumbly, while his mouth stood half-open ready to swallow the first word like a dumpling.

But Patsyuk was still silent.

Then Vakula noticed that there were neither dumplings nor a tub before him; but two wooden bowls were standing on the floor instead—one was filled with turnovers, the other with some cream. His thoughts and his eyes unconsciously fastened on these dainties. "Let us see," he said to himself, "how Patsyuk will eat the turnovers. He certainly won't want to bend down to lap them up like the dumplings; besides he couldn't—he must first dip the turnovers in the cream."

He had hardly time to think this when Patsyuk opened his mouth, looked at the turnovers, and opened his mouth wider still. At that moment a turnover popped out of the bowl, splashed into the cream, turned over on the other side, leaped upward, and flew straight into his mouth. Patsyuk ate it and opened his mouth again, and another turnover went through the same performance. The only trouble he took was to munch it up and swallow it.

"What a miracle!" thought the blacksmith, his mouth dropping open with surprise, and at the same moment he was aware that a turnover was creeping toward him and was already smearing his mouth with cream. Pushing away the turnover and wiping his lips, the blacksmith began to reflect what marvels there are in the world and to what subtle devices the evil spirit may lead a man, saying to himself at the same time that no one but Patsyuk could help him.

"I'll bow to him once more; maybe he will explain properly. . . . He's a devil, though! Why, today is a fast day and he is eating turnovers with meat in them! What a fool I am, really. I am standing here and preparing to sin! Back . . . !" And the pious blacksmith ran headlong out of the hut.

But the devil, sitting in the sack and already gloating over his prey, could not endure letting such a glorious capture slip through his fingers. As soon as the blacksmith put down the sack the devil skipped out of it and straddled his neck.

A cold shudder ran over the blacksmith's skin; pale and scared, he did not know what to do; he was on the point of crossing himself. . . . But the devil, putting his snout down to Vakula's right ear, said: "It's me, your friend; I'll do anything for a friend and comrade! I'll give you as much money as you like," he squeaked into his left ear. "Oksana shall be yours this very day," he whispered, turning his snout again to the right ear. The blacksmith stood still, hesitating.

"Very well," he said at last; "for such a price I am ready to be yours!"

The devil clasped his hands in delight and began galloping up and down on the blacksmith's neck. "Now the blacksmith is done for!" he thought to himself: "now I'll pay you back, my sweet fellow, for all your paintings and false tales thrown up at the devils! What will my comrades say now when they learn that the most pious man of the whole village is in my hands!"

Here the devil laughed with joy, thinking how he would taunt all the long-tailed crew in hell, how furious the lame devil, who was considered the most resourceful among them, would be.

"Well, Vakula!" piped the devil, not dismounting from his neck, as though afraid he might escape, "you know nothing is done without a contract."

"I am ready!" said the blacksmith. "I have heard that among you contracts are signed with blood. Wait. I'll get a nail out of my pocket!"

And he put his hand behind him and caught the devil by the tail.

"What a man you are for a joke!" cried the devil, laughing. "Come, let go, that's enough mischief!"

"Wait a minute, friend!" cried the blacksmith, "and what do you think of this?" As he said that he made the sign of the cross and the devil became as meek as a lamb. "Wait a minute," said the blacksmith, pulling him by the tail to the ground: "I'll teach you to entice good men and honest Christians into sin."

Here the blacksmith leaped on the devil and lifted his hand to make the sign of the cross.

"Have mercy, Vakula!" the devil moaned piteously; "I will do anything you want, anything; only let me off with my life: do not lay the terrible cross upon me!"

"Ah, so that's your tone now, you damned German! Now I know what to do. Carry me at once on your back! Do you hear? And fly like a bird!"

"Where?" asked the miserable devil.

"To Petersburg, straight to the Czarina!" And the blacksmith almost fainted with terror as he felt himself soaring into the air.

Oksana stood for a long time pondering on the strange words of the blacksmith. Already an inner voice was telling her that she had treated him too cruelly. "What if he really does make up his mind to do something dreadful! I wouldn't be surprised! Perhaps his sorrow will make him fall in love with another girl, and in his anger he will begin calling her the greatest beauty in the village. But no, he loves me. I am so beautiful! He will not give me up for anything; he is playing, he is pretending. In ten minutes he will come back to look at me, for certain. I really was angry. I must, as though it were against my will, let him kiss me. Won't he be delighted!" And the frivolous beauty went back to jesting with her companions.

"Stop," said one of them, "the blacksmith has forgotten his sacks: look what fat sacks! He has made more by his carol singing than we have. I bet they must have put here at least a quarter of a sheep, and I am sure that there are no end of sausages and loaves in them. Wonderful! we shall have enough to feast on all Christmas week!"

"Are they the blacksmith's sacks?" asked Oksana. "We had better drag them to my hut and have a good look at what he has put in them."

All the girls laughingly approved of this proposal.

"But we can't lift them!" the whole group cried, trying to move the sacks.

"Wait a minute," said Oksana; "let us run for a sled and take them away on it!"

And the crowd of girls ran out to get a sled.

The captives were terribly bored with staying in the sacks, although the sexton had poked a fair-sized hole to peep through. If there had been no one about, he might have found a way to creep out; but to creep out of a sack in front of everybody, to be a laughingstock . . . that thought restrained him, and he made up his mind to wait, only uttering a slight groan under Chub's ill-mannered boots.

Chub himself was no less eager for freedom, feeling that there was something under him that was terribly uncomfortable to sit upon. But as soon as he heard his daughter's plan, he felt relieved and did not want to creep out, reflecting that it must be at least a hundred paces and perhaps two hundred to his hut; if he crept out, he would have to rearrange himself, button up his sheepskin, fasten his belt—such a lot of trouble! Besides, his winter cap had been left at Solokha's. Let the girls drag him in the sled.

But things turned out not at all as Chub was expecting. Just when the girls were running to fetch the sled, his lean neighbor, Panas, came out of the tavern, upset and ill-humored. The woman who kept the tavern could not be persuaded to serve him on credit. He thought to sit on in the tavern in the hope that some godly gentleman would come along and treat him; but as ill-luck would have it, all the gentlefolk were staying at home and like good Christians were eating rice and honey in the bosom of their families. Meditating on the degeneration of manners and the hard heart of the Jewess who kept the tavern, Panas made his way up to the sacks and stopped in amazement. "My word, what sacks somebody has flung down in the road!" he said, looking about him in all directions. "I'll bet there is pork in them. Some carol singer is in luck to get so many gifts of all sorts! What fat sacks! Suppose they are only stuffed full of buckwheat cake and biscuits, that's worth having; if there should be nothing but biscuits in them, that would be welcome, too; the Jewess would give me a dram of vodka for each cake. Let's make haste and get them away before anyone sees."

Here he flung on his shoulder the sack with Chub and the sexton in it, but felt it was too heavy. "No, it'll be too heavy for one to carry," he said; "and here by good luck comes the weaver Shapuvalenko. Good evening, Ostap!"

"Good evening!" said the weaver, stopping.

"Where are you going?"

"Oh, nowhere in particular."

"Help me carry these sacks, good man! Someone has been singing carols, and has dropped them in the middle of the road. We'll share the things."

"Sacks? sacks of what? White loaves or biscuits?"

"Oh, all sorts of things, I expect."

They hurriedly pulled some sticks out of the fence, laid the sack on them, and carried it on their shoulders.

"Where shall we take it? To the tavern?" the weaver asked on the way.

"That's just what I was thinking; but, you know, the damned Jewess won't trust us, she'll think we have stolen it somewhere; besides, I have only just come from the tavern. We'll take it to my hut. No one will hinder us there; the wife's not at home."

"Are you sure she is not at home?" the cautious weaver inquired.

"Thank God that I am not quite a fool yet," said Panas; "the devil would hardly take me where she is. I'm sure she will be trailing around with the other women till daybreak."

"Who is there?" shouted Panas' wife, opening the door of the hut as she heard the noise in the porch made by the two friends with the sack. Panas was dumbfounded.

"Well, that's it!" said the weaver, letting his hands fall.

Panas' wife was a treasure of a kind that is not uncommon in this world. Like her husband, she hardly ever stayed at home, but almost every day visited various cronies and well-to-do old women, flattered them, and ate with good appetite at their expense; she only quarreled with her husband in the mornings, as it was only then that she sometimes saw him. Their hut was twice as old as the district clerk's trousers; there was no straw in places on their thatched roof. Only the remnants of a fence could be seen, for everyone, as he went out of his house, thought it unnecessary to take a stick for the dogs, relying on passing by Panas' vegetable garden and pulling one out of his fence. The stove was not heated for three days at a time. Whatever the tender wife managed to beg from good Christians she hid as far as possible out of her husband's reach, and often robbed him of his gains if he had not had time to spend them on drink. In spite of his habitual imperturbability Panas did not like to give way to her, and consequently left his house every day with both eyes blackened, while his better half, sighing and groaning, waddled off to tell her old friends of her husband's unmannerliness and the blows she had to put up with from him.

Now you can imagine how disconcerted were the weaver and Panas by this unexpected apparition. Dropping the sack, they stood before it, and concealed it with the skirts of their coats, but it was already too late: Panas' wife, though she did not see well with her old eyes, had observed the sack.

"Well, that's good!" she said, with a face which betrayed the joy of a vulture. "That's good, that you have gained so much singing carols! That's how it always is with good Christians; but no, I'm sure you have stolen it somewhere. Show me your sack at once, do you hear, show me this very minute!"

"The bald devil may show you, but we won't," said Panas, assuming a dignified air.

"What's it to do with you?" said the weaver. "We've sung the carols, not you."

"Yes, you will show me, you wretched drunkard!" screamed the wife, striking her tall husband on the chin with her fist and forcing her way toward the sack. But the weaver and Panas manfully defended the sack and compelled her to beat a retreat. Before they recovered themselves the wife ran out again with a poker in her hands. She nimbly hit her husband a blow on the arms and the weaver one on his back and reached for the sack.

"Why did we let her pass?" said the weaver, regaining his senses.

"Yes, we let her pass! Why did you let her pass?" said Panas coolly.

"Your poker is made of iron, it seems!" said the weaver after a brief silence, rubbing his back. "My wife bought one last year at the fair, gave twenty-five kopeks; that one's all right . . . it doesn't hurt . . ."

Meanwhile the triumphant wife, setting a lamp on the floor, untied the sack and peeped into it.

But her old eyes, which had so well described the sack, this time certainly deceived her.

"Oh, but there is a whole pig lying here!" she shrieked, clapping her hands in glee.

"A pig! Do you hear, a whole pig!" The weaver nudged Panas. "And it's all your fault."

"It can't be helped!" replied Panas, shrugging his shoulders.

"Can't be helped! Why are we standing still? Let us take away the sack! Here, come on! Go away, go away, it's our pig!" shouted the weaver, stepping forward.

"Move away, move away, you devilish woman! It's not your property!" said Panas, approaching.

His wife picked up the poker again, but at that moment Chub crawled out of the sack and stood in the middle of the room, stretching like a man who has just waked up from a long sleep.

Panas' wife shrieked, slapping her skirts, and they all stood with open mouths.

"Why did she say it was a pig, the ass! It's not a pig!" said Panas, staring open-eyed.

"God! What a man has been dropped into a sack!" said the weaver, staggering back in alarm. "You may say what you please, you can burst if you like, but the foul fiend has had a hand in it. Why, he would not go through a window!"

"It's Chub!" cried Panas, looking more closely.

"Why, who did you think it was?" said Chub, laughing. "Well, haven't I played you a fine trick? I'll bet you meant to eat me as pork! Wait a minute, I'll console you: there is something in the sack; if not a whole pig, it's certainly a little porker or some live beast. Something kept moving under me."

The weaver and Panas flew to the sack, the lady of the house clutched at the other side of it, and the battle would have been renewed had not the sexton, seeing that now he had no chance of concealment, scrambled out of the sack of his own accord.

The woman, astounded, let go of the leg by which she was beginning to drag the sexton out of the sack.

"Here's another of them!" cried the weaver in horror, "the devil knows what has happened to the world. . . . My head's going around. . . . Men are put into sacks instead of cakes or sausages!"

"It's the sexton!" said Chub, more surprised than any of them. "Well, then! You're a nice one, Solokha! To put one in a sack . . . I thought at the time her hut was very full of sacks. . . . Now I understand it all: she had a couple of men hidden in each sack. While I thought it was only me she . . . So now you know her!"

The girls were a little surprised on finding that one sack was missing.

"Well, there is nothing we can do, we must be content with this one," murmured Oksana.

The mayor made up his mind to keep quiet, reasoning that if he called out to them to untie the sack and let him out, the foolish girls would run away in all directions; they would think that the devil was in the sack—and he would be left in the street till next day. Meanwhile the girls, linking arms together, flew like a whirlwind with the sled over the crunching snow. Many of them sat on the sled for fun; others even clambered on top of the mayor. The mayor made up his mind to endure everything.

At last they arrived, threw open the door into the outer room of the hut, and dragged in the sack amid laughter.

"Let us see what is in it," they all cried, hastening to untie it.

At this point the hiccup which had tormented the mayor became so much worse that he began hiccuping and coughing loudly.

"Ah, there is someone in it!" they all shrieked, and rushed out of doors in horror.

"What the devil is it? Where are you tearing off to as though you were all possessed?" said Chub, walking in at the door.

"Oh, Daddy!" cried Oksana, "there is someone in the sack!"

"In the sack? Where did you get this sack?"

"The blacksmith threw it in the middle of the road," they all said at once.

"So that's it; didn't I say so?" Chub thought to himself. "What are you frightened at? Let us look. Come now, my man—I beg you won't be offended at our not addressing you by your proper name —crawl out of the sack!"

The mayor did crawl out.

"Oh!" shrieked the girls.

"So the mayor got into one, too," Chub thought to himself in bewilderment, scanning him from head to foot. "Well, I'll be damned!" He could say nothing more.

The mayor himself was no less confused and did not know how to begin. "I think it is a cold night," he said, addressing Chub.

"There is a bit of a frost," answered Chub. "Allow me to ask you what you rub your boots with, goose fat or tar?" He had not meant to say that; he had meant to ask: "How did you get into that sack, mayor?" and he did not himself understand how he came to say something utterly different.

"Tar is better," said the mayor. "Well, good night, Chub!" And pulling his winter cap down over his head, he walked out of the hut.

"Why was I such a fool as to ask him what he rubbed his boots with?" said Chub, looking toward the door by which the mayor had gone out.

"Well, Solokha is a fine one! To put a man like that in a sack . . . ! My word, she is a devil of a woman! While I, poor fool . . . But where is that damned sack?"

"I flung it in the corner, there is nothing more in it," said Oksana.

"I know all about that; nothing in it, indeed! Give it here; there is another one in it! Shake it well . . . What, nothing? My word, the cursed woman! And to look at her she is like a saint, as though she had never tasted anything but lenten fare . . . !"

But we will leave Chub to pour out his anger at leisure and will go back to the blacksmith, for it must be past eight o'clock.

At first it seemed dreadful to Vakula, particularly when he rose up from the earth to such a height that he could see nothing below, and flew like a fly so close under the moon that if he had not bent down he would have caught his cap in it. But in a little while he gained confidence and even began mocking the devil. (He was extremely amused by the way the devil sneezed and coughed when he took the little cyprus-wood cross off his neck and held it down to him. He purposely raised his hand to scratch his head, and the devil, thinking he was going to make the sign of the cross over him, flew along more swiftly than ever.) It was quite light at that height. The air was transparent, bathed in a light silvery mist. Everything was visible, and he could even see a sorcerer whisk by them like a hurricane, sitting in a pot, and the stars gathering together to play hide-and-seek, a whole swarm of spirits whirling away in a cloud, a devil dancing in the light of the moon and taking off his cap at the sight of the blacksmith galloping by, a broom flying back home, from which evidently a witch had just alighted at her destination. . . . And they met many other nasty things. They all stopped at the sight of the blacksmith to stare at him for a moment, and then whirled off and went on their way again. The blacksmith flew on till all at once Petersburg flashed before him, glittering with lights. (For a certain reason the city was illuminated that day.) The devil, flying over the city gate, turned into a horse and the blacksmith found himself mounted on a fiery steed in the middle of the street.

My goodness! the clatter, the uproar, the brilliant light; the walls rose up, four stories on each side; the thud of the horses' hoofs and the rumble of the wheels echoed and resounded from every quarter; houses seemed to pop up out of the ground at every step; the bridges trembled; carriages raced along; sled drivers and postilions shouted; the snow crunched under the thousand sleds flying from all parts; people passing along on foot huddled together, crowded under the houses which were studded with little lamps, and their immense shadows flitted over the walls with their heads reaching the roofs and the chimneys.

The blacksmith looked about him in amazement. It seemed to him as though all the houses had fixed their innumerable fiery eyes upon him, watching. Good Lord! he saw so many gentlemen in cloth fur-lined overcoats that he did not know whom to take off his cap to. "Good God, how many gentlemen are here!" thought the blacksmith. "I think everyone who comes along the street in a fur coat is the assessor and again the assessor! And those who are driving about in such wonderful chaises with glass windows, if they are not police captains they certainly must be commissars or perhaps something even more important." His words were cut short by a question from the devil:

"Am I to go straight to the Czarina?"

"No, I'm frightened," thought the blacksmith. "The Dnieper Cossacks, who marched in the autumn through Dikanka, are stationed here, where I don't know. They came from the camp with papers for the Czarina; anyway, I might ask their advice. Hey, Satan! creep into my pocket and take me to the Dnieper Cossacks."

And in one minute the devil became so thin and small that he had no difficulty creeping into the blacksmith's pocket. And before Vakula had time to look around he found himself in front of a big house, went up a staircase, hardly knowing what he was doing, opened a door, and drew back a little from the brilliant light on seeing the smartly furnished room; but he regained confidence a little when he recognized the Cossacks who had ridden through Dikanka and now, sitting on silk-covered sofas, their tar-smeared boots tucked under them, were smoking the strongest tobacco, usually called "root."

"Good day to you, gentlemen! God be with you, this is where we meet again," said the blacksmith, going up to them and tossing off a low bow.

"What man is that?" the one who was sitting just in front of the blacksmith asked another who was further away.

"You don't know me?" said the blacksmith. "It's me, Vakula the blacksmith! When you rode through Dikanka in the autumn you stayed nearly two days with me. God give you all health and long years! And I put a new iron hoop on the front wheel of your chaise!"

"Oh!" said the same Cossack, "it's that blacksmith who paints so well. Good day to you, neighbor! How has God brought you here?"

"Oh, I just wanted to have a look around. I was told . . ."

"Well, neighbor," said the Cossack, drawing himself up with dignity and wishing to show he could speak Russian too, "well, it's a big city."

The blacksmith, too, wanted to preserve his reputation and not to seem like a novice. Moreover, as we have had occasion to see before, he too could speak as if from a book.

"A considerable town!" he answered casually. "There is no denying the houses are very large, the pictures that are hanging up are uncommonly good. Many of the houses are painted exuberantly with letters in gold leaf. The configuration is superb, there is no other word for it!"

The Dnieper Cossacks, hearing the blacksmith express himself in such a manner, drew the most flattering conclusions in regard to him.

"We will have a little more talk with you, neighbor; now we are going at once to the Czarina."

"To the Czarina? Oh, be so kind, gentlemen, as to take me with you!"

"You?" a Cossack pronounced in the tone in which an old man speaks to his four-year-old charge when the latter asks to be seated on a real, big horse. "What would you do there? No, we can't do that. We are going to talk about our own affairs to the Czarina." And his face assumed an expression of great significance.

"Please take me!" the blacksmith persisted.

"Ask them to!" he whispered softly to the devil, banging on the pocket with his fist.

He had hardly said this, when another Cossack said: "Let's take him, friends!"

"Yes, let's take him!" others joined in.

"Put on the same clothing as we are wearing, then."

The blacksmith was hastily putting on a green coat when all at once the door opened and a man covered with gold braid said it was time to go.

Again the blacksmith was moved to wonder, as he was whisked along in an immense coach swaying on springs, as four-storied houses raced by him on both sides and the rumbling pavement seemed to be moving under the horses' hoofs.

"My goodness, how light it is!" thought the blacksmith to himself. "At home it is not so light as this in the daytime."

The coaches stopped in front of the palace. The Cossacks got out, went into a magnificent vestibule, and began ascending a brilliantly lighted staircase.

"What a staircase!" the blacksmith murmured to himself, "it's a pity to trample it with one's feet. What decorations! They say the stories are untrue! The devil they are! My goodness! what banisters, what workmanship! At least fifty rubles must have been spent on the iron alone!"

When they had mounted the stairs, the Cossacks walked through the first drawing room. The blacksmith followed them timidly, afraid of slipping on the parquet at every footstep. They walked through three drawing rooms, the blacksmith still overwhelmed with admiration. On entering the fourth, he could not help going up to a picture hanging on the wall. It was the Holy Virgin with the Child in her arms.

"What a picture! What a wonderful painting!" he thought. "It seems to be speaking! It seems to be alive! And the Holy Child! It's pressing its little hands together and laughing, poor thing! And the colors! My goodness, what colors! I think there is not a kopek-worth of ochre on it; it's all emerald green and crimson lake. And the blue simply glows! A fine piece of work! I'm sure the background was put in with the most expensive white lead. Wonderful as that painting is, though, this copper handle," he went on, going up to the door and fingering the lock, "is even more wonderful. Ah, what a fine finish! That's all done, I imagine, by German blacksmiths, and it must be terribly expensive."

Perhaps the blacksmith would have gone on reflecting for a long time, if a flunkey in livery had not nudged his arm and reminded him not to lag behind the others. The Cossacks passed through two more rooms and then stopped. They were told to wait in the third, in which there was a group of several generals in gold-braided uniforms. The Cossacks bowed in all directions and stood together.

A minute later, a rather thickset man of majestic stature, wearing the uniform of a Hetman and yellow boots, walked in, accompanied by a retinue. His hair was in disorder, he squinted a little, his face wore an expression of haughty dignity, and the habit of command could be seen in every movement. All the generals, who had been walking up and down rather superciliously in their gold uniforms, bustled about and seemed with low bows to be hanging on every word he uttered and even on his slightest gesture, so as to fly at once to carry out his wishes. But the Hetman did not even notice all that: he barely nodded to them and went up to the Cossacks.

The Cossacks all bowed low, to the ground.

"Are you all here?" he asked deliberately, speaking a little through his nose.

"All, little father!" answered the Cossacks, bowing again.

"Don't forget to speak as I have told you!"

"No, little father, we will not forget."

"Is that the Czar?" asked the blacksmith of one of the Cossacks.

"Czar, indeed! It's Potiomkin[9] himself," answered the other.

Voices were heard in the other room, and the blacksmith did not know which way to look for the number of ladies who walked in, wearing satin gowns with long trains, and courtiers in gold-laced coats with their hair tied in a tail at the back. He could see a blur of brilliance and nothing more.

The Cossacks all bowed down at once to the floor and cried out with one voice: "Have mercy, little mother, mercy!"

The blacksmith, too, though seeing nothing, stretched himself very zealously on the floor.

"Get up!" An imperious and at the same time pleasant voice sounded above them. Some of the courtiers bustled about and nudged the Cossacks.

"We will not get up, little mother! We will not get up! We will die, but we will not get up!" they shouted.

Potiomkin bit his lips. At last he went up himself and whispered sternly to one of the Cossacks. They rose to their feet.

Then the blacksmith, too, ventured to raise his head, and saw standing before him a short and, indeed, rather stout woman with blue eyes, and at the same time with that majestically smiling air which was so well able to subdue everything and could only belong to a queen.

---

[9] Grigory Aleksandrovich Potiomkin (1739-91), of a noble but impoverished Polish family, attracted the notice of Catherine II while serving in the Russian army, and in 1774 became her recognized favorite, and, in fact, directed Russian policy. (ed.)

"His Excellency has promised to make me acquainted today with my people whom I have not seen before," said the lady with the blue eyes, scrutinizing the men with curiosity.

"Are you well cared for here?" she went on, going nearer to them.

"Thank you, little mother! The provisions they give us are excellent, though the mutton here is not at all like what we have in Zaporozhye . . . What does our daily fare matter . . . ?"

Potiomkin frowned, seeing that the Cossacks were saying something quite different from what he had taught them. . . .

One of them, drawing himself up with dignity, stepped forward:

"Be gracious, little mother! How have your faithful people angered you? Have we taken the hand of the vile Tartar? Have we come to agreement with the Turk? Have we been false to you in deed or in thought? How have we lost your favor? First we heard that you were commanding fortresses to be built everywhere against us; then we heard you mean to turn us into carbineers; now we hear of new oppressions. How are your Zaporozhye troops in fault? In having brought your army across the Perekop and helped your generals to slaughter the Tartars in the Crimea . . . ?"

Potiomkin casually rubbed with a little brush the diamonds with which his hands were studded and said nothing.

"What is it you want?" Catherine asked anxiously.

The Cossacks looked meaningly at one another.

"Now is the time! The Czarina asks what we want!" the blacksmith said to himself, and he suddenly flopped down on the floor.

"Your Imperial Majesty, do not command me to be punished! Show me mercy! Of what, be it said without offense to your Imperial Graciousness, are the little slippers made that are on your feet? I think there is no Swede nor a shoemaker in any kingdom in the world who can make them like that. Merciful heavens, if only my wife could wear such slippers!"

The Empress laughed. The courtiers laughed too. Potiomkin frowned and smiled at the same time. The Cossacks began nudging the blacksmith under the arm, wondering whether he had not gone out of his mind.

"Stand up!" the Empress said graciously. "If you wish to have slippers like these, it is very easy to arrange it. Bring him at once the very best slippers with gold on them! Indeed, this simpleheartedness greatly pleases me! Here you have a subject worthy of your witty pen!" the Empress went on, turning to a gentleman with a full but rather pale face, who stood a little apart from the others and whose modest coat with big mother-of-pearl buttons on it showed that he was not one of the courtiers.

"You are too gracious, your Imperial Majesty. It needs a La Fontaine[10] at least to do justice to it!" answered the man with the mother-of-pearl buttons, bowing.

"I tell you sincerely, I have not yet got over my delight at your *Brigadier*.[11] You read so wonderfully well! I have heard, though," the Empress went on, turning again to the Cossacks, "that none of you are married in your camp." [12]

"What next, little mother! Why, you know yourself, a man cannot live without a wife," answered the same Cossack who had talked to the blacksmith, and the blacksmith wondered, hearing him address the Czarina, as though purposely, in coarse language, speaking like a peasant, as it is commonly called, though he could speak as if from a book.

"They are sly fellows!" he thought to himself. "I'll bet he does not do that for nothing."

"We are not monks," the Cossack went on, "but sinful folk. Ready like all honest Christians to fall into sin. There are among us many who have wives, but do not live with them in the camp. There are some who have wives in Poland; there are some who have wives in the Ukraine; there are some who have wives even in Turkey."

At that moment they brought the blacksmith the slippers.

"God, what fine embroidery!" he cried joyfully, taking the slippers. "Your Imperial Majesty! If the slippers on your feet are like this—and in them Your Honor, I expect, goes skating on the ice—what must the feet themselves be like! They must be made of pure sugar at least, I should think!"

The Empress, who had in fact very well-shaped and charming feet, could not help smiling at hearing such a compliment from the

---

[10] French poet (1621-95); author of popular fables. (ed.)
[11] She is speaking to Denis Fonvizin (1744-92). *Brigadier* is his famous comedy. (ed.)
[12] *Sech*, Cossack military camp established in a clearing near the Dnieper River. A full description of a *sech* is given in *Taras Bulba*. (ed.)

lips of a simplehearted blacksmith, who in his Dnieper Cossack uniform might be considered a handsome fellow in spite of his swarthy face.

Delighted with such gracious attention, the blacksmith would have liked to question the pretty Czarina thoroughly about everything: whether it was true that Czars eat nothing but honey, fat bacon, and such; but, feeling that the Cossacks were digging him in the ribs, he made up his mind to keep quiet. And when the Empress, turning to the older men, began questioning them about their manner of life and customs in the camp, he, stepping back, stooped down to his pocket, and said softly: "Get me away from here, quickly!" And at once he found himself outside the city gates.

"He is drowned! I swear he is drowned! May I never leave this spot if he is not drowned!" lisped the weaver's fat wife, standing with a group of Dikanka women in the middle of the street.

"Why, am I a liar, then? Have I stolen anyone's cow? Have I put the evil eye on someone, that I am not to be believed?" shouted a purple-nosed woman in a Cossack coat, waving her arms. "May I never want to drink water again if old Dame Pereperchikha didn't see with her own eyes the blacksmith hanging himself!"

"Has the blacksmith hanged himself? Well, I never!" said the mayor, coming out of Chub's hut, and he stopped and pressed closer to the group.

"You had better say, may you never want to drink vodka, you old drunkard!" answered the weaver's wife. "He must be as crazy as you to hang himself! He drowned himself! He drowned himself in the hole in the ice! I know that as well as I know that you were in the tavern just now."

"You disgrace! See what she throws up at me!" the woman with the purple nose retorted wrathfully. "You had better hold your tongue, you wretch! Do you think I don't know that the sexton comes to see you every evening?"

The weaver's wife flared up.

"What about the sexton? Whom does he go to? What lies are you telling?"

"The sexton?" piped the sexton's wife, squeezing her way up to the combatants, in an old blue cotton coat lined with hareskin. "I'll let the sexton know! Who was it said the sexton?"

"Well, this is the lady the sexton visits!" said the woman with the purple nose, pointing to the weaver's wife.

"So it's you, you bitch!" said the sexton's wife, stepping up to the weaver's wife. "So it's you, is it, witch, who cast a spell over him and gave him foul poison to make him come to you!"

"Get behind me, Satan!" said the weaver's wife, staggering back.

"Oh, you cursed witch, may you never live to see your children! Wretched creature! Tfoo!"

Here the sexton's wife spat straight into the other woman's face.

The weaver's wife tried to do the same, but spat instead on the unshaven chin of the mayor, who had come close to the combatants so that he might hear the quarrel better.

"Ah, nasty woman!" cried the mayor, wiping his face with the skirt of his coat and lifting his whip.

This gesture sent them all flying in different directions, cursing loudly.

"How disgusting!" repeated the mayor, still wiping his face. "So the blacksmith is drowned! My goodness! What a fine painter he was! What good knives and reaping hooks and plows he could forge! What a strong man he was! Yes," he went on musing; "there are not many fellows like that in our village. To be sure, I did notice while I was in that damned sack that the poor fellow was very much depressed. So that is the end of the blacksmith! He was and is not! And I was meaning to have my dapple mare shod . . . !" And filled with such Christian reflections, the mayor quietly made his way to his own hut.

Oksana was much troubled when the news reached her. She put little faith in the woman Pereperchikha's having seen it and in the women's talk; she knew that the blacksmith was too pious a man to bring himself to send his soul to perdition. But what if he really had gone away, intending never to return to the village? And, indeed, in any place it would be hard to find as fine a fellow as the blacksmith. And how he had loved her! He had endured her whims longer than any one of them. . . . All night long the beauty turned over from her right side to her left and her left to her right, and could not fall asleep. Naked, she tossed sensuously in the darkness of her room. She reviled herself almost aloud; grew peaceful; made up her mind to think of nothing—and kept thinking all the time. She was in a perfect fever, and by the morning head over ears in love with the blacksmith.

Chub expressed neither pleasure nor sorrow at Vakula's fate. His thoughts were absorbed by one subject: he could not forget the treachery of Solokha and never stopped abusing her even in his sleep.

Morning came. Even before daybreak the church was full of people. Elderly women in white linen wimples, in white cloth tunics, crossed themselves piously at the church porch. Ladies in green and yellow blouses, some even in dark blue overdresses with gold streamers behind, stood in front of them. Girls who had a whole shopful of ribbons twined on their heads, and necklaces, crosses, and coins around their necks, tried to make their way closer to the icon-stand. But in front of all stood the gentlemen and humble peasants with mustaches, with forelocks, with thick necks and newly shaven chins, for the most part wearing hooded cloaks, below which peeped a white or sometimes a dark blue jacket. Wherever one looked every face had a festive air. The mayor was licking his lips in anticipation of the sausage with which he would break his fast; the girls were thinking how they would skate with the boys on the ice; the old women murmured prayers more zealously than ever. All over the church one could hear the Cossack Sverbiguz bowing to the ground. Only Oksana stood feeling unlike herself: she prayed without praying. So many different feelings, each more amazing, each more distressing than the other, crowded upon her heart that her face expressed nothing but overwhelming confusion; tears quivered in her eyes. The girls could not think why it was and did not suspect that the blacksmith was responsible. However, not only Oksana was concerned about the blacksmith. All the villagers observed that the holiday did not seem like a holiday, that something was lacking. To make things worse, the sexton was hoarse after his travels in the sack and he wheezed scarcely audibly; it is true that the chorister who was on a visit to the village sang the bass splendidly, but how much better it would have been if they had had the blacksmith too, who used always when they were singing *Our Father* or the *Holy Cherubim* to step up into the choir and from there sing it with the same chant with which it is sung in Poltava. Moreover, he alone performed the duty of a churchwarden. Matins were already over; after matins mass was over. . . . Where indeed could the blacksmith have vanished to?

It was still night as the devil flew even more swiftly back with the blacksmith, and in a flash Vakula found himself inside his own hut. At that moment the cock crowed.

"Where are you off to?" cried the blacksmith, catching the devil by his tail as he was about to run away. "Wait a moment, friend, that's not all: I haven't thanked you yet." Then, seizing a switch, he gave him three lashes, and the poor devil started running like a peasant who has just had a beating from the tax assessor. And so, instead of tricking, tempting, and fooling others, the enemy of mankind was fooled himself. After that Vakula went into the outer room, made himself a hole in the hay, and slept till dinnertime. When he woke up he was frightened at seeing that the sun was already high. "I've overslept myself and missed matins and mass!"

Then the worthy blacksmith was overwhelmed with distress, thinking that no doubt God, as a punishment for his sinful intention of damning his soul, had sent this heavy sleep, which had prevented him from even being in church on this solemn holiday. However, comforting himself with the thought that next week he would confess all this to the priest and that from that day he would begin making fifty genuflections a day for a whole year, he glanced into the hut; but there was no one there. Apparently Solokha had not yet returned.

Carefully he drew out from the breast of his coat the slippers and again marveled at the costly workmanship and at the wonderful adventure of the previous night. He washed and dressed himself in his best, put on the very clothes which he had got from the Dnieper Cossacks, took out of a chest a new cap of good astrakhan with a dark blue top not once worn since he had bought it while staying in Poltava; he also took out a new girdle of rainbow colors; he put all this together with a whip in a kerchief and set off straight to see Chub.

Chub opened his eyes wide when the blacksmith walked into his hut, and did not know what to wonder at most: the blacksmith's having risen from the dead, the blacksmith's having dared to come to see him, or the blacksmith's being dressed up as such a dandy, like a Dnieper Cossack. But he was even more astonished when Vakula untied the kerchief and laid before him a new cap and a girdle such as had never been seen in the village, and then fell down on his knees before him, and said in a tone of entreaty: "Have mercy, father! Be not angry! Here is a whip; beat me as much as your heart may desire. I give myself up, I repent of everything! Beat, but only be not angry. You were once a comrade of my father's, you ate bread and salt together and drank the cup of good-will."

It was not without secret satisfaction that Chub saw the black-smith, who had never bowed to anyone in the village and who could twist five-kopek pieces and horseshoes in his hands like pancakes, lying now at his feet. In order to maintain his dignity still further, Chub took the whip and gave him three strokes on the back. "Well, that's enough; get up! Always obey the old! Let us forget everything that has passed between us. Come, tell me now what is it that you want?"

"Give me Oksana for my wife, father!"

Chub thought a little, looked at the cap and the girdle. The cap was delightful and the girdle, too, was not inferior to it; he thought of the treacherous Solokha and said resolutely: "Good! send the matchmakers!"

"Aie!" shrieked Oksana, as she crossed the threshold and saw the blacksmith, and she gazed at him with astonishment and delight.

"Look, what slippers I have brought you!" said Vakula, "they are the same as the Czarina wears!"

"No, no! I don't want slippers!" she said, waving her arms and keeping her eyes fixed upon him. "I am ready without slippers . . ." She blushed and could say no more.

The blacksmith went up to her and took her by the hand; the beauty looked down. Never before had she looked so exquisitely lovely. The enchanted blacksmith gently kissed her; her face flushed crimson and she was even lovelier.

The bishop of blessed memory was driving through Dikanka. He admired the site on which the village stands, and as he drove down the street stopped before a new hut.

"And whose is this hut so gaily painted?" asked his Reverence of a beautiful woman, who was standing near the door with a baby in her arms.

"The blacksmith Vakula's!" Oksana, for it was she, told him, bowing.

"Splendid! splendid work!" said his Reverence, examining the doors and windows. The windows were all outlined with a ring of red paint; everywhere on the doors there were Cossacks on horseback with pipes in their teeth.

But his Reverence was even warmer in his praise of Vakula when he learned that by way of church penance he had painted free of charge the whole of the left choir in green with red flowers.

But that was not all. On the wall, to one side as you go in at the church, Vakula had painted the devil in hell—such a loathsome figure that everyone spat as he passed. And the women would take a child up to the picture, if it would go on crying in their arms, and would say: "There, look! What a *kaka!*" [13] And the child, restraining its tears, would steal a glance at the picture and nestle closer to its mother.

❖❖❖❖❖❖❖❖❖❖❖❖❖❖❖❖❖❖❖❖❖❖❖❖❖

A TERRIBLE VENGEANCE

I

There was a bustle and an uproar in a quarter of Kiev: Gorobets, Captain of the Cossacks, was celebrating his son's wedding. A great many people had come as guests to the wedding. In the old days they liked good food, better still liked drinking, and best of

---

[13] Literally, "defecator," but this hardly does justice to the original which, being Gogol at his outrageous best, has a marvelously funny ring to it: "*Yaka kaka!*" (What a *kaka!*) (ed.)

all they liked merrymaking. Among others the Dnieper Cossack Mikitka came on his sorrel horse straight from a riotous orgy at the Pereshlay Plain, where for seven days and seven nights he had been entertaining the Polish king's soldiers with red wine. The Captain's adopted brother, Danilo Burulbash, came too, with his young wife Katerina and his year-old son, from beyond the Dnieper where his farmstead lay between two mountains. The guests marveled at the fair face of the young wife Katerina, her eyebrows as black as German velvet, her beautiful cloth dress and underskirt of blue silk, and her boots with silver heels; but they marveled still more that her old father had not come with her. He had been living in that region for scarcely a year, and for twenty-one years before nothing had been heard of him and he had only come back to his daughter when she was married and had borne a son. No doubt he would have many strange stories to tell. How could he fail to have them, after being so long in foreign parts! Everything there is different: the people are not the same and there are no Christian churches. . . . But he had not come.

They brought the guests spiced vodka with raisins and plums in it and wedding bread on a big dish. The musicians began on the bottom crust, in which coins had been baked, and put their fiddles, cymbals, and tambourines down for a brief rest. Meanwhile the girls and young women, after wiping their mouths with embroidered handkerchiefs, stepped out again to the center of the room, and the young men, putting their arms akimbo and looking haughtily about them, were on the point of going to meet them, when the old Captain brought out two icons to bless the young couple. These icons had come to him from the venerable hermit, Father Varfolomey. They had no rich setting, there was no gleam of gold or silver on them, but no evil power dare approach the man in whose house they stand. Raising the icons on high the Captain was about to deliver a brief prayer . . . when all at once the children playing on the ground cried out in terror, and the people drew back, and everyone pointed with their fingers in alarm at a Cossack who was standing in their midst. Who he was nobody knew. But he had already danced splendidly and had diverted the people standing around him. But when the Captain lifted up the icons, at once the Cossack's face completely changed: his nose grew longer and twisted to one side, his rolling eyes turned from brown to green, his lips turned blue, his chin quivered and grew pointed like a spear, a tusk peeped out of his mouth, a hump appeared behind his head, and the Cossack turned into an old man.

"It is he! It is he!" shouted the crowd, huddling close together.

"The sorcerer has appeared again!" cried the mothers, snatching up their children.

Majestically and with dignity the Captain stepped forward and, turning the icons toward him, said in a loud voice: "Away, image of Satan! This is no place for you!" And, hissing and clacking his teeth like a wolf, the strange old man vanished.

Talk and conjecture arose among the people and the hubbub was like the roar of the sea in bad weather.

"What is this sorcerer?" asked the young people, who knew nothing about him.

"There will be trouble!" muttered their elders, shaking their heads. And everywhere about the spacious courtyard folks gathered in groups listening to the story of the dreadful sorcerer. But almost everyone told it differently and no one could tell anything certain about him.

A barrel of mead was rolled out and many gallons of Greek wine were brought into the yard. The guests regained their lightheartedness. The orchestra struck up—the girls, the young women, the gallant Cossacks in their gay-colored coats flew around in the dance. After a glass, old folks of ninety, of a hundred, began dancing too, remembering the years that had passed. They feasted till late into the night and feasted as none feast nowadays. The guests began to disperse, but only a few made their way home; many of them stayed to spend the night in the Captain's wide courtyard; and even more Cossacks dropped to sleep uninvited under the benches, on the floor, by their horses, by the stables; wherever the tipplers stumbled, there they lay, snoring for the whole town to hear.

II

There was a soft light all over the earth: the moon had come up from behind the mountain. It covered the steep bank of the Dnieper as with a costly damask muslin, white as snow, and the shadows drew back further into the pine forest.

A boat, hollowed out of an oak tree, was floating in the Dnieper. Two young Cossacks were sitting in the bow; their black Cossack caps were cocked on one side; and the drops flew in all directions from their oars as sparks fly from a flint.

Why were the Cossacks not singing? Why were they not telling of the Polish priests who go about the Ukraine forcing the Cossack people to turn Catholic, or of the two days' fight with the Tartars at the Salt Lake? How could they sing, how could they tell of gallant deeds? Their lord, Danilo, was deep in thought, and the sleeve of his crimson coat hung out of the boat and was dipped in the water; their mistress, Katerina, was softly rocking her child and keeping her eyes fixed upon it, while her beautiful gown was made wet by the spray which fell like fine gray dust.

Sweet it is to look from mid-Dnieper at the lofty mountains, at the broad meadows, at the green forests! Those mountains are not mountains; they end in peaks below, as above, and both under and above them lie the high heavens. Those forests on the hills are not forests: they are the hair that covers the shaggy head of the wood demon. Down below he washes his beard in the water, and under his beard and over his head lie the high heavens. Those meadows are not meadows: they are a green girdle encircling the round sky; and above and below the moon hovers over them.

Lord Danilo looks not about him; he looks at his young wife. "Why are you so deep in sadness, my young wife, my golden Katerina?"

"I am not deep in sadness, Danilo! I am full of dread at the strange tales of the sorcerer. They say when he was born he was terrible to look at . . . and not one of the children would play with him. Listen, Danilo, what dreadful things they say: he thought all were mocking him. If he met a man in the dark he thought that he opened his mouth and grinned at him; and next day they found that man dead. I marveled and was frightened hearing those tales," said Katerina, taking out a kerchief and wiping the face of the sleeping child. The kerchief had been embroidered by her with leaves and fruits in red silk.

Lord Danilo said not a word, but looked into the darkness where far away beyond the forest there was the dark ridge of an earthen wall and beyond the wall rose an old castle. Three lines furrowed his brow; his left hand stroked his gallant mustaches.

"It is not that he is a sorcerer that is cause for fear," he said, "but that he is here for some evil. What whim has brought him here? I have heard it said that the Poles mean to build a fort to cut off our way to the Dnieper Cossacks. That may be true. . . . I will scatter that devil's nest if any rumor reaches me that he harbors our foes there. I will burn the old sorcerer so that even the crows will find nothing to peck at. And I think he lacks not store of gold and wealth of all kinds. It's there the devil lives! If he has gold . . . We shall soon row by the crosses—that's the graveyard! There lie his evil forefathers. I am told they were all ready to sell themselves to Satan for a brass coin—soul and threadbare coat and all. If truly he has gold, there is no time to lose: there is not always booty to be won in war. . . ."

"I know what you are planning: my heart tells me no good will come from your meeting him. But you are breathing so hard, you are looking so fierce, your brows are knitted so angrily above your eyes . . ."

"Hold your tongue, woman!" said Danilo wrathfully. "If one has dealings with you, one will turn into a woman, oneself. You, give me a light for my pipe!" Here he turned to one of the rowers who, knocking some hot ash from his pipe, began putting it into his master's. "She would scare me with the sorcerer!" Danilo went on. "A Cossack, thank God, fears neither devil nor Catholic priest. What should we come to if we listened to women? No good, should we, boys? The best wife for us is a pipe and a sharp sword!"

Katerina sat silent, looking down into the slumbering river; and the wind ruffled the water into eddies and all the Dnieper shimmered with silver like a wolf's skin in the night.

The boat turned and hugged the wooded bank. A graveyard came into sight; tumbledown crosses stood huddled together. No guelder rose grows among them, no grass is green there; only the moon warms them from the heavenly heights.

"Do you hear the shouts? Someone is calling for our help!" said Danilo, turning to his oarsmen.

"We hear shouts, and they are coming from that bank," the two young men cried together, pointing to the graveyard.

But all was still again. The boat turned, following the curve of the projecting bank. All at once the rowers dropped their oars and stared before them without moving. Danilo stopped too: a chill of horror surged through the Cossack's veins.

A cross on one of the graves tottered and a withered corpse rose slowly up out of the earth. Its beard reached to its waist; the nails on its fingers were longer than the fingers themselves. It slowly raised its hands upward. Its face was all twisted and distorted. One could see it was suffering terrible torments. "I am stifling, stifling!" it moaned in a strange, inhuman voice. Its voice seemed to scrape on the heart like a knife, and suddenly it disappeared under the earth. Another cross tottered and again a dead body came forth, more frightening and taller than the one before; it was all hairy, with a beard to its knees and even longer claws. Still more terribly it shouted: "I am stifling!" and vanished into the earth. A third cross tottered, a third corpse appeared. It seemed like a skeleton rising from the earth; its beard reached to its heels; the nails on its fingers pierced the ground. Terribly it raised its hands toward the sky as though it would seize the moon, and shrieked as though someone were sawing its yellow bones. . . .

The child asleep on Katerina's lap screamed and woke up; the lady screamed too; the oarsmen let their caps fall in the river; even their master shuddered.

Suddenly it all vanished as though it had never been; but it was a long time before the rowers took up their oars again. Burulbash looked anxiously at his young wife who, panic-stricken, was rocking the screaming child in her arms; he pressed her to his heart and kissed her on the forehead.

"Fear not, Katerina! Look, there is nothing!" he said, pointing around. "It is the sorcerer who frightens people so that they will not break into his foul lair. He only scares women! Let me hold my son!"

With those words Danilo lifted up his son and kissed him. "Why, Ivan, you are not afraid of sorcerers, are you? Say: 'No, Daddy, I'm a Cossack!' Stop crying! soon we shall be home! Then Mother will give you your porridge, put you to bed in your cradle, and sing:

> Lullaby, my little son,
> Lullaby to sleep!
> Play about and grow a man!
> To the glory of the Cossacks
> And destruction of our foes.

Listen, Katerina! It seems that your father will not live at peace with us. He was sullen, gloomy, as though angry, when he came. . . . If he doesn't like it, why come? He would not drink to Cossack freedom! He has never fondled the child! At first I would have trusted him with all that lay in my heart, but I could not do it; the words stuck in my throat. No, he has not a Cossack heart! When

Cossack hearts meet, they almost leap out of the breast to greet each other! Well, my friends, is the bank near? I will give you new caps. You, Stetsko, I will give one made of velvet and gold. I took it from a Tartar with his head; I got all his gear, too; I let nothing go but his soul. Well, here is land! Here, we are home, Ivan, but still you cry! Take him, Katerina . . . !"

They all got out. A thatched roof came into sight behind the mountain: it was Danilo's ancestral home. Beyond it was another mountain, and then the open plain, and there you might travel a hundred miles and not see a single Cossack.

III

Danilo's farm lay between two mountains in a narrow valley that ran down to the Dnieper. It was a low-pitched house like the hut of an ordinary Cossack, and there was only one large room in it; but he and his wife and their old maidservant and ten picked young Cossacks all had their places in it. There were oak shelves running around the walls at the top. Bowls and cooking pots were piled upon them. Among them were silver goblets and drinking cups mounted in gold, gifts or booty brought from the war. Lower down hung costly swords, guns, spears; willingly or unwillingly, they had come from the Tartars, the Turks, and the Poles, and many a dent there was in them. Looking at them, Danilo was reminded of his encounters. At the bottom of the wall were smooth-planed oak benches; beside them, in front of the stove, the cradle hung on cords from a ring fixed in the ceiling. The whole floor of the room was leveled and plastered with clay. On the benches slept Danilo and his wife; on the stove the old maidservant; the child played and was lulled to sleep in the cradle; and on the floor the young Cossacks slept in a row. But a Cossack likes best to sleep on the flat earth in the open air; he needs no feather bed or pillow; he piles fresh hay under his head and stretches at his ease upon the grass. It rejoices his heart to wake up in the night and look up at the lofty sky spangled with stars and to shiver at the chill of night which refreshes his Cossack bones; stretching and muttering through his sleep, he lights his pipe and wraps himself more closely in his sheepskin.

Burulbash did not wake early after the merrymaking of the day before; when he woke he sat on a bench in a corner and began sharpening a new Turkish saber, for which he had just bartered something; and Katerina set to work embroidering a silken towel with gold thread.

All at once Katerina's father came in, angry and frowning, with an outlandish pipe in his teeth; he went up to his daughter and began questioning her sternly, asking what was the reason she had come home so late the night before.

"It is not her but me you should question about that, father-in-law! Not the wife but the husband is responsible. That's our way here, don't be disturbed about it," said Danilo, going on with his work. "Perhaps in infidel lands it is not so—I don't know."

The color came into the father-in-law's face; there was an ominous gleam in his eye. "Who, if not a father, should watch over his daughter!" he muttered to himself. "Well, I ask you: where were you roving so late at night?"

"Ah, that's it at last, dear father-in-law! To that I will answer that I have left swaddling clothes behind me long ago. I can ride a horse, I can wield a sharp sword, and there are other things I can do . . . I can refuse to answer to anyone for what I do."

"I know, I see, Danilo, you seek a quarrel! A man who is not frank has some evil in his mind."

"You may think as you please," said Danilo, "and I will think as I please. Thank God, I've had no part in any dishonorable deed so far; I have always stood for the Orthodox faith and my fatherland, not like some vagabonds who go tramping God knows where while good Christians are fighting to the death, and afterward come back to reap the harvest they have not sown. They are worse than the Uniats: they never go into the Church of God. It is such men that should be strictly questioned as to where they have been."

"Ah, Cossack! Do you know . . . I am no great shot; my bullet only pierces the heart at seven hundred feet; I am nothing to boast of at swordplay either: I leave bits of my opponent behind, though in truth, the pieces are smaller than the grains you use for porridge."

"I am ready," said Danilo jauntily, making the sign of the cross in the air with the saber, as though he knew what he had sharpened it for.

"Danilo!" Katerina cried aloud, seizing him by the arm and hanging on it, "think what you are doing, madman, see against whom you are lifting your hand! Father, your hair is white as snow, but you have flown into a rage like a senseless boy!"

"Wife!" Danilo cried menacingly, "you know I will have no interference! You mind your woman's business!"

There was a terrible clatter of swords; steel hacked steel and the Cossacks sent sparks flying like dust. Katerina went out weeping into another room, flung herself on the bed, and covered her ears that she might not hear the clash of the swords. But the Cossacks did not fight so faintheartedly that she could smother the sound of their blows. Her heart was ready to break; she seemed to hear all over her the clank of the swords. "No, I cannot bear it, I cannot bear it. . . . Perhaps the red blood is already flowing out of his white body; maybe by now my dear one is helpless, and I am lying here!" And pale all over, scarcely breathing, she went back.

A terrible and even fight it was; neither of the Cossacks was winning the day. At one moment Katerina's father attacked and Danilo seemed to give way; then Danilo attacked and the sullen father seemed to yield; and again they were equal. They boiled with rage, they swung their swords . . . Ough! The swords clashed . . . and with a clatter the blades flew out of the handles.

"Thank God!" said Katerina, but she screamed again when she saw that the Cossacks had picked up their muskets. They put in the flints and drew the triggers.

Danilo fired and missed. Her father took aim . . . He was old, he did not see so well as the younger man, but his hand did not tremble. A shot rang out . . . Danilo staggered; the red blood stained the left sleeve of his Cossack coat.

"No!" he cried, "I will not yield so easily. Not the left but the right hand is master. I have a Turkish pistol hanging on the wall: never yet has it failed me. Come down from the wall, old comrade! Do your friend a service!" Danilo stretched out his hand.

"Danilo!" cried Katerina in despair, clutching his hands and falling at his feet. "Not for myself I beseech you. There is but one end for me: unworthy is the wife who will outlive her husband; Dnieper, the cold Dnieper, will be my grave. . . . But look at your son, Danilo, look at your son! Who will cherish the poor child? Who will be kind to him? Who will teach him to race on the black stallion, to fight for faith and freedom, to drink and carouse like a Cossack? You must perish, my son, you must perish! Your father will not think of you! See how he turns away his head. Oh, I know you now! You are a wild beast and not a man! You have the heart of a wolf and the mind of a crafty reptile! I thought there was a drop of pity in you, that there was human feeling in your breast of stone. I have been terribly deceived! This will be a delight to you. Your bones will dance in the grave with joy when they hear the foul brutes of Poles throwing your son into the flames, when your son shrieks under the knife or the scalding water. Oh, I know you! You would be glad to rise up from the grave and fan the flames under him with your cap!"

"Stop, Katerina! Come, my precious Ivan, let me kiss you! No, my child, no one shall touch a hair of your head. You shall grow up to the glory of your fatherland; like a whirlwind you shall fly at the head of the Cossacks with a velvet cap on your head and a sharp sword in your hand. Give me your hand, Father! Let us forget what has been between us! For what wrong I have done you I ask pardon. Why do you not give me your hand?" said Danilo to Katerina's father, who stood without moving, with no sign of anger nor of reconciliation on his face.

"Father!" cried Katerina, embracing and kissing him, "don't be merciless, forgive Danilo: he will never offend you again!"

"For your sake only, my daughter, I forgive him!" he answered, kissing her with a strange glitter in his eyes.

Katerina shuddered faintly: the kiss and the strange glitter seemed uncanny to her. She leaned her elbows on the table, at which Danilo was bandaging his wounded hand, while he wondered if he had acted like a Cossack in asking pardon when he had done no wrong.

IV

The day broke, but without sunshine: the sky was overcast and a fine rain was falling on the plains, on the forest, and on the broad Dnieper. Katerina woke up, but not joyfully: her eyes were tear-stained, and she was restless and uneasy.

"My dear husband, my precious husband! I have had a strange dream!"

"What dream, my sweet wife Katerina?"

"I had a strange dream, and as vivid as though it were real, that my father was that very monster whom we saw at the Captain's.

But I beg you, do not put faith in the dream: one dreams all manner of foolishness. I dreamed that I was standing before him, was trembling and frightened, my whole body racked with pain at every word he said. If only you had heard what he said . . .''

"What did he say, my darling Katerina?"

"He said: 'Look at me, Katerina, how handsome I am! People are wrong in saying I am ugly. I should make you a fine husband. See what a look there is in my eyes!' Then he turned his fiery eyes upon me. I cried out and woke up . . .''

"Yes, dreams tell many a true thing. But do you know that all is not quiet beyond the mountain? I believe the Poles may have begun to show themselves again. Gorobets sent me a message to keep alert, but he need not have troubled—I am not asleep as it is. My Cossacks have piled up a dozen barricades during the night. We will treat Poland to leaden plums and the Poles will dance to our sticks."

"And Father, does he know of this?"

"Your father is a burden on my back! I'll be damned if I can understand him. Perhaps he has committed many sins in foreign lands. What other reason can there be? Here he has lived with us more than a month and not once has he made merry like a true Cossack! He would not drink mead! Do you hear, Katerina, he would not drink the mead which I wrung out of the Jews at Brest. Boy!" cried Danilo, "run to the cellar, boy, and bring me the Jews' mead! He won't even drink vodka! What do you make of that? I believe, my lády Katerina, that he does not believe in Christ. Eh, what do you think?"

"God forgive you for what you are saying, my lord Danilo!"

"Strange, wife!" Danilo went on, taking the earthenware mug from the Cossack, "even the damned Catholics have a weakness for vodka; it is only the Turks who do not drink. Well, Stetsko, have you had a good sip of mead in the cellar?"

"I just tried it, sir."

"You are lying, you son of a bitch! See how the flies have settled on your mustache! I can see from your eyes that you have gulped down half a pailful. Oh, you Cossacks! What reckless fellows! Ready to give all else to a comrade, but he keeps his drink to himself. It is a long time, my lady Katerina, since I have been drunk. Eh?"

"A long time indeed! Why, last . . .''

"Don't be afraid; don't be afraid, I won't drink more than a mugful! And here is the Turkish abbot at the door!" he muttered through his teeth, seeing his father-in-law stooping to come in.

"What's this, my daughter!" said the father, taking his cap off his head and adjusting his girdle where hung a saber set with precious stones; "the sun is already high and your dinner is not ready."

"Dinner is ready, my lord and father, we will serve it at once! Bring out the pot of dumplings!" said the young mistress to the old maidservant who was wiping the wooden bowls. "Stop, I had better get it out myself, while you call the men."

They all sat down on the floor in a ring; facing the icons sat the father, on his left Danilo, on his right Katerina, and ten of Danilo's most trusted Cossacks in blue and yellow coats.

"I don't like these dumplings!" said the father, laying down his spoon after eating a little. "There is no flavor in them!"

"I know you like Jewish noodles better," thought Danilo. "Why do you say there is no flavor in the dumplings, father-in-law? Are they badly made or what? My Katerina makes dumplings such as the Hetman does not often taste. And there is no need to despise them: it is a Christian dish! All holy people and godly saints have eaten dumplings!"

Not a word from the father. Danilo, too, said no more.

They served roast boar with cabbage and plums.

"I don't like pork," said Katerina's father, picking out a spoonful of cabbage.

"Why don't you like pork?" said Danilo. "It is only Turks and Jews who won't eat pork."

The father frowned more angrily than ever.

He ate nothing but some baked flour pudding with milk over it, and instead of vodka drank some black liquid from a bottle he took out of his bosom.

After dinner Danilo slept like a hero and only woke toward evening. He sat down to write to the Cossack troops, while his young wife sat on the stove, rocking the cradle with her foot. The lord Danilo sat there, his left eye on his writing while his right eye looked out of the window. From the window far away he could see the shining mountains and the Dnieper; beyond the Dnieper lay the dark blue forest; overhead glimmered the clear night sky. But the lord Danilo was not gazing at the faraway sky and the blue forest; he was watching the projecting tongue of land on which stood the old castle. He thought that a light gleamed at a narrow little window in the castle. But everything was still; it must have been his imagination. All he could hear was the hollow murmur of the Dnieper down below and, from three sides, the resounding splash of the waves suddenly awakening. It was not in turmoil. Like an old man, it merely muttered and grumbled, finding nothing that pleased it. Everything about it had changed; it was feuding with the mountains, the woods, and the meadows on its banks, carrying its complaints to the Black Sea.

And now on the wide expanse of the Dnieper the black speck of a boat appeared and again there was a gleam of light in the castle. Danilo gave a low whistle and the faithful servant ran in at the sound.

"Make haste, Stetsko, bring with you a sharp sword and a musket, and follow me!"

"Are you going out?" asked Katerina.

"I am, wife. I must inspect everything and see that all is in order."

"But I am afraid to be left alone. I am weary with sleep: what if I should have the same dream again? And, indeed, I am not sure it was a dream—it was all so vivid."

"The old woman will stay with you, and there are Cossacks sleeping in the porch and in the courtyard."

"The old woman is asleep already, and somehow I put no trust in the Cossacks. Listen, Danilo: lock me in the room and take the key with you. Then I shall not be so afraid; and let the Cossacks lie before the door."

"So be it!" said Danilo, wiping the dust off his musket and loading it with powder.

The faithful Stetsko stood ready with all the Cossack's equipment. Danilo put on his astrakhan cap, closed the window, bolted and locked the door, and stepping between his sleeping Cossacks, went out of the courtyard toward the mountains.

The sky was almost completely clear again. A fresh breeze blew lightly from the Dnieper. But for the wail of a gull in the distance all was silent. But a faint rustle stirred . . . Burulbash and his faithful servant stealthily hid behind the brambles that screened a barricade of felled trunks. Someone in a scarlet coat, with two pistols and a sword at his side, came down the mountainside. "It's my father-in-law," said Danilo, watching him from behind the bushes.

"Where is he going at this hour, and what is he up to? Be alert, Stetsko: keep a sharp watch which road your mistress's father takes."

The man in the scarlet coat went down to the riverbank and turned toward the jutting tongue of land.

"Ah, so that is where he is going," said Danilo. "Tell me, Stetsko, hasn't he gone to the sorcerer's den?"

"Nowhere else, for certain, my lord Danilo! Or we should have seen him on the other side; but he disappeared near the castle."

"Wait a minute: let us get out and follow his track. There is some secret in this. Yes, Katerina, I told you your father was an evil man; he does nothing like a good Christian."

Danilo and his faithful servant leaped out on the tongue of land. Soon they were out of sight; the slumbering forest around the castle hid them. A gleam of light came into an upper window; the Cossacks stood below wondering how to climb to it; no gate nor door was to be seen; doubtless there was a door in the courtyard, but how could they climb in? They could hear in the distance the clanking of chains and the stirring of dogs.

"Why am I wasting time?" said Danilo, seeing a big oak tree by the window. "Stay here, friend! I will climb up the oak; from it I can look straight into the window."

With this he took off his girdle, put down his sword so that it might not jingle, and gripping the branches, lifted himself up. There was still a light at the window. Sitting on a branch close to the window, he held on to the tree and looked in: it was light in the room but there was no candle. On the wall were mysterious symbols; weapons were hanging there, but all were strange—not such as are worn by Turks or Tartars or Poles or Christians or the gallant Swedish people. Bats flitted to and fro under the ceiling and their shadows flitted to and fro over the floor, the doors, and the walls. Then the door noiselessly opened. Someone in a scarlet coat walked in and went straight up to the table, which was covered with a white cloth. "It is he; it is my father-in-law!" Danilo crept a little lower down and huddled closer to the tree.

But his father-in-law had no time to look whether anyone were peeping in at the window. He came in, morose and ill-humored; he drew the cloth off the table, and at once the room was filled with transparent blue light, but the waves of pale golden light with which the room had been filled, eddied and dived, as in a blue sea, without mingling with it, and ran through it in streaks like the lines in marble. Then he set a pot upon the table and began scattering some herbs in it.

Danilo looked more attentively and saw that he was no longer wearing the scarlet coat; and that now he had on wide trousers, such as Turks wear, with pistols in his girdle, and on his head a strange cap embroidered all over with letters that were neither Russian nor Polish. As he looked at his face the face began to change: his nose grew longer and hung right down over his lips; in one instant his mouth stretched to his ears; a crooked tooth peeped out beyond his lips; and Danilo saw before him the same sorcerer who had appeared at the Captain's wedding feast. "Your dream was true, Katerina!" thought Burulbash.

The sorcerer began pacing around the table; the symbols on the wall began changing more rapidly, the bats flitted more swiftly up and down and to and fro. The blue light grew dimmer and dimmer and at last seemed to fade away. And now there was only a dim pinkish light in the room. It spread through the room and a faint ringing sound was heard. The light seemed to flood every corner, and suddenly it vanished and all was darkness. Nothing was heard but a murmur like the wind in the quiet evening hour when hovering over the mirrorlike water it bends the silvery willows lower into its depths. And it seemed to Danilo as though the moon were shining in the room, the stars were moving, there were vague glimpses of the bright blue sky within it, and he even felt the chill of night coming from it. And Danilo imagined (he began fingering his mustaches to make sure he was not dreaming) that it was no longer the sky but his own hut he was seeing through the window; his Tartar and Turkish swords were hanging on the walls; around the walls were the shelves with pots and pans; on the table stood bread and salt; the cradle hung from the ceiling . . . but hideous faces appeared where the icons should have been; on the stove . . . but a thick mist hid all and it was dark again. And accompanied by a faint ringing sound the rosy light flooded the room again, and again the sorcerer stood motionless in his strange turban. The sounds grew louder and deeper, the delicate rosy light shone more brilliant, and something white like a cloud hovered in the middle of the room; and it seemed to Danilo that the cloud was not a cloud, but that a woman was standing there; but what was she made of? Surely not of air? Why did she stand without touching the floor, without leaning on anything, why did the rosy light and the magic symbols on the wall show through her? And now she moved her transparent head; a soft light shone in her pale blue eyes; her hair curled and fell over her shoulders like a pale gray mist; a faint flush colored her lips like the scarcely perceptible crimson glimmer of dawn glowing through the white transparent sky of morning; the brows darkened a little . . . Ah, it was Katerina! Danilo felt his limbs turned to stone; he tried to speak, but his lips moved without uttering a sound.

The sorcerer stood without moving. "Where have you been?" he asked, and the figure standing before him trembled.

"Oh, why did you call me up?" she moaned softly. "I was so happy. I was in the place where I was born and lived for fifteen years. Ah, how good it was there! How green and fragrant was the meadow where I used to play in childhood! The darling wild flowers were the same as ever, and our hut and the garden! Oh, how my dear mother embraced me! How much love there was in her eyes! She caressed me, she kissed my lips and my cheeks, combed out my fair hair with a fine comb . . . Father!" Then she bent her pale eyes on the sorcerer. "Why did you murder my mother?"

The sorcerer shook his finger at her menacingly. "Did I ask you to speak of that?" And the ethereal beauty trembled. "Where is your mistress now?"

"My mistress Katerina has fallen asleep and I was glad of it: I flew up and darted off. For long years I have longed to see my mother. I was suddenly fifteen again, I felt light as a bird. Why have you sent for me?"

"You remember all I said to you yesterday?" the sorcerer said, so softly that it was hard to catch the words.

"I remember, I remember! But what would I not give to forget them. Poor Katerina, there is much she doesn't know that her soul knows!"

"It is Katerina's soul," thought Danilo, but still he dared not stir.

"Repent, Father! Is it not dreadful that after every murder you commit the dead rise up from their graves?"

"You are at your old tune again!" said the sorcerer menacingly. "I will have my way, I will make you do as I will. Katerina shall love me . . ."

"Oh, you are a monster and not my father!" she moaned. "No,

your will shall not be done! It is true that by your foul spells you have power to call up and torture her soul; but only God can make her do what He wills. No, never shall Katerina, so long as I am living in her body, bring herself to so ungodly a deed. Father, a terrible judgment is at hand! Even if you were not my father, you would never make me false to my faithful and beloved husband. Even if my husband were not true and dear to me, I would not betray him, for God detests souls that are faithless and false to their vows."

Then she fixed her pale eyes on the window under which Danilo was sitting, and was silent and still as death.

"What are you looking at? Whom do you see there . . . ?" cried the sorcerer.

The wraith of Katerina trembled. But already Danilo was on the ground and with his faithful Stetsko making his way to his mountain home. "Terrible, terrible!" he murmured to himself, feeling a thrill of fear in his Cossack heart, and he rapidly crossed his courtyard, in which the Cossacks slept as soundly as ever, all but one who sat on guard smoking a pipe.

The sky was all studded with stars.

V

"How glad I am you have awakened me!" said Katerina, wiping her eyes with the embroidered sleeve of her nightgown and looking intently at her husband as he stood facing her. "What a terrible dream I have had! I could hardly breathe! Ough . . . ! I thought I was dying. . . ."

"What was your dream? Was it like this?" And Burulbash told his wife all that he had seen.

"How did you know it, husband?" asked Katerina in amazement. "But no, many things you tell me I did not know. No, I did not dream that my father murdered my mother; I did not dream of the dead. No, Danilo, you have not told the dream right. Oh, what a terrible man my father is!"

"And it is no wonder that you have not dreamed of that. You do not know a tenth part of what your soul knows. Do you know your father is the Antichrist? Only last year when I was getting ready to go with the Poles against the Crimean Tartars (I was still allied with that faithless people then), the Father Superior of the

Bratsky Monastery (he is a holy man, wife) told me that the Antichrist has the power to call up every man's soul; for the soul wanders freely when the body is asleep and flies with the archangels about the dwelling of God. I disliked your father's face from the first. I would not have married you had I known you had such a father; I would have given you up and not have taken upon myself the sin of being allied to the brood of Antichrist."

"Danilo!" cried Katerina, hiding her face in her hands and bursting into tears. "In what have I been to blame? Have I been false to you, my beloved husband? How have I roused your wrath? Have I not served you truly? Do I say a word to cross you when you come back merry from a drinking bout? Have I not borne you a black-browed son?"

"Do not weep, Katerina; now I know you and nothing would make me abandon you. The sin all lies at your father's door."

"No, do not call him my father! He is not my father. God is my witness I disown him, I disown my father! He is Antichrist, a rebel against God! If he were perishing, if he were drowning, I would not hold out a hand to save him; if his throat were parched by some magic herb I would not give him a drop of water. You are my father!"

VI

In a deep underground cellar at Danilo's the sorcerer lay bound in iron chains behind a door with three locks, while his devilish castle above the Dnieper was on fire and the waves, glowing red as blood, splashed and surged around the ancient walls. It was not for sorcery, it was not for ungodly deeds that the sorcerer lay in the underground cellar—for his wickedness God was his judge; it was for secret treachery that he was imprisoned, for plotting with the foes of Orthodox Russia to sell to the Catholics the Ukrainian people and burn Christian churches. The sorcerer was gloomy; thoughts black as night strayed through his mind; he had but one day left to live and on the morrow he would take leave of the world; his punishment was awaiting him on the morrow. It was no light one: it would be an act of mercy if he were boiled alive in a cauldron or his sinful skin were flayed from him. The sorcerer was sad, his head was bowed. Perhaps he was already repenting on the eve of death; but his sins were not such as God would forgive. Above him was a little window covered with an iron grating. Clanking his chains, he stood to look out of the window and see whether his daughter were passing. She was gentle and forgiving as a dove; would she not have mercy on her father . . . ? But there was no one. The road ran below the window; no one passed along it. Beneath it rippled the Dnieper; it cared for no one; it murmured, and it splashed monotonously, drearily.

Then someone appeared upon the road—it was a Cossack! And the prisoner heaved a deep sigh. Again the road was empty. In the distance someone was coming down the hill . . . a green overskirt flapped in the wind . . . a golden headdress glittered on her head . . . It was she! He pressed still closer to the window. Now she was coming nearer . . .

"Katerina, daughter! Have pity on me, be merciful!"

She was silent, she would not listen, she did not turn her eyes toward the prison, and had already passed, already vanished. The whole world was empty; dismally the Dnieper murmured; it made hearts sad; but did the sorcerer know anything of such sadness?

The day was drawing to a close. Now the sun was setting; now it had vanished. Now it was evening, it was cool; an ox was lowing somewhere; sounds of voices floated from afar: people doubtless going home from their work and making merry; a boat flashed into sight on the Dnieper . . . no one thought of the prisoner. A silver crescent gleamed in the sky; now someone came along the road in the opposite direction; it was hard to tell the figure in the darkness; it was Katerina coming back.

"Daughter, for Christ's sake! even the savage wolf cubs will not tear their mother in pieces—daughter, give one look at least to your guilty father!"

She heeded not but walked on.

"Daughter, for the sake of your unhappy mother . . ."

She stopped.

"Come close and hear my last words!"

"Why do you call me, enemy of God? Do not call me daughter! There is no kinship between us. What do you want of me for the sake of my unhappy mother?"

"Katerina, my end is near; I know that your husband means to tie me to the tail of a wild mare and send it racing in the open country, and maybe he will invent an end more dreadful yet . . ."

"But is there in the world a punishment bad enough for your sins? You may be sure no one will plead for you."

"Katerina! It is not punishment in this world that I fear but in the next. . . . You are innocent, Katerina; your soul will fly about God in paradise; but your ungodly father's soul will burn in a fire everlasting and never will that fire be quenched; it will burn more and more hotly; no drop of dew will fall upon it, nor will the wind breathe on it . . ."

"I can do nothing to ease that punishment," said Katerina, turning away.

"Katerina, stay for one word! You can save my soul! You know not yet how good and merciful is God. Have you heard of the Apostle Paul, what a sinful man he was—but afterward he repented and became a saint?"

"What can I do to save your soul?" said Katerina. "It is not for a weak woman like me to think of that."

"If I could but get out, I would abandon everything. I will repent, I will go into a cave, I will wear a hair shirt next to my skin and spend day and night in prayer. I will give up not only meat, but even fish I will not taste! I will lay nothing under me when I lie down to sleep! And I will pray without ceasing, pray without ceasing! And if God's mercy does not release me from at least a hundredth part of my sins, I will bury myself up to the neck in the earth or entomb myself in a wall of stone; I will take neither food nor drink and perish; and I will give all my goods to the monks that they may sing a requiem for me for forty days and forty nights."

Katerina pondered. "If I were to unlock you I could not undo your fetters."

"I do not fear chains," he said. "You say that they have fettered my hands and feet? No, I threw a mist over their eyes and held out a dry tree instead of hands. Here, see: I have not a chain upon me now!" he said, walking into the middle of the cellar. "I should not have been contained by these walls either; but your husband does not know what walls these are: they were built by a holy hermit, and no evil power can deliver a prisoner from them without the very key with which the hermit used to lock his cell. Just such a cell will I build for myself, incredible sinner that I have been, when I am free again."

"Listen, I will let you out; but what if you deceive me," said Katerina, standing still at the door, "and instead of repenting, again become the devil's comrade?"

"No, Katerina, I have not long left to live; my end is near even if I am not put to death. Can you believe that I will give myself up to eternal punishment?"

The key grated in the lock.

"Farewell! God in His mercy keep you, my child!" said the sorcerer, kissing her.

"Do not touch me, you fearful sinner; make haste and go . . ." said Katerina.

But he was gone.

"I let him out!" she said to herself, terror-stricken, looking wildly at the walls. "What answer shall I give my husband now? I am undone. There is nothing left but to bury myself alive!" and sobbing she almost fell upon the block on which the prisoner had been sitting. "But I have saved a soul," she said softly. "I have done a godly deed; but my husband . . . I have deceived him for the first time. Oh, how terrible, how hard it will be for me to lie to him! Someone is coming! It is he! my husband!" She uttered a desperate shriek and fell senseless on the ground.

VII

"It is I, my daughter! It is, I, my darling!" Katerina heard, as she revived and saw the old maidservant before her. The woman bent down and seemed to whisper to her, and stretching out her withered old hand, sprinkled her with water.

"Where am I?" said Katerina, sitting up and looking around her. "The Dnieper is splashing before me, behind me are the mountains . . . Where have you taken me, granny?"

"I have taken you out; I have carried you in my arms from the stifling cellar; I locked up the cellar again that you might not be in trouble with my lord Danilo."

"Where is the key?" asked Katerina, looking at her girdle. "I don't see it."

"Your husband has taken it, to have a look at the sorcerer, my child."

"To look! Granny, I am lost!" cried Katerina.

"God mercifully preserve us from that, my child! Only hold your peace, my little lady, no one will know anything."

"He has escaped, the cursed Antichrist! Do you hear, Katerina, he has escaped!" said Danilo, coming up to his wife. His eyes flashed fire; his sword hung clanking at his side. His wife was like one dead.

"Has someone let him out, dear husband?" she brought out trembling.

"Yes, someone has—you are right: the devil. Look, where he was is a log chained to the wall. It is God's pleasure, it seems, that the devil should not fear a Cossack's hands! If any one of my Cossacks had dreamed of such a thing and I knew of it . . . I could find no punishment bad enough for him!"

"And if I had done it?" Katerina could not resist saying, and she stopped, panic-stricken.

"If you had done it you would be no wife to me. I would sew you up in a sack and drown you in mid-Dnieper . . . !"

Katerina could hardly breathe and she felt the hair stand up on her head.

VIII

On the frontier road the Poles had gathered at a tavern and feasted there for two days. There were not a few of the rabble. They had doubtless met for some raid: some had muskets; there was jingling of spurs and clanking of swords. The nobles made merry and boasted; they talked of their marvelous deeds; they mocked at the Orthodox Christians, calling the Ukrainian people their serfs, and insolently twirled their mustaches and sprawled on the benches. There was a Catholic priest among them, too; but he was like them and had not even the semblance of a Christian priest; he drank and caroused with them and uttered shameful words with his foul tongue. The servants were no better than their masters: tucking up the sleeves of their tattered coats, they walked about with a swagger as though they were of consequence. They played cards, struck each other on the nose with cards; they had brought with them other men's wives; there was shouting, quarreling . . . ! Their masters were at the height of their revelry, playing all sorts of tricks; pulling the Jewish tavern keeper by the beard, painting a cross on his impious brow, shooting blanks at the women, and dancing the *Cracovienne* with their impious priest. Such sinfulness had never been seen on Russian soil even among the Tartars; it was God's chastisement, seemingly, for the sins of Russia that she should be put to so great a shame! In the midst of the bedlam, talk could be heard of lord Danilo's farmstead above the Dnieper, of his lovely wife . . . The gang of thieves was plotting foul deeds!

IX

The lord Danilo sat at the table in his house, leaning on his elbow, thinking. The lady Katerina sat on the stove, singing.

"I am sad, my wife!" said lord Danilo. "My head aches and my heart aches. I feel weighed down. It seems my death is hovering not far away."

"Oh, my precious husband! lean your head upon me! Why do you cherish such black thoughts?" thought Katerina, but dared not utter the words. It was bitter to her, feeling her guilt, to receive her husband's caresses.

"Listen, wife!" said Danilo, "do not desert our son when I am no more. God will give you no happiness either in this world or the next if you forsake him. Sad it will be for my bones to rot in the damp earth; sadder still it will be for my soul!"

"What are you saying, my husband? Was it not you who mocked at us weak women? And now you are talking like a weak woman yourself. You must live many years yet."

"No, Katerina, my heart feels death near at hand. The world has become a sad place; cruel days are coming. Ah, I remember, I remember the good years—they will not return! He was living then, the honor and glory of our army, old Konashevich! The Cossack regiments pass before my eyes as though it were today. Those were golden days, Katerina! The old Hetman sat on a black stallion; his mace shone in his hand; the soldiers stood around him, and on each side moved the red sea of the Dnieper Cossacks. The Hetman began to speak—and all stood as though turned to stone. The old man wept when he told us of old days and battles long ago. Ah, Katerina, if only you knew how we fought in those days with the Turks! The scar on my head shows even now. Four bullets pierced me in four places and not one of the wounds has quite healed. How much gold we took in those days! The Cossacks filled their caps with precious stones. What horses, Katerina! If you only knew, what horses, Katerina, we drove away with us! Ah, I shall never fight like that! One would think I am not old and I am strong in body, yet the sword drops out of my hand, I live doing nothing and know not what I live for. There is no order in the Ukraine: the colonels and the captains quarrel like dogs: there is no chief over them all. Our gentry imitate Polish fashions and have copied their sly ways . . . they have sold their souls, accepting the Uniat faith. The Jews are oppressing the poor. Oh, those days, those days! Those days that are past! Whither have you fled, my years? Go to the cellar, boy, and bring me a jug of mead! I will drink to the life of the past and to the years that have gone!"

"How shall we receive our guests, lord Danilo? The Poles are coming from the direction of the meadow," said Stetsko, coming into the hut.

"I know what they are coming for," said Danilo. "Saddle the horses, my faithful men! Put on your harness! Bare your swords! Don't forget to take your rations of lead: we must do honor to our guests!"

But before the Cossacks had time to saddle their horses and load their guns, the Poles covered the mountainside as leaves cover the ground in autumn.

"Ah, here we have foes to try our strength with!" said Danilo, looking at the stout Poles swaying majestically on their gold-harnessed steeds in the front ranks. "It seems it is my lot to have one more glorious jaunt! Take your pleasure, Cossack soul, for the last time! Go ahead, Cossacks, the festival for which we waited has come!"

And the festival was kept on the mountains and great was the merrymaking: swords were playing, bullets flying, horses neighing and prancing. The shouting dazed the brain; the smoke blinded the eye. All was confusion, but the Cossack knew where was friend, where was foe; whenever a bullet whistled a gallant rider dropped from the saddle, whenever a sword flashed—a head fell to the ground, babbling meaningless words.

But the red crest of Danilo's Cossack cap could always be seen in the crowd; the gold girdle of his dark blue coat gleamed bright, the mane on his black horse fluttered in the breeze. Like a bird he flew here and there, shouting and waving his Damascus sword and hacking to right and to left. Hack away, Cossack, make merry! Cheer your gallant heart; but look not at the gold trappings and tunics: trample under foot the gold and jewels! Stab, Cossack! Wreak your will, Cossack! But look back: already the godless Poles are setting fire to the huts and driving away the frightened cattle. And like a whirlwind Danilo turned around, and the cap with the red crest gleamed now by the huts while the crowd about him scattered.

Hour after hour the Poles fought with the Cossacks; there were not many left of either; but lord Danilo did not slacken; with his long spear he thrust Poles from the saddle and his spirited steed trampled them under foot. Already his courtyard was almost cleared, already the Poles were flying in all directions; already the Cossacks were stripping the golden coats and rich trappings from the slain; already Danilo was setting off in pursuit, when he looked around to call his men together . . . and was overwhelmed with fury: he saw Katerina's father. There he stood on the hillside aiming his musket at him. Danilo urged his horse straight upon him . . . Cossack, you go to your doom! Then came the crack of a shot —and the sorcerer vanished behind the hill. Only the faithful Stetsko caught a glimpse of the scarlet coat and the strange hat. The Cossack staggered and fell to the ground. The faithful Stetsko flew to his master's aid: his lord lay stretched on the ground with his bright eyes closed while the red blood spurted from his breast. But he became aware of his faithful servant's presence; slowly he raised his eyelids and his eyes gleamed: "Farewell, Stetsko! Tell Katerina not to forsake her son! And do not you, my faithful servant, forsake him either!" and he ceased. His gallant soul flew from his noble body; his lips turned blue; the Cossack slept, never to wake again.

His faithful servant sobbed and beckoned to Katerina: "Come, lady, come! deeply has your lord been carousing; in drunken sleep he lies on the damp earth; and long will it be before he awakens!"

Katerina wrung her hands and fell like a sheaf of wheat on the dead body: "Husband, is it you lying here with closed eyes? Rise up, stretch out your hand! Stand up! Look, if only once, at your Katerina, move your lips, utter one word . . . ! But you are mute, you are mute, my noble lord! You have turned blue as the Black Sea. Your heart is not beating! Why are you so cold, my lord? It seems my tears are not scalding, they have no power to warm you! It seems my weeping is not loud, it will not waken you! Who will lead your regiments now? Who will gallop on your black horse, loudly calling, and lead the Cossacks, waving your sword? Cossacks, Cossacks, where is your honor and glory? Your honor and glory is lying with closed eyes on the damp earth. Bury me, bury me with him! Throw earth upon my eyes! Press the maple boards upon my white breasts! My beauty is useless to me now!"

Katerina grieved and wept; while the distant horizon was covered with dust: the old Captain Gorobets was galloping to the rescue.

X

Lovely is the Dnieper in tranquil weather when, freely and smoothly, its waters glide through forests and mountains. Not a sound, not a ripple is stirring. You look and cannot tell whether its majestic expanse moves or does not move; and it might be of molten crystal and like a blue road made of mirror, immeasurably broad, endlessly long, twining and twisting about the green world. Sweet it is then for the burning sun to peep at itself from the heights and to plunge its beams in the cool of its glassy waves, and for the forests on the banks to watch their bright reflections in the water. Wreathed in green, they press with the wild flowers close to the river's edge, and bending over look in and are never tired of gazing and admiring their bright reflection, and smile and greet it with nodding branches. In mid-Dnieper they dare not look: none but the sun and the blue sky gaze into it; rarely a bird flies to the middle of the river. Glorious it is! No river like it in the world! Lovely too is the Dnieper on a warm summer night when all are sleeping— man, beast, and bird—while God alone majestically surveys earth and heaven and majestically shakes His robe, showering stars that glow and shine above the world and are all reflected together in the Dnieper. All of them the Dnieper holds in its dark bosom; not one escapes it till quenched in the sky. The black forests dotted with sleeping crows and the mountains cleft asunder in ages past strive, hanging over, to conceal the river in their long shadows, but in vain! There is nothing in the world that could hide the Dnieper. Deep, deep blue it flows, spreading its waters far and wide at midnight as at midday; it is seen far, far away, as far as the eye of man can see. Shrinking from the cold of night and huddling closer to the bank, it leaves behind a silver trail gleaming like the blade of a Damascus sword, while the deep blue water slumbers again. Lovely then, too, is the Dnieper, and no river is like it in the world! When dark blue storm clouds pile in masses over the sky, the dark forest totters to its roots, the oaks creak, and the lightning slashing through the storm clouds suddenly lights up the whole world—terrible then is the Dnieper! Then its mountainous billows roar, flinging themselves against the hillside, and flashing and moaning rush back and wail and lament in the distance. So the old mother laments as she lets her Cossack son go to the war. Bold and reckless, he rides his black stallion, arms akimbo and jaunty cap on one side, while she, sobbing, runs after him, seizes him by the stirrup, catches the bridle, and wrings her hands over him, bathed in bitter tears.

Strange and black are the burnt tree stumps and stones on the jutting bank between the warring waves. And the landing boat is beaten against the bank, thrown upward, and flung back again. What Cossack dared row out in a boat when the old Dnieper was raging? Surely he knew not that the river swallows men like flies.

The boat reached the bank; out of it stepped the sorcerer. He was in no happy mood: bitter to him was the funeral feast which the Cossacks had kept over their slain master. Heavily had the Poles paid for it: forty-four of them in all their harness and thirty-three servants were hacked to pieces, while the others were captured with their horses to be sold to the Tartars.

He went down stone steps between the burnt stumps to a place where he had a cave dug deep in the earth. He went in softly, not letting the door creak, put a pot on the table that was covered with a cloth, and began with his long hands strewing into it some strange herbs; he took a ladle made of some rare wood, scooped up some water with it, and poured it out, moving his lips and repeating an incantation. The cave was flooded with rosy light and his face was terrible to look upon: it seemed covered with blood, only the deep wrinkles showed up black upon it, and his eyes blazed as though they were on fire. Foul sinner! His beard was gray, his face was lined with wrinkles, he was shriveled with age, and still he persisted in his godless design. A white cloud began to hover in the cave and something like joy gleamed in his face; but why did he suddenly stand motionless with his mouth open, not daring to stir; why did his hair rise up on his head? The features of a strange face appeared to him from the cloud. Unbidden, uninvited it had come to visit him; it grew more distinct and fastened its eyes immovably upon him. The features, eyebrows, eyes, lips—all were unfamiliar; never in his life had he seen them. And there was nothing terrible, seemingly, about it, but he was overwhelmed with horror. The strange, marvelous face still looked fixedly at him from the cloud. Then the cloud vanished, but the unfamiliar face was more distinct than ever and the piercing eyes were still riveted on him. The sorcerer turned white as a sheet; he shrieked in a wild, unnatural voice and overturned the pot . . . The face disappeared.

XI

"Take comfort, my dear sister!" said old Captain Gorobets. "Rarely do dreams come true!"

"Lie down, sister," said his young daughter-in-law. "I will fetch a wise woman; no evil power can stand against her; she will help you."

"Fear nothing!" said his son, touching his sword. "No one shall harm you!"

Gloomily and with dull eyes Katerina looked at them all and found no word to say.

"I myself brought about my ruin: I let him out!" she said at last. "He gives me no peace! Here I have been ten days with you in Kiev and my sorrow is no less. I thought that at least I could bring up my son to avenge . . . I dreamed of him, looking terrible! God forbid that you should ever see him like that! My heart is still throbbing. 'I will kill your child, Katerina,' he shouted, 'if you do not marry me . . . ' " And she flung herself sobbing on the cradle; and the frightened child stretched out its little hands and cried.

The Captain's son was boiling with anger as he heard such words.

The Captain himself was roused. "Let him try coming here, the accursed Antichrist; he will learn whether there is still strength in the old Cossack's arm. God sees," he said, turning his keen eyes to heaven, "whether I did not hasten to give a hand to brother Danilo. It was His holy will! I found him lying on the cold bed upon which so many, many Cossacks have been laid. But what a funeral feast we had for him! We did not leave a single Pole alive! Be comforted, my child. No one shall dare to harm you, so long as I or my son live."

As he finished speaking the old Cossack captain approached the cradle, and the child saw hanging from a strap his red pipe set in silver and the pouch with the shiny flints, and stretched out its arms toward him and laughed. "He takes after his father," said the old captain, unfastening the pipe and giving it to the child. "He is not out of the cradle, but he is thinking of a pipe already!"

Katerina heaved a sigh and fell to rocking the cradle. They agreed to spend the night together and soon afterward they were all asleep; Katerina, too, fell asleep.

All was quiet in the courtyard; everyone slept but the Cossacks who were keeping watch. Suddenly Katerina woke with a scream, and the others woke too. "He is slain, he is murdered!" she cried, and flew to the cradle. All surrounded the cradle and were numb with horror when they saw that the child in it was dead. None uttered a sound, not knowing what to think of so horrible a crime.

XII

Far from the Ukraine, beyond Poland and the populous town of Lemberg, run ranges of high mountains. Mountain after mountain, like chains of stone flung to the right and to the left over the land, they fetter it with layers of rock to keep out the resounding turbulent sea. These stony chains stretch into Wallachia and the Sedmigrad region and stand like a huge horseshoe between the Galician and Hungarian peoples. There are no such mountains in our country. The eye shrinks from viewing them and no human foot has climbed to their tops. They are a wonderful sight. Were they perhaps caused by some angry sea that broke away from its wide shores in a storm and threw its monstrous waves aloft only to have them turn to stone, and remain motionless in the air? Or did heavy storm clouds fall from heaven and cumber up the earth? For they have the same gray color and their white crests flash and sparkle in the sun.

Until you get to the Carpathian Mountains you may hear Russian speech, and just beyond the mountain there are still here and there echoes of our native tongue; but further beyond, faith and speech are different. The numerous Hungarian people live there; they ride, fight, and drink like any Cossack, and do not grudge gold pieces from their pockets for their horses' trappings and costly coats. There are great wide lakes among the mountains. They are still as glass and reflect bare mountaintops and the green slopes below like mirrors.

But who rides through the night on a huge black horse whether stars shine or not? What hero of superhuman stature gallops under the mountains, above the lakes, is mirrored with his gigantic horse in the still waters and throws his vast reflection on the mountains?

His plated armor glitters; his saber rattles against the saddle; his helmet is tilted forward; his mustaches are black; his eyes are closed, his eyelashes are drooping—he is asleep and drowsily holds the reins; and on the same horse sits with him a young child, and he too is asleep and drowsily holds on to the hero. Who is he, where goes he, and why? Who knows? Not one day nor two has he been traveling over the mountains. Day breaks, the sun shines, and he is seen no more; only from time to time the mountain people behold a long shadow flitting over the mountains, though the sky is bright and there is no cloud upon it. But as soon as night brings back the darkness, he appears again and is reflected in the lakes and his quivering shadow follows him. He has crossed many mountains and at last he reaches Krivan. There is no mountain in the Carpathians higher than this one; it towers like a monarch above the others. There the horse and his rider halted and sank into even deeper slumber and the clouds descended and covered them and hid them from view.

XIII

"Hush . . . don't knock like that, nurse: my child is asleep. My baby cried a long time, now he is asleep. I am going to the forest, nurse! But why do you look at me like this? You are hideous: there are iron pincers coming out of your eyes . . . ugh, how long they are, and they blaze like fire! You must be a witch! Oh, if you are a witch, go away! You will steal my son. How absurd the Captain is; he thinks it is enjoyable for me to live in Kiev. No, my husband and my son are here. Who will look after the house? I went out so quietly that even the dog and the cat did not hear me. Do you want to grow young again, nurse? That's not hard at all; you need only dance. Look, how I dance."

And uttering these incoherent sentences Katerina began dancing, looking wildly about her and putting her arms akimbo. With a shriek she tapped with her feet; her silver heels clanked regardless of time or tune. Her black tresses floated loose about her white neck. Like a bird she flew around without resting, waving her hands and nodding her head, and it seemed as though she must either fall helpless to the ground or soar away from earth altogether.

The old nurse stood mournfully, her wrinkled face wet with tears; the trusty Cossacks had heavy hearts as they looked at their mistress. At last she was exhausted and languidly tapped with her feet on the same spot, imagining that she was dancing. "I have a necklace, lads," she said, stopping at last, "and you have not . . . ! Where is my husband?" she cried suddenly, drawing a Turkish dagger out of her girdle. "Oh, this is not the knife I need." With that, tears of grief came into her eyes. "My father's heart is far away; it will not reach it. His heart is wrought of iron; it was forged by a witch in the furnace of hell. Why does not my father come? Does not he know that it is time to stab him? He wants me to come myself, it seems . . ." and breaking off she laughed strangely. "A funny story came into my mind: I remembered how my husband was buried. He was buried alive, you know . . . It did make me laugh . . . ! Listen, listen!" and instead of speaking she began to sing:

> A bloodstained cart races on,
> A Cossack lies upon it
> Shot through the breast, stabbed to the heart.
> In his right hand he holds a spear
> And blood is trickling from it,
> A stream of blood is flowing.
> A plane tree stands over the river,
> Above the tree a raven croaks.
> A mother is weeping for the Cossack.
> Weep not, mother, do not grieve!
> For your son is married.
> He chose a pretty lady for his bride,
> A mound of earth in the bare fields
> Without a door or window.
> And this is how my story ends.
> A fish was dancing with a crab,
> And may a fever take his mother
> If he will not love me!

This was how she muddled lines from different songs. She had been living two days in her own house and would not hear of Kiev. She would not say her prayers, refused to see anyone, and wandered from morning till night in the dark oak thickets. Sharp twigs scratched her white face and shoulders; the wind fluttered her loose hair; the autumn leaves rustled under her feet—she looked at nothing. At the hour when the glow of sunset dies away and before the stars come out or the moon shines, it is frightening to walk in the forest: unbaptized infants claw at the trees and clutch at the branches; sobbing and laughing, they hover over the road and the expanses of nettles; maidens who have lost their souls rise up one after the other from the depths of the Dnieper, their green tresses stream over their shoulders, the water drips splashing to the ground from their long hair; and a maiden shines through the water as through a veil of crystal; her lips smile mysteriously, her cheeks glow, her eyes bewitch the soul . . . as though she might burn with love, as though she might kiss one to death. Flee, Christian! Her lips are ice, her bed—the cold water; she will drag you under water. Katerina looked at no one; in her frenzy she had no fear of the water sprites; she wandered at night with her knife, seeking her father.

In the early morning a visitor arrived, a man of handsome appearance in a scarlet coat, and inquired for the lord Danilo; he heard all the story, wiped his tear-stained eyes with his sleeves, and shrugged his shoulders. He said that he had fought side by side with Burulbash; side by side they had done battle with the Turks and the Crimeans; never had he thought that the lord Danilo would meet with such an end. The visitor told them many other things and wanted to see the lady Katerina.

At first Katerina heard nothing of what the guest said; but afterward she began to listen to his words as though understanding. He told her how Danilo and he had lived together like brothers; how once they had hidden under a dam from the Crimeans . . . Katerina listened and kept her eyes fixed upon him.

"She will recover," the Cossacks thought, looking at her, "this guest will heal her! She is listening like one who understands!"

The visitor began meanwhile describing how Danilo had once, in a confidential conversation, said to him: "Listen, brother Kopryan, when it is God's will that I am gone, you take Katerina, take her for your wife . . ."

Katerina looked piercingly at him. "Aie!" she shrieked, "it is he, it is my father!" and she flew at him with her knife.

For a long time he struggled, trying to snatch the knife from her; at last he snatched it away, raised it to strike—and a terrible deed was done: the father killed his crazed daughter.

The astounded Cossacks rushed at him, but the sorcerer had already leaped upon his horse and was gone.

XIV

An extraordinary marvel appeared outside Kiev. All the nobles and the hetmans assembled to see the miracle: in all directions even the ends of the earth had become visible. Far off was the dark blue of the mouth of the Dnieper and beyond that the Black Sea. Men who had traveled recognized the Crimea jutting like a mountain out of the sea and the marshy Sivash. On the right could be seen the Galician land.

"And what is that?" people asked the old men, pointing to white and gray crests looming far away in the sky, looking more like clouds than anything else.

"Those are the Carpathian Mountains!" said the old men. "Among them are some that are forever covered with snow, and the clouds cling to them and hover there at night."

Then a new miracle happened: the clouds vanished from the highest peak and on the top of it appeared a horseman, in full knightly armor, with his eyes closed, and he could be distinctly seen as though he were standing close to them.

Then among the marveling and fearful people, one leaped on a horse, and looking wildly about him as though to see whether he were pursued, hurriedly set his horse galloping at its utmost speed. It was the sorcerer. Why was he so panic-stricken? Looking in terror at the marvelous knight, he had recognized the face which had appeared to him when he was working his spells. He could not have said why his whole soul was thrown into confusion at this sight, and looking fearfully about him, he raced till he was overtaken by night and the stars began to come out. Then he turned homeward, perhaps to ask the Evil One what was meant by this marvel. He was just about to leap with his horse over a stream which lay across his path when his horse suddenly stopped in full gallop, looked around at him—and, marvelous to relate, laughed aloud! Two rows of white teeth gleamed horribly in the darkness. The sorcerer's hair stood up on his head. He uttered a wild scream, wept like one frantic, and turned his horse straight for Kiev. He felt as though he were being pursued on all sides: the trees that surrounded him in the dark forest strove to strangle him, nodding their black beards and stretching out their long branches; the stars seemed to be racing ahead of him and pointing to the sinner; the very road seemed to be flying after him.

The desperate sorcerer fled to the holy places in Kiev.

XV

A holy hermit sat alone in his cave before a little lamp and did not take his eyes off the holy book. It was many years since he had first shut himself up in his cave; he had already made himself a coffin in which he would lie down to sleep. The holy man closed his book and fell to praying. . . . Suddenly a man of a strange and terrible aspect ran into the cave. At first the holy hermit was astounded and stepped back upon seeing such a man. He was trembling all over like an aspen leaf; his eyes rolled in their sockets, a light of terror gleamed in them; his hideous face made one shudder.

"Father, pray! pray!" he shouted desperately, "pray for a lost soul!" and he sank to the ground.

The holy hermit crossed himself, took up his book, opened it, and stepped back in horror, dropping the book: "No, incredible sinner! There is no mercy for you! Away! I cannot pray for you!"

"No?" the sorcerer cried frantically.

"Look! the letters in the holy book are dripping with blood. . . . There has never been such a sinner in the world!"

"Father! you are mocking me!"

"Away, accursed sinner! I am not mocking you. I am overcome with fear. It is not good for a man to be with you!"

"No, no! You are mocking, say not so . . . I see that your lips are smiling and the rows of your old teeth are gleaming white!"

And like one possessed he flew at the holy hermit and killed him.

A terrible moan was heard and echoed through the forest and the fields. Dry withered arms with long claws rose up from beyond the forest; they trembled and disappeared.

And now he felt no fear. All was confusion: there was a noise in his ears, a noise in his head as though he were drunk, and everything before his eyes was veiled as though by spiders' webs. Leaping on his horse he rode straight to Kanev, thinking from there to go through Cherkassy direct to the Crimean Tartars, though he knew not why. He rode one day and a second and still Kanev was not in sight. The road was the same; he should have reached it long before, but there was no sign of Kanev. Far away there gleamed the cupolas of churches; but that was not Kanev but Shumsk. The sorcerer was amazed to find that he had traveled the wrong way. He

turned back toward Kiev, and a day later a town appeared—not
Kiev but Galich, a town further from Kiev than Shumsk and not
far from Hungary. At a loss what to do he turned back, but felt
again that he was going backward as he went on. No one in the
world could tell what was in the sorcerer's mind; and had anyone
seen and known, he would never have slept peacefully at night or
laughed again in his life. It was not malice, not terror, and not fierce
anger. There is no word in the world to say what it was. He was
burning, scalding; he would have liked to trample the whole country from Kiev to Galich with all the people and everything in it
and drown it in the Black Sea. But it was not from malice he would
do it: no, he knew not why he wanted it. He shuddered when he
saw the Carpathian Mountains and lofty Krivan, its crest capped
with a gray cloud; the horse still galloped on and now was racing
among the mountains. The clouds suddenly lifted, and facing him
appeared the horseman in his terrible majesty. . . . The sorcerer
tried to stop, he tugged at the rein; the horse neighed wildly, tossed
its mane, and dashed toward the horseman. Then the sorcerer felt
everything die within him, while the motionless horseman stirred
and suddenly opened his eyes, saw the sorcerer flying toward him,
and roared with laughter. The wild laugh echoed through the
mountains like a clap of thunder and resounded in the sorcerer's
heart, setting his whole body throbbing. He felt that some mighty
being had taken possession of him and was moving within him,
hammering on his heart and his veins . . . so fearfully did that
laugh resound within him!

The horseman stretched out his mighty hand, seized the sorcerer,
and lifted him into the air. The sorcerer died instantly and he
opened his eyes after his death: but he was dead and looked out of
dead eyes. Neither the living nor the risen from the dead have such
a terrible look in their eyes. He rolled his dead eyes from side to
side and saw dead men rising up from Kiev, from Galicia and the
Carpathian Mountains, exactly like him.

Pale, very pale, one taller than another, one bonier than another,
they thronged around the horseman who held this awful prey in
his hand. The horseman laughed once more and dropped the sorcerer down a precipice. And all the corpses leaped into the precipice and fastened their teeth in the dead man's flesh. Another, taller
and more terrible than all the rest, tried to rise from the ground
but could not—he had not the power, he had grown so immense in

the earth; and if he had risen he would have overturned the Carpathians and the whole of the Sedmigrad and the Turkish lands. He only stirred slightly, but that set the whole earth quaking, and overturned many huts and crushed many people.

And often in the Carpathians a sound is heard as though a thousand mills were churning up the water with their wheels: it is the sound of the dead men gnawing a corpse in the endless abyss which no living man has seen for none dares to approach it. It sometimes happens that the earth trembles from one end to another: that is said by the learned men to be due to a mountain near the sea from which flames issue and hot streams flow. But the old men who live in Hungary and Galicia know better, and say that it is the dead man who has grown so immense in the earth trying to rise that makes the earth quake.

XVI

A crowd had gathered around an old bandore player in the town of Glukhov and had been listening for an hour to the blind man's playing. No bandore player sang so well and such marvelous songs. First he sang of the leaders of the Dnieper Cossacks in the old days, of Sagaydachny and Khmelnitzky. Times were different then: the Cossacks were at the height of their glory, they trampled their foes underfoot and no one dared to mock them. The old man sang merry songs too, and looked about at the crowd as though his eyes could see, and his fingers with little sheaths of bone fixed to them danced like flies over the strings, and it seemed that the strings themselves were playing; and the crowd, the old people looking down and the young staring at the singer, dared not even whisper.

"Now," said the old man, "I will sing to you of what happened long ago." The people pressed closer and the blind man sang:

"In the days of Stepan, prince of Sedmigrad (the prince of Sedmigrad was also king of the Poles), there lived two Cossacks: Ivan and Petro. They lived together like brothers: 'See here, Ivan,' said Petro, 'whatever you gain, let us go halves; when one is merry, the other is merry too; when one is sad, the other is sad too; when one wins booty, we share it; when one gets taken prisoner, the other sells everything to ransom him or else goes himself into captivity.'

And, indeed, whatever the Cossacks gained they shared equally: if they drove away herds of cattle or horses—they shared them.

"King Stepan waged war on the Turks. He had been fighting with the Turks three weeks and could not drive them out. And the Turks had a Pasha who with a few janissaries could slaughter a whole regiment. So King Stepan proclaimed that if a brave warrior could be found to bring him the Pasha dead or alive he would give him a reward equal to the pay of the whole army.

" 'Let us go and catch the Pasha, brother,' said Ivan to Petro. And the two Cossacks set off, one one way, one the other.

"Whether Petro would have been successful or not there is no telling; but Ivan brought the Pasha with a lasso around his neck to the King. 'Brave fellow!' said King Stepan, and he commanded that he should be given a sum equal to the pay of the whole army, and that he should be given land wherever he chose and as many cattle as he pleased. As soon as Ivan received the reward from the King, he shared the money that very day with Petro. Petro took half of the King's money, but could not bear the thought that Ivan had been so honored by the King, and he hid deep in his heart desire for vengeance.

"The two Cossacks were journeying to the land beyond the Carpathians that the King had granted to Ivan. Ivan had set his son on the horse behind him, tying the child to himself. The boy had fallen asleep; Ivan, too, began to doze. A Cossack should not sleep, the mountains paths are perilous . . . ! But the Cossack had a horse who knew the way; it would not stumble or leave the path. There is a precipice between the mountains; no one has ever seen the bottom of it; it is deep as the sky is high. The road passed just above the precipice; two men could ride abreast on it, but for three it was too narrow. The horse began stepping cautiously with the slumbering Cossack on its back. Petro rode beside him; he trembled all over and was breathless with joy. He looked around and thrust his sworn brother into the precipice; and the horse, the Cossack, and the baby fell into the abyss.

"But Ivan grasped a branch and only the horse dropped to the bottom. He began scrambling up with his son upon his back. He looked up when he was nearly at the top and saw that Petro was holding a lance ready to push him back. 'Merciful God! better I had never raised my eyes again than I should see my own brother holding a lance ready to push me back . . . ! Dear brother, stab me if that is my fate, but take my son: what has the innocent child done that he should be doomed to so cruel a death?' Petro laughed and thrust at him with the lance; the Cossack fell with his child to the bottom. Petro took all his goods and began to live like a Pasha. No one had such droves of horses as Petro; no one had such flocks of sheep. And Petro died.

"After he was dead, God summoned the two brothers, Ivan and Petro, to the judgment seat. 'This man is a great sinner,' said God. 'Ivan, it will take me long to find a punishment for him; you select a punishment for him!' For a long time Ivan pondered what punishment to fix and at last he said:

" 'That man did me a great injury: he betrayed his brother like a Judas and robbed me of my honorable name and offspring. And a man without honorable name and offspring is like a seed of wheat dropped into the earth only to die there. If it does not sprout, no one knows that the seed has been dropped into the earth.

" 'Let it be, O Lord, that none of his descendants may be happy upon earth; that the last of his race may be the worst criminal that has ever been seen, and that at every crime he commits, his ancestors, unable to rest in their graves and suffering torments unknown to the world of the living, should rise from the tomb! And that the Judas, Petro, should be unable to rise and that hence he should suffer pain all the more intense; that he should bite the earth like one possessed and writhe in the ground in anguish!

" 'And when the time comes that that man's wickedness has reached its full measure, let me, O Lord God, rise on my horse from the precipice to the highest peak of the mountains, and let him come to me and I will throw him from that mountain into the deepest abyss. And let all his dead ancestors, wherever they lived in their lifetime, come from various parts of the earth to gnaw him for the sufferings he inflicted upon them, and let them gnaw him forever, and I shall rejoice looking at his sufferings. And let the Judas, Petro, be unable to rise out of the earth. Let him lust to gnaw but be forced to gnaw himself, and let his bones grow bigger and bigger as time goes on, so that his pain may be the greater. That torture will be worse for him than any other, for there is no greater torture for a man than to long for vengeance and be unable to accomplish it.'

" 'A terrible punishment thou has devised, O man . . . !' God said. 'All shall be as thou hast said; but thou shalt sit forever on thy horse there and shalt not enter the kingdom of heaven!' And so it all was fulfilled; the strange horseman still sits on his steed in the Carpathians and sees the dead men gnawing the corpse in the bottomless abyss and feels how the dead Petro grows larger under the earth, gnaws his bones in dreadful agony, and sets the earth quaking fearfully."

The blind man had finished his song; he began thrumming the strings again and singing amusing ballads about Khoma and Yerioma and Stkyar Stokoza. . . . But his listeners, old and young, could not rouse themselves from reverie; they still stood with bowed heads, thinking of the terrible story of long ago.

IVAN FIODOROVICH SHPONKA AND HIS AUNT

There is a story about this story: we were told it by Stepan Ivanovich Kurochka, who came over from Gadyach. You must know that my memory is incredibly poor: you may tell me a thing or not tell it, it is all the same. It is just pouring water into a sieve. Being aware of this weakness, I purposely begged him to write the story down in a notebook. Well, God give him good health, he was always a kind man to me, he began to work and wrote it down. I put it in the little table; I believe you know it: it stands in the corner as you come in by the door. . . . But there, I forgot that you had never been in my house. My old woman, with whom I have lived thirty years, has never learned to read—no use hiding one's shortcomings. Well, I noticed that she baked the pies on paper of some sort. She bakes pies beautifully, dear readers; you will never taste better pies anywhere. I happened to look on the underside of a pie —what did I see? Written words! My heart seemed to tell me at once: I went to the table; only half the book was there! All the other pages she had carried off for the pies. What could I do? There is no fighting at our age!

Last year I happened to be passing through Gadyach. Before I reached the town I purposely tied a knot in my handkerchief so that I might not forget to ask Stepan Ivanovich about it. That was not all: I vowed to myself that as soon as ever I sneezed in the town I would be sure to think of it. It was all no use. I drove through the town and sneezed and blew my nose too, but still I forgot it; and I only thought of it nearly six miles after I had passed through the town gate. Well, it couldn't be helped, I had to publish it without the end. However, if anyone particularly wants to know what happened later on in the story, he need only go on purpose to Gadyach and ask Stepan Ivanovich. He will be glad to tell the story all over again from the beginning. He lives not far from the brick church. There is a little lane close by, and as soon as you turn into the lane it is the second or third gate. Or better still, when you see a big post with a quail on it in the yard and coming to meet you a fat peasant woman in a green skirt (you should know, he is a bachelor), that is his yard. Though you may also meet him in the market, where he is to be seen every morning before nine o'clock, choosing fish and vegetables for his table and talking to Father Antip or the Jewish contractor. You will know him at once, for there is no one else who has trousers of printed linen and a yellow cotton coat. And another thing to help you recognize him—he always swings his arms as he walks. Denis Petrovich, the assessor, now deceased, always used to say when he saw him in the distance: "Look, look, here comes our windmill!"

I

IVAN FIODOROVICH SHPONKA

It is four years since Ivan Fiodorovich retired from the army and came to live on his farm Vytrebenki. When he was still Vanyusha,[1] he was at the Gadyach district school, and I must say he was a very well-behaved and industrious boy. Nikifor Timofeevich Deeprichastie[2] the teacher of Russian grammar, used to say that if all the boys had been as anxious to do their best as Shponka, he would not have brought into the classroom the maplewood ruler with which, as he confessed, he was tired of hitting the lazy and mischievous boys' hands. Vanyusha's exercise book was always neat, with a ruled margin, and not the tiniest blot anywhere. He always sat quietly with his arms folded and his eyes fixed on the teacher, and he never used to stick scraps of paper on the back of the boy sitting in front of him, never cut the bench, and never played at shoving the other boys off the bench before the teacher came in. If anyone wanted a penknife to sharpen his quill, he immediately asked Ivan Fiodorovich, knowing that he always had a penknife, and Ivan Fiodorovich, then called simply Vanyusha, would take it out of a little leather case attached to a buttonhole of his gray coat, and would only request that the sharp edge should not be used for scraping the quill, pointing out that there was a blunt side for the purpose. Such good conduct soon attracted the attention of the Latin teacher, whose cough in the passage was enough to reduce the class to terror, even before his frieze coat and pockmarked face had appeared in the doorway. This terrifying teacher, who always had two birches lying on his desk and half of whose pupils were always on their knees, made Ivan Fiodorovich monitor, although there were many boys in the class of much greater ability. Here I cannot omit an incident which had an influence on the whole of his future life. One of the boys entrusted to his charge tried to induce his monitor to write *scit*[3] on his report, though he had not learned his lesson, by bringing into class a pancake soaked in butter and wrapped in paper. Though Ivan Fiodorovich was usually conscientious, on this occasion he was hungry and could not resist the

---

1 Diminutive of Ivan, i.e., a child. (ed.)
2 "Participle," i.e., Nikifor Timofeevich Participle. (ed.)
3 Latin for "knows," i.e., a good grade. (ed.)

temptation; he took the pancake, held a book up before him, and began eating it, and he was so absorbed in this occupation that he did not observe that a deathly silence had fallen upon the class. He woke up with horror only when a terrible hand protruding from a frieze overcoat seized him by the ear and dragged him into the middle of the room. "Hand over that pancake! Hand it over, I tell you, you rascal!" said the terrifying teacher; he seized the buttery pancake in his fingers and flung it out of the window, sternly forbidding the boys running about in the yard to pick it up. Then he proceeded on the spot to whack Ivan Fiodorovich very painfully on the hands; and quite rightly—the hands were responsible for taking it and no other part of the body. Anyway, the timidity which had always been characteristic of him was more marked from that time forward. Possibly the same incident was the explanation of his feeling no desire to enter the civil service, having learned by experience that one is not always successful in hiding one's misdeeds.

He was very nearly fifteen when he advanced to the second class,[4] where instead of the four rules of arithmetic and the abridged catechism, he went on to the unabridged one, the book describing the duties of man, and fractions. But seeing that the further you went into the forest the thicker the wood became, and receiving the news that his father had departed this life, he stayed only two years longer at school, and with his mother's consent went into the P—— infantry regiment.

The P—— infantry regiment was not at all of the class to which many infantry regiments belong, and, although it was for the most part stationed in villages, it was in no way inferior to many cavalry regiments. The majority of the officers drank hard and were really as good at dragging Jews around by their earlocks as any Hussars; some of them even danced the mazurka, and the colonel of the regiment never missed an opportunity of mentioning the fact when he was talking to anyone in company. "Among my officers," he used to say, patting himself on the belly after every word, "a number dance the mazurka, quite a number of them, really a great number of them indeed." To show our readers the degree of culture of the P—— infantry regiment, we must add that two of the officers were passionately fond of the game of bank[5] and used to

---

[4] Ivan was not too bright. He should have advanced to the second class—roughly equivalent to the sixth grade—at eleven. (ed.)

[5] *Shtoss*, a variation of faro. (ed.)

gamble away their uniforms, caps, overcoats, sword knots, and even their underclothes, which is more than you could say about every cavalry regiment.

Contact with such comrades did not, however, diminish Ivan Fiodorovich's timidity; and as he did not drink hard liquor, preferring instead a wineglassful of ordinary vodka before dinner and supper, did not dance the mazurka or play bank, naturally he was bound to be always left alone. And so it came to pass that while the others were driving about with hired horses, visiting the less important landowners, he, sitting at home, spent his time in pursuits peculiar to a mild and gentle soul: he either polished his buttons, or read a fortunetelling book[6] or set mousetraps in the corners of his room, or failing everything he would take off his uniform and lie on his bed.

On the other hand, no one in the regiment was more punctual in his duties than Ivan Fiodorovich, and he drilled his platoon in such a way that the commander of the company always held him up as a model to the others. Consequently in a short time, only eleven years after becoming an ensign, he was promoted to be a second lieutenant.

During that time he had received the news that his mother was dead, and his aunt, his mother's sister, whom he only knew from her bringing him in his childhood—and even sending him when he was at Gadyach—dried pears and extremely nice honeycakes which she made herself (she was on bad terms with his mother and so Ivan Fiodorovich had not seen her in later years), this aunt, in the goodness of her heart, undertook to look after his little estate and in due time informed him of the fact by letter.

Ivan Fiodorovich, having the fullest confidence in his aunt's good sense, continued to perform his duties as before. Some men in his position would have grown conceited at such promotion, but pride was a feeling of which he knew nothing, and as lieutenant he was the same Ivan Fiodorovich as he had been when an ensign. He spent another four years in the regiment after his promotion, an event of great importance to him, and was about to leave the Mogiliov district for Great Russia with his regiment when he received a letter as follows:

---

[6] Fortunetelling and dream-interpreting books were enormously popular throughout Russia. (ed.)

My Dear Nephew, Ivan Fiodorovich,

I am sending you some linen: five pairs of socks and four shirts of fine linen; and what is more I want to talk to you of something serious; since you have already a rank of some importance, as I suppose you are aware, and have reached a time of life when it is fitting to take up the management of your land, there is no reason for you to remain longer in military service. I am getting old and can no longer see to everything on your farm; and in fact there is a great deal that I want to talk to you about in person.

Come, Vanyusha! Looking forward to the real pleasure of seeing you, I remain your very affectionate aunt

Vasilisa Tsupchevska

P.S.—There is a wonderful turnip in our vegetable garden, more like a potato than a turnip.

A week after receiving this letter Ivan Fiodorovich wrote an answer as follows:

Honored Madam, Auntie, Vasilisa Kashporovna,

Thank you very much for sending the linen. My socks especially are very old; my orderly has darned them four times and that has made them very tight. As to your views in regard to my service in the army, I completely agree with you, and the day before yesterday I sent in my papers. As soon as I get my discharge I will engage a chaise. As to your commission in regard to the wheat seed and Siberian grain, I cannot carry it out; there is none in all the Mogiliov province. Pigs here are mostly fed on brewers' grains together with a little beer when it has grown flat. With the greatest respect, honored madam and auntie, I remain your nephew

Ivan Shponka

At last Ivan Fiodorovich received his discharge with the grade of lieutenant, hired for forty rubles a Jew to drive from Mogiliov to Gadyach, and set off in the chaise just at the time when the trees are clothed with young and still scanty leaves, the whole earth is bright with fresh green, and there is the fragrance of spring over all the fields.

II

THE JOURNEY

Nothing of great interest occurred on the journey. They traveled more than two weeks. Ivan Fiodorovich might have arrived a little sooner than that, but the devout Jew kept the Sabbath on the Saturdays and, putting his horse blanket[7] over his head, prayed the whole day. Ivan Fiodorovich, however, as I have had occasion to mention already, was a man who did not give way to being bored. During these intervals he undid his trunk, took out his underclothes, inspected them thoroughly to see whether they were properly washed and folded; carefully removed the fluff from his new uniform, which had been made without epaulets, and repacked it all in the best possible way. He was not fond of reading in general; and if he did sometimes look into a fortunetelling book, it was because he liked to find again what he had already read several times. In the same way one who lives in the town goes every day to the club, not for the sake of hearing anything new there, but in order to meet there friends with whom it has been his habit to chat at the club from time immemorial. In the same way a government clerk will read a directory of addresses with immense satisfaction several times a day with no ulterior object; he is simply entertained by the printed list of names. "Ah! Ivan Gavrilovich So-and-so . . ." he murmurs mutely to himself. "And here again am I! h'm . . . !" and next time he reads it over again with exactly the same exclamations.

After a two-week journey Ivan Fiodorovich reached a little village some eighty miles from Gadyach. This was on Friday. The sun had long set when with the chaise and the Jew he reached an inn.

This inn differed in no respects from other little village inns. As a rule the traveler is zealously regaled in them with hay and oats, as though he were a posthorse. But should he want to lunch as decent people lunch, he keeps his appetite intact for some future opportunity. Ivan Fiodorovich, knowing all this, had provided himself beforehand with two bundles of pretzels and a sausage, and asking for a glass of vodka, of which there is never a shortage in any inn, he began his supper, sitting down on a bench before an oak table which was fixed immovably in the clay floor.

Meanwhile he heard the rattle of a chaise. The gates creaked but it was a long while before the chaise drove into the yard. A loud voice was engaged in scolding the old woman who kept the inn. "I will drive in," Ivan Fiodorovich heard, "but if I am bitten by a

---

[7] I.e., prayer shawl. (ed.)

single bug in your inn, I will beat you, I swear I will, you old witch! and I won't give you anything for your hay either!"

A minute later the door opened and there walked—or rather squeezed himself—in a fat man in a green coat. His head rested immovably on his short neck, which seemed even thicker because of a double chin. To judge from his appearance, he belonged to that class of men who do not trouble their heads about trifles and whose whole life has passed easily.

"I wish you good day, honored sir!" he pronounced on seeing Ivan Fiodorovich.

Ivan Fiodorovich bowed in silence.

"Allow me to ask, to whom have I the honor of speaking?" the fat newcomer continued.

At such a question Ivan Fiodorovich involuntarily got up and stood at attention as he usually did when the colonel asked him a question. "Retired Lieutenant Ivan Fiodorovich Shponka," he answered.

"And may I ask what place you are bound for?"

"My own farm Vytrebenki."

"Vytrebenki!" cried the stern questioner. "Allow me, honored sir, allow me!" he said, going toward him, and waving his arms as though someone were hindering him or as though he were making his way through a crowd, he folded Ivan Fiodorovich in an embrace and kissed him first on the right cheek and then on the left and then on the right again. Ivan Fiodorovich was much gratified by this kiss, for his lips were pressed against the stranger's fat cheeks as though against soft cushions.

"Allow me to make your acquaintance, my dear sir!" the fat man continued: "I am a landowner of the same district of Gadyach and your neighbor; I live not more than four miles from your Vytrebenki in the village of Khortyshche; and my name is Grigory Grigorievich Storchenko. You really must, sir, you really must pay me a visit at Khortyshche. I won't speak to you if you don't. I am in haste now on business . . . Why, what's this?" he said in a mild voice to his lackey, a boy in a Cossack coat with patched elbows and a bewildered expression, who came in and put bundles and boxes on the table. "What's this, what's the meaning of it?" and by degrees Grigory Grigorievich's voice grew more and more threatening. "Did I tell you to put them here, my good lad? Did I tell you to put them here, you rascal? Didn't I tell you to heat the chicken up first, you dirty scoundrel? Get out!" he shouted stamping. "Wait, you ugly rogue! Where's the basket with the bottles? Ivan Fiodorovich!" he said, pouring out a glass of liqueur, "I beg you to take some cordial!"

"Oh, really, I cannot . . . I have already had occasion . . ." Ivan Fiodorovich began hesitatingly.

"I won't hear a word, sir!" the gentleman raised his voice, "I won't hear a word! I won't budge till you drink it. . . ."

Ivan Fiodorovich, seeing that it was impossible to refuse, not without gratification emptied the glass.

"This is a chicken, sir," said the fat Grigory Grigorievich, carving it in its wooden box. "I must tell you that my cook Yavdokha is fond of a drop at times and so she makes things too dry. Hey, boy!" here he turned to the boy in the Cossack coat who was bringing in a feather bed and pillows, "make my bed on the floor in the middle of the room! Make sure you put plenty of hay under the pillow! And pull a bit of hemp from the woman's spindle to stop up my ears for the night! I must tell you, sir, that I have the habit of stopping up my ears at night ever since the damned occasion when a cockroach crawled into my left ear in a Great Russian inn. Those damned Russians, as I found out afterward, eat their soup with cockroaches in it. Impossible to describe what happened to me; there was such a tickling, such a tickling in my ear . . . I was almost mad! I was cured by a simple old woman in our district, and by what, do you suppose? Simply by charming it. What do you think, my dear sir, about doctors? What I think is that they simply hoax us and make fools of us: some old women know a dozen times as much as all these doctors."

"Indeed, what you say is perfectly true, sir. There certainly are cases . . ." Here Ivan Fiodorovich paused as though he could not find the right word. It may not be improper to mention here that he was at no time lavish of words. This may have been due to timidity, or it may have been due to a desire to express himself elegantly.

"Shake up the hay properly, shake it up properly!" said Grigory Grigorievich to his servant. "The hay is so bad around here that you may come upon a twig in it any minute. Allow me, sir, to wish you a good night! We shall not see each other tomorrow. I am setting off before dawn. Your Jew will keep the Sabbath because to-

morrow is Saturday, so it is no good for you to get up early. Don't
forget my invitation; I won't speak to you if you don't come to see
me at Khortyshche."

At this point Grigory Grigorievich's servant pulled off his coat
and high boots and gave him his dressing gown instead, and Grigory
Grigorievich stretched on his bed, and it looked as though one
huge feather bed were lying on another.

"Hey, boy! where are you, rascal? Come here and arrange my
quilt. Hey, boy, prop up my head with hay! Have you watered the
horses yet? Some more hay! here, under this side! And arrange the
bedspread properly, you rascal! That's right, more! Ough . . . !"

Then Grigory Grigorievich heaved two sighs and filled the
whole room with a terrible whistling through his nose, snoring so
loudly at times that the old woman who was snoozing on the stove,
suddenly waking up, looked about her in all directions, but seeing
nothing, subsided and went to sleep again.

When Ivan Fiodorovich woke up next morning, the fat gentleman was no longer there. This was the only noteworthy incident
that occurred on the journey. Two days later he drew near his little
farm.

He felt his heart begin to throb when the windmill waving its
sails peeped out and, as the Jew drove his nag up the hill, the row of
willows came into sight below. The pond gleamed bright and shining through them and a breath of freshness rose from it. Here he
used to bathe in the old days; in that pond he used to wade with the
peasant lads up to his neck after crayfish. The covered cart mounted
the dam and Ivan Fiodorovich saw the little old house thatched
with reeds, and the apple trees and cherry trees which he used to
climb on the sly as a boy. He had no sooner driven into the yard
than dogs of all kinds, brown, black, gray, spotted, ran up from
every side. Some flew under the horse's hoofs, barking; others ran
behind the cart, noticing that the axle was smeared with bacon fat;
one, standing near the kitchen and keeping his paw on a bone, uttered a volley of shrill barks; and another barked from the distance,
running to and fro wagging his tail and seeming to say: "Look, good
Christians! What a fine young fellow I am!" Boys in dirty shirts
ran out to stare. A sow who was promenading in the yard with sixteen little pigs lifted her snout with an inquisitive air and grunted
louder than usual. In the yard a number of hempen sheets were lying on the ground covered with wheat, millet, and barley drying

in the sun. A good many different kinds of herbs, such as wild chicory and hawkweed, were drying on the roof.

Ivan Fiodorovich was so occupied looking at all this that he was only roused when a spotted dog bit the Jew on the calf of his leg as he was getting down from the box. The servants who ran out, that is, the cook and another woman and two girls in woolen petticoats, after the first exclamations: "It's our young master!" informed him that his aunt was sowing sweet corn together with the girl Palashka and Omelko the coachman, who often performed the duties of a gardener and watchman also. But his aunt, who had seen the covered cart in the distance, was already on the spot. And Ivan Fiodorovich was astonished when she almost lifted him from the ground in her arms, hardly able to believe that this could be the aunt who had written to him of her old age and infirmities.

III

THE AUNT

Aunt Vasilisa Kashporovna was at this time about fifty. She had never married, and commonly declared that she valued her maiden state above everything. Though, indeed, to the best of my memory, no one ever courted her. This was due to the fact that all men were rather timid in her presence, and never had the courage to make her an offer. "A girl of great character, Vasilisa Kashporovna!" all the young men used to say, and they were quite right, too, for there was no one Vasilisa Kashporovna could not get the better of. With her own manly hand, tugging every day at his forelock, she could, unaided, turn the drunken miller, a worthless fellow, into a perfect treasure. She was of almost gigantic stature and her breadth and strength were fully in proportion. It seemed as though nature had made an unpardonable mistake in condemning her to wear a dark brown gown with little flounces on weekdays and a red cashmere shawl on Sunday and on her name day, though a dragoon's mustaches and high topboots would have suited her better than anything. On the other hand, her pursuits completely corresponded with her appearance: she rowed the boat herself and was more skillful with the oars than any fisherman; shot game; stood over the mowers all the while they were at work; knew the exact number of the melons, of all kinds, in the vegetable garden; took a toll of five kopeks from every wagon that crossed her dam; climbed the trees and shook down the pears; beat lazy vassals with her terrible hand and with the same menacing hand bestowed a glass of vodka on the deserving. Almost at the same moment she was scolding, dyeing yarn, racing to the kitchen, brewing kvass, making jam with honey; she was busy all day long and everywhere in the nick of time. The result of all this was that Ivan Fiodorovich's little property, which had consisted of eighteen serfs at the last census, was flourishing in the fullest sense of the word. Moreover, she had a very warm affection for her nephew and carefully saved kopeks for him.

From the time of his arrival at his home Ivan Fiodorovich's life was completely changed and took an entirely different turn. It seemed as though nature had designed him expressly for looking after an estate of eighteen serfs. His aunt observed that he would make an excellent farmer, though she did not yet permit him to meddle in every branch of the management. "He's still a child," she used to say, though Ivan Fiodorovich was in fact not far from forty. "How should he know it all?"

However, he was always in the fields with the reapers and mowers, and this was a source of unutterable pleasure to his gentle heart. The sweep of a dozen or more gleaming scythes in unison; the sound of the grass falling in even swathes; the caroling songs of the reapers at intervals, at one time joyous as the welcoming of a guest, at another mournful as a parting; the calm pure evening—and what an evening! How free and fresh the air! How everything revived; the steppe flushed red, then turned dark blue and gleamed with flowers; quails, bustards, gulls, grasshoppers, thousands of insects, and all of them whistling, buzzing, chirping, calling, and suddenly blending into a harmonious chorus; nothing was silent for an instant, while the sun set and was hidden. Oh, how fresh and delightful it was! Here and there about the fields campfires were built and cauldrons set over them, and around the fires the mowers sat down; the steam from the dumplings floated upward; the twilight turned grayer. . . . It is hard to say what passed in Ivan Fiodorovich at such times. When he joined the mowers, he forgot to try their dumplings, though he liked them very much, and stood motionless, watching a gull disappear in the sky or counting the sheaves of wheat dotted over the field.

In a short time Ivan Fiodorovich was spoken of as a great farmer.

His aunt never tired of rejoicing over her nephew and never lost an opportunity of boasting of him. One day—it was just after the end of the harvest, that is, at the end of July—Vasilisa Kashporovna took Ivan Fiodorovich by the arm with a mysterious air, and said she wanted now to speak to him of a matter which had long been on her mind.

"You are aware, dear Ivan Fiodorovich," she began "that there are eighteen serfs on your farm, though, indeed, that is by the census register, and in reality they may amount to more, they may be twenty-four. But that is not the point. You know the copse that lies behind our vegetable ground, and no doubt you know the broad meadow behind it; there are very nearly sixty acres in it; and the grass is so good that it is worth a hundred rubles every year, especially if, as they say, a cavalry regiment is to be stationed at Gadyach."

"To be sure, Auntie, I know: the grass is very good."

"You needn't tell me the grass is very good, I know it; but do you know that all that land is by rights yours? Why do you look so surprised? Listen, Ivan Fiodorovich! You remember Stepan Kuzmich? What am I saying: 'you remember'! You were so little that you could not even pronounce his name. Yes, indeed! How could you remember! When I came on the very eve of Christmas and took you in my arms, you almost ruined my dress; luckily I was just in time to hand you to your nurse, Matryona; you were such a horrid little thing then . . . ! But that is not the point. All the land beyond our farm, and the village of Khortyshche itself belonged to Stepan Kuzmich. I must tell you that before you were in this world he used to visit your mama—though, indeed, only when your father was not at home. Not that I say it to blame her—God rest her soul!—though your poor mother was always unfair to me! But that is not the point. Be that as it may, Stepan Kuzmich made a gift to you of that same estate of which I have been speaking. But your poor mama, in confidence, was a very strange character. The devil himself (God forgive me for the nasty word!) would have been puzzled trying to understand her. What she did with that deed —God only knows. It's my opinion that it is in the hands of that old bachelor, Grigory Grigorievich Storchenko. That potbellied scoundrel has got hold of the whole estate. I'd bet anything you like that he has hidden that deed."

"Allow me to ask, Auntie: isn't he the Storchenko whose acquaintance I made at the inn?" Here Ivan Fiodorovich described his meeting with Storchenko.

"Who knows," said his aunt after a moment's thought, "perhaps he is not a rascal. It's true that it's only six months since he came to live among us; there's no finding out what a man is in that time. The old lady, his mother, is a very sensible woman, so I hear, and they say she is a great hand at pickling cucumbers; her own serf girls can make wonderful rugs. But as you say he gave you such a friendly welcome, go and see him; perhaps the old sinner will listen to his conscience and will give up what is not his. If you like you can go in the chaise, only those confounded brats have pulled out all the nails at the back; we must tell the coachman, Omelko, to nail the leather on better everywhere."

"What for, Auntie? I will take the trap that you sometimes go out shooting in."

With that the conversation ended.

IV

THE DINNER

It was about dinnertime when Ivan Fiodorovich drove into the hamlet of Khortyshche, and he felt a little timid as he approached the country house. It was a long house, not thatched with reeds like the houses of many of the neighboring landowners, but with a wooden roof. Two barns in the yard also had wooden roofs: the gate was of oak. Ivan Fiodorovich felt like a dandy who, on arriving at a ball, sees everyone more smartly dressed than himself. He stopped his horse by the barn as a sign of respect and went on foot toward the front door.

"Ah, Ivan Fiodorovich!" cried the fat man Grigory Grigorievich, who was crossing the yard in his coat but without necktie, vest, and suspenders. But apparently this attire weighed oppressively on his bulky person, for the perspiration was streaming down him.

"Why, you said you would come as soon as you had seen your aunt, and all this time you have not been here?" After these words Ivan Fiodorovich's lips found themselves again in contact with the same cushions.

"I've been busy looking after the land . . . I have come just for a minute to see you on business. . . ."

"For a minute? Well, that won't do. Hey, boy!" shouted the fat gentleman, and the same boy in the Cossack coat ran out of the kitchen. "Tell Kasian to shut the gate tight, do you hear! make it fast! And unharness this gentleman's horse this minute. Please come indoors; it is so hot out here that my shirt's soaked."

On going indoors Ivan Fiodorovich made up his mind to lose no time and in spite of his shyness to act with decision.

"My aunt had the honor . . . she told me that a deed of the late Stepan Kuzmich's . . ."

It is difficult to describe the unpleasant grimace made by the broad face of Grigory Grigorievich at these words.

"Oh dear, I hear nothing!" he responded. "I must tell you that a cockroach got into my left ear (those damned Russians breed cockroaches in all their huts); no pen can describe what agony it was, it kept tickling and tickling. An old woman cured me by the simplest means . . ."

"I meant to say . . ." Ivan Fiodorovich ventured to interrupt, seeing that Grigory Grigorievich was intentionally changing the subject; "that in the late Stepan Kuzmich's will mention is made, so to speak, of a deed . . . According to it I ought . . ."

"I know; so your aunt has told you that story already. It's a lie, I swear it is! My uncle made no deed. Though, indeed, some such thing is referred to in the will. But where is it? No one has produced it. I tell you this because I sincerely wish you well. I assure you it is a lie!"

Ivan Fiodorovich said nothing, reflecting that possibly his aunt really might be mistaken.

"Ah, here comes Mother with my sisters!" said Grigory Grigorievich, "so dinner is ready. Let us go!"

And he drew Ivan Fiodorovich by the hand into a room in which vodka and snacks were on a table.

At the same time a short little old lady, a coffeepot in a cap, with two young ladies, one fair and one dark, came in. Ivan Fiodorovich, like a well-bred gentleman, went up to kiss the old lady's hand and then to kiss the hands of the two young ladies.

"This is our neighbor, Ivan Fiodorovich Shponka, Mother," said Grigory Grigorievich.

The old lady looked intently at Ivan Fiodorovich, or perhaps it only seemed that she looked intently at him. She was good-natured simplicity itself, though; she looked as though she would like to ask Ivan Fiodorovich: "How many cucumbers has your aunt pickled for the winter?"

"Have you had some vodka?" the old lady asked.

"You can't be yourself, Mother," said Grigory Grigorievich. "Who asks a visitor whether he has had anything? You offer it to him, that's all. Whether he wants to drink or not is his business. Ivan Fiodorovich! the centaury-flavored vodka or the Trofimov brand? Which do you prefer? And you, Ivan Ivanovich, why are you standing there?" Grigory Grigorievich said, turning around, and Ivan Fiodorovich saw the gentleman so addressed approaching the vodka, in a frock coat and an immense stand-up collar, which covered the whole back of his head, so that his head sat in it, as though it were a chaise.

Ivan Ivanovich went up to the vodka and rubbed his hands, carefully examined the wineglass, filled it, held it up to the light, and poured all the vodka at once into his mouth. He did not, however, swallow it at once, but rinsed his mouth thoroughly with it first before finally swallowing it, and then after eating some bread and salted mushrooms, he turned to Ivan Fiodorovich.

"Is it not Ivan Fiodorovich, Mr. Shponka, I have the honor of addressing?"

"Yes, certainly," answered Ivan Fiodorovich.

"You have changed a great deal, sir, since I saw you last. Why!" he continued, "I remember you when you were that high!" As he spoke he held his hand a yard from the floor. "Your poor father, God grant him the kingdom of heaven, was a rare man. He used to have melons such as you never see anywhere now. Here, for instance," he went on, drawing him aside, "they'll set melons before you on the table—such melons! You won't care to look at them! Would you believe it, sir, he used to have watermelons," he pronounced with a mysterious air, flinging out his arms as if he were about to embrace a stout tree trunk, "God bless me, they were as big as this!"

"Come to dinner!" said Grigory Grigorievich, taking Ivan Fiodorovich by the arm.

Grigory Grigorievich sat down in his usual place at the end of the table, draped with an enormous tablecloth which made him resemble the Greek heroes depicted by barbers on their signs. Ivan Fiodorovich, blushing, sat down in the place assigned to him, facing the two young ladies; and Ivan Ivanovich did not let slip the chance of sitting down beside him, inwardly rejoicing that he had someone to whom he could impart his various bits of information.

"You shouldn't take the end, Ivan Fiodorovich! It's a turkey!" said the old lady, addressing Ivan Fiodorovich, to whom the village waiter in a gray frock coat patched with black was offering a dish. "Take the back!"

"Mother! no one asked you to interfere!" commented Grigory Grigorievich. "You may be sure our visitor knows what to take himself! Ivan Fiodorovich! take a wing, the other one there with the gizzard! But why have you taken so little? Take a leg! Why do you gape at him?" he asked the waiter holding the dish. "Ask him! Go down on your knees, rascal! Say, at once, 'Ivan Fiodorovich, take a leg!'"

"Ivan Fiodorovich, take a leg!" the waiter bawled, kneeling down.

"H'm! do you call this a turkey?" Ivan Ivanovich muttered in a low voice, turning to his neighbor with an air of disdain. "Is that what a turkey ought to look like? If you could see my turkeys! I assure you there is more fat on one of them than on a dozen of these. Would you believe me, sir, they are really a repulsive sight when they walk about my yard, they are so fat . . . !"

"Ivan Ivanovich, you are telling lies!" said Grigory Grigorievich, overhearing these remarks.

"I tell you," Ivan Ivanovich went on talking to his neighbor, affecting not to hear what Grigory Grigorievich had said, "last year when I sent them to Gadyach, they offered me fifty kopeks apiece for them, and I wouldn't take even that."

"Ivan Ivanovich! I tell you, you are lying!" observed Grigory Grigorievich, dwelling on each syllable for greater distinctness and speaking more loudly than before.

But Ivan Ivanovich behaved as though the words could not possibly refer to him; he went on as before, but in a much lower voice: "Yes, sir, I would not take it. There is not a gentleman in Gadyach . . ."

"Ivan Ivanovich! You are a fool, and that's the truth," Grigory Grigorievich said in a loud voice. "Ivan Fiodorovich knows all about it better than you do, and doesn't believe you."

At this Ivan Ivanovich was really offended: he said no more, but began downing the turkey, even though it was not so fat as those that were a repulsive sight.

The clatter of knives, spoons, and plates took the place of conversation for a time, but loudest of all was the sound made by Grigory Grigorievich, smacking his lips over the marrow of the mutton bones.

"Have you," inquired Ivan Ivanovich after an interval of silence, poking his head out of the chaise, "read *The Travels of Korobeynikov to Holy Places*? [8] It's a real delight to heart and soul! Such books aren't published nowadays. I very much regret that I did not notice in what year it was written."

Ivan Fiodorovich, hearing mention of a book, applied himself diligently to taking sauce.

"It is truly marvelous, sir, when you think that a humble artisan visited all those places: over two thousand miles, sir! over two thousand miles! Truly, it was divine grace that enabled him to reach Palestine and Jerusalem."

"So you say," said Ivan Fiodorovich, who had heard a great deal about Jerusalem from his orderly, "that he visited Jerusalem."

"What are you saying, Ivan Fiodorovich?" Grigory Grigorievich inquired from the end of the table.

"I had occasion to observe what distant lands there are in the world!" said Ivan Fiodorovich, genuinely gratified that he had succeeded in uttering so long and difficult a sentence.

"Don't you believe him, Ivan Fiodorovich!" said Grigory Grigorievich, who had not quite caught what he said. "He always tells fibs!"

Meanwhile dinner was over. Grigory Grigorievich went to his own room, as his habit was, for a little nap; and the visitors followed their aged hostess and the young ladies into the drawing room, where the same table on which they had left vodka when they went out to dinner was now as though by some magical transformation covered with little saucers of jam of various sorts and dishes of cherries and different kinds of melons.

The absence of Grigory Grigorievich could be seen in everything: the old lady became more disposed to talk and, of her own

---

[8] I.e., *The Travels of a Moscow Merchant, Trifon Korobeynikov, and His Comrades to Jerusalem, Egypt, and Mount Sinai in 1583*, which first saw print in 1783, was frequently reprinted. (ed.)

accord, without being asked, revealed several secrets in regard to the making of apple cheese and the drying of pears. Even the young ladies began talking; though the fair one, who looked some six years younger than her sister and who was apparently about twenty-five, was rather silent.

But Ivan Ivanovich was more talkative and livelier than anyone. Feeling secure that no one would snub or contradict him, he talked of cucumbers and of planting potatoes and of how much more sensible people were in the old days—no comparison with what people are now!—and of how as time goes on everything improves and the most intricate inventions are discovered. He was, indeed, one of those persons who take great pleasure in relieving their souls by conversation and will talk of anything that possibly can be talked about. If the conversation touched upon grave and solemn subjects, Ivan Ivanovich sighed after each word and nodded his head slightly: if the subject were of a more domestic character, he would pop his head out of his chaise and make faces from which one could almost, it seemed, read how to make pear kvass, how large were the melons of which he was speaking, and how fat were the geese that were running about in his yard.

At last, with great difficulty and not before evening, Ivan Fiodorovich succeeded in taking his leave, and although he was usually ready to give way and they almost kept him for the night by force, he persisted in his intention of going—and went.

V

HIS AUNT'S NEW PLANS

"Well, did you get the deed out of the old reprobate?" Such was the question with which Ivan Fiodorovich was greeted by his aunt, who had been expecting him for some hours in the porch and had at last been unable to resist going out to the gate.

"No, Auntie," said Ivan Fiodorovich, getting out of the trap: "Grigory Grigorievich has no deed!"

"And you believed him? He was lying, the damned scoundrel! Some day I'll come across him and I will give him a drubbing with my own hands. Oh, I'd get rid of some of his fat for him! Though perhaps we ought first to consult our court assessor and see if we couldn't get the law on him. . . . But that's not the point now. Well, was the dinner good?"

"Very . . . yes, excellent, Auntie!"

"Well, what did you have? Tell me. The old lady, I know, is a great hand at looking after the cooking."

"Curd fritters with sour cream, Auntie; a stew of stuffed pigeons . . ."

"And a turkey with pickled plums?" asked his aunt, for she was herself very skillful in the preparation of that dish.

"Yes, there was a turkey, too . . . ! Very handsome young ladies, Grigory Grigorievich's sisters, especially the fair one!"

"Ah!" said Auntie, and she looked intently at Ivan Fiodorovich, who dropped his eyes, blushing. A new idea flashed into her mind. "Come, tell me," she said eagerly and with curiosity, "what are her eyebrows like?" We should note that the aunt considered fine eyebrows as the most important item in a woman's looks.

"Her eyebrows, Auntie, are exactly like what you described yours as being when you were young. And there are little freckles all over her face."

"Ah," commented his aunt, well pleased with Ivan Fiodorovich's observation, though he had had no idea of paying her a compliment. "What sort of dress was she wearing? Though, indeed, it's hard to get good material nowadays, such as I have here, for instance, in this dress. But that's not the point. Well, did you talk to her about anything?"

"Talk . . . how do you mean, Auntie? Perhaps you are imagining . . ."

"Well, what of it, there would be nothing strange in that! Such is God's will! It may have been ordained at your birth that you should make a match of it."

"I don't know how you can say such a thing, Auntie. That shows that you don't know me at all. . . ."

"Well, well, now he is offended," said his aunt. "He's still only a child!" she thought to herself: "he knows nothing! We must bring them together—let them get to know each other!"

The aunt went to have a look at the kitchen and left Ivan Fiodorovich alone. But from that time on she thought of nothing but seeing her nephew married as soon as possible and fondling his little ones. Her brain was absorbed in making preparations for the wedding, and it was noticeable that she bustled about more busily than ever, though the work was the worse rather than the better for it. Often when she was making the pies, a job which she never left to the cook, she would forget everything, and imagining that a tiny great-nephew was standing by her asking for some pie, would absently hold out her hands with the nicest bit for him, and the watchdog, taking advantage of this, would snatch the dainty morsel and by its loud munching rouse her from her reverie, for which it was always beaten with the poker. She even abandoned her favorite pursuits and did not go out shooting, especially after she shot a crow by mistake for a partridge, a thing which had never happened to her before.

At last, four days later, everyone saw the chaise brought out of the carriage house into the yard. The coachman Omelko (he was also the gardener and the watchman) had been hammering from early morning, nailing on the leather and continually chasing away the dogs who licked the wheels. I think it my duty to inform my readers that this was the very chaise in which Adam used to drive; and therefore, if anyone tries to convince you that some other chaise was Adam's, it is an absolute lie, and his chaise is certainly not the genuine article. It is impossible to say how it survived the Flood. It must be supposed that there was a special carriage house for it in Noah's Ark. I am very sorry that I cannot give a vivid picture of it for my readers. It is enough to say that Vasilisa Kashporovna was very well satisfied with its structure and always expressed regret that the old style of carriages had gone out of fashion. The chaise had been constructed a little on one side, that is, the right half was much higher than the left, and this pleased her particularly, because, as she said, a fat person could sit on one side and a tall person on the other. Inside the chaise, however, there was room for five small persons or three as big as the aunt.

About midday Omelko, having finished with the chaise, brought out of the stable three horses that were only a little younger than the chaise, and began harnessing them to the magnificent vehicle with a rope. Ivan Fiodorovich and his aunt, one on the left side and the other on the right, stepped in and the chaise drove off. The peasants they met on the road, seeing this sumptuous chaise (Vasilisa Kashporovna rarely drove out in it), stopped respectfully, taking off their caps and bowing low.

Two hours later the chaise stopped at the front door—I think I need not say—of Storchenko's house. Grigory Grigorievich was not at home. His old mother and the two young ladies came into the dining room to receive the guests. The aunt walked in with a majestic step, with a great air stopped short with one foot forward, and said in a loud voice:

"I am delighted, dear madam, to have the honor to offer you my respects in person; and at the same time to thank you for your hospitality to my nephew, who has been warm in his praises of it. Your buckwheat is very good, madam—I saw it as we drove into the village. May I ask how many sheaves you get to the acre?"

After that followed kisses all around. As soon as they were seated in the drawing room, the old lady began:

"About the buckwheat I cannot tell you: that's Grigory Grigorievich's department: it's long since I have had anything to do with the farming; indeed I am not equal to it, I am old now! In the old days I remember the buckwheat stood up to my waist; now goodness knows what it is like, though they do say everything is better now." At that point the old lady heaved a sigh, and some observers would have heard in that sigh the sigh of a past age, of the eighteenth century.

"I have heard, madam, that your own serf girls can make excellent carpets," said Vasilisa Kashporovna, and with that touched on the old lady's most sensitive nerve; at those words she seemed to brighten up, and she talked readily of the way to dye the yarn and prepare the thread.

From carpets the conversation passed easily to the pickling of cucumbers and drying of pears. In short, before the end of an hour the two ladies were talking together as though they had been friends all their lives. Vasilisa Kashporovna had already said a great deal to her in such a low voice that Ivan Fiodorovich could not hear what she was saying.

"Yes, would you like to have a look at them?" said the old lady, getting up.

The young ladies and Vasilisa Kashporovna also got up and all moved toward the serf girls' room. The aunt signaled, however, to Ivan Fiodorovich to remain, and whispered something to the old lady.

"Mashenka," said the latter, addressing the fair-haired young lady, "stay with our visitor and talk with him, so that he doesn't become bored!"

The fair-haired young lady remained and sat down on the sofa. Ivan Fiodorovich sat on his chair as though on thorns, blushed and cast down his eyes; but the young lady appeared not to notice this and sat unconcernedly on the sofa, carefully scrutinizing the windows and the walls, or watching the cat timorously running around under the chairs.

Ivan Fiodorovich grew a little bolder and would have begun a conversation; but it seemed as though he had lost all his words on the way. Not a single idea came into his mind.

The silence lasted for nearly a quarter of an hour. The young lady went on sitting as before.

At last Ivan Fiodorovich plucked up his courage.

"There are a great many flies in summer, madam!" he said in a half-trembling voice.

"A very great many!" answered the young lady. "My brother has made a swatter out of an old slipper of Mama's but there are still lots of them."

Here the conversation stalled again, and Ivan Fiodorovich was utterly unable to find anything to say.

At last the old lady and his aunt and the dark-haired young lady came back again. After a little more conversation, Vasilisa Kashporovna took leave of the old lady and her daughters in spite of their entreaties that they stay the night. The three ladies came out on the steps to see their visitors off, and continued for some time nodding to the aunt and nephew, as they looked out of the chaise.

"Well, Ivan Fiodorovich, what did you talk about when you were alone with the young lady?" his aunt asked him on the way home.

"Maria Grigorievna is a modest and well-behaved young lady!" said Ivan Fiodorovich.

"Listen, Ivan Fiodorovich, I want to talk seriously to you. Here you are thirty-eight, thank God; you have obtained a good rank in the service—it's time to think about children! You must have a wife . . ."

"What, Auntie!" cried Ivan Fiodorovich, panic-stricken, "a wife! No, Auntie, for goodness' sake . . . You make me quite ashamed . . . I've never had a wife . . . I wouldn't know what to do with her!"

"You'll find out, Ivan Fiodorovich, you'll find out," said his aunt, smiling, and she thought to herself: "What next, he is a perfect baby, he knows nothing!" "Yes, Ivan Fiodorovich!" she went on aloud, "we could not find a better wife for you than Maria Grigorievna. Besides, you are very much attracted by her. I have had a good talk with the old lady about it: she'll be delighted to see you her son-in-law. It's true that we don't know what that old scoundrel Grigorievich will say to it; but we won't consider him, and if he takes it into his head not to give her a dowry, we'll have the law on him. . . ."

At that moment the chaise drove into the yard and the ancient nags grew more lively, feeling that their stable was not far off.

"Listen, Omelko! Let the horses have a good rest first, and don't take them down to drink the minute they are unharnessed; they are overheated."

"Well, Ivan Fiodorovich," his aunt went on as she got out of the chaise, "I advise you to think it over carefully. I must run to the kitchen: I forgot to tell Solokha what to get for supper, and I expect the wretched girl won't have thought of it herself."

But Ivan Fiodorovich stood as though thunderstruck. It was true that Maria Grigorievna was a very nice-looking young lady; but to get married . . . ! It seemed to him so strange, so peculiar, he couldn't think of it without horror. Living with a wife . . . ! Unthinkable! He would not be alone in his own room, but they would always have to be together . . . ! Perspiration came out on his face as he sank more deeply into meditation.

He went to bed earlier than usual but in spite of all his efforts he could not go to sleep. But at last sleep, that universal comforter, came to him; but such sleep! He had never had such incoherent dreams. First, he dreamed that everything was whirling noisily around him, and he was running and running, as fast as his legs could carry him . . . Now he was at his last gasp . . . All at once someone caught him by the ear. "Aie! who is it?" "It is I, your wife!" a voice resounded loudly in his ear—and he woke up. Then he imagined that he was married, that everything in their little house was so peculiar, so strange: a double bed stood in his room instead of a single one; his wife was sitting on a chair. He felt strange; he did not know how to approach her, what to say to her, and then he noticed that she had the face of a goose. He turned aside and saw another wife, also with the face of a goose. Turning in another direction, he saw still a third wife; and behind him was still another. Then he was seized by panic: he dashed away into the garden; but there it was hot. He took off his hat, and—saw a wife sitting in it. Drops of sweat came out on his face. He put his hand in his pocket for his handkerchief and in his pocket too there was a wife; he took some cotton out of his ear—and there too sat a wife. . . . Then he suddenly began hopping on one leg, and his aunt, looking at him, said with a dignified air: "Yes, you must hop on one leg now, for you are a married man." He went toward her, but his aunt was no longer an aunt but a belfry, and he felt that someone was dragging him by a rope up the belfry. "Who is it pulling me?" Ivan Fiodorovich asked plaintively. "It is I, your wife. I am pulling you because you are a bell." "No, I am not a bell, I am Ivan Fiodorovich," he cried. "Yes, you are a bell," said the colonel of the P—— infantry regiment, who happened to be passing. Then he suddenly dreamed that his wife was not a human being at all but a sort of woolen material, and that he went into a shop in Mogiliov. "What sort of material would you like?" asked the shopkeeper. "You had better take a wife, that is the most fashionable material! It wears well! Everyone is having coats made of it now." The shopkeeper measured and cut off his wife. Ivan Fiodorovich put her under his arm and went off to a Jewish tailor. "No," said the Jew, "that is poor material! No one has coats made of that now. . . ."

Ivan Fiodorovich woke up in terror, not knowing where he was; he was dripping with cold perspiration.

As soon as he got up in the morning, he went at once to his fortunetelling book, at the end of which a virtuous bookseller had in the goodness of his heart and unselfishness inserted an abridged dream interpreter. But there was absolutely nothing in it that remotely resembled this incoherent dream.

Meanwhile a new scheme, of which you shall hear more in the following chapter, matured in his aunt's brain.

A BEWITCHED PLACE

A True Story Told by the Sexton

I swear, I am sick of telling stories! Why, what would you expect? It really is tiresome; one goes on telling stories and there is no getting out of it! Oh, very well, I will tell you a story, then; only remember, it is for the last time. Well, we were talking about a man's being able to get the better, as the saying is, of the devil. To be sure, if it comes to that, all sorts of things do happen in this world. . . . Better not say so, though: if the devil wants to bamboozle you he will, I swear he will. . . . Now, you see, my father had the four of us; I was only a moron then, I wasn't more than eleven, no, not yet eleven. I remember as though it were today when I was running on all fours and began barking like a dog, my dad shouted at me, shaking his head: "Aie, Foma, Foma, you are almost old enough to be married and you are as foolish as a young mule."

My grandfather was still living then and fairly—may his hiccup ease up in the other world—strong on his legs. At times he would imagine things . . . But how am I to tell a story like this? Here one of you has been raking an ember for his pipe out of the stove for the last hour and the other has run behind the cupboard for something. It's too much . . . ! It wouldn't bother me if you didn't want to hear what I had to say, but you kept annoying me for a story . . . If you want to listen, then listen!

Just at the beginning of spring Father went with the wagons to the Crimea to sell tobacco; but I don't remember whether he loaded two or three wagons; tobacco brought a good price in those days. He took my three-year-old brother with him to train him early as a dealer. Grandad, Mother, and I and a brother and another brother were left at home. Grandad had sown melons on a bit of ground by the roadway and went to stay at the shanty there; he took us with him, too, to scare the sparrows and the magpies away from the garden. I can't say we didn't enjoy it: sometimes we'd eat so many cucumbers, melons, turnips, onions, and peas that I swear, you would have thought there were cocks crowing in our stomachs. Well, to be sure, it was profitable too: travelers jog along the road, everyone wants to treat himself to a melon, and, besides that, from the neighboring farms they would often bring us fowls, turkeys, eggs, to exchange for our vegetables. We did very well.

But what pleased Grandad more than anything was that some fifty dealers would pass with their wagonloads every day. They are people, you know, who have seen life: if one of them wants to tell you anything, you would do well to perk up your ears, and to Grandad it was like dumplings to a hungry man. Sometimes there would be a meeting with old acquaintances—everyone knew Grandad—and you know yourself how it is when old folks get together: it is this and that, and so then and so then, and so this happened and that happened . . . Well, they just go on. They remember things that happened, God knows when.

One evening—why, it seems as though it might have happened today—the sun had begun to set. Grandad was walking about the garden removing the leaves with which he covered the watermelons in the day to save them from being scorched by the sun.

"Look, Ostap," I said to my brother, "here come some wagoners!"

"Where are the wagoners?" said Grandad, as he put a mark on the big melon so that the boys wouldn't eat it by accident.

There were, as a fact, six wagons trailing along the road; a wagoner, whose mustache had gone gray, was walking ahead of them. He was still—what shall I say?—ten paces off, when he stopped.

"Good day, Maxim, so it has pleased God we should meet here."

Grandad screwed up his eyes. "Ah, good day, good day! Where do you come from? And Bolyachka here, too! Good day, good day, brother! What the devil! why, they are all here: Krutotryshchenko too! and Pecherytsya! and Koveliok and Stetsko! Good day! Ha, ha, ho, ho . . . !" And they began kissing each other.

They took the oxen out of the shafts and let them graze on the grass; they left the wagons on the road and they all sat down in a circle in front of the shanty and lit their pipes. Though they had no thought for their pipes; well, between telling stories and chattering, I don't believe they smoked a pipe apiece.

After supper Grandad began regaling his visitors with melons. So, taking a melon each, they trimmed it neatly with a knife (they were all old hands, had been about a good deal, and knew how to eat in company—I daresay they would have been ready to sit down even at a gentleman's table); after cleaning the melon well, everyone made a hole with his finger in it, drank the juice, and began cutting it up into pieces and putting them into his mouth.

"Why are you standing there gaping, boys?" said my grandfather. "Dance, you sons of bitches! Where's your pipe, Ostap? Now then, the Cossack dance! Foma, arms akimbo! Come, that's it, hey, hop!"

I was an energetic boy in those days. Cursed old age! Now I can't move like that; instead of cutting capers, my legs can only trip and stumble. For a long time Grandad watched us as he sat with the dealers. I noticed that his legs wouldn't keep still; it was as though something was tugging at them.

"Look, Foma," said Ostap, "if the old fellow isn't going to dance."

What do you think, he had hardly uttered the words when the old man could resist it no longer! He wanted, you know, to show off in front of the dealers.

"Now, you little bastards, is that the way to dance? This is the way to dance!" he said, getting up on his feet, stretching out his arms, and tapping with his heels.

Well, there is no denying that he did dance; he couldn't have danced better if it had been with the Hetman's wife. We stood aside and the old man went whirling all over the flat area beside the cucumber beds. But as soon as he had got halfway through the dance and wanted to do his best and cut some more capers, his feet wouldn't lift from the ground, no matter what he did! "What a plague!" He moved backwards and forwards again, got to the middle of the dance again, but he couldn't go on with it! Whatever he did—he couldn't do it, and he didn't do it! His legs were stiff as though made of wood. "Look, the place is bewitched, look, it is a spell of Satan! The enemy of mankind has a hand in it!" Well, he couldn't disgrace himself before the dealers like that, could he? He made a fresh start and began cutting tiny trifling capers, a joy to see; up to the middle—then no! it wouldn't be danced, and that is all!

"Ah, you damned Satan! I hope you choke on a rotten melon, that you perish before you grow up, you son of a bitch. See what shame he has brought me to in my old age . . . !" And indeed someone did laugh behind his back.

He looked around: no melon garden, no dealers, nothing; behind, in front, on both sides was a flat field. "Ay! Sss! . . . Well, I never!" he began screwing up his eyes—the place doesn't seem quite unfamiliar: on one side a copse, behind the copse some sort of post sticking up which can be seen far away against the sky. Damn it all! but that's the dovehouse in the priest's garden! On the other side, too, there is something grayish; he looked closer: it was the district clerk's threshing barn. So this was where the devil had dragged him! Going around in a circle, he found a little path. There was no moon; instead of it a white blur glimmered through a dark cloud.

"There will be a high wind tomorrow," thought Grandad. All at once there was the gleam of a light on a little grave to one side of the path. "Well, I never!" Grandad stood still, put his arms akimbo, and stared at it. The light went out; far away and a little further yet, another twinkled. "A treasure!" cried Grandad. "I'll bet anything it's a treasure!" And he was just about to spit on his hands to begin digging when he remembered that he had no spade or shovel with him. "Oh, what a pity! Well—who knows?— maybe I've only to lift the turf and there it lies, the precious dear! Well, there's nothing I can do; I'll mark the place anyway so as not to forget it afterwards."

So pulling along a large branch that must have been broken off by a high wind, he laid it on the little grave where the light gleamed and then he continued along the path. The young oak copse grew thinner; he caught a glimpse of a fence. "There, didn't I say that it was the priest's garden?" thought Grandad. "Here's his fence; now it is not three-quarters of a mile to the melon patch."

It was pretty late, though, when he came home, and he wouldn't have any dumplings. Waking my brother Ostap, he only asked him whether it was long since the dealers had gone, and then rolled himself up in his sheepskin. And when Ostap started to ask him: "And what did the devils do with you today, Grandad?" "Don't ask," he said, wrapping himself up tighter than ever, "don't ask, Ostap, or your hair will turn gray!"

And he began snoring so that the startled sparrows which had been flocking together to the melon patch rose up in the air and flew away. But how was it that he could sleep? There's no denying, he was a sly beast. God give him the kingdom of heaven, he could always get out of any scrape; sometimes he would pitch such a yarn that you would have to bite your lips.

Next day as soon as it began to get light Grandad put on his coat, fastened his belt, took a spade and shovel under his arm, put on his cap, drank a mug of kvass, wiped his lips with the skirt of his coat, and went straight to the priest's vegetable garden. He passed both the hedges and the low oak copse, and there was a path winding out between the trees and coming out into the open country; it seemed the same. He came out of the copse and the place seemed exactly the same as yesterday. He saw the dovehouse sticking out, but he could not see the threshing barn. "No, this isn't the place, it must be a little farther; it seems I must turn a little toward the threshing barn!" He turned back a little and began going along another path—then he could see the barn but not the dovehouse. Again he turned, and a little nearer to the dovehouse the barn was hidden. As though to spite him it began to drizzle. He ran again toward the barn—the dovehouse vanished; toward the dovehouse—the barn vanished.

"You damned Satan, may you never live to see your children!" he cried. And the rain came down in buckets.

Taking off his new boots and wrapping them in a handkerchief, so that they might not be warped by the rain, he ran off at a trot like some gentleman's saddle horse. He crept into the shanty, drenched through, covered himself with his sheepskin, and began grumbling between his teeth and cursing the devil with words such as I had never heard in my life. I must admit I would really have blushed if it had happened in broad daylight.

Next day I woke up and looked; Grandad was walking about the melon patch as though nothing had happened, covering the melons with burdock leaves. At dinner the old man began talking again and scaring my young brother, saying he would trade him for a fowl instead of a melon; and after dinner he made a pipe out of a bit of wood and began playing on it; and to amuse us gave us a melon which was twisted in three coils like a snake; he called it a Turkish one. I don't see such melons anywhere nowadays; it is true he got the seed from somewhere far away. In the evening, after supper, Grandad went with the spade to dig a new bed for late pumpkins. He began passing that bewitched place and he couldn't resist saying, "Cursed place!" He went into the middle of it, to the spot where he could not finish the dance the day before, and in his anger struck it with his spade. In a flash—that same field was all around him again: on one side he saw the dovehouse and on the other the threshing barn. "Well, it's a good thing I brought my spade. And there's the path, and there is the little grave! And there's the branch lying on it, and there, see there, is the light! If only I have made no mistake!"

He ran up stealthily, holding the spade in the air as though he were going to hit a hog that had poked its nose into a melon patch, and stopped before the grave. The light went out. On the grave lay a stone overgrown with weeds. "I must lift up that stone," thought Grandad, and tried to dig around it on all sides. The damned stone was huge! But planting his feet on the ground he shoved it off the grave. "Goo!" it rolled down the slope. "That's the right road for you to take! Now we'll get things done quickly!"

At this point Grandad stopped, took out his horn, sprinkled a little snuff in his hand, and was about to raise it to his nose when all at once—"Tchee-hee!" something sneezed above his head so that the trees shook and Grandad's face was spattered all over. "You might at least turn aside when you want to sneeze," said Grandad, wiping his eyes. He looked around—there was no one there. "No, it seems the devil doesn't like the snuff," he went on, putting back the horn in his bosom and picking up his spade. "He's a fool! Neither his grandfather nor his father ever had a pinch of snuff like that!" He began digging; the ground was soft, the spade had no trouble biting into it. Then something clanked. Pushing aside the earth he saw a cauldron.

"Ah, you darling, here you are!" cried Grandad, thrusting the spade under it.

"Ah, you darling, here you are!" piped a bird's beak, pecking the cauldron.

Grandad looked around and dropped the spade.

"Ah, you darling, here you are!" bleated a sheep's head from the top of the trees.

"Ah, you darling, here you are!" roared a bear, poking its snout out from behind a tree. A shudder ran down Grandad's back.

"Why, one is afraid to say a word here!" he muttered to himself.

"One is afraid to say a word here!" piped the bird's beak.

"Afraid to say a word here!" bleated the sheep's head.

"To say a word here!" roared the bear.

"Hm!" said Grandad, and he felt terrified.

"Hm!" piped the beak.

"Hm!" bleated the sheep.

"Hm!" roared the bear.

Grandad turned around in astonishment. Heaven help us, what a night! No stars nor moon; pits all around him, a bottomless precipice at his feet and a crag hanging over his head and looking every minute as though it would break off and come down on him. And Grandad imagined that a horrible face peeped out from behind it. "Oo! Oo!" a nose like a blacksmith's bellows. You could pour a bucket of water into each nostril! Lips like two logs! Red eyes seemed to be popping out, and a tongue was thrust out too, and jeering. "The devil take you!" said Grandad, flinging down the cauldron. "Damn you and your treasure! What an ugly snout!" And he was just going to cut and run, but he looked around and stopped, seeing that everything was as before. "It's only the damned devil trying to frighten me!"

He set to work at the cauldron again. No, it was too heavy! What was he to do? He couldn't leave it now! So exerting himself to his utmost, he clutched at it. "Come, heave ho! again, again!" and he dragged it out. "Ough, now for a pinch of snuff!"

He took out his horn. Before shaking any out, though, he took a good look around to be sure there was no one there. He thought there was no one; but then it seemed to him that the trunk of the tree was gasping and blowing, ears made their appearance, there were red eyes, puffing nostrils, a wrinkled nose and it seemed on the point of sneezing. "No, I won't have a pinch of snuff!" thought Grandad, putting away the horn. "Satan will be spitting in my eyes again!" He made haste to snatch up the cauldron and began running as fast as his legs could carry him; only he felt something behind him scratching on his legs with twigs. . . . "Aie, aie, aie!" was all that Grandad could cry as he ran as fast as he could; and it was not till he reached the priest's vegetable garden that he paused for breath.

"Where can Grandad be gone?" we wondered, waiting three hours for him. Mother had come from the farm long ago and brought a pot of hot dumplings. Still no sign of Grandad! Again we had supper without him. After supper Mother washed the pot and was looking for a spot to throw the dishwater because there were melon beds all around, when she saw a barrel rolling straight toward her! It was quite dark. She felt sure one of the boys was hiding behind it in mischief and shoving it toward her. "That's right, I'll throw the water at him," she said, and flung the hot dishwater at the barrel.

"Aie!" shouted a bass voice. Imagine that: Grandad! Well, who would have known him! I swear we thought it was a barrel coming up! I must admit, though it was a sin, we really thought it funny when Grandad's gray head was all drenched in the dishwater and decked with melon peelings.

"Oh, you devil of a woman!" said Grandad, wiping his head with the skirt of his coat. "What a hot bath she has given me, as though I were a pig before Christmas! Well, boys, now you will have something for pretzels! You'll go about dressed in gold jackets, you puppies! Look what I have brought you!" said Grandad, and opened the cauldron.

What do you suppose there was in it? Come, think, make a guess! Eh? Gold? Well now, it wasn't gold—it was filth, slop, I am ashamed to say what it was. Grandad spat, dropped the cauldron, and washed his hands.

And from that time forward Grandad made us two swear never to trust the devil. "Don't you believe it!" he would often say to us. "Whatever the foe of our Lord Christ says, he is always lying, the son of a bitch! There isn't a kopek's worth of truth in him!" And if ever the old man heard that things were not right in some place: "Come, boys, let's cross ourselves! That's it! That's it! Properly!" and he would begin making the sign of the cross. And that accursed place where he couldn't finish the dance he fenced in, and he asked that we fling all the garbage there, all the weeds and litter which he raked off the melon patch.

So you see how the devil fools a man. I know that bit of ground well; later on some neighboring Cossacks hired it from Dad for a melon patch. It's marvelous ground and there is always a wonderful crop on it; but there has never been anything good on that bewitched place. They may sow it properly, but there's no saying what it is that comes up: not a melon—not a pumpkin—not a cucumber, the devil only knows what to make of it.

MIRGOROD

OLD-WORLD LANDOWNERS

I am very fond of the modest manner of life of those solitary owners of remote villages, who in Little Russia are commonly called "old-fashioned," who are like tumbledown picturesque little houses, delightful in their simplicity and complete unlikeness to the new smooth buildings whose walls have not yet been discolored by the rain, whose roof is not yet covered with green lichen, and whose porch does not display its red bricks through the peeling stucco. I like sometimes to enter for a moment into that extraordinarily secluded life in which not one desire flits beyond the palisade surrounding the little courtyard, beyond the hurdle of the orchard filled with plum and apple trees, beyond the village huts surrounding it, lying all aslant under the shade of willows, elders, and pear trees. The life of their modest owners is so quiet, so quiet, that for a moment one is lost in forgetfulness and imagines that those passions, desires, and restless promptings of the evil spirit that trouble the world have no real existence, and that you have only beheld them in some lurid dazzling dream. I can see now the low-pitched little house with the gallery of little blackened wooden posts running right around it, so that in hail or storm they could close the shutters without being wetted by the rain. Behind it a fragrant bird-cherry, rows of dwarf fruit trees, drowned in a sea of red cherries and amethyst plums, covered with lead-colored bloom; a spreading maple in the shade of which a rug is laid to rest on; in front of the house a spacious courtyard of short fresh grass with a little pathway trodden from the storehouse to the kitchen and from the kitchen to the master's apartments; a long-necked goose drinking water with young goslings soft as down around her; a palisade hung with strings of dried pears and apples and rugs put out to air; a cartful of melons standing by the storehouse; an unharnessed ox lying lazily beside it—they all have an inexpressible charm for me, perhaps because I no longer see them and because everything from which we are parted is dear to us.

Be that as it may, at the very moment when my chaise was driving up to the steps of that little house, my soul passed into a wonderfully sweet and serene mood; the horses galloped merrily up to the steps; the coachman very tranquilly clambered down from the box and filled his pipe as though he had reached home; even the barking set up by the phlegmatic Rovers, Pontos, and Neros was pleasant to my ears. But best of all I liked the owners of these modest little nooks—the little old men and women who came out solicitously to meet me. I can see their faces sometimes even now among fashionable dress coats in the noise and crowd, and then I sink into a half-dreaming state, and the past rises up before me. Their faces always betray such kindness, such hospitality and singleheartedness, that unconsciously one renounces, for a brief spell at least, all ambitious dreams, and imperceptibly passes with all one's heart into this humble bucolic life.

To this day, I cannot forget two old people of a past age, now, alas! no more. To this day I am full of regret, and it sends a strange pang to my heart when I imagine myself going sometime again to their old, now deserted dwelling, and seeing the heap of ruined huts, the pond choked with weeds, an overgrown ditch on the spot where the little house stood—and nothing more. It is sad! I am sad at the thought ! But let me turn to my story.

Afanasy Ivanovich Tovstogub and his wife Pulkheria Ivanovna, as the neighboring peasants called her, were the old people of whom I was beginning to tell you. If I were a painter and wanted to portray Philemon and Baucis[1] on canvas, I could choose no other models. Afanasy Ivanovich was sixty. Pulkheria Ivanovna was fifty-five. Afanasy Ivanovich was tall, always wore a camlet-covered sheepskin, used to sit bent over, and was invariably almost smiling, even though he was telling a story or simply listening. Pulkheria Ivanovna was rather grave and scarcely ever laughed; but in her face and eyes there was so much kindness, so much readiness to regale you with the best of all they had, that you would certainly have found a smile superfluously sweet for her kind face. The faint wrinkles on their faces were drawn so charmingly that an artist would surely have stolen them; it seemed as though one could read in them their whole life, clear and serene—the life led by the old, typically Little Russian, simplehearted and at the same time wealthy families, always such a contrast to the meaner sort of Little Russians who, struggling up from making tar and petty trading, swarm like locusts in the law courts and public offices, fleece their fellow villagers of their last kopek, inundate Petersburg with pettifogging attorneys, make their pile at last, and solemnly add V to surnames ending in O.[2] No, they, like all the old-fashioned, primitive Little Russian families, were utterly different from such paltry contemptible creatures.

One could not look without sympathy at their mutual love. They never addressed each other familiarly, but always with formality. "Was it you who broke the chair, Afanasy Ivanovich?" "Never mind, don't be cross, Pulkheria Ivanovna, it was I." They had had no children, and so all their affection was concentrated on each other. At one time in his youth Afanasy Ivanovich was in the service and had been a lieutenant major; but that was very long ago, that was all over, Afanasy Ivanovich himself scarcely ever recalled it. Afanasy Ivanovich was married at thirty when he was a fine fellow and wore an embroidered coat; he even eloped rather neatly with Pulkheria Ivanovna, whose relations opposed their

---

[1] The devoted couple, in Greek legend, who graciously supplied food and shelter to Zeus and Hermes after they had been turned away by others, and, as a result of their kindness, survived the flood Zeus unleashed to destroy their neighbors. (ed.)

[2] In an effort to be considered a Great Russian. Ukrainian surnames usually end in "o," Russian names in "v." (ed.)

marriage, but he thought very little about that now—at any rate, he never spoke of it.

All these faraway extraordinary adventures had been followed by a peaceful and secluded life, by the soothing and harmonious dreams that you enjoy when you sit on a wooden balcony overlooking the garden while a delicious rain keeps up a luxurious sound pattering on the leaves, flowing in gurgling streams, and inducing a drowsiness in your limbs, while a rainbow hides behind the trees and in the form of a half-broken arch gleams in the sky with seven soft colors—or when you are swayed in a carriage that drives between green bushes while the quail of the steppes calls and the fragrant grass mingled with ears of wheat and wild flowers thrusts itself in at the carriage doors, flicking you pleasantly on the hands and face.

Afanasy Ivanovich always listened with a pleasant smile to the guests who visited him; sometimes he talked himself, but more often he asked questions. He was not one of those old people who bore one with everlasting praise of old days or denunciation of the new: on the contrary, as he questioned you, he showed great interest and curiosity about the circumstances of your own life, your failures and successes, in which all kindhearted old people show an interest, though it is a little like the curiosity of a child who examines the seal on your watch at the same time as he talks to you. Then his face, one may say, was breathing with kindliness.

The rooms of the little house in which our old people lived were small and low-pitched, as they usually are in the houses of old-world people. In each room there was an immense stove which covered nearly a third of the floor space. These rooms were terribly hot, for both Afanasy Ivanovich and Pulkheria Ivanovna liked warmth. The stoves were all heated from the outer room, which was always filled almost up to the ceiling with straw, commonly used in Little Russia instead of firewood.[3] The crackle and flare of this burning straw made the outer room exceedingly pleasant on a winter's evening when ardent young men, chilled with the pursuit of some dark charmer, ran in, rubbing their hands. The walls of the room were adorned with a few pictures in old-fashioned narrow frames. I am convinced that their owners had themselves long ago forgotten what they represented, and if some of them had been

---

[3] *Kiziak,* pressed brick of manure and straw, was the common fuel. (ed.)

taken away, they would probably not have noticed it. There were two big portraits painted in oils. One depicted a bishop, the other Peter III; a flyblown Duchesse de La Vallière[4] looked out from a narrow frame. Around the windows and above the doors there were numbers of little pictures which one grew used to looking upon as spots on the wall and so never examined them. In almost all the rooms the floor was of clay but cleanly painted and kept with a neatness with which probably no parquet floor in a wealthy house, lazily swept by sleepy gentlemen in livery, has ever been kept.

Pulkheria Ivanovna's room was all surrounded with chests and boxes, big and little. Numbers of little bags and sacks of flower seeds, vegetable seeds, and melon seeds hung on the walls. Numbers of balls of different-colored wools and rags of old-fashioned gowns made half a century ago were stored in the little chests and between the little chests in the corners. Pulkheria Ivanovna was a notable housewife and saved everything, though sometimes she could not herself have said to what use it could be put afterwards.

But the most remarkable thing in the house was the singing of the doors. As soon as morning came, the singing of the doors could be heard all over the house. I cannot say why it was they sang— whether the rusty hinges were to blame for it or whether the mechanic who made them had concealed some secret in them—but it was remarkable that each door had its own voice. The door leading to the bedroom sang in the thinnest falsetto, and the door into the dining room in a husky bass; but the one on the outer room gave out a strange cracked and at the same time moaning sound, so that as one listened to it one heard distinctly: "Holy Saints! I am freezing!" I know that many people very much dislike this sound; but I am very fond of it, and if here I sometimes happen to hear a door creak, it seems at once to bring me a whiff of the country: the low-pitched little room lighted by a candle in an old-fashioned candlestick; supper already on the table; a dark May night peeping in from the garden through the open window at the table laid with knives and forks; the nightingale flooding garden, house, and far-away river with its trilling song; the tremor and rustle of branches, and, my God! what a long string of memories stretches before me then! . . .

The chairs in the room were massive wooden ones such as were

---

[4] (1644-1710), mistress of Louis XIV. (ed.)

common in the old days; they all had high carved backs and were without any kind of varnish or stain; they were not even upholstered, and were rather like the chairs on which bishops sit to this day. Little triangular tables in the corners and square ones before the sofa, and the mirror in its thin gold frame carved with leaves which the flies had covered with black spots; in front of the sofa a rug with birds on it that looked like flowers and flowers that looked like birds: that was almost all the furnishing of the unpretentious little house in which my old people lived. The maids' room was packed full of young girls, and girls who were not young, in striped petticoats; Pulkheria Ivanovna sometimes gave them some trifling sewing or set them to prepare the fruit, but for the most part they ran off to the kitchen and slept. Pulkheria Ivanovna thought it necessary to keep them in the house and looked strictly after their morals; but, to her great surprise, many months never passed without the waist of some girl or other growing much larger than usual. This seemed the more surprising as there was scarcely a bachelor in the house with the exception of the house-boy, who used to go about barefoot in a gray tail coat, and, if he were not eating, was sure to be asleep. Pulkheria Ivanovna usually scolded the erring damsel and punished her severely so that it might not happen again.

A terrible number of flies were always buzzing on the window-panes, above whose notes rose the deep bass of a bumblebee, sometimes accompanied by the shrill plaint of a wasp; then, as soon as candles were brought, the swarm went to bed and covered the whole ceiling with a black cloud.

Afanasy Ivanovich took very little interest in farming his land, though he did drive out sometimes to the mowers and reapers and watched their labors rather attentively; the whole burden of management rested upon Pulkheria Ivanovna. Pulkheria Ivanovna's housekeeping consisted in continually locking up and unlocking the storeroom, and in salting, drying, and preserving countless masses of fruits and vegetables. Her house was very much like a chemical laboratory. There was always a fire built under an apple tree; and a cauldron or a copper pan of jam, jelly, or fruit cheese made with honey, sugar, and I don't remember what else, was scarcely ever taken off the iron tripod on which it stood. Under another tree the coachman was forever distilling in a copper retort vodka with peach leaves, or bird-cherry flowers or centaury or cherry stones, and at the end of the process was utterly unable to control his tongue, jabbered such nonsense that Pulkheria Ivanovna could make nothing of it, and had to go away to sleep it off in the kitchen. Such a quantity of all this stuff was boiled, salted, and dried that the whole courtyard would probably have been drowned in it at last (for Pulkheria Ivanovna always liked to prepare a store for the future in addition to all that was thought necessary for use) if the larger half of it had not been eaten up by the serf girls, who, stealing into the storeroom, would overeat themselves so frightfully that they were moaning and complaining of stomach-ache all day. Pulkheria Ivanovna had little chance of looking after the tilling of the fields or other branches of husbandry. The steward, in conjunction with the village elder, robbed them in a merciless fashion. They had adopted the habit of treating their master's forest land as though it were their own; they made numbers of sleds and sold them at the nearest fair; moreover, all the thick oaks they sold to the neighboring Cossacks to be cut down for building mills. On only one occasion did Pulkheria Ivanovna desire to inspect her forests. For this purpose a chaise was brought out with immense leather aprons which, as soon the coachman shook the reins, and the horses, who had served in the militia, set off, filled the air with strange sounds, so that a flute and a tambourine and a drum all seemed suddenly audible; every nail and iron bolt clanked so loudly that even at the mill it could be heard that the mistress was driving out of the yard, though the distance was fully a mile and a half. Pulkheria Ivanovna could not help noticing the terrible devastation in the forest and the loss of the oaks, which even in childhood she had known to be a hundred years old.

"Why is it, Nichipor," she said, addressing her steward who was present, "that the oaks have been so thinned? Mind that the hair on your head does not grow so thin."

"Why is it?" the steward said. "They have fallen down! They have simply fallen: struck by lightning, gnawed by maggots—they have fallen, lady." Pulkheria Ivanovna was completely satisfied with this answer, and on arriving home merely gave orders that the watch should be doubled in the garden near the Spanish cherry trees and the big winter pears.

These worthy rulers, the steward and the elder, considered it quite superfluous to take all the flour to their master's granaries; they thought that the latter would have quite enough with half, and what is more they took to the granaries the half that had begun to grow moldy or had got wet and been rejected at the fair. But however much the steward and the elder stole; however gluttonously everyone on the place ate, from the housekeeper to the pigs, who guzzled an immense number of plums and apples and often pushed the tree with their snouts to shake a perfect rain of fruit down from it; however much the sparrows and crows pecked; however many presents all the servants carried to their friends in other villages, even hauling off old linen and yarn from the storerooms, all of which went into the everflowing stream, that is, to the tavern; however much was stolen by visitors, phlegmatic coachmen, and flunkeys, yet the blessed earth produced everything in such abundance, and Afanasy Ivanovich and Pulkheria Ivanovna wanted so little, that this terrible robbery made no perceptible impression on their prosperity.

Both the old people were very fond of good food, as was the old-fashioned tradition of old-world landowners. As soon as the sun had risen (they always got up early) and as soon as the doors began their varied concert, they were sitting down to a little table, drinking coffee. When he had finished his coffee Afanasy Ivanovich would go out into the porch and, shaking his handkerchief, say: "Kish, kish! Get off the steps, geese!" In the yard he usually came across the steward. As a rule he entered into conversation with him, questioned him about the field labors with the greatest minuteness, made observations, and gave orders which would have impressed anyone with his extraordinary knowledge of farming; and no novice would have dared to dream that he could steal from such a sharp-eyed master. But the steward was a wily old bird: he knew how he must answer, and, what is more, he knew how to manage the land.

After this Afanasy Ivanovich would go back indoors, and going up to his wife would say: "Well, Pulkheria Ivanovna, isn't it time perhaps for a snack of something?"

"What would you like to have now, Afanasy Ivanovich? Would you like biscuits with lard or poppy-seed pies, or perhaps salted mushrooms?"

"Perhaps mushrooms or pies," answered Afanasy Ivanovich; and the table would at once be laid with a cloth, pies, and mushrooms.

An hour before dinner Afanasy Ivanovich would have another snack, would empty an old-fashioned silver goblet of vodka, would

eat mushrooms, various sorts of dried fish, and so on. They sat down
to dinner at twelve o'clock. Besides the dishes and sauce bowl
there stood on the table numbers of pots with closely covered lids
so that no appetizing masterpiece of old-fashioned cookery might
be spoiled. At dinner the conversation usually turned on subjects
closely related to the dinner. "I think this porridge," Afanasy
Ivanovich would say, "is a little bit burned. Don't you think so,
Pulkheria Ivanovna?" "No, Afanasy Ivanovich. You put a little
more butter in it, then it won't taste burned, or have some of this
mushroom sauce; pour that over it!" "Perhaps," said Afanasy
Ivanovich, passing his plate. "Let us try how it would be."

After dinner Afanasy Ivanovich went to lie down for an hour,
after which Pulkheria Ivanovna would take a sliced watermelon
and say: "Taste what a nice melon, Afanasy Ivanovich."

"Don't you be so sure of it, Pulkheria Ivanovna, because it is red
in the middle," Afanasy Ivanovich would say, taking a good slice.
"There are some that are red and are not nice."

But the melon quickly disappeared. After that Afanasy Ivanovich would eat a few pears and go for a walk in the garden with
Pulkheria Ivanovna. On returning home Pulkheria Ivanovna would
go to look after household affairs, while he sat under an awning
turned toward the courtyard and watched the storeroom continually displaying and concealing its interior and the serf girls pushing
one another as they brought in or carried out heaps of trifles of all
sorts in wooden boxes, sieves, trays, and other receptacles for holding fruit. A little afterward he sent for Pulkheria Ivanovna, or went
himself to her and said: "What shall I have to eat, Pulkheria Ivanovna?"

"What would you like?" Pulkheria Ivanovna would say. "Shall I
go and tell them to bring you the fruit dumpling I ordered them to
keep especially for you?"

"That would be nice," Afanasy Ivanovich would answer.

"Or perhaps you would like some jelly?"

"That would be good too," Afanasy Ivanovich would answer.
Then all this was promptly brought him and duly eaten.

Before supper Afanasy Ivanovich would have another snack of
something. At half past nine they sat down to supper. After supper
they at once went to bed, and complete stillness reigned in this
active and at the same time tranquil home.

The room in which Afanasy Ivanovich and Pulkheria Ivanovna

slept was so hot that not many people could have stayed in it for several hours; but Afanasy Ivanovich, in order to be even hotter, used to sleep on the platform of the stove, though the intense heat made him get up several times in the night and walk about the room. Sometimes Afanasy Ivanovich would moan as he walked about the room. Then Pulkheria Ivanovna would ask: "What are you groaning for, Afanasy Ivanovich?"

"Goodness only knows, Pulkheria Ivanovna; I feel as though I have a little stomach-ache," said Afanasy Ivanovich.

"Hadn't you better eat something, Afanasy Ivanovich?"

"I don't know whether it would be good, Pulkheria Ivanovna! What should I eat, though?"

"Sour milk or some dried stewed pears."

"Perhaps I might try it, anyway," said Afanasy Ivanovich.

A sleepy serf girl went off to rummage in the cupboards, and Afanasy Ivanovich would eat a plateful, after which he usually said: "Now it does seem to be better."

Sometimes, if it was fine weather and rather warm indoors, Afanasy Ivanovich, being in good spirits, liked to make fun of Pulkheria Ivanovna and talk of something.

"Pulkheria Ivanovna," he would say, "what if our house were suddenly burned down, where should we go?"

"Heaven forbid!" Pulkheria Ivanovna would say, crossing herself.

"But suppose our house were burned down, where should we go then?"

"God knows what you are saying, Afanasy Ivanovich! How is it possible that our house could be burned down? God will not permit it."

"Well, but if it were burned down?"

"Oh, then we would move into the kitchen. You should have for the time the little room that the housekeeper has now."

"But if the kitchen were burned too?"

"What next! God will preserve us from such a calamity as having both house and kitchen burned down at the same time! Well, then we would move into the storeroom while a new house was being built."

"And if the storeroom were burned?"

"God knows what you are saying! I don't want to listen to you! It's a sin to say it, and God will punish you for saying such things!"

And Afanasy Ivanovich, pleased at having made fun of Pulkheria Ivanovna, sat smiling in his chair.

But the old couple seemed most of all interesting to me on the occasions when they had guests. Then everything in their house assumed a different aspect. These good-natured people lived, one may say, for visitors. The best of everything they had was all brought out. They vied with each other in trying to regale you with everything their husbandry produced. But what pleased me most of all was that in their solicitude there was no trace of unctuousness. This hospitality and readiness to please was so gently expressed in their faces, was so in keeping with them, that the guests could not help falling in with their wishes, which were the expression of the pure serene simplicity of their kindly guileless souls. This hospitality was something quite different from the way in which a clerk of some government office who has been helped in his career by your efforts entertains you, calling you his benefactor and cringing at your feet. The visitor was on no account to leave on the same day: he absolutely had to stay the night. "How could you set off on such a long journey at so late an hour!" Pulkheria Ivanovna always said. (The guest usually lived two or three miles away.)

"Of course not," Afanasy Ivanovich said. "You never know what may happen: robbers or other evil-minded men may attack you."

"God preserve us from robbers!" said Pulkheria Ivanovna. "And why talk of such things at night? It's not a question of robbers, but it's dark, it's not fit for driving at all. Besides, your coachman . . . I know your coachman, he is so frail, and such a little man, any horse would be too much for him; and besides he has probably had a drop by now and is asleep somewhere." And the guest was forced to remain; but the evening spent in the low-pitched hot room, the kindly, warming and soporific talk, the steam rising from the food on the table, always nourishing and cooked in first-rate fashion, was compensation for him. I can see as though it were today Afanasy Ivanovich sitting bent in his chair with his invariable smile, listening to his visitor with attention and even delight! Often the talk touched on politics. The guest, who also very rarely left his village, would often with a significant air and a mysterious expression trot out his conjectures, telling them that the French had a secret agreement with the English to let Bonaparte out again in order to attack Russia, or would simply prophesy war in the near future; and then Afanasy Ivanovich, pretending not to look at

Pulkheria Ivanovna, would often say: "I think I shall go to the war myself; why shouldn't I go to the war?"

"There he goes again!" Pulkheria Ivanovna interrupted. "Don't you believe him," she said, turning to the guest. "How could an old man like him go to the war! The first soldier would shoot him. Yes, he would! He'd simply take aim and shoot him."

"Well," said Afanasy Ivanovich, "and I'll shoot him."

"Just hear how he talks!" Pulkheria Ivanovna interrupted. "How could he go to the war! And his pistols have been rusty for years and are lying in the cupboard. You should just see them: why, they'd explode from the gunpowder before they'd fire a shot. And he'd blow off his hands and disfigure his face and be miserable for the rest of his days!"

"Well," said Afanasy Ivanovich, "I'd buy myself new weapons; I'll take my saber or a Cossack lance."

"That's all nonsense. An idea comes into his head and he begins talking!" Pulkheria Ivanovna interrupted with some annoyance. "I know he is only joking, but yet I don't like to hear it. That's the way he always talks; sometimes one listens and listens till it frightens one."

But Afanasy Ivanovich, pleased at having scared Pulkheria Ivanovna a little, laughed sitting bent in his chair. Pulkheria Ivanovna was most attractive to me when she was taking a guest in to lunch. "This," she would say, taking a cork out of a bottle, "is vodka distilled with milfoil and sage—if anyone has a pain in the shoulder blades or loins, it is very good; now this is distilled with centaury— if anyone has a ringing in the ears or a rash on the face, it is very good; and this now is distilled with peach stones—take a glass, isn't it a delicious smell? If anyone getting up in the morning knocks his head against a corner of the cupboard or a table and a bump comes up on his forehead, he has only to drink one glass of it before dinner and it takes it away entirely; it all passes off that very minute, as though it had never been there at all." Then followed a similar account of the other bottles, which all had some healing properties. After burdening the guest with all these remedies she would lead him up to a number of dishes. "These are mushrooms with wild thyme! These are with cloves and hazelnuts! A Turkish woman taught me to salt them in the days when we still had Turkish prisoners here. She was such a nice woman, and it was not noticeable at all that she professed the Turkish religion: she went about almost exactly as we do; only she wouldn't eat pork; she said it was forbidden somewhere in their law. And these are mushrooms prepared with black-currant leaves and nutmeg! And these are big pumpkins: it's the first time I have pickled them in vinegar; I don't know what they'll be like! I learned the secret from Father Ivan; first of all you must lay some oak leaves in a tub and then sprinkle with pepper and saltpeter and then put in the flower of the hawk-weed, take the flowers and strew them in with stalks uppermost. And here are the little pies; these are cheese pies. And those are the ones Afanasy Ivanovich is very fond of, made with cabbage and buckwheat."

"Yes," Afanasy Ivanovich would add, "I am very fond of them; they are soft and a little sourish."

As a rule Pulkheria Ivanovna was in the best of spirits when she had guests. Dear old woman! She was entirely devoted to her visitors. I liked staying with them, and although I overate fearfully, as indeed all their visitors did, and though that was very bad for me, I was always glad to go and see them. But I wonder whether the very air of Little Russia has not some peculiar property that promotes digestion; for if anyone were to venture to eat in that way here,[5] there is no doubt he would find himself lying in his coffin instead of his bed.

Good old people! But my account of them is approaching a very melancholy incident which transformed forever the life of that peaceful nook. This incident is the more impressive because it arose from such an insignificant cause. But such is the strange order of things; trifling causes have always given rise to great events, and on the other hand great undertakings frequently end in insignificant results. Some military leader rallies all the forces of his state, carries on a war for several years, his generals cover themselves with glory; and in the end it all results in gaining a bit of land in which there is not room to plant a potato; while sometimes two sausage makers of two towns quarrel over some nonsense, and in the end the towns are drawn into the quarrel, then villages, and then the whole kingdom. But let us abandon these reflections: they are out of keeping here; besides I am not fond of reflections, so long as they get no further than being reflections.

Pulkheria Ivanovna had a little gray cat, which almost always lay

---

[5] I.e., St. Petersburg. (ed.)

curled up at her feet. Pulkheria Ivanovna sometimes stroked her and with one finger scratched her neck, which the spoiled cat stretched as high as she could. I cannot say that Pulkheria Ivanovna was excessively fond of her; she was simply attached to her from being used to seeing her about. Afanasy Ivanovich, however, often teased her about her affection for it.

"I don't know, Pulkheria Ivanovna, what you find in the cat: what use is she? If you had a dog, then it would be a different matter: one can take a dog out shooting, but what use is a cat?"

"Oh, be quiet, Afanasy Ivanovich," said Pulkheria Ivanovna. "You are simply fond of talking and nothing else. A dog is not clean, a dog makes a mess, a dog breaks everything, while a cat is a quiet creature: she does no harm to anyone."

Cats and dogs were all the same to Afanasy Ivanovich, however; he only said it to tease Pulkheria Ivanovna a little.

Beyond their garden they had a big forest which had been completely spared by the enterprising steward, perhaps because the sound of the ax would have reached the ears of Pulkheria Ivanovna. It was wild and neglected, the old tree stumps were covered with overgrown nut bushes and looked like the feathered legs of trumpeter pigeons. Wild cats lived in this forest. Wild forest cats must not be confused with the bold rascals who run about on the roofs of houses; in spite of their fierce disposition the latter, being in cities, are far more civilized than the inhabitants of the forest. Unlike the town cats, the latter are for the most part shy and gloomy creatures; they are always gaunt and lean; they mew in a coarse, uncultured voice. They sometimes scratch their way underground into the very storehouses and steal bacon; they even penetrate into the kitchen, springing suddenly in at the open window when they see that the cook has gone off into the high grass.

In fact, they are unacquainted with any noble sentiments; they live by plunder, and murder little sparrows in their nests. These cats had for a long time past sniffed through a hole under the storehouse at Pulkheria Ivanovna's gentle little cat and at last they enticed her away, as a company of soldiers entices a silly peasant girl. Pulkheria Ivanovna noticed the disappearance of the cat and sent to look for her; but the cat was not found. Three days passed; Pulkheria Ivanovna was sorry to lose her, but at last forgot her. One day when she was inspecting her vegetable garden and was returning with fresh green cucumbers plucked by her own hand for

Afanasy Ivanovich, her ear was caught by a most pitiful mew. As though by instinct she called: "Puss, puss!" and all at once her gray cat, lean and skinny, came out from the high grass; it was evident that she had not tasted food for several days. Pulkheria Ivanovna went on calling her, but the cat stood mewing and did not venture to come close; it was clear that she had grown very wild during her absence. Pulkheria Ivanovna still went on calling the cat, who timidly followed her right up to the fence. At last, seeing the old familiar places, she even went indoors. Pulkheria Ivanovna at once ordered milk and meat to be brought her and, sitting before her, enjoyed the greediness with which her poor little favorite swallowed piece after piece and lapped up the milk. The little gray fugitive grew fatter almost before her eyes and soon did not eat so greedily. Pulkheria Ivanovna stretched out her hand to stroke her, but the ungrateful creature had evidently grown too much accustomed to the ways of wild cats, or had adopted the romantic principle that poverty with love is better than life in a palace (and, indeed, the wild cats were as poor as church mice); anyway, she sprang out of a window and not one of the house serfs could catch her.

The old lady sank into thought. "It was my death coming for me!" she said to herself, and nothing could distract her mind. All day she was sad. In vain Afanasy Ivanovich joked and tried to find out why she was so melancholy all of a sudden. Pulkheria Ivanovna made no answer, or answered in a way that could not possibly satisfy Afanasy Ivanovich. Next day she was perceptibly thinner.

"What is the matter with you, Pulkheria Ivanovna? You must be ill."

"No, I am not ill, Afanasy Ivanovich! I want to tell you something strange; I know that I shall die this summer: my death has already come to fetch me!"

Afanasy Ivanovich's lips twitched painfully. He tried, however, to overcome his gloomy feeling and with a smile said: "God knows what you are saying, Pulkheria Ivanovna! You must have drunk some peach vodka instead of the concoction you usually drink."

"No, Afanasy Ivanovich, I have not drunk peach vodka," said Pulkheria Ivanovna. And Afanasy Ivanovich was sorry that he had so teased her; he looked at her and a tear hung on his eyelash.

"I beg you, Afanasy Ivanovich, to carry out my wishes," said Pulkheria Ivanovna; "when I die, bury me by the church fence.

Put my gray dress on me, the one with the little flowers on a brown background. Don't put on me my satin dress with the crimson stripes; a dead woman has no need of such a dress—what use is it to her?—while it will be of use to you: have a fine dressing gown made of it, so that when visitors are here you can show yourself and welcome them, looking decent."

"God knows what you are saying, Pulkheria Ivanovna!" said Afanasy Ivanovich. "Death may be a long way off, but you are frightening me already with such sayings."

"No, Afanasy Ivanovich, I know now when my death will come. Don't grieve for me, though: I am an old woman and have lived long enough, and you are old, too; we shall soon meet in the other world."

But Afanasy Ivanovich was sobbing like a child.

"It's a sin to weep, Afanasy Ivanovich! Do not be sinful and anger God by your sorrow. I am not sorry that I am dying; there is only one thing I am sorry about"—a heavy sigh interrupted her words for a minute—"I am sorry that I do not know in whose care to leave you, who will look after you when I am dead. You are like a little child. You need somebody who loves you to look after you."

At these words there was an expression of such deep, such distressed heartfelt pity on her face that I doubt whether anyone could have looked at her at that moment unmoved.

"Be careful, Yavdokha," she said, turning to the housekeeper for whom she had purposely sent, "that when I die you look after your master; watch over him like the apple of your eye, like your own child. Make certain that what he likes is always cooked for him in the kitchen; that you always give him clean linen and clothes; that when visitors come you dress him in his best, or else maybe he will sometimes come out in his old dressing gown, because even now he often forgets when it's a holiday and when it's a working day. Don't take your eyes off him, Yavdokha; I will pray for you in the next world and God will reward you. Do not forget, Yavdokha, you are old, you have not long to live—do not take a sin upon your soul. If you do not look after him you will have no happiness in life. I myself will beseech God not to give you a happy end. And you will be unhappy yourself and your children will be unhappy, and all your family will not have the blessing of God in anything."

Poor old woman! At that minute she was not thinking of the great moment awaiting her, nor of her soul, nor of her own future life; she was thinking only of her poor companion with whom she had spent her life and whom she was leaving helpless and forlorn. With extraordinary efficiency she arranged everything, so that Afanasy Ivanovich should not notice her absence when she was gone. Her conviction that her end was at hand was so strong, and her state of mind was so attuned to it, that she did in fact take to her bed a few days later and could eat nothing. Afanasy Ivanovich never left her bedside and was all solicitude. "Perhaps you would eat a little of something, Pulkheria Ivanovna," he said, looking with anxiety into her eyes. But Pulkheria Ivanovna said nothing. At last, after a long silence, she seemed trying to say something, her lips stirred—and her breathing ceased.

Afanasy Ivanovich was absolutely overwhelmed. It seemed to him so uncanny that he did not even weep; he looked at her with dull eyes as though not grasping the significance of the corpse.

The dead woman was laid out on the table in the dress she had herself decided upon, her arms were crossed and a wax candle put in her hand—he looked at all this impassively. Numbers of people of all kinds filled the courtyard; numbers of guests came to the funeral; long tables were laid out in the courtyard; they were covered with masses of funeral rice, of homemade beverages and pies. The guests talked and wept, gazed at the dead woman, discussed her qualities, and looked at him; but he himself looked peculiarly at it all. The coffin was carried out at last, the people crowded after it, and he followed it. The priests were in full vestments, the sun was shining, babies were crying in their mothers' arms, larks were singing, and children raced and skipped about the road. At last the coffin was put down above the grave; he was asked to approach and kiss the dead woman for the last time. He went up and kissed her; there were tears in his eyes, but they were somehow apathetic tears. The coffin was lowered, the priest took the spade and first threw in a handful of earth; the deep rich voices of the deacon and the two sextons sang "Eternal Memory" under the pure cloudless sky; the laborers took their spades, and soon the earth covered the grave and made it level. At that moment he pressed forward; everyone stepped aside and made way for him, anxious to know what he meant to do. He raised his eyes, looked at them vacantly, and said: "So you have buried her already! What for?" He broke off and said no more.

But when he was home again, when he saw that his room was

empty, that even the chair Pulkheria Ivanovna used to sit on had been taken away—he sobbed, sobbed violently, inconsolably, and tears flowed from his lusterless eyes like a river.

Five years have passed since then. What grief does not time bear away? What passion survives in the unequal combat with it? I knew a man in the flower of his youth and strength, full of true nobility of character. I knew him in love, tenderly, passionately, madly, fiercely, humbly; and before me, and before my eyes almost, the object of his passion, a tender creature, lovely as an angel, was struck down by merciless death. I have never seen such awful depths of spiritual suffering, such frenzied poignant grief, such devouring despair as overwhelmed the luckless lover. I had never imagined that a man could create for himself such a hell with no shadow, no shape, no semblance of hope. . . . People tried not to leave him alone; all weapons with which he might have killed himself were hidden from him. Two weeks later he suddenly mastered himself, and began laughing and jesting; he was given his freedom, and the first use he made of it was to buy a pistol. One day his family were terrified by the sudden sound of a shot; they ran into the room and saw him stretched on the floor with a shattered skull. A doctor, who happened to be there at the time and whose skill was famous, saw signs of life in him, found that the wound was not absolutely fatal; and, to the amazement of everyone, the young man recovered. The watch kept on him was stricter than ever. Even at dinner a knife was not laid for him and everything was removed with which he could have hurt himself; but in a short time he found another opportunity and threw himself under the wheels of a passing carriage. An arm and a leg were broken; but again he recovered. A year after that I saw him in a roomful of people: he was sitting at a table saying, gaily, *"Petite ouverte,"* [6] as he covered a card, and behind him, with her elbows on the back of his chair, was standing his young wife, turning over his chips.

At the end of the five years after Pulkheria Ivanovna's death I was in those parts and drove to Afanasy Ivanovich's little farm to visit my old neighbor, in whose house I used at one time to spend the day pleasantly and always to overeat myself with the choicest masterpieces of its hospitable mistress.

As I approached the courtyard the house seemed to me twice as

---

[6] "Small bid." (ed.)

old as it had been: the peasants' huts were lying completely on one side, as no doubt their owners were too; the fence and the hurdle around the yard were completely broken down, and I myself saw the cook pull sticks out of it to heat the stove, though she need have only taken two steps further to reach the fagot stack. Sadly I drove up to the steps; the same old Neros and Trustys, by now blind or lame, barked, wagging their fluffy tails covered with burdocks. An old man came out to greet me. Yes, it was he! I knew him at once; but he stooped twice as much as before. He knew me and greeted me with the old familiar smile. I followed him indoors. It seemed as though everything was as before. But I noticed a strange disorder in everything, an unmistakable absence of something. In fact I experienced the strange feelings which come upon us when for the first time we enter the house of a widower whom we have known in old days inseparable from the wife who has shared his life. The feeling is the same when we see a man crippled whom we have always known in health. In everything the absence of careful Pulkheria Ivanovna was visible: on the table a knife was laid without a handle; the dishes were not cooked with the same skill. I did not want to ask about the farm; I was afraid even to look at the farm buildings. When we sat down to dinner, a maid tied a napkin around Afanasy Ivanovich, and it was good that she did so, as without it he would have spilled sauce all over his dressing gown. I tried to entertain him and told him various items of news; he listened with the same smile, but from time to time his eyes were completely vacant, and his thoughts did not stray, they vanished. Often he lifted a spoonful of porridge and instead of putting it to his mouth put it to his nose; instead of sticking his fork into a piece of chicken, he prodded the decanter, and then the maid, taking his hand, directed it back to the chicken. We sometimes waited several minutes for the next course.

Afanasy Ivanovich himself noticed it and said: "Why is it they are so long bringing the food?" But I saw through the crack of the door that the boy who carried away our plates was asleep and nodding on a bench, not thinking of his duties at all.

"This is the dish," said Afanasy Ivanovich, when we were handed curd cakes with sour cream; "this is the dish," he went on, and I noticed that his voice began quivering and a tear was ready to drop from his leaden eyes, but he did his utmost to restrain it: "This is the dish which my . . . my . . . dear . . . my dear . . ." And all at once he burst into tears; his hand fell on the plate, the plate turned upside down, slipped, and was smashed, and the sauce was spilled all over him. He sat vacantly, vacantly held the spoon; and tears like a stream, like a ceaselessly flowing fountain, flowed and flowed on the napkin that covered him.

"My God!" I thought, looking at him, "five years of all-destroying time—an old man already apathetic, an old man whose life one would have thought had never once been stirred by a strong feeling, whose whole life seemed to consist in sitting on a high chair, in eating dried fish and pears, in telling good-natured stories—and such long, such bitter grief! What is stronger in us—passion or habit? Or are all the violent impulses, all the whirl of our desires and boiling passions, only the consequence of our ardent age, and is it only through youth that they seem deep and shattering?"

Be that as it may, at that moment all our passions seemed like child's play beside this effect of long, slow, almost insensible habit. Several times he struggled to utter his wife's name, but, halfway through the word, his quiet and ordinary face worked convulsively and his childish weeping cut me to the very heart. No, those were not the tears with which old men are usually so lavish, as they complain of their pitiful position and their troubles; they were not the tears which they drop over a glass of punch either. No! They were tears which brimmed over uninvited, from the accumulated rankling pain of a heart already turning cold.

He did not live long after that. I heard lately of his death. It is strange, though, that the circumstances of his end had some resemblance to those of Pulkheria Ivanovna's death. One day Afanasy Ivanovich ventured to take a little walk in the garden. As he was pacing slowly along a path with his usual absent-mindedness, without a thought of any kind in his head, he had a strange adventure. He suddenly heard someone behind him pronounce in a fairly distinct voice: "Afanasy Ivanovich!" He turned around but there was absolutely nobody there; he looked in all directions, he peered into the bushes—no one anywhere. It was a still day and the sun was shining. He pondered for a minute; his face seemed to brighten and he brought out at last: "It's Pulkheria Ivanovna calling me!"

It has, no doubt, happened to you, some time or other, to hear a voice calling you by name, which simple people explain as a soul grieving for a human being and calling him; and after that, they say, death follows inevitably. I must admit I was always frightened by that mysterious call. I remember that in childhood I often heard it. Sometimes suddenly someone behind me distinctly uttered my name. Usually on such occasions it was a very bright and sunny day; not one leaf in the garden was stirring; the stillness was death-like; even the grasshopper left off churring for the moment; there was not a soul in the garden. But I confess that if the wildest and most tempestuous night had lashed me with all the fury of the elements, alone in the middle of an impenetrable forest, I should not have been so terrified as by that awful stillness in the midst of a cloudless day. I usually ran out of the garden in a great panic, hardly able to breathe, and was only reassured when I met some person, the sight of whom dispelled the terrible spiritual loneliness.

Afanasy Ivanovich surrendered completely to his inner conviction that Pulkheria Ivanovna was calling him; he submitted with the readiness of an obedient child, wasted away, coughed, melted like a candle, and at last flickered out, as a candle does when there is nothing left to sustain its feeble flame. "Lay me beside Pulkheria Ivanovna" was all he said before his end.

His desire was carried out and he was buried near the church beside Pulkheria Ivanovna's grave. The guests were fewer at the funeral, but there were just as many beggars and peasants. The little house was now completely emptied. The enterprising steward and the elder hauled away to their huts all that were left of the old-fashioned goods and furniture, which the housekeeper had not been able to carry off. Soon there arrived, I cannot say from where, a distant kinsman, the heir to the estate, who had been a lieutenant, I don't know in what regiment, and was a terrible reformer. He saw at once the great slackness and disorganization in the management of the land; he made up his mind to change all that radically, to improve things and bring everything into order. He bought six splendid English sickles, pinned a special number on each hut, and managed so well that within six months his estate was put under the supervision of a board of trustees.

The sage trustees (consisting of an ex-assessor and a lieutenant in a faded uniform) had within a very short time left no fowls and eggs. The huts, which were almost lying on the earth, fell down completely; the peasants gave themselves up to drunkenness and most of them ran away. The real owner, who got on, however, pretty comfortably with his trustees and used to drink punch with them, very rarely visited his estate and never stayed long. To this day he drives about to all the fairs in Little Russia, carefully inquiring the prices of all sorts of produce sold wholesale, such as flour, hemp, honey, and so on; but he only buys small trifles such as flints, a nail to clean out his pipe, in fact nothing which exceeds at the utmost a ruble in price.

☒◄C◆◄C◆◄C◆◄C◆◄C◆◄C◆◄C◆◄C◆◄C◆◄C◆◄C◆◄C◆◄C◆◄C◆◄C◆☒

TARAS BULBA[1]

I

"Turn around, son! What a sight you are! Are those priests' cassocks you are wearing? And do they all go about like that at the seminary?"

With these words old Bulba greeted his two sons, who had been studying at the Kiev seminary and had come home to their father.

His sons had just dismounted from their horses. They were two sturdy young men who still looked sullenly from under their brows, as befits seminarists fresh from school. Their strong, healthy faces were covered with the first down of beard not yet touched by

1 This highly romantic story is not to be confused with history. It is essentially an imaginative recreation of the tone and quality of an historical period written in the epic tradition. To add to its verisimilitude, Gogol uses several names and situations that existed in fact, yet the story contains anachronisms (e.g., Bulba, we are told, could only have lived in the fifteenth century, yet his sons return home from a seminary which did not exist until the beginning of the seventeenth century). But Gogol's description of Cossacks and their affairs seems, from all accounts, remarkably accurate, if romanticized. A community of Cossacks was established, in the location described by Gogol, as early as the first half of the fifteenth century, apparently to defend the Ukraine against Tartar raiding parties and, after 1659, to defend Ukrainian sovereignty against the Poles. (ed.)

the razor. They were much disconcerted at this reception from their father and stood motionless with their eyes on the ground.

"Stand still, stand still! Let me have a good look at you," he went on, turning them around: "what long frocks you have on! Strange frocks! Such frocks have never been seen before. One of you take a little run! I'd like to see whether he won't fall flat on the ground, entangled in his skirts."

"Don't taunt, don't taunt, Father!" the elder of them said at last.

"My, what a precious fellow! And why not taunt?"

"You may be my father, but by God I'll beat you if you go on taunting us!"

"What! You're a nice sort of son! Your father?" said Taras Bulba, retreating a few paces in surprise.

"Yes, though you are my father. If I am insulted it makes no difference to me who does the insulting."

"How do you want to fight with me? With fists?"

"Any way you like."

"Well, let it be with fists!" said Bulba, rolling up his sleeves: "I'll see what you are worth with your fists!"

And, instead of a welcome after their long separation, father and son began punching each other in the ribs and the back and the chest, stepping apart and looking about them and then beginning again.

"Look, good people! The old man is crazy! He's gone off his head!" said their pale, thin, and kindly mother, who stood in the doorway and had not yet succeeded in embracing her precious children. "The boys have come home, we've not seen them for over a year; and a peculiar whim takes him: a fist fight!"

"But he fights very well!" said Bulba, stopping. "I swear he does!" he went on, rearranging his disheveled clothing. "One doesn't want too much of it! He will make a good Cossack! Well, how are you, son? Give us a kiss!" And father and son kissed each other. "Bravo, son! You whack everyone as you thumped me; don't let anyone off! But it is an absurd outfit, though. What's that cord hanging? And you, you fool, why do you stand doing nothing?" he said, turning to the younger. "Why don't you try me, you son of a bitch?"

"What will he think of next!" said the mother, who was meanwhile embracing the younger boy. "Has anyone heard of such a thing as a child hitting his own father! And as though he were fit for that now: the child is young, he has had such a journey, he is tired out . . ." (the child was over twenty and more than six foot) "he needs to rest now and have something to eat, and here you are forcing him to fight."

"Well, you are a dainty fellow, I see!" said Bulba. "Don't heed your mother, son: she is a woman, she knows nothing. What do you want with spoiling? What you want is the open plain and a good horse: that's the best treat for you! And you see this saber here? That's the mother for you! It's all nonsense—what they have been stuffing your heads with: and the seminaries and all the books and vocabularies and philosophies, and all that rubbish. I'd spit on it all!" Here Bulba finished up with a word which is positively inadmissible in print. "I'll tell you what, I'd better send you this very week to the camp of the Dnieper Cossacks. That's the place for learning! That's the school for you; it's only there you'll pick up sense."

"And are they to be only one week at home?" said the thin old mother piteously, with tears in her eyes: "and they won't have time to enjoy themselves, poor dears; they won't have time to get to know their own home, and I won't have time to look at them!"

"Stop whining, stop whining, old woman! A Cossack's not for hanging about with women. You'd hide them both under your petticoat and sit on them as though they were hen's eggs. Go along, go along, quickly, and set all you have on the table for us. We don't want doughnuts, honey buns, poppy cakes, and other dainties; bring us a whole sheep, serve a goat and forty-year-old mead! And plenty of vodka, not vodka with all sorts of fancies, not with raisins and flavorings, but pure foaming vodka, that hisses and bubbles like mad."

Bulba led his sons into the parlor where two pretty serf girls in necklaces made of coins were busy. They scurried out, apparently alarmed at the entrance of young masters who were not in the habit of leaving people alone, or perhaps they simply wanted to observe feminine tradition by shrieking and rushing headlong at the sight of a man, and then hiding their faces in their sleeves from bashfulness. The room was decorated in the taste of that time—of which hints have survived only in the songs and popular ballads, no longer sung in the Ukraine by old bearded blind men to the gently tinkling bandore, while a crowd stood around to listen—in the taste of those turbulent troubled times when the struggles and battles for

the union of Russia and the Ukraine were beginning. Everything
was clean and covered with colored clay. On the walls were sabers,
whips, bird nets, fishing tackle, and guns, an elaborately worked
horn for powder, a golden bridle for a horse, and a harness with
silver disks. The windows in the parlor were small, with dingy
round panes such as are only seen nowadays in old-fashioned
churches, so that one could only look out by raising the movable
pane. Around the windows and doors were red sills and lintels. On
the shelves in the corners stood jugs, bottles, and flasks of green or
of dark blue glass, ornamental silver mugs, gilt goblets of various
patterns—Venetian, Turkish, and Circassian—that had come into
Bulba's parlor by devious routes after passing through several
hands, as such things often did in those lawless days. Birchbark
benches ran all around the room; an immense table stood in the
center under the icons; a wide stove with cozy projections and
nooks covered with bright-colored tiles. All this was very familiar
to our two young men who walked home for the summer holidays
every year—walked because they had then no horses and because
it was not customary to allow students to ride on horseback. They
wore long forelocks which any Cossack carrying a weapon had the
right to pull. Only just before they had left the seminary for good
had Bulba sent them a pair of young stallions from his herd of
horses.

In honor of his sons' arrival, Bulba had bidden all the officers of
the regiment who were on the spot to be summoned; and when two
of them and his old comrade, Captain Dmitro Tovkach, arrived, he
presented his sons to them at once, saying: "Here, look what fine
lads! I shall soon send them to the Cossack camp." The guests congratulated both Bulba and the two young men, and told them they
were doing the right thing and that there was no better training
for a young man than the Zaporozhsky camp.

"Well, friends, sit down each where he likes best at the table.
Come, sons! First of all, a drink of vodka!" said Bulba. "God bless
you! To your health, sons: yours, Ostap, and yours, Andrei! God
grant that you may always be successful in war! That you may beat
everyone—pagans, Turks, Tartars, and that when the Poles begin
attacking our Church, you may beat the Poles. Come, pass up your
goblet; well, is the vodka good? And what's vodka in Latin? They
were morons, you know, the Latins, son; they did not even know
there was such a thing as vodka in the world. What is his name, who

wrote Latin verses? I am not strong in literature, and so I don't know; Horace, was it?"

"What a fellow Father is!" the elder son Ostap thought to himself. "The old man knows it all, the dog, and feigns ignorance, too."

"I expect the archimandrite didn't let you have a sniff of vodka," Taras went on. "Confess, sons, they whipped you soundly with birch rods and a fresh cherry switch on the back and everything else a Cossack has? And perhaps since you became too intelligent, you were lashed with whips, too? Not only on Saturdays, I bet, but on Wednesdays and Thursdays too, you caught it?"

"No need to recall the past, Father," Ostap answered coolly, "the past is over!"

"Let him try it now!" said Andrei: "let anybody dare touch me now. If only some Tartar gang would turn up now, they would learn what a Cossack saber is like!"

"Good, son! I swear that's good! And since it's come to that, I'll go with you! Yes, I will. Why the devil should I stay here? To sow buckwheat and mind the house, to look after the sheep and the swine, and to drag about with my wife? Plague take her; I am a Cossack, I won't allow it! What if there is no war? I'll go with you anyway to the Cossack camp for a little junketing. I swear, I will!" And little by little old Bulba grew hotter and hotter till at last he worked himself into a fury, got up from the table, and drawing himself up to his full height, stamped on the floor.

"We'll go tomorrow! Why put it off? What enemy can we hatch out here? What do we want with this house? What use is it all to us? What are these pots for?" Saying this he began flinging down and smashing the pots and bottles.

The poor old woman, accustomed to such outbursts from her husband, sat on the bench mournfully looking on. She dared say nothing; but hearing of this terrible decision she could not refrain from tears; she looked at her children from whom she was threatened to be parted so soon—and no one could describe the mute bitterness of the sadness which seemed quivering in her eyes and her tightly compressed lips.

Bulba was terribly stubborn. He was one of those characters which could only appear in that half-nomadic corner of Europe, in the cruel fifteenth century when all primitive South Russia, abandoned by its princes, had been laid waste and burned to ashes by the ruthless onslaughts of the Mongol hordes; when, deprived of home and shelter, men here grew bold and daring; when they settled on the ashes of their burned villages, in sight of menacing neighbors and perpetual danger, and grew accustomed to looking them straight in the face, forgetting that there was such a thing as fear in the world; when the inherently peaceful Slav character was tempered in the flames of warfare, and the Cossack organization arose—the expression of the broad dashing recklessness of Russian nature. By every ferry, at every fording place, every strip by a riverbank, every convenient spot, there were countless Cossacks, whose bold comrades properly answered the Sultan when he wanted to know how many there were: "Who knows! They are spread all over the steppe: wherever there's a hillock there's a Cossack!" It was truly a marvelous manifestation of Russian strength: it was struck out of the heart of the people by the flint and steel of calamity. In place of the old districts and little towns filled with huntsmen, in place of the unimportant princes who were always fighting and selling their towns, there sprang up strong Cossack villages and districts, settlements bound together by a common danger and a common hatred of the heathen savages. Everyone knows from history how their turbulent life and perpetual struggle saved Europe from the ruthless onslaughts which threatened to destroy it. The Polish kings who found themselves, in place of the district princes, sovereigns of these wide though remote and weak lands, saw the importance of the Cossacks and their value as soldiers and guards. They encouraged them and flattered their warlike disposition. Under their remote authority the Hetmans, elected from the Cossacks themselves, transformed the villages and districts into regiments and divisions. It was not a regular standing army; no one would have noticed it; but in case of war and general uprising, within a week or less, every man appeared on his horse, fully equipped, receiving only one gold coin of pay from the King, and within a fortnight an army was assembled, such as no drafting of recruits could have raised. When the campaign was over the warrior went back to his meadows and his plowlands, to his ferry over the Dnieper, caught fish, traded, brewed beer, and was a free Cossack. Foreign contemporaries rightly marveled at his wonderful capacities. There was no craft which the Cossack did not know: distilling spirits, building carts, making gunpowder, doing blacksmith's and carpenter's work, and in addition doing all that carousing with reckless gaiety, drinking, and merrymaking that only a Russian can—it all came easy to him. Besides the registered Cossacks who considered it their duty to appear in wartime, it was possible at any time of urgent necessity to collect whole crowds of volunteer cavalry: the esauls (or captains) had only to go about the fairs and markets of all the villages and hamlets and standing in a cart shout at the top of their voices: "Hey, you beer swillers and brewers! Drop your brewing and lolling about the stove, feeding the flies with your fat bodies! Come and win knightly glory and honor! You plowmen sowing buckwheat, minding your flocks, and running after the wenches! Enough of following the plow, muddying your yellow boots on the land, running after women, and losing your knightly valor! It is high time to win a Cossack's fame!" And those words were like sparks falling on dry wood. The brewers and distillers threw down their casks and broke their barrels, the craftsmen and the tradesmen sent craft and shop to the devil, broke the pots in the hut—and everyone mounted his horse. In fact, here the Russian character found the full outlet for its expression.

Taras was one of the original old colonels: he was created for the excitement of battle and was distinguished by the coarse directness of his character. In those days the influence of Poland was already beginning to be apparent in the Russian nobility. Many of them were already adopting Polish manners, introducing luxurious habits, keeping a magnificent retinue of servants, hawks, and hunting dogs, giving banquets, laying out courtyards. All that was not to Taras' taste. He liked the simple life of the Cossacks and quarreled with those of his comrades who were disposed to follow the Warsaw fashion, calling them the servingmen of the Polish lords. Always tireless, he regarded himself as the authorized champion of the Russian Orthodox Church. At his own initiative he would go into villages where there were complaints by people against their landlords or of new taxes being laid on each chimney. He would with his Cossacks deal with the oppressors, and made it a rule always to have recourse to the sword in three cases: namely, when the commissars showed any lack of respect for the elders and did not take off their caps while standing before them; when the Orthodox faith was insulted and the traditions of their forefathers were disregarded; and lastly, when the enemies were Turks or pagans, against whom he always thought it permissible to lift his sword to the glory of Christianity.

Now he was already gloating over the thought of arriving with his two sons at the Zaporozhye camp and saying: "Here, look what fine fellows I have brought you!" He thought how he would present them to all his old battle-seasoned comrades; how he would watch their first feats of arms and their carousing, which he regarded as also one of the chief distinctions of a warrior. He had meant at first to send them off alone; but at the sight of their youth and vigor, their sturdy handsomeness, his warlike spirit flared up and he resolved to go with them next day himself, though the only necessity for doing so was his own stubborn desire. He was already busily engaged giving orders, selecting horses and their trappings for his young sons, superintending preparations in the stables and the storehouses, and picking out the servants who were to go with them the next day. He handed over his authority to Captain Tovkach along with a stern injunction to come at once with the whole regiment if he should send a summons from the camp. Though he had been drinking heavily and the fumes were still in his head, yet he forgot nothing; he even remembered to order that the horses should be given drink and that the best wheat should be put in their mangers. He came in tired from his exertions. "Well, children, now you must sleep and tomorrow we shall do as God wills. But don't make up a bed for us! We need no bed; we will sleep in the open air."

Night was only just embracing the heavens, but Bulba always lay down to sleep early. He stretched himself on a rug, and covered himself with a sheepskin, because the night air was rather fresh and because he liked to be wrapped up warmly when he was at home. He soon began snoring, and the whole courtyard followed his example; everywhere in the different corners there was snoring and whistling. The watchman was the first to fall asleep, for he had drunk more than any in honor of the young masters' arrival.

Only the poor mother did not sleep. She stooped down to the pillow of her precious sons who were lying side by side; she combed out their carelessly matted youthful locks and wetted them with her tears. She gazed at them, and her whole being, every feeling was in that gaze, she was entirely absorbed in it and could not gaze enough. She had nursed them at her own breast; she had petted and tended them as they grew—and now only for one minute could she see them. "My sons, my darling sons! What will happen to you? What awaits you?" she said, and tears lingered in the wrinkles that transformed her once lovely face. She was indeed to be pitied, like every woman of that fierce age. For only a moment had she lived in love, in the first fever of passion, in the first fever of youth, and then her harsh lover forsook her for his sword, for his comrades, for carousing. She would see her husband for two or three days in a year and then hear nothing of him for years. And, indeed, when she did see him, when they did live together, what was her life? She endured insults, even blows; the only caresses she knew were given as a favor; she was an alien creature in this crowd of wifeless warriors, on whom the reckless life of the Dnieper Cossack had put its harsh stamp. Her youth had flashed by without joy, and her lovely fresh cheeks and bosom had withered without kisses and were covered with premature wrinkles. All love, every emotion, all that is tender and passionate in woman had in her turned into the one feeling of motherhood. With fervor, with passion, with tears, she hovered like a gull of the steppes over her children. Her sons, her darling sons were being taken from her—she might never see them again! Who knows, perhaps in their first battle the Tartars would hack off their heads and she would not know where lay their forsaken bodies, pecked by the wild birds on the roadside; and for each drop of their blood she would have given all of hers. Sobbing, she looked into their eyes, as an overpowering drowsiness was beginning to close them, and thought: "Maybe when Bulba wakes he may put off their going for a day or two; perhaps he thought of going so soon only because he had drunk so much."

For hours the moon high up in the heavens had flooded with light the yard filled with sleepers, the thick bush of willows, and the tall weeds in which the fence that surrounded the yard was lost. Still she sat by the pillow of her darling sons and never for a moment took her eyes from them nor thought of sleep. Already the horses, scenting the dawn, lay down on the grass and stopped grazing; the top leaves of the willows began whispering, and little by little the whisper ran eddying down them to the lowest branches. She sat till daylight, feeling no weariness and inwardly longing for the night to last on and on. The ringing neigh of a foal floated from the steppe; red streaks gleamed brightly in the sky.

Bulba suddenly woke and leaped up. He remembered very well the orders he had given the day before. "Come, boys, wake up! It's time, high time! Water the horses! And where's the old woman?"

(This was his usual name for his wife.) "Look alive, old woman, prepare food for us; a great journey lies before us!"

The poor old mother, deprived of her last hope, dragged herself dejectedly into the hut. While she was tearfully preparing what was wanted for breakfast, Bulba was giving orders, looking after things in the stables, and picking out his best equipment for his sons.

The seminary students were transformed; instead of their muddy boots, they had boots of red morocco with silver taps; trousers as wide as the Black Sea, with thousands of folds and pleats, were drawn in with a golden cord; to the cord were attached long straps with tassels and various trifles for a pipe. A Cossack coat of crimson cloth bright as fire was girt with a gaily patterned sash; embossed Turkish pistols were thrust into this sash and a saber clanked about their legs. Their faces, still scarcely sunburned, looked handsomer and fairer; their young black mustaches seemed to emphasize the whiteness of their skins and the healthy vigorous hue of youth; they were handsome under their black, gold-topped astrakhan caps. Poor mother! As she looked at them she could not utter a word; tears stood in her eyes.

"Well, sons, everything is ready! There's no need to linger!" Bulba pronounced at last. "Now, as is the Christian custom, we must all sit down before the journey."

All sat down, even the young men who had been standing respectfully at the doors.

"Now, mother, bless your children!" said Bulba; "pray that they may fight bravely, that they may ever defend the honor of knighthood; that they may ever champion the Christian faith, and that if they don't—that they be dead and leave no trace behind them. Go up to your mother, children: a mother's prayer brings safety on land and on sea!"

The mother, weak as a mother, embraced them and, bringing out two small icons, put them on their necks, sobbing as she did so. "May the Mother of God . . . keep you . . . don't forget your mother . . . send me just a word of news . . ." She could say no more.

"Well, come along, children!" said Bulba.

Saddled horses were standing at the steps. Bulba leaped on his Devil, which reared wildly, feeling a terrific weight on the saddle, for Taras was exceedingly thickset and heavy.

When the mother saw that her sons were mounted on their horses, she flew up to the younger one, whose features betrayed more of something like tenderness; she clutched his stirrup, she clung to his saddle, and with despair in her eyes held him tight in her arms. Two strong Cossacks took her carefully and bore her away into the hut. But when they rode out at the gate, she ran out with the nimbleness of a wild goat, hardly believable at her years, and with startling force stopped the horse and embraced one of her sons with blind frenzied fervor. She was taken away again.

The young Cossacks rode on in embarrassment, restraining their tears for fear of their father, who for his part was a little troubled, too, though he tried not to show it. It was a gray day; the green leaves and grass glittered brightly; the birds chirped discordantly. After riding on they looked back; their home seemed to have sunk into the earth; nothing was to be seen above ground but two chimneys of their modest little hut and the tops of the trees, on the branches of which they had climbed in old days like squirrels. There still lay stretched before them the meadow which might have recalled to them the whole story of their lives, from the age when they used to roll on its dewy grass to the age when they waited in it for the black-browed Cossack girl who timidly fluttered across it on her swift young feet. And now only the post over the well with a cart wheel fastened to the top stood out forlornly against the sky; by now the plain which they were riding through looked in the distance like a mountain and hid everything from sight. Farewell to childhood, to play, and to everything, everything!

II

All three rode in silence. Old Taras was thinking of long ago: before his mind passed his youth, those years, those bygone years, always regretted by the Cossack, who would like this whole life to be youth. He wondered whom he would meet of his old comrades at the camp. He tried to recall which were dead, which were still living. Tears slowly gathered in his eyes and his gray head drooped mournfully.

His sons were occupied with other thoughts. But we must say a little more about those sons. They had been sent in their twelfth year to the seminary in Kiev, for all persons of consequence in those days thought it necessary to give their sons an education even if they were only to forget it completely afterwards. They were then, like all who came to the seminary, wild creatures reared in freedom, and in the seminary the boys commonly acquired a certain polish and gained a common quality which made them resemble each other. The elder boy, Ostap, began his career by running away in his first year. He was brought back, severely flogged, and sent back to his books. Four times he buried his reading text in the earth and four times after beating him inhumanly they bought him a new one. And he would undoubtedly have done the same again for the fifth time, if his father had not solemnly given his word that he would keep him for twenty full years as a lay brother in a monastery, and sworn that he should never see the Cossack camp in his life if he did not learn all his lessons at the seminary. It is curious that this was said by Taras Bulba, who abused all learning and, as we have seen already, advised his sons to pay no attention to it at all. From that time Ostap began studying the tedious book with extraordinary diligence and was soon on a level with the best of the scholars. The kind of education in vogue in those days was terribly divorced from the manner of life: these scholastic, grammatical, rhetorical, and logical subtleties had absolutely no relation with the times, and were never applied or repeated in life. Those who studied them could not connect their acquirements, even the least pedantic, with anything in their lives. The most learned men in those days were more ignorant than the rest, because they were entirely removed from experience. Moreover, the democratic organization of the seminary, the immense numbers of young, sturdy, healthy fellows, were bound to impress upon them a reality absolutely remote from their studies. Sometimes their poor fare, sometimes their frequent punishments by hunger, sometimes the many cravings that spring up in a fresh, strong, healthy lad, and all these in conjunction, aroused in them that spirit of enterprise which was afterward developed in the Cossack camp. The hungry students lounged about the streets of Kiev and forced everyone to be on his guard. The market women always covered their pies, their pretzels, and their pumpkin seeds with their hands, as eagles cover their young, as soon as they saw a student coming. The monitor, bound by his duty to watch over the colleagues committed to his charge, had such enormous pockets in his trousers that he could have stuffed them with the entire shop of an unwary market woman. These seminary students made up a separate world; they were not admitted into the higher circles consisting of Polish and Russian noblemen. Even the military governor, Adam Kisel, in spite of his patronage of the seminary, did not admit them into society, and gave orders that they should be disciplined as strictly as possible. This injunction was quite superfluous, however, for the rector and the monk-professors did not spare the rod and the whip, and often the lictors, by their orders, thrashed the monitors so cruelly that the latter were rubbing their trousers for weeks afterward. To many of them this was a matter of little importance, hardly more stinging than good vodka with pepper in it; others became fearfully sick at last of these incessant drubbings, and they ran away to the Cossack camp, if they could find the road and were not caught on the way. Though Ostap Bulba began with great diligence studying logic and even theology, he did not escape the merciless rod. It was natural that all this should in a way toughen the character and give it the hardness that has always characterized the Cossacks. Ostap was always considered one of the best of the comrades. He did not often take the lead in rash enterprises, such as plundering an orchard or a vegetable garden, but he was always one of the first to follow the lead of an enterprising student, and never under any circumstances betrayed his comrades; no rods nor lashes could make him do that. He suppressed any interests other than fighting and carousing; anyway he scarcely ever thought of anything else. He was frank with his equals. He was kindhearted as far as that was possible with such a character and in those times. He was genuinely touched by the tears of his poor mother, and her grief was the only thing that troubled him and made his head lower pensively.

His younger brother Andrei had rather refined and as it were more sensitive feelings. He studied more eagerly and without the effort with which a man of plodding mind usually sets to work. He was more inventive than his brother, more frequently took the lead in rather a dangerous enterprise, and sometimes, thanks to his resourceful wit, managed to escape punishment, while his brother Ostap, without a second thought, slipped off his jacket and lay down on the floor, not dreaming of asking for mercy. Andrei, too, was boiling with the desire for adventure, but at the same time his soul was open to other feelings also. A yearning for love flamed hotly in him after he had reached his eighteenth year; woman was more often the subject of his ardent dreams; as he listened to philosophic arguments he saw her every minute, fresh, black-eyed, tender. Her firm breasts, her lovely, delicate naked arms were continually flitting before his eyes; the very dress that clung to her maidenly and yet strong limbs had in his dreams a fragrance of inexpressible sensuousness. He carefully concealed from his comrades these emotions of his passionate youthful soul, for in those days it was a shame and a dishonor for a Cossack to think of woman and love before he had seen any fighting. Of late years he had less often been leader of a rowdy gang; more often he sauntered alone in some solitary Kiev lane drowned in a sea of cherry trees between narrow little houses that looked appealingly into the road. Sometimes he also wandered into the street of the aristocrats in what is now Old Kiev, where the Little Russian and Polish nobles lived, and where the houses were built with a certain pretentious taste.

One day when he was not looking, the coach of some Polish nobleman almost drove over him, and the coachman, with terrific mustaches, lashed at him from the box with good aim. The young student flew into a rage: recklessly he clutched the hind wheel in his powerful hands and stopped the coach. But the coachman, dreading retaliation, whipped up the horses, they dashed forward—and Andrei, who luckily just had time to snatch away his hands, fell face downward in the mud. A most musical and melodious laugh rang out above him. He raised his eyes and saw standing at a window the loveliest creature he had seen in his life, with black eyes and a skin white as snow when it is lighted up by the flush of the dawning sun. She was laughing heartily, and her laughter gave a sparkling brilliance to her dazzling beauty. He was disconcerted. He gazed at her, completely overwhelmed, while he absent-mindedly rubbed the mud off his face, smearing it the more as he did so. Who could this beauty be? He tried to find out from the servants who stood in expensive livery at the gate listening to a young bandore player. But the servants laughed when they saw his muddy face and did not choose to answer. At last he found out that she was the daughter of the Kovno military governor who had come on a visit to Kiev. The very next night, with the audacity of which only seminary students are capable, he climbed over the fence into the garden, and climbed up a tree, the branches of which reached the very roof of the house; from the tree he jumped up on the roof and climbing down through the chimney of the open fireplace, made his way straight into the bedroom of the beauty who was at the moment sitting in front of a candle and removing her expensive earrings. The lovely Polish girl was so frightened at seeing an unknown man suddenly confronting her that she could not utter a word; but when she noticed that the student was standing with downcast eyes, too shy to move a hand, when she recognized in him the youth who had tumbled into the mud before her eyes, she was overcome with laughter again. Moreover, there was nothing alarming in Andrei's face: he was very handsome. She laughed with genuine mirth and for a long time amused herself at his expense. The beauty was as lighthearted as Polish girls are; but her eyes, her wonderful, piercingly bright eyes looked at him steadily. The seminary student could not stir a limb, but stood stiffly as though tied in a sack, while the military governor's daughter went boldly up to him, put her glittering diadem on his head, hung earrings on his lips, and threw over him a transparent muslin chemisette with ruffles embroidered in gold. She dressed him up, and, with the naughty childlike ease characteristic of frivolous Polish girls, played a thousand silly pranks with him, and this put the poor student into even greater confusion. He was a ridiculous sight standing with his mouth open, staring into her dazzling eyes. A knock at the door at this moment alarmed her. She told him to hide under the bed, and as soon as the interruption was over, called her maid, a Tartar captive, and gave her orders to guide him cautiously to the garden and from there to help him over the fence. But this time our student did not climb over the fence so successfully: the watchman, waking up, caught him firmly by the legs and the assembled servants gave him a good beating, pursuing him even after he was in the street, where only his swift legs saved him. After this it was very dangerous to go near the house, for there were a great many servants in the governor's household. He met the daughter once more at church; she saw him and smiled to him very graciously, as to an old friend. He caught a passing glimpse of her once again; but soon after that the Kovno general went away, and, instead of the lovely black-eyed Polish girl, an unknown fat face looked out of the window. This was what Andrei was thinking of as he rode on with hanging head and eyes fixed on his horse's mane.

Meanwhile the steppe had long since wrapped them in its green embraces, the high grass hid them from sight, and only glimpses of their black Cossack caps showed from time to time among its flowering spikes.

"Aie, aie, aie! Why are you so quiet, lads?" said Bulba at last, rousing himself from his reverie. "As though you were monks! Come, to the devil with all brooding! Take your pipes between your teeth, let us light up and spur on our horses and fly so that no bird can overtake us!"

And the Cossacks, bending forward on their horses, disappeared in the grass. Now even their black caps could not be seen; only the lines of crushed grass showed the track of their swift course.

The sun had long since risen in the clear sky and was flooding the steppe with its warm, life-giving light. Every trace of trouble and drowsiness in the soul of the Cossacks vanished in an instant; their hearts were fluttering like birds.

The further they went, the lovelier the steppe became. In those days the vast expanse which makes up the southern part of Russia, right down to the Black Sea, was green virgin wilderness. Never had plow cut through the immense waves of its wild flowers; they were only trampled by the horses who were hidden in them as in a forest. Nothing in nature could be fairer; the whole surface of the earth was an ocean of green and gold, glittering with millions of different flowers. Through the high slender stalks of grass slipped the pale blue, indigo, and lilac cornflowers; the yellow broom thrust up its pyramidal crest; the white meadowsweet studded the surface with its umbrella-shaped plumes; an ear of wheat, brought God knows whence, was ripening among them. Among their slender stems partridges scurried about craning their necks. The air was filled with a thousand different bird calls. Hawks hovered motionless in the sky with wings outspread and eyes fixed immovably on the grass. The cries of a flock of wild geese moving off echoed from God knows what faraway lake. A gull rose with measured sweep of its wings from the grass and luxuriously bathed in the blue ocean of the air. Now she vanished in the heights, passing into a tiny black dot; now she turned over and gleamed in the sun. . . . How lovely are the steppes, damn them!

Our travelers only halted for a few minutes for dinner, when the escort of ten Cossacks who accompanied them dismounted and untied the wooden kegs of vodka and the pumpkin shells which were used instead of bowls. They ate nothing but bread and lard, or biscuits, drank only one cupful of vodka to keep up their strength, for Taras Bulba never permitted drinking on the road, and then went on till the evening. Toward nightfall the whole steppe was completely transformed; all its multicolored surface was flooded with the last bright glow of the sun and gradually darkened, so that the shadow could be seen creeping over it and turning it dark green; the odors that arose were richer; every flower, every blade of grass exhaled fragrance, and the whole steppe was bathed in sweet scent. Over the dark blue sky broad streaks of rosy gold were flung as though by a gigantic brush; light and transparent clouds made white drifts here and there; and the freshest breath of wind, alluring as a wave of the sea, faintly stirred the tops of the grass and gently caressed the cheek. All the music that had resounded in the day was hushed and replaced by another. The spotted marmots crept out of their holes, stood upon their hind paws, and made the steppe resound with their whistling. The churring of the grasshoppers grew louder. At times from some secluded lake came the cry of a swan, ringing like silver in the air.

The travelers halted in the middle of the open steppe, picked out a resting place, made a fire, and set on it a cauldron in which they cooked a stew; the steam rose and floated slanting through the air. After supper the Cossacks lay down to sleep, leaving their fettered horses grazing in the grass. They stretched themselves on their jackets. The midnight stars looked straight at them. They heard the innumerable world of insects that filled the grass, their whirr and buzz and churring; all resounded musically in the night, grew clearer in the fresh air, and lulled the drowsy ear. If one of them rose and stood up for a moment, he saw the steppe dotted with the gleaming sparks of fireflies. Here and there the night sky was lighted up by the faraway glow of dry reeds being burned here and there in the meadows and by the rivers, and a dark string of swans flying to the north would suddenly gleam with silvery pink light, and then it looked as though red handkerchiefs were flying through the dark sky.

The travelers rode on without incident. They nowhere came upon trees: everywhere the same boundless, free, lovely steppe. But at times they saw on one side the dark blue tops of the faraway forest that stretches along the bank of the Dnieper. Only once did Taras point out to his sons a little black dot far away in the grass, saying: "Look, boys, there's a Tartar galloping there!" A little head fixed its narrow eyes straight upon them in the distance, sniffed the air above its mustaches like a hunting dog, and like an antelope vanished on seeing that the Cossacks were thirteen in number.

"Well now, lads, you may try to overtake the Tartar! But better not try, you'll never catch him: his horse is swifter than my Devil." Bulba, however, took precautions, fearing an ambush concealed somewhere. They galloped up to the Tatarka, a little stream that falls into the Dnieper, plunged into the water with their horses, and for a long time swam along to conceal their tracks, then clambered out onto the bank and went on their way.

Three days after that they were not far from the place which was the goal of their journey. There was a sudden chill in the air; they felt that the Dnieper was near. Then it gleamed in the distance and stood out, a dark streak against the horizon. A chill breath arose from its cold waves, and it stretched nearer and nearer, and at last covered half the surface of the land. It was that part of the Dnieper where, after being narrowed into rapids, it at last takes its own way, and, roaring like the sea, flows in freedom, where the islands scattered in mid-river force it still further from the banks, and its waters spread themselves wide over the land, meeting no crags or heights. The Cossacks dismounted from their horses, embarked on a ferry, and after three hours' sailing reached the shores of the Island of Khortitsa, where at that time the camp, which so often changed its location, was situated.

A group of people were wrangling with the ferrymen on the bank. The Cossacks looked after their horses. Taras drew himself up with dignity, tightened his belt, and haughtily stroked his mustaches. His young sons, too, looked themselves up and down with a sort of apprehension and vague pleasure, and all of them rode together into the outer village, which is half a mile from the camp. As they rode in, they were deafened by fifty smiths' hammers clanging upon twenty-five anvils covered with turf and sunk in the earth. Powerful leatherworkers were sitting under their porches in the street; they were kneading bulls' skins with their powerful arms. Hucksters were sitting in shanties with heaps of flints, tinder, and powder; an Armenian had hung out costly kerchiefs; a Tartar was turning upon spits fillets of mutton dipped in dough; a Jew, craning his head forward, was drawing vodka out of a barrel. But the first man they came across was a Dnieper Cossack asleep in the middle of the road, his arms and legs stretched out. Taras Bulba could not help stopping and admiring him. "Ah, how grandly he is sprawling! I swear, he is an impressive figure!" he said, stopping his horse. It was indeed a rather bold picture; the

Cossack lay full length like a lion in the road; his forelock, tossed proudly back, covered half a yard of ground; his trousers of expensive crimson cloth were smeared with tar, showing his complete disregard for them. After admiring him, Bulba made his way further along the narrow street, which was encumbered by craftsmen carrying on their trades there, and men of all nations, who crowded this outer village of the camp, which was like a fair and which clothed and fed the Cossacks, who could do nothing but carouse and shoot.

At last they had passed the outer village and saw a few scattered barracks,[2] roofed with turf or, in the Tartar fashion, with felt. There were cannons standing about some of them. Nowhere were fences to be seen, nor little low-pitched huts with porches on low wooden posts such as were in the outer village. A small rampart and barricade, not guarded by anyone, showed their fearful recklessness. A few sturdy Cossacks, lying with their pipes in their teeth, right on the road, looked at them rather unconcernedly and did not move. Taras rode carefully between them with his sons, saying: "Good health to you, gentlemen!"

"Good health to you too!" answered the Cossacks. Everywhere picturesque groups were dotted about the plain. From their tanned faces it could be seen that they all had been hardened in battle and had passed through privations of all sorts. So this was it, the camp! This was the nest from which all those heroes came forth as proud and vigorous as lions. This was the source from which freedom and Cossack chivalry flowed over the whole of the Ukraine!

The travelers came out into a spacious square where the Council[3] usually assembled. On a big cask turned upside down a Cossack was sitting without his shirt; he had it in his hands and was slowly mending the holes in it. Their way was barred again by a crowd of musicians in whose midst a young Cossack was dancing and flinging up his arms, his cap jauntily thrust on one side. He only shouted: "Play faster, musicians! Foma, don't grudge vodka to good Christians!" And Foma, who had a black eye, was ladling out an enormous mugful to every comer at random. Four old Cossacks near the young one were working their legs rather mincingly, flinging themselves like a whirlwind almost on the musicians'

---

[2] *Kurens*, a group of buildings within the camp (*sech*); a fortified village. Also applied to a detachment of men, a military unit. (ed.)

[3] *Rada*, assembly of Cossack elders. (ed.)

heads, and suddenly dropping into a squatting position, they flew around, stamping with their silver heels vigorously and resoundingly on the hard beaten ground. The earth resounded with a hollow echo far around and the air was ringing with the dance tunes struck out by the clinking heels of their boots. One more eager than the rest kept uttering shrieks and flying after the others in the dance. His long forelock fluttered in the wind, his powerful chest was revealed; but he was wearing a warm winter sheepskin and the sweat was dripping from him as from a pail.

"At least take off your sheepskin!" said Taras at last. "You see how hot it is!"

"I can't!" cried the Cossack.

"Why not?"

"I cannot; if I fling a thing off I swap it for drink; that's my way." The young warrior had long been without cap or girdle, or embroidered kerchief; all had gone the same road.

The crowd grew larger; others joined the dancers, and no one could have watched without being held spellbound by that most free, most furious dance the world has ever seen, the *Kozatchok*, named after its originators.

"Oh, if it weren't for my horse," cried Taras, "I'd join in, I'd really join in the dance!"

And meanwhile they began coming upon gray-headed old veterans who had more than once been elders and were respected by all in the camp for their services. Taras soon met a number of old acquaintances. Ostap and Andrei heard nothing but greetings. "Ah, is that you, Pecheritsa! Good day, Kozolup!" "From where has God brought you, Taras?" "How did you come here, Doloto? Good health to you, Kirdiaga! Good health to you, Gusty! I never thought to see you, Remen!" And warriors, gathered from all the turbulent world of South Russia, kissed each other, and questions followed at once. "And what of Kasian? Where's Borodavka? What news of Kolopior? What's Pidsyshok doing?" And all Taras Bulba heard in reply was that Borodavka had been hanged at Tolopan, that Kolopior had been flayed near Kizikirmen, that Pidsyshok's head had been pickled in a barrel and sent to Constantinople. Old Bulba's head drooped as he said pensively: "They were good Cossacks!"

III

Taras Bulba had been living with his sons for about a week in the camp. Ostap and Andrei were not much occupied in studying the military art. The Cossacks did not care to trouble themselves with drill or to waste time in maneuvers: the young men were taught and trained only by experience in the heat of battle, which was therefore almost continuous. The Cossacks thought it tedious to employ the intervals in practicing any sort of discipline except perhaps firing at a target and occasionally horse racing and hunting wild beasts in the steppes and the meadows. All the rest of the time was given up to revelry—the outward manifestation of the breadth and vigor of their unfettered spirits. The camp presented an extraordinary spectacle; it was an uninterrupted festivity, a ball that began noisily and never ended. Some of its inmates practiced crafts, others kept shops and traded; but the majority caroused from morning till evening, if the jingle in their pockets made it possible, and the booty they had won had not yet passed into the hands of dealers and tavern keepers. There was a fascinating charm in this carousing. It was not a gathering of people drinking to drown sorrow, but simply the frenzied recklessness of gaiety. Everyone who came here forgot and forsook everything that had occupied him before. He spat, one may say, upon his past, and carelessly abandoned himself to freedom and the companionship of other reckless revelers like himself, who had no kindred, no home nor family, nothing but the open sky and the eternal festivity. This produced a wild gaiety that could spring from no other source. The talk and storytelling among the crowd lazily resting on the ground was often so amusing, so full of life and vigor, that all the cool composure of the Cossacks was needed to maintain an unmoved expression without the twitch of a mustache —a conspicuous characteristic by which the Russian of the South is still distinguished from his fellow countrymen. The gaiety was drunken and noisy, but for all that it was not the gaiety of the gloomy tavern where a man seeks forgetfulness in dreary and depraving hilarity; it was like an intimate club of school comrades. The only difference was that instead of sitting spelling out words and listening to the dull teaching of a schoolmaster, they rode out on five thousand horses to the attack; instead of a field to play ball in, they had unguarded, insecure frontiers, over which the swift

Tartar showed his head and the Turk in his green turban looked steadily and menacingly. The difference was that, instead of being compulsorily kept at school, they had of their own free will forsaken their fathers and mothers and run away from their homes; that here there were men who had had the noose around their necks and who, escaping pale death, had plunged into life, and life in all its festive fullness; that here there were men whose honorable tradition it was never to keep a kopek in their pockets; that here there were men who had till then considered a gold coin a fortune, whose pockets, thanks to the Jewish leaseholders, might have been turned inside out without risk of losing anything. Here there were all the students who could not endure the floggings of the seminary and who had not learned one letter of the alphabet in school; but with them there were also men here who knew something of Horace, Cicero, and the Roman Republic. Here were many of the officers who afterward distinguished themselves in the Polish army; here, too, were numbers of experienced guerillas who had the conviction that it did not matter where they fought so long as they fought, since it was improper for a gentleman not to be engaged in warfare. There were many here, too, who had come to the camp in order to say afterward that they had been there, and were seasoned warriors. Who was not to be found there? The strange republic was a necessity of the age. Lovers of the military life, lovers of gold goblets, rich brocades, gold coins, could find work here at any time. Only those devoted to women could find nothing here, for not one woman dared to show herself even in the outer village of the camp.

To Ostap and Andrei it seemed exceedingly strange that numbers of people arrived at the camp and no one asked where these men came from, who they were, and what were their names. They came here as though returning to their own home which they had left but an hour before. The newcomer merely showed himself to the leader,[4] who usually said: "Good health to you! Do you believe in Christ?"

"I do!" answered the newcomer.

"And do you believe in the Holy Trinity?"

"I do!"

"And do you go to church?"

---

[4] *Koshevoy*, head of a camp. (ed.)

"I do!"

"Well, then, cross yourself!" The newcomer crossed himself.

"Good!" answered the leader. "Go to the unit which you choose."

With that the whole ceremony ended. And all of the camp prayed in one church and was ready to defend it to the last drop of their blood, though they would not hear of fasting and abstinence. Only Jews, Armenians, and Tartars, moved by intense desire of gain, ventured to live and trade in the outer village, for the Cossacks never liked bargaining and paid just as much money as their hand happened to pull out of their pockets. The lot of these covetous traders was most pitiful, however; they were like the villagers who live at the foot of Vesuvius, for as soon as the Cossacks had spent all their money, they smashed the dealers' stalls and took their goods for nothing.

The camp consisted of over sixty military units, which were very much like separate independent republics and still more like a children's boarding school or a seminary. No one kept anything to himself: everything was in the hands of the chief of the unit, who because of that was commonly addressed as "Father." He kept the money, the clothes, all the provisions, the boiled grain, the porridge, and even the fuel; the Cossacks gave him their money to take care of. Frequently a quarrel sprang up between one unit and another, and this at once led to a fight. Their inmates crowded the square and belabored each other's ribs with their fists, until at last one party proved the stronger and gained the upper hand; then followed a wild drinking party. Such was the camp which had such a fascination for young men.

Ostap and Andrei plunged with all the ardor of youth into this sea of reckless gaiety and instantly forgot their father's house and their seminary, and all that had stirred their hearts before this; they surrendered entirely to their new life. Everything interested them, the festive customs of the camp and the not very complicated rules and regulations which sometimes, indeed, struck them as too severe in such an independent republic. If a Cossack were a thief and stole any trifle, it was regarded as a disgrace to the whole body of Cossacks: he was bound to the whipping post as a thief, and beside him was laid an oak club with which each Cossack was obliged to deal him a blow, until in this way he was beaten to death. If a man did not pay his debts, he was chained to a cannon, where he had to remain until one of his comrades was moved to buy him off by paying the debt for him. But Andrei was most impressed by the fearful punishment laid down for murder. He saw a pit dug on the spot and the murderer lowered into it alive, and above him the coffin containing the body of his victim was laid, and then both were covered with earth. Long afterward he was haunted by this horrible form of punishment and kept picturing the man buried alive with the horrible coffin.

Soon the two young Cossacks were quite at home in the camp. Often with other comrades of their unit and sometimes with the whole of their unit and the neighboring ones, they went out to shoot immense numbers of the various wild birds of the steppe, of stags and goats; or they visited the lakes, rivers, and streams which were assigned by lot to the different units, dropped in their tackle and their nets, and drew out vast shoals of fish to supply their comrades. Though there were no maneuvers in which a Cossack could show his mettle, they had already attracted notice among the other young men by their reckless boldness and success in everything. They shot quickly and accurately at the target, and swam across the Dnieper against the current—a feat which wins for the novice a triumphant reception into Cossack circles.

But old Taras was preparing a different kind of activity for them. Such an idle life was not to his taste—he longed for action. He was always pondering how he could rouse the camp to some bold enterprise in which a warrior might fittingly enjoy himself. At last one day he went to the leader and said to him plainly: "Well, it's high time for the Dnieper Cossacks to go on an adventure."

"There's nowhere for them to have it," answered the leader, taking a little pipe out of his mouth and spitting aside.

"Nowhere? We could move against the Turks or the Tartars."

"We cannot go into Turkey nor to the Tartars," answered the leader, coolly putting his pipe back into his mouth.

"Why can't we?"

"Well, we promised the Sultan peace."

"But you know he is a pagan, and God and the Holy Scriptures bid us beat the infidels."

"We have not the right. If we had not sworn by our faith, then perhaps we might have; but now we cannot, it's impossible."

"How impossible? How can you say we have not the right? Here I have two sons, both young men. Neither has ever been once in battle, and you say we have not the right; and you say the Cossacks must not go to war."

"Well, it's not right to do so."

"Then it is right for the strength of the Cossacks to be wasted, for a man to rot like a dog without deeds of valor, for neither fatherland nor Christianity to get any good from him, is it? Then what the hell are we living for? Explain that to me. You're a clever man, it was not for nothing they chose you leader: explain what we are living for?"

The leader made no answer to this question. He was an obstinate Cossack. He was silent for a little while and then said:

"There won't be war, anyway."

"So there won't be war?" Taras asked him.

"No."

"So it's no use thinking about it?"

"It's no use even thinking about it."

"You wait, you tight-fisted devil!" said Bulba to himself: "I'll let you know!" And he determined on the spot to revenge himself on the leader.

After talking to one and then to another, he set up a drinking feast for them all, and several drunken Cossacks went straight to the square where, tied to posts, there were kettledrums on which they used to beat to summon the assembly. Not finding the sticks, which were always kept at the drummer's, they each snatched up a block of wood and began beating the drums. The first to run up at the sound was the drummer, a tall man with only one eye, and that one looking terribly sleepy.

"Who dares beat the drums?" he shouted.

"Hold your tongue! Take your drumsticks and beat the drum when you are told!" they answered.

The drummer at once took out of his pocket the sticks which he had brought with him, knowing well how such incidents ended. At the rat-a-tat of the drums, dark groups of Cossacks began swarming into the square like bees. They all gathered in a circle, and after a third tattoo had been beaten on the drums, the elders showed themselves at last: the leader with his mace, the badge of office, in his hand, the judge with the official seal, the clerk with his inkpot, and the captain with his staff. The leader and the other officials took off their caps and bowed in all directions to the Cossacks, who stood proudly with their arms akimbo.

"What is the meaning of this assembly? What do you want, comrades?" said the leader. The shouts and abuse would not let him go on.

"Put down your mace! Put down your mace this minute, son of the devil! We'll have no more of you!" the Cossacks shouted from the crowd. Some of the sober units wanted, it seemed, to protest, but the drunken and the sober came to blows. The noise and uproar became general.

The leader tried to speak, but knowing that the determined crowd, once roused to fury, might beat him to death for it (which almost always happened on such occasions), he made a very low bow, put down his mace, and disappeared into the crowd.

"Do you bid us, too, to put down our badge of office, comrades?" said the judge, the clerk, and the captain, and they made ready at once to lay down the inkpot, the seal, and the staff.

"No, you remain!" the crowd shouted. "We only wanted to throw out the leader because he is a woman and we want a man for a leader."

"Whom do you elect leader now?" asked the judge and the captain.

"Choose Kukubenko!" shouted some.

"We won't have Kukubenko!" shouted others. "It's too soon for him, the milk is not dry on his lips."

"Let Shilo be leader!" shouted some.

"A Shilo[5] in your back!" the crowd shouted with oaths. "A fine Cossack when he thieves like a Tartar, the son of a bitch! Into the devil's sack with drunken Shilo!"

"Borodaty, let us make Borodaty leader!"

"We won't have Borodaty! The devil's mother take him!"

"Shout Kirdiaga!" whispered Taras Bulba to several.

"Kirdiaga! Kirdiaga!" shouted the crowd. "Borodaty! Borodaty! Kirdiaga! Kirdiaga! Shilo! The hell with Shilo! Kirdiaga!"

All the candidates, hearing their names called, at once stepped out of the crowd to avoid giving any grounds for supposing that they were taking any personal part in their election.

"Kirdiaga! Kirdiaga!" sounded louder than the rest.

"Borodaty!" The question was put to a show of hands and Kirdiaga was the victor.

---

[5] "Bradawl." (ed.)

"Go and fetch Kirdiaga!" they shouted.

A dozen Cossacks, some hardly able to stand, they had drunk so heavily, moved out of the crowd and went at once to tell Kirdiaga of his election. Kirdiaga, a clever though rather elderly Cossack, had been sitting for some time in his barracks, as though he knew nothing of what was taking place.

"What is it, comrades? What do you want?" he asked.

"Come along, you have been elected leader!"

"Mercy on us!" said Kirdiaga. "How can I be worthy of such an honor? How can I be leader? Why, I haven't sense enough to fill such an office. Could no one better be found in the whole camp?"

"Come along, we tell you!" shouted the Cossacks. Two of them took him by the arms and, although he resisted, he was at last dragged along to the square, accompanied by abuse, punches in the back, kicks, and exhortations. "Don't resist, you son of a bitch! Accept the honor, you dog, when it's given to you!" In this way Kirdiaga was led into the circle of Cossacks.

"Well, comrades!" those who led him boomed out to the crowd: "do you agree that this Cossack should be our leader?"

"We all agree!" roared the crowd, and the whole plain resounded to their shout.

One of the elders picked up the mace of office and took it to the newly elected leader. Kirdiaga, as the custom was, at once refused it. It was brought him a second time, and only at the third time he at last accepted it. A shout of approval rang out through the whole crowd, and again the whole plain echoed far and wide from the Cossacks' shout. Then four of the oldest Cossacks, with gray mustaches and gray forelocks (there were no very old men in the camp, for no Dnieper Cossack died a natural death) stepped forward out of the crowd, and each, taking a handful of earth which had been turned into mud by recent rain, laid it on Kirdiaga's head. The wet earth trickled from his head over his mustache and cheeks, and his whole face was smeared with mud. But Kirdiaga stood without moving and thanked the Cossacks for the honor shown him.

Thus ended the noisy meeting. Bulba was very pleased with the results, perhaps more than the others: it was his revenge on the former leader; moreover, Kirdiaga was an old comrade of his and had been with him on campaigns by land and sea, sharing the toils and hardships of war. The crowd dispersed at once to celebrate the election, and a riotous debauch followed, such as Ostap and Andrei had not before seen. The drinking booths were smashed; mead, vodka, and beer were simply seized, without payment; the booth keepers were glad to get off alive. The whole night was spent in shouting and singing songs celebrating their exploits, and the rising moon for hours witnessed crowds of musicians parading through the streets with bandores, drums, and round balalaikas, together with church choristers who were kept at the camp to sing in church and to glorify the deeds of the Cossacks. At last drink and exhaustion overcame their stubborn heads. And here and there a Cossack was seen falling to the ground; another, embracing a comrade and even weeping with sentimentality, would roll over with him. Here a whole group were lying in a heap; here a Cossack looking out for the best place to lie down ended by lying on a block of wood. The last whose head was most stubborn still uttered incoherent words; at last he too was felled by the power of drink, he too fell sprawling—and all of the camp sank into slumber.

IV

Next day Taras Bulba was conferring with the new leader as to how to rouse the Cossacks to some deed of valor. The leader was a clever and crafty Cossack, he knew the Cossacks through and through, and at first he said: "We cannot go beyond our oath, it can't be done," but after a pause he added: "No matter, it can be done; we will not break our oath, but we will think of something. Only let the people assemble, but not at my command, but simply at their own pleasure—you know how to manage that—and we and the elders will hasten to the square, as though we knew nothing about it."

Not an hour after their conversation the kettledrums were sounding again. Both drunken and reckless Cossacks suddenly popped up. Thousands of Cossacks were hurrying at once to the square. Questions were asked: "Who? What for? Why is a meeting called?" No one answered. At last, first in one corner and then in another, men were heard saying: "Here the strength of the Cossacks is being wasted; there is no war! Here our elders have grown sluggish, their eyes are buried in fat! It seems there is no justice in the world!" Other Cossacks listened at first, and then they too began saying: "Indeed, there is no justice in the world!" The elders seemed astounded at these sayings. At last the leader stepped forward and said: "Allow me, comrades, to speak!"

"Speak!"

"What we have to discuss now, honorable sirs, and you, maybe, know this better than I do, is that many Cossacks are so deeply in debt to the Jews at the taverns and to their comrades that not even the devil will give them credit. Then again there are many fellows who have never seen what war is with their eyes, while no young man—you know it very well, comrades—can exist without war. What sort of Cossack will he make if he has not once fought a pagan?"

"He speaks well," thought Bulba.

"Don't imagine though, comrades, that I say this to break the peace. God forbid! I merely state it. Moreover we have a church—it's a disgrace to say what it's like: here by the grace of God the camp has been established so many years, and up to now not only the outside of the church but even the icons are devoid of adornment; someone might at least have thought to make them a silver frame; they have only received what some Cossacks have bequeathed, and indeed their offerings were poor, because they had drunk up almost everything they had in their lifetime. I am saying this not to urge the beginning of war with the heathens: we have promised the Sultan peace, and it would be a great sin for us, because we have taken an oath in accordance with our law."

"Why is he making such a muddle?" said Bulba to himself.

"So, as you see, comrades, it is not possible to begin a war: knightly honor forbids. So this is what in my poor judgment I suggest: let the young ones go alone with the boats, let them make a little visit to the shores of Anatolia.[6] What do you think, comrades?"

"Take us all, take us all!" the crowd shouted from all sides: "we are ready to lay down our lives for our faith."

The leader was alarmed; he had not at all wanted to arouse all the Cossacks: to break the peace seemed to him in this case to be wrong. "Will you allow me, comrades, to speak again?"

"Enough!" exclaimed the Cossacks. "You'll say nothing better."

"If that's how it is, so be it. I am the servant of your will. We all know, we know it from Scripture, that the voice of the people is the voice of God. Nothing wiser can be thought of than what the people has thought. But there is this: you know, comrades, that

---

[6] The Asiatic part of Turkey. (ed.)

the Sultan will not let our young men's diversion go unpunished. And by that time we should be ready and our strength would be fresh and we should be afraid of nobody. And while we are absent the Tartars may attack: they won't face us, the Turkish dogs, and dare not come to the house when the master is at home, but will bite our heels from behind and bite hard too. And if it has come to telling the whole truth, we have not boats enough in store nor powder enough ground for all to go. So be it: I am the servant of your will."

The crafty leader ceased speaking. The Cossacks began talking in groups, the chiefs of each unit consulted together; fortunately few were drunk, and so they decided to listen to the counsels of prudence.

That very hour several men set off to the opposite bank of the Dnieper to the treasury, where in inaccessible secret places, under water and in the reeds, the treasury of the army and some of the weapons taken from the enemy lay hidden. All the others rushed to the boats to overhaul them and get them ready for the journey. The bank was instantly crowded with men. Some carpenters arrived with axes in their hands. Old weather-beaten, broad-shouldered, sturdy-legged Cossacks, some with grizzled mustaches, some with black ones, tucking up their trousers, stood knee-deep in the water and dragged the boats with a strong rope from the shore. Others hauled dry logs and trees of all sorts. Here men were mending the boats with boards; here they had turned one upside down and were calking and tarring it; here, as the custom was with the Cossacks, they were binding bundles of long reeds to the sides of boats so that they would not be sunk by the sea waves; further up, camp-fires had been built all along the bank and tar was being boiled in copper cauldrons for tarring the vessels. The old and experienced directed the young. The tapping of hammers and the shouts of the workmen sounded all over the place; the whole bank was heaving with life and movement.

At that moment a big ferryboat began floating toward the bank. A group of men standing on it waved their hands from afar. They were Cossacks in tattered jackets. Their disordered dress—many had nothing but their shirt and the short pipe in their teeth—showed that they had just escaped from some disaster, or that they had been drinking so deeply that they had squandered everything that they had had upon them. A short, broad-shouldered Cossack of about fifty stepped out from among them and stood in front. He shouted and waved his arms more vigorously than the rest; but his words could not be heard above the hammering and shouts of the workmen.

"What has brought you?" asked the leader, when the ferryboat reached the bank. All the workmen stopped their work and with ax and chisel in the air stared in expectation.

"Trouble!" the short Cossack shouted from the ferry.

"What trouble?"

"Will you allow me to speak, Cossack?"

"Speak!"

"Or maybe you will call the assembly?"

"Speak, we are all here."

They all crowded around.

"Can you have heard nothing of what is being done in the Hetman's land?"

"Why, what?" one of the unit chiefs asked.

"Ah! What? It seems the Tartars have glued up your ears that you have heard nothing?"

"Tell us what is happening there?"

"Such doings have never been seen since we were born and christened."

"But do tell us what has happened, you son of a bitch!" shouted someone from the crowd, evidently losing patience.

"Such times have come that now even the holy churches are not ours."

"How do you mean, not ours?"

"Nowadays they are leased out to the Jews. If you don't pay the Jew beforehand, you cannot serve mass."

"What are you talking about?"

"And if a Jewish dog does not put a stamp with his unbaptized hand on the Holy Easter Cake, one cannot consecrate the cake."

"He is lying, comrades; it cannot be that an unbaptized Jew puts a stamp on the Holy Easter Cake."

"Listen! I've more to tell you: and the Catholic priests are driving now all over the Ukraine in their two-wheeled carts. And the trouble is not that they ride in their carriages, but that Orthodox Christians and not horses pull them. Listen! There's more to tell: they say the Jewesses are making themselves petticoats out of the priests' vestments. These are the things that are going on in the Ukraine, comrades! And you sit here in the camp and enjoy yourselves, and it seems the Tartar has given you such a fright that you have neither ears nor eyes—and you don't hear what is going on in the world."

"Stop, stop!" broke in the leader, who had stood till then with his eyes on the ground like all the Dnieper Cossacks, who in important matters never give way to their first impulse, but remain mute and let the power of their indignation accumulate in silence.

"Stop! I too will say a word. And what were you—may the devil beat your father all over!—what were you doing yourselves? Hadn't you swords, or what? How was it you allowed such lawlessness?"

"Aye, how did we allow such lawlessness . . . ! You should have tried it when there were fifty thousand Poles and—indeed, no use to hide a sin—there were dogs too among our own men who had already accepted their Roman faith."

"And your Hetman and the chiefs, what were they about?"

"What the chiefs were about God grant no man may see again!"

"How so?"

"Why, so that now the Hetman lies in Warsaw roasted in a copper pot, and the arms and heads of the chiefs are being carried about at the fairs as a show. That's what has come of our chiefs' deeds!"

The whole crowd heaved. At first a silence fell over the whole riverside such as is common before a violent storm, then all at once voices arose and the whole riverside was talking:

"What! Jews renting out the Orthodox churches! Polish priests harnessing Orthodox Christians! What! Allow such tortures in Russia at the hands of the cursed infidels? Let them treat the chiefs and Hetman like that? But that shall not be, that shall never be!" Such sayings flew from one end of the crowd to another. The Dnieper Cossacks were in an uproar and felt their strength. This was not the excitement of frivolous people; it was the excitement of slow strong characters who do not soon get hot, but, when they are hot, long and obstinately retain that inner fire.

"Hang all the Jews!" was heard from the crowd. "Don't let them make the priests' vestments into petticoats for the Jewesses! Don't let them put stamps on the Holy Easter Cakes! Drown them all, the heathens, in the Dnieper!" These words uttered by someone in the crowd flashed like lightning through the heads of all, and the crowd rushed to the outer village, intending to cut the throats of all the Jews.

The poor sons of Israel, losing what little courage they had, hid in empty vodka barrels, in ovens, and even crept under the skirts of their wives; but the Cossacks found them everywhere.

"Illustrious masters!" cried one tall Jew as long as a stick, thrusting his pitiful face, distorted by terror, from among a group of his companions: "Illustrious masters! A word, only let us say one word! We'll tell you something you have never heard before—so important that there is no saying how important!"

"Well, let them speak," said Bulba, who always liked to hear the accused.

"Noble lords!" the Jew articulated. "Such lords have never before been known, upon my soul, never! Such kind, good, valiant gentlemen have never been in the world before!" His voice failed and shook with terror. "How could we think any harm to the Dnieper Cossacks! Those who are leaseholders in the Ukraine are not our people at all! By God, they are not! They are not Jews at all! The devil knows what they are: such that one can but spit upon them and turn them out! Here they will say the same. Isn't it true, Shloma, or you, Shmuel?"

"By God, it's true!" answered Shloma and Shmuel from among the crowd, in tattered caps, both white as clay.

"We have never had any dealings with the enemy," the tall Jew went on, "and we don't want to know anything of the Catholics: may they dream of the devil! We have been like brothers with you. . . ."

"What? The Dnieper Cossacks are your brothers?" one of the crowd shouted. "You'll never see that, you damned Jews! Into the Dnieper with them, comrades, drown all the heathens!"

These words were the signal. They seized the Jews by their arms and began flinging them into the water. Pitiful cries rang out on all sides, but the hardhearted Cossacks only laughed at the sight of the Jews' legs in slippers and stockings kicking in the air.

The poor orator who had called down trouble on his own head, slipped out of the long coat by which he was being held, and in nothing but a narrow spotted jacket clutched at Bulba's feet and in a piteous voice besought him: "Great lord, illustrious master! I knew your brother, the lamented Dorosh! He was a warrior who brought honor to all knighthood. I gave him eight hundred sequins, when he had to be ransomed from the Turks. . . ."

"You knew my brother?" asked Taras.

"By God, I did! A greathearted gentleman he was."

"And what is your name?"

"Yankel."

"Good," said Taras, and after a moment's thought he turned to the Cossacks and said: "There will always be time to hang the Jew when need be; but today give him to me."

Saying this, Taras led him to his wagons beside which his Cossacks were standing; "Come, crawl under the cart, lie there and don't move, and you, boys, don't let the Jew go."

Then he started to the square, for the whole crowd had for some time been assembled there. Everyone had instantly abandoned the riverbank and the equipment of the boats, for now an expedition by land and not by sea was before them, and not boats and Cossack "sea gulls" but carts and horses were needed. Now all wanted to join, old and young; everyone, with the assent of all the elders, the unit chiefs, and by the will of all the Dnieper Cossacks, resolved to go straight to Poland, to revenge all the wrong and shame done to their faith and to the Cossack fame, to plunder the towns, to burn the villages and crops, and to spread their glory far and wide over the steppe. All were at once belted and armed. The leader seemed to have grown several feet taller. He was no longer the timid servant of the frivolous desires of the free people; he was an absolute ruler, he was a despot who knew how to command. All the independent and reveling warriors stood in orderly ranks respectfully looking down, not daring to raise their eyes when the leader gave an instruction: he gave them quietly without haste or shouting, like an old Cossack, much experienced in action, who was not for the first time carrying out a well-planned enterprise.

"Inspect yourselves, all of you. Inspect yourselves!" he said. "See that the baggage wagons and kegs of tar are in order; try your weapons. Do not take much clothing with you: a shirt and two pairs of trousers for each Cossack, and a pot of porridge and of crushed millet—let no one take more! Everything that is needed will be in the store-wagons. Let every Cossack have a pair of horses! And take two hundred oxen, for oxen will be needed at the fords and slippery places. And keep discipline, comrades, above everything. I know there are some among you who, as soon as

God sends them any booty, go at once tearing up cotton stuff and expensive velvets for leg wrappers. Give up that wretched habit, don't touch petticoats of any sort, but only take a weapon if you can get hold of a good one, and gold or silver pieces, for they go a long way and are of use in every emergency. And here, comrades, I tell you beforehand: if anyone gets drunk on the campaign, there will be no trial for him; I will have him tied by the collar to a wagon, whoever he may be, even though it should be the most valiant Cossack of the whole army; like a dog, he will be shot at once and left without burial for the birds to peck, for a man drunk on a campaign does not deserve Christian burial. Young men, obey your elders in everything! If you are grazed by a bullet or get a scratch on the head from a saber or anything else, don't pay much attention to it; mix a charge of powder in a goblet of vodka, drink it off at one breath, and it will all pass off, there will be no fever even; and on the wound, if it is not too big, simply put earth, mixing it with spittle in the palm of your hand, and the wound will dry up. Well, now to work, to work, lads, and without haste; do the thing thoroughly!"

So spoke the leader and as soon as he had finished his speech, all the Cossacks set to work at once. The whole camp was sober, and not a single drunken man could be found anywhere; it was as though there had never been any among the Cossacks. Some were mending the hoops of the wheels and changing the axles in the carts; some were carrying sacks of provisions to the wagons or heaping weapons on them; some were driving in horses and oxen. From all sides was heard the tramp of horses' hoofs, the firing of guns to test them, the clank of swords, the bellowing of bulls, the creaking of wagons being turned upside down, talk and loud shouting and driving. And soon the Cossack camp stretched in a long, long string over the whole plain. And anyone wanting to run from the head to the tail of it would have had to run a great way. In the little wooden church the priests conducted a service and sprinkled all with holy water; everyone kissed the cross. When they started off and filed out of the camp all the Cossacks looked back. "Farewell, our Mother!" they said almost in the same words: "May God keep thee from all calamity!"

As he rode through the outer village Taras Bulba saw that his Jew, Yankel, had already rigged up a sort of booth and was selling flints, screwdrivers, powder, and various military equipment necessary for the journey, even loaves and rolls. "What a devil of a Jew!" Taras thought to himself, and riding up to him on his horse said: "Fool, why are you sitting here? Do you want to be shot like a sparrow?"

Yankel, in answer to this, went closer up to him and, making a gesture with both hands as though he wanted to tell him something mysterious, said: "Let only my lord keep silent and say nothing to anyone: among the Cossack wagons is one wagon of mine; I am taking stores of everything necessary for the Cossacks, and on the way I will furnish provisions of all sorts at a cheaper price than any Jew has sold them yet; by God, yes; by God, yes!"

Taras Bulba shrugged his shoulders, marveled at the spontaneous resourcefulness of the Jewish character, and rode off to join the others.

V

Soon all the southwest of Poland was a prey to terror. From all sides flew the rumor: "The Dnieper Cossacks! The Dnieper Cossacks have appeared!" Everyone who could escape, escaped. All rose up and ran in different directions, after the manner of that reckless unorganized age, when nobody built fortresses or castles, but a man put up his thatched dwelling anyhow for a time. He thought: "Useless to waste labor and money on a hut when it will be carried off by invading Tartars anyway!" All was in commotion: some bartered oxen and plow for horse and gun and set off to join the troops; some went into hiding, driving away their cattle and carrying away what could be carried away. Sometimes they were met upon the way by men who greeted their visitors with weapons, but more often by others who had made their escape sooner. Everyone knew that it was hard to deal with the turbulent and warlike crowd that went under the name of the Dnieper Cossack army, which, for all its external freedom and lack of organization, had a discipline adapted for times of warfare. The horsemen rode on, not overstraining or overheating their horses; those on foot marched soberly behind the wagons; and the whole body moved only by night, resting by day and choosing for that purpose uninhabited places and forests, of which there were plenty in those days. Spies and scouts were sent on ahead to find out and learn where, what, and how. And often they suddenly appeared in places where they could least be expected, and then everyone there took leave of life: villages were wrapped in flames, what cattle and horses were not driven off with the troops were slaughtered on the spot. It seemed as though they were carousing rather than carrying on a campaign. One's hair stands on end nowadays at the terrible evidence of the ferocity of that half-savage age displayed everywhere by the Dnieper Cossacks. Slaughtered babes, women with breasts cut off, men set free with the skin flayed from their feet to their knees—in fact, the Cossacks paid off their old scores with interest. The prelate of one monastery, hearing of their approach, sent two monks to tell them that they were not behaving as they should, that there was an agreement between the Dnieper Cossacks and the Government, that they were guilty of a breach of their duty to the Polish King and at the same time infringing all the people's rights. "Tell the bishop from me and all the Dnieper Cossacks," said the leader, "not to be afraid: so far the Cossacks are only lighting their pipes." And soon the stately monastery was wrapped in flames and its colossal Gothic windows looked out sullenly through waves of fire. The fleeing crowds of monks, Jews, and women flooded the towns, where there was at least some hope from the garrison and armed defense of the town. The belated help sent from time to time by the Government, consisting of a few regiments, either could not find the enemy or feared them, turned their backs at the first encounter, and fled on their swift steeds. Sometimes it happened that many of the Polish generals who had been victorious in previous wars resolved on joining their forces and setting up a united front against the Cossacks. And then it was that the young Cossacks proved themselves, shunning plunder, gain, and helpless enemies, and burning to show what they could do before their older comrades and to measure themselves in single combat with some alert and boastful Pole, flaunting on his proud steed, with his wide sleeves and cloak flying in the wind. It was diverting practice; they carried off plenty of horses, trappings, expensive swords, and guns. In one month the callow fledglings had grown hardy and been completely transformed; they had become men, their features in which a youthful softness had till then been perceptible were now fierce and vigorous. And old Taras was glad to see that his two sons were among the foremost. It seemed as though Ostap were destined from birth for the career of arms and the hard discipline of warlike deeds. Never losing his head nor being disconcerted by any emergency, with a coolness almost unnatural in a lad of twenty-two, he could in one instant gauge all the hazards and circumstances of the situation, could on the spot find the means of escaping it, and in such a way as to overcome it more surely afterwards. His movements began to be marked by the confidence of experience, and the qualities of a future leader were apparent in them. His whole body was charged with energy, and there was a breadth and lionlike power about his knightly qualities. "Ah, that one with time will make a good colonel!" said old Taras to himself. "Aie, aie, he will make a good colonel and one that will outshine his father!"

Andrei was entirely absorbed in the fascinating music of the bullets and the swords. He did not know what it meant to consider or calculate, or to measure his own strength and that of others beforehand. He found in battle a wild thrill and enchantment; he seemed imbued with a joyous feeling in those moments when a man's mind is aflame, when all flits in confusion before his eyes, when heads are flying and horses falling to the earth with a crash, while he dashes, as though drunk, amid the whizz of bullets and the glitter of swords, and deals blows on all sides and does not feel those dealt him. More than once the father marveled at Andrei too, seeing how, urged on only by passionate enthusiasm, he rushed upon what a cool and prudent man would not have risked, and merely by his furious impetus achieved marvels at which veteran warriors could not but wonder. Old Taras was surprised and said: "And he is a good one too—may the devil not take him—he's not Ostap, but he's a good warrior too!"

It was decided to march straight upon the town of Dubno, where, so it was rumored, there were many wealthy inhabitants and plenty of treasure. In a day and a half the march was accomplished and the Cossacks appeared before the town. The inhabitants resolved to defend themselves to the last, and preferred to die in their squares and streets and at their thresholds, rather than admit the enemy into their homes. A high rampart of earth surrounded the town; where the rampart was lower a stone wall jutted out or a house that served as a battery or an oak palisade. The garrison was strong and felt the gravity of the position. The Cossacks eagerly tried to clamber on the rampart but were met with volleys of grapeshot. The tradespeople and inhabitants apparently did not care to remain idle and they stood in crowds on the rampart. A spirit of desperate

resistance could be discerned in their eyes; the women, too, resolutely assisted, and stones, barrels, and pots flew down on the heads
of the Cossacks, followed by boiling liquid and finally by sacks of
sand which blinded them. The Cossacks did not like to deal with
fortified places; besieging was not in their line. The leader ordered
them to retreat, and said: "It is no matter, comrades, our retreating; may I be an unclean Tartar and not a Christian if we let a
single one of them out of the town. Let them all rot with hunger,
the dogs!" The troops, retreating, surrounded the whole town, and,
having nothing better to do, spent their time in devastating the surrounding neighborhood, burning the villages and shocks of uncar-
ried wheat, turning their droves of horses into the crops yet un-
touched by the sickle, where, as luck would have it, the waving
ears were heavy with grain, the fruit of an extraordinarily good
season, that should have brought a lavish reward to all the peasants.
The besieged saw with horror from the town the destruction of the
means of their subsistence. Meanwhile the Cossacks, after drawing a
double ring with their carts around the whole town, settled down
as though at the camp in units, smoked their pipes, exchanged the
weapons they had carried off as plunder, played leapfrog or odd
and even, and looked with exasperating unconcern at the town. At
night they lighted campfires; the cooks in each unit boiled porridge
in immense copper cauldrons; a guard stood watch by the fires
which burned all night. But soon the Cossacks began to be bored by
their inactivity and prolonged sobriety, now unaccompanied by action. The leader indeed ordered the ration of drink to be doubled,
a concession sometimes made when no difficult exploits or maneuvers were required of the troops. The young men, especially the
sons of Taras Bulba, disliked such a life. Andrei was unmistakably
bored. "Silly fellow," Taras said to him, "be patient as a Cossack
and you will be a leader! He is not a good warrior who keeps up
his spirits only in affairs of great moment; he is a good warrior who
is not weary in idleness, who endures everything and will still
stick to his point, do what you will to him." But a fiery youth
cannot be like an old man: their characters are different and they
look with different eyes on the same thing.

Meanwhile Taras' regiment arrived, led by Tovkach; with him
there were two other captains, a clerk, and other officers; all the
Cossacks made up over four thousand. Among them were not a
few volunteers who had joined of their own free will without a

summons, as soon as they heard what was doing. The captains brought Taras' sons a blessing from their old mother and a cypruswood icon to each of them from the Mezhigorsky Monastery at Kiev. Both the brothers put the holy images around their necks and could not help being sad as they thought of their old mother. What did that blessing predict and tell them? Was it a blessing for victory over the enemy and then a joyous return home with booty and everlasting glory in the songs of the bandore players, or . . . ? But the future is unknown, and it stands before man like the autumn fog that rises from the swamp; in it the birds fly senselessly up and down flapping their wings, not recognizing one another, the dove not seeing the hawk, the hawk not seeing the dove, and not one knowing how far he is flying from his doom.

Ostap was already busily employed and had long ago gone off to his unit; but Andrei felt a vague depression at heart, though he could not have said why. Already the Cossacks had finished their supper. The evening had long ago faded into dusk, the air was enfolded in the marvelous night of July; but still Andrei did not go to his unit, he did not lie down to sleep, but still unconsciously he gazed at the picture spread out before him. Stars innumerable twinkled with a delicate bright gleam in the sky. The plain was covered far and wide with the wagons scattered about it with hanging pails of pitch and with all sorts of goods and provisions taken from the enemy. Beside the carts, under the carts, and at a little distance from them everywhere, the Cossacks stretched on the grass. They were all sleeping in picturesque attitudes: one with a bag for a pillow under his head, another with a cap, another simply using the ribs of a comrade. A saber, a matchlock gun, a short pipe with copper disks, a metal rod and tinder lay invariably by each Cossack. The heavy oxen lay, their legs bent under them, like great whitish masses, and might in the distance have been taken for gray rocks scattered about the slopes of the steppe. On all sides the bass snore of the sleeping warriors rose up from the grass, and the horses, indignant at their hobbled legs, answered it with resounding neighs from the steppe. Meanwhile something grand and sinister was mingled with the beauty of the July night. This was the glow of the burning villages in the distance. In one place the flame spread calmly and majestically over the sky; in another, meeting something inflammable and at once flaring up, it hissed and flew whirling upward to the very stars, and shreds of flame flickered out in the faraway sky. Here a charred and blackened monastery stood fiercely like a grim Carthusian monk, displaying its gloomy magnificence at every flash; there the monastery garden was burning; it seemed as though one could hear the trees hissing amid the coils of smoke, and, when the flame leaped up, it threw a phosphorescent purplish light on ripe clusters of plums, or turned the yellow pears to red gold, and, hanging on the wall or the branch of a tree, the body of a poor Jew or monk who had perished with the building in the flames made a patch of black among them. Above the flames the birds hovered in the distance, looking like a heap of tiny dark crosses upon a field of fire. The besieged town, it seemed, was sleeping; its spires and roofs and the palisade and the walls were all glowing with the reflection of the faraway fires.

Andrei made the round of the Cossack lines. The campfires, by which guards were sitting, were every minute on the point of going out, and the guards themselves were asleep after a meal eaten with Cossack appetite. He wondered a little at such carelessness, thinking: "It's as well that no powerful enemy is near and there is nothing to be afraid of." At last, he too went up to one of the wagons, clambered on it, and lay down on his back with his hands folded under his head; but he could not go to sleep, and lay a long time gazing at the sky: it was all open before him; the air was pure and limpid; the multitude of stars that make up the Milky Way and lie like a slanting stripe across the sky were all bathed in light. At times Andrei seemed to sink into forgetfulness and a light mist of drowsiness screened the sky from him for a minute; then it grew clear and all was visible again.

At that moment he imagined that the strange image of a human face flitted before him. Thinking that it was simply an illusion of sleep, which would at once vanish, he opened his eyes wide and saw that a wan emaciated face was really bending down to him and looking straight into his eyes. Long coal-black hair hung in loose disorder from under the dark veil flung over the head; and the strange glitter in the eyes and the deathly pallor of the dark face with its sharp features made him think that it was a ghost. He unconsciously put his hand on his gun, and said almost with a shudder: "Who are you? If you are an evil spirit, begone; if a living man, you have chosen an ill time for a jest—I will kill you with one shot."

In answer to this, the apparition put its finger to its lips and seemed to be imploring silence. He dropped his hand and looked more closely at it. From the long hair and from the neck and dark half-naked bosom he saw it was a woman. But she was not a native of those parts: her face was swarthy, wasted, and wan; her broad cheekbones stood out sharply above the sunken cheeks; her narrow eyes slanted upward. The more he gazed at her features the more he fancied something familiar in them. At last he could not refrain from asking: "Tell me, who are you? It seems to me that I know you, or have seen you somewhere."

"Two years ago in Kiev."

"Two years ago in Kiev," repeated Andrei, trying to ransack all that remained in his memory of his old student life. He looked at her intently once more and all at once cried out aloud: "You are the Tartar woman! The servant of the Polish lady, the governor's daughter . . ."

"Hush!" the Tartar woman said, folding her hands with a supplicating air, trembling all over, and at the same time turning her head to see whether anyone had been awakened by the loud cry uttered by Andrei.

"Tell me, tell me, why are you here?" Andrei, almost breathless, asked in a whisper broken by emotion. "Where is your lady? Is she still living?"

"She is here, in the town."

"In the town?" he repeated, almost crying out again, and he felt all his blood rush to his heart. "How is it she is in the town?"

"Because the old master is in the town: he has been commander in Dubno for the last year and a half."

"Is she married? But tell me—how strange you are!—how is she now . . . ?"

"She has had nothing to eat for two days."

"What?"

"None of the inhabitants have had a bit of bread for a long time, for a long time they have eaten nothing but earth."

Andrei was stunned.

"My lady saw you with the Cossacks from the town rampart. She said to me: 'Go tell him, if he remembers me, to come to me; and, if he does not, to give you a piece of bread for my old mother, for I do not want to see my mother die before my eyes. Let me die first and her after me. Clasp his knees and his feet and entreat him; he, too, has an old mother—let him for her sake give us bread!' "

Many and varied feelings woke up and burned in the youthful heart of the Cossack.

"But how is it you are here? How did you come?"

"By an underground way."

"Is there an underground way?"

"There is."

"Where?"

"You will not betray us, sir?"

"I swear by the Holy Cross!"

"Going down the steep bank and crossing the stream there among the reeds."

"And it comes out in the town?"

"Straight to the town monastery."

"Let us go, let us go at once!"

"But, for the sake of Christ and Holy Mary, a bit of bread."

"Good, you shall have it. Stay here by the wagon, or, better still, lie down on it; nobody will see you, all are asleep. I will be back at once."

And he went off to the wagon where the provisions belonging to his unit were kept. His heart was throbbing. All the past, all that had been stifled by the Cossack bivouacking, by the harsh life of warfare—all floated to the surface again, in its turn drowning the present. Again there rose up before him, as though from the depths of a dark sea, the proud girl; her lovely hands, her eyes, her laughing lips, her thick dark nut-brown hair that fell in curls over her firm breasts, and all the supple harmonious lines of her girlish figure flashed in his memory again. No, they had never died away, they had never vanished from his heart, they had merely been laid aside for a time to make room for other powerful feelings; but often, very often, the deep sleep of the young Cossack had been troubled by them, and often waking up he had lain sleepless on his bed, though he had not fully understood the cause.

He walked on, while the throbbing of his heart grew more and more violent at the mere thought that he would see her again, and his strong young knees trembled. When he reached the wagons, he had entirely forgotten what he came for: he put his hand to his forehead and stood rubbing it, trying to remember what he had to do. At last he started, filled with horror: it suddenly came into his mind that she was dying of hunger. He rushed to a wagon and put under his arm several big black loaves; but at once wondered whether that food, well fitted for a strong and by no means dainty Cossack, would not be coarse and unsuitable for her tender constitution. Then he remembered that the leader had yesterday blamed the cooks for boiling all the buckwheat flour at once for porridge when there was fully enough for three meals. In the full conviction that he would find enough in the cauldrons, he pulled out his father's field cauldron and went with it to the cook of their unit who was asleep by two immense cauldrons, under which the embers were still warm. Glancing into them, he was amazed to see that both were empty. Superhuman powers were needed to eat all they had contained, especially as there were fewer men in their unit than in the others. He glanced into the cauldrons of the other units—nothing anywhere. He could not help recalling the saying, "The Dnieper Cossacks are like children: when there is little they eat it all, when there is much they leave nothing either." What was he to do? There was somewhere, he thought, in the stores of his father's regiment a sack of white bread which they had found when plundering the bakehouse of a monastery. He went at once to his father's wagon, but it was no longer on the wagon. Ostap had taken it for a pillow and, stretched on the ground near by, he was snoring for all the plain to hear. Andrei seized the sack with one hand and pulled it away so suddenly that Ostap's head fell on the ground and he sat up half-asleep, and, with his eyes still closed, shouted at the top of his voice:

"Hold him, hold the Polish bastard and catch his horse, catch his horse!"

"Be quiet, I'll kill you!" Andrei cried in terror, swinging the sack at him. But Ostap would not have gone on speaking anyway; he subsided with a snore which set the grass quivering where he lay. Andrei looked about him timidly to see whether Ostap's outbreak in his sleep had wakened any of the Cossacks. One head with a shock of hair was raised in the next unit, but after looking around it dropped back again on the ground at once.

After waiting a few minutes, he set off with his burden. The Tartar woman was lying, hardly daring to breathe. "Get up, let us go! All are asleep, do not fear! Can you lift just one of those loaves, if I can't carry all?" Saying this, he heaped up sacks on his back and, passing by a wagon, dragged out another sack of millet, even took in his hands the loaves which he had meant to give the Tartar woman to carry, and, somewhat bowed under the weight, walked boldly between the rows of sleeping Cossacks.

"Andrei!" said old Bulba, as his son passed him. The young man's heart sank; he stood still and, trembling all over, asked softly "What is it?"

"There's a woman with you! Aye, I'll skin you when I get up! Women will bring you to no good!" Saying this he propped his head on his elbow and stared intently at the Tartar woman, muffled in her veil. Andrei stood more dead than alive and had not the courage to glance at his father's face. When at last he raised his eyes and looked at him, he saw that old Bulba was asleep again, his head lying on his open hand.

He crossed himself. The panic flew from his heart as quickly as it had swooped down upon it. When he turned to look toward the Tartar woman, she was standing before him like a statue of dark granite, all muffled in her veil, and the glow of the faraway fire flaring up gleamed only in her eyes, which looked lifeless as those of a corpse. He pulled her by the sleeve and they set off together, continually looking back, and at last went down the slope to a low hollow—almost a ravine, such as is called in some places a creek—at the bottom of which a stream trickled amid tufts of grass and sedge. Going down into this hollow, they were completely concealed from the view of the whole plain on which the Cossack camp was pitched. Anyway, when Andrei looked around he saw that the slope behind him rose up like a steep wall above the height of a man; at the top of it some stalks of wild flowers were swaying, and above them the moon was rising in the sky like a slanting sickle of bright red gold. A slight breeze rising from the steppe announced that the dawn was not far off. But nowhere was a cock-crow heard in the distance: neither in the town nor in the ruined villages around it was there one cock left. They crossed the water on a small log; the opposite bank seemed higher than the one they left behind and rose up like a cliff. It seemed as though this place was in itself a strong and trustworthy point of the town fortification; the earthen rampart was lower here and no garrison was looking out behind it. But at a little distance there rose up the thick wall of the monastery. The steep bank was all overgrown with rough grass, and in the little glade between it and the water tall reeds stood almost as high as a man. At the top of the steep bank the remains of a fence which had once enclosed a vegetable garden could be seen; in front of it were broad burdock leaves, behind it rose goosefoot, wild prickly thistle, and a sunflower tossing its head higher than them all. Here the Tartar woman slipped off her shoes and walked barefoot, pulling up her skirt, for the place was marshy and full of water. Making their way through the reeds, they stopped before a heap of brushwood and fagots. Moving aside the brushwood they found an opening in the earth—an opening hardly bigger than the doorway of a bread oven. The Tartar woman, bending her head, went in first; Andrei followed her, bending down as low as he could do to creep in with his sacks, and soon they found themselves in complete darkness.

VI

Andrei moved slowly in the dark and narrow underground passage, following the woman and carrying the sacks of bread. "Soon we shall be able to see," said his guide. "We are near the spot where I left the candlestick." And in fact the dark earthen walls began to be lighted up with a faint glimmer. They reached a rather wider place which seemed to be a chapel of sorts; anyway there was a little narrow table like an altar fixed to the wall, and a faded, almost completely effaced image of a Catholic Madonna could be discerned above it. A little silver lamp hanging before it gave a faint glimmer. The Tartar woman bent down and picked up from the ground a tall thin copper candlestick, with snuffers, a skewer to push up the wick, and an extinguisher hanging on little chains about it. Picking it up, she lighted it from the little lamp. The light grew brighter and, walking on together, now throwing a brilliant light, now casting a coal-black shadow, they were like a Gherardo delle notti.[7] The fresh handsome face of the young Cossack, brimming over with health and youth, was a striking contrast to the wan pale face of his companion. The passage grew a little wider so that it was possible for Andrei to stand a little more upright. He looked with curiosity at the earthen walls, which reminded him of the Kiev catacombs. Here, just as in the Kiev catacombs, there were recesses in the walls and coffins stood here and there; in places there were even human bones softened by the damp and dropping into powder. It

---

[7] Italian name ("Gherardo of the nights") of a Dutch painter, Gerard van Honthorst (1590-1656), who was fond of painting interiors dimly lighted. (ed.)

seemed that here, too, there had been holy men, who had hidden themselves from the turmoils, sorrows, and temptations of the world. The passage was in places very damp: sometimes there was standing water under their feet. Andrei had often to stop to let his companion rest, for she was continually overcome by weariness. Her stomach, unaccustomed to food, could not digest the small piece of bread she had swallowed, and often she stood still, motionless for several minutes.

At last a little iron door appeared before them. "Well, thank God, we have arrived!" said the Tartar in a faint voice, and she lifted her hand to knock, but had not the strength to do it. Andrei instead struck a violent blow on the door; there was a hollow echo which showed that there was a big open space beyond it. The sound changed in tone, resounding against the lofty domes. Two minutes later there was the jingle of keys and someone seemed to come down a staircase. At last the door was unlocked; they were met by a monk standing on a narrow flight of stairs with keys and a candle in his hands. Andrei involuntarily stood still at the sight of the Catholic monk, a figure that aroused hatred and contempt in the Cossacks, who treated monks more inhumanly than Jews. The monk too stepped back a little on seeing a Cossack; but a word indistinctly uttered by the Tartar woman reassured him. He locked the door after them and led them up the stairs; they found themselves under the dark lofty arches of the monastery church. At one of the altars decked with tall candlesticks and candles a priest was kneeling and praying in a low voice. Two young choristers in purple robes with white lace capes over them knelt on each side of him with censers in their hands. He prayed that a miracle might take place so that the town might be saved, so that the failing spirit of the people might be fortified, so that patience might be strengthened and the tempter confounded when he incited the people to utter weak-spirited and cowardly lamentations over their earthly misfortunes. A few women, looking like ghosts, knelt leaning with their weary heads sunk on the backs of chairs and dark wooden benches in front of them; a few men too knelt mournfully propped against the columns and pillars which supported the vaulted roof. The stained-glass window above the altar was lighted up with the pink flush of morning, and circles of light of blue, yellow, and many other hues fell from it on the floor, casting a sudden brightness into the dark church. The whole altar in its faraway recess seemed all at once bathed in brilliance; the smoke of the incense hovered in the air in a cloud of rainbow light. Andrei, from his dark corner, gazed not without wonder at the marvelous effect of light. At that moment the majestic strains of the organ suddenly filled the whole church; they grew richer and richer, swelling out and spreading out, changing into resounding peals of thunder; then, suddenly transformed into heavenly music, floated aloft under the arched roof, the melodious notes recalling the high-pitched voices of girls; then, changing again to a bass roar and thunder, died away. And the thundering echoes still floated quivering under the roofs, and Andrei, with his mouth open, marveled at the majestic music.

At that moment he felt someone pull him by the lower half of his jacket. "Come!" said the Tartar woman. They crossed the church unnoticed by anyone, and then came out into the market place which lay before it. The dawn had long been red in the sky. Everything proclaimed the rising of the sun. The market place, which was square in shape, was completely empty; there were still wooden tables standing in the middle of it showing that here, only perhaps a week before, a provision market had been held. The street—in those days there was no pavement—was simply heaped with dry mud. The market place was surrounded by little one-story stone and clay houses with wooden posts and pillars visible in their walls all the way up, with slanting crosspieces of wood, as men usually built their houses in those days and as they may be seen even today in some parts of Lithuania and Poland. They were all topped with disproportionately high roofs, and had numbers of dormer windows and apertures in the walls. On one side, almost next to the church, rose a higher building, quite different from the rest, probably the town hall or some government office. It was a two-story building, and above it there was a belvedere built in two arches, and inside it a sentry standing watch. There was a big clock face under the roof. The market place looked dead, but Andrei thought he heard a faint moan. Looking more closely, he noticed on the other side a group of two or three men lying on the ground completely motionless. He looked steadily to find out whether they were asleep or dead, and at that moment stumbled over something lying at his feet. It was the dead body of a woman, apparently a Jewess. She seemed to be young, though there was no trace of youth in her distorted and emaciated features. There was a red silk handkerchief on her head; two rows of pearls or beads adorned the lappets over her ears; two or three long curls fell below them on her wasted neck on which the veins stood out. Beside her lay a baby convulsively clutching her thin breast and pinching it with his fingers in unconscious anger at finding no milk. He no longer screamed or cried, and only from the slow heaving of his body it could be seen he was not dead or was perhaps just now expiring. They turned into the streets and were suddenly stopped by a frenzied figure, who, seeing Andrei's precious burden, flew at it like a tiger and clutched at him, shouting "Bread!" but his strength was not equal to his fury; Andrei pushed him away; he fell to the ground. Moved by compassion, he thrust on him one loaf, on which the poor wretch fell like a mad dog, gnawing at it, eating it up, and on the spot in the street expired in terrible convulsions through having been so long without food. Almost at every step they met the dreadful victims of famine. It seemed as though, unable to support their agonies within doors, many had run out into the streets in hope of finding something to sustain them. At the gate of a house sat an old woman, and no one could have said whether she was asleep or dead, or simply lost in forgetfulness; anyway she heard nothing and saw nothing, but sat motionless with her head sunk on her breast. A wasted body was hanging in a noose from the roof of another house: the poor wretch, unable to endure the agonies of hunger, had preferred to hasten his end by suicide. At the sight of this horrible evidence of starvation, Andrei could not refrain from asking the Tartar woman: "Surely they could have found something to maintain life? If a man is brought to the last extremity, then there is nothing he can do, he ought to eat what he has before looked upon with disgust: he can feed on the animals forbidden by law; anything can be turned into food at such a time."

"All are eaten up," said the Tartar woman: "every creature; you will find not a horse nor a dog nor even a mouse in the town. We have never kept stores in reserve in the town; everything used to be brought us from the villages."

"But how can you, when you are dying such a cruel death, still think of defending the town?"

"Well, maybe the commander would surrender, but yesterday morning the colonel, who is not far away, sent a hawk into the town with a note tied to it, telling us not to surrender the town, and saying that he was coming to save us with a regiment and only waiting for another colonel that they may come together. And now they are expected every minute . . . but here we are at the house."

Andrei had already from the distance seen the house, which was unlike the others and designed, so it seemed, by an Italian architect; it was built of fine red bricks and was of two stories. The windows of the lower story were set in high, jutting granite cornices; the upper story consisted of small arches forming a gallery; between them was a trellis with heraldic crests on it; there were crests too on the corners of the house. A wide outer staircase of painted bricks led into the market place itself. At the bottom of the staircase were two sentries, one on each side, who picturesquely and symmetrically leaned with one hand on the halberd standing beside them, and with the other supported their bowed heads, and so looked more like carved images than living creatures. They were not asleep nor dozing, but seemed insensible to everything. They did not even notice who went up the steps. At the top of the stairs they found a sumptuously equipped and dressed soldier holding a prayer book in his hand. He raised his weary eyes to look at them, but the Tartar woman said one word to him, and he dropped them again on the open pages of his prayer book. They went into the first room, a rather large one, which served as a waiting room, or simply as a vestibule; it was filled with people sitting in different positions around the walls; soldiers, servants, secretaries, butlers, and all the retinue required to display the grandeur of a great Polish nobleman, who was not only a soldier but also a landowner. There was the smell of a smoldering candle; two others were still burning in two immense candlesticks almost as tall as a man, standing in the middle of the room, although the morning light had for some time been looking into the broad latticed window. Andrei would have gone straight up to a broad oak door decorated with a crest and a number of carved ornaments; but the Tartar woman pulled him by the sleeve and pointed to a little door in the side wall. By this door they came out into the corridor and then into a room which he began to scrutinize attentively. The light coming through a crack in the shutter fell on something—a crimson curtain, a gilt cornice, and a picture on the wall. Here the Tartar woman bade Andrei wait, and opened the door into another room from which there came a gleam of light. He heard a whisper and a soft voice which thrilled him through and through. He caught through the open door a rapid glimpse of a graceful feminine figure with a wealth of long hair which fell on her raised arm. The Tartar woman came back and told him to go in. He had no memory of how he went in and how the door closed behind him. In the room two candles were burning and a little lamp glimmered before the holy image; under it, after the Catholic fashion, stood a tall table with steps to kneel on during prayer. But this was not what his eyes were seeking. He glanced around and saw a woman who looked as though frozen or turned to stone in rapid movement. It seemed as though her whole figure had been darting toward him and had suddenly stopped. And he, too, stood still before her in bewilderment. It was not like this that he had imagined seeing her; this was not she, not the lady he had known before; nothing in her was the same, but now she was twice as beautiful and marvelous as before; then there had been something unfinished, incomplete in her, now she was the perfect picture to which the artist has given the finishing touch. That had been a charming, frivolous girl; this was a lovely woman in all the perfection of her beauty. Every depth of feeling was expressed in her lifted eyes, not traces, not hints of feeling, but its fullest intensity. The tears not yet dry upon them veiled them with a brilliant mist which pierced the heart; her bosom, neck, and shoulders had the lovely lines of perfectly developed beauty; her hair, which had floated before in light curls about her face, was now a thick luxuriant mass, part of which was done up and part of which hung loose over the full length of her arm, and in delicate, long, beautifully curling tresses fell over her bosom. It seemed as though every one of her features was transformed. In vain he strove to find one of those which had haunted his memory—not one was the same. Terrible as was her paleness, it had not dimmed her incredible beauty; on the contrary, it seemed to give it an intense, invincibly triumphant quality. And Andrei felt awed and stood motionless before her. She, too, seemed impressed at the sight of the ruggedly handsome and manly Cossack; even though his limbs were motionless his figure seemed to reveal the ease and freedom of his movements; his eyes flashed with clear firmness, the velvety eyebrows rose in a bold arch, the tanned cheeks glowed with all the brightness of youth, and the thin black mustache shone like silk.

"No, I have not the strength to thank you fittingly, generous knight," she said, and the silvery notes of her voice quivered.

"Only God can reward you; it's not for me, a weak woman . . ." She dropped her eyes; like lovely semicircles of snow, the eyelids, edged with lashes long as arrows, hid them; her lovely face was bowed, and a faint flush suffused it. Andrei could say nothing to this; he longed to utter all that was in his heart, to utter it with all the ardor which was in his heart, and could not. He felt something sealing his lips; the sound died away from the word; he felt that it was not for him, bred in the seminary and the rough life of the camp, to answer such words, and he raged inwardly at his Cossack nature.

At that moment the Tartar woman came into the room. She had already cut the loaf brought by the young knight into slices; she brought it on a golden dish and set it before her mistress. The beauty glanced at her, at the bread, and raised her eyes to Andrei and much was said in those eyes. That softened gaze that betrayed the helplessness and inability to express the feelings that were overwhelming her was easier for Andrei to understand than any words. His heart grew light at once; he felt that the knot in it was unraveled. The feelings and emotions of his soul, which had been as though shackled, now felt released and longed to find vent in a ceaseless flow of words, when the beauty, turning to the Tartar, asked her uneasily: "And Mother? Have you taken her some?"

"She is asleep."

"And Father?"

"Yes; he said that he would come himself to thank the knight."

She took the bread and raised it to her lips. With unutterable pleasure Andrei watched her break it with her gleaming white fingers and eat. All at once he remembered the man frenzied with hunger who had expired before his eyes after swallowing a piece of bread. He turned pale, and clutching her by the arm cried:

"Enough! Do not eat more! You have eaten nothing for so long, bread will be poison to you now." And she dropped her hand at once, laid the bread on the dish and, like an obedient child, looked into his eyes. And if but some word could tell . . . but no sculptor's chisel nor painter's brush nor the lofty might of words has power to express what is sometimes seen in the eyes of a maiden, nor the tenderness which overwhelms one who looks into them.

"My queen!" cried Andrei, his heart and soul and whole being brimming over. "What do you need, what do you wish? Command me! Set me the most impossible task in the world—I will hasten to carry it out! Tell me to do what no man can do—I will do it; I will go to perdition for you! I will, I will! And to perish for you, I swear by the Holy Cross, is so sweet for me . . . but I do not know how to say this! I have three farms, half of my father's herds, everything that my mother brought my father, what she even conceals from him—all is mine. No one of the Cossacks has weapons now like mine: for the handle of my sword alone they would give me the best herd of horses and three thousand sheep. And all that I renounce, I cast aside, I throw away, I fling into the fire or the water at one word from your lips, or one sign from your delicate black eyebrow! But I know that I may be uttering foolish words and out of season, and that all this is not fitting here; that it is not for me, who have spent my life in the seminary and in the camp, to speak as men speak in the company of kings, princes, and all who are foremost in the world of knighthood. I see that you are a different creation from all of us, and all other wives and daughters of boyars are far beneath you. We are not fit to be your slaves; only the heavenly angels can serve you."

Mutely attentive, hanging on each word, the maiden heard with growing amazement the frank earnest words in which a youthful soul brimming over with strength was reflected as in a mirror. And every simple word of that speech, uttered in a voice that came straight from the heart, was full of strength. And, her lovely face thrust forward, she flung back her unruly hair, opened her mouth, and gazed at him with parted lips. Then she tried to say something, and suddenly stopped short and remembered that the knight was bound to other duties, that his father, his brother, and all his fellow countrymen stood behind him like cruel avengers; that the terrible besiegers of the town were the Cossacks, that all of them, with their town, were doomed to a cruel death . . . and her eyes suddenly filled with tears. She quickly seized her silk-embroidered handkerchief, put it to her face, and in a minute it was all wet; and a long time she sat, her lovely head thrown back, biting her lower lip with her snow-white teeth—as though suddenly stung by a poisonous snake—and keeping the handkerchief to her face that he might not see her heart-rending grief.

"Say one word to me!" said Andrei, taking her by her hand, which was soft as satin. The touch of it sent fire thrilling through his veins, and he pressed the hand that lay lifeless in his. But still she stayed motionless and neither spoke nor took the handkerchief from her face.

"Why is it you are so sorrowful? Tell me, why is it you are so sorrowful?"

She threw away her handkerchief, flung back the long hair that crept into her eyes, and poured out pitiful words, uttering them in a soft, soft voice, like the breeze that rises on a fair evening and suddenly passes over the thick reeds by the waterside; they stir, they rustle, and all at once mournful whispers rise, and the wayfarer stands still to catch them with inexplicable sadness, heeding not the fading eventide, nor the gay songs of the peasants on their homeward way from harvest and field labor, nor the faraway rumble of some passing cart.

"Do I not deserve everlasting compassion? Is not the mother unhappy who brought me into the world? Is it not a bitter fate that has fallen to my lot? A cruel torturer is my harsh destiny! It brought all men to my feet: the foremost noblemen of all Poland, the wealthiest lords, counts, foreign barons, and all the flower of our knighthood. All of them were free to love me, and every one of them would have deemed my love great happiness. I had but to lift my finger, and any one of them, the fairest, the noblest in face and in family, would have been my husband. But not for one of them has my cruel fate bewitched my heart; passing by the noblest knights of our land, my heart is lost to a stranger, to our foe. Wherefore, Holy Mother of God, for what sins, for what terrible crimes dost Thou so harshly and mercilessly chastise me? My days have been spent in abundance and luxury; the best and costliest dishes and sweet wines have been my fare. And what has it all been for? To what end? Is it to die at last a bitter death, such as the poorest beggar in the land does not die? And it is not enough that I am destined to this dreadful doom; not enough that before my own end I must see dying in insufferable agonies the father and mother to save whom I would gladly give my life twenty times over; all that is not enough: before my end I must see and hear words and love such as I have never known. He must rend my heart with his words that my bitter lot may be bitterer still, that I may grieve the more for my young life, that death may seem to me more terrible, and that I may reproach more bitterly my cruel fate and Thee —forgive my transgression—Holy Mother of God!" And when she ceased, a feeling of utter hopelessness was reflected in her face;

every feature told of gnawing grief, and everything, from the mournfully bowed brow and downcast eyes to the tears lingering and drying on her flushed cheeks, all seemed saying, "There is no happiness in this face!"

"It is unheard of, it cannot be," said Andrei, "that the fairest and best of women should suffer a fate so bitter, when she is born for everything that is best in the world to bow down before her as before a shrine. No, you shall not die! It is not for you to die; I swear by my birth and all that is dear to me in the world—you shall not die! If it comes to that, if nothing—no strength, no prayer, no valor, can turn aside the bitter fate, we will die together and I will die first; I will die before you at your lovely knees, and even in death they shall not part me from you."

"Do not deceive yourself and me," she said, softly, shaking her lovely head. "I know, and to my great sorrow know too well, that you must not love me; and I know what is your sacred duty: your father, your comrades, your country are calling you, while we are your foes."

"And what are father, comrades, and country to me?" said Andrei, tossing his head and drawing his whole figure erect like a poplar. "If that is it, then let me tell you I have no one! No one, no one!" he repeated with the voice and movement of his hand with which the buoyant, indomitable Cossack expresses determination in face of a deed incredible and impossible for another. "Who says that my country is the Ukraine? Who gave it to me for my country? Our country is what our soul seeks, what is most precious of all things to it. My country is you! Here is my country! And I shall bear it in my heart, I shall bear it in my heart to the day of my death, and we shall see, let any Cossack tear it from me! And I will give up everything in the world, renounce all, and perish for this country!"

For an instant, petrified like a lovely statue, she gazed into his eyes, then suddenly, with the exquisite feminine impulsiveness of which only a spontaneously generous-hearted woman created for noble emotion is capable, she threw herself on his neck, flinging her exquisite snow-white arms about him, and broke into sobs. At that instant there came from the street the sound of confused shouts, accompanied by the blowing of trumpets and beating of drums: but he heard them not; he felt nothing but the fragrant warmth with which her exquisite lips breathed upon him, the tears that streamed on his face, and the sweetly perfumed hair in which he was held as in a net of dark and shining silk.

Then the Tartar woman ran in with a joyful cry. "Saved, saved!" she cried, beside herself. "Our soldiers are entering the town, they have brought bread, millet, flour, and Cossack prisoners!" But neither of them heard what soldiers had come into the town, what they had brought with them, and what Cossacks were prisoners. Full of emotions transcending all things earthly, Andrei kissed the fragrant lips that pressed his cheek, and warmly those lips responded. And in that mutual kiss they felt what man feels but once in a lifetime.

And ruined is the Cossack! He is lost for all the chivalry of the Cossacks! He will see the camp no more; nor his father's farms, nor the church of God. The Ukraine will see no more of the bravest of the sons who undertook to defend her. Old Taras will tear the gray hair from his head and curse the day and hour when he begot such a son to shame him.

VII

There was noise and confusion in the camp of the Cossacks. At first no one could explain how the Polish troops had succeeded in entering the town. Then it appeared that all the men of the Pereiaslav unit, stationed in front of the side gate of the town, were dead drunk; so there was no cause for wonder that half of them had been killed and the other half taken prisoner before they all understood what was happening. While the next units, awakened by the noise, were seizing their weapons, the troops were already entering the town, and their rear guard drove off with their fire the sleepy and only half-sober Cossacks, who were pursuing them in disorder.

The leader gave the order for all to assemble, and, when all were standing in a circle and had taken off their caps, amid general silence he said: "See, comrades, what has come to pass during this night; see what drunkenness leads to! See what a disgrace the enemy has done us! If you are allowed a double portion, it's your way, it seems, to get so drunk that the enemy of Christ's army pull off your trousers and even sneeze in your face without your noticing it."

All the Cossacks stood hanging their heads, knowing that they were to blame; only one, Kukubenko, the chief of the Nezamai-kovsky unit, replied. "Wait a moment, little father!" he said, "though it is not the rule to make reply when the leader speaks before the face of the whole company; but the thing was not so, and one must say it. You have upbraided the Christian soldiers not quite justly. The Cossacks would be to blame and deserving of death if they had been drunk on the march, in the field, or at hard heavy labor; but we were sitting with nothing to do, idly sauntering to and fro before the town. There was no fast nor other Christian ordinance: what was there to prevent a man drinking in idleness? There is no sin in that. We had much better show them what it costs to attack innocent people. Before this we fought well, but now let us fight so that there will be nothing left of them."

The chief's speech pleased the Cossacks. They raised their hanging heads and many nodded approval, saying: "Well said, Kukubenko!" And Taras Bulba, standing not far from the leader, said: "Well, it seems Kukubenko has spoken the truth? What do you say to it?"

"What do I say? I say blessed the father who begot such a son: there is no great wisdom in uttering words of blame, but great wisdom in uttering a word which instead of upbraiding a man after misfortune cheers him up and gives him courage, as the spur gives courage to the horse, refreshed by a drink of water. I myself meant to say a word of comfort to you afterwards, but Kukubenko has forestalled me."

"The leader has spoken well, too!" resounded among the ranks of the Cossacks. "Well said!" repeated others. And even the elders, gray-headed like pigeons, nodded, and, twitching their gray mustaches, said quietly: "Well said!"

"Listen, comrades!" the leader went on. "To take fortresses, to scale walls and mine under them, as the German craftsmen of foreign lands do—may the devil confound them!—is not a task befitting Cossacks. But seemingly the enemy has entered the town with no great stores. They had but few carts with them. The people in the town are hungry, so they will eat it all up in no time, and there's hay which the horses need, too . . . of course I don't know, maybe some saint of theirs will pitch it to them from heaven . . . God knows about that; but their priests are good but for words. For that cause or another they will come out of the town. Divide into three detachments and stand on the three roads before the three gates. Before the chief gate five units, before each of the other gates three units. The Diadkivsy and Korsunsky units into ambush! The Tytarevsky and Tymoshevsky units to the reserve on the right side of the wagons! The Sherbinovsky and upper Steblikivsky units to the left side! And you fine fellows who are most violent in speech, step out of the ranks to provoke the enemy! The Poles are an empty-headed lot; they can't stand abuse, and maybe they will all come out of the gates this very day. Chiefs of the units, each inspect his men: if you are short of men, fill up your ranks with what are left of the Pereiaslavsky. Inspect everything anew! Give every man a cupful to sober him, and a loaf to every Cossack, though I dare say they all had enough yesterday, for, to tell the truth, they all overate themselves, till it's a wonder no one burst in the night. And here is one more warning: if any Jewish tavern owner sells a Cossack a single mug of vodka, I'll nail a pig's ear to the dog's forehead, and will hang him upside down! To work, brothers! Get to work!"

Such were the leader's orders, and all bowed low to him and went bareheaded to their wagons and their horses, and not till they were quite a long way off did they put on their caps again. All began arming themselves: they tested their sabers and their double-edged swords, poured powder from the sacks into their powder pouches, rolled the wagons to their proper places, and picked out their horses.

Going off to his regiment, Taras wondered in vain what had become of Andrei: "Was he captured with the rest and bound when he was asleep? But no, Andrei is not a man to let himself be taken prisoner alive." He was not to be seen among the slain Cossacks either. Taras was greatly perplexed, and he marched at the head of his regiment without noticing that someone had been for a good time calling him by name. "Who needs me?" he said at last, coming to himself. The Jew Yankel stood before him.

"Noble colonel, noble colonel!" the Jew said in a hurried and broken voice, as though he wanted to communicate a matter not quite unimportant: "I have been in the town, noble colonel." Taras looked at the Jew and wondered how he had managed to get into the town.

"What devil took you there?"

"I'll tell you at once," said Yankel. "As soon as I heard the uproar at dawn and the Cossacks began firing, I caught up my long coat and ran there without putting it on! I only put my arms in the sleeves on the way, because I wanted to find out as quickly as I could the reason of the uproar, the reason that the Cossacks were firing at daybreak. I ran up to the town gates at the moment when the last company was entering the town. I look, and at the head of a division, I see the standard bearer Galiandovich. He is a man I know; for the last three years he has owed me a hundred gold pieces. I followed him with the notion of getting him to pay me, and went into the town together with them."

"How could you go into the town and expect them to pay you, too?" said Bulba. "And didn't he order you to be hanged on the spot like a dog?"

"Oh, dear, yes, he meant to hang me," answered the Jew. "His servants caught me and put the rope around my neck; but I besought the gentleman; I said that I would wait for the money as long as the gentleman wished, and promised to lend him more if only he would help me to get from the other knights what they owe me; for Galiandovich—I am telling you everything, noble sir—has not a single gold piece in his pocket, though he has farms and estates and four castles and steppe land right up to the Shklov; like a Cossack he has nothing, not a kopek, and now, if the Jews of Breslau had not equipped him, he would have had nothing to go to the war in. That is why he was at the Diet. . . ."

"What were you doing in the town? Did you see our men?"

"To be sure! There are lots of our men there: Yitzchak, Rachum, Shmuel, the Jewish contractor . . ."

"Confound them, the bastards!" cried Taras, flying into a rage. "Why do you foist your scurvy kindred on me? I am asking you about our Cossacks."

"Our Cossacks I did not see; I saw only the lord Andrei."

"You saw Andrei?" cried Bulba. "What are you saying? Where did you see him? In a dungeon? In a pit? Dishonored? Bound?"

"Who would dare bind the lord Andrei? Now he is such a great knight . . . My word, yes! I did not know him! And his shoulderpieces are of gold and his armguards of gold and his breastplate is of gold and his cap is of gold and there is gold on his belt and everywhere gold and all gold. So that he is all shining in gold, like the sun in the spring when every bird chirps and sings in the garden and the wild flowers smell sweet. And the general has given him the very best horse to ride; the horse alone cost two hundred gold pieces."

Bulba was dumbfounded.

"Why has he put on other dress?"

"Because it is better, that's why he has put it on. And he is riding about and the others are riding about; and he is teaching them and they are teaching him, like the richest Polish nobleman!"

"Who has forced him to do it?"

"I don't know that anyone has forced him. Does my lord not know that he has gone over to them of his own will?"

"Who has gone over?"

"Why, the lord Andrei!"

"Gone over? Where?"

"Gone over to their side; he is one of them now."

"You are lying, you swine!"

"How can I be lying? Am I a fool to tell you a lie? Would I tell a lie to my own ruin? Don't I know that a Jew will be hanged like a dog if he tells a lie to a gentleman?"

"So according to you, then, he has sold his fatherland and his faith?"

"I don't say he has sold anything; I only said that he has gone over to them!"

"You are lying, you devil of a Jew! Such a thing has never been in a Christian land! You are mistaken, you dog!"

"May the grass grow on the threshold of my house if I am. May everyone spit on the tomb of my father and my mother, of my father-in-law, and the father of my father and the father of my mother if I am mistaken. If my lord wishes I will even tell him why he has gone over to them."

"Why?"

"The general has a beautiful daughter. Holy God, what a beauty!" Here the Jew did his utmost to portray her beauty in his own face, flinging wide his arms, screwing up his eyes, and twisting his mouth as though tasting something.

"Well, what of that?"

"It is for her sake he has done it all and has gone over. If a man is in love he is like the sole of a shoe: when it has been soaked in water, take and bend it, it will bend."

Bulba pondered deeply. He remembered how great is the power of weak woman, how many strong men she has ruined, how susceptible Andrei's nature was on that side; and for some time he stood without moving from the spot as though struck dumb.

"If my lord will listen, I will tell him more," the Jew went on. "As soon as I heard the uproar and saw that they were going in at the town gates, I snatched up a string of pearls in case of need, for there are noble and beautiful ladies in the town; and if there are noble and beautiful ladies, I said to myself, though they have nothing to eat, yet they will buy pearls. And when the gentleman's servants let me go, I ran to the general's courtyard to sell the pearls. I questioned the Tartar servingwoman. 'There will be a wedding directly,' she said, 'as soon as they drive off the Cossacks. The lord Andrei has promised to drive back the Cossacks!'"

"And you did not kill him on the spot, the son of a bitch?" cried Bulba.

"What for? He has gone over of his own will. How is the man to blame? He is happier there, so he has gone over there."

"And you saw him face to face?"

"Oh dear, yes! Such a glorious warrior! The most splendid of them all. God give him good health, he knew me at once; and when I went up to him, he said at once . . ."

"What did he say?"

"He said—first he beckoned with his finger, and then he said: 'Yankel!' 'Lord Andrei?' said I. 'Yankel! Tell my father, tell my brother, tell all the Cossacks, tell everyone that my father is no father to me now, my brother is no brother, my comrade no comrade, and that I will fight against all of them, all of them I will fight!'"

"You are lying, damned Judas!" Taras shouted, beside himself. "You are lying, you son of a bitch! You crucified Christ, you man accursed of God! I will kill you—you bastard! Be off—or you will meet your death!" Taras snatched up his sword as he said it. The terrified Jew took to his heels and fled as fast as his thin spare legs would carry him. For a long time he ran without looking back, through the Cossack camp and far away over the open plain, though Taras did not pursue him, reflecting that it was senseless to vent his fury on the first comer. Now he remembered that on the previous night he had seen Andrei walking about the camp with some woman, and he bowed his gray head and still refused to believe that so great a disgrace could have come to pass and that his own son had sold his faith and soul.

At last he led his regiment into ambush and concealed himself with them behind a wood, the only one not yet burned by the Cossacks.

Meanwhile the Dnieper Cossacks, both on foot and on horse, came out on the three roads to the three gates of the city. One after the other the chiefs filed by: the Umansky, the Popovichevsky, the Kanevsky, the Steblikivsky, the Nezamaikovsky, the Gurguziv, the Tytarevsky, and the Tymoshevsky. Only the Pereiaslavsky unit was absent. The Cossacks of that unit had drunk deep and drunk away their lives. Some awoke, bound in the foes' hands; some, without waking, had passed asleep into the damp earth; and Khlib, their chief, himself, without his trousers and upper attire, was in the Polish camp.

The Cossacks' movements were heard in the city. All streamed out on the rampart, and a picture came alive before the Cossacks; the Polish knights, one handsomer than the other, stood on the wall. Copper helmets flashed like the sun, plumed with feathers white as the swan's. Others wore light caps of pink and blue, with the tops bent over on one side, full coats with hanging sleeves embroidered with gold and garnished with little cords; some had sabers and weapons in sumptuous settings, for which their masters had paid great sums—and there were many other sumptuous things of all sorts. Foremost of all stood the colonel of the new troops in a red cap decked with gold. The colonel was a heavy man, taller and stouter than any, and the ample folds of his costly full coat barely met around him. On the other side, almost at the side gate, stood another colonel, a small dried-up man: but his keen little eyes looked out sharply from under his overhanging brows, and he turned rapidly from side to side, pointing briskly with his thin sinewy hand, and giving orders; it could be seen that in spite of his frail body he was well versed in the arts of war. Near him stood a standard bearer, a tall lanky figure with thick mustaches, with no lack of color in his face: he was a man fond of strong mead and carousing. And behind them there were many Polish nobles of all sorts, some equipped at the cost of their own gold pieces, some at the Crown's expense, some by loans from Jews, after pledging all that was left in their ancestral castles. There were not a few also of the various parasites, whom the senators used to take with them to banquets to add to their own consequence, and who stole silver goblets from the table and the sideboards, and, after being gentlemen one day, would be sitting on the coachman's box the next. There were some of all sorts. There were some who at times had not a drop to drink, but all had been equipped for the war.

The Cossack ranks stood silent before the walls. There was no gold on any one of them; there was but a gleam of it here and there on the hilts of swords and stocks of guns. The Cossacks did not like to be richly attired for battle; they wore plain coats of mail and jackets, and far into the distance could be seen the black astrakhan and red tops of their caps.

Two Cossacks rode out in front of their ranks: one quite young, the other older, both bitter in speech and not bunglers in action: Okhrim Nash and Mykyta Golokopytenko. After them rode out Demid Popovich, too, a powerful Cossack who had been at the camp for years, had been at Adrianopolis and suffered many hardships in his day—he had been burned in the fire and escaped to the camp with his head singed and blackened and his mustaches burned off—but Popovich had regained his strength, grown a love-lock over his ear, and thick pitch-black mustaches. And a bitter and biting tongue had Popovich.

"Ah, red coats on all the troops, but I should like to know whether there is any red blood in the soldiers?"

"I'll show you!" the stout colonel shouted from above. "I'll bind you all! Hand over your guns and horses, you peasants. Have you seen how I've bound your fellows captive? Bring the Cossacks onto the rampart to show them!"

And they led the Cossacks out on the rampart tightly bound with ropes. Foremost of them was the chief of a unit, Khlib, without his trousers and shirt, just as they had captured him drunk. The chief hung his head, ashamed of being naked before his own Cossacks and of having been caught like a dog, asleep. And his head had turned gray in a single night.

"Don't grieve, Khlib! We will rescue you!" the Cossacks shouted to him from below.

"Don't grieve, old friend!" the unit chief Borodaty called out: "you're not to blame that you were taken naked; a misfortune may happen to any man; the shame is theirs for displaying your nakedness."

"Your soldiers are brave at fighting men asleep, it seems," said Golokopytenko, looking up at the rampart.

"You wait a bit, we'll shave off your forelocks!" they shouted from above.

"I should like to see them shave off our forelocks," said Popovich, turning to face them on his horse, and then looking at his own men, he said: "But maybe the Poles are right: if that fat man there leads them they will all have a good defense."

"Why do you think they'll have a good defense?" said the Cossacks, knowing that Popovich doubtless had some sally ready.

"Because they can all hide behind him and no lance could get at them behind his belly!"

All the Cossacks laughed; and long afterward many of them shook their heads, saying: "Well, he is something, Popovich! If anyone can twist a word, well . . ." But what the Cossacks meant by "well" they did not say.

"Move back, move back at once from the walls!" cried the leader; for the Poles seemed exasperated by the sarcasm and the colonel waved his hand.

Scarcely had the Cossacks moved aside when there came a volley of grapeshot from the rampart. There was a stir and bustle; the gray-headed commander in chief rode up himself on his horse. The gates were opened and the troops marched out. Foremost in straight ranks the embroidered hussars rode out on their horses; after them came men in coats of mail and then those in plated armor with lances, then others in copper helmets; then the Poles of the highest nobility rode apart, each dressed after his own taste. The proud nobles would not mingle in the ranks with the others, and those of them who were not in command rode apart with their servants. Then again came rows of soldiers, followed by Galiandovich; after him came ranks of soldiers again and then the stout colonel, and in the rear the little short colonel rode last of all.

"Don't let them! Don't let them form into ranks!" shouted the leader. "All units press upon them at once! Leave all the other gates! Tytarevsky unit, attack on the flank! Diadkiv unit, attack on the other flank! Bear on them in the rear, Kukubenko, Palyvoda! Harass them, harass them and keep them apart!"

And the Cossacks rushed from all sides, attacked the Poles and threw them into disorder, and were thrown into disorder themselves. They did not even let it come to firing; the fighting was with swords and lances. All were thrown together in confusion, and every man had a chance to show his mettle.

Demid Popovich stabbed three of the rank and file with his lance and threw two Polish noblemen from their horses, saying: "Those are good horses! I've wanted to get hold of such for a long time." And he drove the horses far away into the plain, shouting to the Cossacks standing there to catch them. Then he forced his way back into the turmoil and again set upon the Poles he had thrown from their horses; one he killed, on the neck of the other he flung a noose, tied him to his saddle, and dragged him across the field, taking from him a saber with a costly hilt, and untying from his belt a whole pouch of gold pieces.

Kobita, a brave, still young Cossack, engaged in combat with one of the most valiant of the Polish army, and long they struggled. They fought hand to hand. The Cossack had already nearly vanquished his assailant and, knocking him down, stabbed him with a sharp Turkish knife in the breast: but he did not escape himself; at the same instant a hot bullet struck him on the temple. He was felled by one of the most illustrious, most handsome of the Polish knights, of an ancient princely family. Swaying like a slender poplar, he darted hither and thither on his dun-colored steed. And many more feats of knightly valor he performed: two Cossacks he hacked in pieces; he threw Fiodor Korzh, a brave Cossack, to the ground, horse and all, fired at the horse, and struck the Cossack behind the horse with his lance; he smote off many a head and many a hand, and he it was that felled the Cossack Kobita with a bullet in his head.

"That's the man I would try my strength with!" shouted Kukubenko, the chief of the Nezamaikovsky unit. Giving his horse the rein, he pounced straight upon him from behind, uttering a loud scream so that all standing by shuddered at the unnatural sound. The Pole tried to turn his horse and face him; but the horse would not obey. Terrified by the dreadful scream, he started to one side, and Kukubenko caught him with a bullet from his gun. The molten lead passed in between his shoulder blades and he fell from his horse. But even then the Pole would not yield, he still strove to deal a blow at his foe; but the hand that held the sword sank powerless to the ground. And Kukubenko, taking his heavy lance in both hands, drove it right between his blanching lips; the pike knocked out two teeth, white as sugar, cleft the tongue in twain, smashed the neckbone, and drove far into the earth. So he pinned him there to the damp earth forever. The noble blood, crimson as the guelder-rose berry, spurted up in streams and stained his yellow gold-embroidered jacket all red. Kukubenko left him and made his way with his Nezamaikovsky Cossacks to another group.

"Oh, what precious trappings he has left unstripped!" said Borodaty, the chief of the Umansky unit, riding away from his followers to the spot where lay the Pole slain by Kukubenko. "Seven Poles have I killed with my own hand, but such trappings I have not seen yet on any." And Borodaty coveted them: he bent down to take the costly armor from the dead Pole; already he had pulled out a Turkish knife, set with gems all of one hue, and untied a pouch of gold pieces from the belt, and lifted from the breast a knapsack containing fine linen, sumptuous silver, and a maiden's curl, carefully treasured in remembrance. And Borodaty did not hear the red-nosed standard bearer, whom he had thrown down once from the saddle and at whom he had had a good slash, fly up behind him. The standard bearer swung his sword and smote him on the neck as he bowed down. Greed brought the Cossack to no good; the mighty head flew off and the dead man fell headless, wetting the earth with blood far and wide. Up into the heights flew the stern Cossack's soul, frowning and indignant, and at the same time marveling that it had so quickly parted from so strong a body. The standard bearer had not time to seize the chief's head by the forelock to tie it to his saddle before a fierce avenger was upon him.

As a hawk, soaring in the sky and circling around and around on its powerful wings, suddenly hovers suspended on one spot and then darts like an arrow on the quail calling to its mate, so Taras' son Ostap pounced on the standard bearer and cast a rope about his neck. The Pole's red face flushed a deeper crimson as the cruel noose tightened upon his throat. He gripped his pistol, but his convulsively twitching hand could not guide the shot and the bullet flew at random into the plain. In an instant Ostap untied from the man's own saddle the silken cord which the standard bearer took for binding prisoners, and with his own silken cord tied his hands and his feet, fastened the end of the cord to the saddle, and dragged him across the battlefield, calling loudly to the Cossacks of the Umansky unit to go and pay the last honors to their chief.

When the Umansky Cossacks heard that their chief, Borodaty, was among the dead, they left the battlefield and ran to take his body; and on the spot began discussing whom to choose to succeed him. At last they said: "But why discuss it? We could not find a better chief than Bulba's son Ostap: it is true he is younger than all of us, but he has the good sense of an old man."

Ostap, taking off his cap, thanked all his Cossack comrades for the honor done him; he did not urge his youth nor his inexperience, knowing that they were fighting and it was no time for that, but at once led them back to the fray and showed them that they had not been wrong to choose him as chief. The Poles felt that the battle was growing too fierce; they retreated, and were racing across the plain to rally at its other end. And the short colonel waved to four fresh divisions standing apart by the very gate, and from them came a volley of grapeshot into the Cossacks: but few were hit; the bullets struck the Cossacks' cattle who were staring wildly at the battle. The panic-stricken cattle bellowed, turned toward the Cossack encampment, broke the carts, and trampled many underfoot. But at that moment Taras, bursting out of ambush with his regiment, rushed with a loud shout to intercept them. All the frantic herd turned back, terrified by his shout, and stampeded the Polish regiments, scattering the cavalry and trampling and dispersing all.

"Oh, thanks to you, oxen!" shouted the Cossacks. "You did your work on the march and now you've done fighting service, too!" And they struck at the enemy with fresh energy. They overcame many of their foes at that time. Many Cossacks showed their mettle: Metelitsia, Shilo, the two Pysarenkos, Vovtuzenko, and many others. The Poles saw that things were going badly indeed; they lowered their standards and began shouting for the city gates to be opened. The ironshod gates opened with a creak and received the exhausted and dust-covered horsemen who crowded in like sheep into a fold. Many of the Cossacks would have pushed them, but Ostap checked his men, saying: "Keep back, keep back from the walls, comrades! You must not go close to them." And true were the words he spoke, for the enemy hurled and flung down from the walls anything they could lay their hands on, and many were struck. At that moment, the leader rode up and praised Ostap, saying: "Here is a new unit chief, but he leads his troops as though he were a veteran!" Old Bulba turned around to look what new chief was there and saw Ostap on his horse at the head of all the Umansky unit, with his cap crushed on one side and the commander's staff in his hand.

"What a son you are!" he said, looking at him; and the old man was happy, and began thanking all of the troops of the unit for the honor they had shown his son.

The Cossacks retreated once more, making ready to go to the camps; and again the Poles appeared on the city rampart, this time with tattered cloaks. There were stains of gore on many costly coats, and the handsome copper helmets were thick with dust.

"Well, did you bind us?" the Cossacks shouted to them from below.

"I've this for you!" the stout colonel kept shouting from above, showing a rope; and the dusty, weary warriors still went on hurling threats, and the more defiant on both sides flung biting words at one another.

At last they all dispersed. Some, worn out with the fight, went to rest. Others sprinkled earth on their wounds and tore into bandages the kerchiefs and costly garments taken from the slain foe. Others, who were a little less weary, began gathering up the dead and paying them the last honors; with broadswords and lances they dug graves; they brought earth in their caps and jackets; they laid out their comrades' bodies with respect and scattered fresh earth upon them that the crows and fierce eagles should not peck their eyes. But the bodies of the Poles they bound by dozens to the tails of wild horses and set them loose to race over the plain, and for a long way pursued them, lashing them all the time. The frantic horses galloped over ridges and hillocks, across the hollows and watercourses, and the dead bodies of the Poles were battered on the earth and covered with blood and dust.

Then all the Cossacks sat down in circles to supper, and long they talked of the deeds and feats that had fallen to the lot of each to make an everlasting tale for strangers and posterity. It was long before they lay down to sleep; and old Taras sat wakeful longer than all, pondering what it could mean that Andrei had not been among the enemy. Had the Judas been ashamed to come out to fight against his comrades, or had the Jew deceived him, and was his son simply a prisoner? But then he remembered that Andrei's heart was excessively susceptible to women's words. He was overcome with grief, and inwardly vowed vengeance against the Polish woman who had ensnared his son. And he would have carried out his vow: he would not have heeded her beauty; he would have dragged her by her thick luxuriant hair and have hauled her across the plain among all the Cossacks. And her marvelous breasts and shoulders, dazzling as the unmelting snows that cover the mountain heights, would have been crushed on the earth, blood-stained and covered with dust. He would have torn her glorious lovely body limb from limb. But Bulba knew not what God prepares for man on the morrow, and he began sinking into slumber and at last fell asleep. But the Cossacks still talked together, and all night long the guard, sober and wakeful, stood on watch by the fires, gazing intently in all directions.

VIII

The sun had not yet reached the zenith when all the Cossacks gathered in circles. News had come from the camp that in the absence of the Cossacks the Tartars had plundered everything in it, had dug out the goods which the Cossacks kept hidden underground, had overwhelmed and taken prisoner all who were left behind, and with all the herds of cattle and droves of horses had set off straight for Perekop. Only one Cossack, Maxim Golodukha, had torn himself out of the Tartars' hands on the way, stabbed the guard, unfastened his bag of sequins, and on a Tartar horse, in Tartar dress, ridden away from his pursuers for a day and a half and two nights, ridden the horse to death, mounted another on the road, crippled that one too, and on a third reached the camp, having learned on the way that the Cossacks were at Dubno. He could only tell them that this misfortune had happened; but how it had come to pass, whether the men left behind had been carousing after the Cossack habit and been taken prisoner when they were drunk, and how the Tartars had found the spot where the treasury was buried—that he did not tell them. The Cossack was terribly exhausted, he was swollen all over, his face was burned and chapped by the wind; he sank down on the spot and fell into a deep sleep.

In such cases it was the custom with Dnieper Cossacks to pursue the raiders instantly, trying to overtake them on the road; for the prisoners might immediately be carried to the markets of Asia Minor, to Smyrna or Crete, and there was no telling in what places their Cossack heads with the long forelocks might not be seen. This was why they had assembled. They all, to the last man, stood with their caps on, for they had not come to listen to the commands of their superiors, but to consult together as equals. "Let the elders give counsel first!" they shouted in the crowd. "Let the leader give counsel!" said the others.

Then the leader, taking off his cap, not as their commanding officer but as their comrade, thanked all the Cossacks for the honor, and said: "Many among us are older and wiser in counsel, but, since you have done me the honor, my advice is not to lose time, comrades, but to pursue the Tartars; for you know yourselves what a Tartar is; they will not stand still with their plunder to await our arrival, but will dispose of it instantly, so that no trace may be found. So my advice is, go. We have had our fling here. The Poles know what the Cossacks are; we have avenged our faith so far as was in our power; there is little to be gained from the starved city. And so my advice is to go."

"Go!" rang out loudly in the Cossack ranks. But these words were not to Taras Bulba's taste, and he knitted his frowning black eyebrows, sprinkled with white, like bushes growing on the high crag of a mountainside with their tops always covered with the hoarfrost of the north.

"No, your counsel is not right," he said. "You are wrong; you seem to have forgotten that our comrades seized by the Poles are left in captivity. You would seemingly have us disregard the first sacred law of comradeship, would have us leave our mates to be flayed alive, or to be quartered and their Cossack limbs sent about from town to village, as the Poles did with the Hetman and the foremost Russian noblemen in the Ukraine. Have they not insulted our holy things enough? What are we made of? I ask you all. What is the Cossack worth who leaves a comrade in misfortune, leaves him like a dog to perish among aliens? If it has come to the point that Cossack honor is meaningless, that you will allow people to spit into your gray mustaches, to reproach you with words of infamy, then I will not risk such upbraiding. I will remain alone!"

All the standing Cossacks wavered.

"But have you forgotten, brave colonel," the leader said then, "that we have comrades in the Tartars' hands, also, that if we do not rescue them now they will be sold into lifelong slavery to heathens, which is worse than any cruel death? Have you forgotten that they have now all our treasure paid for with Christian blood?"

All the Cossacks hesitated and did not know what to say. No one of them was willing to face dishonor. Then Kasian Bovdiug, the oldest in years of all the army, stepped forward. He was held in honor by all the Cossacks; twice he had been elected leader, and in battle, too, had been a good Cossack, but for years now he had been too old to take part in any campaigns. He did not like to give advice either; what the old warrior liked best was lying on his side by the Cossack campfire, listening to tales of the adventures and campaigns of years gone by. He never took part in their talk, but only listened, pressing down with his finger the ash in his short pipe, which he never took out of his mouth. And for hours afterward he would sit screwing up his eyes, and the Cossacks did not know whether he was asleep, or still listening. He always remained behind them when there were campaigns, but this time something had roused the old man. Waving his hand in Cossack fashion, he had said: "Well! come what may! I'm coming too; perhaps I may be of some use to the Cossack cause!"

All the Cossacks sank into silence when he stepped out now before the assembly, for it was long since they had heard a word from him. Everyone wanted to know what Bovdiug would say.

"My turn has come to say a word, comrades!" was how he began. "Listen to an old man, children. The leader uttered words of wisdom; and, as the head of the Cossack army in duty bound to guard its safety and to take care of the army treasury, he could have said nothing better. I tell you that! Let that be my first speech! And now listen to what my second speech tells you. This is what my second speech tells you: Taras, the colonel, God grant him long years and may there be more colonels like him in the Ukraine, spoke a greater truth! The first duty and the chief honor of the Cossack is to be true to his comrades. Long as I have lived I have never, brothers, heard of a Cossack deserting or betraying his comrade. And both these and the others are our comrades— whether there are more or fewer of them does not matter—all are comrades, all are dear to us. So this is my counsel: let those who care more for the prisoners seized by the Tartars set off in pursuit of the Tartars, and those who care more for the friends who have been taken prisoners by the Poles, and who do not want to leave their true task, remain. The leader is in duty bound to go with the one half after the Tartars, while the other half will choose another leader. And that leader, if you care to listen to a white-headed comrade, could be no one but Taras Bulba. No one of us is his equal in valor."

So said Bovdiug and ceased; and all the Cossacks were pleased that the old man had brought them to sense like this. They all flung up their caps and shouted: "Thanks, old man! For years you have sat silent, but here at last you have spoken; well might you say when you set off on the march that you would be of use to the Cossack cause: so it has come to pass."

"Well, do you agree to it?" asked the leader.

"We all agree!" shouted the Cossacks.

"Then is the assembly over?"

"The assembly is over!" shouted the Cossacks.

"Then now listen to my orders," said the leader, and he stepped forward and put on his hat, while all the Cossacks took off their caps and stood with uncovered heads and downcast eyes, as was always done among the Cossacks when a superior officer was about to address them. "Now you must divide, comrades. Those who want to go, step to the right; those who want to remain, step to the left! Each unit chief will go where the greater number of his unit go; the lesser half of the unit will join other units."

And they all began to cross over, some to the right, some to the left. The leader passed over to the side to which the greater number of his unit had passed; the rest of the unit joined other units; and it turned out that the numbers to the right and to the left were almost equal. Among those who wanted to remain were almost the whole of the Nezamaikovsky unit, the larger part of the Popovichev-sky unit, the whole Umansky unit, the whole Kanevsky unit, the greater part of the Steblikivsky unit, the greater part of the Tymo-shevsky unit. All the others chose to go in pursuit of the Tartars. There were many brave and stalwart Cossacks on both sides. Among those who decided to go after the Tartars were: Cherevaty, a good old Cossack, Pokotypole, Lemish, Khoma Prokopovich; Demid Popovich, too, went to the right because he was a Cossack of a very restless character and would never stay long in one place; he had already tried his strength with the Poles and wanted to try it with the Tartars. The chiefs of the units were Nostiugan, Po-kryshka, Nevylychsky; and many other famous and valiant Cos-sacks longed to try their sword and mighty arm in combat with the

Tartars. There were many extremely good Cossacks also who chose to remain: the unit chiefs Demytrovich, Kukubenko, Vertykhvist, Balaban, and Ostap Bulba. Then there were many other renowned and bold Cossacks: Vovtuzenko, Cherevychenko, Stepan Guska, Okhrim Guska, Mykola Gusty, Zadorozhny, Metelitsia, Ivan Zakrutyguba, Mosy Shilo, Diogtiarenko, Sydorenko, Pysarenko, and then the second Pysarenko and the third Pysarenko, and there were many other good Cossacks. All were men who had traveled far and wide; they had marched about the Anatolian coasts, about the salt marshes and steppes of the Crimea, along all the streams big and little which fall into the Dnieper, about all the pools and islands of that river; they had been in the Moldavian, Wallachian, and Turkish lands, and navigated all the Black Sea in the double-ruddered Cossack boats; in fifty such boats drawn up in a row they had attacked richly laden ships; they had sunk not a few of the Turkish galleys, and much powder they had fired in their day. Many a time they had torn up expensive silks and velvets for leg wrappers; many a time they had stuffed the purses in their trousers' girdles with sequins of pure gold. And there is no reckoning the wealth, enough to last another man a lifetime, which each one of them had squandered on drink and debauchery. They threw everything away in Cossack style, treating everybody and hiring musicians that everything in the world might be gay. Yet even now few of them had no hoard of wealth buried—mugs, silver ladles, and bracelets—under the reeds on the isles of the Dnieper that the Tartars might not succeed in finding it, if by ill-luck they made an unexpected attack on the camp; but it would be hard for the Tartars to find it, for the owner himself had by now almost forgotten where it was buried. Such were the Cossacks who prepared to remain and take vengeance on the Poles for their trusty comrades and the Christian faith.

The old Cossack Bovdiug, too, preferred to remain with them, saying: "I'm too old to pursue the Tartars, but this is the place in which to die a good Cossack death. Long have I prayed to God that when my time comes to end my life I may end it warring for a holy and Christian cause. And so it has come to pass. There could be in no other place a more glorious end for an old Cossack."

When all were divided and standing in two rows on opposite sides, the leader passed between them and said: "Well, comrades, is the one side content with the other?"

"All are content, old man!" answered the Cossacks.

"Well, then, kiss each other and say farewell, for God knows whether it will be your lot to meet again in this life. Obey your chief and do what you know yourselves: you know yourselves what Cossack honor dictates."

And all the Cossacks kissed one another. First the chiefs began, and, holding aside their gray mustaches, kissed each other three times, took each other's hands, and held them tight; each wanted to ask the other: "Well, comrade, shall we see each other again?" But they did not ask, they were silent, and both gray-headed warriors sank into thought. And all the Cossacks said farewell to one another knowing there was much work ahead for both; they could not, however, separate at once, but they had to wait for the darkness of night that the enemy might not see that their numbers were diminished. Then they all went off to dinner with their separate units.

After dinner all who had the journey before them lay down to rest and had a long sound sleep, as though feeling that it might be the last time they could sleep so freely. They slept till sunset: when the sun had gone down and it was beginning to get dark, they began greasing the cart wheels. After equipping themselves they sent the baggage on ahead and, taking off their caps once more to their comrades, set off quietly after the wagons; the cavalry quietly, with no shouting or whistling to the horses, tramped lightly after the foot soldiers, and quickly they vanished in the darkness. Only the hollow ring of the horses' hoofs and the creaking of the wheels, which had perhaps not been properly greased, resounded in the darkness of the night.

Their comrades, left behind, still waved their hands though nothing could be seen. And when they turned and went back to their places, when, as the stars came out, they saw that half the carts were gone, that many, many comrades were lost to them, everyone felt sad at heart, and none could help growing melancholy, and bowing their reckless heads.

Taras saw how troubled were the Cossack ranks and how a gloom, unseemly in the brave, was slowly overcoming them, but he said nothing; he wanted to give them time to get over the sadness of parting from their comrades. Meanwhile in silence he prepared himself to rouse them all at one moment by uttering the Cossack battle cry, so that courage might come back anew to the heart of each with greater force than before, a revitalization of which only the Slav race is capable, that richly endowed, vigorous race which, compared with all others, is as the ocean to shallow rivers; in time of tempest it is all uproar and commotion, tossing and flinging up billows as no impotent river can; in calm, still weather it stretches far and wide its limitless glassy surface, fairer than any river, an endless joy to the eye.

And Taras bade his servants unload one of the wagons that stood apart from the rest. It was larger and stronger than any of the others; its thick wheels were covered with strong double bands of iron; it was heavily laden, covered with horsecloths and strong ox-leathers and bound with stiffly tarred ropes. In the wagon were barrels and kegs of excellent old wine which had lain long in Bulba's cellars. He had held it in reserve for a solemn occasion, so that, if a great moment came and some deed worthy to be handed down to posterity should be awaiting them, every single Cossack should have a drink of precious wine, so that at a great moment a man might rise to the occasion. Hearing their colonel's command, the servants rushed to the wagon; with their broadswords they cut the strong cords, took off the stout ox-leathers and the horsecloths, and brought out the barrels and the kegs.

"All of you take as much as you want," said Bulba. "Each use what he has, ladle or bowl with which he waters his horse, or gauntlet, or cap, and if there's nothing better, then simply cup your hands."

One Cossack used a ladle, one a bowl for giving drink to the horses, another a gauntlet, another a cap, while some simply cupped their hands. Bulba's servants, going back and forth between the ranks, poured out from the barrels and the kegs for all. But Taras bade them await the signal for all to drink at once. They could see that he wanted to say something. Taras knew that strong as the good old wine was in itself and well fitted to fortify the spirit, yet if the right word went with it, the power of the wine and the spirit would be doubly strengthened.

"I am treating you, comrades!" said Bulba, "not in honor of your having made me your commander, great as such an honor is, nor in honor of our leave-taking from our comrades; no, at another time either would have been fitting, but a very different moment awaits us now. Deeds of great endeavor, of great Cossack valor, are awaiting us! And so, comrades, let us drink all together, let us drink, first of all, to the holy Orthodox faith, that the time may come at last when it will spread over the whole world and everywhere there may be one holy religion and all the pagans on earth will become Christian! And at the same time let us drink, too, to the camp, that long it may stand to the destruction of all the heathen world, that it may send out everywhere young heroes, each better, each finer than the last. And let us drink, too, to our own glory, that our grandsons and their sons after them may tell how once there were men who were not false to their comrades and did not betray them. So to our faith, comrades, to our faith!"

"To our faith!" all who stood in the front ranks boomed out with their deep voices. "To our faith!" Those further away took it up—and all, old and young, drank to their faith.

"To the camp!" said Taras, and raised his hand high above his head.

"To the camp!" came the deep echo in the foremost ranks. "To the camp!" the old men said quietly, twitching their gray mustaches; and with a flutter like young falcons the young Cossacks repeated: "To the camp!" And the plain heard far away the Cossacks honoring their camp.

"Now the last drink, comrades, to glory and to all the Christians in the world!"

And all the Cossacks to the last man tossed off the last drop to glory and to all Christians in the world. Long afterward it was repeated through all the ranks among all the units: "To all the Christians there are in the world!"

By now their drinking vessels were empty and still the Cossacks stood with their hands raised; though the eyes of all, sparkling with the wine, looked gay, yet they were full of brooding thought; it was not of gain and the booty of war that they were thinking now, nor were they wondering who would be lucky in winning gold pieces, costly weapons, embroidered coats, and Circassian horses. They were looking into the future, like eagles sitting on the topmost crags of rocky mountains, high precipitous mountains, from which they can see the boundless expanse of the ocean, dotted with galleys, ships, and all manner of vessels like tiny birds in the sky, and bordered by faintly visible strips of coast with towns on the shore like tiny insects, and sloping forests like fine grass. Like eagles they scanned all the plain around them and looked into their future that grew blacker in the distance. The whole plain with its fields and roads will be covered with their bleaching bones, be richly bathed in their Cossack blood and strewn with broken wagons, shattered swords, and splintered lances; far and wide will lie, scattered, their heads with hanging mustaches and long forelocks tangled and stiff with blood; the eagles will fly down to peck and tear out their Cossack eyes. But there will be great comfort in a deathbed so spacious and free! Not one noble deed will perish, and the Cossack glory will not be lost like the little grain of powder from the musket barrel. The bandore player will come with the gray beard over his chest, a white-headed old man, though maybe still full of ripe manhood, prophetic in spirit, and he will say his rich powerful word about them. And the tale of them will race over the whole world, and all who are born hereafter will talk of them: for a mighty word resounds far and wide like the sonorous copper of the bell into which the craftsman has blended much pure precious silver, that its lovely chime may ring out afar through cities, hovels, palaces, and plains, calling all alike to join in holy prayer.

IX

No one in the city had learned that half of the Cossacks had set off in pursuit of the Tartars. From the tower of the town hall the sentinels only noticed that some of the wagons were moving out beyond the forest, but they thought that the Cossacks were preparing to make an ambush; the French engineer thought the same. Meanwhile the leader's words were coming true, and a shortage of provisions was being felt in the city: as was common in past times the soldiers had not considered how much they would need. They tried to make a sortie, but half of the bold men who took part in it were slain on the spot by the Cossacks, and the other driven back into the city without having gained anything. The Jews, however, took advantage of the sortie and sniffed out information: where the Cossacks had gone and for what purpose, and under which leaders, and how many of them had departed and how many of them had been left behind, and what they were thinking of doing —in fact, within a few minutes everything was known in the town. The commanders recovered their spirits and prepared to give battle: Taras saw it at once from the commotion and uproar in the city, and he worked zealously, drew up his men, gave orders, and stationed the units in three camps, surrounding them with the wagons by way of barricades—a form of battle in which the Dnieper Cossacks were invincible; he commanded two units to prepare an ambush; he covered part of the plain with short stakes, broken weapons, and splinters of lances, intending if possible to drive the enemy cavalry there. And when all was done that was needed, he made a speech to the Cossacks, not to encourage them and renew their vigor, but simply because he desired to utter all that was in his heart.

"I want to tell you, friends, what is meant by our comradeship. You have heard from your fathers and your grandfathers in what honor our land was once held among all men; she let the Greeks see what she could do, and took tribute from Constantinople, and her cities were rich, and her temples, and her princes were of Russian birth, her own princes and not Catholic heretics. All that was taken by the infidels, all was lost. We were left destitute, and, like a widow when her strong husband is dead, our country was destitute as we were! It was in those days that we, comrades, clasped our hands in brotherhood! It is on that that our comradeship stands! Nothing is holier than the love of comrades. The father loves his child, the mother loves her child, the child loves its father and mother; but that is not the same, brothers; the wild beast too loves its offspring, but only man can be akin in soul, though not in blood. There have been comrades in other lands, too, but such comrades as in Russia there have never been. More than one of you has had occasion to be for a little while in foreign lands; you see that there, too, are men! God's creatures, too, and you speak with them as with your own fellows; but when it comes to uttering a word from the heart—no! You see they are clever people, but not the same; they are men like us but not the same! No, comrades, to love as the Russian heart can love—to love not with the mind or anything else, but with all that God has given you, all that is in you —Ah! . . ." said Taras, and he waved his hand while his gray head trembled and his mustache twitched. "No!" he said. "No one can love like that! I know that mean ways have come into our land now; men think only of having sheaves of grain and stacks of wheat and of their droves of horses, and of their mead sealed up safe in their cellars. The devil knows what pagan habits they are adopting; they disdain their own language, they do not care to talk with their own people; they sell their own countrymen, as men sell a soulless beast in the market. The favor of an alien king, and, indeed, not of a king, but the paltry favor of a Polish nobleman who kicks them in the face with his yellow boot, is more precious to them than any brotherhood. But even the lowest wretch, whatever he may be, even though he may be groveling in grime and servility, even he, comrades, has a grain of Russian feeling; it will awaken one day—and he, poor wretch, will clasp his hands in horror, will clutch at his head cursing aloud his abject life, ready by tortures to expiate his shameful deeds. Let them all know what comradeship means in Russia! If it comes to dying, not one of them will have the luck to meet with such a death! Not one, not one! Mice like them can't rise to that!"

So spoke the chief and, when he ended his speech, his head which had grown silvery in Cossack service still trembled. All who stood around were deeply moved by such a speech, which went straight to their hearts; the eldest in the ranks stood motionless, their gray heads bowed; a tear quietly gathered in their old eyes; they slowly wiped it away with their sleeve. And then all, as though by common agreement, waved their hands at the same instant and tossed their heads. Clearly old Taras had brought back to them much that was familiar and best in those who had gained wisdom by sorrow, toils, daring, and all the hardships of life, and stirred those whose youthful souls, pure as a pearl, understood much instinctively, to the everlasting joy of the old parents who gave them life.

Already the enemy's troops were marching out of the city to the din of drums and the blowing of trumpets, and the Polish nobles, with their arms akimbo, rode forth, surrounded by innumerable servants. The stout colonel was giving orders. As they began in close ranks to advance upon the Cossack camps, with flashing eyes and glittering copper armor, they took aim with their rifles. As soon as the Cossacks saw that they had come within reach of their guns, they all fired in return, unceasingly. The clamor floated over all the surrounding fields and meadows, blending into one continuous roar: the smoke covered the whole plain. The Cossacks still fired without taking breath; those in the rear did nothing but load and hand the weapons to those in the front ranks, so that the enemy were amazed and could not understand how the Cossacks fired without loading their guns. By now nothing could be seen for the dense smoke in which both armies were wrapped; no one could see how first one and then another dropped in the ranks. But the Poles felt that the bullets were flying thickly and that things were getting hot; and when they staggered back to move out of the smoke and look about them, many were missing from their ranks; while of the Cossacks only perhaps two or three were killed out of a hundred. And still the Cossacks went on firing without stopping. Even the French engineer marveled and had never seen the like, saying on the spot before all of them: "They are gallant fellows, the Dnieper Cossacks! That's how others should fight in other lands!" And he advised the Poles to turn their cannon at once upon the camp. Loud was the roar from the throats of the iron cannon; the earth trembled, resounding afar, and twice as much smoke rolled over the plain. Men smelled the gunpowder in the squares and streets of cities far and near. But the Poles aimed too high, the blazing hot balls made too wide a sweep; tearing through the air, they flew over the heads of those in the camp and sank deeply into the ground, ripping and flinging up the black earth. The French engineer tore at his hair at such blundering and began firing the cannon himself, disregarding the incessant hail of bullets from the Cossacks.

Taras saw from a distance the danger threatening the Nezamaikovsky and Steblikivsky units, and he shouted in a booming voice: "Quickly, away from the wagons! and let each man mount his horse!" But the Cossacks would not have had time to carry out either command if Ostap had not rushed into the very midst of the Polish gunners; he beat out the fuses of six gunners, but four he could not cope with; the Poles drove him back. Meanwhile the Frenchman himself took a fuse in his hand to fire off the biggest cannon, which no one of the Cossacks had seen before. Terrible it looked with its huge throat, and a thousand deaths looked down from it: and when it boomed out, and after it three others, making the earth shake four times with hollow echo, terrible was the destruction they dealt! Many an old mother will sob for her Cossack son, beating her bony hands on her aged bosom; many a widow will be left in Glukhov, Nemirov, Chernigov, and other cities. She will run out every day to the market place, scanning all who pass by, looking into the face of each one of them, seeking for one dearer than all; but many warriors will pass through the town and never will she find among them the one dearer than all.

It was as though half of the Nezamaikovsky unit had never been! As suddenly as a field, where every ear of wheat shines bright as a heavy gold piece, is beaten down by the hail, so they were beaten down and laid low.

How the Cossacks raged! How they all rushed to the rescue! How the chief Kukubenko boiled with fury seeing that more than half of his unit was no more! With those who were left he fought his way into the midst of the fray. In his wrath he chopped into mincemeat the first Pole he came upon; many he flung down from their horses, driving his lance through rider and horse; he made his way to the gunners and carried off one cannon. Then he saw the Umansky chief was busy, and Stepan Guska was already capturing the chief cannon. He left those Cossacks and returned with his men to another part where the enemy were thickest: where the Nezamaikovsky Cossacks passed they left an open way, where they turned there was an open space! It could be seen that the ranks were thinner and that the Poles had fallen in stacks. Vovtuzenko was by the wagons, while Cherevychenko was in front, and Diogtiavenko was at the furthest wagons, and beyond him was the chief Vertykhvist. Diogtiavenko had tossed two Poles on his lance, but fell at last on a third who was not easy to overcome. The Pole was resourceful and stalwart, he was adorned with sumptuous accouterments, and brought with him no less than fifty servants. He pressed Diogtiavenko hard, felled him to the ground, and as he swung his sword over him, shouted: "There is not one among you, dogs of Cossacks, who would dare to face me in combat!"

"Here is one!" said Mosy Shilo, and he stepped forward. He was a mighty Cossack; more than once he had been in command on the sea and had suffered many hardships. The Turks had captured him with his followers at Trebizond and had taken them all as galley slaves, had kept them with iron chains on their arms and legs, given them no grain for weeks at a time, and nothing to drink but putrid seawater. The poor prisoners had suffered and endured it all rather than give up their Orthodox faith. But their chief, Mosy Shilo, could not hold out; he trampled underfoot the holy law, bound the unholy turban around his sinful head, gained the confidence of the Pasha, became the steward on the ship, and was put in charge of all the prisoners. Greatly the poor captives grieved over it, for they knew that, if their own comrade would betray his faith and go over to the oppressors, their lot would be harder and more bitter in his power than under any other infidel; and so indeed it came to pass. Mosy Shilo put them all into fresh chains, three in a row, bound them with cords that cut them to their very bones; he beat them with blows upon their necks. And when the Turks, delighted at having gained such a servant, began feasting and, forgetting their own religious law, all got drunk, he took all the sixty-four keys and gave them to the prisoners that they might unlock their fetters, cast them with their chains into the sea, take up swords instead, and slaughter the Turks. The Cossacks took much booty then and returned with glory to their country, and long afterward the bandore players sang the praises of Mosy Shilo. He would have been elected leader, but he was a peculiar Cossack. Sometimes he performed exploits such as the best of them would not have dreamed of; at other times some crazy whim took possession of him. He squandered everything in drink and revelry, was in debt to everyone in the camp, and stole, moreover, like a gutter thief; he would by night carry off all the equipment of a Cossack from another unit and pawn it. For such a shameful deed he was tied to a post in the market place and an oak cudgel was put beside him, so that every man might deal him a blow according to his strength: but there was not one among all the Cossacks who would lift the cudgel against him, for they all remembered his services in the past. Such was the Cossack Mosy Shilo.

"There are men who can destroy you, dog!" he said, setting upon him. And how they hacked at each other then! And the shoulderpieces and breastplates of both were dented by the blows. The Polish foe cleft Shilo's coat of mail, driving the blade right into his body; the Cossack's shirt was stained red. But Shilo heeded it not; he swung his sinewy arm (he had a powerful muscular arm) and dealt the Pole a blow upon the head. The copper helmet flew in pieces, the Pole staggered and fell with a thud, and Shilo began hacking and quartering the stunned foe. Slay him not, Cossack, but rather turn around! The Cossack did not turn, and one of the slain man's servants stabbed him in the neck with a knife. Shilo turned and the bold fellow would have been badly handled, but he vanished in the smoke. From all sides came the sound of guns. Shilo staggered, and felt that his wound was mortal. He fell to the ground, put his hand on his wound, and said, turning to his comrades: "Farewell, comrades! May Holy Russia live forever, and may her glory be eternal!" And he closed his dimming eyes, and his Cossack soul soared out of his rough body. But by then Zadorozhny had ridden out with his men, Vertykhvist had broken the ranks, and Balaban had moved forward.

"Well, comrades," said Taras, calling to the leaders of the units, "is there powder left in your flasks? Has the Cossack might failed? Are the Cossacks giving way?"

"We have powder still in our flasks, old man; the Cossack might has not failed yet! The Cossacks are not giving way!"

And the Cossacks pressed hard; all the enemy's ranks were thrown into confusion. The short colonel sounded a rallying call, and ordered eight painted standards to be unfurled to gather his men, who were scattered far and wide over the plain. All the Poles hastened to the standards, but before they had time to form into ranks again the chief Kukubenko with his Nezamaikovsky Cossacks dashed into their midst and flew straight for the fat colonel. The colonel could not hold out, but, turning his horse, put it into a gallop; and Kukubenko pursued him far into the plain, not letting him join his regiment. Seeing this from a unit on the flank, Stepan Guska galloped to intercept him, a noose in his hand, riding with his head on his horse's neck, and seizing the moment, with one throw he cast the noose about the Pole's neck. The colonel turned crimson, clutching at the rope with both hands and struggling to tear it apart, but a mighty thrust drove the fatal lance straight into his stomach. There he was left pinned to the earth. But Guska fared no better! The Cossacks hardly had time to look around when they saw Stepan Guska lifted on four lances. The poor Cossack had only breath to say: "Down with all foes, and may Russia rejoice forever and ever!" And with that he gave up his soul.

The Cossacks looked around, and on one side the Cossack Metelitsia was entertaining the Poles, knocking down one and then another; while on the other side the chief Nevylychky and his Cossacks were pressing them hard; while at the wagons Zakrutyguba was turning the enemy and beating them; while Pysarenko the third had already driven back a whole crowd from the furthest wagons. In another place there was hand-to-hand fighting on the wagons.

"Well, comrades," their chief Taras shouted to them as he rode ahead of them all, "have you still powder left in the flasks? Is the Cossack force still strong? The Cossacks are not giving way yet?"

"We've still powder left in our flasks; the Cossack force is still strong; the Cossacks are not giving way yet!"

But Bovdiug had fallen from the wagon. The bullet had caught him just under the heart; yet the old man rallied all his strength and said: "I am not sorry to part with life. God grant every man such a death! May Russia be glorious to the end of time!" And Bovdiug's soul fled to the heavenly heights to tell the old men who had departed long before how men can fight in Russia and, better still, how they can die for their holy faith.

Balaban also fell to the ground soon after. Three mortal wounds were dealt him from a spear, from a bullet, and from a heavy broadsword. He was one of the most valiant Cossacks; many exploits he had performed when in command of expeditions by sea, but most famous of all was his raid on the coasts of Anatolia. That time the Cossacks carried off many sequins, precious Turkish possessions, robes and trappings of all sorts, but they met with trouble on their homeward way: they came, poor fellows, under Turkish fire. When the ship fired at them, half the boats whirled around and turned over, throwing more than one Cossack into the water; but the reeds bound to the sides saved the boats from sinking. Balaban rowed off as fast as he could, steered straight toward the sun, and so could not be seen by the Turkish ship. All the night after, with ladles and with their caps they baled out the water, stuffing up the broken places; from their Cossack trousers they cut out sails, and so sailed off and escaped from the swift Turkish ship. And not only did they reach the camp unharmed, but brought with them a gold embroidered chasuble for the Archimandrite of the Mezhigorsky Monastery at Kiev, and for the icon of the Church of the Intercession at camp they brought a setting of pure silver. And long afterward the bandore players celebrated the Cossacks' success.

Now he bowed his head, feeling the death agonies, and said quietly: "It seems to me, comrades, I am dying a fine death: seven have I slain with the sword, nine I have stabbed with the lance, I have trampled under my horse's hoofs plenty, and I know not how many I have shot. May Russia flourish forever . . ." And his soul fled from his body.

Cossacks! Cossacks! abandon not the flower of your army! By now Kukubenko was surrounded: only seven men were left of the Nezamaikovsky unit, and by now they were overpowered; already their chief's garments were stained with blood. Taras himself, seeing his plight, hastened to his assistance. But the Cossacks were too late: a lance had stabbed him to the heart before the enemy surrounding him were driven off. Slowly he sank into the arms of the Cossacks who supported him, and the young blood spurted out in a stream like precious wine brought in a glass vessel from the cellar by careless servants who slip at the entrance and shatter the costly flagon, the wine spilling upon the ground; and the master, running up, clutches his head in despair, since he has kept it for the best moment of his life, so that, if God should grant in his old age a meeting with the comrades of his youth, they might celebrate together those old other days when men made merry otherwise and better. . . . Kukubenko looked around and said: "I thank God that it is my lot to die before your eyes, comrades! May men better than we live after us, and may Russia, beloved of Christ, flourish forever . . . !" And his young soul fled. The angels received it in their arms and bore it to heaven. It will be good for him there. "Sit at my right, Kukubenko!" Christ will say to him, "thou hast not betrayed thy comrades; thou hast wrought no deed of dishonor; thou hast forsaken no man in trouble; thou hast guarded and saved My Church."

Kukubenko's death was a blow to everyone. The Cossack ranks were by now very thin; many, very many valiant men were missing; but still the Cossacks stood firm and held their own.

"Well, comrades," Taras shouted to the units that were left, "is there still powder in your flask? Are not your sabers blunted? Is not the Cossack force weary? Have not the Cossacks given way?"

"We still have powder, old man; our sabers are still sharp; the Cossack force is not weary; the Cossacks have not given way yet!"

And the Cossacks charged again as though they had suffered no losses. By now only three leaders of the units were left alive; streams of blood ran red on every side; the mounds of Cossack and Polish dead rose high. Taras glanced at the sky and already a string of vultures stretched across it. Well, there would be a harvest for someone! And over there Metelitsia was tossed on a lance, and the head of one of the Pysarenkos rolled to the ground, severed from the body, and Okhrim Guska, overwhelmed and thrown to the earth, was hacked in quarters. "Now!" said Taras, and waved his handkerchief. Ostap understood the signal and, dashing out of ambush, charged the cavalry. The Poles could not stand against his furious onslaught, and Ostap chased and drove them straight to the place where stakes and broken lances were driven into the ground. The horses stumbled and fell and the Poles flew over their heads. At the same moment the Cossacks who stood last behind the wagons, seeing that the Poles were within range, opened fire. All the Poles were overwhelmed and thrown into confusion, and the Cossacks' spirits rose. "Victory is ours," the voices of Cossacks rang out on all sides, trumpets were sounded, and a banner of victory was unfurled. The defeated Poles were running in all directions seeking cover.

"Oh, no, not quite victory yet!" said Taras, looking toward the city gates, and he was right.

The gates were flung open and a regiment of hussars, the flower of all the cavalry regiments, darted out. All were mounted on dun-colored stallions, all alike; at their head rode a young noble more alert and handsomer than any; his black hair strayed from under his copper helmet; a costly scarf embroidered by the hands of the greatest beauty in the city was twisted around his arm. Taras was thunderstruck when he saw that it was Andrei. And Andrei, meanwhile, caught up in the fire and ardor of battle, eager to be worthy of the gift tied to his arm, bounded forward like a young wolf-hound, the handsomest, swiftest, and youngest of the pack. The practiced huntsman calls to him—and he races on, his legs forming one straight line in the air, his whole body slanting sideways as he flings up the snow and a dozen times runs beyond the hare in the heat of his course. Old Taras stood still and looked at the way in which he cleared a road before him, dispersing the Cossacks, hacking and dealing blows to right and to left. Taras could not stand it and shouted: "What? Your own men? You are striking your comrades, you devil's son?" But Andrei saw not who was before him, he knew not whether they were his comrades or others; he saw nothing. Tresses, long tresses were all that he saw, and a breast like a river swan and a snowy neck and shoulders, and all that is created for wild embraces.

"Hey, Cossacks! Lure him into the wood, lure him!" shouted Taras. And at once thirty of the swiftest Cossacks undertook to lure him there. And, setting straight their high caps, they galloped on their horses right across the path of the hussars. They struck the foremost on the flank and threw them into confusion, parted them from those behind, dealt a blow to two or three, while Golo-kopytenko dealt Andrei a blow flat on the back, and at once the Cossacks galloped away from them at their utmost speed. How Andrei flew at them! How the young blood boiled in all his veins! Driving his sharp spurs into his horse, he dashed full speed after

the Cossacks, not looking back, not seeing that only twenty men
were following him; while the Cossacks galloped like the wind
and made straight for the wood. Andrei overtook them and had
almost caught Golokopytenko, when suddenly a mighty hand
clutched at his horse's bridle. Andrei looked around: Taras was
facing him! The young man trembled all over and turned pale, as a
schoolboy who has heedlessly been teasing a companion and has
been struck by him on the forehead with a ruler flares up, leaps
from the bench in a rage and chases his terrified schoolfellow,
ready to tear him to pieces, when he suddenly stumbles against
the teacher as he is entering the classroom: instantly his rage is over
and his impotent fury subsides. So Andrei's anger passed away instantly, as though it had never been. And he was aware of no one
but his terrifying father.

"Well, what are we going to do now?" said Taras, looking him
straight in the face. But Andrei stood with downcast eyes and said
nothing in reply.

"Well, son, have your Poles helped you?"

Andrei was speechless.

"So you would betray? Betray your faith? Betray your comrades? Stop! Dismount!"

Obediently, like a child, Andrei slipped off his horse and stood
more dead than alive before Taras.

"Stand still and do not stir! I begot you. I will kill you!" said
Taras, and stepping back he took the gun from his shoulder. Andrei
was pale as a sheet; his lips could be seen to move and he uttered a
name, but it was not the name of his country, nor of his mother or
brother; it was the name of the Polish beauty. Taras fired.

Like a stalk of wheat cut by the sickle, like a young lamb with
the deadly steel at its heart, Andrei hung his head and sank upon
the grass, not uttering one word.

His murderer stood still, and long he gazed at the lifeless corpse.
He was handsome even in death; his manly face, lately so full of
strength and irresistible charm for women, was still magnificent;
the black eyebrows like mourning velvet cast a shadow over his
blanching features.

"What a Cossack he might have been!" said Taras. "Tall in
stature and black-browed and a face like a nobleman, and his arm
was strong in battle! He has perished! Dying shamefully like a vile
dog!"

"Father, what have you done! Was it you who killed him?" said Ostap, riding up.

Taras bowed his head.

Steadily Ostap gazed into the dead man's eyes. He grieved for his brother and said at once: "Let us give him honorable burial, father, that the enemy may not cast ignominy upon him, nor birds of prey tear his body."

"They will bury him without our help!" said Taras. "There will be plenty to weep and mourn for him!"

And for two minutes he pondered whether to leave him to be torn by the wolves or to honor in him the knightly valor which a brave man ought to respect in anyone, when he saw Golokopytenko galloping up to him: "Bad news: the Poles are reinforced, fresh troops have come to their support!" Before Golokopytenko had finished speaking, Vovtuzenko galloped up: "Bad news: more reinforcements are coming . . . !" Before Vovtuzenko had finished Pysarenko ran up without his horse, crying: "Where are you? The Cossacks are looking for you, the chief Nevylychsky is slain, Zadorozhny is slain, Cherevychenko is slain; but the Cossacks stand firm. They do not want to die without looking at your face; they want you to glance at them before the hour of death."

"Mount, Ostap!" said Taras, and he made haste that he might find the Cossacks still there, that he might yet look upon them and that they might see their chief again before their death. But they had not ridden out of the wood before the forces of the enemy had surrounded the wood on all sides, and everywhere between the trees horsemen appeared with swords and lances.

"Ostap! Ostap! Do not surrender!" shouted Taras, and drawing his sword he began to tackle the first he came upon. But six had pounced on Ostap all at once. But it was an unlucky hour for them, it seemed: the head of the first flew off; the second was sent whirling back; the third had a thrust from a lance in his ribs; the fourth was more daring: he bent his head to escape a bullet and the lead went into his horse's chest—the frenzied beast reared, fell to the earth, and crushed his rider under him. "Well done, son! Well done, Ostap!" shouted Taras; "here I am behind you!" And he still beat off his assailants. Taras struggled and slashed away, dealt blows on many a head, while he gazed before him at Ostap and saw that he was attacked again by almost eight at once.

"Ostap! Ostap! Do not surrender!" But by now Ostap was overpowered; by now one had cast a noose about his neck; they were binding him, carrying him off.

"Oh, Ostap, Ostap!" shouted Taras, struggling to him and making mincemeat of all he met.

"Oh, Ostap, Ostap . . . !" But at that very minute something like a heavy stone struck him. Everything went around in a whirl before his eyes. For an instant he had a confused vision of heads, lances, smoke, gleams of fire, branches covered with leaves, flashing before his eyes. Then he sank to the earth like a felled oak. And a mist covered his eyes.

X

"I have had a long sleep!" said Taras, waking as from a heavy drunken slumber, and trying to recognize the objects around him. A terrible weakness overpowered his limbs. The walls and corners of an unfamiliar room seemed hovering before him. At last he saw that Tovkach was sitting before him and seemed to be listening to every breath he took.

"Yes," thought Tovkach to himself, "you might perhaps have slept forever!" But he said nothing, only held up his finger and gestured to him to be silent.

"But tell me, where am I now?" asked Taras, racking his brains and trying to remember what had happened.

"Be silent!" his comrade shouted sternly at him. "What more do you want to know? Don't you see you are covered with wounds? For the last two weeks we have been galloping with you, not stopping to take breath, and you have been raving in fever and delirium. This is the first time you have waked up quietly. Be quiet if you don't want to do yourself harm."

But Taras kept on striving and struggling to remember what had happened. "But didn't the Poles surround me altogether and seize me? There was no possibility of my fighting my way out of the crowd, was there?"

"Be quiet, I tell you, son of a devil!" shouted Tovkach angrily, as a nurse driven out of all patience shouts at a disobedient child. "What good is it to you to know how you escaped? It's enough that you have escaped. There were men who would not abandon you—well, and that's enough for you! We have many a night yet to gallop together. You think they rate you a simple Cossack? No, they have set a price of two thousand gold pieces on your head."

"And Ostap?" Taras cried suddenly. He had striven his utmost to remember, and suddenly he recalled that Ostap had been captured and bound before his eyes and now was in the hands of the Poles. And the old man's mind was overwhelmed with grief. He tore and pulled off all the bandages on his wounds; he flung them far away, tried to say something aloud, but fell to raving instead. Fever and delirium overpowered him again and senseless babble flowed incoherently from his lips. And meanwhile his faithful comrade stood before him, cursing and uttering harsh words of reproach. At last he seized him by the hands and feet, rolled him up like a baby, fixed all his bandages, wrapped him in a wolf skin, bound him in splints of bark and, fastening him with cords to his saddle, galloped along the road with him again.

"I will bring you home even dead! I will not let the Poles dishonor your Cossack name, tear your body to pieces, and fling it into the water. If an eagle is to peck out your eyes, let it be at least our eagle of the steppes and not the Polish one, not the one that flies from Poland. Even though dead, I will bring you to the Ukraine."

So spake his faithful comrade. He galloped on day and night without resting and brought Taras unconscious to the camp of the Dnieper Cossacks. There he began treating him persistently with herbs and ointments; he found a wise Jewess who for a month gave him potions to drink, and at last Taras was better. Whether it was the treatment or his iron strength that gained the day, within six weeks he was on his legs again; the wounds had healed, and only the scars left by the sword showed how deeply once the old Cossack had been wounded. But he had grown noticeably gloomy and melancholy. Three sorrowful lines furrowed his brow and never left it. He looked about him now: all was new at the camp, all his old comrades were dead. Not one was left of those who had fought for justice, for faith, and for brotherhood. And those who had gone with the leader in pursuit of the Tartars—those, too, had long passed away. All had laid down their lives, all had perished; some had been killed honorably in battle, others had perished from lack of food and water in the salt wastes of the Crimea; some had perished in captivity, unable to bear disgrace; the old leader himself was no more, not one of his old comrades was left, and the strong Cossacks that had once been brimming over with life had long been laid to rest under the grass. All he felt was that there had been a mighty feast, a noisy feast: all the drinking vessels had been smashed to bits; not one drop of wine was left; the guests and the servants had carried off all the costly goblets and drinking bowls —and the giver of the feast was left at home in confusion, thinking: "Better had there never been that feast." All efforts to entertain and to cheer Taras were in vain; in vain the gray-headed, bearded bandore players, who passed by in twos and in threes, sang the praises of his Cossack feats. He looked with gloom and indifference at everything, and his passive face bore traces of hopeless grief and suffering, as with bowed head he murmured: "My son! My Ostap!"

The Cossacks made ready for an expedition by sea. Two hundred boats were lowered into the Dnieper and Asia Minor saw them with shaven heads and long forelocks putting her flourishing coasts to fire and sword; she saw the turbans of her Moslem inhabitants scattered like her innumerable flowers on the blood-soaked fields and floating on her shores. She saw many Cossack trousers smeared with tar, many muscular arms holding black whips. The Cossacks devoured and laid waste all the vineyards; they left dung heaps in the mosques; they used costly Persian shawls for leg wrappers and encircled their mud-stained jackets with them. For years afterward their short pipes were picked up in those parts. Gaily they set sail back; a Turkish ship with ten cannon pursued them and dispersed their light canoes like birds with a volley from all ten at once. A third of their number were drowned in the depths of the sea; but the rest met together again at the mouth of the Dnieper with twelve barrels full of sequins. But Taras cared nothing for all this now. He went off into the water meadows and the steppes as if to go hunting, but his gun was not discharged. And laying it on the ground he would sit on the seashore, full of grief. For hours he would sit there with bowed head, murmuring: "My Ostap! My Ostap!" Before him the Black Sea stretched sparkling; the sea gull called in the faraway reeds; his white mustache glistened like silver as one tear after another dropped on it.

At last Taras could bear it no longer: "Come what may, I will go to find out what has happened to him, whether he is alive or in the tomb, or whether there is no trace of him, even in the grave. Come what may, I will find out!" he said.

And a week later he was in the town of Uman on his horse, fully armed, with a lance and a sword, a bottle at his saddle, a pot of porridge, cartridges, horse's harness, and other equipment. He rode straight up to a dirty, mud-stained little hut whose little windows were so begrimed that they could scarcely be seen; the chimney was stuffed up with a rag, and the roof was full of holes and covered with sparrows. A garbage heap lay before the very door. The face of a Jewess wearing a headpiece adorned with faded pearls peeped out of the window.

"Is your husband at home?" said Bulba, dismounting and tying the reins to an iron hook in the doorpost.

"Yes," said the Jewess, and made haste to come out with grain in a ladle for the horse and a bottle of beer for the horseman.

"Where is your Jew?"

"He is in the other room, saying his prayers," said the Jewess, bowing and wishing Bulba good health as he lifted the bottle to his lips.

"Stay here, feed and water my horse, while I will go and speak with him alone. I have business with him."

This Jew was our friend Yankel. By now he rented a bit of land and kept a little tavern; he had by degrees got all the gentry and nobility of the neighborhood into his hands, had gradually extracted almost all their money, and the presence of this Jew was having a profound influence in the district. For three miles in every direction there was not a single hut left in decent condition; they were all tumbling down and falling into ruins; everything was being squandered in drink, and nothing was left but poverty and rags; the whole countryside was laid bare as though by fire or pestilence. And if Yankel had stayed there another ten years, he would certainly have laid bare the whole province.

Taras went into the inner room. The Jew was saying his prayers, covered with his rather dirty blanket,[8] and in accordance with the rites of his religion turned to spit for the last time, when his eyes suddenly fell on Bulba standing behind him. First of all, the two thousand gold pieces promised as a reward for Bulba's head seemed to leap up before the Jew's eyes; but he was ashamed of his greed and strove to conquer the everlasting thought of gold which twines like a worm about the soul of a Jew.

"Listen, Yankel," said Taras to the Jew, who began by bowing

---

[8] I.e., prayer shawl. (ed.)

down before him, and then carefully locked the door that they might not be seen. "I saved your life—the Cossacks would have torn you to pieces like a dog. Now it is your turn: now do me a service!"

The Jew's face clouded over a little.

"What service? If it is something I can do, why not do it?"

"Say nothing. Take me to Warsaw."

"To Warsaw? How, to Warsaw?" said Yankel. His eyebrows and his shoulders jerked in amazement.

"Don't tell me anything. Take me to Warsaw. Come what may, I want to see him once more, to say one word to him."

"Say one word to whom?"

"To him, Ostap, my son."

"Has not his honor heard that . . ."

"I know, I know all about it; they offered two thousand gold pieces for my head. They give it a value, the fools! I'll give you five thousand. Here are two thousand on the spot"—Bulba shook two thousand gold pieces out of his leather purse—"and the rest when I come back."

The Jew instantly seized a towel and covered the gold pieces with it.

"Aie, the wonderful money! Aie, the gold coin!" he said, turning a gold piece over in his hands and trying it with his teeth. "I expect that the man from whom your honor seized such good gold pieces did not live another hour, he went at once to the river and drowned himself there, after losing such splendid gold pieces."

"I would not have asked you. I could, perhaps, have found the road to Warsaw by myself; but the damned Poles may recognize me somehow and seize me; for I am not good at strategy, while you Jews have been created for it. You can cheat the very devil; you know every dodge; so that's why I have come to you! And indeed I should gain nothing in Warsaw by myself. Bring out your cart at once and take me!"

"And does your honor expect me to harness the nag right away and say 'Hey, gee up!' Does your honor suppose that I can take your honor just as he is without hiding him?"

"Well then, hide me, hide me as best you can, in an empty barrel or something."

"Aie, aie! And does your honor think he could be hidden in a barrel? Surely your honor knows that everyone supposes that there is vodka in a barrel."

"Well, let them suppose that there is vodka in it."

"What? Let them suppose there is vodka!" said the Jew, and he seized his earlocks in both hands and then threw up both hands in dismay.

"Why, what are you so worked up about?"

"Why, surely your honor knows that God created vodka for everyone to taste it. They are all greedy and fond of dainties there; a Polish gentleman would run four miles after a barrel, pierce a hole in it on the spot and see at once that nothing runs out, and say: 'A Jew doesn't carry a barrel empty; there is sure to be something in it! Seize the Jew, bind the Jew, take all the Jew's money, throw the Jew into prison!' For everyone wicked pounces on the Jew; everyone takes a Jew for a dog, for they think he is not a man, if he's a Jew!"

"Well, then, put me in a load of fish!"

"I can't, your honor, I really can't. The folks are hungry as dogs now through all Poland, and they'll steal the fish and feel your honor under them."

"Well, take me to the devil, only take me."

"Listen, listen, your honor!" said the Jew, tucking up the cuffs of his sleeves and going up to him with outspread hands. "This is what we will do. Fortresses and castles are being built everywhere now; French engineers have come from Germany, and so lots of bricks and stones are being carted along the road. Let your honor lie at the bottom of the cart and I'll lay the bricks above; your honor looks strong and sturdy and so he won't mind if it's a little heavy; and I'll make a hole in the load below to pass food to your honor."

"Do as you like, only take me!"

And an hour later a brick cart was driven out of Uman with two horses in the shafts. On one of them sat lanky Yankel, and his long curly earlocks danced under his Jewish skullcap as he jolted up and down on the horse, looking as thin as a signpost.

XI

At the time when the events described took place there were as yet none of the customs officials and excise officers who are such a terrible menace to enterprising people now, and so everyone could take any goods he thought fit anywhere. If somebody made a raid upon them and inspected them, he did so mostly for his own satisfaction, especially if there were objects alluring to the eye among the goods, and if his own arm was of fair weight and strength. But bricks aroused no covetousness and were driven without hindrance through the principal gate of the town. Bulba, in his narrow cage, could hear only the noise of the traffic, the shouts of wagoners, and nothing more. Yankel, jogging up and down on his short-shanked dusty nag, turned, after taking several roundabout ways, into a dark narrow thoroughfare, known by the name of Mud Street and also Jew Street, because almost all the Jews of Warsaw were to be found there. This street was very much like a backyard turned inside out. It seemed as though the sun never entered it at all. The completely blackened wooden houses, with numbers of poles stretched from the windows, made the street even darker. At rare intervals a brick wall showed red between them, and even that had turned black in many places. Only here and there the stucco top of a wall, catching the sunlight, made a glaring patch of white that hurt the eyes. Here there was a striking selection of articles: pipes, rags, shells, broken pots. Everyone flung into the street whatever was of no use to him, so affording the passer-by the agreeable possibility of thrilling his esthetic sensibility. A man on horseback could almost reach with his hand the poles which were stretched across the street from one house to another with long Jewish stockings, short trousers, and a smoked goose hanging on them. Sometimes the rather attractive face of a Jewess, adorned with tarnished beads, peeped out of a decrepit window. A group of muddy, tattered Jew boys with curly heads shouted and lolled in the mud. A red-haired Jew with freckles all over his face, which made him look like a sparrow's egg, peeped out of a window; at once he addressed Yankel in his unintelligible jargon, and Yankel at once drove into a yard. Another Jew came down the street, stopped, and also entered into conversation; and when Bulba emerged at last from under the bricks, he saw three Jews talking with great animation.

Yankel turned to him and said that everything would be arranged, that his Ostap was in the city dungeon, and that though it would be a hard task to persuade the guards, yet he hoped to obtain an interview for him.

Bulba went with the three Jews into the house.

The Jews began talking among themselves again in their incomprehensible language. Taras looked at each one of them. It seemed as though he were deeply moved; an overmastering flame of hope —that hope which sometimes visits a man in the utmost depths of despair—gleamed in his harsh and apathetic face; his old heart began beating as violently as a young man's.

"Listen, Jews!" he said. And there was something of passion in his words. "You can do anything in the world, you can dig a thing up from the bottom of the sea, and there is an old saying that a Jew will steal himself if he can steal nothing else. Set free my Ostap for me! Give him a chance to escape from the devil's hands. Here, I've promised this man twelve thousand gold pieces; I will add another twelve. Everything I have, costly goblets and gold buried in the earth, my house and my last garment I will sell, and will make a contract with you for all my life that whatever I take in war I will share it in equal halves with you."

"Oh, it can't be done, your honor, it can't be done!" Yankel said with a sigh.

"No, it can't!" said another of the Jews.

All three of them looked at one another.

"We might try," said the third, looking sheepishly at the other two. "Maybe God will help us."

The three Jews began talking in German.[9] Though Bulba strained his ears he could make out nothing; he could only distinguish the word "Mordechai" uttered several times.

"Listen, your honor!" said Yankel. "We must take counsel with a man the like of whom has never been seen in this world. Oo, oo! He is as wise as Solomon, and if he can do nothing no one in the world can do it. Stay here; here is the key and don't let anyone in."

The Jews went out into the street. Taras locked the door and looked through the little window at the filthy scene. The three Jews had stopped in the middle of the street and had begun talking rather excitedly; they were soon joined by a fourth and finally by a fifth. He heard "Mordechai, Mordechai," repeated again. The Jews kept continually looking toward one side of the street; at last from a wretched-looking house at the end of it a foot appeared in a Jewish slipper, and he saw the flutter of the skirts of a long coat. "Ah! Mordechai! Mordechai!" the Jews all cried with one voice. A

---

[9] Yiddish. (ed.)

scrawny Jew, somewhat shorter than Yankel and far more wrinkled, with an immense upper lip, drew near the impatient group;
and all the Jews vied with one another in hurriedly telling him the
story, while Mordechai glanced several times toward the little
window. Mordechai gesticulated, listened, interrupted, often spat
to one side, and lifting up the skirts of his coat, thrust his hand into
his pocket and drew out some jingling coins, displaying his very
shabby trousers. At last all the Jews set up such an uproar that the
one who was standing on the lookout had to signal to them to be
silent, and Taras was beginning to be anxious about his own safety,
till, remembering that Jews can discuss nothing except in the
street, and that the devil himself could not understand their language, he felt reassured. Two minutes later the Jews came into the
room together. Mordechai went up to Taras, patted him on the
shoulder, and said: "When we and God mean to do a thing, it will
come out right."

Taras looked at this Solomon, the like of whom had never been
seen in the world, and some hope revived in him. His appearance
was certainly calculated to inspire some confidence. His upper lip
was something fearful to look at; its thickness was undoubtedly
not all due to nature. This Solomon only had fifteen hairs in his
beard—and those on the left side. His face bore so many traces of
blows he had received for his temerity, that he had doubtless lost
count of them long ago and grown used to regarding them as something natural.

Mordechai went away with the companions who were so filled
with wonder at his wisdom. Bulba was left alone. He was in a
strange and novel situation; for the first time in his life he was
conscious of anxiety. His soul was in a feverish state. He was not
the same man as of old, inflexible, unwavering, steadfast as an oak;
he was timid, he was weak now. He shuddered at every rustle, at
every fresh figure of a Jew appearing at the end of the street. In
this condition he spent the whole day; he neither ate nor drank,
and never took his eyes off the little window looking on the street.
At last, late in the evening, Mordechai and Yankel appeared. Taras'
heart stood still.

"Well? Successful?" he asked them with the restive eagerness of
a wild horse. But, before the Jews had recovered breath to answer,
Taras noticed that Mordechai was without one of his earlocks
which had hung down in ringlets somewhat untidily below his

skullcap. It could be seen that he wanted to say something, but he mumbled out such drivel that Taras could make nothing of it. And Yankel himself kept putting his hand to his mouth, as though he were suffering from a cold.

"Oh! Honored sir!" said Yankel. "Now it is utterly impossible! I swear it is! Such wicked people that one ought to spit on their heads. Here, Mordechai will tell you. Mordechai did what no one in the world has done yet; but it is not God's will it should be so. Three thousand soldiers are stationed there, and tomorrow all the prisoners will be executed."

Taras looked into the Jew's eyes; there was no impatience or anger in his face now.

"And if your honor wants to see him you must go early tomorrow before the sun has risen. The guards have agreed, and one officer has promised. But may they have no happiness in the world to come! *Oy weh mir!*[10] What greedy folks they are! There are none such even among us: fifty gold pieces I gave to each one of them and to the officer . . ."

"Very good, take me to him!" Taras pronounced resolutely, and all his firmness came back to him. He agreed to Yankel's proposal that he should be disguised as a foreign count who had arrived from Germany. The farsighted Jew had already provided clothes for the purpose. By now it was night. The master of the house, the red-haired, freckled Jew whom the reader knows already, pulled out a thin mattress covered with a sort of sacking and laid it on a bench for Bulba. Yankel lay down on the floor on a similar mattress. The red-haired Jew drank a small goblet of some beverage, threw off his full coat, and, looking in his slippers and stockings rather like a chicken, retreated with his Jewess into a sort of cupboard. Two little Jew boys lay down on the floor beside the cupboard like two little puppies. But Taras did not sleep; he sat motionless, faintly drumming with his fingers on the table; he kept his pipe in his mouth and blew out smoke, which started the Jew sneezing in his sleep and tucking his nose into the quilt. The sky was hardly touched by the first pale glimmer of dawn when he poked Yankel with his foot. "Get up, Jew," he said, "and give me the disguise."

In an instant he had dressed himself; he blackened his mustache and his eyebrows, put a little dark cap on his head, and not one of

---

[10] A common Yiddish expression: "Woe is me!" (ed.)

the Cossacks who knew him best could have recognized him. He
did not look more than thirty-five. A ruddy flush of health played
on his cheeks, and the scars on his face gave it a commanding air.
The gold-embroidered coat was very becoming to him.

The streets were still asleep. Not a single figure with a tradesman's basket was yet to be seen in the town. Bulba and Yankel
reached a building which looked like a nesting heron. It was low-
pitched, broad, huge, blackened, and on one side of it a long narrow tower like the neck of a stork was thrust up with a bit of roof
sticking up on the top of it. This building served a number of different purposes: in it were barracks, a prison, and even a court of justice. Our friends went in at the gate and found themselves in the
middle of a spacious hall or covered court. About a thousand men
were asleep in it. Directly opposite the entrance was a low door
before which two sentinels were sitting, playing a sort of game
which consisted in one of them striking the other on the palm of
the hand with two fingers. They only turned their heads when
Yankel said: "It's us; listen, gentlemen, it's us."

"Go in!" said one of them, opening the door with one hand
while he held out the other to his comrade to receive his blows.
They went into a dark, narrow corridor, which led them again into
a similar hall with little windows high up.

"Who goes there?" shouted several voices, and Taras saw a considerable number of soldiers fully armed. "We are forbidden to
admit anyone," they said.

"It's us!" shouted Yankel. "Us, noble gentlemen!" But no one
would listen to him. Luckily at that moment there walked in a fat
man who was apparently a commanding officer, for he swore louder
than any.

"Noble sir, here we are; you know us, and his honor the count
will show his gratitude too."

"Let them in, you damned bastards! And admit no one else. And
let no one take off his sword nor make a mess on the floor . . ."

The rest of his eloquent orders our friends did not hear. "You
know us, it's me; we are your own people!" said Yankel to everyone he met.

"Well, can we go in now?" he asked one of the guards when
they had at last reached the end of the corridor.

"You can, only I don't know whether they'll admit you right

into the prison. Jan is not there now; there's another man on guard in his place," answered the sentry.

"Aie, aie," the Jew pronounced softly. "That's bad, your honor!"

"Lead the way!" Taras pronounced stubbornly. The Jew obeyed.

At the door of the dungeon, which ran up to a point at the top, stood a soldier with mustaches in three stories. The upper story of the mustaches turned backward, the second straight forward, the third downward, which made him look very much like a tomcat.

The Jew approached him, cringing, and almost sideways. "Your Serene Highness! Illustrious lord!"

"Are you speaking to me, Jew?"

"To you, your high nobility."

"Hm . . . and I am just a simple soldier!" said he with the mustaches, his eyes beginning to twinkle.

"Why, upon my word, I thought you were the general himself. Aie, aie, aie . . . !" With this the Jew wagged his head and twiddled his fingers. "Aie, how grand you look! Upon my word, a colonel, a regular colonel! Another touch and he'd be a colonel! Your honor only needs to be mounted on a horse as swift as a fly and to drill the regiments!"

The soldier stroked the lowest tier of his mustaches, while his eyes gleamed with pleasure.

"What fine fellows soldiers are!" the Jew went on. "*Oy weh mir*, what splendid fellows! The gold lacings and brass plates, they fairly glitter like the sun; and the girls—as soon as they see the soldiers . . . Aie, aie . . . !" The Jew wagged his head again.

The soldier twisted the upper stage of his mustaches and let out through his teeth a sound not unlike the neigh of a horse.

"I beg your honor to do me a service!" the Jew said. "This prince here has come from foreign lands, he wants to have a look at the Cossacks. He has never in his life seen what the Cossacks are like."

The arrival of foreign counts and barons was a fairly common event in Poland; they were often attracted solely by curiosity to see this half-Asiatic corner of Europe; they looked upon Muscovy and the Ukraine as almost a part of Asia. And so the soldier, making a rather low bow, thought proper to add a few words from himself.

"I don't know, Your Highness," he said, "why you care to look at them. They are dogs, not men, and their religion is one that everyone despises."

"You lie, you bastard!" said Bulba. "You are a dog yourself! How dare you say our faith is despised? It's your heretical belief that is despised!"

"Ah, ha!" said the soldier. "I know, friend, who you are; you are one of the same lot I have in prison. Wait while I call our men here."

Taras saw his indiscretion, but obstinacy and some annoyance prevented him from thinking how to correct it. Happily Yankel intervened instantly.

"Your High Nobility! How could the count be a Cossack? And if he were a Cossack, how could he come to be dressed and look like a count?"

"Tell that to others . . . !" And the soldier was opening his mouth to shout.

"Your Royal Majesty! Hush, for God's sake!" cried Yankel. "Don't speak! We will pay you for it beyond anything you have even seen. We'll give you two gold pieces."

"Ah, ha! Two gold pieces! Two gold pieces are nothing to me; I pay the barber that for shaving only half my chin. A hundred gold pieces, Jew!" Here the soldier twisted his mustache. "And if you don't give the hundred I'll call at once!"

"And why so much?" said the Jew, mournfully, untying his leather purse. He had turned quite pale, but he was glad there was no more in his purse, and that the soldier could not count beyond a hundred.

"Your honor, your honor! Let us make haste and go! You see what bad people they are!" said Yankel, observing that the soldier was fingering the money, as though regretting he had not asked more.

"Why, you Polish swine," said Bulba, "you have taken the money and you don't intend to show me the prisoners? No, you must show me. Since you've taken the money you have no right to refuse now."

"Go along, go to hell! Or I'll call out this minute and then you'll . . . Look sharp and be off, I tell you!"

"Your honor, let us go, do let us go! Curse them! May they spit with horror in their dreams!" cried poor Yankel.

Slowly, with bowed head, Bulba turned and walked back, followed by reproaches from Yankel, who was consumed by grief at the thought of the wasted gold pieces.

"And what did he get them for! Let him swear, the dog, they are folk that always must be swearing! *Oy!* What luck God sends some people! A hundred gold pieces simply for turning us out! While the likes of us have our hair torn off and our faces made unfit to look at and no one gives us a hundred gold pieces. Oh, my God! Merciful God!"

But their failure had far more effect on Bulba; it was shown in the violently burning flame in his eyes.

"Let us go!" he said suddenly as though shaking himself. "Let us go to the market place. I want to see how they will torture him."

"*Oy*, your honor! Why go? That will be no good to us now, you know."

"Come along!" said Bulba, stubbornly; and the Jew, sighing, trailed after him like a nurse.

It was not difficult to find the square in which the execution was to take place; people were flocking to it from all sides. In that brutal age such occasions were regarded as among the most interesting spectacles not only by the ignorant mob but even by the upper classes. Numbers of old women, most devout; numbers of young girls and young women, so timid that all night afterward they dreamed of blood-stained corpses and cried out in their sleep as loudly as a drunken hussar, never missed a chance of satisfying their curiosity. "Oh, what torture!" many of them cried with hysterical frenzy, shutting their eyes and turning away, yet they would go on standing, often for hours. One man stood with his mouth open and his arms stretched out before him, as though he meant to leap on the heads of the crowd to get a better view. A butcher thrust his fat face above the mass of narrow, small, and ordinary heads; he watched the whole process with the air of a connoisseur and talked in monosyllables with a gunsmith, whom he addressed as "old friend," because on some holiday he had been drinking with him in the same tavern. Some of the people kept up an eager discussion, others were even making bets; but the majority were the sort of people who look at the whole world and everything that happens in it and go on picking their noses. In the front, close to the whiskered warriors who made up the town guard, was standing a young gentleman, or youth who looked like a gentleman in military uniform, who had put on absolutely everything he had, so that nothing was left in his lodging but a tattered shirt and an old pair of boots. Two chains with some sort of coin on them hung about his neck, one above the other. He was standing with his sweetheart, and was continually looking around for fear someone should soil her silk dress. He explained everything to her so thoroughly that not a word could have been added: "All these people that you see, Juzysya darling," he told her, "have come to look at the execution of criminals. And this man, darling, who is holding an ax and other instruments in his hand, is the executioner, and he will punish them. And when he begins to break them on the wheel and inflict other tortures, the criminal will still be alive; but when his head is cut off, he will die at once, darling. At first he will scream and move, but as soon as his head is cut off then he will not be able to scream nor eat nor drink, because he won't have any head, darling." And the girl heard it all with awe and curiosity.

The roofs of the houses were dotted with people. Strange faces decked with whiskers or wearing something like a cap were poked out of attic windows. The aristocracy sat on the balconies under awnings. The pretty little hand of a Polish lady, smiling and sparkling, lay white as sugar on the railing. Illustrious nobles, rather stout, gazed at the scene with a dignified air. A footman in gorgeous livery with flowing sleeves was handing them various beverages and edibles. Often a black-eyed roguish girl would seize a cake or fruit in her little white hand and throw it into the crowd. A throng of hungry knights held out their caps to catch it, and a tall one, whose head stood out above the crowd, in a faded red coat with tarnished gold braid on it, was the first to catch one, thanks to his long fingers; he kissed the prize, pressed it to his heart, and then put it in his mouth. A falcon, hanging in a gilt cage under the balcony, was also a spectator; with his beak on one side and one claw in the air, he too scrutinized the people attentively from his perch. But all at once a stir passed through the crowd, and voices were heard on all sides:

"They are bringing them! The Cossacks!"

They came, bareheaded, with long forelocks and beards that had been left to grow. They moved with no sign of fear nor sullenness, but with a sort of quiet pride; their garments of costly cloth were worn threadbare and hung in ancient rags about them; they did not greet the people nor look at them. Foremost of all walked Ostap.

What were old Taras' feelings when he saw his Ostap? What passed in his heart? He gazed at him from the crowd, not one movement escaped him. The Cossacks drew near the scaffold. Ostap stopped. He was to be the first to face the terrible ordeal. He looked at his comrades, raised his hand, and pronounced in a loud voice: 'O God! grant that none of the heretics standing here may hear, the unclean wretches, how a Christian is tortured! That not one of us may utter one word!" After this he went up to the scaffold.

"Good, son, good!" said Bulba softly, and he bowed his gray head.

The executioner stripped Ostap of his old rags; his arms and legs were bound in a frame made for the purpose and . . . We will not horrify our readers with a picture of the fiendish tortures, which would make their hair stand on end. These atrocities were the product of that coarse, savage age, when man led a bloody life spent entirely in violence, and his heart was hardened by this till he lost all sense of humanity. In vain some few, who stand out as exceptions in their age, opposed these horrors. In vain the King and many nobles of enlightened heart and intelligence urged that such cruel punishments could only inflame the vengeance of the Cossacks. But the influence of the King and of wise counsels was of no avail beside the turbulence and unbridled violence of the nobles, whose imprudent, incredible lack of foresight, childish vanity, and trivial pride turned the Diet into a parody of government.

Ostap bore the tortures and agonies like a hero. No cry or moan was heard, even when the bones of his arms and legs were being broken, when the awful cracking sound made by them was heard by the farthest spectators in the deathly silence of the crowd, while the Polish ladies turned away their eyes—there was no flinching in his face, nothing like a moan broke from his lips. Taras stood in the crowd with bowed head, though he proudly raised his eyes, and only said approvingly: "Good, son, good!"

But when Ostap was brought to the last mortal agonies, it seemed as though his strength was beginning to give way. And he turned his eyes in all directions about him: good God! all unknown, all alien faces! If only someone akin to him could have been present at his death! He did not wish to hear the sobs and desolation of a weak mother, or the frantic wails of a wife tearing her hair and beating her white breasts; he longed now to see a strong man who with a word of wisdom might have strengthened and comforted him at his end. And his heart failed him and he cried out:

"Father, where are you, do you hear all this . . . ?"

"I hear!" rang forth out of the absolute stillness, and all the thousands of people shuddered. A division of cavalry dashed to make a careful inspection of the crowd. Yankel turned pale as death; and when the cavalry moved on a little way from him, he turned around in horror to glance at Taras. But Taras was no longer beside him; all trace of him had vanished.

XII

Taras had reappeared. A hundred and twenty thousand Cossacks appeared on the frontiers of the Ukraine. This was no small division, no company that had come out in search of booty or in pursuit of the Tartars. No, the whole nation had risen up, for the patience of the people was exhausted; they had risen up to avenge the flouting of their rights, the disgraceful mockery of their customs, the outraging of the faith of their forefathers and their sacred traditions, the desecrating of their churches, the licentiousness of the foreign nobles, the religious persecutions, the shameful domination of Jews in a Christian land: everything that had accumulated from old days and swollen the sum of sullen hatred in the Cossacks. The young but stouthearted headman Ostranitsa[11] was in command of the vast numbers of Cossacks. His old experienced comrade and adviser, Gunia, was conspicuous at his side. Eight colonels commanded regiments of twelve thousand each. Two captains and another staff-bearing officer rode after the headman. The chief standard bearer was in command of the principal flag; many other flags and banners fluttered in the distance; the assistant staff-bearing officers bore the badges of office. There were many of other grades in the regiments: quartermaster and transport officers, regimental clerks, and with them detachments of cavalry and infantry; there were almost as many volunteers as there were regular enrolled Cossacks. The Cossacks had risen up from all sides: from Chigirin, from Pereiaslav, from Baturin, from Glukhov, from the Lower Dnieper, and from all the districts and islands about its upper reaches. Horses beyond number and immense cavalcades of carts trailed over the fields. And among those Cossacks, and among those eight regiments, was one regiment finer than all the rest; and

---

[11] Several of the secondary characters are based on historical figures. Ostranitsa, for example, was a leader of the Cossacks who was beheaded by the Poles in 1638. (ed.)

that regiment was commanded by Taras Bulba. Everything gave him the foremost place—his age, his experience, his skill in moving his troops, and his hatred of the foe, more intense than anyone's. His ruthless ferocity and cruelty seemed excessive even to the Cossacks. The gray-headed warrior would set no punishment but the fire and the gallows, and his voice in the military councils was always for slaughter.

No need to describe the battles in which the Cossacks displayed their bravery, nor the course of the campaign in detail; all that is recorded in the pages of the chronicles. We all know what war waged for religion is like in Russia; no force is stronger than faith. It is as fierce and invincible as the unhewn rock in the midst of the stormy, ever treacherous sea. From the very midst of the ocean depths it raises to the heavens its indestructible walls, all fashioned of one single stone. It can be seen from all sides, and it looks straight in the face of the racing billows. And woe to the ship which falls foul of it! Its weak masts and rigging fly into chips, everything in it is smashed to atoms, and the shuddering air resounds with the pitiful screams of the drowning.

The chronicles give a detailed picture of the flight of the Polish garrisons from the towns set free by the Cossacks; of the hanging of the shameless Jewish contractors; of the weakness of the Polish commander, Nikolai Pototsky, with his immense army, against the invincible force of the Cossacks; of the way in which, defeated and pursued, he lost the greater part of his army in a little river, and the fierce Cossacks besieged him in the little town of Polonnoe; and how the Polish commander in the last extremity solemnly vowed in the name of the King and the nobles that the Cossacks should be satisfied in full and all their rights and privileges should be restored. But the Cossacks were not such fools as to be taken in by that; they knew what Polish vows were worth. And Pototsky would not have flaunted again on his six-thousand-ruble racehorse, the mark for all the great ladies and the envy of the nobles; he would not have made a noise at the Diets and given gorgeous banquets to the senators, had he not been saved by the Russian clergy of the district. When all the priests in their shining gold chasubles, bearing crosses and icons, and the bishop at the head of them in his pastoral miter, cross in hand, came out to meet the Cossacks, they all bowed and took off their caps. They would have disregarded anyone at that time, even the King himself; but they dared not oppose their Orthodox Church and they revered their clergy. The Cossack leader and his colonel agreed together to release Pototsky, taking from him a solemn oath to leave all Orthodox churches in freedom, to renounce his old enmity, and to do nothing to harm the Cossack power. Only one colonel would not agree to such a peace. That one was Taras. He tore a handful of hair from his head and cried:

"Aie, leaders, colonels! Do no such womanish deed! Trust not the Poles; they will betray you, the dogs!"

When the regimental clerk presented the terms of the peace, and the leader signed it, Taras took off his trusty blade, a costly Turkish saber of the finest steel, broke it in two like a stick, and flung the parts far away in different directions, saying: "Farewell! As the two parts of that sword cannot be united and make up one blade again, so shall we comrades never meet again in this world! Remember my farewell words . . ." (At this word his voice rose higher, gathering uncanny strength, and all were confounded at his prophetic words.) "You will remember me at your dying hour! Do you think you have bought peace and tranquillity; do you think you are going to live at ease? A strange sort of ease you will enjoy: they will flay the skin from your head, leader, they will stuff it with chaff, and for years it will be seen at the fairs! Nor will you Cossacks keep your heads! You will perish in damp dungeons, buried within stone walls, if you are not all boiled alive in cauldrons like sheep!

"And you, lads!" he went on, turning to his followers: "who among you wants to die a genuine death, not on the stove or on a woman's bed, or drunk under a tavern fence like any carcass, but an honest Cossack death, all in one bed like bride and bridegroom? Or maybe you will go back home and turn infidels and carry the Catholic priests upon your backs?"

"We're with you, we're with you, colonel! We'll follow you!" cried all who were in Taras' regiment, and many others hastened to join them.

"Since you will follow me, then follow me!" said Taras, pulling his cap down on his head; he looked fiercely at all those who stayed behind, straightened himself on his horse, and shouted to his men: "No one shall insult us with words of reproach! And now, lads, off to pay a visit to the Catholics!" And then he lashed his horse, and a string of a hundred wagons trailed behind him, and with him were many Cossacks on horse and foot; and he turned around to look menacingly at those who stayed behind, and his eyes were full of wrath. No one dared to stop them. The regiment marched off in sight of the whole army, and for a long way Taras still turned and gazed menacingly back.

The leader and the colonels stood confounded, all sank into thought, and were silent as though oppressed by some gloomy foreboding. Taras' prophecy was not an idle one: everything came true as he had predicted. A little later, after the treachery at Kanev, the leader's head was stuck upon a pole, and many of the foremost commanders shared his fate.

And what of Taras? Taras marched all over Poland with his regiment, burned eighteen villages and nearly forty churches, and arrived as far as Cracow. He slaughtered numbers of Poles of all sorts, and sacked the finest and wealthiest castles; the Cossacks unsealed and poured away barrels of mead and wine hundreds of years old that had been carefully preserved in Polish noblemen's cellars; they slashed to bits and burned the sumptuous cloth of garments and the vessels that were in the storerooms. "Spare nothing!" was all Taras said. The Cossacks did not spare the black-browed damsels, the white-bosomed, fair-faced maidens; even at the altar they could find no safety; Taras burned them together with the altars. More than once snow-white arms were raised from the flames to the heavens accompanied with pitiful cries which would have moved the very earth and set the grass of the steppes shuddering with pity. But the cruel Cossacks heeded nothing; picking up the babes from the streets on their lances, they flung them too into the flames. "That's for you, accursed Poles, in memory of Ostap!" Taras would say. And such sacrifices he made to Ostap's memory in every village, until the Polish government saw that Taras' exploits were something more than common brigandage, and the same Pototsky was sent with five regiments to capture Taras.

For six days the Cossacks retreated by byroads from their pursuers; their horses saved them, but they were almost worn out by this headlong flight. But this time Pototsky was equal to the charge laid upon him; he pursued them without flagging and overtook them on the bank of the Dniester, where Bulba had halted to rest in a deserted ruined fortress.

It stood conspicuous above the precipitous bank at the edge of the Dniester, with its broken rampart and dilapidated walls. The topmost crag, that looked on the point of breaking off and flying down, was strewn with rubble and broken bricks. The Polish commander Pototsky assailed him here on the two sides that looked out to the open plain. For four days the Cossacks fought and struggled, beating back the Poles with bricks and stones. But their stores and their strength were exhausted, and Taras decided to fight his way through the ranks of the foe. And the Cossacks were making their way through, and their swift horses would perhaps have served them faithfully once more, when suddenly Taras stopped in full flight and shouted: "Stop! I've dropped my pipe; I won't have even my pipe fall into the hands of the accursed Poles!" And the old chief bent down and began looking in the grass for the pipe which had been his inseparable companion, by land and by sea, on the march, and at home. And at that moment a gang suddenly dashed up and seized him under his mighty shoulders. He struggled with every limb, but the soldiers who had captured him were not thrown to the ground, as had happened in the past.

"Ah, old age, old age!" he said, and the stout old Cossack burst into tears. But old age was not to blame; his strength was overcome by greater strength. There were nearly thirty men hanging on to his arms and legs. "The crow is caught!" cried the Poles. "Now we've only to think how best to do him honor, the dog." And with Pototsky's sanction they decided to burn him alive in the sight of all. A leafless tree which had been struck by lightning stood at hand. They dragged him by iron chains to the tree trunk, nailed his hands to it, and raising him on high so that he could be seen from all parts, began to build a fire under the tree. But Taras looked not at the pile, he thought not of the fire by which they were going to burn him; he looked where the Cossacks were making a stand; from his height he could see everything plainly.

"Make for the mountain, Cossacks, make swiftly for the mountain beyond the forest," he shouted, "they will not reach you there!" But the wind did not carry his words. "They will be lost for nothing!" he said in despair, and glanced below where the Dniester sparkled. Joy gleamed in his eyes. He saw four boats peeping out from behind the bushes, and, straining his voice to the utmost, he shouted: "To the river! To the river, Cossacks, go down by the path on the left. There are boats by the bank; take all, that they may not pursue!"

This time the wind blew from the other quarter and all he said was heard by the Cossacks. But for such counsel he was given a blow on the head which made everything hazy.

The Cossacks raced full gallop by the path downhill with the Poles in full pursuit just behind them. They saw that the path turned and twisted, going around and around. "Ah, comrades! here goes!" they all said; they halted for an instant, raised their whips, whistled, and their Tartar steeds, rising from the earth and stretching themselves in the air like snakes, flew over the precipice and splashed into the Dniester. Only two fell short of the river, and they were dashed on the rocks, and perished there with their horses, without time to cry out. The rest were swimming with their horses in the river and unmooring the boats. The Poles stopped short at the precipice, marveling at the incredible feat of the Cossacks, and hesitating whether to leap down or not. One young colonel, an eager, hot-blooded fellow, the brother of the lovely lady who had bewitched poor Andrei, did not hesitate but rushed headlong on his horse after the Cossacks: he turned over three times in the air and fell straight upon the jagged rocks. He was torn to pieces falling over the precipice, and his brains, mixed with blood, bespattered the bushes that covered the rugged walls of the cliff.

When Taras Bulba recovered from the blow and looked at the Dniester, the Cossacks were in their boats and rowing hard; bullets were flying after them from above, but did not reach them. And the old chief's eyes glittered joyfully.

"Farewell, comrades!" he shouted to them. "Remember me and come here again next spring and have a fine time of it! What have you gained, you Polish bastards? Think you there is anything in the world that a Cossack would fear? Wait a while, the time is coming, the time is at hand when you will learn what the Orthodox Russian faith can do! Already the nations far and near have an inkling that their ruler will rise up from Russia, and there will be no power on earth that will not submit to him . . . !"

By now the fire was rising about his legs, and wrapping the tree in flames. . . . But there are no fires, no tortures in the world, no force indeed that can break the Russian spirit!

The Dniester is no small river, and many are the backwaters, the thick sedges, the sandbanks, and the deep pools in it; the river glimmers like a mirror, resounding with the ringing cry of the swans, and the proud golden-eye duck soars swiftly above it, and many marsh birds, and red-breasted sandpipers and other wildfowl abound among its reeds and on its banks. The Cossacks plied their oars in unison, moved rapidly in their narrow boats, and cautiously avoided the sandbanks, rousing the fluttering birds and talking of their chief.

⋆⋆⋆⋆⋆⋆⋆⋆⋆⋆⋆⋆⋆⋆⋆⋆⋆⋆⋆⋆⋆⋆⋆⋆⋆⋆⋆⋆⋆⋆⋆⋆⋆⋆⋆⋆⋆

VIY [1]

As soon as the rather lilting seminary bell which hung at the gate of the Bratsky Monastery rang out every morning in Kiev, schoolboys and students hurried there in crowds from all parts of the town. Students of grammar, rhetoric, philosophy, and theology trudged to their classrooms with exercise books under their arms. The grammarians were very small boys: they shoved each other as they went along and quarreled in a shrill alto; they almost all wore muddy or tattered clothes, and their pockets were full of all manner of garbage, such as knucklebones, whistles made of feathers, or a half-eaten pie, sometimes even little sparrows, one of whom, suddenly tweeting at an exceptionally quiet moment in the classroom, would cost its owner some sound whacks on both hands and sometimes a thrashing. The rhetoricians walked with more dignity; their clothes were often quite free from holes; on the other hand, their faces almost all bore some decoration: either one eye

---

[1] Viy is a colossal creation of the popular imagination. It is the name among the Little Russians for the chief of the gnomes, whose eyelids droop down to the earth. This whole story is folklore. I was unwilling to change it, and I tell it almost in the simple words in which I heard it. (N. Gogol) [Gogol probably never heard it at all. No discovery has been made of the folklore source of Viy. (ed.)]

had sunk right under the forehead, or there was a monstrous swelling in place of a lip, or some other disfigurement. They talked and swore among themselves in tenor voices. The philosophers conversed an octave lower in the scale; they had nothing in their pockets but strong, cheap tobacco. They prepared no provisions of any sort but ate on the spot anything they came across; they smelled of pipes and vodka to such a distance that a passing workman would sometimes stop a long way off and sniff the air like a hound.

As a rule the market was just beginning to stir at that hour, and the women with pretzels, rolls, melon seeds, and poppy cakes would tug at the skirts of those whose coats were of fine cloth or some cotton material.

"This way, young gentlemen, this way!" they kept saying from all sides: "here are pretzels, poppy cakes, twists, good white rolls. They are really good! Made with honey! I baked them myself."

Another woman, lifting up a sort of long twist made of dough, would cry: "Here's a pretzel! Buy my pretzel, young gentlemen!"

"Don't buy anything from her: see what a disgusting woman she is, her nose is horrible and her hands are dirty. . . ."

But the women were afraid to bother the philosophers and the theologians, for the latter were fond of taking samples, and always a good handful.

On reaching the seminary, the crowd dispersed to their various classes, which were held in low-pitched but fairly large rooms with little windows, wide doorways, and dirty benches. The classroom was at once filled with all sorts of buzzing sounds: the "auditors" heard their pupils repeat their lessons; the shrill alto of a grammarian rang out, and the windowpane responded with almost the same note; in a corner a rhetorician, whose mouth and thick lips should have belonged at least to a student of philosophy, was droning something in a bass voice, and all that could be heard at a distance was "Boo, boo, boo . . ." The "auditors," as they heard the lesson, kept glancing with one eye under the bench, where a roll or a cheesecake or some pumpkin seeds were peeping out of a scholar's pocket.

When this learned crowd managed to arrive a little too early, or when they knew that the professors would be later than usual, then by general consent they got up a fight, and everyone had to take part in it, even the monitors whose duty it was to maintain discipline and look after the morals of all the students. Two theologians usually settled the arrangements for the battle: whether each class was to defend itself individually, or whether all were to be divided into two parties, the bursars and the seminarists.[2] In any case, the grammarians first began the attack, and, as soon as the rhetoricians entered the fray, they ran away and stood at points of vantage to watch the contest. Then the devotees of philosophy, with long black mustaches, joined in, and finally those of theology, very thick in the neck and attired in shocking trousers, took part. It commonly ended in theology beating all the rest, and the philosophers, rubbing their ribs, would be forced into the classroom and sat down on the benches to rest. The professor, who had himself at one time taken part in such battles, could, on entering the class, see in a minute from the flushed faces of his audience that the battle had been a good one, and, while he was caning a rhetorician on the fingers, in another classroom another professor would be smacking philosophy's hands with a ruler. The theologians were dealt with in quite a different way: they received, to use the expression of a professor of theology, "a peck of peas apiece"—in other words, a liberal drubbing with short leather thongs.

On holidays and ceremonial occasions the bursars and the seminarists went from house to house as mummers. Sometimes they acted a play, and then the most distinguished figure was always some theologian, almost as tall as the belfry of Kiev, who took the part of Herodias or Potiphar's wife.[3] They received in payment a piece of linen, a sack of millet, or half a boiled goose, or something of the sort. All in this crowd of students—the seminarists as well as the bursars, with whom they maintained a hereditary feud—were exceedingly badly off for means of subsistence, and at the same time had extraordinary appetites, so that to reckon how many dumplings each of them tucked away at supper would be utterly impossible, and therefore the voluntary offerings of prosperous citizens could not be sufficient for them. Then the "senate" of the philosophers and theologians dispatched the grammarians and rhet-

---

[2] Both bursars and seminarists studied for the priesthood. Bursars were partly sponsored by the government and partly by private donations; they lived on the premises of the seminary. Seminarists were fully sponsored by the state and did not necessarily reside on the premises. (ed.)

[3] Herodias was the wife of Herod, ruler of Palestine at the time of Christ's death. Potiphar's wife falsely accused Joseph of attempting to seduce her (Genesis 39). (ed.)

oricians, under the supervision of a philosopher (who sometimes took part in the raid himself), with sacks on their shoulders to plunder the vegetable gardens—and pumpkin porridge was made in the bursars' quarters. The members of the "senate" ate such masses of melons that the next day their "auditors" heard two lessons from them instead of one, one coming from their lips, another muttering in their stomachs. Both the bursars and the seminarists wore long garments resembling frock coats, "prolonged to the utmost limit," a technical expression signifying below their heels.

The most important event for the seminarists was the coming of the vacation: it began in June, when they usually dispersed to their homes. Then the main road was dotted with philosophers, grammarians, and theologians. Those who had nowhere to go went to stay with some comrade. The philosophers and theologians took a situation, that is, undertook the tutoring of the children in some prosperous family, and received in payment a pair of new boots or sometimes even a coat. The whole crowd trailed along together like a gypsy encampment, boiled their porridge, and slept in the fields. Everyone hauled along a sack in which he had a shirt and a pair of leg wrappers. The theologians were particularly careful and precise: to avoid wearing out their boots, they took them off, hung them on sticks, and carried them on their shoulders, particularly if it was muddy; then, tucking their trousers up above their knees, they splashed fearlessly through the puddles. When they saw a village, they turned off the main road and, going up to any house that seemed a little better looking than the rest, stood in a row before the windows and began singing a chant at the top of their voices. The master of the house, some old Cossack villager, would listen to them for a long time, his head propped on his hands; then he would sob bitterly and say, turning to his wife: "Wife! What the scholars are singing must be very profound. Bring them bacon and anything else that we have." And a whole bowl of dumplings was emptied into the sack; a big piece of bacon, several flat loaves, sometimes a trussed hen, would go into it, too. Fortified with such supplies, the grammarians, rhetoricians, philosophers, and theologians went on their way again. Their numbers lessened, however, the further they went. Almost all wandered off toward their homes, and only those were left whose parental homes were further away.

Once, at the time of such a migration, three students turned off the main road in order to replenish their store of provisions at the first homestead they could find, for their sacks had long been empty. They were the theologian Khaliava, the philosopher Khoma Brut, and the rhetorician Tibery Gorobets.

The theologian was a tall, broad-shouldered fellow; he had an extremely odd habit—anything that lay within his reach he invariably stole. In other circumstances, he was of an excessively gloomy temper, and when he was drunk he used to hide in the rank grass, and the seminarists had a lot of trouble finding him there.

The philosopher, Khoma Brut, was of a cheerful temper, he was very fond of lying on his back, smoking a pipe; when he was drinking he always engaged musicians and danced the *trepak*. He often had a taste of the "peck of peas" but took it with perfect philosophical indifference, saying that there is no escaping what has to be. The rhetorician, Tibery Gorobets, had not yet the right to wear a mustache, to drink vodka, and to smoke a pipe. He only wore a curl around his ear, and so his character was as yet hardly formed; but, judging from the big bumps on the forehead, with which he often appeared in class, it might be presumed that he would make a good fighter. The theologian, Khaliava, and the philosopher, Khoma, often pulled him by the forelock as a sign of their favor, and employed him as their messenger.

It was evening when they turned off the main road; the sun had only just set and the warmth of the day still lingered in the air. The theologian and the philosopher walked along in silence smoking their pipes; the rhetorician, Tibery Gorobets, kept knocking off the heads of the wayside thistles with his stick. The road ran between scattered groups of oak and nut trees standing here and there in the meadows. Sloping uplands, little hills, green and round as cupolas, were interspersed here and there about the plain. The fields of ripening wheat, which came into view in two places, showed that some village must soon be seen. However, it was more than an hour since they had passed the wheatfields and still they had come upon no dwelling. The sky was now completely wrapped in darkness, and only in the west was there a pale streak left of the glow of sunset.

"What the hell does it mean?" said the philosopher, Khoma Brut. "It looked as though a village would appear in a minute."

The theologian did not speak; he gazed at the surrounding country, then put his pipe back in his mouth, and they continued on their way.

"I swear!" the philosopher said, stopping again, "not even the fist of a devil is to be seen."

"Maybe some village will turn up further on," said the theologian, not removing his pipe.

But meantime night had come on, and a rather dark night it was. Small storm clouds increased the gloom, and by every sign they could expect neither stars nor moon. The students noticed that they had lost their way and for a long time had been walking off the road.

The philosopher, after feeling about with his feet in all directions, said at last, abruptly: "Where's the road?"

The theologian did not speak for a while, then after pondering, he said: "Yes, it is a dark night."

The rhetorician walked off to one side and tried on his hands and knees to feel for the road, but his hands came upon nothing but foxes' holes. On all sides of them there was the steppe, which, it seemed, no one had ever crossed.

The travelers made another effort to press on a little, but there was the same wilderness in all directions. The philosopher tried shouting, but his voice seemed completely lost on the steppe, and met with no reply. All they heard was, a little afterward, a faint moaning like the howl of a wolf.

"What are we to do?" said the philosopher.

"Why, stop and sleep in the open!" said the theologian, and he felt in his pocket for flint and tinder to light his pipe again. But the philosopher could not agree to this: it was always his habit at night to put away a quarter-loaf of bread and four pounds of bacon, and he was conscious on this occasion of an insufferable sense of loneliness in his stomach. Besides, in spite of his cheerful temper, the philosopher was rather afraid of wolves.

"No, Khaliava, we can't," he said. "What, stretch out and lie down like a dog, without having eaten anything? Let's make another try for it; maybe we'll stumble on some dwelling place and get at least a drink of vodka for supper."

At the word "vodka" the theologian spat to one side and said: "Well, of course, it's no use staying in the open."

The students walked on, and to their intense delight, they caught the sound of barking in the distance. Listening which way it came from, they walked on more boldly and a little later saw a light.

"A village! It really is a village!" said the philosopher.

He was not mistaken in his supposition; in a little while they actually saw a small homestead consisting of only two huts looking into the same farmyard. There was a light in the windows; a dozen plum trees stood by the fence. Looking through the cracks in the gates made of paling the students saw a yard filled with carts of merchants. Stars peeped out here and there in the sky at the moment.

"Look, fellows, let's not be put off! We must get a night's lodging somehow!"

The three learned gentlemen banged on the gates together and shouted, "Open!"

The door of one of the huts creaked, and a minute later they saw before them an old woman in sheepskin.

"Who is there?" she cried, with a hollow cough.

"Give us a night's lodging, granny; we have lost our way; a night in the open is as bad as a hungry belly."

"What manner of folks may you be?"

"Oh, harmless folks: Khaliava, a theologian; Brut, a philosopher; and Gorobets, a rhetorician."

"I can't," grumbled the old woman. "The yard is crowded with folk and every corner in the hut is full. Where am I to put you? And such great hulking fellows, too! Why, it would knock my hut to pieces if I put such fellows in it. I know these philosophers and theologians; if one began taking in these drunken fellows, there'd soon be no home left. Be off, be off! There's no place for you here!"

"Have pity on us, granny! How can you let Christian souls perish for no rhyme or reason? Put us where you please; and if we do anything wrong or anything else, may our arms be withered, and God only knows what befall us—so there!"

The old woman seemed somewhat softened.

"Very well," she said, as though reconsidering. "I'll let you in, but I'll put you all in different places; for my mind won't be at rest if you are all together."

"That's as you please; we'll make no objection," answered the students.

The gate creaked and they went into the yard.

"Well, granny," said the philosopher, following the old woman, "how would it be, as they say . . . I swear I feel as though somebody were driving a cart in my stomach: not a morsel has passed my lips all day."

"What next will he want!" said the old woman. "No, I've nothing to give you, and the oven's not been heated today."

"But we'd pay for it all," the philosopher went on, "tomorrow morning, in hard cash. Yes!" he added in an undertone, "the devil you'll get!"

"Go in, go in! and you must be satisfied with what you're given. Fine young gentlemen the devil has brought us!"

Khoma the philosopher was thrown into utter dejection by these words, but his nose was suddenly aware of the odor of dried fish; he glanced toward the trousers of the theologian, who was walking at his side, and saw a huge fishtail sticking out of his pocket. The theologian had already succeeded in requisitioning a whole carp from a wagon. And as he had done this from no selfish motive but simply from habit, and, quite forgetting his carp, was already looking about for anything else he could carry off, having no mind to miss even a broken wheel, the philosopher slipped his hand into his friend's pocket, as though it were his own, and pulled out the carp.

The old woman put the students in their several places: the rhetorician she kept in the hut, the theologian she locked in an empty closet, the philosopher she assigned a sheep's pen, also empty.

The latter, on finding himself alone, instantly devoured the carp, examined the walls of the pen, kicked an inquisitive pig that woke up and thrust its snout in from the next pen, and turned over on his right side to fall into a sound sleep. All at once the low door opened, and the old woman, bending down, stepped into the pen.

"What is it, granny, what do you want?" said the philosopher.

But the old woman came toward him with outstretched arms.

"Aha, ha!" thought the philosopher. "No, my dear, you are too old!"

He turned away a little, but the old woman unceremoniously approached him again.

"Listen, granny!" said the philosopher. "It's a fast time now; and I am a man who wouldn't sin in a fast for a thousand gold pieces."

But the old woman opened her arms and tried to catch him without saying a word.

The philosopher was frightened, especially when he noticed a strange glitter in her eyes. "Granny, what is it? Go—go away— God bless you!" he cried.

The old woman said not a word, but tried to clutch him in her arms.

He leaped to his feet, intending to escape; but the old woman stood in the doorway, fixed her glittering eyes on him, and again began approaching him.

The philosopher tried to push her back with his hands but, to his surprise, found that his arms would not rise, his legs would not move, and he perceived with horror that even his voice would not obey him: words hovered on his lips without a sound. He heard nothing but the beating of his heart. He saw the old woman approach him. She folded his arms, bent his head down, leaped with the swiftness of a cat upon his back, and struck him with a broom on the side; and he, prancing like a horse, carried her on his shoulders. All this happened so quickly that the philosopher scarcely knew what he was doing. He clutched his knees in both hands, trying to stop his legs from moving, but, to his extreme amazement, they were lifted against his will and executed capers more swiftly than a Circassian racer. Only when they had left the farm, and the wide plain lay stretched before them with a forest black as coal on one side, he said to himself: "Aha! she's a witch!"

The waning crescent of the moon was shining in the sky. The timid radiance of midnight lay mistily over the earth, light as a transparent veil. The forests, the meadows, the sky, the dales, all seemed as though slumbering with open eyes; not a breeze fluttered anywhere; there was a damp warmth in the freshness of the night; the shadows of the trees and bushes fell on the sloping plain in pointed wedge shapes like comets. Such was the night when Khoma Brut, the philosopher, set off galloping with a mysterious rider on his back. He was aware of an exhausting, unpleasant, and at the same time, voluptuous sensation assailing his heart. He bent his head and saw that the grass which had been almost under his feet seemed growing far below him, and that above it there lay water, transparent as a mountain stream, and the grass seemed to be at the bottom of a clear sea, limpid to its very depths; anyway, he saw clearly in it his own reflection with the old woman sitting on his back. He saw shining there a sun instead of the moon; he heard the bluebells ringing as they bent their little heads; he saw a water sprite float out from behind the reeds, there was the gleam of her leg and back, rounded and firm, all brightness and shimmering. She turned toward him and now her face came nearer, with eyes clear, sparkling, keen, with singing that pierced the heart; now it was on the surface, and shaking with sparkling laughter it moved away; and now she turned on her back, and her cloudlike breasts, dead white like unglazed china, gleamed in the sun at the edges of their white, soft, and supple roundness. Little bubbles of water like beads bedewed them. She was all quivering and laughing in the water. . . .

Did he see this or did he not? Was he awake or dreaming? But what was that? The wind or music? It was ringing, ringing and reverberating and coming closer and piercing his heart with an insufferable thrill. . . .

"What does it mean?" the philosopher wondered, looking down as he flew along, full speed. The sweat was streaming from him. He was aware of a fiendishly voluptuous feeling; he felt a stabbing, exhaustingly terrible delight. It often seemed to him as though his heart had melted away, and with terror he clutched at it. Worn out, desperate, he began trying to recall all the prayers he knew. He went through all the exorcisms against evil spirits, and all at once felt somewhat refreshed; he felt that his step was growing slower, the witch's hold upon his back seemed feebler, thick grass touched him, and now he saw nothing extraordinary in it. The clear, crescent moon was shining in the sky.

"Good!" the philosopher Khoma thought to himself, and he began repeating the exorcisms almost aloud. At last, quick as lightning, he sprang from under the old woman and in his turn leaped on her back. The old woman, with a tiny tripping step, ran so fast that her rider could scarcely breathe. The earth flashed by under him; everything was clear in the moonlight, though the moon was not full; the ground was smooth, but everything flashed by so rapidly that it was confused and indistinct. He snatched up a piece of wood that lay on the road and began whacking the old woman with all his might. She uttered wild howls; at first they were angry and menacing, then they grew fainter, sweeter, clearer, then rang out gently like delicate silver bells that went straight to his heart; and the thought flashed through his mind: was it really an old woman?

"Oh, I can do no more!" she murmured, and sank exhausted on the ground.

He stood up and looked into her face (there was the glow of sunrise, and the golden domes of the Kiev churches were gleaming in the distance): before him lay a beautiful girl with luxuriant tresses all in disorder and eyelashes as long as arrows. Senseless, she tossed her bare white arms and moaned, looking upward with eyes full of tears.

Khoma trembled like a leaf on a tree; he was overcome by pity and a strange emotion and timidity, feelings he could not himself explain. He began running, full speed. His heart throbbed uneasily as he went, and he could not account for the strange new feeling that had taken possession of it. He did not want to go back to the farm; he hastened to Kiev, thinking all the way of this incomprehensible adventure.

There was scarcely a student left in the town. All had dispersed about the countryside, either to jobs as tutors, or simply without them; because in the villages of Little Russia they could get dumplings, cheese, sour cream, and puddings as big as a hat without paying a kopek for them. The big rambling house in which the students were lodged was absolutely empty, and although the philosopher rummaged in every corner, and even felt in all the holes and cracks in the roof, he could not find a bit of bacon or even a stale roll such as were commonly hidden there by the students.

The philosopher, however, soon found means to improve his lot: he walked whistling three times through the market, finally winked at a young widow in a yellow bonnet who was selling ribbons, shot, and wheels—and was that very day regaled with wheat dumplings, a chicken . . . in short, there is no telling what was on the table laid for him in a little mud hut in the middle of a cherry orchard.

The same evening the philosopher was seen in a tavern; he was lying on the bench, smoking a pipe as his habit was, and in the sight of all he flung the Jew who kept the tavern a gold coin. A mug stood before him. He looked at all that came in and went out with cool, contented eyes, and thought no more of his extraordinary adventure.

Meanwhile rumors were circulating everywhere that the daughter of one of the richest Cossack captains,[4] who lived nearly forty miles from Kiev, had returned one day from a walk, terribly injured, hardly able to crawl home to her father's house, was lying at the point of death, and had expressed a wish that one of the Kiev seminarists, Khoma Brut, should read the prayers over her and the psalms for three days after her death. The philosopher heard of this from the rector himself, who summoned him to his room and informed him that he was to set off on the journey without any delay, that the Cossack captain had sent servants and a carriage to fetch him.

The philosopher shuddered from an unaccountable feeling which he could not have explained to himself. A dark presentiment told him that something evil was awaiting him. Without knowing why, he bluntly declared that he would not go.

"Listen, Domine Khoma!" said the rector. (On some occasions he expressed himself very courteously with those under his authority.) "Who the hell is asking you whether you want to go or not? All I have to tell you is that if you go on flaunting your wit and making trouble, I'll order you such a whacking with a young birch tree, on your back and the rest of you, that there will be no need for you to go to the bath[5] after."

The philosopher, scratching behind his ear, went out without uttering a word, proposing at the first suitable opportunity to put his trust in his heels. Plunged in thought he went down the steep staircase that led into a yard shut in by poplars, and stood still for a minute, hearing quite distinctly the voice of the rector giving orders to his butler and someone else—probably one of the servants sent to fetch him by the officer.

"Thank his honor for the grain and the eggs," the rector was saying: "and tell him that as soon as the books about which he writes are ready I will send them at once, I have already given them to a scribe to be copied, and don't forget, my good man, to mention to his honor that I know there are excellent fish at his place, especially sturgeon, and he might on occasion send some; here in

---

[4] *Sotniks,* Cossack officers who commanded one hundred troops originally, a greater number in later times. (ed.)
[5] *Bania,* a bathhouse where birch twigs are used to massage and cleanse the skin. (ed.)

the market the fish are bad and expensive. And you, Yavtukh, give the young fellows a cup of vodka each, and tie up the philosopher or he'll run off directly."

"There, the devil's son!" the philosopher thought to himself. "He got wind of it, the long-legged charlatan!" He went down and saw a covered chaise, which he almost took at first for a baker's oven on wheels. It was, indeed, as deep as the oven in which bricks are baked. It was only the ordinary Cracow carriage in which Jews travel fifty together with their wares to all the towns where they smell out a fair. Six healthy and powerful Cossacks, no longer young, were waiting for him. Their coats of fine cloth, with tassels, showed that they belonged to a rather important and wealthy master; some small scars proved that they had at some time been in battle, not ingloriously.

"What's to be done? What is to be must be!" the philosopher thought to himself and, turning to the Cossacks, he said aloud: "Good day to you, comrades!"

"Good health to you, master philosopher," some of the Cossacks replied.

"So I am to get in with you? It's a large chaise!" he went on, as he clambered in, "we need only hire some musicians and we might dance here."

"Yes, it's a carriage of ample proportions," said one of the Cossacks, seating himself on the box beside the coachman, who had tied a rag over his head to replace the cap which he had managed to leave behind at a tavern. The other five and the philosopher crawled into the recesses of the chaise and settled themselves on sacks filled with various purchases they had made in the town. "It would be interesting to know," said the philosopher, "if this chaise were loaded up with goods of some sort, salt for instance, or iron wedges, how many horses would be needed then?"

"Yes," the Cossack sitting on the box said after a pause, "it would need a sufficient number of horses."

After this satisfactory reply the Cossack thought himself entitled to hold his tongue for the remainder of the journey.

The philosopher was extremely desirous of learning more in detail, who this captain was, what he was like, what had been heard about his daughter who in such a strange way returned home and was found on the point of death, and whose story was now connected with his own, what was being done in the house, and how things were there. He addressed the Cossacks with inquiries, but no doubt they too were philosophers, for by way of a reply they remained silent, smoking their pipes and lying on their backs. Only one of them turned to the driver on the box with a brief order: "Take care, Overko, you old buzzard, when you are near the tavern on the Chukhrailovski road, don't forget to stop and wake me and the other fellows if any should happen to drop asleep."

After this he fell asleep rather noisily. These instructions were, however, quite unnecessary, for as soon as the gigantic chaise drew near the tavern all the Cossacks shouted together: "Stop!" Moreover, Overko's horses were already trained to stop themselves at every tavern.

In spite of the hot July day, they all got out of the chaise and went into the low-pitched dirty room, where the Jew who kept the tavern hastened to receive his old friends with every sign of delight. The Jew brought from under the skirt of his coat some ham sausages, and putting them on the table, turned his back at once on this food forbidden by the Talmud. All the Cossacks sat down around the table; earthenware mugs were set for each of the guests. Khoma had to take part in the general festivity, and, as Little Russians infallibly begin kissing each other or weeping when they are drunk, soon the whole room resounded with smacks. "Come, Spirid, a kiss." "Come here, Dorosh, I want to embrace you!"

One Cossack with gray mustaches, a little older than the rest, propped his cheek on his hand and began sobbing bitterly at the thought that he had no father nor mother and was all alone in the world. Another one, much given to moralizing, persisted in consoling him, saying: "Don't cry; please don't cry! What is there in it . . . ? The Lord knows best, you know."

The one whose name was Dorosh became extremely inquisitive, and, turning to the philosopher Khoma, kept asking him: "I should like to know what they teach you in the seminary. Is it the same as what the deacon reads in church, or something different?"

"Don't ask!" the sermonizing Cossack said emphatically: "let it be as it is. God knows what is wanted, God knows everything."

"No, I want to know," said Dorosh, "what is written there in those books? Maybe it is quite different from what the deacon reads."

"Oh, my goodness, my goodness!" said the sermonizing worthy, "and why say such a thing; it's as the Lord wills. There is no changing what the Lord has willed!"

"I want to know all that's written. I'll go to the seminary, I will. Do you suppose I can't learn? I'll learn it all, all!"

"Oh my goodness . . . !" said the sermonizing Cossack, and he dropped his head on the table, because he was utterly incapable of supporting it any longer on his shoulders. The other Cossacks were discussing their masters and the question of why the moon shone in the sky. The philosopher, seeing the state of their minds, resolved to seize his opportunity and make his escape. To begin with he turned to the gray-headed Cossack who was grieving for his father and mother.

"Why are you blubbering, uncle?" he said. "I am an orphan myself! Let me go in freedom, fellows! What do you want with me?"

"Let him go!" several responded. "Why, he is an orphan, let him go where he likes."

"Oh, my goodness, my goodness!" the moralizing Cossack articulated, lifting his head. "Let him go!"

"Let him go where he likes!"

And the Cossacks meant to lead him out into the open air themselves, but the one who had displayed his curiosity stopped them, saying: "Don't touch him. I want to talk to him about the seminary: I am going to the seminary myself. . . ."

It is doubtful, however, whether the escape could have taken place, for when the philosopher tried to get up from the table his legs seemed to have become wooden, and he began to perceive such a number of doors in the room that he could hardly discover the real one.

It was evening before the Cossacks realized that they had further to go. Clambering into the chaise, they trailed along the road, urging on the horses and singing a song of which nobody could have made out the words or the sense. After trundling on for the greater part of the night, continually straying off the road, though they knew every inch of the way, they drove at last down a steep hill into a valley, and the philosopher noticed a fence that ran alongside, low trees and roofs peeping out behind it. This was a big village belonging to the captain. By now it was long past midnight; the sky was dark, but there were little stars twinkling here and there. No light was to be seen in a single hut. To the accompaniment of the barking of dogs, they drove into the courtyard. Thatched barns and little houses came into sight on both sides; one of the latter, which stood exactly in the middle opposite the gates, was larger than the others, and was apparently the officer's residence. The chaise drew up before a little shed that served as a barn, and our travelers went off to bed. The philosopher, however, wanted to inspect the outside of the officer's house; but, though he stared his hardest, nothing could be seen distinctly; the house looked to him like a bear; the chimney turned into the rector. The philosopher gave up the idea and went to sleep.

When he woke up, the whole house was in commotion: the captain's daughter had died during the night. Servants were hurriedly running back and forth; some old women were crying; an inquisitive crowd was looking through the fence at the house, as though something might be seen there. The philosopher began leisurely examining the objects he could not discern in the night. The captain's house was a little, low-pitched building, such as was usual in Little Russia in old days; its roof was of thatch; a small, high, pointed gable with a little window that looked like an eye turned upward, was painted in blue and yellow flowers and red crescents; it was supported on oak posts, rounded above and hexagonal below, with carving at the top. Under the gable was a little porch with seats on each side. There were verandas around the house resting on similar posts, some of them carved in spirals. A tall pyramidal pear tree, with trembling leaves, made a patch of green in front of the house. Two rows of barns for storing grain stood in the middle of the yard, forming a sort of wide street leading to the house. Beyond the barns, close to the gate, stood facing each other two three-cornered storehouses, also thatched. Each triangular wall was painted in various designs and had a little door in it. On one of them was depicted a Cossack sitting on a barrel, holding a mug above his head with the inscription: "I'll drink it all!" On the other, there was a bottle, flagons, and at the sides, by way of ornament, a horse upside down, a pipe, a tambourine, and the inscription: "Wine is the Cossack's comfort!" A drum and brass trumpets could be seen through the huge window in the loft of one of the barns. At the gates stood two cannons. Everything showed that the master of the house was fond of merrymaking, and that the yard often resounded with the shouts of revelers. There were two windmills outside the gate. Behind the house stretched gardens, and through the treetops the dark caps of chimneys were all that could be seen of huts smothered in green bushes. The whole village lay on the broad sloping side of a hill. The steep side, at the very foot of which lay the courtyard, made a screen from the north. Looked at from below, it seemed even steeper, and here and there on its tall top uneven stalks of rough grass stood out black against the clear sky; its bare aspect was somehow depressing; its clay soil was hollowed out by the fall and trickle of rain. Two huts stood at some distance from each other on its steep slope; one of them was overshadowed by the branches of a spreading apple tree, banked up with soil and supported by short stakes near the root. The apples, knocked down by the wind, were falling right into the master's courtyard. The road, coiling about the hill from the very top, ran down beside the courtyard to the village. When the philosopher scanned its terrific steepness and recalled their journey down it the previous night, he came to the conclusion that either the captain had very clever horses or that the Cossacks had very strong heads to have managed, even when drunk, to escape flying head over heels with the immense chaise and baggage. The philosopher was standing on the highest point in the yard. When he turned and looked in the opposite direction he saw quite a different view. The village sloped away into a plain. Meadows stretched as far as the eye could see; their brilliant verdure was deeper in the distance, and whole rows of villages looked like dark patches in it, though they must have been more than fifteen miles away. To the right of the meadowlands was a line of hills, and a hardly perceptible streak of flashing light and darkness showed where the Dnieper ran.

"Ah, a wonderful spot!" said the philosopher, "this would be the place to live, fishing in the Dnieper and the ponds, birdcatching with nets, or shooting kingsnipe and little bustards. Though I do believe there would be a few great bustards too in those meadows! One could dry lots of fruit, too, and sell it in the town, or, better still, make vodka of it, for there's no drink to compare with fruit vodka. But it would be just as well to consider how to slip away from here."

He noticed outside the fence a little path completely overgrown with weeds; he was mechanically setting his foot on it with the idea of simply going first out for a walk, and then stealthily passing between the huts and dashing out into the open country, when he suddenly felt a rather strong hand on his shoulder.

Behind him stood the old Cossack who had on the previous evening so bitterly bewailed the death of his father and mother and his own solitary state.

"It's no good your thinking of running away, Mr. Philosopher!" he said: "this isn't the sort of establishment you can run away from; and the roads are bad, too, for anyone on foot; you had better come to the master: he's been expecting you for a long time in the parlor."

"Let's go! To be sure . . . I'm delighted," said the philosopher, and he followed the Cossack.

The officer, an elderly man with gray mustaches and an expression of gloomy sadness, was sitting at a table in the parlor, his head propped on his hands. He was about fifty; but the deep despondency on his face and its wan pallor showed that his soul had been crushed and shattered at one blow, and all his old gaiety and noisy merrymaking had disappeared forever. When Khoma went in with the old Cossack, he removed one hand from his face and gave a slight nod in response to their low bows.

Khoma and the Cossack stood respectfully at the door.

"Who are you, where do you come from, and what is your calling, good man?" said the captain, in a voice neither friendly nor ill-humored.

"A bursar, student in philosophy, Khoma Brut . . ."

"Who was your father?"

"I don't know, honored sir."

"Your mother?"

"I don't know my mother either. It is reasonable to suppose, of course, that I had a mother; but who she was and where she came from, and when she lived—I swear, good sir, I don't know."

The old man paused and seemed to sink into a reverie for a minute.

"How did you come to know my daughter?"

"I didn't know her, honored sir, I swear, I didn't. I have never had anything to do with young ladies, never in my life. Bless them, begging your pardon!"

"Why did she select you and no other to read the psalms over her?"

The philosopher shrugged his shoulders. "God knows how to explain that. It's a well-known thing, the gentry are forever taking fancies that the most learned men couldn't explain, and the proverb says: 'The devil himself must dance at the master's bidding.' "

"Are you telling the truth, philosopher?"

"May I be struck down by thunder on the spot if I'm not."

"If she had only lived one brief moment longer," the captain said to himself mournfully, "I should have learned all about it. 'Let no one else read over me, but send, Father, at once to the Kiev Seminary and fetch the bursar, Khoma Brut; let him pray three nights for my sinful soul. He knows . . . !' But what he knows, I did not hear: she, poor darling, could say no more before she died. You, good man, are no doubt well known for your holy life and pious works, and she, maybe, heard tell of you."

"Who? I?" said the philosopher, stepping back in amazement. "I —holy life!" he articulated, looking straight in the officer's face. "God be with you, sir! What are you talking about! Why—though it's not a decent thing to speak of—I paid the baker's wife a visit on Holy Thursday."

"Well . . . I suppose there must be some reason for selecting you. You must begin your duties this very day."

"As to that, I would tell your honor . . . Of course, any man versed in Holy Scripture may, as far as in him lies . . . but a deacon or a sacristan would be better fitted for it. They are men of understanding, and know how it is all done, while I . . . Besides I haven't the right voice for it, and I myself am good for nothing. I'm not the figure for it."

"Well, say what you like, I shall carry out all my darling's wishes; I will spare nothing. And if for three nights from today you duly recite the prayers over her, I will reward you; if not . . . I don't advise the devil himself to anger me!"

The last words were uttered by the captain so vigorously that the philosopher fully grasped their significance.

"Follow me!" said the captain.

They went out into the hall. The captain opened the door into another room, opposite the first. The philosopher paused a minute in the hall to blow his nose and crossed the threshold with unaccountable apprehension.

The whole floor was covered with red cotton material. On a high table in the corner under the holy images lay the body of the dead girl on a coverlet of dark blue velvet adorned with gold fringe and tassels. Tall wax candles, entwined with sprigs of guelder rose, stood at her feet and head, shedding a dim light that was lost in the brightness of daylight. The dead girl's face was hidden from him by the inconsolable father, who sat down facing her with his back to the door. The philosopher was impressed by the words he heard:

"I am grieving, my dearly beloved daughter, not that in the flower of your age you have left the earth, to my sorrow and mourning, without living your allotted span; I grieve, my darling, that I know not him, my bitter foe, who was the cause of your death. And if I knew the man who could but dream of hurting you, or even saying anything unkind of you, I swear to God he should not see his children again, if he be old as I, nor his father and mother, if he be of that time of life, and his body should be cast out to be devoured by the birds and beasts of the steppe! But my grief it is, my wild marigold, my bird, light of my eyes, that I must live out my days without comfort, wiping with the skirt of my coat the trickling tears that flow from my old eyes, while my enemy will be making merry and secretly mocking the feeble old man. . . ."

He came to a standstill, due to an outburst of sorrow, which found vent in a flood of tears.

The philosopher was touched by such inconsolable sadness; he coughed, uttering a hollow sound in the effort to clear his throat. The captain turned around and pointed him to a place at the dead girl's head, before a small lectern with books on it.

"I shall get through three nights somehow," thought the philosopher: "and the old man will stuff both my pockets with gold pieces for it."

He drew near, and clearing his throat once more, began reading, paying no attention to anything else and not venturing to glance at the face of the dead girl. A profound stillness reigned in the room. He noticed that the captain had withdrawn. Slowly he turned his head to look at the dead, and . . .

A shudder ran through his veins: before him lay a beauty whose like had surely never been on earth before. Never, it seemed, could features have been formed in such striking yet harmonious beauty. She lay as though living: the lovely forehead, fair as snow, as silver, looked deep in thought; the even brows—dark as night in the midst of sunshine—rose proudly above the closed eyes; the eyelashes, that fell like arrows on the cheeks, glowed with the warmth of secret desires; the lips were rubies, ready to break into the laugh of bliss, the flood of joy . . . But in them, in those very features, he saw something terrible and poignant. He felt a sickening ache stirring in his heart, as though, in the midst of a whirl of gaiety and dancing crowds, someone had begun singing a funeral dirge. The rubies of her lips looked like blood surging up from her heart. All at once he was aware of something dreadfully familiar in her face. "The witch!" he cried in a voice not his own, as, turning pale, he looked away and fell to repeating his prayers. It was the witch that he had killed!

When the sun was setting, they carried the corpse to the church. The philosopher supported the coffin swathed in black on his shoulder, and felt something cold as ice on it. The captain walked in front, with his hand on the right side of the dead girl's narrow coffin. The wooden church, blackened by age and overgrown with green lichen, stood disconsolately, with its three cone-shaped domes, at the very end of the village. It was evident that no service had been performed in it for a long time. Candles had been lighted before almost every image. The coffin was set down in the center opposite the altar. The old captain kissed the dead girl once more, bowed down to the ground, and went out with the coffin bearers, giving orders that the philosopher should have a good supper and then be taken to the church. On reaching the kitchen all the men who had carried the coffin began putting their hands on the stove, as the custom is with Little Russians, after seeing a dead body.

The hunger of which the philosopher began at that moment to be conscious made him for some minutes entirely oblivious of the dead girl. Soon all the servants began gradually assembling in the kitchen, which in the captain's house was something like a club, where all the inhabitants of the yard gathered together, including even the dogs, who, wagging their tails, came to the door for bones and scraps. Wherever anybody might be sent, and with whatever duty he might be charged, he always went first to the kitchen to rest for at least a minute on the bench and smoke a pipe. All the unmarried men in their smart Cossack coats lay there almost all day long, on the bench, under the bench, or on the stove—anywhere, in fact, where a comfortable place could be found. Then everybody invariably left behind in the kitchen either his cap or a whip to keep stray dogs off or some such thing. But the biggest crowd always gathered at suppertime, when the coachman who had taken the horses to the paddock, and the herdsman who had brought the cows in to be milked, and all the others who were not to be seen during the day, came in. At supper, even the most taciturn tongues were moved to loquacity. It was then that all the news was discussed: who had got himself new trousers, and what was hidden in the bowels of the earth, and who had seen a wolf. There were witty talkers among them; indeed, there is no lack of them anywhere among the Little Russians.

The philosopher sat down with the others in a big circle in the open air before the kitchen door. Soon a peasant woman in a red bonnet popped out, holding in both hands a steaming bowl of dumplings, which she set down in their midst. Each pulled out a wooden spoon from his pocket, or, for lack of a spoon, a wooden stick. As soon as their jaws began moving more slowly, and the wolfish hunger of the whole party was somewhat assuaged, many of them began talking. The conversation naturally turned on the dead maiden.

"Is it true," said a young shepherd who had put so many buttons and copper disks on the leather strap on which his pipe hung that he looked like a small haberdasher's shop, "is it true that the young lady, pardon the expression, was on friendly terms with the Evil One?"

"Who? The young mistress?" said Dorosh, a man our philosopher already knew, "why, she was a witch! I'll take my oath she was a witch!"

"Hush, hush, Dorosh," said another man, who had shown a great disposition to soothe the others on the journey, "that's no business of ours, forget it. It's no good talking about it."

But Dorosh was not at all inclined to hold his tongue; he had just been to the cellar on some job with the butler, and, having applied his lips to two or three barrels, he had come out extremely merry and talked away without ceasing.

"What do you mean? Me to be quiet?" he said. "Why, I've been ridden by her myself! I swear I have!"

"Tell us, uncle," said the young shepherd with the buttons, "are there signs by which you can tell a witch?"

"No, you can't," answered Dorosh, "there's no way of telling; you might read through all the psalm books and you couldn't tell."

"Yes, you can, Dorosh, you can; don't say that," the former com-

forter objected; "it's with good purpose God has given every creature its peculiar habit; folks that have studied say that a witch has a
little tail."

"When a woman's old, she's a witch," the gray-headed Cossack
said coolly.

"Oh! you're a nice bunch!" retorted the peasant woman, who
was at that instant pouring a fresh lot of dumplings into the empty
pot; "regular fat hogs!"

The old Cossack, whose name was Yavtukh and nickname Kov-
tun, gave a smile of satisfaction, seeing that his words had cut the
old woman to the quick; while the herdsman gave vent to a guffaw,
like the bellowing of two bulls as they stand facing each other.

The beginning of the conversation had aroused the philosopher's
curiosity and made him intensely anxious to learn more details about
the captain's daughter, and so, wishing to bring the conversation
back to that subject, he turned to his neighbor with the words: "I
should like to ask why all the folk sitting at supper here look upon
the young mistress as a witch? Did she do mischief to anybody or
bring anybody to harm?"

"There were all sorts of doings," answered one of the company,
a man with a flat face strikingly resembling a spade. "Everybody
remembers the huntsman Mikita and the . . ."

"What about the huntsman Mikita?" said the philosopher.

"Stop! I'll tell about the huntsman Mikita," said Dorosh.

"I'll tell about him," said the coachman, "for he was a great
crony of mine."

"I'll tell about Mikita," said Spirid.

"Let him, let Spirid tell it!" shouted the company.

Spirid began: "You didn't know Mikita, Mr. Philosopher Khoma.
Ah, he was a man! He knew every dog as well as he knew his own
father. The huntsman we've got now, Mikola, who's sitting next
but one from me, isn't worth the sole of his shoe. Though he
knows his job, too, but beside the other he's trash, garbage."

"You tell the story well, very well!" said Dorosh, nodding his
head approvingly.

Spirid went on: "He'd see a hare quicker than you'd wipe the
snuff from your nose. He'd whistle: 'Here, Breaker! Here, Swift-
foot!' and he in full gallop on his horse; and there was no saying
which would outrace the other, he the dog, or the dog him. He'd
toss off a mug of vodka without winking. He was a fine huntsman!"

Only a little time back he began to be always staring at the young mistress. Whether he had fallen in love with her, or whether she had simply bewitched him, anyway the man was done for, he became stupid; the devil only knows what he turned into . . . pfoo! No decent word for it. . . ."

"That's good," said Dorosh.

"As soon as the young mistress looks at him, he drops the bridle out of his hand, calls Breaker 'Bushybrow,' is all of a fluster and doesn't know what he's doing. One day the young mistress comes into the stable where he is rubbing down a horse.

" 'Mikita,' says she, 'let me put my little foot on you.' And he, foolish fellow, is pleased at that. 'Not your foot only,' says he, 'you may sit on me altogether.' The young mistress lifted her foot, and, as soon as he saw her bare, plump white leg, he went fairly crazy, so he said. He bent his back, silly fellow, and clasping her bare legs in his hands, ran galloping like a horse all over the countryside. And he couldn't say where he was driven, but he came back more dead than alive, and from that time he withered up like a chip of wood; and one day when they went into the stable, instead of him they found a heap of ashes lying there and an empty pail; he had burned up entirely, burned up by himself. And he was a huntsman such as you couldn't find another all the world over."

When Spirid had finished his story, reflections upon the rare qualities of the deceased huntsman followed from all sides.

"And haven't you heard tell of Sheptun's wife?" said Dorosh, addressing Khoma.

"No."

"Well, well! You are not taught with too much sense, it seems, in the seminary. Listen, then. There's a Cossack called Sheptun in our village—a good Cossack! He is given to stealing at times, and telling lies when there's no occasion, but . . . he's a good Cossack. His place is not so far from here. Just about the very hour that we sat down this evening at the table, Sheptun and his wife finished their supper and lay down to sleep, and, as it was fine weather, his wife lay down in the yard, and Sheptun in the hut on the bench; or no . . . it was the wife lay indoors on the bench and Sheptun in the yard . . ."

"Not on the bench; she was lying on the floor," said a peasant woman, who stood in the doorway with her cheek propped in her hand.

Dorosh looked at her, then looked down, then looked at her again, and after a brief pause, said: "When I strip off your petticoat before everybody, you won't be pleased."

This warning had its effect; the old woman held her tongue and did not interrupt the story again.

Dorosh went on: "And in the cradle hanging in the middle of the hut lay a baby a year old—whether of the male or female sex I can't say. Sheptun's wife was lying there when she heard a dog scratching at the door and howling fit to make you run out of the hut. She was scared, for women are such foolish creatures that, if toward evening you put your tongue out at one from behind a door, her heart's in her mouth. However, she thought: 'Well, I'll go and give that damned dog a whack on its nose, and maybe it will stop howling,' and taking the poker she went to open the door. She had hardly opened it when a dog dashed in between her legs and straight to the baby's cradle. She saw that it was no longer a dog, but the young mistress, and, if it had been the young lady in her own shape as she knew her, it would not have been so bad. But the peculiar thing is that she was all blue and her eyes glowing like coals. She snatched up the child, bit its throat, and began sucking its blood. Sheptun's wife could only scream: 'Oh, horror!' and rushed toward the door. But she sees the door's locked in the passage; she flies up to the loft and there she sits trembling, the foolish woman; and then she sees the young mistress coming up to her in the loft; she pounced on her, and began biting the foolish woman. When Sheptun pulled his wife down from the loft in the morning she was bitten all over and had turned black and blue; and next day the foolish woman died. So you see what uncanny and wicked doings happen in the world! Though it is of the gentry's breed, a witch is a witch."

After telling the story, Dorosh looked about him complacently and thrust his finger into his pipe, preparing to fill it with tobacco. The subject of the witch seemed inexhaustible. Each in turn hastened to tell some tale of her. One had seen the witch in the form of a haystack come right up to the door of his cottage; another had had his cap or his pipe stolen by her; many of the girls in the village had had their hair cut off by her; others had lost several quarts of blood which she had sucked from them.

At last they pulled themselves together and saw that they had been chattering too long, for it was quite dark in the yard. They all began wandering off to their sleeping places, which were either in the kitchen, or the barns, or the middle of the courtyard.

"Well, Mr. Khoma! now it's time for us to go to the deceased lady," said the gray-headed Cossack, addressing the philosopher; and with Spirid and Dorosh they set off to the church, lashing with their whips at the dogs, of which there were a great number in the road, and which gnawed their sticks angrily.

Though the philosopher had managed to fortify himself with a good mugful of vodka, he felt a fearfulness creeping stealthily over him as they approached the lighted church. The stories and strange tales he had heard helped to work upon his imagination. The darkness under the fence and the trees grew less thick as they came into the more open place. At last they went into the church enclosure and found a little yard, beyond which there was not a tree to be seen, nothing but open country and meadows swallowed up in the darkness of night. The three Cossacks and Khoma mounted the steep steps to the porch and went into the church. Here they left the philosopher with the best wishes that he might carry out his duties satisfactorily, and locked the door after them, as their master had bidden them.

The philosopher was left alone. First he yawned, then he stretched, then he blew into both hands, and at last he looked about him. In the middle of the church stood the black coffin; candles were gleaming under the dark images; the light from them only lit up the icon stand and shed a faint glimmer in the middle of the church; the distant corners were wrapped in darkness. The tall, old-fashioned icon stand showed traces of great antiquity; its carved fretwork, once gilt, only glistened here and there with splashes of gold; the gilt had peeled off in one place, and was completely tarnished in another; the faces of the saints, blackened by age, had a gloomy look. The philosopher looked around him again. "Well," he said, "what is there to be afraid of here? No living man can come in here, and to guard me from the dead and ghosts from the other world I have prayers that I have but to read aloud to keep them from laying a finger on me. It's all right!" he repeated with a wave of his hand, "let's read." Going up to the lectern he saw some bundles of candles. "That's good," thought the philosopher; "I must light up the whole church so that it may be as bright as daylight. Oh, it is a pity that one must not smoke a pipe in the temple of God!"

And he proceeded to stick up wax candles at all the cornices, lecterns, and images, not stinting them at all, and soon the whole church was flooded with light. Only overhead the darkness seemed somehow more profound, and the gloomy icons looked even more sullenly out of their antique carved frames, which glistened here and there with specks of gilt. He went up to the coffin, looked timidly at the face of the dead—and could not help closing his eyelids with a faint shudder: such terrible, brilliant beauty!

He turned and tried to move away; but with the strange curiosity, the self-contradictory feeling, which dogs a man especially in times of terror, he could not, as he withdrew, resist taking another look. And then, after the same shudder, he looked again. The striking beauty of the dead maiden certainly seemed terrible. Possibly, indeed, she would not have overwhelmed him with such fear if she had been a little less lovely. But there was in her features nothing faded, tarnished, dead; her face was living, and it seemed to the philosopher that she was looking at him with closed eyes. He even fancied that a tear was oozing from under her right eyelid, and, when it rested on her cheek, he saw distinctly that it was a drop of blood.

He walked quickly away to the lectern, opened the book, and to give himself more confidence began reading in a very loud voice. His voice beat upon the wooden church walls, which had so long been deaf and silent; it rang out, forlorn, unechoed, in a deep bass in the absolutely dead stillness, and seemed somehow uncanny even to the reader himself. "What is there to be afraid of?" he was saying meanwhile to himself. "She won't rise up out of her coffin, for she will fear the word of God. Let her lie there! And a fine Cossack I am, if I should be scared. Well, I've drunk a drop too much—that's why it seems dreadful. I'll have a pinch of snuff!" However, as he turned over the pages, he kept taking sidelong glances at the coffin, and an involuntary feeling seemed whispering to him: "Look, look, she is going to get up! See, she'll sit up, she'll look out from the coffin!"

But the silence was deathlike; the coffin stood motionless; the candles shed a perfect flood of light. A church lighted up at night with a dead body in it and no living soul near is full of terror!

Raising his voice, he began singing in various keys, trying to drown the fears that still lurked in him, but every minute he turned his eyes to the coffin, as though asking, in spite of himself: "What if she does sit up, if she gets up?"

But the coffin did not stir. If there had but been some sound! some living creature! There was not so much as a cricket churring in the corner! There was nothing but the faint sputter of a distant candle, the soft sound of a drop of wax falling on the floor.

"What if she were to get up . . . ?"

She was raising her head . . .

He looked at her wildly and rubbed his eyes. She was, indeed, not lying down now, but sitting up in the coffin. He looked away, and again turned his eyes with horror on the coffin. She stood up . . . she was walking about the church with her eyes shut, moving her arms back and forth as though trying to catch someone.

She was coming straight toward him. In terror he drew a circle around him; with an effort he began reading the prayers and pronouncing the exorcisms which had been taught him by a monk who had all his life seen witches and evil spirits.

She stood almost on the very line; but it was clear that she had not the power to cross it, and she turned livid all over like one who has been dead for several days. Khoma had not the courage to look at her; she was terrifying. She ground her teeth and opened her dead eyes; but, seeing nothing, turned with fury— that was apparent in her quivering face—in another direction, and flinging her arms, clutched in them each column and corner, trying to catch Khoma. At last, she stood still, holding up a menacing finger, and lay down again in her coffin.

The philosopher could not recover his self-possession, but kept gazing at the narrow coffin of the witch. At last the coffin suddenly sprang up from its place and with a hissing sound began flying all over the church, zigzagging through the air in all directions.

The philosopher saw it almost over his head, but at the same time he saw that it could not cross the circle he had drawn, and he redoubled his exorcisms. The coffin dropped down in the middle of the church and stayed there without moving. The corpse got up out of it, livid and greenish. But at that instant the crow of the cock was heard in the distance; the corpse sank back in the coffin and closed the lid.

The philosopher's heart was throbbing and the sweat was

streaming down him; but, emboldened by the cock's crowing, he read on more rapidly the pages he ought to have read through before. At the first streak of dawn the sexton came to relieve him, together with old Yavtukh, who was at that time performing the duties of a beadle.

On reaching his distant sleeping place, the philosopher could not for a long time get to sleep; but weariness gained the upper hand at last and he slept on till it was time for dinner. When he woke up, all the events of the night seemed to him to have happened in a dream. To keep up his strength he was given a mug of vodka.

Over dinner he soon grew lively, made a remark or two, and devoured a rather large sucking pig almost unaided; but some feeling he could not have explained made him unable to bring himself to speak of his adventures in the church, and to the inquiries of the inquisitive he replied, "Yes, all sorts of strange things happened." The philosopher was one of those people who, if they are well fed, are moved to extraordinary benevolence. Lying down with his pipe in his teeth, he watched them all with a sweet look in his eyes and kept spitting to one side.

After dinner the philosopher was in excellent spirits. He went around the whole village and made friends with almost everybody; he was kicked out of two huts; indeed, one good-looking young woman caught him a good smack on the back with a spade when he took it into his head to feel her chemise and skirt, and inquire what stuff they were made of. But as evening approached the philosopher grew more pensive. An hour before supper almost all the servants gathered together to play *kragli*—a sort of skittles in which long sticks are used instead of balls, and the winner has the right to ride on the loser's back. This game became very entertaining for the spectators; often the coachman, a man as broad as a pancake, was mounted on the swineherd, a feeble little man, who was nothing but wrinkles. Another time it was the coachman who had to bow his back, and Dorosh, leaping on it, always said: "What a fine bull!" The more dignified of the company sat in the kitchen doorway. They looked on very gravely, smoking their pipes, even when the young people roared with laughter at some witty remark from the coachman or Spirid. Khoma tried in vain to give himself up to this game; some gloomy thought stuck in his head like a nail. At supper, in spite of his efforts to be merry, terror grew within him as the darkness spread over the sky.

"Come, it's time to start, Mr. Seminarist!" said his friend, the gray-headed Cossack, getting up from the table with Dorosh; "let us go to our task."

Khoma was taken to the church again in the same way; again he was left there alone and the door was locked upon him. As soon as he was alone, fear began to take possession of him again. Again he saw the dark icons, the gleaming frames, and the familiar black coffin standing in menacing stillness and immobility in the middle of the church.

"Well," he said to himself, "now there's nothing amazing to me in this marvel. It was only alarming the first time. Yes, it was only rather alarming the first time, and even then it wasn't so alarming; now it's not alarming at all."

He made haste to take his stand at the lectern, drew a circle around him, pronounced some exorcisms, and began reading aloud, resolving not to raise his eyes from the book and not to pay attention to anything. He had been reading for about an hour and was beginning to cough and feel rather tired; he took his horn out of his pocket and, before putting the snuff to his nose, stole a timid look at the coffin. His heart turned cold; the corpse was already standing before him on the very edge of the circle, and her dead, greenish eyes were fixed upon him. The philosopher shuddered, and a cold chill ran through his veins. Dropping his eyes to the book, he began reading the prayers and exorcisms more loudly, and heard the corpse again grinding her teeth and waving her arms trying to catch him. But, with a sidelong glance out of one eye, he saw that the corpse was feeling for him where he was not standing, and that she evidently could not see him. He heard a hollow mutter, and she began pronouncing terrible words with her dead lips; they gurgled hoarsely like the bubbling of boiling pitch. He could not have said what they meant; but there was something fearful in them. The philosopher understood with horror that she was making an incantation.

A wind blew through the church at her words, and there was a sound as of multitudes of flying wings. He heard the beating of wings on the panes of the church windows and on the iron window frames, the dull scratching of claws upon the iron, and numberless evil creatures thundering on the doors and trying to break in. His heart was throbbing violently all this time; closing his eyes, he kept reading prayers and exorcisms. At last there was a sudden shrill sound in the distance; it was a distant cock crowing. The philosopher, utterly spent, stopped and took breath.

When they came in to fetch him, they found him more dead than alive; he was leaning with his back against the wall while, with his eyes almost popping out of his head, he stared at the Cossacks as they came in. They could scarcely get him along and had to support him all the way back. On reaching the courtyard, he pulled himself together and bade them give him a mug of vodka. When he had drunk it, he stroked down the hair on his head and said: "There are lots of foul things of all sorts in the world! And the fright they give one, there . . ." With that the philosopher waved his hand in despair.

The company sitting around him bowed their heads, hearing such sayings. Even a small boy, whom everybody in the servants' quarters felt himself entitled to depute in his place when it was a question of cleaning the stables or fetching water, even this poor youngster stared openmouthed at the philosopher.

At that moment the old cook's assistant, a peasant woman, not yet past middle age, a terrible coquette, who always found something to pin to her cap—a bit of ribbon, a carnation, or a little paper, if she had nothing better—passed by, in a tightly tied apron, which displayed her round, sturdy figure.

"Good day, Khoma!" she said, seeing the philosopher. "Aie, aie, aie! what's the matter with you?" she shrieked, clasping her hands.

"Why, what is it, silly woman?"

"Oh, my goodness! Why, you've become quite gray!"

"Aha! why, she's right!" Spirid pronounced, looking attentively at the philosopher. "Why, you have really become as gray as our old Yavtukh."

The philosopher, hearing this, ran headlong to the kitchen, where he had noticed on the wall a fly-spattered triangular bit of mirror before which were stuck forget-me-nots, periwinkles, and even wreaths of marigolds, testifying to its importance for the toilet of the finery-loving coquette. With horror he saw the truth of their words: half of his hair had in fact turned white.

Khoma Brut hung his head and abandoned himself to reflection.

"I will go to the master," he said at last. "I'll tell him all about it and explain that I cannot go on reading. Let him send me back to Kiev straight away."

With these thoughts in his mind he bent his steps toward the porch of the house.

The captain was sitting almost motionless in his parlor. The same hopeless grief which the philosopher had seen in his face before was still apparent. Only his cheeks were more sunken. It was evident that he had taken very little food, or perhaps had not eaten at all. The extraordinary pallor of his face gave it a look of stony immobility.

"Good day!" he pronounced on seeing Khoma, who stood, cap in hand, at the door. "Well, how goes it with you? All satisfactory?"

"It's satisfactory, all right; such devilish doings that one can but pick up one's cap and take to one's heels."

"How's that?"

"Why, your daughter, your honor . . . Looking at it reasonably, she is, to be sure, of noble birth, nobody is going to deny it; only, if I may, God rest her soul . . ."

"What of my daughter?"

"She had dealings with Satan. She gives one such horrors that there's no reading Scripture at all."

"Read away! read away! She did well to send for you; she took much care, poor darling, about her soul and tried to drive away all evil thoughts with prayers."

"That's your right to say, your honor; but I swear I cannot go on with it!"

"Read away!" the captain persisted in the same persuasive voice, "you have only one night left; you will do a Christian deed and I will reward you."

"But whatever rewards . . . Do as you please, your honor, but I will not read!" Khoma declared resolutely.

"Listen, philosopher!" said the captain, and his voice grew firm and menacing. "I don't like these pranks. You can behave like that in your seminary, but with me it is different. When I flog, it's not the same as your rector's flogging. Do you know what good leather whips are like?"

"I should think I do!" said the philosopher, dropping his voice; "everybody knows what leather whips are like: in a large dose, they're quite unendurable."

"Yes, but you don't know yet how my fellows can lay them on!" said the captain menacingly, rising to his feet, and his face assumed an imperious and ferocious expression that betrayed the unbridled violence of his character, only subdued for the time by sorrow.

"Here they first give a sound flogging, then sprinkle with vodka, and begin over again. Go along, go along, finish your task! If you don't—you'll never get up again. If you do—a thousand gold pieces!"

"Oho, ho! he's a rough one!" thought the philosopher as he went out: "he's not to be trifled with. Wait a moment friend; I'll cut and run, so that you and your hounds will never catch me."

And Khoma made up his mind to run away. He only waited for the hour after dinner when all the servants were accustomed to lie about in the hay in the barns and to give vent to such snores and wheezing that the back yard sounded like a factory.

The time came at last. Even Yavtukh closed his eyes as he lay stretched out in the sun. With fear and trembling, the philosopher stealthily made his way into the garden, from which he thought he could more easily escape into the open country without being observed. As is usual with such gardens, it was dreadfully neglected and overgrown, and so made an extremely suitable setting for any secret enterprise. Except for one little path, trodden by the servants on their tasks, it was entirely hidden in a dense thicket of cherry trees, elders, and burdock, which thrust up their tall stems covered with clinging pinkish burs. A network of wild hop was flung over this medley of trees and bushes of varied hues, forming a roof over them, clinging to the fence and falling, mingled with wild bellflowers, from it in coiling snakes. Beyond the fence, which formed the boundary of the garden, there came a perfect forest of tall grass and weeds, which looked as though no one cared to peep enviously into it, and as though any scythe would be broken to bits trying to mow down the stout stubbly stalks.

When the philosopher tried to get over the fence, his teeth chattered and his heart beat so violently that he was frightened at it. The skirts of his long coat seemed to stick to the ground as though someone had nailed them down. As he climbed over, he fancied he heard a voice shout in his ears with a deafening hiss: "Where are you off to?" The philosopher dived into the long grass and started running, frequently stumbling over old roots and trampling upon moles. He saw that when he came out of the tall weeds he would have to cross a field, and that beyond it lay a dark thicket of blackthorn, in which he thought he would be safe. He expected after making his way through it to find the road leading straight to Kiev. He ran across the field at once and found himself in the thicket.

He crawled through the prickly bushes, paying a toll of rags from his coat on every thorn, and came out into a little hollow. A willow with spreading branches bent down almost to the earth. A little brook sparkled pure as silver. The first thing the philosopher did was to lie down and drink, for he was insufferably thirsty. "Good water!" he said, wiping his lips; "I might rest here!"

"No, we had better go straight ahead; they'll be coming to look for you!"

These words rang out above his ears. He looked around— before him was standing Yavtukh. "Curse Yavtukh!" the philosopher thought in his wrath; "I could take you and fling you . . . And I could batter in your ugly face and all of you with an oak post."

"You needn't have gone such a long way around," Yavtukh went on, "you'd have done better to keep to the road I have come by, straight by the stable. And it's a pity about your coat. It's a good cloth. What did you pay a yard for it? But we've walked far enough; it's time to go home."

The philosopher trudged after Yavtukh, scratching himself. "Now the cursed witch will give it to me!" he thought. "Though, after all, what am I thinking about? What am I afraid of? Am I not a Cossack? Why, I've been through two nights, God will help me the third also. The cursed witch committed a fine lot of sins, it seems, since the Evil One makes such a fight for her."

Such were the reflections that absorbed him as he walked into the courtyard. Keeping up his spirits with these thoughts, he asked Dorosh, who through the patronage of the butler sometimes had access to the cellars, to pull out a keg of vodka; and the two friends, sitting in the barn, put away not much less than half a pailful, so that the philosopher, getting on his feet, shouted: "Musicians! I must have musicians!" and without waiting for the latter fell to dancing a jig in a clear space in the middle of the yard. He danced till it was time for the afternoon snack, and the servants who stood around him in a circle, as is the custom on such occasions, at last spat on the ground and walked away, saying: "Good gracious, how long the fellow keeps it up!" At last the philosopher lay down to sleep on the spot, and a good dousing with cold water was needed to wake him up for supper. At supper he talked of what it meant to be a Cossack, and how he should not be afraid of anything in the world.

"Time is up," said Yavtukh, "let us go."

"A splinter through your tongue, you damned hog!" thought the philosopher, and getting to his feet he said: "Come along."

On the way the philosopher kept glancing from side to side and made faint attempts at conversation with his companions. But Yavtukh said nothing; and even Dorosh was disinclined to talk. It was a hellish night. A whole pack of wolves was howling in the distance, and even the barking of the dogs had a dreadful sound.

"I imagine something else is howling; that's not a wolf," said Dorosh. Yavtukh was silent. The philosopher could find nothing to say.

They drew near the church and stepped under the decaying wooden domes that showed how little the owner of the place thought about God and his own soul. Yavtukh and Dorosh withdrew as before, and the philosopher was left alone.

Everything was the same, everything wore the same sinister familiar aspect. He stood still for a minute. The horrible witch's coffin was still standing motionless in the middle of the church.

"I won't be afraid; by God, I will not!" he said, and, drawing a circle around himself as before, he began recalling all his spells and exorcisms. There was an awful stillness; the candles spluttered and flooded the whole church with light. The philosopher turned one page, then turned another, and noticed that he was not reading what was written in the book. With horror he crossed himself and began chanting. This gave him a little more courage; the reading made progress, and the pages turned rapidly one after the other.

All of a sudden . . . in the midst of the stillness . . . the iron lid of the coffin burst with a crash and the corpse rose up. It was more terrible than the first time. Its teeth clacked horribly against each other, its lips twitched convulsively, and incantations came from them in wild shrieks. A whirlwind swept through the church, the icons fell to the ground, broken glass came flying down from the windows. The doors were burst from their hinges and a countless multitude of monstrous beings flew into the church of God. A terrible noise of wings and scratching claws filled the church. All flew and raced about looking for the philosopher.

All trace of drink had disappeared, and Khoma's head was quite clear now. He kept crossing himself and repeating prayers at random. And all the while he heard evil creatures whirring around him, almost touching him with their loathsome tails and the tips of their wings. He had not the courage to look at them; he only saw a huge monster, the whole width of the wall, standing in the shade of its matted locks as of a forest; through the tangle of hair two eyes glared horribly with eyebrows slightly lifted. Above it something was hanging in the air like an immense bubble with a thousand claws and scorpion stings stretching from the center; black earth hung in clods on them. They were all looking at him, seeking him, but could not see him, surrounded by his charmed circle. "Bring Viy! Fetch Viy!" he heard the corpse cry.

And suddenly a stillness fell upon the church; the wolves' howling was heard in the distance, and soon there was the thud of heavy footsteps resounding through the church. With a sidelong glance he saw they were bringing a squat, thickset, bandy-legged figure. He was covered all over with black earth. His arms and legs grew out like strong sinewy roots. He trod heavily, stumbling at every step. His long eyelids hung down to the very ground. Khoma saw with horror that his face was of iron. He was supported under the arms and led straight to the spot where Khoma was standing.

"Lift up my eyelids. I do not see!" said Viy in a voice that seemed to come from deep in the earth, and all the creatures flew to raise his eyelids.

"Do not look!" an inner voice whispered to the philosopher. He could not restrain himself, and he looked.

"There he is!" shouted Viy, and thrust an iron finger at him. And all pounced upon the philosopher together. He fell expiring to the ground, and his soul fled from his body in terror.

There was the sound of a cock crowing. It was the second cockcrow; the first had been missed by the gnomes. In panic they rushed to the doors and windows to fly out; but they could not; and so they remained there, stuck in the doors and windows.

When the priest went in, he stopped short at the sight of this defamation of God's holy place, and dared not serve the requiem on such a spot. And so the church was left forever, with monsters stuck in the doors and windows, overgrown with forest trees, roots, rough grass, and wild thorns, and no one can now find the way to it.

When the rumors of this reached Kiev, and the theologian, Khaliava, heard at last of the fate of the philosopher Khoma, he spent a whole hour plunged in thought. Great changes had befallen him during that time. Fortune had smiled on him; on the conclusion of his course of study, he was made bellringer of the very highest belfry, and he was almost always to be seen with a damaged nose, as the wooden staircase to the belfry had been extremely carelessly made.

"Have you heard what has happened to Khoma?" Tibery Gorobets, who by now was a philosopher and had a newly grown mustache, asked, coming up to him.

"Such was the lot God sent him," said Khaliava the bellringer. "Let us go to the tavern and drink to his memory!"

The young philosopher, who was beginning to enjoy his privileges with the ardor of an enthusiast, so that his full trousers and his coat and even his cap reeked of spirits and coarse tobacco, instantly signified his readiness.

"He was a fine fellow, Khoma!" said the bellringer, as the lame tavern keeper placed the third mug before him. "He was a fine man! And he came to grief for nothing."

"I know why he came to grief: it was because he was afraid; if he had not been afraid, the witch could not have done anything to him. You have only to cross yourself and spit right on her tail, and nothing will happen. I know all about it. Why, the old women who sit in our market in Kiev are all witches."

To this the bellringer bowed his head in token of agreement. But, observing that his tongue was incapable of uttering a single word, he cautiously got up from the table, and, lurching to right and to left, went to hide in a remote spot in the rough grass; from the force of habit, however, he did not forget to carry off the sole of an old boot that was lying on the bench.

THE TALE OF HOW IVAN IVANOVICH QUARRELED WITH IVAN NIKIFOROVICH

CHAPTER I

IVAN IVANOVICH AND IVAN NIKIFOROVICH

Ivan Ivanovich has a splendid coat.[1] Superb! And what astrakhan! Phew, damn it all, what astrakhan! Purplish-gray with a frost on it! I'll bet anything you please that nobody can be found with one like it! Now just look at it—particularly when he is standing talking to somebody—look from the side: isn't it delicious? There is no finding words for it. Velvet! Silver! Fire! Merciful Lord! St. Nikolai the Wonder-Worker, Holy Saint! Why don't I have a coat like that! He had it made before Agafya Fedoseevna went to Kiev. You know Agafya Fedoseevna, who bit off the tax assessor's ear?

An excellent man is Ivan Ivanovich! What a house he has in Mirgorod! There's a porch all round it on oak posts, and there

---

[1] *Bekesha,* a short hunting coat made of fur or astrakhan. (ed.)

are seats under the porch everywhere. When the weather is too hot, Ivan Ivanovich casts off his coat and his underwear, remaining in nothing but his shirt, and rests under his porch watching what is passing in the yard and in the street. What apple trees and pear trees he has under his very windows! You need only open the window—and the branches thrust themselves into the room. That is just in the front of the house; but you should see what he has in the garden at the back! What hasn't he got there? Plums, white and black cherries, vegetables of all sorts, sunflowers, cucumbers, melons, peas, even a threshing barn and a forge.

An excellent man is Ivan Ivanovich! He is very fond of a melon: it is his favorite dish. As soon as he has dined and come out into the porch, wearing nothing but his shirt, he at once bids Gapka bring him two melons, and with his own hands cuts them into slices, collects the seeds in a special piece of paper, and begins eating them. And then he tells Gapka to bring the inkstand, and with his own hand writes an inscription on the paper containing the seeds: "This melon was eaten on such and such a date." If some visitor happens to be there, he adds: "So and so was present."

The late Mirgorod judge always looked at Ivan Ivanovich's house with admiration. Yes, the little house is very nice. What I like is that barns and sheds have been built on every side of it so that, if you look at it from a distance, there is nothing to be seen but roofs, lying one over another, very much like a plateful of pancakes or even like those funguses that grow upon a tree. All the roofs are thatched with reeds, however; a willow, an oak tree, and two apple trees lean their spreading branches on them. Little windows with carved and whitewashed shutters peep through the trees and even wink into the street.

An excellent man is Ivan Ivanovich! The Poltava Commissar, Dorosh Tarasovich Pukhivochka, knows him too; when he comes from Khorol, he always goes to see him. And whenever the chief priest, Father Piotr, who lives at Koliberda, has half a dozen visitors, he always says that he knows no one who fulfills the duty of a Christian and knows how to live as Ivan Ivanovich does.

Goodness, how time flies! He had been a widower ten years even then. He had no children. Gapka has children and they often run about the yard. Ivan Ivanovich always gives each of them a slice of melon, or a pear. His Gapka carries the keys of the cupboards and cellars; but the key to the big chest standing in his bedroom, and of the middle cupboard, Ivan Ivanovich keeps himself, and he does not like anyone to go to them. Gapka is a sturdy wench, she goes about in a skirt, has fine healthy calves and fresh cheeks.

And what a devout man Ivan Ivanovich is! Every Sunday he puts on his coat and goes to church. When he goes in Ivan Ivanovich bows in all directions and then usually installs himself in the choir and sings a very good bass. When the service is over, Ivan Ivanovich cannot bear to go away without making the round of the beggars. He would, perhaps, not care to go through this tedious task, if he were not impelled to it by his innate kindliness. "Hello, poor woman!" he commonly says, seeking out the most crippled beggar woman in a tattered gown made up of patches. "Where do you come from, poor thing?"

"I've come from the hamlet, kind sir; I've not had a drop to drink or a morsel to eat for three days; my own children turned me out."

"Poor creature! what made you come here?"

"Well, kind sir, I came to ask alms, in case anyone would give me a copper for bread."

"Hm! Then I suppose you want bread?" Ivan Ivanovich usually inquires.

"Yes I do! I am as hungry as a dog."

"Hm!" Ivan Ivanovich usually replies, "so perhaps you would like meat too?"

"Yes and I'll be glad of anything your honor may be giving me."

"Hm! Is meat better than bread?"

"Is it for a hungry beggar to be choosy? Whatever you kindly give will be greatly appreciated." With this the old woman usually holds out her hand.

"Well, go along and God be with you," says Ivan Ivanovich. "What are you staying for? I am not beating you, am I?"

And after addressing similar inquiries to a second and a third, he at last returns home or goes to drink a glass of vodka with his neighbor, Ivan Nikiforovich, or to see the judge or the police captain.

Ivan Nikiforovich is a very good man, too. His garden is next door to Ivan Ivanovich's. They are such friends as the world has never seen. Anton Prokofievich Golopuz,[2] who goes about to this day in his cinnamon-colored coat with light blue sleeves, and dines on Sundays at the judge's, used frequently to say that the devil himself had tied Ivan Nikiforovich and Ivan Ivanovich together with a string; where the one went the other would turn up also.

Ivan Nikiforovich has never been married. Though people used to say he was going to be married, it was an absolute falsehood. I know Ivan Nikiforovich very well and can say that he has never had the faintest idea of getting married. What does all this gossip spring from? For instance, it used to be rumored that Ivan Nikiforovich was born with a tail. But this invention is so absurd, and at the same time disgusting and improper, that I do not even think it necessary to disprove it to enlightened readers, who must doubtless be aware that none but witches, and only very few of them, in fact, have a tail. Besides, witches belong rather to the female than to the male sex.

In spite of their great affection, these rare friends were not at all alike. Their characters can be best understood by comparison. Ivan Ivanovich has a marvelous gift for speaking extremely pleasantly. Goodness! How he speaks! Listening to him can only be compared with the sensation you have when someone is searching in your hair for lice, or gently passing a finger over your heel. One listens and listens and grows drowsy. It is pleasant! Extremely pleasant! Like a nap after bathing. Ivan Nikiforovich, on the other hand, is rather silent. But if he does rap out a word, one must look out, that's all! He is more cutting than any razor. Ivan Ivanovich is thin and tall; Ivan Nikiforovich is a little shorter, but makes up for it in breadth. Ivan Ivanovich's head is like a radish, tail downwards; Ivan Nikiforovich's head is like a radish, tail upwards. Ivan Ivanovich only lies in the porch in his shirt after dinner; in the evening he puts on his coat and goes off somewhere, either to the town shop which he supplies with flour, or into the country to catch quail. Ivan Nikiforovich lies all day long on his steps, usually with his back to the sun—if it is not too hot a day—and he does not care to go anywhere. If the whim takes him in the morning, he will walk about the yard, see how things are going in the garden and the house, and then go back to rest again. In the old days he used to go around to Ivan Ivanovich sometimes. Ivan Ivanovich is an ex-

---

[2] "Naked Belly." (ed.)

ceedingly refined man, he never utters an improper word in gentlemanly conversation, and takes offense at once if he hears one. Ivan Nikiforovich is sometimes not so prudent. On those occasions Ivan Ivanovich usually gets up from his seat and says: "That's enough, that's enough, Ivan Nikiforovich; we had better make haste out into the sun instead of uttering such ungodly words." Ivan Ivanovich is very angry if a fly gets into his borsht: he is quite beside himself then—he will throw the plate and his host is sure to catch hell! Ivan Nikiforovich is exceedingly fond of bathing and, when he is sitting up to his neck in water, he orders the table and the samovar to be set in the water too, and is very fond of drinking tea in such refreshing coolness. Ivan Ivanovich shaves his beard twice a week; Ivan Nikiforovich only once. Ivan Ivanovich is exceedingly inquisitive. God forbid that you should begin to tell him about something and not finish the story! If he is displeased with anything, he lets you know it. It is extremely difficult to tell from Ivan Nikiforovich's face whether he is pleased or angry; even if he is delighted at something he will not show it. Ivan Ivanovich is rather of a meek character. Ivan Nikiforovich, on the other hand, wears trousers with such ample folds that if they were blown out you could put the whole courtyard with the barns and the outhouses into them. Ivan Ivanovich has big expressive snuff-colored eyes and a mouth like the letter V; Ivan Nikiforovich has little yellowish eyes completely lost between his thick eyebrows and chubby cheeks, and a nose that looks like a ripe plum. If Ivan Ivanovich offers you snuff, he always first licks the lid of the snuffbox, then taps on it with his finger, and offering it to you, says, if you are someone he knows: "May I make so bold as to ask you to help yourself, sir?" Or if you are someone he does not know: "May I make so bold as to ask you to help yourself, sir, though I have not the honor of knowing your name and your father's and your rank in the service?"

Ivan Nikiforovich puts his horn of snuff straight into your hands and merely adds: "Help yourself." Both Ivan Ivanovich and Ivan Nikiforovich greatly dislike fleas, and so neither Ivan Ivanovich nor Ivan Nikiforovich ever let a Jew with his merchandise pass without buying from him various little bottles of an elixir protecting them from those insects, though they abuse him soundly for professing the Jewish faith. In spite of some dissimilarities, however, both Ivan Ivanovich and Ivan Nikiforovich are excellent people.

CHAPTER II

FROM WHICH MAY BE LEARNED
THE OBJECT OF IVAN IVANOVICH'S DESIRE,
THE SUBJECT OF A CONVERSATION BETWEEN
IVAN IVANOVICH AND IVAN NIKIFOROVICH,
AND IN WHAT WAY IT ENDED

One morning—it was in July—Ivan Ivanovich was lying under his porch. The day was hot, the air was arid and vibrating. Ivan Ivanovich had already been out into the country to see the hay cutters and the farm, and had already asked the peasants and the women he met from where they had come, where they were going, how, and when, and why; he was terribly tired and lay down to rest. As he lay down, he looked around at the storehouses, the yard, the barns, the hens running about the yard, and thought to himself: "Good Lord, what a manager I am! What is there that I have not got? Fowls, buildings, barns, everything I want, herb and berry vodka; pears and plum trees in my orchard; poppies, cabbage, peas in my vegetable garden . . . What is there that I have not got? . . . I should like to know what there is I have not got?"

After putting so profound a question to himself, Ivan Ivanovich sank into thought; meanwhile his eyes were in search of a new object, and, passing over the fence into Ivan Nikiforovich's yard, were involuntarily caught by a curious spectacle. A lean peasant woman was carrying out clothes that had been stored away, and was hanging them out on a line to air. Soon an old uniform with frayed facings stretched its sleeves out in the air and embraced a brocade blouse; after it, a gentleman's dress coat with a crest on the buttons and a moth-eaten collar displayed itself behind it; white cashmere trousers, covered with stains, which had once been drawn over the legs of Ivan Nikiforovich, though now they could scarcely have been drawn on his fingers. After them other garments in the shape of an inverted V were suspended, then a dark blue Cossack coat which Ivan Nikiforovich had had made twenty years before when he had been preparing to enter the military and was already letting his mustaches grow. At last, to put the finishing touch, a sword was displayed that looked like a spire sticking up in the air. Then the tails of something resembling a coat fluttered, grass-green in color and with copper buttons as big as a five-kopek piece. From behind peeped a vest trimmed with gold braid and cut low in front. The vest was soon concealed by the old petticoat of a deceased grandmother with pockets in which one could have stowed a watermelon. All this taken together made up a very interesting spectacle for Ivan Ivanovich, while the sunbeams, catching here and there a blue or a green sleeve, a red cuff or a bit of gold brocade, or playing on the sword that looked like a spire, turned it into something extraordinary, like the show played in the villages by strolling vagrants, when a crowd of people closely packed looks at King Herod in his golden crown or at Anton leading the goat.[3] Behind the scenes[4] the fiddle squeaks; a gypsy claps his hands on his lips by way of a drum, while the sun is setting and the fresh coolness of the southern night imperceptibly creeps closer to the fresh shoulders and full bosoms of the plump village women.

Soon the old woman emerged from the storeroom, sighing and groaning as she hauled along an old-fashioned saddle with broken stirrups, with shabby leather cases for pistols, and a saddlecloth that had once been crimson, embroidered in gold and with copper disks. "That's a stupid woman!" thought Ivan Ivanovich, "next she'll pull out Ivan Nikiforovich and air him!"

And indeed Ivan Ivanovich was not entirely mistaken in this surmise. Five minutes later Ivan Nikiforovich's nankeen trousers were swung up, and filled almost half of the courtyard. After that she brought out his cap and his gun.

"What is the meaning of it?" thought Ivan Ivanovich. "I have never seen a gun at Ivan Nikiforovich's. What does he want with that? He never shoots, but keeps a gun! What use is it to him? But it is a nice thing! I have been wanting to get one like that for a long time past. I should very much like to have that gun; I like to amuse myself with a little gun. Hey, woman!" Ivan Ivanovich shouted, nodding with his finger.

The old woman went up to the fence.

"What's that you have got there, granny?"

"You see yourself—a gun."

---

[3] King Herod and Anton were common figures on the puppet stage. (ed.)
[4] Of the puppet stage. Puppet shows were extremely popular, and the puppet theater was carried from town to town in a large wooden box. The puppet tradition influenced Gogol considerably, most especially in the earliest volume. (ed.)

"What sort of gun?"

"Who can say what sort! If it were mine, I might know, maybe, what it is made of; but it is the master's."

Ivan Ivanovich got up and began examining the gun from every point of view, and even forgot to scold the old woman for hanging it and the sword out to air.

"It's made of iron, one would think," the old woman went on.

"Hm! made of iron. Why is it made of iron?" Ivan Ivanovich said to himself. "Has your master had it long?"

"Maybe he has."

"It's a fine thing!" Ivan Ivanovich went on. "I'll ask him for it. What can he do with it? Or I'll trade him something for it. Granny, is your master at home?"

"Yes."

"What is he doing, lying down?"

"Yes."

"Well, that's all right, I'll come and see him."

Ivan Ivanovich dressed, took his gnarled stick to keep off the dogs, for there are many more dogs in the streets of Mirgorod than there are men, and went out.

Though Ivan Nikiforovich's courtyard was next to Ivan Ivanovich's and one could climb over the fence from one into the other, Ivan Ivanovich went by way of the street. From the street he had to pass into an alley which was so narrow that, if two one-horse carts happened to meet in it, they could not pass, but had to remain in that position until they were each dragged by their back wheels in the opposite direction into the street; as for anyone on foot, he was as apt to be adorned with burdocks, as with flowers. Ivan Ivanovich's cart shed looked into this lane on the one side, and Ivan Nikiforovich's barn, gates, and dovehouse on the other. Ivan Ivanovich went up to the gate and rattled the latch. Dogs began barking from within, but soon a crowd of dogs of various colors ran up, wagging their tails on seeing that it was a person they knew. Ivan Ivanovich crossed the courtyard in which Indian pigeons, fed by Ivan Nikiforovich with his own hand, melon rinds, with here and there green stuff or a broken wheel or a hoop off a barrel, or a boy sprawling in a soiled shirt—made up a picture such as painters love! The shadow cast by the garments on the clothesline covered almost the whole courtyard and gave it some degree of coolness. The woman met him with a bow and stood still, gaping.

Before the house a little porch was adorned with a roof on two oak posts—an unreliable shelter from the sun which at that season in Little Russia shines in deadly earnest and bathes a pedestrian from head to foot in scalding sweat. From this can be seen how strong was Ivan Ivanovich's desire to obtain the indispensable article, since he had even brought himself to break his invariable rule of walking only in the evening by going out at this hour in such weather!

The room into which Ivan Ivanovich stepped was quite dark, because the shutters were closed and the sunbeam that penetrated through a hole in the shutter was broken into rainbow hues and painted upon the opposite wall a multicolored landscape of thatched roofs, trees, and clothes hanging in the yard, but all upside down. This made an uncanny twilight in the whole room.

"God's blessing!" said Ivan Ivanovich.

"Ah, good day, Ivan Ivanovich!" answered a voice from the corner of the room. Only then did Ivan Ivanovich observe Ivan Nikiforovich lying on a rug spread out upon the floor.

"You must excuse my being in a state of nature." Ivan Nikoforovich was lying without anything on, not even his shirt.

"Never mind. Have you slept well today, Ivan Nikiforovich?"

"I have. And have you slept, Ivan Ivanovich?"

"I have."

"So now you have just got up?"

"Just got up? Good gracious, Ivan Nikiforovich! How could I sleep till now! I have just come from the farm. The wheatfields along the roadside are splendid! Magnificent! And the hay is so high and soft and golden!"

"Gorpina!" shouted Ivan Nikiforovich, "bring Ivan Ivanovich some vodka and some pies with sour cream."

"It's a very fine day."

"Don't praise the weather, Ivan Ivanovich. The devil take it! There's no doing anything for the heat!"

"So you must bring the devil in. Aie, Ivan Nikiforovich! you will remember my words, but then it will be too late; you will suffer in the next world for your ungodly language."

"What have I done to offend you, Ivan Ivanovich? I've not referred to your father or your mother. I don't know in what way I have offended you!"

"That's enough, that's enough, Ivan Nikiforovich!"

"I swear I have done nothing to offend you, Ivan Ivanovich!"

"It's strange that the quails still don't come at the birdcall."

"You may think what you like, but I have done nothing to offend you."

"I don't know why it is they don't come," said Ivan Ivanovich as though he did not hear Ivan Nikiforovich; "whether it is not quite time yet . . . though the weather one would think is just right."

"You say the wheatfields are good . . ."

"Magnificent! Magnificent!"

Then followed a silence.

"How is it you are hanging the clothes out, Ivan Nikiforovich?" Ivan Ivanovich said at last.

"Yes, that damned woman has let splendid clothes, almost new, get mildewy; now I am airing them; it's excellent fine cloth, they only need turning and I can wear them again."

"I liked one thing there, Ivan Nikiforovich."

"What's that?"

"Tell me, please, what do you want that gun for that's been hung out to air with the clothes?" At this point Ivan Ivanovich held out a snuffbox. "May I beg you to help yourself?"

"Not at all, you help yourself. I'll take a pinch of my own." With this Ivan Nikiforovich felt about him and got hold of his horn. "There's a stupid woman! So she has hung the gun out, too, has she? Wonderful snuff the Jew makes in Sorochintsy. I don't know what he puts in it, but it's so fragrant! It's a little like balsam. Here, take some, chew a little in your mouth. Isn't it like balsam? Do take some, help yourself!"

"Please tell me, Ivan Nikiforovich, I am still talking of the gun; what are you going to do with it? It's no use to you, you know."

"No use to me, but what if I go shooting?"

"Lord bless you, Ivan Nikiforovich, whenever will you go shooting? At the Second Coming, perhaps? You have never yet killed a single duck as far as I know and as others tell me, and you have not been created by the Lord for shooting. You have a dignified figure and deportment. How could you go trailing about the bogs when that article of your apparel which it is not quite proper to mention is in holes on every occasion as it is? What would it be like then? No, what you want is rest and peace." (Ivan Ivanovich, as we have mentioned already, was extremely picturesque in his speech when he wanted to persuade anyone. How he talked! Goodness, how he talked!) "Yes, you must behave accordingly. Listen, give it to me!"

"What an idea! It's an expensive gun. You can't get guns like that nowadays. I bought it from a Turk when I was going into the military; and to think of giving it away now all of a sudden! Impossible! It's an indispensable thing!"

"What is it indispensable for?"

"What for? Why, if burglars should break into the house . . . Not indispensable, indeed! Now, thank God, my mind is at rest and I am afraid of nobody. And why? Because I know I have a gun in my cupboard."

"A fine gun! Why, Ivan Nikiforovich, the lock is ruined."

"What if it is ruined? It can be repaired; it only needs a little hemp oil to get the rust off."

"I see no kind feeling for me in your words, Ivan Nikiforovich. You won't do anything to show your goodwill."

"What do you mean, Ivan Ivanovich, saying I show you no goodwill? Aren't you ashamed? Your oxen graze on my meadow and I have never once interfered with them. When you go to Poltava you always ask me for my cart, and have I ever refused it? Your little boys climb over the fence into my yard and play with my dogs—I say nothing. Let them play, so long as they don't touch anything! Let them play!"

"Since you don't care to give it to me, perhaps you might exchange it for something?"

"What will you give me for it?" With this Ivan Nikiforovich sat up, leaning on his elbow, and looked at Ivan Ivanovich.

"I'll give you the gray sow, the one that I fed up in the sty. A splendid sow! You'll see if she won't give you a litter of suckling pigs next year."

"I don't know how you can suggest that, Ivan Ivanovich. What use is your sow to me? Am I going to give a banquet at the devil's wake?"

"Again! You must keep bringing the devil in! It's a sin, it really is a sin, Ivan Nikiforovich!"

"How could you really, Ivan Ivanovich, give me for the gun the devil knows what—a sow?"

"Why is she the devil knows what, Ivan Nikiforovich?"

"Why is she? I should think you might know that for yourself.

This is a gun, a thing everyone knows; while that—the devil only knows what to call it—is a sow! If it had not been you speaking, I might have taken it as an insult."

"What fault have you found in the sow?"

"What do you take me for? That I should take a pig . . . ?"

"Sit still, sit still! I will say no more. . . . You may keep your gun, let it rust and rot standing in the corner of the cupboard—I don't want to speak of it again."

A silence followed upon that.

"They say," began Ivan Ivanovich, "that three kings have declared war on our Czar."

"Yes, Piotr Fiodorovich told me so. What does it mean? And what's the war about?"

"There is no saying for certain, Ivan Nikiforovich, what it's about. I imagine that the kings want us all to accept the Turkish faith."

"My word, the fools, what a thing to want!" Ivan Nikiforovich commented, raising his head.

"So you see, and our Czar has declared war on them for that. 'No,' he says, 'you accept the Orthodox faith!'"

"Well, our men will beat them, Ivan Ivanovich, won't they?"

"They certainly will. So you won't trade the gun, Ivan Nikiforovich?"

"I'm surprised at you, Ivan Ivanovich: I believe you are a man noted for your culture and education, but you talk like a boy. Why should I be such a fool . . . ?"

"Sit still, sit still. Forget it! Plague take it; I won't speak of it again."

At that moment some lunch was brought in. Ivan Ivanovich drank a glass of vodka and ate a pie with sour cream.

"I say, Ivan Nikiforovich, I'll give you two sacks of oats besides the sow; you have not sown any oats, you know. You would have to buy oats this year, anyway."

"I swear, Ivan Ivanovich, one should talk to you only after eating beans." (That was nothing; Ivan Nikiforovich would let off phrases worse than that.) "Who has ever heard of swapping a gun for two sacks of oats? I'll bet you won't offer your coat."

"But you forget, Ivan Nikiforovich, I am giving you the sow, too."

"What, two sacks of oats and a sow for a gun!"

"Why, isn't it enough?"

"For the gun?"

"Of course for the gun!"

"Two sacks for a gun?"

"Two sacks, not empty, but full of oats; and have you forgotten the sow?"

"You can go and kiss your sow or the devil, if you prefer him!"

"Oh! You'll see, your tongue will be pierced with red-hot needles for such ungodly sayings. One has to wash one's face and hands and fumigate oneself after talking to you."

"Excuse me, Ivan Ivanovich: a gun is a gentlemanly thing, a very interesting entertainment, besides being a very agreeable ornament to a room . . ."

"You go on about your gun, Ivan Nikiforovich, like a crazy child with a new toy," said Ivan Ivanovich with annoyance, for he was really beginning to feel angry.

"And you, Ivan Ivanovich, are a regular gander."

If Ivan Nikiforovich had not uttered that word, they would have quarreled and have parted friends as they always did; but now something quite different happened. Ivan Ivanovich turned crimson.

"What was that you said, Ivan Nikiforovich?" he asked, raising his voice.

"I said you were like a gander, Ivan Ivanovich!"

"How dare you, sir, forget propriety and respect for a man's rank and family and insult him with such an infamous name?"

"What is there infamous about it? And why are you waving your hands about like that, Ivan Ivanovich?"

"I repeat, how dare you, regardless of every rule of propriety, call me a gander?"

"I sneeze on your head, Ivan Ivanovich. What are you cackling about?"

Ivan Ivanovich could no longer control himself; his lips were quivering; his mouth lost its usual resemblance to the letter V and was transformed into an O; his eyes blinked until it was positively alarming. This was extremely rare with Ivan Ivanovich; he had to be greatly exasperated to be brought to this pass. "Then I beg to inform you," Ivan Ivanovich articulated, "that I do not want to know you."

"No great loss! Upon my word, I won't weep for that!" answered Ivan Nikiforovich.

He was lying, I swear he was! He was very much upset by it.

"I will never set foot in your house again."

"Aha, ah!" said Ivan Nikiforovich, so vexed that he did not know what he was doing, and, contrary to his habit, he rose to his feet. "Hey, woman, boy!" At this the same lean old woman and a small boy muffled in a long and full coat appeared in the doorway.

"Take Ivan Ivanovich by the arms and lead him out of the door!"

"What! A gentleman!" Ivan Ivanovich cried out indignantly, full of a sense of injured dignity. "You only dare! You approach! I will annihilate you together with your stupid master! Even the crows will not find your pieces!" (Ivan Ivanovich used to speak with extraordinary force when his soul was agitated.)

The whole group presented a striking picture: Ivan Nikiforovich, standing in the middle of the room in full beauty completely unadorned! The servingwoman, with her mouth wide open and an utterly senseless terror-stricken expression on her face! Ivan Ivanovich, as the Roman tribunes are depicted, with one arm raised! It was an extraordinary moment, a magnificent spectacle! And meanwhile there was but one spectator: that was the boy in an enormous coat, who stood very tranquilly picking his nose.

At last Ivan Ivanovich took his cap.

"Very nice behavior on your part, Ivan Nikiforovich! Excellent! I will not let you forget it!"

"Go along, Ivan Ivanovich, go along! And mind you don't cross my path. If you do, I will smash your ugly mug, Ivan Ivanovich!"

"So much for that, Ivan Nikiforovich," answered Ivan Ivanovich, making a fig and slamming the door, which squeaked loudly and sprang open again.

Ivan Nikiforovich appeared in the doorway and tried to add something, but Ivan Ivanovich flew out of the yard without looking back.

CHAPTER III

WHAT HAPPENED AFTER THE QUARREL OF IVAN IVANOVICH AND IVAN NIKIFOROVICH

And so two worthy men, the honor and ornament of Mirgorod, had quarreled! And over what? Over a trifle, over a gander. They refused to see each other, and broke off all relations, though they had before this been known as the most inseparable friends! Before this Ivan Ivanovich and Ivan Nikiforovich had sent every day to inquire after each other's health, and used often to converse together from their respective balconies and would say such agreeable things to each other than it warmed the heart to hear them.

On Sundays, Ivan Ivanovich in his cloth coat and Ivan Nikiforovich in his yellowish-brown nankeen Cossack coat used to set off to church almost arm in arm. And if Ivan Ivanovich, who had extremely sharp eyes, first noticed a puddle or filth of any sort in the middle of the street—a thing which sometimes does happen in Mirgorod—he would always say to Ivan Nikiforovich: "Be careful, don't put your foot down here, for it is unpleasant." Ivan Nikiforovich for his part, too, showed the most touching signs of affection, and, however far off he might be standing, always stretched out his hand with his horn of snuff and said: "Help yourself!" And how wonderfully they both managed their lands . . . ! And now these two friends . . . I was thunderstruck when I heard of it! For a long time I refused to believe it. Merciful Heavens! Ivan Ivanovich has quarreled with Ivan Nikiforovich! Such important men! Is there anything in this world one can depend on after that?

When Ivan Ivanovich reached home he was for a long time in a state of violent agitation. It was his habit to go first of all to the stable to see whether the mare was eating her oats (Ivan Ivanovich had a roan mare with a bald patch on her forehead, a very good little beast); then to feed the turkeys and suckling pigs with his own hand; and only then to go indoors, where he either would make wooden bowls (he was very skillful, as good as a turner, at carving things out of wood), or would read a book published by Liuby, Gary, and Popov[5] (Ivan Ivanovich did not remember the title of it, because the servant had long ago torn off the upper part of the title page to amuse a child with it), or would rest in the porch. Now he paid no heed to any of his usual occupations. Instead of doing so, on meeting Gapka he began scolding her for dawdling about doing nothing, though she was dragging grain into the kitchen; he shook his stick at the cock which came to the front steps for its usual tribute; and when a grubby little boy in a tattered shirt ran up to him, shouting, "Daddy, daddy! give me a

---

[5] Early nineteenth-century publishers of popular literature, i.e., cheap illustrated books for the half-literate. (ed.)

cake!" he threatened him and stamped his foot so alarmingly that the terrified boy fled.

At last, however, he recovered himself and began to follow his usual pursuits. He sat down to dinner late, and it was almost evening when he lay down to rest under the porch. The good borsht with pigeons in it which Gapka had cooked completely erased the incident of the morning. Ivan Ivanovich began to look after his garden and household with pleasure again. At last his eyes rested on the neighboring courtyard and he said to himself: "I haven't been to see Ivan Nikiforovich today: I'll go around to him." Saying this, Ivan Ivanovich took his stick and his cap and was going out into the street; but he had scarcely walked out of the gate when he remembered the quarrel, spat on the ground, and turned back. Almost the same action took place in Ivan Nikiforovich's yard. Ivan Ivanovich saw the servingwoman put her foot on the fence with the intention of climbing over into his yard, when suddenly the voice of Ivan Nikiforovich was audible, shouting: "Come back, come back! No need!"

· Ivan Ivanovich felt very dreary, however. It might very well have happened that these worthy men would have been reconciled the very next day, had not a particular event in the house of Ivan Nikiforovich destroyed every hope of reconciliation and poured oil on the fire of resentment when it was on the point of going out.

On the evening of the very same day Agafya Fedoseevna arrived on a visit to Ivan Nikiforovich. Agafya Fedoseevna was neither a relative nor a sister-in-law, nor, indeed, any connection of Ivan Nikiforovich's. One would have thought that she had absolutely no reason to visit him, and he was, indeed, not particularly pleased to see her. She did visit him, however, and used to stay with him for whole weeks at a time and occasionally longer. Then she carried off the keys and took the whole housekeeping into her own hands. This was very disagreeable to Ivan Nikiforovich, but, strange to say, he obeyed her like a child and, though he attempted sometimes to quarrel with her, Agafya Fedoseevna always got the best of it.

I must admit I do not understand why it has been ordained that women should take us by the nose as easily as they take hold of the handle of a teapot: either their hands are so created or our noses are fit for nothing better. And, although Ivan Nikiforovich's nose was rather like a plum, she took him by that nose and made him follow her about like a little dog. Indeed, he reluctantly changed his whole manner of life when she was there: he did not lie so long in the sun, and, when he did lie there, it was not in a state of nature; he always put on his shirt and his trousers, though Agafya Fedoseevna was far from insisting upon it. She was not one to stand on ceremony and, when Ivan Nikiforovich had a feverish attack, she used to rub him herself with her own hands from head to foot with vinegar and turpentine. Agafya Fedoseevna wore a cap on her head, three warts on her nose, and a coffee-colored jacket with yellow flowers on it. Her whole figure resembled a tub, and it was as hard to find her waist as it is to see one's nose without a mirror. Her legs were very short and shaped on the pattern of two cushions. She used to talk scandal and eat pickled beetroot in the mornings, and was a wonderful hand at scolding; and through all these varied pursuits, her face never for one moment changed its expression, a strange peculiarity only found as a rule in women.

As soon as she arrived, everything was turned upside down. "Don't you be reconciled with him, Ivan Nikiforovich, and don't you beg his pardon; he wants to be your ruin; he is that sort of man! You don't know him!" The damned woman went on whispering and whispering, till she brought Ivan Nikiforovich to such a state that he would not hear Ivan Ivanovich's name.

Everything assumed a different aspect. If the neighbor's dog ran into the yard, it was whacked with whatever was handy; if the children climbed over the fence, they came back howling with their little grubby shirts held up and marks of a switch on their backs. Even the servingwoman, when Ivan Ivanovich would have asked her some question, was so rude that Ivan Ivanovich, a man of extreme refinement, could only spit and say: "What a nasty woman! Worse than her master!"

At last, to put the finishing touches to all his offenses, the detested neighbor put up directly opposite, at the spot where the fence was usually climbed, a goose pen, as though specially planned to emphasize the insult. This revolting pen was put up with diabolical rapidity in a single day.

This excited fury and a desire for revenge in Ivan Ivanovich. He did not, however, show any sign of annoyance, although part of the pen was actually on his land; but his heart throbbed so violently that it was extremely hard for him to maintain this outward composure.

So he spent the day. Night came on. . . . Oh, if I were a painter, how wonderfully I could portray the charm of the night! I would picture all Mirgorod sleeping; the countless stars looking down on it immovably; the quiet streets resounding with the barking of the dogs far and near; the lovesick sexton hastening by them and climbing over a fence with chivalrous fearlessness; the white walls of the houses still whiter in the moonlight, while the trees that canopy them are darker, the shadows cast by the trees blacker, the flowers and silent grass more fragrant; while from every corner the crickets, the tireless minstrels of the night, set up their churring song in unison. I would describe how in one of those low-pitched clay houses a black-browed maiden, tossing on her lonely bed, dreams with heaving young breasts of a hussar's spurs and mustache, while the moonlight smiles on her cheeks. I would describe how the black shadow of a bat that settled on the white chimneys flits across the white road. . . . But even so I could hardly have depicted Ivan Ivanovich as he went out that night with a saw in his hand, so many were the different emotions written on his face! Quietly, stealthily, he slunk up and crept under the goose pen. Ivan Nikiforovich's dogs knew nothing as yet of the quarrel between them, and so allowed him as a friend to approach the pen, which stood firmly on four oak posts. Creeping up to the nearest post, he put the saw to it and began sawing. The noise of the saw made him look around every minute, but the thought of the insult revived his courage. The first post was sawn through; Ivan Ivanovich set to work on the second. His eyes were burning and could see nothing because of terror. All at once he uttered a cry and almost fainted; he thought he saw a corpse, but soon he recovered on perceiving that it was the goose, craning its neck at him. Ivan Ivanovich spat with indignation and went on with his work again. The second post, too, was sawn through; the goose house tottered. Ivan Ivanovich's heart began beating so violently as he attacked the third post, that several times he had to stop. More than half of the post was sawn through when all at once the tottering pen lurched violently. . . . Ivan Ivanovich barely had time to leap aside when it came down with a crash. Snatching up the saw in a terrible panic, he ran home and flung himself on his bed, without even courage to look out of the window at the results of his terrible act. He imagined that all Ivan Nikiforovich's household were assembled: the old servingwoman, Ivan Nikiforovich, the boy in the immense overcoat, were all led by Agafya Fedoseevna, coming with clubs to break down and smash his house.

Ivan Ivanovich passed all the following day in a kind of fever. He kept thinking that in revenge his detested neighbor would at least set fire to his house; and so he gave Gapka orders to keep a continual lookout to see whether dry straw had been put down anywhere. At last, to anticipate Ivan Nikiforovich, he made up his mind to be ahead of him and to lodge a complaint against him in the Mirgorod district court. What this meant the reader may learn from the following chapter.

CHAPTER IV

OF WHAT TOOK PLACE IN THE MIRGOROD DISTRICT COURT

A delightful town is Mirgorod! There are all sorts of buildings in it. Some thatched with straw and some with reeds, some even with a wooden roof. A street to the right, a street to the left, everywhere an excellent fence; over it twines the hop, upon it hang pots and pans, behind it the sunflower displays its sunlike head and one catches glimpses of red poppies and fat pumpkins. . . . Splendid! The fence is always adorned with objects which make it still more picturesque—a checked petticoat stretched out on it or a smock or trousers. There is no thieving nor robbery in Mirgorod, and so everyone hangs on his fence what he thinks fit. If you come from the square, you will certainly stop for a moment to admire the view. There is a pool in it—a wonderful pool! You have never seen one like it! It fills up almost the whole square. A lovely pool! The houses, which might in the distance be taken for haystacks, stand around admiring its beauty.

But to my thinking there is no better house than the district court. Whether it is built of oak or birch wood does not matter to me, but, honored friends, there are eight windows in it! Eight windows in a row, looking straight on the square and onto that stretch of water of which I have spoken already and which the police captain calls the lake! It is the only one painted the color of granite; all the other houses in Mirgorod are simply whitewashed. Its roof is all made of wood, and would, indeed, have been painted red, if the oil intended for that purpose had not been eaten by the office clerks with onions, for, as luck would have it, it was Lent, and so the roof was left unpainted. There are steps leading out to the square, and the hens often run up them, because there are almost always grains or other things eatable scattered on the steps; this is not done on purpose, however, but simply from the carelessness of the petitioners coming to the court. The building is divided into two parts: in one there is the court, in the other there is the jail. In the first part, there are two clean, whitewashed rooms; one the outer room for petitioners to wait in, while in the other there is a table adorned with five inkstands; on the table stands the image of the two-headed eagle, the symbol of office; there are four oak chairs with high backs, and along the walls stand ironbound chests in which the records of the lawsuits of the district are piled up. On one of these chests a polished boot was standing at the moment.

The court had been sitting since early morning. The judge, a rather stout man, though considerably thinner than Ivan Nikiforovich, with a good-natured face and a greasy vest, was talking over a pipe and a cup of tea with the court assessor. The judge's lips were close under his nose, and so his nose could sniff his upper lip to his heart's content. This upper lip served him instead of a snuffbox, for the snuff aimed at his nose almost always settled upon it. And so the judge was talking to the court assessor. At one side a barefooted wench was holding a trayful of cups. At the end of the table the secretary was reading the summing up of a case, but in such a monotonous and depressing tone that the very man whose case it was would have fallen asleep listening to him. The judge would no doubt have been the first to do so if he had not been engaged in an interesting conversation.

"I purposely tried to find out," said the judge, taking a sip of tea, though the cup was by now cold, "how they manage to make them sing so well. I had a wonderful blackbird two years ago. And do you know, it suddenly went off completely and began singing God knows what; and the longer it went on, the worse it got; it took to lisping, wheezing—good for nothing! And you know it was the merest trifle! I'll tell you how it's done. A little pimple no bigger than a pea grows under the throat; this must be pricked with a needle. I was told that by Zakhar Prokofievich, and if you like I'll tell you just how it happened: I was going to see him . . ."

"Am I to read the second, Demyan Demyanovich?" the secretary, who had finished reading some minutes before, broke in.

"Oh, have you finished it already? Imagine, how quick you have been! I haven't heard a word of it! But where is it? Give it here! I'll sign it! What else have you got there?"

"The case of the Cossack Bokitko's stolen cow."

"Very good, read away! Well, so I arrived at his house . . . I can even tell you exactly what he gave me. With the vodka some sturgeon was served, unique! Yes, not like the sturgeon . . ." (At this the judge put out his tongue and smiled, while his nose sniffed his invariable snuffbox) ". . . to which our Mirgorod shop treats us. I didn't taste the herring because, as you are aware, it gives me heartburn; but I tried the caviar—splendid caviar! there can be no two words about it, superb! Then I drank peach vodka distilled with centaury. There was saffron vodka, too; but, as you are aware, I never touch it. It's very nice, you know; it whets the appetite before a meal, they say, and puts a finishing touch afterwards . . . Ah! what do my ears hear, what do my eyes behold . . . !" the judge cried out all at once on seeing Ivan Ivanovich walk in.

"God be with you! I wish you good health!" Ivan Ivanovich pronounced, bowing in all directions with the urbanity which was his peculiar characteristic. My goodness, how he could fascinate us all with his manners! I have never seen such refinement anywhere. He was very well aware of his own consequence, and so looked upon the universal respect in which he was held as his due. The judge himself handed Ivan Ivanovich a chair; his nose drew in all the snuff from his upper lip, which was always a sign with him of great satisfaction.

"What may I offer you, Ivan Ivanovich?" he inquired. "Will you take a cup of tea?"

"No, thank you very much!" answered Ivan Ivanovich; and he bowed and sat down.

"Oh, please do, just a cup!" repeated the judge.

"No, thank you. Very grateful for your hospitality!" answered Ivan Ivanovich. He bowed and sat down.

"Just one cup!" repeated the judge.

"Oh, do not trouble, Demyan Demyanovich!" At this Ivan Ivanovich bowed and sat down.

"One little cup?"

"Well, perhaps just one cup!" pronounced Ivan Ivanovich, and he put out his hand to the tray.

Merciful heavens! The height of refinement in that man! There is no describing the pleasing impression made by such manners!

"May I offer you another cup?"

"No, thank you very much!" answered Ivan Ivanovich, putting the cup turned upside down upon the tray and bowing.

"To please me, Ivan Ivanovich!"

"I cannot; I thank you!" With this Ivan Ivanovich bowed and sat down.

"Ivan Ivanovich! Come now, as a friend, just one cup!"

"No, very much obliged for your kindness!" Saying this, Ivan Ivanovich bowed and sat down.

"Just one cup! One cup!"

Ivan Ivanovich put out his hand to the tray and took a cup.

Bless me! How that man could keep up his dignity!

"I have," said Ivan Ivanovich, after drinking the last drop, "urgent business with you, Demyan Demyanovich: I wish to lodge a complaint." With this Ivan Ivanovich put down his cup and took from his pocket a sheet of stamped paper covered with writing. "A complaint against my enemy, my sworn foe."

"Against whom is that?"

"Against Ivan Nikiforovich Dovgochkhun!"

At these words the judge almost fell off his chair. "What are you saying!" he articulated, flinging up his hands; "Ivan Ivanovich! is this you?"

"You see for yourself it is I!"

"The Lord be with you and all the Holy Saints! What! You, Ivan Ivanovich, have become the enemy of Ivan Nikiforovich! Was it your lips that uttered those words? Say it again! Was not someone hiding behind you and speaking with your voice . . . ?"

"What is there so incredible in it? I cannot bear the sight of him: he has done me a deadly injury, he has insulted my honor!"

"Holy Trinity! How shall I ever tell my mother? She, poor old dear, says every day when my sister and I quarrel: 'You live like cats and dogs, children. If only you would take example from Ivan Ivanovich and Ivan Nikiforovich: once friends, always friends! To be sure they are friends! To be sure they are excellent people!' Fine friends after all! Tell me, what's it all about? How is it?"

"It's a delicate matter, Demyan Demyanovich! It cannot be told by word of mouth: better bid your secretary read my petition. Take it in that way; it would be more proper here."

"Read it aloud, Taras Tikhonovich!" said the judge, turning to the secretary. Taras Tikhonovich took the petition and, blowing his nose as all secretaries in district courts do blow their noses, that is, with the help of two fingers, began reading:

"From Ivan, son of Ivan Pererepenko, gentleman and landowner of the Mirgorod district, a petition; whereof the following points ensue:

"(1) Whereas the gentleman Ivan, son of Nikifor Dovgochkhun, notorious to all the world for his godless lawfully-criminal actions which overstep all bounds and provoke aversion, did, on the seventh day of July of the present year 1810, perpetrate a deadly insult upon me, both personally affecting my honor and likewise for the humiliation and confusion of my rank and family. The said gentleman is, moreover, of loathsome appearance, has a quarrelsome temper, and abounds with blasphemous and abusive words of every description . . ."

Here the reader made a slight pause to blow his nose again, while the judge folded his arms with a feeling of reverence and said to himself: "What a clever pen! Lord have mercy on us! How the man does write!"

Ivan Ivanovich begged the secretary to read on, and Taras Tikhonovich continued:

"The said gentleman, Ivan, son of Nikifor Dovgochkhun, when I went to him with friendly propositions, called me publicly by an insulting name derogatory to my honor, to wit, 'gander,' though it is well known to all the district of Mirgorod that I have never had the name of that disgusting animal and do not intend to be so named in the future. The proof of my gentle origin is the fact that in the register in the church of the Three Holy Bishops, there is recorded both the day of my birth and likewise the name given me in baptism. A 'gander,' as all who have any knowledge whatever of science are aware, cannot be inscribed in the register, seeing that a 'gander' is not a man but a bird, a fact thoroughly well known to everyone, even though he may not have been to a seminary. But the aforesaid pernicious gentleman, though fully aware of all this, abused me with the aforesaid foul name for no other purpose than to inflict a deadly insult to my rank and station.

"(2) This same unmannerly and ungentlemanly gentleman has inflicted damage, moreover, upon my private property, inherited by me from my father of the clerical calling, Ivan of blessed memory, son of Onisy Pererepenko, inasmuch as in contravention of every law he has moved a goose pen precisely opposite my front entrance, which was done with no other design but to emphasize the insult paid me, forasmuch as the said goose pen had till then been standing in a suitable place and was fairly solid. But the abominable plan of the aforesaid gentleman was solely to compel me to witness unseemly incidents: forasmuch as it is well known that no man goes into a pen, above all a goose pen, for any proper purpose. In carrying out this illegal action the two foremost posts have trespassed upon my private property, which passed into my possession in the lifetime of my father, Ivan of blessed memory, son of Onisy Pererepenko, which runs in a straight line from the barn to the place where the women wash their pots.

"(3) The gentleman described above, whose very name inspires aversion, cherishes in his heart the wicked design of setting fire to me in my own house. Whereof unmistakable signs are manifest from what follows: in the first place, the said pernicious gentleman has taken to emerging frequently from his apartments, which he never did in the past by reason of his slothfulness and the repulsive corpulence of his person; in the second place, in the servants' quarters adjoining the very fence which is the boundary of my land inherited by me from my late father, Ivan of blessed memory, son of Onisy Pererepenko, there is a light burning every day and for an exceptional length of time, which same is manifest proof thereof; inasmuch as hitherto through his niggardly stinginess not only the tallow candle but even the little oil lamp was always put out.

"And therefore I petition that the said gentleman, Ivan, son of Nikifor Dovgochkhun, as being guilty of arson, of insulting my rank, name, and family, and of covetously appropriating my property, and above all for the vulgar and reprehensible coupling with my name the title of 'gander,' be condemned to the payment of a fine together with all costs and expenses, and himself be thrown into fetters as a lawbreaker, and put in the prison of the town, and that this my petition may meet with prompt and immediate attention. Written and composed by Ivan, son of Ivan Pererepenko, gentleman and landowner of Mirgorod."

When the petition had been read, the judge drew nearer to Ivan Ivanovich, took him by a button, and began addressing him in somewhat this fashion: "What are you doing, Ivan Ivanovich? Have some fear of God! Drop the petition, the devil take it! (Let Satan enjoy it!) Much better shake hands with Ivan Nikiforovich and kiss him, and buy some santurin or nikopol wine or simply make some punch and invite me! We'll have a good drink together and forget it all!"

"No, Demyan Demyanovich, this is not a matter," said Ivan Ivanovich with the dignity which always suited him so well, "this is not a matter which admits of an amicable settlement. Goodbye! Goodbye to you, too, gentlemen!" he continued with the same dignity, turning to the rest of the company: "I trust that the necessary steps will in due course be taken in accordance with my petition." And he went out, leaving everyone present in amazement.

The judge sat without saying a word; the secretary took a pinch of snuff; the clerks upset the broken bottle which served them for an inkstand, and the judge himself was so absent-minded that he enlarged the pool of ink on the table with his finger.

"What do you say to this, Dorofei Trofimovich?" said the judge after a brief silence, turning to the assessor.

"I say nothing," said the assessor.

"What things people do!" the judge went on. He had hardly uttered the words when the door creaked and the front half of Ivan Nikiforovich landed in the office—the remainder of him was still in the hall. That Ivan Nikiforovich should appear, and in the court, too, seemed so extraordinary that the judge cried out, the secretary interrupted his reading, one clerk, in a frieze semblance of a dress coat, put his pen in his lips, while another swallowed a fly. Even the veteran with a stripe on his shoulder who discharged the duties of messenger and house porter, and who had before this been standing at the door scratching himself under his dirty shirt—even he gaped and stepped on somebody's foot.

"What fate has brought you? How and why? How are you, Ivan Nikiforovich?"

But Ivan Nikiforovich was more dead than alive, for he had become stuck in the doorway and could not take a step backwards or forwards. In vain the judge shouted to anyone who might be in the waiting room to shove Ivan Nikiforovich from behind into the court. There was nobody in the waiting room but an old woman who had come with a petition, and in spite of all her efforts she could do nothing with her skinny hands. Then one of the clerks, a broad-shouldered fellow with thick lips and a thick nose, with a drunken look in his squinting eyes, and ragged elbows, approached the foremost half of Ivan Nikiforovich, folded the latter's arms across his chest as though he were a baby, and winked to the veteran, who shoved with his knee in Ivan Nikiforovich's belly, and in spite of the latter's piteous moans he was squeezed out into the waiting room. Then they drew back the bolts and opened the second half of the door, during which operation the united efforts and heavy breathing of the clerk and his assistant, the veteran, diffused such a powerful odor about the room that the court seemed transformed for a time into a tavern.

"I hope you are not hurt, Ivan Nikiforovich? I'll tell my mother and she'll send you a lotion; you only rub it on your back and it will all pass off."

But Ivan Nikiforovich flopped into a chair, and except for prolonged sighs and groans could say nothing. At last in a faint voice hardly audible from exhaustion he said: "Would you like some?" and taking his snuff horn from his pocket added: "take some, help yourself!"

"Delighted to see you," answered the judge, "but still I cannot imagine what has led you to take so much trouble and to oblige us with such an agreeable surprise."

"A petition . . ." was all Ivan Nikiforovich could articulate.

"A petition? What sort of petition?"

"A complaint . . ." (Here breathlessness led to a prolonged pause.) "Oh! . . . a complaint against that scoundrel . . . Ivan Ivanovich Pererepenko!"

"Good Lord! You at it too! Such rare friends! A complaint against such an exemplary man . . . !"

"He is the devil himself!" Ivan Nikiforovich pronounced abruptly.

The judge crossed himself.

"Take my petition, read it!"

"There is nothing we can do, read it aloud, Taras Tikhonovich," said the judge, addressing the secretary with an expression of displeasure, though his nose unconsciously sniffed his upper lip, which it commonly did only from great satisfaction. Such perversity on the part of his nose caused the judge even more vexation: he took out his handkerchief and swept from his upper lip all the snuff, to punish its insolence.

The secretary, after going through his usual performance, which he invariably did before beginning to read, that is, blowing his nose without the assistance of a handkerchief, began in his ordinary voice, as follows:

"The petition of Ivan, son of Nikifor Dovgochkhun, gentleman of the Mirgorod district, whereof the following points ensue:

"(1) Whereas by his spiteful hatred and undisguised ill-will, the self-styled gentleman, Ivan, son of Ivan Pererepenko, is committing all sorts of mean, injurious, malicious, and shocking actions against me, and yesterday, like a robber and a thief, broke—with axes, saws, screwdrivers, and all sorts of carpenter's tools—at night into my yard and into my private pen situate therein, and with his own hand, and infamously hacked it to pieces, whereas on my side I had given no cause whatever for so lawless and burglarious a proceeding.

"(2) The said gentleman Pererepenko has designs upon my life, and, concealing the said design until the seventh of last month, came to me and began in cunning and friendly fashion begging from me a gun, which stands in my room, and with his characteristic meanness offered me for it many worthless things such as a gray sow and two measures of oats. But, guessing his criminal design at the time, I tried in every way to dissuade him therefrom; but the aforesaid blackguard and scoundrel, Ivan, son of Ivan Pererepenko, swore at me like a peasant and from that day has cherished an implacable hostility toward me. Moreover, the often aforementioned ferocious gentleman and brigand, Ivan, son of Ivan Pererepenko, is of a very ignoble origin: his sister was known to all the world as a strumpet, and left the place with the regiment of light cavalry stationed five years ago at Mirgorod and registered her husband as a peasant; his father and mother, too, were exceedingly lawless people, and both were incredible drunkards. But the aforementioned gentleman and robber, Pererepenko, has surpassed all his family in his beastly and reprehensible behaviour, and under a show of piety is guilty of the most profligate conduct: he does not keep the fasts, seeing that on St. Philip's Eve the godless man bought a sheep and next day bade his illegitimate wench Gapka slaughter it, alleging that he had need at once for tallow for lamps and candles.

"Wherefore I petition that the said gentleman may, as guilty of robbery, sacrilege, and cheating, and caught in the act of theft and burglary, be thrown into fetters and cast into the jail of the town or prison of the province, and there as may seem best, after being deprived of his grades and nobility, be soundly flogged and be sent to hard labor in Siberia if need be, and be ordered to pay all costs and expenses, and that this my petition may receive immediate attention. To this petition, Ivan, son of Nikifor Dovgochkhun, gentleman of the Mirgorod district, herewith puts his hand."

As soon as the secretary had finished reading, Ivan Nikiforovich picked up his cap and bowed with the intention of going away.

"Where are you off to, Ivan Nikiforovich?" the judge called after him. "Stay a little! Have some tea! Oryshko! Why are you standing there, foolish girl, winking at the clerks? Go and bring some tea!"

But Ivan Nikiforovich, terrified at having come so far from home and having endured so dangerous a quarantine, was already through the doorway saying: "Don't put yourself out, with pleasure I'll . . ." and he shut the door after him, leaving all the court in amazement.

There was no helping the situation. Both petitions had been received and the case seemed likely to awaken considerable interest, when an unforeseen circumstance gave it an even more remarkable character. When the judge had gone out of the court, accompanied by the assessor and the secretary, and the clerks were stowing away into a sack the various fowls, eggs, pies, rolls, and other trifles brought by the petitioners, the gray sow ran into the room and, to the surprise of all present, seized—not a pie or a crust of bread, but Ivan Nikiforovich's petition, which was lying at the end of the table with its pages hanging over the edge. Snatching up the petition, the gray grunter ran out so quickly that not one of the clerks could overtake her, in spite of the rulers and inkpots that were thrown after her.

This extraordinary incident caused a terrible commotion, because they had not taken a copy of the petition. The judge, his secretary, and the assessor spent a long time arguing over this unprecedented event; at last it was decided to write a report on it to the police captain, since proceedings in this matter were more the concern of the city police. The report, No. 389, was sent to him the same day and led to rather an interesting explanation, of which the reader may learn from the next chapter.

CHAPTER V

IN WHICH IS DESCRIBED A CONSULTATION BETWEEN TWO PERSONAGES HIGHLY RESPECTED IN MIRGOROD

Ivan Ivanovich had only just seen after his household duties and gone out, as his habit was, to lie down in the porch, when to his unutterable surprise he saw something red at the garden gate. It was the police captain's red cuff which, like his collar, had acquired a glaze, and at the edges was being transformed into polished leather. Ivan Ivanovich thought to himself: "It's just as well that Piotr Fiodorovich has come for a little talk"; but he was much surprised to see the police captain walking extremely fast and waving his hands, which he did not do as a rule. There were eight buttons on the police captain's uniform; the ninth had been torn off during the procession at the consecration of the church two years before, and the police constables had not yet been able to find it; though when the superintendents presented the police captain with their daily reports he invariably inquired whether the button had been found. These eight buttons had been sewn on as peasant women sow beans, one to the right and the next to the left. His left leg had been struck by a bullet in his last campaign, and so, as he limped along, he flung it so far to one side that it almost canceled all the work done by the right leg. The more rapidly the police captain forced the march the less he advanced, and so, while he was approaching the porch, Ivan Ivanovich had time enough to lose himself in conjecture why the police captain was waving his arms so vigorously. This interested him all the more as he thought the latter's business must be of exceptional importance, since he was actually wearing his new sword.

"Good day, Piotr Fiodorovich!" cried Ivan Ivanovich, who, as we have said already, was very inquisitive and could not restrain his impatience at the sight of the police captain attacking the step, still not raising his eyes, but struggling with his unruly legs which were utterly unable to take the step at one assault.

"A very good day to my dear friend and benefactor, Ivan Ivanovich!" answered the police captain.

"Pray be seated. You are tired I see, for your wounded leg hinders . . ."

"My leg!" cried the police captain, casting upon Ivan Ivanovich a glance such as a giant casts on a pigmy or a learned pedant on a dancing master. With this he stretched out his foot and stamped on the floor with it. This display of valor, however, cost him dear, for his whole person lurched forward and his nose pecked the railing; but the sage guardian of order, to preserve appearances, at once righted himself and felt in his pocket as though to get out his snuffbox.

"I can assure you, my dearest friend and benefactor, Ivan Ivanovich, that I have made worse marches in my time. Yes, seriously I have. For instance during the campaign of 1807 . . . Ah, I'll tell you how I climbed over a fence to visit a pretty German." With this the police captain screwed up one eye and gave a fiendishly sly smile.

"Where have you been today?" asked Ivan Ivanovich, desirous of cutting the police captain short and bringing him as quickly as possible to the occasion of his visit. He would very much have liked to ask what it was the police captain intended to tell him; but a refined *savoir faire* made him feel the impropriety of such a question, and Ivan Ivanovich was obliged to control himself and to wait for the solution of the mystery, though his heart was throbbing with unusual violence.

"By all means, I will tell you where I have been," answered the police captain; "in the first place I must tell you that it is beautiful weather today . . ."

The last words were almost too much for Ivan Ivanovich.

"But excuse me," the police captain went on, "I've come to you today about an important matter." Here the police captain's face and deportment resumed the anxious expression with which he had attacked the steps. Ivan Ivanovich revived, and trembled as though he were in a fever, though as his habit was, he promptly asked:

"What is it? Important? Is it really important?"

"Well, you will see: first of all, I must hasten to inform you, dear friend and benefactor, Ivan Ivanovich, that you . . . for my part kindly observe I say nothing, but the laws of government, the laws of government demand it: you have committed a breach of public order!"

"What are you saying, Piotr Fiodorovich? I don't understand a word of it."

"I swear, Ivan Ivanovich! How can you say you don't understand a word of it? Your own beast has carried off a very important legal document, and after that you say you don't understand a word of it!"

"What beast?"

"If I may say so, your own gray sow."

"And how am I to blame? Why did the court porter open the door?"

"But, Ivan Ivanovich, the beast is your property; so you are to blame."

"I am very much obliged to you for putting me on a level with a sow."

"Come, I did not say that, Ivan Ivanovich! Dear me, I did not say that! Kindly consider the question yourself with an open mind. You are undoubtedly aware that, in accordance with the laws of government, unclean animals are prohibited from walking about in the town, especially in the principal streets. You must admit that that's prohibited."

"God knows what you are talking about. As though it mattered a sow going out into the street!"

"Allow me to put to you, allow me, allow me, Ivan Ivanovich; it's utterly impossible. What can we do? It's the will of the government, we must obey. I do not dispute the fact that fowls and geese sometimes run into the street and even into the square—fowls and geese, mind; but even last year I issued a proclamation that pigs and goats were not to be allowed in public squares, and I ordered that proclamation to be read aloud before the assembled people."

"Well, Piotr Fiodorovich, I see nothing in all this but that you are trying to insult me in every way possible."

"Oh, you can't say that, my dear friend and benefactor, you can't say that I am trying to insult you! Think yourself: I didn't say a word to you last year when you put up a roof fully a yard higher than the legal height. On the contrary, I pretended I hadn't noticed it at all. Believe me, dearest friend, on this occasion, too, I would absolutely, so to speak . . . but my duty, my office, in fact, requires me to look after public cleanliness. Only consider when all at once there rushes into the main street . . ."

"Your main street, indeed! Why, every peasant woman goes there to fling away what she does not want."

"Allow me to say, Ivan Ivanovich, that it's you who are insulting me! It is true it does happen at times, but mostly under a fence, or behind barns or sheds; but that a sow in farrow should run into the main street, the square, is a thing that . . ."

"Good gracious, Piotr Fiodorovich! Why, a sow is God's creation!"

"Agreed. All the world knows that you are a learned man, that you are versed in the sciences and all manner of subjects. Of course, I have never studied any sciences at all. I began to learn to write only when I was thirty. You see, I rose from the ranks, as you are aware."

"Hm!" said Ivan Ivanovich.

"Yes," the police captain went on, "in 1801 I was in the forty-second regiment of light cavalry, an ensign in the fourth company. Our company commander was—if you will allow me to say so—Captain Eremeev." At this the police captain put his finger into the snuffbox which Ivan Ivanovich held open and fiddled with the snuff. Ivan Ivanovich answered: "Hm."

"But my duty," the police captain went on, "is to obey the commands of government. Are you aware, Ivan Ivanovich, that anyone who steals a legal document in a court of law is liable like any other criminal to be tried in a criminal court?"

"I am so well aware of it that if you like I will teach you. That applies to human beings; for instance, if you were to steal a document; but a sow is an animal, God's creation."

"Quite so, but the law says one guilty of stealing . . . I beg you to note attentively, one guilty! Nothing is here defined as to species, sex, or calling; therefore an animal, too, may be guilty. Say what you like, but until sentence is passed on it, the animal ought to be handed over to the police, as guilty of a breach of order."

"No, Piotr Fiodorovich," retorted Ivan Ivanovich coolly, "that will not be so!"

"As you like, but I am bound to follow the regulations of government."

"Why are you threatening me? I suppose you mean to send the

one-armed soldier for her? I'll bid my servant girl show him out with the poker; his remaining arm will be broken."

"I will not venture to argue with you. In that case, if you will not hand her over to the police, make what use you like of her; cut her up, if you like, for Christmas, and make her into ham or eat her as fresh pork. Only I should like to ask you, if you will be making sausages, to send me just a couple of those your Gapka makes so nicely of the blood and fat. My Agrafena Trofimovna is very fond of them."

"Certainly I'll send you a couple of sausages."

"I shall be very grateful to you, dear friend and benefactor. Now allow me to say just one more word. I am charged by the judge and, indeed, by all our acquaintances, so to speak, to reconcile you with your friend, Ivan Nikiforovich."

"What! That boor! Reconcile me with that ruffian! Never! That will never be! Never!" Ivan Ivanovich was in an extremely resolute mood.

"Have it your own way," answered the police captain, regaling both nostrils with snuff. "I will not venture to advise you; however, allow me to put it to you: here you are now on bad terms, while if you are reconciled . . ."

But Ivan Ivanovich began talking about catching quails, which was his usual resource when he wanted to change the subject.

And so the police captain was obliged to go about his business without having achieved any success whatever.

CHAPTER VI

FROM WHICH THE READER MAY EASILY
LEARN ALL THAT IS CONTAINED THEREIN

In spite of all the efforts of the court to conceal the affair, the very next day all Mirgorod knew that Ivan Ivanovich's sow had carried off Ivan Nikiforovich's petition. The police captain himself, in a moment of forgetfulness, first let slip a word. When Ivan Nikiforovich was told of it, he made no comment; he only asked: "Wasn't it the gray one?"

But Agafya Fedoseevna, who was present at the time, began needling Ivan Nikiforovich again: "What are you thinking about, Ivan Nikiforovich? You'll be laughed at as a fool if you let it pass!

A fine gentleman you'll be after this! You'll be lower than the peasant woman who sells the doughnuts you are so fond of."

And the pertinacious woman talked him around! She picked up a swarthy middle-aged man with pimples all over his face, in a dark blue coat with patches on the elbows, a typical scribbling pettifogger! He smeared his high boots with tar, wore three pens in his ear and a glass bottle by way of an inkpot tied on a string to a button. He would eat nine pies at a sitting and put the tenth in his pocket, and would write so much of all manner of legal chicanery on a single sheet of stamped paper that nobody could read it aloud straight off without intervals of coughing and sneezing. This little image of a man rummaged about, racked his brains and wrote, and at last concocted the following document:

"To the Mirgorod district court from the nobleman Ivan, son of Nikifor Dovgochkhun.

"Concerning the aforesaid my petition the which was from me, the gentleman Ivan, son of Nikifor Dovgochkhun, relating to the gentleman Ivan, son of Ivan Pererepenko, wherein which the district court of Mirgorod has manifested its partiality. And the same brash arbitrariness of the gray sow which was kept a secret and has reached our ears from persons in no way concerned therewith. Whereto the partiality and connivance, as of evil intention, falls within the jurisdiction of the law; inasmuch as the aforesaid sow is a foolish creature and thereby the more apt for the stealing of papers. Wherefrom it is evidently apparent that the sow frequently aforementioned, could not otherwise than have been incited to the same by the opposing party, the self-styled gentleman, Ivan, son of Ivan Pererepenko, the same having been already detected in housebreaking, attempted murder, and sacrilege. But the aforesaid Mirgorod court with its characteristic partiality manifested its tacit connivance; without the which connivance the aforesaid sow could by no manner of means have been admitted to the stealing of the paper, inasmuch as the Mirgorod district court is well provided with service; to which intent it is sufficient to name one soldier present on all occasions in the reception room, who, though he has a cross-eye and a somewhat useless arm, is yet fully capable of driving out a sow and striking her with a stick. Wherefrom the connivance of the aforesaid Mirgorod court thereto is proven and the partition of the ill-gotten profits therefrom on mutual terms is abundantly evident. The aforesaid robber and gentleman, Ivan, son of Ivan Pererepenko, is manifestly the scoundrelly accomplice therein. Wherefore, I, the gentleman Ivan, son of Nikifor Dovgochkhun, do herewith inform the said district court that if the petition above-mentioned shall not be recovered from the aforesaid gray sow, or from the gentleman Pererepenko, her accomplice, and if proceedings shall not be taken upon it in accordance with justice and in my favor, then I, the gentleman, Ivan, son of Nikifor, will lodge a complaint with the higher court concerning such illegal connivance of the aforesaid district court, transferring the case thereto with all due formalities.

"Ivan, son of Nikifor Dovgochkhun, gentleman of the Mirgorod district."

This petition produced its effect. The judge, like good-natured people as a rule, was a man of cowardly disposition. He appealed to the secretary. But the secretary emitted a bass "Hm" through his lips, while his face wore the expression of unconcern and diabolical ambiguity which appears only on the face of Satan when he sees the victim who has appealed to him lying at his feet. One resource only was left: to reconcile the two friends. But how approach that when all attempts had up to now been unsuccessful? However, they decided to try again; but Ivan Ivanovich declared point-blank that he would not hear of it, and was, indeed, very much incensed. Ivan Nikiforovich turned his back instead of answering, and did not utter a word. Then the case went forward with the extraordinary rapidity for which our courts of justice are so famous. A document was registered, inscribed, docketed, filed, copied, all in one and the same day; and then the case was laid on a shelf, where it lay and lay and lay for one year and a second and a third. Numbers of young girls had time to get married; a new street was laid down in Mirgorod, the judge lost one molar and two side teeth; more small children were running about Ivan Ivanovich's yard than before (goodness only knows where they sprang from); to spite Ivan Ivanovich, Ivan Nikiforovich built a new goose pen, though a little further away than the first, and so completely screened himself from Ivan Ivanovich that these worthy gentlemen scarcely ever saw each others' faces—and still the case lay in perfect order, in the cupboard which had been turned to marble by inkstains.

Meanwhile there occurred an event of the greatest importance in Mirgorod. The police captain was giving a party! Where can I find brushes and colors to paint the variety of the assembly and the magnificence of the entertainment? Take a clock, open it, and look what is going on there! Terribly confusing, isn't it? Now imagine as many if not more wheels standing in the police captain's courtyard. What chaises and traveling carriages were not there! One had a wide back and a narrow front; another a narrow back but a wide front. One was a chaise and a covered trap both at once; another was neither chaise nor trap; one was like a huge haystack or a fat merchant's wife; another was like a disheveled Jew or a skeleton that had not quite got rid of its skin. One was in profile exactly like a pipe with a long mouthpiece; another a strange creation, utterly shapeless and fantastic, was unlike anything in the world. From the midst of this chaos of wheels and box seats rose the semblance of a carriage with a window like that of a room, with a thick bar right across it. The coachmen in gray Cossack coats, tunics, and gray jerkins, in sheepskin hats and caps of all patterns, with pipes in their hands, led the unharnessed horses about the courtyards. What a party it was that the police captain gave! Allow me, I will enumerate all who were there: Taras Tarasovich, Evpl Akinfovich, Evtikhy Evtikhievich, Ivan Ivanovich—not *the* Ivan Ivanovich, but the other—Savva Gavrilovich, our Ivan Ivanovich, Elevfery Elevferievich, Makar Nazaryevich, Foma Grigorievich . . . I cannot go on! It is too much for me! My hand is tired from writing! And how many ladies there were! Dark and fair, and long and short, stout as Ivan Nikiforovich, and so thin that it seemed as though one could hide each one of them in the scabbard of the police captain's sword. What hats! What dresses! Red, yellow, coffee-colored, green, blue, new, turned and remade —fichus, ribbons, reticules! Goodbye to my poor eyes! They will be no more use after that spectacle. And what a long table was drawn out! And how everybody talked; what an uproar there was! A mill with all its clappers, grindstones, and wheels going is nothing to it! I cannot tell you for certain what they talked about, but it must be supposed that they discussed many interesting and important topics, such as the weather, dogs, ladies' hats, wheat, horses. At last Ivan Ivanovich—not *the* Ivan Ivanovich but the other one who squinted—said: "I am very much surprised that my right eye" (the squinting Ivan Ivanovich always spoke ironically of himself) "does not see Ivan Nikiforovich."

"He would not come!" said the police captain.

"How is that?"

"Well, it's two years, thank God, since they had a quarrel, that is, Ivan Ivanovich and Ivan Nikiforovich, and wherever one goes the other won't come on any account!"

"What are you telling me!" At this the squinting Ivan Ivanovich turned his eyes upward and clasped his hands together.

"Well, now, if men with good eyes don't live in peace, how am I to see eye to eye with anyone!"

At these words everyone laughed heartily. We were all very fond of the squinting Ivan Ivanovich, because he used to make jokes that were precisely in the taste of the day. Even a tall lean man in a wadded overcoat with a plaster on his nose who had before this been sitting in the corner without the slightest change in the expression of his face, even when a fly flew up his nose—even this gentleman rose from his seat and moved nearer to the crowd surrounding the squinting Ivan Ivanovich.

"Do you know what," the latter said when he saw a goodly company standing around him, "instead of gazing at my cross-eye, as you are now, let us reconcile our two friends! At this moment Ivan Ivanovich is conversing with the ladies—let us send on the sly for Ivan Nikiforovich and bring them together."

All agreed with Ivan Ivanovich's suggestion and decided to send at once to Ivan Nikiforovich's house to beg him most particularly to come to dine with the police captain. But the important question to whom to entrust this weighty commission puzzled everyone. They discussed at length who was most capable and most skillful in the diplomatic line; at last, it was unanimously resolved to confide the task to Anton Prokofievich Golopuz.

But we must first make the reader a little acquainted with this remarkable person. Anton Prokofievich was a perfectly virtuous man in the full meaning of that word; if any of the worthy citizens of Mirgorod gave him a scarf or a pair of trousers, he thanked them; if any gave him a slight flip on the nose, he thanked them even then. If he were asked: "Why is it your frock coat is brown, Anton Prokofievich, but the sleeves are blue?" he almost always answered: "And you haven't one at all! Wait a little while, it will soon be shabby and then it will be all alike!" And in fact the blue cloth began, from the effect of the sun, to turn brown, and now it goes perfectly well with the color of the coat. But what is strange is that Anton Prokofievich has the habit of wearing cloth clothes in the summer and cotton in the winter. He has no house of his own. He used to have one at the end of the town, but he sold it and with the money he got for it he bought three bay horses and a small chaise, in which he used to ride about visiting the neighboring landowners. But as the horses gave him a great deal of trouble, and besides he needed money to buy them oats, Anton Prokofievich swapped them for a fiddle and a serf girl, receiving a twenty-five ruble note in the bargain. Then Anton Prokofievich sold the fiddle and swapped the girl for a morocco purse set with gold, and now he has a purse the like of which no one else possesses. He pays for this gratification by not being able to drive about the countryside, and is forced to remain in town and to spend his nights at different houses, especially those of the gentlemen who derive pleasure from flipping him on the nose. Anton Prokofievich is fond of good food and plays pretty well at "Fools" and "Millers." [6] Obedience has always been his natural element, and so, taking his cap and his stick, he set off immediately.

But as he went, he began thinking how he was to make Ivan Nikiforovich come to the reception. The somewhat harsh character of that otherwise estimable individual made his task almost an impossible one. And, indeed, how could he be induced to come when even to get out of bed was a very great effort for him? And even supposing that he did get up, was he likely to go where —as he undoubtedly knew—his irreconcilable enemy was to be found? The more Anton Prokofievich considered the subject, the more difficulties he found. The day was sultry; the sun was scorching; the perspiration poured down him in streams. Anton Prokofievich, though he was flipped on the nose, was rather a wily man in many ways. It was only in swapping that he was rather unlucky. He knew very well when he had to pretend to be a fool, and sometimes knew how to hold his own in circumstances and cases in which a clever man cannot often steer his course.

While his resourceful mind was thinking out means for persuading Ivan Nikiforovich, and he was going valiantly to face

---

[6] *Durak* and *melnik*, popular card games. (ed.)

the worst, an unexpected circumstance somewhat disconcerted him. It will not be amiss at this juncture to inform the reader that Anton Prokofievich had, among other things, a pair of trousers with the strange peculiarity of attracting all the dogs to bite his calves whenever he put them on. As ill-luck would have it, he had put on those trousers that day, and so he had hardly abandoned himself to meditation when a terrible barking in all directions beat on his ears. Anton Prokofievich set up such a shout (no one could shout louder than he) that not only our friend the serving-woman and the inmate of the immense overcoat ran out to meet him, but even the urchins from Ivan Ivanovich's courtyard raced to him, and, though the dogs only succeeded in biting one leg, this greatly cooled his enthusiasm, and he went up the steps with a certain timidity.

CHAPTER VII

AND LAST

"Ah, good day! What have you been teasing my dogs for?" said Ivan Nikiforovich, on seeing Anton Prokofievich; for no one ever addressed the latter except humorously.

"Plague take them all! Who's teasing them?" answered Anton Prokofievich.

"That's a lie."

"I swear it isn't. Piotr Fiodorovich asks you to dinner."

"Hm!"

"I swear! I can't tell you how earnestly he begs you to come. 'What's the meaning of it?' he said. 'Ivan Nikiforovich avoids me as though I were an enemy; he will never come for a little chat or to sit a bit.' "

Ivan Nikiforovich stroked his chin.

" 'If Ivan Nikiforovich will not come now,' he said, 'I don't know what to think: he must have something in his mind against me! Do me the favor, Anton Prokofievich, persuade Ivan Nikiforovich!' Come, Ivan Nikiforovich, let us go! There is a delightful group there now!"

Ivan Nikiforovich began scrutinizing a cock, who was standing on the steps crowing his loudest.

"If only you knew, Ivan Nikiforovich," the zealous delegate

continued, "what oysters, what fresh caviar has been sent to Piotr Fiodorovich!"

At this Ivan Nikiforovich turned his head and began listening attentively.

This encouraged the delegate.

"Let us make haste and go; Foma Grigorievich is there, too! What are you doing?" he added, seeing that Ivan Nikiforovich was still lying in the same position. "Well, are we going or not?"

"I don't want to."

That "I don't want to" was a shock to Anton Prokofievich; he had already imagined that his urgent representations had completely prevailed on this really worthy man; but he heard instead a resolute "I don't want to."

"Why don't you want to?" he asked almost with annoyance, a feeling he very rarely displayed, even when he had burning paper put on his head, which was a trick the judge and the police captain were particularly fond of.

Ivan Nikiforovich took a pinch of snuff.

"It's your business, Ivan Nikiforovich, but I don't know what prevents you."

"Why should I go?" Ivan Nikiforovich said at last. "The ruffian will be there!" That was what he usually called Ivan Ivanovich now . . . Merciful heavens! And not long ago . . .

"I swear, he won't! By all that's holy he won't! May I be struck dead on the spot with a thunderbolt!" answered Anton Prokofievich, who was ready to take this oath a dozen times in an hour. "Let us go, Ivan Nikiforovich!"

"But you are lying, Anton Prokofievich, he is there, isn't he?"

"He's not! May I never leave the spot if he is! And think yourself what reason have I to tell a lie! May my arms and legs be withered! . . . What, don't you believe me even now? May I drop here dead at your feet! May neither father nor mother nor myself ever see the kingdom of heaven! Do you still disbelieve me?"

Ivan Nikiforovich was completely appeased by these assurances, and bade his valet in the enormous overcoat to bring him his trousers and his nankeen Cossack coat.

I imagine that it is quite superfluous to describe how Ivan Nikiforovich put on his trousers, how his cravat was tied, and how, finally, he put on his Cossack coat which had split under the left sleeve. It is enough to say that during that time he maintained a decorous composure and did not answer one word to Anton Prokofievich's proposition that he should swap something with him for his Turkish purse.

Meanwhile the assembled company were, with impatience, awaiting the decisive moment when Ivan Nikiforovich would make his appearance, and the universal desire that these worthy men should be reconciled might at last be gratified. Many were almost positive that Ivan Nikiforovich would not come. The police captain even offered to take a wager with squinting Ivan Ivanovich that he would not come, and only gave it up because the latter insisted that the police captain should stake his wounded leg and he his cross-eye—at which the police captain was extremely offended and the company laughed on the sly. No one had yet sat down at the table, though it was long past one o'clock—an hour at which people have got some way with their dinner at Mirgorod, even on grand occasions.

Anton Prokofievich had hardly appeared at the door when he was instantly surrounded by all. In answer to all questions he shouted one decisive phrase: "Won't come!" He had scarcely uttered this, and a shower of reproaches and abuse and possibly flips, too, was about to descend on his head for the failure of his mission, when the door opened suddenly and—Ivan Nikiforovich walked in.

If Satan himself or a corpse had suddenly appeared he would not have produced such amazement as that into which Ivan Nikiforovich's entrance plunged the whole company; while Anton Prokofievich went off into guffaws of laughter, holding his sides with glee that he had so taken them in.

Anyway, it was almost incredible to everyone that Ivan Nikiforovich could, in so short a time, have dressed as befits a gentleman. Ivan Ivanovich was not present at this moment; he had left the room. Recovering from their stupefaction, all the company showed their interest in Ivan Nikiforovich's health and expressed their pleasure that he had grown stouter. Ivan Nikiforovich kissed everyone and said: "Much obliged."

Meanwhile the smell of borsht floated through the room and agreeably tickled the nostrils of the starving guests. All streamed into the dining room. A string of ladies, talkative and silent, lean and stout, filed in ahead, and the long table was dotted with every hue. I am not going to describe all the dishes on the table! I shall say nothing of the cheese cakes and sour cream, nor of the sweet-bread served in the borsht, nor of the turkey stuffed with plums and raisins, nor of the dish that looked very much like a boot soaked in kvass, nor of the sauce which is the swansong of the old cook, the sauce which is served in flaming spirit to the great diversion, and, at the same time, terror of the ladies. I am not going to talk about these dishes because I greatly prefer eating them to expatiating on them in conversation.

Ivan Ivanovich was very much pleased with the fish prepared with horse-radish sauce. He was entirely engrossed in the useful and nutritious exercise of eating it. Picking out the smallest fish-bones, he laid them on the plate, and somehow chanced to glance across the table. Heavenly Creator! How strange it was! Opposite him was sitting Ivan Nikiforovich!

At the very same instant Ivan Nikiforovich looked up, too . . . ! No . . . ! I cannot! Give me another pen! My pen is feeble, dead; it has too thin a point for this picture! Their faces were as though turned to stone with amazement reflected on them. Each saw the long-familiar face, at the sight of which, one might suppose, each would advance as to an unexpected friend, offering his snuffbox with the words: "Help yourself," or, "I venture to ask you to help yourself"; and yet that very face was terrible as some evil portent! Drops of sweat rolled down the faces of Ivan Ivanovich and Ivan Nikiforovich.

All who were sitting at the table were mute with attention and could not take their eyes off the friends of days gone by. The ladies, who had till then been absorbed in a rather interesting conversation on the method of preparing capons, suddenly ceased talking. All was hushed! It was a picture worthy of the brush of a great artist.

At last Ivan Ivanovich took out his handkerchief and began to blow his nose, while Ivan Nikiforovich looked around and rested his eyes on the open door.

The police captain at once noticed this movement and bade the servant shut the door securely. Then each of the friends began eating, and they did not once glance at each other again.

As soon as dinner was over, the two old friends rose from their seats and began looking for their caps to slip away. Then the police captain gave a wink, and Ivan Ivanovich—not *the* Ivan Ivanovich but the other, the one who squinted—stood behind Ivan Nikiforovich's back while the police captain went up behind Ivan Ivanovich's back, and both began shoving them from behind so as to push them toward each other and not to let them go till they had shaken hands. Ivan Ivanovich, the one who squinted, though he shoved Ivan Nikiforovich a little askew, yet pushed him fairly successfully to the place where Ivan Ivanovich was standing; but the police captain took a line too much to one side, because again he could not cope with his unruly leg which, on this occasion, would heed no command, and, as though to spite him, lurched a long way off in quite the opposite direction (this may possibly have been due to the number of liqueurs on the table), so that Ivan Ivanovich fell against a lady in a red dress who had been compelled by curiosity to thrust herself into their midst. Such an incident boded nothing good. However, to mend matters, the judge took the police captain's place and, sniffing up all the snuff from his upper lip, shoved Ivan Ivanovich in the other direction. This is the usual means of bringing about a reconciliation in Mirgorod; it is not unlike a game of ball. As soon as the judge gave Ivan Ivanovich a shove, the Ivan Ivanovich who squinted pushed with all his strength and shoved Ivan Nikiforovich, from whom the sweat was dropping like rain water from a roof. Although both friends resisted stoutly, they were thrust together, because both sides received considerable support from the other guests.

Then they were closely surrounded on all sides and not allowed to go until they consented to shake hands.

"God bless you, Ivan Nikiforovich and Ivan Ivanovich! Tell us truthfully now: what did you quarrel about? Wasn't it something trifling? Aren't you ashamed before men and before God!"

"I don't know," said Ivan Nikiforovich, panting with exhaustion (it was noticeable that he was by no means averse to reconciliation). "I don't know what I have done to Ivan Ivanovich; why did he cut down my goose pen and plot my ruin?"

"I am not guilty of any such evil designs," said Ivan Ivanovich, not looking at Ivan Nikiforovich. "I swear before God and before you, honorable gentlemen, I have done nothing to my enemy. Why does he defame me and cast ignominy on my rank and name?"

"How have I cast ignominy on you, Ivan Ivanovich?" said Ivan Nikiforovich. Another moment of explanation—another moment of reconciliation—and the long-standing feud was on the point of dying out. Already Ivan Nikiforovich was feeling in his pocket to get out his snuff horn and say: "Help yourself."

"Was it not damage," answered Ivan Ivanovich without raising his eyes, "when you, sir, insulted my rank and name with a word which it would be unseemly to repeat here?"

"Let me tell you as a friend, Ivan Ivanovich!" (At this Ivan Nikiforovich put his finger on Ivan Ivanovich's button, which was a sign of his complete goodwill.) "You took offense over the devil knows what, over my calling you a 'gander' . . ."

Ivan Nikiforovich was instantly aware that he had committed an indiscretion in uttering that word; but it was too late: the word had been uttered. All was ruined! Since Ivan Ivanovich had been beside himself and had flown into a rage, such as God grant one may never see, at the utterance of that word in private—think, dear readers, what it was now when this murderous word had been uttered in a company among whom there were a number of ladies, in whose society Ivan Ivanovich liked to be particularly punctilious. Had Ivan Nikiforovich acted otherwise, had he said "bird" and not "gander," the position might still have been saved. But—all was over!

He cast on Ivan Nikiforovich a glance—and what a glance! If that glance had been endowed with the power of action it would have reduced Ivan Nikiforovich to ashes. The guests understood that glance, and of their own accord made haste to separate them. And that man, a paragon of gentleness, who never let one beggar woman pass without questioning her, rushed out in a terrible fury. How violent are the tempests aroused by the passions!

For a whole month nothing was heard of Ivan Ivanovich. He shut himself up in his house. The sacred chest was opened, from the chest were taken—what? Silver rubles! Old ancestral silver rubles! And these silver rubles passed into the inky hands of scribblers. The case was transferred to the higher court. And when Ivan Ivanovich received the joyous tidings that it would be decided on the morrow, only then he looked out at the world and made up his mind to go out. Alas! for the next ten years the higher court informed him daily that the case would be settled on the morrow!

Five years ago I was passing through the town of Mirgorod. It was a bad time for traveling. Autumn had set in with its gloomy, damp weather, mud, and fog. A sort of unnatural greenness—the work of the tedious, incessant rains—lay in a thin network over the meadows and wheatfields, on which it seemed no more becoming than mischievous tricks in an old man, or roses on an old woman. In those days weather had a great effect upon me: I was depressed when it was dreary. But in spite of that I felt my heart beating eagerly as I drove into Mirgorod. Goodness, how many memories! It was twelve years since I had seen Mirgorod. Here, in those days, lived in touching friendship two unique men, two unique friends. And how many distinguished persons had died! The judge, Demyan Demyanovich, was dead by then; Ivan Ivanovich, the one who squinted, had taken leave of life, too. I drove into the principal street: posts were standing everywhere with wisps of straw tied to their tops: they were altering the streets! Several huts had been removed. Remnants of hurdles and fences remained standing disconsolately.

It was a holiday. I ordered my sack-covered chaise to stop before the church, and went in so quietly that no one turned around. It is true there was no one to do so: the church was deserted; there were scarcely any people about; evidently even the most devout were afraid of the mud. In the dull, or rather, sickly weather the candles were somehow strangely unpleasant; the dark side chapels were gloomy; the long windows with their round panes were streaming with tears of rain. I walked out into the side chapel and addressed an old man with grizzled hair. "Allow me to ask, is Ivan Nikiforovich living?" At that moment the lamp before the icon flared up and the light fell directly on the old man's face. How surprised I was when looking closely at it I saw familiar features! It was Ivan Nikiforovich himself! But how he had changed!

"Are you quite well, Ivan Nikiforovich? You look much older!"

"Yes, I am older. I have come today from Poltava," answered Ivan Nikiforovich.

"Good gracious! You have been to Poltava in such dreadful weather?"

"I was forced to! My lawsuit . . ."

At this I could not help dropping a sigh.

Ivan Nikiforovich noticed that sigh and said: "Don't be anxious: I have positive information that the case will be settled next week and in my favor."

I shrugged my shoulders and went to find out something about Ivan Ivanovich.

"Ivan Ivanovich is here!" someone told me. "He is in the choir."

Then I caught sight of a thin, wasted figure. Was that Ivan Ivanovich? The face was covered with wrinkles, the hair was completely white. But the coat was still the same. After the first greetings, Ivan Ivanovich, addressing me with the good-humored smile which so well suited his funnel-shaped face, said: "Shall I tell you my pleasant news?"

"What news?" I asked.

"Tomorrow my case will positively be settled; the court has told me so for certain."

I sighed still more heavily, and made haste to say goodbye—because I was traveling on very important business—and got into my chaise.

The lean horses, known in Mirgorod by the name of the post-express horses, set off, making an unpleasant sound as their hoofs sank into the gray mass of mud. The rain poured in streams onto the Jew who sat on the box covered with a sack. The damp pierced me through and through. The gloomy gate with the sentry box, in which a veteran was cleaning his gray equipment, slowly passed by. Again the same fields, in places black and furrowed and in places covered with green, the drenched cows and crows, the monotonous rain, the tearful sky without one gleam of light in it. —It is a dreary world, gentlemen.

ARABESQUES

NEVSKY PROSPEKT[1]

There is nothing finer than Nevsky Prospekt, not in Petersburg anyway: it is the making of the city. What splendor does it lack, that fairest of our city thoroughfares? I know that not one of the poor clerks that live there would trade Nevsky Prospekt for all the blessings of the world. Not only the young man of twenty-five summers with a fine mustache and a splendidly cut coat, but even the veteran with white hairs sprouting on his chin and a head as smooth as a silver dish is enthusiastic over Nevsky Prospekt. And the ladies! Nevsky Prospekt is even more attractive to the ladies. And indeed, to whom is it not attractive? As soon as you step into Nevsky Prospekt you are in an atmosphere of gaiety. Though you may have some necessary and important business, yet as soon as you are there you forget all about it. This is the one place where people put in an appearance without being forced to, without being driven there by the needs and commercial interests that swallow up all Petersburg. A man met on Nevsky Prospekt seems

---

[1] Nevsky Avenue. (ed.)

less of an egoist than in the other streets where greed, selfishness, and covetousness are apparent in all who walk or drive along them. Nevsky Prospekt is the general channel of communication in Petersburg. The man who lives on the Petersburg or Viborg Side who hasn't seen his friend at Peski[2] or at the Moscow Gate for years may be sure to meet him on Nevsky Prospekt. No directory list at an information bureau supplies such accurate information as Nevsky Prospekt. All-powerful Nevsky Prospekt! Sole place of entertainment for the poor man in Petersburg! How wonderfully clean are its surfaces, and, my God, how many feet leave their traces on it! The clumsy, dirty boots of the ex-soldier, under whose weight the very granite seems to crack, and the miniature, ethereal little shoes of the young lady who turns her head toward the glittering shop windows as the sunflower turns to the sun, and the rattling saber of the ambitious lieutenant which marks a sharp scratch along it—all print the scars of strength or weakness on it! What changes pass over it in a single day! What transformations it goes through between one dawn and the next!

Let us begin with earliest morning, when all Petersburg smells of hot, freshly baked bread and is filled with old women in ragged clothes who are making their raids on the churches and on compassionate passers-by. At such a time, Nevsky Prospekt is empty: the stout shopkeepers and their assistants are still asleep in their linen shirts or soaping their noble cheeks and drinking their coffee; beggars gather near the doors of the cafe where the drowsy Ganymede,[3] who the day before flew around with the cups of chocolate like a fly, crawls out with no necktie on, broom in hand, and throws stale pies and scraps at them. Working people move through the streets: sometimes peasants cross the avenue, hurrying to their work, in high boots caked with mortar which even the Ekaterieninsky Canal, famous for its cleanness, could not wash off. At this hour it is not proper for ladies to walk out, because Russian people like to explain their meaning in rude expressions such as they would not hear even in a theater. Sometimes a drowsy government clerk trudges along with a portfolio under his arm, if the way to his department lies through Nevsky Prospekt. It may be confidently stated that at this period, that is, up to twelve o'clock,

---

[2] A St. Petersburg district. (ed.)
[3] Mythological figure: a beautiful boy carried to Olympus by the eagle of Zeus to be cupbearer of the gods. (ed.)

Nevsky Prospekt is not the goal for any man, but simply the means of reaching it: it is filled with people who have their occupations, their anxieties, and their annoyances, and are not thinking about the avenue. Peasants talk about ten kopeks or seven coppers; old men and women wave their hands or talk to themselves, sometimes with very striking gesticulations, but no one listens to them or laughs at them with the exception perhaps of street boys in homespun smocks, streaking like lightning along Nevsky Prospekt with empty bottles or pairs of boots from the cobblers in their arms. At that hour you may put on what you like, and even if you wear a cap instead of a hat, or the ends of your collar stick out too far from your necktie, no one notices it.

At twelve o'clock tutors of all nationalities descend upon Nevsky Prospekt with their young charges in fine cambric collars. English Joneses and French Cocos walk arm in arm with the nurslings entrusted to their parental care, and with becoming dignity explain to them that the signboards over the shops are put there so that people may know what is to be found within. Governesses, pale Misses, and rosy Mademoiselles walk majestically behind their light and nimble charges, telling them to hold themselves more upright or not to drop their left shoulder; in short, at this hour Nevsky Prospekt plays its pedagogic part. But as two o'clock approaches, the governesses, tutors, and children are fewer; and finally are crowded out by their tender papas walking arm in arm with their highstrung wives in gaudy dresses of every possible color. Gradually these are joined by all who have finished their rather important domestic duties, such as talking to the doctor about the weather and the pimple that has come out on their nose, inquiring after the health of their horses and their promising and gifted children, reading in the newspaper a leading article and the announcements of the arrivals and departures, and finally drinking a cup of tea or coffee. They are joined, too, by those whose enviable destiny has called them to the blessed vocation of clerks on special duties, and by those who serve in the Department of Foreign Affairs and are distinguished by the dignity of their pursuits and their habits. My God! What splendid positions and duties there are! How they elevate and sweeten the soul! But, alas, I am not in the service and am denied the pleasure of watching the refined behavior of my superiors. Everything you meet on the Nevsky Prospekt is brimming over with propriety: the men in long jackets with their hands in their pockets, the ladies in pink, white, or pale blue satin coats and stylish hats. Here you meet unique whiskers, drooping with extraordinary and amazing elegance below the necktie, velvety, satiny whiskers, as black as sable or as coal, but alas! invariably the property of members of the Department of Foreign Affairs. Providence has denied black whiskers to clerks in other departments; they are forced, to their great disgust, to wear red ones. Here you meet marvelous mustaches that no pen, no brush could do justice to, mustaches to which the better part of a life has been devoted, the objects of prolonged care by day and by night; mustaches upon which enchanting perfumes are sprinkled and on which the rarest and most expensive kinds of pomade are lavished; mustaches which are wrapped up at night in the most expensive vellum; mustaches to which their possessors display the most touching devotion and which are the envy of passers-by. Thousands of varieties of hats, dresses, and kerchiefs, flimsy and bright-colored, for which their owners feel sometimes an adoration that lasts two whole days, dazzle everyone on Nevsky Prospect. A whole sea of butterflies seem to have flown up from their flower stalks and to be floating in a glittering cloud above the beetles of the male sex. Here you meet waists of a slim delicacy beyond dreams of elegance, no thicker than the neck of a bottle, and respectfully step aside for fear of a careless nudge with a discourteous elbow; your heart beats with apprehension lest an incautious breath snap in two the exquisite products of art and nature. And the ladies' sleeves that you meet on Nevsky Prospekt! Ah, how exquisite! They are like two balloons and the lady might suddenly float up into the air, were she not held down by the gentleman accompanying her; for it would be as easy and agreeable for a lady to be lifted into the air as for a glass of champagne to be lifted to the lips. Nowhere do people bow with such dignity and ease as on Nevsky Prospekt. Here you meet with a unique smile, a smile that is the acme of art, that will sometimes melt you with pleasure, sometimes make you bow your head and feel lower than the grass, sometimes make you hold it high and feel loftier than the Admiralty spire.[4] Here you meet people conversing about a concert or the weather with extraordinary dignity and sense of their own importance. Here you meet a thousand incredible types

---

[4] At that time, the tallest building in St. Petersburg. (ed.)

and figures. Good heavens! what strange characters are met on
Nevsky Prospekt! There are numbers of people who, when they
meet you, invariably stare at your boots, and when they have
passed, turn around to have a look at the skirts of your coat. I have
never been able to discover the reason for it. At first I thought
they were bootmakers, but they're not: they are for the most part
clerks in various departments and many of them are very good at
referring a case from one department to another; or they are people
who spend their time walking about or reading the paper in res-
taurants—in fact they are usually very respectable people. In this
blessed period between two and three o'clock in the afternoon,
when everyone seems to be walking on Nevsky Prospekt, there is
a display of all the finest things the genius of man has produced.
One displays a smart overcoat with the best beaver on it, the second
—a lovely Greek nose, the third—superb whiskers, the fourth—a
pair of pretty eyes and a marvelous hat, the fifth—a signet ring on
a jaunty forefinger, the sixth—a foot in a bewitching shoe, the
seventh—a necktie that excites wonder, and the eighth—a mustache that reduces one to stupefaction. But three o'clock strikes
and the display is over, the crowd grows less thick . . . At three
o'clock there is a fresh change. Suddenly it is like spring on Nevsky
Prospekt; it is covered with government clerks in green uniforms.
Hungry titular, lower court, and other councilors do their best to
quicken their pace. Young collegiate registrars and provincial and
collegiate secretaries are in haste to be in time to parade on Nevsky
Prospekt with a dignified air, trying to look as if they had not been
sitting in an office for the last six hours. But the elderly collegiate
secretaries and titular and lower court councilors walk quickly
with bowed heads: they are not disposed to amuse themselves by
looking at the passers-by; they have not yet completely torn themselves away from their office cares; in their heads is a full list of
work begun and not yet finished; for a long time, instead of the
signboards, they seem to see a cardboard rack of papers or the full
face of the head of their office.

From four o'clock Nevsky Prospekt is empty, and you hardly
meet a single government clerk. Some seamstress from a shop runs
across Nevsky Prospekt with a box in her hands. Some pathetic
victim of a benevolent attorney, cast adrift in a frieze overcoat;
some eccentric visitor to whom all hours are alike; a tall, lanky
Englishwoman with a handbag and a book in her hand; a foreman

in a high-waisted coat of cotton with a narrow beard, a ramshackle figure, back, arms, head, and legs all twisting and turning as he walks deferentially along the pavement; sometimes a humble craftsman . . . those are the only people that we meet at that hour on Nevsky Prospekt.

But as soon as dusk descends upon the houses and streets and the policeman covered with a piece of coarse material climbs up his ladder to light the lamp, and engravings which do not venture to show themselves by day peep out of the lower windows of the shops, Nevsky Prospekt revives again and begins to stir. Then comes that mysterious time when the street lamps throw a marvelous alluring light upon everything. You meet a great number of young men, for the most part bachelors, in warm frock coats and overcoats. There is a suggestion at this time of some aim, or rather something like an aim, something extremely unaccountable; the steps of all are more rapid and altogether very uneven; long shadows flit over the walls and pavement and their heads almost reach the Police Bridge. Young collegiate registrars, provincial and collegiate secretaries walk up and down for hours, but the elderly collegiate registrars, the titular and lower court secretaries are for the most part at home, either because they are married, or because the German cook living in their house gives them a very good dinner. Here you may meet some of the respectable-looking old gentlemen who with such dignity and propriety walked on Nevsky Prospekt at two o'clock. You may see them now racing along like the young government clerks to peep under the hat of some lady spotted in the distance, whose thick lips and fat cheeks plastered with rouge are so attractive to many, and above all to the shopmen, workmen, and shopkeepers, who promenade in crowds, always in coats of German cut and usually arm in arm.

"Hey!" cried Lieutenant Pirogov on such an evening, nudging a young man who walked beside him in a dress coat and cloak. "Did you see her?"

"I did; lovely, a perfect Bianca of Perugino." [5]

"But which do you mean?"

"The lady with the dark hair . . . And what eyes! Good God, what eyes! Her attitude and stunning figure and the lines of the face . . . exquisite!"

---

[5] Umbrian painter (1445-1523?) whose real name was Pietro di Cristoforo Vannuccio. Pupil of da Vinci. "Bianca" is his most famous painting. (ed.)

"I am talking of the blonde who passed after her on the other side. Why don't you go after the brunette if you find her so attractive?"

"Oh, how can you!" cried the young man in the dress coat, turning crimson. "As though she were one of the women who walk on Nevsky Prospekt at night. She must be a very distinguished lady," he went on with a sigh. "Why, her cloak alone is worth eighty rubles."

"You fool!" cried Pirogov, giving him a violent shove in the direction in which the brilliant cloak was fluttering. "Move on, you idiot, don't waste time. I'll follow the blonde."

"We know what you all are," Pirogov thought to himself, with a self-satisfied and confident smile, convinced that no beauty could withstand him.

The young man in the dress coat and cloak with timid and tremulous step walked in the direction in which the bright-colored cloak was fluttering, at one moment shining brilliantly as it approached a street lamp, at the next shrouded in darkness as it moved further away. His heart throbbed and he unconsciously quickened his pace. He dared not even imagine that he could have a claim on the attention of the beauty who was retreating into the distance, and still less could he admit the evil thought suggested by Lieutenant Pirogov. All he wanted was to see the house, to discover where this exquisite creature lived who seemed to have flown straight down from heaven onto the Nevsky Prospekt, and who would probably fly away, no one could tell where. He darted along so fast that he was continually jostling dignified, gray-whiskered gentlemen off the pavement. This young man belonged to a class which is a great exception among us, and he no more belonged to the common run of Petersburg citizens than a face that appears to us in a dream belongs to the world of actual fact. This exceptional class is very rare in the town where all are officials, shopkeepers, or German craftsmen. He was an artist. A strange phenomenon, is it not? A Petersburg artist. An artist in the land of snows. An artist in the land of the Finns where everything is wet, flat, pale, gray, foggy. These artists are utterly unlike the Italian artists, proud and ardent as Italy and her skies. The Russian artist on the contrary is, as a rule, mild, gentle, retiring, carefree, and quietly devoted to his art; he drinks tea with a couple of friends in his little room, modestly discusses his favorite subjects, and does not trouble his head at all about anything superfluous. He frequently employs some old beggar woman, and makes her sit for six hours on end in order to transfer to canvas her pitiful, almost inanimate countenance. He draws a sketch in perspective of his studio with all sorts of artistic litter lying about, copies plaster-of-Paris hands and feet, turned coffee-colored by time and dust, a broken easel, a palette lying upside down, a friend playing the guitar, walls smeared with paint, with an open window through which there is a glimpse of the pale Neva and poor fishermen in red shirts. Almost all these artists paint in gray, muddy colors that bear the unmistakable imprint of the north. For all that, they all work with instinctive enjoyment. They are often endowed with real talent, and if only they were breathing the fresh air of Italy, they would no doubt develop as freely, broadly, and brilliantly as a plant at last brought from indoors into the open air. They are, as a rule, very timid; stars and thick epaulets reduce them to such a confused state that they ask less for their pictures than they had intended. They are sometimes fond of dressing smartly, but anything smart they wear always looks too startling and rather like a patch. You sometimes meet them in an excellent coat and a muddy cloak, an expensive velvet vest and a coat covered with paint, just as on one of their unfinished landscapes you sometimes see the head of a nymph, for which the artist could find no other place, sketched on the background of an earlier work which he had once painted with pleasure. Such an artist never looks you straight in the face; or, if he does look at you, it is with a vague, indefinite expression. He does not transfix you with the vulturelike eye of an observer or the hawklike glance of a cavalry officer. This is because he sees at the same time your features and the features of some plaster-of-Paris Hercules standing in his room, or because he is imagining a picture which he dreams of producing later on. This makes him often answer incoherently, sometimes quite incomprehensibly, and the muddle in his head increases his shyness. To this class belonged the young man we have described, an artist called Piskarev, retiring, shy, but carrying in his soul sparks of feeling, ready at a fitting opportunity to burst into flame. With secret dread he hastened after the lady who had made so strong an impression on him, and he seemed to be surprised at his audacity. The unknown girl who had so captured his eyes, his thoughts, and his feelings suddenly turned her head and glanced at him.

Good God, what divine features! The dazzling whiteness of the exquisite brow was framed by hair lovely as an agate. They curled, those marvelous tresses, and some of them strayed below the hat and caressed the cheek, flushed by the chill of evening with a delicate fresh color. A swarm of exquisite visions hovered about her lips. All the memories of childhood, all the visions that rise from dreaming and quiet inspiration in the lamplight—all seemed to be blended, mingled, and reflected on her delightful lips. She glanced at Piskarev and his heart quivered at that glance; her glance was severe, a look of anger came into her face at the sight of this impudent pursuit; but on that lovely face even anger was bewitching. Overcome by shame and timidity he stood still, dropping his eyes; but how could he lose this divine being without discovering the sanctuary in which she was enshrined? Such was the thought in the mind of the young dreamer, and he resolved to follow her. But, to avoid her notice, he fell back a good distance, looked aimlessly from side to side, and examined the signboards on the shops, yet he did not lose sight of a single step the unknown lady took. Passers-by were less frequent; the street became quieter. The beauty looked around and he fancied that her lips were curved in a faint smile. He trembled all over and could not believe his eyes. No, it was the deceptive light of the street lamp which had thrown that trace of a smile upon her lips; no his own imagination was mocking him. But he held his breath and everything in him quivered, all his feelings were ablaze and everything before him was lost in a sort of mist; the pavement seemed to be moving under his feet, carriages drawn by trotting horses seemed to stand still, the bridge stretched out and seemed broken in the center, the houses were upside down, a sentry box seemed to be reeling toward him, and the sentry's halberd, and the gilt letters of the signboard and the scissors painted on it, all seemed to be flashing across his very eyelash. And all this was produced by one glance, by one turn of a pretty head. Hearing nothing, seeing nothing, understanding nothing, he followed the light traces of the lovely feet, trying to moderate the swiftness of his own steps which moved in time with the throbbing of his heart. At moments he was overcome with doubt whether the look on her face was really so gracious; and then for an instant he stood still; but the beating of his heart, the irresistible violence and turmoil of his feelings drove him forward. He did not even notice a four-storied house that loomed before him; four rows of windows, all lighted up, burst upon him all at once, and he was brought to a sudden stop by striking against the iron railing of the entrance. He saw the lovely stranger fly up the stairs, look around, lay a finger on her lips, and make a sign for him to follow her. His knees trembled, his feelings, his thoughts were aflame. A thrill of joy, unbearably acute, flashed like lightning through his heart. No, it was not a dream! Good God, what happiness in one instant! What a lifetime's rapture in two minutes!

But was it not all a dream? Could it be true that this girl for whom he would gladly have given his life for one heavenly glance, that she who made him feel such bliss just to be near the house where she lived, could she really have been so kind and attentive to him? He flew up the stairs. He was conscious of no earthly thought; he was not aflame with earthly passion. No, at that moment he was pure and chaste as a virginal youth burning with the vague spiritual craving for love. And what would have awakened base thoughts in a dissolute man, in him made them still holier. This confidence, shown him by a weak and lovely creature, laid upon him the sacred duty of chivalrous austerity, the sacred duty to carry out all her commands. All that he desired was that those commands should be as difficult, as hard to carry out as possible, so that more effort be required to overcome all obstacles. He did not doubt that some mysterious and at the same time important circumstance compelled the unknown lady to confide in him; that she would certainly require some important service from him, and he felt in himself enough strength and resolution for anything.

The staircase went around and around, and his thoughts whirled around and around with it. "Be careful!" a voice rang out like a harpstring, sending a fresh thrill through him. On the dark landing of the fourth floor the blonde stranger knocked at a door; it was opened and they went in together. A woman of rather attractive appearance met them with a candle in her hand, but she looked so strangely and impudently at Piskarev that he dropped his eyes. They went into the room. Three female figures in different corners of the room met his eye. One was laying out cards; another was sitting at the piano and with two fingers strumming out a pitiful travesty of an old polonaise; the third was sitting before a mirror combing her long hair, and had apparently no intention of discontinuing her toilette because of the arrival of an unknown visitor. An unpleasant untidiness, usually only seen in the neglected rooms of bachelors, was everywhere apparent. The furniture, which was fairly good, was covered with dust. Spiders' webs stretched over the carved cornice; through the open door of another room he caught the gleam of a spurred boot and the red edging of a uniform; a man's loud voice and a woman's laugh rang out without restraint.

Good God, where had he come! At first he would not believe it, and began looking more attentively at the objects that filled the room; but the bare walls and uncurtained windows betrayed the absence of a careful housewife; the faded faces of these pitiful creatures, one of whom was sitting just under his nose and staring at him as coolly as though he were a spot on someone's dress—all convinced him that he had come into one of those revolting places in which the pitiful vice that springs from a poor education and the terrible overpopulation of a great town finds shelter, one of those places in which man sacrilegiously tramples and derides all that is pure and holy, all that makes life beautiful, where woman, the beauty of the world, the crown of creation, is transformed into a strange, equivocal creature, where she loses with her purity of her heart all that is womanly, revoltingly adopts the swagger and impudence of man, and ceases to be the delicate, the lovely creature, so different from us. Piskarev looked at her from head to foot with troubled eyes, as though trying to make sure whether this was really she who had so enchanted him and had brought him flying from Nevsky Prospekt. But she stood before him lovely as ever; her eyes were even more heavenly. She was fresh, not more than seventeen; it could be seen that she had not long been in the grip of vice; it had as yet left no trace upon her cheeks, they were fresh and faintly flushed with color; she was lovely.

He stood motionless before her and was ready to allow himself to be once again deceived. But the beautiful girl was tired of this long silence and gave a meaning smile, looking straight into his eyes. That smile was full of a sort of pitiful insolence; it was so strange and as incongruous with her face as a sanctimonious air with the brutal face of a bribetaker or a manual of bookkeeping with a poet. He shuddered. She opened her lovely lips and began saying something, but all that she said was so stupid, so vulgar . . . As though intelligence were lost with innocence! He wanted to hear no more. He was absurd! Simple as a child! Instead of taking advantage of such graciousness, instead of rejoicing at such an opportunity, as anyone else in his place would probably have done, he dashed away like a wild antelope and ran out into the street.

He sat in his room with his head bowed and his hands hanging loose, like a poor man who has found a precious pearl and at once dropped it into the sea. "Such a beauty, such divine features! And where? In such a place . . ." That was all that he could say.

Nothing, indeed, moves us to such pity as the sight of beauty touched by the putrid breath of vice. Ugliness may go with it, but beauty, tender beauty . . . In our thoughts it blends with nothing but purity and innocence. The beauty who had so enchanted poor Piskarev really was a rare and extraordinary exception. Her presence in those vile surroundings seemed even more incredible. All her features were so purely molded, the whole expression of her lovely face wore the stamp of such nobility, that it was impossible to think that vice already held her in its grip. She should have been the priceless pearl, the whole world, the paradise, the wealth of a devoted husband; she should have been the lovely, gentle star of some quiet family circle, and with the faintest movement of her lovely lips should have given her sweet commands there. She would have been a divinity in the crowded ballroom, on the glistening parquet, in the glow of candles surrounded by the silent adoration of a crowd of admirers; but, alas! by some terrible machination of the fiendish spirit, eager to destroy the harmony of life, she had been flung with satanic laughter into this horrible swamp.

Exhausted by heartbreaking pity, he sat before a candle that was burned low in the socket. Midnight was long past, the belfry chime rang out half-past twelve, and still he sat without stirring, neither asleep nor fully awake. Sleep, abetted by his stillness, was beginning to steal over him, and already the room was beginning to disappear, and only the light of the candle still shone through the dreams that were overpowering him, when all at once a knock at the door made him start and wake up. The door opened and a footman in gorgeous livery walked in. Never had a gorgeous livery peeped into his lonely room. At such an hour of the night! . . . He was amazed, and with impatient curiosity looked intently at the footman who entered.

"The lady," the footman pronounced with a deferential bow, "whom you visited some hours ago bade me invite you and sent the carriage to fetch you."

Piskarev was speechless with amazement: the carriage, a footman in livery! . . . No, there must be some mistake. . . . .

"My good man," he said timidly, "you must have come to the wrong door. Your mistress must have sent you for someone else and not for me."

"No, sir, I am not mistaken. Did you not accompany my mistress home? It's in Liteyny Street, on the fourth floor."

"I did."

"Then, if so, please make haste; my mistress is very anxious to see you, and begs you come straight to her house."

Piskarev ran down the stairs. A carriage was, in fact, standing in the courtyard. He got into it, the door was slammed, the cobbles of the pavement resounded under the wheels and the hoofs, and the illuminated panorama of houses and lamps and signboards passed by the carriage windows. Piskarev pondered all the way and could not explain this adventure. A house of her own, a carriage, a footman in gorgeous livery . . . He could not reconcile all this with the room on the fourth floor, the dusty windows, and the jangling piano. The carriage stopped before a brightly lighted entrance, and he was at once struck by the procession of carriages, the talk of the coachmen, the brilliantly lighted windows, and the strains of music. The footman in gorgeous livery helped him out of the carriage and respectfully led him into a hall with marble columns, with a porter in gold lace, with cloaks and fur coats flung here and there, and a brilliant lamp. An airy staircase with shining banisters, fragrant with perfume, led upward. He was already mounting it; hesitating at the first step and panic-stricken at the crowds of people, he went into the first room. The extraordinary brightness and variety of the scene completely staggered him; it seemed to him as though some demon had crumbled the whole world into bits and mixed all these bits indiscriminately together. The gleaming shoulders of the ladies and the black tailcoats, the chandeliers, the lamps, the ethereal floating gauze, the filmy ribbons, and the fat bass looking out from behind the railing of the orchestra—everything was dazzling. He saw at the same instant such numbers of respectable old or middle-aged men with stars on their evening coats and ladies sitting in rows or stepping so lightly, proudly, and graciously over the parquet floor; he heard so many French and English words; moreover, the young men in black evening clothes were filled with such dignity, spoke or kept silence

with such gentlemanly decorum, were so incapable of saying anything inappropriate, made jokes so majestically, smiled so politely,
wore such superb whiskers, so skillfully displayed their elegant
hands as they straightened their neckties; the ladies were so ethereal, so steeped in perfect self-satisfaction and rapture, so enchant-
ingly cast down their eyes, that . . . but Piskarev's subdued air,
as he leaned timidly against a column, was enough to show that he
was completely overwhelmed. At that moment the crowd stood
around a group of dancers. They whirled around, draped in the
transparent creations of Paris, in garments woven of air itself;
effortlessly they touched the parquet floor with their lovely feet,
as ethereal as though they walked on air. But one among them was
lovelier, more splendid, and more brilliantly dressed than the rest.
An indescribable, subtle perfection of taste was apparent in all her
attire, and at the same time it seemed as though she cared nothing
for it, as though it had come unconsciously, of itself. She looked
and did not look at the crowd of spectators crowding around her,
she cast down her lovely long eyelashes indifferently, and the
gleaming whiteness of her face was still more dazzling when she
bent her head and a light shadow lay on her enchanting brow.

Piskarev did his utmost to make his way through the crowd and
get a better look at her; but to his intense annoyance a huge head
of curly black hair was continually screening her from him; moreover, the crush was so great that he did not dare to press forward
or to step back, for fear of jostling against some privy councilor.
But at last he squeezed his way to the front and glanced at his
clothes, anxious that everything should be neat. Heavenly Creator!
What was his horror! he had on his everyday coat, and it was all
smeared with paint; in his haste to leave he had actually forgotten
to change into suitable clothes. He blushed up to his ears and,
dropping his eyes in confusion, would have gone away, but there
was absolutely nowhere he could go; court chamberlains in brilliant uniforms formed an inexorable compact wall behind him. By
now his desire was to be as far away as possible from the beauty of
the lovely brows and eyelashes. In terror he raised his eyes to see
whether she were looking at him. Good God! she stood facing
him. . . . What did it mean? "It is she!" he cried almost at the top
of his voice. It was really she—the one he had met on Nevsky
Prospekt and had escorted home.

Meanwhile she raised her eyelashes and looked at all with her bright eyes. "Aie, aie, aie, how beautiful! . . ." was all he could say with bated breath. She scanned the faces around her, all eager to catch her attention, but with an air of weariness and indifference she looked away and met Piskarev's eyes. Oh heavens! What paradise! Oh God, for strength to bear this! Life cannot contain it, such rapture tears it asunder and bears away the soul! She made a sign to him, but not by hand nor by inclination of the head; no, it was in her ravishing eyes, so subtle, so imperceptible that no one else could see it, but he saw it! He understood it! The dance lasted a long time; the languorous music seemed to flag and die away and again it broke out, shrill and thunderous; at last the dance was over. She sat down. Her bosom heaved under the light cloud of gossamer, her hand (Oh, heavens! what a wonderful hand!) dropped on her knee, rested on her filmy gown which seemed to be breathing music under her hand, and its delicate lilac hue made that lovely hand look more dazzlingly white than ever. Just to touch it and nothing more! No other desires—they would be insolence. . . . He stood behind her chair, not daring to speak, not daring to breathe. "Have you been bored?" she asked. "I have been bored too. I see that you hate me. . . ." she added, lowering her long eyelashes.

"Hate you? I? . . . I? . . . ?" Piskarev, completely overwhelmed, tried to say something, and he would probably have poured out a stream of incoherent words, but at that moment a court chamberlain with a magnificently curled shock of hair came up making witty and polite remarks. He agreeably displayed a row of rather good teeth, and at every jest his wit drove a sharp nail into Piskarev's heart. At last someone fortunately addressed the court chamberlain with a question.

"How unbearable it is!" she said, lifting her heavenly eyes to him. "I will sit at the other end of the room; be there!" She glided through the crowd and vanished. He pushed his way through the crowd like one possessed, and in a flash was there.

Yes, it was she! She sat like a queen, finer than all, lovelier than all, and her eyes sought him.

"Are you here?" she asked softly. "I will be frank with you: no doubt you think the circumstances of our meeting strange. Can you imagine that I belong to the degraded class of beings among

whom you met me? You think my conduct strange, but I will reveal a secret to you. Can you promise never to betray it?" she asked,
fixing her eyes upon him.

"Oh I will, I will, I will! . . ."

But at that moment an elderly man shook hands with her and
began speaking in a language Piskarev did not understand. She
looked at the artist with an imploring gaze, and gestured to him to
remain where he was and await her return; but much too impatient, he could not obey a command even from her lips. He followed her, but the crowd parted them. He could no longer see
the lilac dress; in consternation he forced his way from room to
room and elbowed all he met mercilessly, but in all the rooms
gentlemen were sitting at whist plunged in dead silence. In a corner of the room some elderly people were arguing about the su-
periority of military to civil service; in another some young men
in superb dress coats were making a few light remarks about the
voluminous works of a poet. Piskarev felt that a gentleman of venerable appearance had taken him by the button of his coat and was
submitting some very just observation to his criticism, but he
rudely thrust him aside without even noticing that he had a very
distinguished order on his breast. He ran into another room—she
was not there; into a third—she was not there either. "Where is
she? Give her to me! Oh, I cannot live without another look at her!
I want to hear what she meant to tell me!" But his search was in
vain. Anxious and exhausted, he huddled in a corner and looked at
the crowd. But everything seemed blurred to his strained eyes. At
last the walls of his own room began to grow distinct. He raised
his eyes: before him stood a candlestick with the light flickering
in the socket; the whole candle had burned away and the melted
wax lay on his table.

So he had been asleep! My God, what a splendid dream! And
why had he awakened? Why had it not lasted one minute longer?
She would no doubt have appeared again! The unwelcome dawn
was peeping in at his window with its unpleasant, dingy light. The
room was in such a gray, untidy muddle . . . Oh, how revolting
was reality! What was it compared to dreams? He undressed
quickly and got into bed, wrapping himself up in a blanket, anxious
to recapture the dream that had flown. Sleep certainly did not take
long to come, but it presented him with something quite different
from what he desired: at one moment Lieutenant Pirogov with his

pipe, then the porter of the Academy, then an actual civil councilor, then the head of a Finnish woman who had sat for him for a
portrait, and such absurd things.

He lay in bed till the middle of the day, longing to dream again,
but she did not appear. If only she had shown her lovely features
for one minute, if only her light step had rustled, if only her hand,
shining white as driven snow, had for one instant appeared before
him.

Dismissing everything, forgetting everything, he sat with a
crushed and hopeless expression, full of nothing but his dream. He
never thought of touching anything; his eyes were fixed in a vacant, lifeless stare upon the windows that looked into the yard,
where a dirty watercarrier was pouring water that froze in the air,
and the cracked voice of a peddler bleated like a goat, "Old clothes
for sale." The sounds of everyday reality rung strangely in his
ears. He sat on till evening in this manner, and then flung himself
eagerly into bed. For hours he struggled with sleeplessness; at
last he overcame it. Again a dream, a vulgar, horrid dream. "God,
have mercy! For one minute, just for one minute, let me see her!"

Again he waited for the evening, again he fell asleep. He dreamed
of a government clerk who was at the same time a government
clerk and a bassoon. Oh, this was intolerable! At last she appeared!
Her head and her curls . . . she gazed at him . . . for—oh, how
brief a moment, and then again mist, again some stupid dream.

At last, dreaming became his life and from that time his life was
strangely turned upside down; he might be said to sleep when he
was awake and to come to life when he was asleep. Anyone seeing
him sitting dumbly before his empty table or walking along the
street would certainly have taken him for a lunatic or a man de-
ranged by drink: his eyes had a perfectly vacant look, his natural
absent-mindedness increased and drove every sign of feeling and
emotion out of his face. He only revived at the approach of night.

Such a condition destroyed his health, and the worst torture for
him was the fact that sleep began to desert him altogether. Anxious
to save the only treasure left him, he used every means to regain
it. He had heard that there were means of inducing sleep—one
need only take opium. But where could he get opium? He thought
of a Persian who sold shawls and, whenever he saw Piskarev, asked
him to paint a beautiful woman for him. He decided to go to him,
assuming that he would be sure to have the drug he wanted.

The Persian received him, sitting on a sofa with his legs crossed under him. "What do you want opium for?" he asked.

Piskarev told him about his sleeplessness.

"Very well, you must paint me a beautiful woman, and I will give you opium. She must be a real beauty: let her eyebrows be black and her eyes be as big as olives; and let me be lying near her smoking my pipe. Do you hear, she must be beautiful! She must be beautiful!"

Piskarev promised everything. The Persian went out for a minute and came back with a little jar filled with a dark liquid; he carefully poured some of it into another jar and gave it to Piskarev, telling him to take not more than seven drops in water. Piskarev greedily clutched the precious little jar, with which he would not have parted for a pile of gold, and dashed home.

When he got home he poured several drops into a glass of water and, swallowing it, lay down to sleep.

Oh God, what joy! She! She again, but now in quite a different world! Oh, how charmingly she sat at the window of a bright little country house! In her dress was the simplicity in which the poet's thought is clothed. And her hair! Merciful heavens! how simple it was and how it suited her. A short shawl was thrown lightly around her graceful throat; everything about her was modest, everything about her showed a mysterious, inexplicable sense of taste. How charming her graceful carriage! How musical the sound of her steps and the rustle of her simple gown! How lovely her arm encircled by a bracelet of hair! She said to him with a tear in her eye: "Don't look down upon me; I am not at all what you take me for. Look at me, look at me more carefully and tell me: am I capable of what you imagine?" "Oh no, no! May he who should dare to think it, may he . . ."

But he awoke, deeply moved, harassed, with tears in his eyes. "Better that you had not existed! had not lived in this world, but had been an artist's creation! I would never have left the canvas, I would have gazed at you forever and kissed you! I would have lived and breathed in you, as in the loveliest of dreams, and then I should have been happy. I should have desired nothing more; I would have called upon you as my guardian angel at sleeping and at waking, and I would have gazed upon you if ever I had to paint the divine and holy. But as it is . . . how terrible life is! What good is it that she lives? Is a madman's life a source of joy to his friends and family who once loved him? My God! what is our life! An eternal battle between dream and reality!" Such ideas absorbed him continually. He thought of nothing, he almost gave up eating, and with the impatience and passion of a lover waited for the evening and his coveted dreams. The continual concentration of his thoughts on one subject at last so completely mastered his whole being and imagination that the coveted image appeared before him almost every day, always in positions that were the very opposite of reality, for his thoughts were as pure as a child's. Through these dreams, the subject of them became in his imagination purer and was completely transformed.

The opium inflamed his thoughts more than ever, and if there ever was a man passionately, terribly, and ruinously in love to the utmost pitch of madness, he was that luckless man.

Of all his dreams one delighted him more than any: he saw himself in his studio. He was in good spirits and sitting happily with the palette in his hand! And she was there. She was his wife. She sat beside him, leaning her lovely elbow on the back of his chair and looking at his work. Her eyes were languid and weary with excess of bliss; everything in his room breathed of paradise; it was so bright, so neat. Good God! she leaned her lovely head on his bosom . . . He had never had a better dream than that. He got up after it fresher, less absent-minded than before. A strange idea came into his mind. "Perhaps," he thought, "she has been drawn into vice by some terrible misfortune, through no will of her own; perhaps her soul is disposed to penitence; perhaps she herself is longing to escape from her awful position. And am I to stand aside indifferently and let her ruin herself when I have only to hold out a hand to save her from drowning?" His thoughts carried him further. "No one knows me," he said to himself, "and no one cares what I do, and I have nothing to do with anyone either. If she shows herself genuinely penitent and changes her mode of life, I will marry her. I ought to marry her, and no doubt will do much better than many who marry their housekeepers or sometimes the most contemptible creatures. My action will be disinterested and very likely a good deed. I shall restore to the world the loveliest of its ornaments!"

Making this reckless plan, he felt the color flushing in his cheek; he went up to the mirror and was frightened at his hollow cheeks and the paleness of his face. He began carefully dressing; he washed, smoothed his hair, put on a new coat, a smart vest, flung on his cloak, and went out into the street. He breathed the fresh air and had a feeling of freshness in his heart, like a convalescent who has gone out for the first time after a long illness. His heart throbbed when he turned into the street which he had not passed through again since that fatal meeting.

He was a long time looking for the house. He walked up and down the street twice, uncertain before which to stop. At last one of them seemed to him to be the one. He ran quickly up the stairs and knocked at the door: the door opened and who came out to meet him? His ideal, his mysterious divinity, the original of his dream pictures—she who was his life, in whom he lived so terribly, so agonizingly, so blissfully—she, she herself, stood before him! He trembled; he could hardly stand on his feet for weakness, overcome by the rush of joy. She stood before him as lovely as ever, though her eyes looked sleepy, though a pallor had crept over her face, no longer quite so fresh; but still she was lovely.

"Ah!" she cried on seeing Piskarev and rubbing her eyes (it was two o'clock in the afternoon); "why did you run away from us that day?"

He sat down in a chair, feeling faint, and looked at her.

"And I am only just awake; I was brought home at seven in the morning. I was quite drunk," she added with a smile.

Oh, better you had been dumb and could not speak at all than uttering such words! She had shown him in a flash the whole panorama of her life. But, in spite of that, struggling with his feelings, he made up his mind to try whether his admonitions would have any effect on her. Pulling himself together, he began in a trembling but ardent voice depicting her awful position. She listened to him with a look of attention and with the feeling of wonder which we display at the insight of something strange and unexpected. She looked with a faint smile toward her friend who was sitting in a corner, and who stopped cleaning a comb and also listened with attention to this new preacher.

"It is true that I am poor," said Piskarev, at last, after a prolonged and persuasive appeal, "but we will work, we will do our best, side by side, to improve our position. Yes, nothing is sweeter than to owe everything to one's own work. I will sit at my pictures, you shall sit by me and inspire my work, while you are busy with sewing or some other handicraft, and we shall not want anything."

"Indeed!" she interrupted his speech with an expression of scorn. "I am not a washerwoman or a seamstress who has to work!"

Oh God! In those words the whole of an ugly, degraded life was portrayed, the life of the true followers of vice, full of emptiness and idleness!

"Marry me!" her friend who had till then sat silent in the corner put in, with a saucy air. "When I am your wife I will sit like this!" As she spoke she pursed up her pitiful face and assumed a silly expression, which greatly amused the beauty.

Oh, that was too much! That was more than he could bear! He rushed away with every thought and feeling in a turmoil. His mind was clouded: stupidly, aimlessly, he wandered about all day, seeing nothing, hearing nothing, feeling nothing. No one could say whether he slept anywhere or not; only next day, by some blind instinct, he found his way to his room, pale and looking terrible, with his hair disheveled and signs of madness in his face. He locked himself in his room and admitted no one, asked for nothing. Four days passed and his door was not once opened; at last a week had passed, and still the door was locked. People went to the door and began calling him, but there was no answer; at last the door was broken open and his corpse was found with the throat cut. A bloodstained razor lay on the floor. From his arms flung out convulsively and his terribly distorted face, it might be concluded that his hand had faltered and that he had suffered in agony before his soul left his sinful body.

So perished the victim of a frantic passion, poor Piskarev, the gentle, timid, modest, childishly simple-hearted artist whose spark of talent might with time have glowed into the full bright flame of genius. No one wept for him; no one was seen beside his dead body except the police inspector and the indifferent face of the town doctor. His coffin was taken to Okhta quickly, without even religious rites; only a soldier who followed it wept, and that only because he had had a glass too many of vodka. Even Lieutenant Pirogov did not come to look at the dead body of the poor luckless artist to whom he had extended his exalted patronage. He had no thoughts to spare for him; indeed, he was absorbed in a very exciting adventure. But let us turn to him. I do not like corpses, and it is always disagreeable to me when a long funeral procession crosses my path and some veteran dressed like a Capuchin monk takes a pinch of snuff with his left hand because he has a torch in his right. I always feel annoyed at the sight of a magnificent catafalque with a velvet pall; but my annoyance is mingled with sadness when I see a cart dragging the red, uncovered coffin of some poor fellow and only some old beggar woman who has met it at the crossways follows it weeping, because she has nothing else to do.

I believe we left Lieutenant Pirogov at the moment when he parted with Piskarev and went in pursuit of the blonde charmer. The latter was a lively, rather attractive little creature. She stopped before every shop and gazed at the sashes, kerchiefs, earrings, gloves, and other trifles in the shop windows, was continually twisting and turning and gazing about her in all directions and looking behind her. "You'll be mine, you darling!" Pirogov said confidently, as he pursued her, turning up the collar of his coat for fear of meeting someone of his acquaintance. We should, however, let the reader know what sort of person Lieutenant Pirogov was.

But before we describe Lieutenant Pirogov, we should say something of the circle to which Lieutenant Pirogov belonged. There are officers who form a kind of middle class in Petersburg. You will always find one of them at every evening party, at every dinner given by a civil councilor or an actual civil councilor who has risen to that grade through forty years of service. A couple of pale daughters, as colorless as Petersburg, some of them already gone to seed, the tea table, the piano, the impromptu dance, are all inseparable from the gay epaulet which gleams in the lamplight between the virtuous young lady and the black coat of her brother or of some old friend of the family. It is extremely difficult to arouse and divert these phlegmatic misses. To do so requires a great deal of skill, or rather perhaps the absence of all skill. One has to say what is not too clever or too amusing and to talk of the trivialities that women love. One must give credit for that to the gentlemen we are discussing. They have a special gift for making these drab beauties laugh and listen. Exclamations, smothered in laughter, of "Oh, do stop! Aren't you ashamed to be so absurd!" are often their highest reward. They rarely, one may say never, get into higher circles: from those regions they are completely crowded out by the so-called aristocrats. At the same time, they pass for well-bred, highly educated men. They are fond of talking about literature;

praise Bulgarin, Pushkin, and Gretch,[6] and speak with contempt
and witty sarcasm of A. A. Orlov.[7] They never miss a public lec-
ture, though it may be on bookkeeping or even forestry. You will
always find one of them at the theater, whatever the play, unless, indeed, it be one of the farces of the "Filatka" class,[8] which greatly
offend their fastidious taste. They are priceless at the theater and
the greatest asset to managers. They are particularly fond of fine
verses in a play, and they are greatly given to calling loudly for the
actors; many of them, by teaching in government establishments or
preparing pupils for them, arrive at the moment when they can
afford a carriage and a pair of horses. Then their circle becomes
wider and in the end they succeed in marrying a merchant's daughter who can play the piano, with a dowry of a hundred thousand,
or something near it, in cash, and a lot of bearded relations. They
can never achieve this honor, however, till they have reached the
rank of colonel at least, for Russian merchants, though there may
still be a smell of cabbage about them, will never consent to see
their daughters married to any but generals or at least colonels.
Such are the leading characteristics of this class of young men. But
Lieutenant Pirogov had a number of talents belonging to him individually. He recited verses from *Dimitry Donsky*[9] and *Woe
from Wit*[10] with great effect, and had a talent for blowing smoke
out of a pipe in rings so successfully that he could string a dozen
of them together in a chain; he could tell a very good story to the
effect that a cannon was one thing and a unicorn was another. It
is difficult to enumerate all the qualities with which fate had endowed Pirogov. He was fond of talking about actresses and dancers, but not quite in such a crude way as young lieutenants commonly hold forth on that subject. He was very much pleased with
his rank in the service, to which he had only lately been promoted,
and although he did occasionally say as he lay on the sofa: "O dear,
vanity, all is vanity. What if I am a lieutenant?" yet his vanity was

---

[6] Russia's greatest poet, Pushkin, is here satirically sandwiched between two
relative mediocrities: F. V. Bulgarin (1789-1859) and N. I. Gretch (1787-
1867), Gogol's contemporaries, who were journalists and editors of *The
Northern Bee*, a St. Petersburg magazine. (ed.)
[7] (1791-1840), author of moralistic tracts for half-literate masses. (ed.)
[8] *Filatka and Miroshka*, popular vaudeville show by P. Grigoriev, performed
in 1831. (ed.)
[9] Tragedy by V. A. Ozerov (1770-1816). (ed.)
[10] Comedy by A. S. Griboedov (1795-1829). (ed.)

secretly much flattered by his new dignity; he often tried in conversation to allude to it in a roundabout way, and on one occasion when he jostled against a copying clerk in the street who struck him as uncivil he promptly stopped him and, in a few but vigorous words, pointed out to him that there was a lieutenant standing before him and not any other kind of officer. He was especially eloquent in his observations because two very nice-looking ladies were passing at the moment. Pirogov displayed a passion for everything artistic in general and encouraged the artist Piskarev; this may have been partly due to a desire to see his manly face portrayed on canvas. But enough of Pirogov's good qualities. Man is such a strange creature that one can never enumerate all his good points, and the more we look into him the more new characteristics we discover and the description of them would be endless. And so Pirogov continued to pursue the unknown blonde, and from time to time he addressed her with questions to which she responded infrequently with abrupt and incoherent sounds. They passed by the dark Kazansky gate into Meshchansky Street—a street of tobacconists and little shops, of German artisans and Finnish nymphs. The fair lady ran faster than ever, and scurried in at the gate of a rather dirty-looking house. Pirogov followed her. She ran up a narrow, dark staircase and went in at a door through which Pirogov boldly followed her. He found himself in a big room with black walls and a grimy ceiling. A heap of iron screws, locksmith's tools, shining tin coffeepots, and candlesticks lay on the table; the floor was littered with brass and iron filings. Pirogov saw at once that this was a workman's lodging. The unknown charmer darted away through a side door. He hesitated for a minute, but, following the Russian rule,[11] decided to push forward. He went into the other room, which was quite unlike the first and very neatly furnished, showing that it was inhabited by a German. He was struck by an extremely strange sight: before him sat Schiller. Not the Schiller who wrote *William Tell* and the *History of the Thirty Years' War*, but the famous Schiller, the ironmonger and tinsmith of Meshchansky Street. Beside Schiller stood Hoffmann—not the writer Hoffmann, but a rather high-class bootmaker who lived in Ofitsersky Street and was a great friend of Schiller's. Schiller was drunk and was sitting on a chair, stamping and saying something excitedly. All

---

[11] When in doubt, plunge ahead. (ed.)

this would not have surprised Pirogov, but what did surprise him was the extraordinary attitude of the two figures. Schiller was sitting with his head upraised and his rather thick nose in the air, while Hoffmann was holding this nose between his finger and thumb and was flourishing the blade of his cobbler's knife over its surface. Both men were talking in German, and so Lieutenant Pirogov, whose knowledge of German was confined to *"Gut Morgen,"* could not make out what was going on. However, what Schiller said amounted to this: "I don't want it, I have no need of a nose!" he said, waving his hands, "I use three pounds of snuff a month on my nose alone. And I pay in a dirty Russian shop, for a German shop does not keep Russian snuff. I pay in a dirty Russian shop forty kopeks a pound—that makes one ruble twenty kopeks, twelve times one ruble twenty kopeks—that makes fourteen rubles forty kopeks. Do you hear, friend Hoffmann? Fourteen rubles forty kopeks on my nose alone! And on holidays I take a pinch of rappee, for I don't care to use that rotten Russian snuff on a holiday. In a year I use two pounds of rappee at two rubles a pound. Six and fourteen makes twenty rubles forty kopeks on snuff alone. It's robbery! I ask you, my friend Hoffmann, isn't it?" Hoffmann, who was drunk himself, answered in the affirmative. "Twenty rubles and forty kopeks! Damn it, I am a Swabian! I have a king in Germany. I don't want a nose! Cut off my nose! Here is my nose."

And had it not been for Lieutenant Pirogov's suddenly appearing, Hoffmann would certainly, for no rhyme or reason, have cut off Schiller's nose, for he already had his knife in position, as though he were going to cut a sole.

Schiller seemed very much annoyed that an unknown and uninvited person should so inopportunely interrupt him. Although he was in a state of intoxication, he felt that it was rather improper to be seen in the presence of an outsider in such a state and engaged in such proceedings. Meanwhile Pirogov made a slight bow and, with his characteristic agreeableness, said: "Excuse me . . . !"

"Get out!" Schiller responded emphatically.

Lieutenant Pirogov was taken aback at this. Such treatment was absolutely new to him. A smile which had begun faintly to appear on his face vanished at once. With a feeling of wounded dignity he said: "I am surprised, sir . . . I suppose you have—not observed . . . I am an officer . . ."

"And what's an officer? I'm a Swabian." (At this Schiller banged the table with his fist.) "I can be an officer; a year and half a cadet, two years a lieutenant, and tomorrow an officer. But I don't want to serve. This is what I'd do to officers: phoo!" Schiller held his open hand before him and spat into it.

Lieutenant Pirogov saw that there was nothing for him to do but withdraw. Such a proceeding, however, was quite out of keeping with his rank, and was disagreeable to him. He stopped several times on the stairs as though trying to rally his forces and to think how to make Schiller feel his impudence. At last he decided that Schiller might be excused because his head was full of beer; besides, he recalled the image of the charming blonde, and he made up his mind to consign the incident to oblivion.

Early next morning Lieutenant Pirogov appeared at the tinsmith's workshop. In the outer room he was met by the blonde charmer, who asked him in a rather severe voice, which went admirably with her little face: "What do you want?"

"Oh, good morning, my cutie! Don't you recognize me? You little rogue, what delicious eyes!"

As he said this Lieutenant Pirogov tried very charmingly to chuck her under the chin; but the lady uttered a frightened exclamation and with the same severity asked: "What do you want?"

"To see you, that's all that I want," answered Lieutenant Pirogov, smiling rather agreeably and going nearer; but noticing that the timid beauty was about to slip through the door, he added: "I want to order some spurs, my dear. Can you make me some spurs? Though indeed no spur is needed to make me love you; a bridle is what one needs, not a spur. What charming little hands!"

Lieutenant Pirogov was particularly agreeable in declarations of this kind.

"I will call my husband at once," cried the German, and went out, and within a few minutes Pirogov saw Schiller come in with sleepy-looking eyes; he had only just waked up after the drunkenness of the previous day. As he looked at the officer he remembered as though in a confused dream what had happened the previous day. He could recall nothing exactly as it was, but felt that he had done something stupid and so received the officer with a very sullen face. "I can't ask less than fifteen rubles[12] for a pair of

---

[12] In nineteenth-century Russia the ruble was worth about fifty-one cents, but, like the nineteenth-century dollar, it bought approximately six or seven times more than it buys today. (ed.)

spurs," he said, hoping to get rid of Pirogov, for as a respectable German he was ashamed to look at anyone who had seen him in an undignified condition. Schiller liked to drink without witnesses, in company with two or three friends, and at such times locked himself in and would not admit even his own workmen.

"Why are they so expensive?" asked Pirogov genially.

"German work," Schiller pronounced coolly, stroking his chin. "A Russian will undertake to make them for two rubles."

"Well, to show you that I like you and should be glad to make your acquaintance, I will pay fifteen rubles."

Schiller pondered for a minute; as a respectable German he felt a little ashamed. Hoping to put him off, he declared that he could not undertake it for a fortnight. But Pirogov, without making any objections, readily agreed to this.

The German mused and began wondering how he could best do the work so as to make it really worth fifteen rubles.

At this moment the blonde charmer came into the room and began looking for something on the table, which was covered with coffeepots. The lieutenant took advantage of Schiller's deep thought, stepped up to her, and pressed her arm, which was bare to the shoulder.

This was very distasteful to Schiller. "*Meine Frau!*" [13]

"*Was wollen Sie doch?*" [14] said the blonde to her husband.

"*Gehn Sie*[15] to the kitchen!" The blonde withdrew.

"In two weeks then?" said Pirogov.

"Yes, in two weeks," replied Schiller, still pondering. "I have a lot of work now."

"Goodbye for now, I will call again."

"Goodbye," said Schiller, closing the door after him.

Lieutenant Pirogov made up his mind not to relinquish his pursuit, though the blonde had so plainly rebuffed him. He could not conceive that anyone could resist him, especially as his politeness and the brilliant rank of a lieutenant gave him a full claim to attention. It must be mentioned also that despite her attractiveness Schiller's wife was extremely stupid. Stupidity, however, adds a special charm to a pretty wife. I have known several husbands, anyway, who were enraptured by the stupidity of their wives and

---

[13] "My wife!" (ed.)

[14] "But what do you want?" (ed.)

[15] "You go . . ." (ed.)

saw in it evidence of childlike innocence. Beauty works perfect miracles. All spiritual defects in a beauty, far from exciting revulsion, become somehow wonderfully attractive; even vice adds an aura of charm to the beautiful; but when beauty disappears, a woman needs to be twenty times as intelligent as a man merely to inspire respect, to say nothing of love. Schiller's wife, however, for all her stupidity was always faithful to her duties, and consequently it was no easy task for Pirogov to succeed in his bold enterprise. But there is always a pleasure in overcoming difficulties, and the blonde became more and more attractive to him every day. He began inquiring pretty frequently about the progress of the spurs, so that at last Schiller was weary of it. He did his utmost to finish the spurs quickly; at last they were done.

"Oh, what splendid workmanship," cried Lieutenant Pirogov on seeing the spurs. "Good Heavens, how well they're made! Our general hasn't spurs like that."

A feeling of self-complacency filled Schiller's soul. His eyes began to sparkle, and he felt inwardly reconciled to Pirogov. "The Russian officer is an intelligent man," he thought to himself.

"So, then, you could make a sheath for a dagger or for anything else?"

"Indeed I can," said Schiller with a smile.

"Then make me a sheath for a dagger. I will bring it you. I have a very fine Turkish dagger, but I want to have another sheath for it."

This was like a bomb dropped upon Schiller. His brows suddenly knitted.

"So that's what you are after," he thought to himself, inwardly swearing at himself for having praised his own work. To refuse it now he felt would be dishonest; besides, the Russian officer had praised his workmanship. Slightly shaking his head, he gave his consent; but the kiss which Pirogov impudently printed on the lips of the pretty wife as he went out reduced the tinsmith to stupefaction.

I think it will not be superfluous to make the reader better acquainted with Schiller himself. Schiller was a real German in the full sense of the word. From the age of twenty, that happy time when the Russian lives without a thought of the next day, Schiller had already mapped out his whole life and did not deviate from his plan under any circumstances. He made it a rule to get up at seven, to dine at two, to be punctual in everything, and to get drunk every Sunday. He set, as a goal, saving fifty thousand in the course of ten years, and all this was as certain and as unalterable as fate, for sooner would a government clerk forget to look in at the porter's lodge of his chief than a German would bring himself to break his word. Never under any circumstances did he increase his expenses, and if the price of potatoes went up much above the ordinary he did not spend one copper more on them but simply diminished the amount he bought, and although he was left sometimes feeling rather hungry, he soon got used to it. His exactitude was such that he made it his rule to kiss his wife twice in twenty-four hours but not more, and that he might not exceed the number he never put more than one small teaspoonful of pepper in his soup; on Sunday, however, this rule was not so strictly kept, for then Schiller used to drink two bottles of beer and one bottle of herb-flavored vodka which, however, he always abused. He did not drink like an Englishman, who locks his doors directly after dinner and gets drunk in solitude. On the contrary, like a German he always drank with inspiration either in the company of Hoffmann the bootmaker or with Kuntz the carpenter, who was also a German and a great drunkard. Such was the disposition of the worthy Schiller, who was indeed placed in a very difficult position. Though he was phlegmatic and a German, Pirogov's behavior excited in him a feeling resembling jealousy. He racked his brains and could not think of how to get rid of this Russian officer. Meanwhile Pirogov, smoking a pipe in the company of his fellow officers—since Providence has ordained that wherever there is an officer there is a pipe—alluded significantly and with an agreeable smile on his lips to his little intrigue with the pretty German, with whom he was, according to his account, already on the best of terms, though as a matter of fact he had almost lost all hope of winning her favor.

One day he was walking along Meshchansky Street looking at the house adorned by Schiller's signboard with coffeepots and samovars on it; to his great joy he caught sight of the blonde charmer's head thrust out of the window watching the passers-by. He stopped, blew her a kiss, and said: "*Gut Morgen.*"

The fair lady bowed to him as to an acquaintance.

"Is your husband at home?"

"Yes," she answered.

"And when is he out?"

"He is not at home on Sundays," said the foolish little German.

"That's not bad," Pirogov thought to himself. "I must take advantage of that."

And the following Sunday he suddenly and unexpectedly stood facing the blonde German. Schiller really was not at home. The pretty wife was frightened; but Pirogov on this occasion behaved rather warily, he was very respectful in his manner, and, making his bows, displayed all the elegance of his supple figure in his close-fitting uniform. He made polite and agreeable jests, but the foolish little German responded with nothing but monosyllables. At last, having made his attack from all sides and seeing that nothing would entertain her, he suggested that they dance. The German agreed immediately, for all German girls are passionately fond of dancing. Pirogov rested great hopes upon this: in the first place it gave her pleasure, in the second place it displayed his figure and dexterity; and thirdly he could get so much closer to her in dancing and put his arm around the pretty German and lay the foundation for everything else; in short, he reckoned on complete success resulting from it. He began humming a gavotte, knowing that Germans must have something sedate. The pretty German walked into the middle of the room and lifted her shapely foot. This attitude so enchanted Pirogov that he flew to kiss her. The lady began to scream, and this only enhanced her charm in Pirogov's eyes. He was showering kisses on her when the door suddenly opened and Schiller walked in, with Hoffmann and Kuntz the carpenter. All these worthy persons were as drunk as cobblers.

But . . . I leave the reader to imagine the wrath and indignation of Schiller.

"Ruffian!" he shouted in the utmost indignation. "How dare you kiss my wife? You are a son of a bitch and not a Russian officer. Go to hell! That's right, isn't it, friend Hoffmann? I am a German and not a Russian swine." (Hoffmann gave him an affirmative answer.) "Oh, I don't want to wear horns! [16] Take him by the collar, friend Hoffmann; I won't have it," he went on, brandishing his arms violently, while his whole face was the color of his red vest. "I have been living in Petersburg for eight years, I have a mother in Swabia and an uncle in Nuremburg. I am a German and

---

[16] I.e., have an unfaithful wife. Reference is to horns worn by a cuckold. (ed.)

not a horned ox. Undress him, my friend Hoffmann. Hold him by his arms and his legs, comrade Kuntz!"

And the Germans seized Pirogov by his arms and his legs.

He tried in vain to get away; these three tradesmen were among the sturdiest people in Petersburg, and they treated him so roughly and disrespectfully that I cannot find words to do justice to this unfortunate incident.

I am sure that next day Schiller was in a high fever, that he was trembling like a leaf, expecting from moment to moment the arrival of the police, that he would have given anything in the world for what had happened on the previous day to be a dream. But what has been cannot be changed. No comparison could do justice to Pirogov's anger and indignation. The very thought of such an insult drove him to fury. He thought Siberia and the lash too slight a punishment for Schiller. He flew home to dress himself and go at once straight to the general to paint for him in the most vivid colors the seditious insolence of the Germans. He meant to lodge a complaint in writing with the general staff; and, if the punishment meted out to the offenders was not satisfactory, to carry the matter to higher authorities.

But all this ended rather strangely; on the way to the general he went into a cafe, ate two cream puffs, read something out of *The Northern Bee* and left the cafe with his wrath somewhat cooled. Then a pleasant fresh evening led him to take a few turns along Nevsky Prospekt; by nine o'clock he had recovered his serenity and decided that he had better not disturb the general on Sunday; especially as he would be sure to be away somewhere. And so he went to spend the evening with one of the directors of the control committee, where he met a very agreeable party of government officials and officers of his regiment. There he spent a very pleasant evening, and so distinguished himself in the mazurka that not only the ladies but even their partners were moved to admiration.

"Marvelously is our world arranged," I thought as I walked two days later along Nevsky Prospekt, and mused over these two incidents. "How strangely, how unaccountably Fate plays with us! Do we ever get what we desire? Do we ever attain what our powers seem specially fitted for? Everything goes contrary to what we expect. Fate gives splendid horses to one man and he drives in his carriage without noticing their beauty, while another who is consumed by a passion for horses has to go on foot, and all the satisfaction he gets is clicking with his tongue when trotting horses are led past him. One has an excellent cook, but unluckily so small a mouth that he cannot take more than two pecks; another has a mouth as big as the arch of the Staff headquarters, but alas, has to be content with a German dinner of potatoes. What strange pranks Fate plays with us!"

But strangest of all are the incidents that take place on Nevsky Prospekt. Oh, do not trust that Nevsky Prospekt! I always wrap myself more closely in my cloak when I pass along it and try not to look at the objects which meet me. Everything is a cheat, everything is a dream, everything is other than it seems! You think that the gentleman who walks along in a splendidly cut coat is very wealthy?—not at all. All his wealth lies in his coat. You think that those two stout men who stand facing the church that is being built are criticizing its architecture?—not at all: they are talking about how peculiarly two crows are sitting facing each other. You think that that enthusiast waving his arms about is describing how his wife was playing ball out of window with an officer who was a complete stranger to him?—not so at all, he is talking of Lafayette. You imagine those ladies . . . but ladies are least of all to be trusted. Do not look into the shop windows; the trifles exhibited in them are delightful but they have an odor of money about them. But God save you from peeping under the ladies' hats! However attractively in the evening a fair lady's cloak may flutter in the distance, nothing would induce me to follow her and try to get a closer view. Keep your distance, for God's sake, keep your distance from the street lamp! and pass by it quickly, as quickly as you can! It is a happy escape if you get off with nothing worse than some of its stinking oil on your foppish coat. But even apart from the street lamp, everything breathes deception. It deceives at all hours, the Nevsky Prospekt does, but most of all when night falls in masses of shadow on it, throwing into relief the white and dun-colored walls of the houses, when all the town is transformed into noise and brilliance, when myriads of carriages roll over bridges, postilions shout and jolt up and down on their horses, and when the devil himself lights the street lamps to show everything in false colors.

DIARY OF A MADMAN

October 3

Today an extraordinary event occurred. I got up rather late in the morning, and when Mavra brought me my cleaned boots I asked her the time. Hearing that it was long past ten I dressed quickly. I admit I wouldn't have gone to the department at all, knowing the sour face the chief of our section will make at me. For a long time past he has been saying to me: "How is it, my man, your head always seems in a muddle? Sometimes you rush about as though you were crazy and do your work so that the devil himself could not make head or tail of it, you write the heading with a small letter, and you don't put in the date or the number." The damned heron! He must be jealous because I sit in the director's room and sharpen quills for his Excellency. In short I wouldn't have gone to the department if I had not hoped to see the cashier and to find out whether maybe I could not get something of my month's salary in advance out of that wretched Jew. That's another creature! Do you suppose he would ever let one have a month's pay in advance? Good gracious! the Last Judgment will come before he'd do it! You may ask till you burst, you may be in your final misery, but the gray-headed devil won't let you have it—and when he is at home his own cook slaps him in the face; everybody knows it. I can't see the advantage of serving in a department; there are absolutely no possibilities in it. In the provincial government, or in the civil and crown offices, it's quite a different matter: there you may see some wretched man squeezed into the corner, copying away, with a disgusting old coat on and such a face that it nearly makes you sick, but look what a villa he rents! It's no use offering him a gilt china cup: "That's a doctor's present," he will say. You must give him a pair of trotting horses or a carriage or a beaver fur coat worth three hundred rubles. He is such a quiet fellow to look at, and says in such a refined way: "Oblige me with a penknife just to sharpen a quill," but he fleeces the petitioners so that he scarcely leaves them a shirt to their backs. It is true that ours is a gentlemanly office; there is a cleanliness in everything such as is never seen in provincial offices, the tables are mahogany, and all our superiors address you formally. . . . I must confess that if it were not for the prestige of the service I should have left the department long ago.

I put on my old overcoat and took my umbrella, because it was pouring buckets. There was no one in the streets; some peasant women pulling their skirts over their heads to cover themselves and some Russian merchants under umbrellas and some messengers met my eye. I saw none of the better class except a fellow clerk. I saw him at the intersection. As soon as I saw him I said to myself: "No, my dear fellow, you are not on your way to the department; you are running after that girl who is racing ahead and you're looking at her legs." What rogues clerks are! I swear, they are as bad as any officer: if any female goes by in a hat they are bound to be after her. While I was making this reflection I saw a carriage driving up to the shop which I was passing. I recognized it at once. It was our director's carriage. "But he can have nothing to go to the shop for," I thought; "I suppose it must be his daughter." I flattened myself against the wall. The footman opened the carriage door and she darted out like a bird. How she glanced from right to left, how her eyes and eyebrows gleamed . . . Good God, I am done for, completely lost! And why does she drive out in such rain! Don't tell me that women have not a passion for these rags. She didn't know me, and, indeed, I tried to muffle myself up all I could, because I had on a very muddy old-fashioned overcoat. Now people wear cloaks with long collars, while I had short collars one above the other, and, indeed, the cloth was not at all rainproof. Her little dog, which had been too slow to dash in at the door, was left in the street. I know the dog—her name is Madgie. I had hardly been there a minute when I heard a thin little voice: "Good morning,

Madgie." "Well, I'll be damned! Who's that speaking?" I looked
around me and saw two ladies walking along under an umbrella:
one old and the other young; but they had passed already and again
I heard beside me: "Shame on you, Madgie!" What the hell! I saw
that Madgie was sniffing at a dog that was following the ladies.
"Aha," I said to myself, "but come, surely I am drunk! Only I
imagine that very rarely happens to me." "No, Fido, you are
wrong there," said Madgie—I saw her say it with my own eyes.
"I have been, wow, wow, I have been very ill, wow, wow, wow!"
"Oh, so it's you, you little dog! Goodness me!" I must confess I
was very much surprised to hear her speaking like a human being;
but afterward, when I thought it all over, I was no longer surprised.
A number of similar instances have as a fact occurred. They say
that in England a fish popped up and uttered two words in such a
strange language that the learned men have been for three years
trying to interpret them and have not succeeded yet. I have also
read in the papers of two cows who went into a shop and asked
for a pound of tea. But I must admit I was much more surprised
when Madgie said: "I did write to you, Fido; Polkan probably
didn't bring you the letter." Damn it all! I never in all my life heard
of a dog being able to write. No one but a gentleman by birth can
write correctly. It's true, of course, that some shopmen and even
serfs can sometimes write a little; but their writing is for the most
part mechanical: they have no commas, no stops, no style.

It amazed me. I must confess that of late I have begun seeing and
hearing things such as no one has ever seen or heard before. "I'll
follow that dog," I said to myself, "and find out what she is like and
what she thinks." I opened my umbrella and set off after the two
ladies. They passed into Gorokhovaya Street, turned into Meshchanskaya and from there into Stolyarnya Street; at last they reached
Kokushkin Bridge and stopped in front of a big house. "I know
that house," I said to myself. "That's Zverkov's Buildings. What a
huge place! All sorts of people live in it: so many cooks, so many
visitors from all parts! and our friends the clerks, one on the top
of another, with a third trying to squeeze in, like dogs. I have a
friend living there, who plays beautifully on the trombone." The
ladies went up to the fifth floor. "Good," I thought, "I won't go
in now, but I will note the place and I will certainly take advantage
of the first opportunity."

October 4

Today is Wednesday, and so I was in our chief's study. I came a little early on purpose and, sitting down, began sharpening quills. Our director must be a very clever man. His whole study is lined with bookshelves. I have read the titles of some of them: they are all learned, so learned that they are really beyond anyone like me—they are all either in French or in German. And just look into his face! Aie! what importance in his eyes! I have never heard him say a word too much. Sometimes when one hands him the papers he'll ask: "What's it like out of doors?" "Damp, your Excellency." Yes, he is a cut above anyone like me! He's a statesman. I notice, however, he is particularly fond of me. If his daughter, too, were . . . Damn it! . . . Never mind, never mind, silence! I read *The Bee*. They are stupid people, the French! What do they want? I'd take the bunch of them, I swear I would, and thrash them all soundly with birch rods! In it I read a very pleasant description of a ball written by a country gentleman of Kursk. The country gentlemen of Kursk write well. Then I noticed it was half-past twelve and that our chief had not come out of his bedroom. But about half-past one an event occurred which no pen could describe. The door opened; I thought it was the director and jumped up from my chair with my papers, but it was she, in person! Holy fathers, how she was dressed! Her dress was white as a swan—aie, how sumptuous! And the look in her eye—like sunshine, I swear, like sunshine. She bowed and said: "Hasn't Papa been here?" Aie, aie, aie, what a voice! A canary, a regular canary. "Your Excellency," I was on the point of saying, "do not ask them to punish me, but if you want to punish, then punish with your own noble hand." But damn it all, my tongue would not obey me, and all I said was: "No, madam." She looked at me, looked at the books, and dropped her handkerchief. I dashed forward, slipped on the damned parquet, and almost smashed my nose but recovered myself and picked up the handkerchief. Holy fathers, what a handkerchief! The most delicate batiste—amber, perfect amber! you would know from the very scent that it belonged to a general's daughter. She thanked me and gave me a faint smile, so that her sugary lips scarcely moved, and after that went away. I stayed on another hour, when the footman came in and said: "You can go home, Aksenty Ivanovich; the master has gone out." I cannot endure the flunkey set: they are always lolling about in the hall and don't even take the trouble to nod to me. That's nothing: once one of these animals had the gall to offer me his snuffbox without even getting up from his seat. Doesn't the fellow know I am a government clerk, that I am a gentleman by birth? However, I took my hat and put on my overcoat myself, for these people never help me on with it, and went off. At home I spent most of the time lying on my bed. Then I copied out some very good verses:

> My love for one hour I did not see,
> And a whole year it seemed to me.

> "My life is now a hated task,
> How can I live this life," I ask.

It must have been written by Pushkin.[1] In the evening, wrapping myself up in my overcoat, I went to the front door of her Excellency's house and waited about for a long time on the chance of her coming out to get into her carriage, so that I might snatch another glimpse of her.

November 6

The head of our section was in a fury today. When I came into the department he called me into his room and began like this: "Come, kindly tell me what you are doing?" "How do you mean?" I said. "I am doing nothing." "Come, think what you are up to!" Why, you are over forty. It's time you had a little sense. What do you imagine yourself to be? Do you suppose I don't know all the tricks you are up to? Why, you are philandering after the director's daughter! Come, look at yourself; just think what you are! Why, you are a nonentity and nothing else! Why, you haven't a copper to bless yourself with. And just look at yourself in the mirror—how could you think of such a thing!" Damn him! Because his face is like a druggist's bottle and he has a shock of hair on his head curled in a tuft, and pomades it into a kind of rosette, and holds his head in the air, he imagines he is the only one who may do anything. I understand, I understand why he is so angry with me. He is envious: he has perhaps seen signs of preference shown to me. But I spit on him! As though a court councilor were of so much importance! He hangs a gold chain on his watch and orders boots at thirty rubles—but to hell with him! Am I a tailor or a son of a

[1] Not quite. It was written by N. P. Nikolev (1758-1815). (ed.)

noncommissioned officer? I am a gentleman. Why, I may rise in the service too. I am only forty-two, a time of life in which a career in the service is really only just beginning. Just wait, my friend! I'll be a colonel and perhaps, please God, something better. I will have a reputation, and better maybe than yours. A peculiar notion you have got into your head that no one is a gentleman but yourself. Give me a fashionably cut coat and let me put on a necktie like yours—and then you wouldn't hold a candle to me. I haven't the means, that's the only trouble.

November 8

I have been to the theater. It was a performance of the Russian fool Filatka.[2] I laughed very much. There was vaudeville too, with some amusing verses about lawyers, and especially about a collegiate registrar, so outspoken that I was surprised that the censor had passed it; and about the merchants they openly said that they cheat the people and that their sons are debauched and ape the gentry. There was a very amusing couplet about the journalists too: saying that they abused everyone and that an author begged the public to defend him against them. The authors do write amusing plays nowadays. I love being at the theater. As soon as I have a coin in my pocket I can't resist going. And among our fellow clerks there are such pigs that they positively won't go to the theater, the peasants; unless perhaps you give them a free ticket. One actress sang very nicely. I thought of the other girl . . . ah, damn it! . . . Never mind, never mind . . . silence!

November 9

At eight o'clock I went to the department. The head of our section put on a look as though he did not see me come in. I, too, behaved as though nothing had passed between us. I looked through and checked some papers. I went out at four o'clock. I walked by the director's house, but no one was to be seen. After dinner, for the most part, I lay on my bed.

November 11

Today I sat in our director's study. I sharpened twenty-three quills for him and for her . . . aie, aie! for her Excellency four

---

[2] See p. 443, n. 8. (ed.)

quills. He likes to have a lot of quills. Oo, he must have a head! He always sits silent, and I expect he is turning over everything in his head. I should like to know what he thinks most about. What is going on in that head? I should like to get a close view of the life of these gentlemen, of all these *équivoques* and court ways. How they go on and what they do in their circle—that's what I should like to find out! I have several times thought of beginning a conversation on the subject with his Excellency, but, damn it all. I couldn't bring my tongue to it; one says it's cold or warm today and can't utter another word. I should like to look into the drawing room, of which one only sees the open door and another room beyond it. Ah, what sumptuous furniture! What mirrors and china! I long to have a look in there, into the part of the house where her Excellency is, that's where I should like to go! Into her boudoir where there are all sorts of little jars, little bottles, and such flowers that one is frightened even to breathe on them, to see her dresses lying scattered about, more like ethereal gossamer than dresses. I long to glance into her bedroom; there I imagine there must be marvels . . . a paradise, such as is not to be found in the heavens. To look at the little stool on which she puts her little foot when she gets out of bed and the way she puts a little snow-white stocking on that little foot . . . Aie, aie, aie! never mind, never mind . . . silence!

But today a light dawned upon me. I remembered the conversation between the two dogs that I heard on Nevsky Prospekt. "Good," I thought to myself, "now I will learn all. I must get hold of the correspondence that these wretched dogs have been carrying on. Then I shall certainly learn something." I must admit I once called Madgie to me and said to her: "Listen, Madgie; here we are alone. If you like I will shut the door too, so that no one shall see you; tell me all you know about your young lady: what she is like and how she behaves. I swear I won't tell anyone." But the sly little dog put her tail between her legs, doubled herself up, and went quickly to the door as though she hadn't heard. I have long suspected that dogs are far more intelligent than men; I am even convinced that they can speak, only there is a certain doggedness about them. They are extremely diplomatic: they notice everything, every step a man takes. Yes, regardless of what happens I will go tomorrow to Zverkov's Buildings. I will question

Fido, and if I am successful I will seize all the letters Madgie has written her.

November 12

At two o'clock in the afternoon I set out determined to see Fido and question her. I can't endure cabbage, the smell of which floats from all the little shops in Meshchanskaya Street; moreover, such a hellish reek rises from under every gate that I raced along at full speed holding my nose. And the nasty workmen let off such a lot of soot and smoke from their workshops that a gentleman cannot stroll there. When I climbed up to the sixth floor and rang the bell, a girl who was not at all bad-looking, with little freckles, came to the door. I recognized her: it was the girl who was with the old lady. She turned a little red, and I said to myself at once: "You are looking for a bridegroom, my dear." "What do you want?" she asked. "I want to have a few words with your dog." The girl was stupid. I saw at once that she was stupid. At that moment the dog ran out barking; I tried to catch hold of her, but the nasty wretch almost snapped at my nose. However, I saw her bed in the corner. Ah, that was just what I wanted. I went up to it, rummaged in the straw in the wooden box, and to my indescribable delight pulled out a packet of little slips of paper. The wretched dog, seeing this, first bit my calf, and then, when she perceived that I had taken her letters, began to whine and fawn on me, but I said: "No, my dear, goodbye," and took to my heels. I believe the girl thought I was a madman, as she was very much frightened. When I got home I wanted to begin at once to decipher the letters, for I don't see very well by candlelight; but Mavra had taken it into her head to wash the floor. These stupid Finnish women always clean at the wrong moment. And so I went out to walk about and think over the incident. Now I shall find out all their doings and ways of thinking, all the hidden springs, and shall get to the bottom of it all. These letters will reveal everything. Dogs are clever creatures, they understand all the diplomatic relations, and so no doubt I shall find there everything about our gentleman: all about his character and behavior. There will be something in them too about her who . . . never mind, silence! Toward evening I came home. For the most part I lay on my bed.

November 13

Well, we shall see! The writing is fairly distinct; at the same time there is something doggy about the handwriting. Let us read:

DEAR FIDO,

I never can get used to your common name. As though they could not have given you a better one? Fido, Rose—what vulgarity! No more about that, however. I am very glad we thought of writing to each other.

The letter is very well written. The punctuation and even the spelling is quite correct. Even the chief of our section could not write like this, though he does talk of having studied at some university. Let us see what comes next.

It seems to me that to share one's ideas, one's feelings, and one's impressions with others is one of the greatest blessings on earth.

H'm! . . . an idea taken from a work translated from the German. I don't remember the name of it.

I say this from experience, though I have not been about the world, beyond the gates of our house. Is not my life spent in comfort? My young lady, whom her papa calls Sophie, loves me passionately.

Aie, aie! never mind, never mind! Silence!

Papa, too, often caresses me. I drink tea and coffee with cream. Ah, *ma chère*, I ought to tell you that I see nothing agreeable at all in big, gnawed bones such as our Polkan crunches in the kitchen. The only bones that are nice are those of game, and then only when the marrow hasn't been sucked out of them by someone. What is very good is several sauces mixed together, only they must be free from capers and green stuff; but I know nothing worse than giving dogs little balls of bread. A gentleman sitting at the table who has been touching all sorts of dirty things with his hands begins with those hands rolling up bread, calls you up, and thrusts the ball upon you. To refuse seems somehow discourteous—well, you eat it—with revulsion, but you eat it. . . .

What the devil's this! What nonsense! As though there were nothing better to write about. Let us look at another page and see if there is nothing more sensible.

I shall be delighted to let you know about everything that happens here. I have already told you something about the chief gentleman, whom Sophie calls Papa. He is a very strange man.

Ah, here we are at last! Yes, I knew it; they have a very political view of everything. Let us see what Papa is like.

> . . . a very strange man. For the most part he says nothing; he
> very rarely speaks. But about a week ago he was continually talking
> to himself: "Shall I get it or shall I not?" He would take a paper in
> one hand and close the other empty hand and say: "Shall I get it or
> shall I not?" Once he turned to me with the question: "What do
> you think, Madgie, shall I get it or not?" I certainly couldn't under-
> stand a word of it; I sniffed at his boots and walked away. A week
> later, *ma chère*, he came in in high glee. All the morning gentlemen
> in uniform were coming to see him and were congratulating him on
> something. At the table he was merrier than I have ever seen him;
> he kept telling stories. And after dinner he lifted me up to his neck
> and said: "Look, Madgie, what's this?" I saw a little ribbon. I sniffed
> it, but could discover no aroma whatever; at last I licked it on the
> sly: it was a little bit salty.

H'm! This dog seems to me to be really too . . . she ought to be
beaten! And so he is ambitious! One must take that into consideration.

> Farewell, *ma chère!* I fly, and so on . . . and so on . . . I will
> finish my letter tomorrow. Well, good day, I am with you again.
> Today my young lady Sophie . . .

Oh come, let us see about Sophie. Damn it! . . . Never mind,
never mind . . . let us go on.

> My young lady Sophie was in a great fluster. She was getting
> ready to go to a ball, and I was delighted that in her absence I could
> write to you. My Sophie is always very glad to go to a ball, though
> she always gets almost angry when she is being dressed. I can't un-
> derstand, *ma chère*, what pleasure there is in going to balls. Sophie
> always comes home from balls at six o'clock in the morning, and I
> can almost always guess from her pale and exhausted face that they
> had given the poor thing nothing to eat. I must confess I couldn't
> live like that. If I didn't get grouse and gravy or the roast wing of
> a chicken, I don't know what would become of me. Gravy is nice
> too with grain in it, but with carrots, turnips, or artichokes it is
> never good.

What an uneven style! You can see at once that it is not a man
writing; it begins as it should and ends with dogginess. Let us look
at one more letter. It's rather long. H'm! and there's no date on it.

Ah, my dear, how one feels the approach of spring! My heart beats as though I were expecting someone. There is always a noise in my ears so that I often stand for some minutes with my foot in the air listening at doors. I must confide to you that I have a number of suitors. I often sit at the window and look at them. Oh, if only you knew what ugly creatures there are among them. One is a very clumsy mongrel, fearfully stupid, stupidity is painted on his face; he walks about the street with an air of importance and imagines that he is a distinguished person and thinks that everybody is looking at him. Don't you believe it! I don't take any notice of him—I behave exactly as though I didn't see him. And what a terrifying Great Dane stops before my window! If he were to stand on his hind legs, which I expect the clod could not do, he would be a whole head taller than my Sophie's papa, who is fairly tall and fat, too. That blockhead must be a terribly insolent fellow. I growled at him, but much he cared; he hardly frowned, he put out his tongue, dangled his huge ears and looked up at the window—such a country bumpkin! But can you suppose, *ma chère*, that my heart makes no response to any overture? Ah no . . . If only you could see one of my suitors climbing over the fence next door, by name Trésor. . . . Ah, *ma chère*, what a face he has! . . .

Pfoo, the devil! . . . What rubbish! How can anyone fill a letter with foolishness! Give me a man! I want to see a man. I want spiritual sustenance—in which my soul might find food and enjoyment; and instead of that I have this nonsense. . . . Let us turn over the page and see whether it gets better!

Sophie was sitting at the table sewing something, I was looking out of the window because I am fond of watching passers-by, when all at once the footman came in and said "Teplov!" "Ask him in," cried Sophie, and rushed to embrace me. "Ah, Madgie, Madgie! If only you knew who that is: a dark young man, a court chamberlain, and eyes black as agates!" And Sophie ran off to her room. A minute later a court chamberlain with black whiskers came in, walked up to the mirror, smoothed his hair, and looked about the room. I growled and sat in my place. Sophie soon came in and bowed gaily in response to his shuffling; and I just went on looking out of the window as though I were noticing nothing. However, I bent my head a little on one side and tried to hear what they were saying. Oh, *ma chère*, the nonsense they talked! They talked about a lady who had mistaken one dance movement for another; and said that someone called Bobov with a ruffle on his shirt looked just like a stork and had almost fallen down on the floor, and that a girl

called Lidina thought that her eyes were blue when they were really
green—and that sort of thing. "Well," I thought to myself, "if one
were to compare that court chamberlain to Trésor, heavens, what
a difference!" In the first place, the court chamberlain has a perfectly flat face with whiskers all around as though he had tied it
up in a black handkerchief; while Trésor has a delicate little countenance with a white patch on the forehead. It's impossible to compare the court chamberlain's figure with Trésor's. And his eyes,
his ways, his manners are all quite different. Oh, what a difference!
I don't know, *ma chère*, what she sees in her Teplov. Why she is so
enthusiastic about him. . . .

Well, I think myself that there is something wrong about it. It's
impossible that she can be fascinated by Teplov. Let us see what
next.

It seems to me that if she is attracted by that court chamberlain
she will soon be attracted by that clerk that sits in Papa's study. Oh,
ma chère, if you knew what an ugly fellow that is! He looks like a
turtle in a bag. . . .

What clerk is this? . . .

He has a very queer surname. He always sits sharpening the
quills. The hair on his head is very much like hay. Papa sometimes
sends him out instead of a servant. . . .

I do believe the nasty little dog is alluding to me. But my hair
isn't like hay!

Sophie can never help laughing when she sees him.

That's a lie, you damned little dog! What an evil tongue! As
though I didn't know that that is the result of jealousy! As though
I didn't know whose tricks were at the bottom of that! This is all
the doing of the chief of my section. The man has sworn eternal
hatred, and here he tries to injure me again and again, at every
turn. Let us look at one more letter, though. Perhaps the thing will
explain itself.

My Dear Fido,
    Forgive me for not writing for so long. I have been in a perfect
ecstasy. How truly has some writer said that love is a second life.
Moreover, there are great changes in the house here. The court
chamberlain is here every day. Sophie is frantically in love with
him. Papa is very happy. I have even heard from our Grigory, who
sweeps the floor and almost always talks to himself, that there will

soon be a wedding because Papa is determined to see Sophie married to a general or a court chamberlain or to a colonel in the army. . . .

Damn it! I can't read any more. . . . It's always a court chamberlain or a general. Everything that's best in the world falls to the court chamberlains or the generals. If you find some poor treasure and think it is almost within your grasp, a court chamberlain or a general will snatch it from you. God damn it! I'd like to become a general myself, not in order to receive her hand and all the rest of it; no, I should like to be a general only to see how they would wriggle and display all their court manners and *équivoques* and then to say to them: I spit on you both. Oh, damn it! I tore the stupid dog's letters to bits.

December 3

It cannot be. It's idle talk! There won't be a wedding! What if he is a court chamberlain? Why, that is nothing but a rank; it's not a visible thing that one could pick up in one's hands. You don't get a third eye in your head because you are a court chamberlain. Why, his nose is not made of gold but is just like mine and everyone else's; he sniffs with it and doesn't eat with it, he sneezes with it and doesn't cough with it. I have often tried to discover what all these differences come from. Why am I a titular councilor and on what grounds am I a titular councilor? Perhaps I am not a titular councilor at all? Perhaps I am a count or a general, and only somehow appear to be a titular councilor. Perhaps I don't know myself who I am. How many instances there have been in history: some simple, humble tradesman or peasant, not even a nobleman, is suddenly discovered to be a great gentleman or a baron, or what do you call it. . . . If a peasant can sometimes turn into something like that, what may not a nobleman turn into? I shall suddenly, for instance, go to see our chief in a general's uniform: with an epaulet on my right shoulder and an epaulet on my left shoulder, and a blue ribbon across my chest; well, my charmer will sing a different tune then, and what will her papa, our director, himself say? Ah, he is very ambitious! He is a Mason, he is certainly a Mason; though he does pretend to be this and that, but I noticed at once that he was a Mason: if he shakes hands with anyone, he only offers him two fingers. Might I not be appointed a governor or a general this very minute or a superintendent, or something of that sort? I should like to know why I am a titular councilor. Why precisely a titular councilor?

December 5

I spent the whole morning reading the newspaper. Strange things are going on in Spain. In fact, I can't really understand it. They write that the throne is vacant, and that they are in a difficult position about choosing an heir, and that, as a consequence, there are insurrections. It seems to me that it is extremely peculiar. How can the throne be vacant? They say that some Donna[3] ought to ascend the throne. A Donna cannot ascend the throne, she cannot possibly. There ought to be a king on the throne. "But," they say, "there is not a king." It cannot be that there is no king. A kingdom can't exist without a king. There is a king, only probably he is in hiding somewhere. He may be there, but either family reasons or danger from some neighboring state, such as France or some other country, may compel him to remain in hiding, or there may be some other reasons.

December 8

I quite wanted to go to the department, but various reasons and considerations detained me. I cannot get the affairs of Spain out of my head. How can it be that a Donna should be made queen? They won't allow it. England in the first place won't allow it. And besides, the politics of all Europe, the Emperor of Austria and our Czar . . . I must admit these events have so overwhelmed and shaken me that I haven't been able to do anything all day. Mavra remarked that I was extremely absent-minded at the table. And I believe I did accidentally throw two plates on the floor, which smashed immediately. After dinner I went for a walk down the hill: nothing edifying. For the most part I lay on my bed and reflected on the affairs of Spain.

2000 A.D., April 43

This is the day of the greatest public rejoicing! There is a king of Spain! He has been discovered. I am that king. I only heard of it this morning. I must confess it burst upon me like a flash of lightning. I can't imagine how I could believe and imagine myself to be

---

[3] I.e., "woman." (ed.)

a titular councilor. How could that crazy, mad idea ever have entered my head? It's a good thing that no one thought of putting me in a madhouse. Now everything has been revealed to me. Now it is all as clear as can be. But until now I did not understand; everything was in a sort of mist. And I believe it all arose from believing that the brain is in the head. It's not so at all; it comes with the wind from the direction of the Caspian Sea. First of all, I told Mavra who I am. When she heard that the King of Spain was standing before her, she clasped her hands and almost died of horror; the ignorant woman had never seen a King of Spain before. I tried to reassure her, however, and in gracious words tried to convince her of my benevolent feelings toward her, saying that I was not angry with her for having sometimes cleaned my boots so badly. Of course they are uncultured people; it is no good talking of elevated subjects to them. She is frightened because she is convinced that all kings of Spain are like Philip II.[4] But I assured her that there was no resemblance between me and Philip II and that I have not even one Capuchin monk. I didn't go to the department . . . the hell with it! No, my friends, you won't entice me there again; I am not going to copy your horrible papers!

Martober 86 between
day and night

Our office messenger arrived today to tell me to go to the department, and to say that I had not been there for more than three weeks. However, I did go to the department just for the fun of it. The head of our section thought that I should bow to him and apologize, but I looked at him indifferently, not too angrily and not too graciously, and sat down in my place as though I did not notice anything. I looked at all the scum of the office and thought: "If only you knew who is sitting among you!" Good gracious! wouldn't there be a commotion! And the head of our section would bow to me as he bows now to the director. They put a paper before me to make some sort of an extract from it. But I didn't touch it. A few minutes later everyone was in an uproar. They said the director was coming. A number of the clerks ran forward to show off for him, but I didn't stir. When he walked through our room they all buttoned up their coats, but I didn't do anything at all.

---

[4] (1527-98), the king under whom the Spanish Inquisition reached its infamous peak. (ed.)

What's a director? Am I going to tremble before him—never! He's a fine director! He is a cork, he is not a director. An ordinary cork, a plain cork and nothing else—such as you cork a bottle with. What amused me most of all was when they put a paper before me to sign. They thought I should write at the bottom of the paper, So-and-so, head clerk of the table—how else should it be! But in the most important place, where the director of the department signs his name, I wrote "Ferdinand VIII." You should have seen the awe-struck silence that followed; but I only waved my hand and said: "I don't insist on any signs of allegiance!" and walked out. From there I walked straight to the director's. He was not at home. The footman did not want to let me in, but I spoke to him in such a way that his hands fell to his sides. I went straight to her bedroom. She was sitting before the mirror; she jumped up and stepped back when she saw me. I did not tell her that I was the King of Spain, however; I only told her that there was a happiness awaiting her such as she could not imagine, and that in spite of the wiles of our enemies we should be together. I didn't care to say more and walked out. Oh, woman is a treacherous creature! I have discovered now what women are. So far no one has found out with whom Woman is in love: I have been the first to discover it. Woman is in love with the devil. Yes, joking apart. Scientific men write nonsense saying that she is this or that—she cares for nothing but the devil. You will see her from a box in the first tier fixing her *lorgnette*. You imagine she is looking at the fat man with decorations. No, she is looking at the devil who is standing behind his back. There he is, hidden in his coat. There he is, beckoning to her! And she will marry him, she will marry him. And all these people, their dignified fathers who fawn on everybody and push their way to court and say that they are patriots and one thing and another: profit, profit is all that these patriots want! They would sell their father and their mother and God for money, ambitious creatures, Judases! All this is ambition, and the ambition is because of a little pimple under the tongue and in it a little worm no bigger than a pin's head, and it's all the doing of a barber who lives in Gorokhovaya Street, I don't remember his name; but I know for a fact that, in collusion with a midwife, he is trying to spread Mohammedanism all over the world, and that is why, I am told, that the majority of people in France profess the Mohammedan faith.

No date. The day
had no date

I walked incognito along Nevsky Prospekt. His Majesty the Czar drove by. All the people took off their caps and I did the same, but I made no sign that I was the King of Spain. I thought it improper to reveal myself so suddenly before everyone, because I ought first to be presented at court. The only thing that has prevented my doing so is the lack of a Spanish uniform. If only I could get hold of a royal mantle. I should have liked to order it from a tailor, but they are perfect asses; besides they neglect their work so, they have given themselves up to speculating and usually end up being employed in laying pavement. I determined to make the mantle out of my new uniform, which I had only worn twice. And so that the scoundrels should not ruin it I decided to make it myself, shutting the door so that no one might see me at it. I ripped it all up with the scissors because the style has to be completely different.

I don't remember the date
There was no month either
The devil knows what to make of it

The mantle is completely finished. Mavra shrieked when she saw me in it. However, I can't make up my mind to present myself at court, for so far the delegation hasn't arrived from Spain. It wouldn't be proper to go without my delegation; there would be nothing to lend weight to my dignity. I expect them any hour.

The 1st

I am extremely surprised at the lateness of the delegation. What can be detaining them? Can it be the machinations of France? Yes, that is the most malignant of states. I went to inquire at the post office whether the Spanish delegates had not arrived; but the postmaster was excessively stupid and knew nothing. "No," he said, "there are no delegates here, but if you care to write a letter I will send it off in accordance with the regulations." Damn it all, what's the use of a letter? A letter is nonsense. Letters are even written by pharmacists. . . .

Madrid, February
thirtieth

And so here I am in Spain, and it happened so quickly that I can hardly believe it. This morning the Spanish delegates arrived and I got into a carriage with them. The extraordinary rapidity of our journey struck me as strange. We went at such a rate that within half an hour we had reached the frontiers of Spain. But of course now there are railroads all over Europe, and ships go very rapidly. Spain is a strange land! When we went into the first room I saw a number of people with shaven heads. I guessed at once that these were either grandees or soldiers because they do shave their heads. I thought the behavior of the High Chancellor, who led me by the hand, extremely strange. He thrust me into a little room and said: "Sit there, and if you persist in calling yourself King Ferdinand, I'll knock the inclination out of you." But knowing that this was only to try me I answered in the negative, whereupon the Chancellor hit me twice on the back with a stick, and it hurt so that I almost cried out, but I restrained myself, remembering that this is the custom of chivalry on receiving any exalted dignity, for customs of chivalry persist in Spain to this day. When I was alone I decided to occupy myself with the affairs of state. I discovered that Spain and China are one and the same country, and it is only through ignorance that they are considered to be different kingdoms. I recommend everyone to try to write Spain on a bit of paper and it will always turn out China. But I was particularly distressed by an event which will take place tomorrow. Tomorrow at seven o'clock a strange phenomenon will occur: the earth will sit on the moon. The celebrated English chemist Wellington has written about it. I must confess that I experience a tremor at my heart when I reflect on the extreme softness and fragility of the moon. You see the moon is usually made in Hamburg, and very badly made too. I am surprised that England hasn't taken notice of it. It was made by a lame barrel maker, and it is evident that the fool had no idea what a moon should be. He put in tarred cord and one part of lamp oil; and that is why there is such a fearful stench all over the world that one has to stop up one's nose. And that's how it is that the moon is such a soft globe that man cannot live on it and that nothing lives there but noses. And it is for that very reason that we can't see our noses, because they are all in the moon. And when I reflected that the earth is a heavy body and when it falls may grind our noses to powder, I was overcome by such uneasiness that, putting on my shoes and stockings, I hastened to the hall of the Imperial Council to give orders to the police not to allow the earth to sit on the moon. The grandees with shaven heads whom I found in great numbers in the hall of the Imperial Council were very intelligent people, and when I said: "Gentlemen, let us save the moon, for the earth is trying to sit upon it!" they all rushed to carry out my sovereign wishes, and several climbed up the walls to try and get at the moon; but at that moment the High Chancellor walked in. Seeing him they all ran in different directions. I as King remained alone. But, to my amazement, the Chancellor struck me with his stick and drove me back to my room! How great is the power of national tradition in Spain!

*January of the same year
which came after February*

So far I have not been able to understand what sort of a country Spain is. The national traditions and the customs of the court are quite extraordinary. I can't understand it, I can't understand it, I absolutely can't understand it. Today they shaved my head, although I shouted at the top of my voice that I didn't want to become a monk. But I can't even remember what happened afterward when they poured cold water on my head. I have never endured such hell. I was almost going frantic, so that they had difficulty in holding me. I cannot understand the meaning of this strange custom. It's a stupid, senseless practice! The lack of good sense in the kings who have not abolished it to this day is beyond my comprehension. Judging from all the circumstances, I wonder whether I have not fallen into the hands of the Inquisition, and whether the man I took to be the Grand Chancellor isn't the Grand Inquisitor. But I cannot understand how a king can be subject to the Inquisition. It can only be through the influence of France, especially of Polignac.[5] Oh, that beast of a Polignac! He has sworn to harm me to the death. And he pursues me and pursues me; but I know, my friend, that you are the tool of England. The English are great politicians. They poke their noses into everything. All the world knows that when England takes a pinch of snuff, France sneezes.

---

[5] (1780-1847), reactionary prime minister of France in 1830. (ed.)

The twenty-fifth

Today the Grand Inquisitor came into my room again, but hearing his steps in the distance I hid under a chair. Seeing I wasn't there, he began calling me. At first he shouted "Poprischin!" I didn't say a word. Then: "Aksenty Ivanov! Titular councilor! Nobleman!" I still remained silent. "Ferdinand VIII, King of Spain!" I was on the point of sticking out my head, but then I thought: "No, my friend, you won't fool me, I know you: you will be pouring cold water on my head again." However, he caught sight of me and drove me from under the chair with a stick. That damned stick does hurt. However, I was rewarded for all this by the discovery I made today. I found out that every cock has a Spain, that it is under his wings [not far from his tail].[6]

The Grand Inquisitor went away, however, very angry, threatening me with some punishment. But I disdain his impotent malice, knowing that he is simply an instrument, a tool of England.

34 ꓘɘqɯnɐſ Yrae 349

No, I haven't the strength to endure more. My God! the things they are doing to me! They pour cold water on my head! They won't listen to me, they won't see me, they won't hear me. What have I done to them? Why do they torture me? What do they want of a poor creature like me? What can I give them? I have nothing. It's too much for me, I can't endure these agonies, my head is burning and everything is going around. Save me, take me away! Give me a troika and horses swift as a whirlwind! Take your seat, my driver, ring out, my bells, fly upward, my steeds, and bear me away from this world! Far away, far away, so that nothing can be seen, nothing. Yonder the sky whirls before me, a star sparkles in the distance; the forest floats by with dark trees and the moon; blue-gray mist lies stretched under my feet; a chord resounds in the mist; on one side the sea, on the other Italy; yonder the huts of Russia can be seen. Is that my home in the distance? Is it my mother sitting before the window? Mother, save your poor son! Drop a tear on his sick head! See how they torment him! Press your poor orphan to your bosom! There is nowhere in the world

---

[6] This phrase does not appear in the Academy edition of Gogol's works. Whether or not it belongs to Gogol at all is moot. (ed.)

for him! he is persecuted! Mother, have pity on your sick child! . . .

And do you know that the Dey of Algiers has a boil just under his nose? [7]

---

[7] This line originally read: "The French king has a boil just under his nose." Since the word for boil in Russian, *shishka,* is a colloquialism for "trouble," the sentence could easily have been interpreted as an irreverent poke at Charles X, who had abdicated in August of 1830, and it is highly probable that Gogol was less than eager to become involved in a postrevolution imbroglio. In its present form, the line refers to the deposal of the last Dey of Algiers, Hussein Pasha, by the French, in 1830. (ed.)

Other Tales

THE NOSE

I

An extraordinarily strange incident took place in Petersburg on the twenty-fifth of March. The barber, Ivan Yakovlevich, who lives on Voznesensky Avenue (his surname is lost, and nothing more appears even on his signboard, where a gentleman is depicted with his cheeks covered with soapsuds, together with an inscription "also lets blood")—the barber Ivan Yakovlevich woke up rather early and was aware of a smell of hot bread. Raising himself in bed he saw his wife, a rather portly lady who was very fond of drinking coffee, engaged in taking out of the oven some freshly baked loaves.

"I won't have coffee today, Praskovia Osipovna," said Ivan Yakovlevich. "Instead I should like some hot bread with onions." (The fact is that Ivan Yakovlevich would have liked both, but he knew that it was utterly impossible to ask for two things at once, for Praskovia Osipovna greatly disliked such caprices.)

"Let the fool have bread: so much the better for me," thought his wife to herself. "There will be an extra cup of coffee left," and she flung one loaf on the table.

For the sake of propriety Ivan Yakovlevich put a jacket over his shirt, and, sitting down at the table, sprinkled some salt, peeled two onions, took a knife in his hand and, assuming an air of importance, began to cut the bread. After dividing the loaf into two halves he looked into the middle of it—and to his amazement saw something there that looked white. Ivan Yakovlevich probed at it carefully with his knife and felt it with his finger: "It's solid," he said to himself. "What in the world is it?"

He thrust in his fingers and pulled it out—it was a nose! . . . Ivan Yakovlevich's hand dropped with astonishment, he rubbed his eyes and felt it: it actually was a nose, and, what's more, it looked to him somehow familiar. A look of horror came into Ivan Yakovlevich's face. But that horror was nothing compared to the indignation with which his wife was overcome.

"Where have you cut that nose off, you monster?" she cried wrathfully. "You scoundrel, you drunkard, I'll go to the police myself to report you! You villain! I have heard from three men that when you are shaving them you pull at their noses till you almost tug them off."

But Ivan Yakovlevich was more dead than alive: he recognized that the nose belonged to none other than Kovaliov, the collegiate assessor whom he shaved every Wednesday and every Sunday.

"Wait, Praskovia Osipovna! I'll wrap it up in a rag and put it in a corner. Let it stay there for a while; I'll return it later on."

"I won't hear of it! As though I would allow a stray nose to lie about in my room. You dried-up biscuit! He can do nothing but sharpen his razors on the strop, but soon he won't be fit to do his duties at all, the gadabout, the good-for-nothing! As though I were going to answer to the police for you. . . . Oh, you dirt, you stupid blockhead. Away with it, away with it! Take it where you like! Don't let me set eyes on it again!"

Ivan Yakovlevich stood as though utterly crushed. He thought and thought, and did not know what to think. "The devil only knows how it happened," he said at last, scratching behind his ear. "Did I come home drunk last night or not? I can't say for certain now. But from all signs it seems that something extraordinary must have happened, for bread is a thing that is baked, while a nose is something quite different. I can't make head or tail of it." Ivan Yakovlevich sank into silence. The thought that the police might make a search there for the nose and throw the blame of it on him reduced him to complete prostration. Already the red collar, beautifully embroidered with silver, the saber, hovered before his eyes, and he trembled all over. At last he got his trousers and his boots, pulled on these wretched objects, and, accompanied by the stern reproaches of Praskovia Osipovna, wrapped the nose in a rag and went out into the street.

He wanted to thrust it out of sight somewhere, under a gate, or somehow accidentally to drop it and then turn off into a side street, but as ill-luck would have it he kept coming across people he knew, who would at once begin asking: "Where are you going?" or "Whom are you going to shave so early?" so that Ivan Yakovlevich could never find a moment to get rid of it. Another time he really did drop it, but a policeman pointed to it with his halberd from a long way off, saying as he did so: "Pick it up, you have dropped something!" and Ivan Yakovlevich was obliged to pick up the nose and put it in his pocket. He was overcome by despair, especially as the number of people in the street was continually increasing as the shops and stalls began to open.

He made up his mind to go to Isakievsky Bridge in the hope of being able to fling it into the Neva. . . . But I am afraid I am a little to blame for not having so far said more about Ivan Yakovlevich, a worthy man in many respects.

Ivan Yakovlevich, like every self-respecting Russian workman, was a terrible drunkard, and though every day he shaved other people's chins, his own went forever unshaven. Ivan Yakovlevich's jacket (he never wore any other shape) was motley, that is, it was black dappled all over with brown and yellow and gray; the collar was shiny, and instead of three buttons there was only one hanging on a thread. Ivan Yakovlevich was a great cynic, and when Kovaliov the collegiate assessor said to him while he was being shaved: "Your hands always stink, Ivan Yakovlevich," the latter would reply with the question: "What should make them stink?" "I can't tell, my good man, but they do stink," the collegiate assessor would say, and, taking a pinch of snuff, Ivan Yakovlevich lathered him for that on his cheeks and under his nose and behind his ears and under his beard—in fact, wherever he chose.

The worthy citizen found himself by now on Isakievsky Bridge. First of all he looked about him, then bent over the parapet as though to look under the bridge to see whether there were a great number of fish racing by, and stealthily flung in the rag with the nose. He felt as though a heavy weight had rolled off his back. Ivan Yakovlevich actually grinned. Instead of going to shave the chins of government clerks, he went to an establishment bearing the inscription "Tea and refreshments" and asked for a glass of punch, when he suddenly observed at the end of the bridge a police inspector of respectable appearance with full whiskers, a three-cornered hat, and a sword. He turned cold, and meanwhile the inspector beckoned to him and said: "Come this way, my good man."

Ivan Yakovlevich, knowing etiquette, took off his hat some way off and, as he approached, said: "I wish your honor good health."

"No, no, old fellow, I am not 'your honor': tell me what you were doing on the bridge?"

"I swear, sir, I was on my way to shave my customers, and I was only looking to see whether the current was running fast."

"That's a lie, that's a lie! You won't get off with that. Kindly answer!"

"I am ready to shave you, gracious sir, two or even three times a week with no conditions whatever," answered Ivan Yakovlevich.

"No, my friend, that is nonsense; I have three barbers to shave me and they think it a great honor, too. But be so kind as to tell me what you were doing there?"

Ivan Yakovlevich turned pale . . . but the incident is completely veiled in obscurity, and absolutely nothing is known of what happened next.

II

Kovaliov the collegiate assessor woke up early next morning and made the sound "brrrr . . ." with his lips as he always did when he woke up, though he could not himself have explained the reason for his doing so. Kovaliov stretched and asked for a little mirror that was standing on the table. He wanted to look at a pimple which had appeared on his nose the previous evening, but to his great astonishment there was a completely flat space where his nose should have been. Frightened, Kovaliov asked for some water and a towel to rub his eyes; there really was no nose. He began feeling with his hand, and pinched himself to see whether he was still asleep: it appeared that he was not. The collegiate assessor jumped out of bed, he shook himself—there was still no nose. . . . He ordered his clothes to be given him at once and flew off straight to the police commissioner.

But meanwhile we must say a word about Kovaliov in order that the reader may have some idea of what kind of collegiate assessor he was. Collegiate assessors who receive that title with the aid of academic diplomas cannot be compared with those who are created collegiate assessors in the Caucasus. They are two quite different species. The erudite collegiate assessors . . . But Russia is such a wonderful country that, if you say a word about one collegiate assessor, all the collegiate assessors from Riga to Kamchatka would certainly think you are referring to them; and it is the same, of course, with all grades and titles. Kovaliov was a collegiate assessor from the Caucasus. He had only been of that rank for the last two years, and so could not forget it for a moment; and to give himself greater weight and dignity he did not call himself simply collegiate assessor but always spoke of himself as a major. "Listen, my dear," he would usually say when he met a woman in the street selling shirt fronts, "you go to my house; I live in Sadovaya Street; just ask, does Major Kovaliov live here? Anyone will show you." If he met some pretty little baggage he would also give her a secret instruction, adding: "You ask for Major Kovaliov's flat, my love." For this reason we will for the future speak of him as the major.

Major Kovaliov was in the habit of walking every day up and down Nevsky Prospekt. The collar of his shirt front was always extremely clean and well starched. His whiskers were such as one may see nowadays on provincial and district surveyors, on architects and army doctors, also on those employed on special commissions, and in general on all such men as have full ruddy cheeks and are very good hands at a game of boston: these whiskers start from the middle of the cheek and go straight up to the nose. Major Kovaliov used to wear a number of cornelian seals, some with crests on them and others on which were carved Wednesday, Thursday, Monday, and so on. Major Kovaliov had come to Petersburg on business, that is, to look for a post befitting his rank: if he were successful, the post of a vice-governor, and failing that, the situation of an executive clerk in some prominent department. Major Kovaliov was not averse to matrimony, but only on condition he could find a bride with a fortune of two hundred thousand. And so the reader may judge for himself what was the major's position when he saw, instead of a nice-looking, well-proportioned nose, an extremely absurd flat space.

As misfortune would have it, not a cab was to be seen in the street, and he was obliged to walk, wrapping himself in his cloak and hiding his face in his handkerchief, as though his nose were bleeding. "But perhaps it was my imagination: it's impossible: I couldn't have been idiotic enough to lose my nose," he thought, and went into a café to look at himself in the mirror. Fortunately there was no one in the shop; some boys were sweeping the floor and arranging all the chairs; others with sleepy faces were bringing in hot pastries on trays; yesterday's papers covered with coffee stains were lying about on the tables and chairs. "Well, thank God, there is nobody here," he thought; "now I can look." He went timidly up to the mirror and looked. "What the hell's the meaning of it? Damn it!" he said, spitting. "If only there had been something instead of a nose, but there is nothing! . . ."

Biting his lips with vexation, he went out of the café and resolved, contrary to his usual practice, not to look or smile at anyone. All at once he stood as though rooted to the spot before the door of a house. Something inexplicable took place before his eyes: a carriage was stopping at the entrance; the carriage door flew open; a gentleman in uniform, bending down, sprang out and ran up the steps. What was the horror and at the same time amazement of Kovaliov when he recognized that this was his own nose! At this extraordinary phenomenon it seemed to him that everything was swimming before his eyes; he felt that he could scarcely stand; but he made up his mind, come what may, to await the gentleman's return to the carriage, and he stood trembling all over as though in a fever. Two minutes later the nose actually did come out. He was in a gold-braided uniform with a high collar; he had on buckskin trousers and at his side was a sword. From his plumed hat it might be inferred that he was of the rank of a civil councilor. Everything showed that he was going somewhere to pay a visit. He looked to both sides, called to the coachman to open the carriage door, got in, and drove off.

Poor Kovaliov almost went out of his mind; he did not know what to think of such a strange occurrence. How was it possible for a nose—which had only yesterday been on his face and could neither drive nor walk—to be in uniform! He ran after the carriage, which luckily did not go far, but stopped before the entrance of Kazansky Cathedral.[1]

He hurried in that direction, made his way through a row of old beggar women with their faces tied up and two slits in place of their eyes at whom he used to laugh so merrily, and went into the church. There were not many people inside the church. Kovaliov felt so upset that he could not pray, and he looked for the gentleman. At last he saw him standing apart from the other worshippers. The nose was hiding his face completely in a high stand-up collar and was saying his prayers in an attitude of complete piety.

"How am I to approach him?" thought Kovaliov. "One can see by everything—from his uniform, from his hat—that he is a civil councilor. Damned if I know how to do it!"

He began by coughing at his side; but the nose never changed his pious attitude for a minute and continued genuflecting.

"Sir," said Kovaliov, inwardly forcing himself to speak confidently. "Sir . . ."

"What do you want?" answered the nose, turning around.

"It seems . . . strange to me, sir. . . . You ought to know your proper place, and all at once I find you in church, of all places! You will admit . . ."

"Excuse me, I cannot understand what you are talking about. . . . Explain."

"How am I to explain to him?" thought Kovaliov, and plucking up his courage he began: "Of course I . . . I am a major, by the way. For me to go about without a nose, you must admit, is improper. An old woman selling peeled oranges on Voskresensky Bridge may sit there without a nose; but having prospects of obtaining . . . and being besides acquainted with a great many ladies in the families of Chekhtariova the civil councilor and others . . . You can judge for yourself . . . I don't know, sir" (at this point Major Kovaliov shrugged his shoulders) ". . . excuse me

---

[1] One of Gogol's squabbles with the omnipresent and omnipotent Russian censor came about as a result of the "sacrilegious" presence of the nose in Kazansky Cathedral. Gogol, always extremely sensitive to criticism (even, at times, before it was delivered), wrote a note to a friend in which he anticipated the adverse reaction of the censor, and, he wrote, if the censor objected to the nose being in an Orthodox church, he might place it in a Catholic church instead. But Gogol yielded to the censor, and the nose found itself before a bazaar. Mrs. Garnett translated from the revised (censor-approved) version. The original text (which now appears in the Academy edition of Gogol's work) appears above. (ed.)

. . . if you look at the matter in accordance with the principles of duty and honor . . . you can understand of yourself . . ."

"I don't understand a word," said the nose. "Explain it more satisfactorily."

"Sir," said Kovaliov, with a sense of his own dignity, "I don't know how to understand your words. The matter appears to me perfectly obvious . . . either you wish . . . Why, you are my own nose!"

The nose looked at the major and his eyebrows slightly quivered.

"You are mistaken, sir. I am an independent individual. Moreover, there can be no sort of close relations between us. I see, sir, from the buttons of your uniform, you must be serving in a different department." Saying this, the nose turned away.

Kovaliov was utterly confused, not knowing what to do or even what to think. Meanwhile they heard the agreeable rustle of a lady's dress: an elderly lady was approaching, all decked out in lace, and with her a slim lady in a white dress which looked very charming on her slender figure, in a straw-colored hat as light as a pastry puff. Behind them stood, opening his snuffbox, a tall footman with big whiskers and a dozen collars.

Kovaliov came nearer, pulled out the cambric collar of his shirt front, arranged the seals on his gold watch chain, and smiling from side to side, turned his attention to the ethereal lady who, like a spring flower, faintly swayed forward and put her white hand with its half-transparent fingers to her brow. The smile on Kovaliov's face broadened when he saw under the hat her round, dazzlingly white chin and part of her cheek flushed with the hues of the first spring rose; but all at once he skipped away as though he had been scalded. He remembered that he had absolutely nothing on his face in place of a nose, and tears oozed from his eyes. He turned away to tell the gentleman in uniform straight out that he was only pretending to be a civil councilor, that he was a rogue and a scoundrel, and that he was nothing else than his own nose. . . . But the nose was no longer there; he had managed to gallop off, probably again to call on someone.

This reduced Kovaliov to despair. He went back and stood for a minute or two under the colonnade, carefully looking in all directions to see whether the nose was anywhere about. He remembered very well that there was plumage in his hat and gold braid on his uniform; but he had not noticed his overcoat nor the color of his carriage, nor his horses, nor even whether he had a footman behind him and if so in what livery. Moreover, such numbers of carriages were driving backwards and forwards and at such a speed that it was difficult even to distinguish them; and if he had distinguished one of them he would have had no means of stopping it. It was a lovely, sunny day. There were masses of people on Nevsky Prospekt; ladies were scattered like a perfect cataract of flowers all over the pavement from Politseysky to the Anichkin Bridge. Here he saw coming toward him a court councilor of his acquaintance whom he used to call "lieutenant colonel," particularly if he were speaking to other people. There he saw Yarygin, a head clerk in the senate, a great friend of his, who always lost points when he went eight at boston. And here was another major who had received the rank of assessor in the Caucasus, beckoning to him. . . .

"Hell!" said Kovaliov. "Hi, cab! drive straight to the police commissioner's."

Kovaliov got into a cab and shouted to the driver:

"Drive like a house on fire."

"Is the commissioner at home?" he cried, going into the hall.

"No," answered the porter, "he has just gone out."

"Well, that's my luck."

"Yes," added the porter, "and he has not been gone so long: if you had come but a tiny minute earlier you might have found him."

Kovaliov, still keeping the handkerchief over his face, got into the cab and shouted in a voice of despair: "Drive on."

"Where?" asked the cabman.

"Drive straight on!"

"How straight on? The street divides here; is it to the right or to the left?"

This question forced Kovaliov to pause, to think, again. In his position he ought first of all to address himself to the department of law and order, not because it had any direct connection with the police but because the intervention of the latter might be far more rapid than any help he could get in other departments. To seek satisfaction from the higher officials of the department in which the nose had announced himself as serving would have been unwise, since from the nose's own answers he had been able to perceive that nothing was sacred to that man and that he might tell lies in this case too, just as he had lied in declaring that he had never seen him before. And so Kovaliov was on the point of telling the cabman to drive to the police station, when again the idea occurred to him that this rogue and scoundrel who had at their first meeting behaved in such a shameless way might seize the opportunity and slip out of town—and then all his searches would be in vain, or might be prolonged, God forbid, for a whole month. At last it seemed that Heaven itself directed him. He decided to go straight to a newspaper office and without loss of time to publish a circumstantial description of the nose, so that anyone meeting it might at once present it to him or at least let him know where it was. And so, deciding upon this course, he told the cabman to drive to the newspaper office, and all the way never stopped hitting him with his fist on the back, saying as he did so, "Faster, you rascal; hurry, you scoundrel!"

"Ugh, sir!" said the cabman, shaking his head and flicking with the reins at the horse, whose coat was as long as a lapdog's. At last the cab stopped and Kovaliov ran panting into a little reception room where a gray-headed clerk in spectacles, wearing an old jacket, was sitting at a table and with a pen between his teeth was counting over some coppers he had before him.

"Who receives inquiries here?" cried Kovaliov. "Ah, good day!"

"I wish you good day," said the gray-headed clerk, raising his eyes for a moment and then dropping them again on the money lying in heaps on the table.

"I want to insert an advertisement . . ."

"Allow me to ask you to wait a minute," the clerk pronounced, with one hand noting a figure on the paper and with the finger of his left hand moving two beads on the abacus. A footman in a braided coat and of rather smart appearance, which betrayed that he had at some time served in an aristocratic family, was standing at the table with a written paper in his hand and thought fit to display his social abilities: "Would you believe it, sir, that the little bitch is not worth eighty kopeks; in fact I wouldn't give eight for it, but the countess is fond of it—my goodness, she is fond of it, and here she will give a hundred rubles to anyone who finds it! To speak politely, as you and I are speaking now, people's tastes are quite incompatible: when a man's a sportsman, then he'll keep a setter or a poodle; he won't mind giving five hundred or a thousand so long as it is a good dog."

The worthy clerk listened to this with a significant air, and at the same time was reckoning the number of letters in the advertisement brought him. Along the sides of the room stood a number of old women, shop assistants, and house porters who had brought advertisements. In one it was announced that a coachman of sober habits was looking for a situation; in the next a secondhand carriage brought from Paris in 1814 was offered for sale; next a maid, aged nineteen, experienced in laundry work and also competent to do other work, was looking for a situation; a strong carriage with only one spring broken was for sale; a spirited, young, dappled gray horse, only seventeen years old, for sale; a new consignment of turnip and radish seed from London; a summer villa with all conveniences, stabling for two horses, and a piece of land that might well be planted with fine birches and pine trees; there was also an appeal to those wishing to purchase old boot soles, inviting such to come for the same every day between eight o'clock in the morning and three o'clock in the afternoon. The room in which all this company was assembled was a small one and the air in it was extremely thick, but the collegiate assessor Kovaliov was incapable of noticing the stench both because he kept his handkerchief over his face and because his nose was goodness knows where.

"Dear sir, allow me to ask you . . . my case is very urgent," he said at last impatiently.

"In a minute, in a minute! . . . Two rubles, forty-three kopeks! . . . This minute! One ruble and sixty-four kopeks!" said the gray-headed gentleman, flinging the old women and house porters the various documents they had bought. "What can I do for you?" he said at last, turning to Kovaliov.

"I want to ask . . ." said Kovaliov. "Some robbery or swindle has occurred; I cannot understand it at all. I only want you to advertise that anyone who brings me the scoundrel will receive a handsome reward."

"Allow me to ask what is your surname?"

"No, why put my surname? I cannot give it to you! I have a large circle of acquaintances: Chekhtariova, wife of a civil councilor, Podtochina, widow of an officer . . . they will find out. God forbid! You can simply put: 'a collegiate assessor,' or better still, 'a person of major's rank.' "

"Is the runaway your house serf, then?"

"A house serf indeed! that would not be so bad! It's my nose . . . has run away from me . . . my own nose."

"H'm, what a strange surname! And is it a very large sum this Mr. Nosov has robbed you of?"

"Nosov! . . . you are on the wrong track. It is my nose, my own nose that has disappeared. I don't know where. The devil wanted to have a joke at my expense."

"But in what way did it disappear? There is something I can't quite understand."

"And indeed, I can't tell you how it happened; the point is that now it is driving about the town, calling itself a civil councilor. And so I beg you to announce that anyone who catches him must bring him at once to me as quickly as possible. Only think, really, how can I manage without such a conspicuous part of my person? It's not like a little toe, the loss of which I could hide in my boot and no one could say whether it was there or not. I go on Thursdays to Chekhtariova's: Podtochina, an officer's widow, and her very pretty daughter are great friends of mine; and you can judge for yourself what a fix I am in now . . . I can't possibly show myself now. . . ."

The clerk pondered, a fact which was obvious from the way he compressed his lips.

"No, I can't put an advertisement like that in the paper," he said at last, after a long silence.

"What? Why not?"

"Well. The newspaper might lose its reputation. If everyone is going to write that his nose has run away, why . . . As it is, they say we print lots of absurd things and false reports."

"But what is there absurd about this? I don't see anything absurd in it."

"You think there is nothing absurd in it? But last week, now, this was what happened. A government clerk came to me just as you have; he brought an advertisement, it came to two rubles seventy-three kopeks, and all the advertisement amounted to was that a poodle with a black coat had strayed. You wouldn't think that there was anything in that, would you? But it turned out to be libelous: the poodle was the cashier of some department, I don't remember which."

"But I am not asking you to advertise about poodles but about my own nose; that is almost the same as about myself."

"No, such an advertisement I cannot insert."

"But since my nose really is lost!"

"If it is lost that is a matter for the doctor. They say there are people who can fit you with a nose of any shape you like. But I observe you must be a gentleman of merry disposition and are fond of having your little joke."

"I swear as God is holy! If you like, since it has come to that, I will show you."

"I don't want to trouble you," said the clerk, taking a pinch of snuff. "However, if it is no trouble," he added, moved by curiosity, "it might be desirable to have a look."

The collegiate assessor took the handkerchief from his face. "It really is extremely strange," said the clerk, "the place is perfectly flat, like a freshly fried pancake. Yes, it's incredibly smooth."

"Will you dispute it now? You see for yourself I must advertise. I shall be particularly grateful to you and very glad this incident has given me the pleasure of your acquaintance."

The major, as may be seen, made up his mind on this occasion to resort to a little flattery.

"To print such an advertisement is, of course, not such a very great matter," said the clerk. "But I do not foresee any advantage to you from it. If you do want to, put it in the hands of someone with a skillful pen, describe it as a rare freak of nature, and publish the little article in *The Northern Bee*" (at this point he once more took a pinch of snuff) "for the benefit of youth" (at this moment he wiped his nose), "or anyway as a matter of general interest."

The collegiate assessor felt quite hopeless. He dropped his eyes and looked at the bottom of the paper where there was an announcement of a theatrical event; his face was ready to break into a smile as he saw the name of a pretty actress, and his hand went to his pocket to feel whether he had a five-ruble note there, for an officer of his rank ought, in Kovaliov's opinion, to have a seat in the orchestra; but the thought of his nose spoiled it all.

Even the clerk seemed touched by Kovaliov's difficult position. Desirous of relieving his distress in some way, he thought befitting to express his sympathy in a few words: "I am really very much grieved that such an incident should have occurred to you. Wouldn't you like a pinch of snuff? it relieves headache and dissipates depression; even in intestinal trouble it is of use." Saying this the clerk offered Kovaliov his snuffbox, rather deftly opening the lid with a portrait of a lady in a hat on it.

This thoughtless act exhausted Kovaliov's patience.

"I can't understand how you can think it proper to make a joke of it," he said angrily; "don't you see that I am without just what I need for sniffing? To hell with your snuff! I can't bear the sight of it now, not merely your miserable Berezinsky stuff but even if you were to offer me rappee itself!" Saying this he walked out of the newspaper office, deeply mortified, and went in the direction of the local police inspector.

Kovaliov walked in at the very moment when he was stretching and clearing his throat and saying: "Ah, I should enjoy a couple of hours' nap!" And so it might be foreseen that the collegiate assessor's visit was not very opportune. The police inspector was a great patron of all arts and manufactures; but he preferred money to everything. "That is a thing," he used to say; "there is nothing better than that thing; it does not ask for food, it takes up little space, there is always room for it in the pocket, and if you drop it, it does not break."

The police inspector received Kovaliov rather coldly and said that after dinner was not the time to make an inquiry, that nature itself had ordained that man should rest a little after eating (the collegiate assessor could see from this that the sayings of the ancient sages were not unfamiliar to the local inspector), and that a respectable man does not have his nose pulled off.

This was adding insult to injury. It must be said that Kovaliov was very easily offended. He could forgive anything said about himself, but could never forgive insult to his rank or his calling. He was even of the opinion that any reference to officers of the higher ranks might be allowed to pass in stage plays, but that no attack ought to be made on those of a lower grade. The reception given him by the local inspector so disconcerted him that he tossed his head and said with an air of dignity and a slight gesture of surprise: "I must observe that after observations so insulting on your part I can add nothing more . . ." and went out.

He went home hardly conscious of the ground under his feet. By now it was dusk. His lodgings seemed to him melancholy or rather utterly disgusting after all these unsuccessful efforts. Going into his hall he saw his valet, Ivan, lying on his dirty leather sofa; he was spitting on the ceiling and rather successfully aiming at the same spot. The nonchalance of his servant enraged him; he hit him

on the forehead with his hat, saying: "You pig, you are always doing something stupid."

Ivan jumped up and rushed headlong to help him off with his
cloak.

Going into his room, weary and dejected, the major threw himself into an easy chair, and at last, after several sighs, said:

"My God, my God! Why has this misfortune befallen me? If I
had lost an arm or a leg it would have been better; but without a
nose a man is goodness knows what: neither fish nor fowl nor human being, good for nothing but to be flung out of the window!
And if only it had been cut off in battle or in a duel, or if I had been
the cause of it myself, but as it is, it is lost for no cause or reason, it
is lost for nothing, absolutely nothing! But no, it cannot be," he
added after a moment's thought; "it's incredible that a nose should
be lost. It must be a dream or an illusion. Perhaps by some mistake
I drank instead of water the vodka I use to rub my chin with after
shaving. Ivan, the idiot, did not remove it and very likely I took it."
To convince himself that he was not drunk, the major pinched
himself so painfully that he shrieked. The pain completely convinced him that he was living and acting in real life. He slowly approached the mirror and at first screwed up his eyes with the idea
that maybe his nose would appear in its proper place; but at the
same minute sprang back, saying: "What a terrible sight!"

It really was incomprehensible; if a button had been lost or a
silver spoon or a watch or anything similar—but to have lost this,
and in one's own apartment too! Thinking over all the circumstances, Major Kovaliov reached the supposition that what might
be nearest the truth was that the person responsible for this could
be no other than Madame Podtochina, who wanted him to marry
her daughter. He himself liked flirting with her, but avoided a definite engagement. When the mother had informed him plainly that
she wished for the marriage, he had slyly put her off with his compliments, saying that he was still young, that he must serve for five
years so as to be exactly forty-two. And that Madame Podtochina
had therefore made up her mind, probably out of revenge, to ruin
him, and had hired for the purpose some peasant witches, because
it was impossible to suppose that the nose had been cut off in any
way; no one had come into his room; the barber Ivan Yakovlevich
had shaved him on Wednesday, and all Wednesday and even all
Thursday his nose had been all right—that he remembered and

was quite certain about; besides, he would have felt pain, and there could have been no doubt that the wound could not have healed so soon and been as flat as a pancake. He formed various plans in his mind: either to summon Madame Podtochina formally before the court or to go to her himself and confront her with it. These reflections were interrupted by a light which gleamed through all the cracks of the door and informed him that a candle had been lighted in the hall by Ivan. Soon Ivan himself appeared, holding it before him and lighting up the whole room. Kovaliov's first movement was to snatch up his handkerchief and cover the place where yesterday his nose had been, so that his really stupid servant might not gape at the sight of anything so peculiar in his master.

Ivan had hardly time to retreat to his lair when there was the sound of an unfamiliar voice in the hall, pronouncing the words: "Does the collegiate assessor Kovaliov live here?"

"Come in, Major Kovaliov is here," said Kovaliov, jumping up hurriedly and opening the door.

A police officer walked in. He was of handsome appearance, with whiskers neither too fair nor too dark, and rather fat cheeks, the same officer who at the beginning of our story was standing at the end of Isakievsky Bridge.

"Did you lose your nose, sir?"

"That is so."

"It is now found."

"What are you saying?" cried Major Kovaliov. He could not speak for joy. He stared at the police officer standing before him, on whose full lips and cheeks the flickering light of the candle was brightly reflected. "How?"

"By extraordinary luck: he was caught almost on the road. He had already taken his seat in the stagecoach and was intending to go to Riga, and had already taken a passport in the name of a government clerk. And the strange thing is that I myself took him for a gentleman at first, but fortunately I had my spectacles with me and I soon saw that it was a nose. You know I am shortsighted. And if you stand before me I only see that you have a face, but I don't notice your nose or your beard or anything. My mother-in-law, that is my wife's mother, doesn't see anything either."

Kovaliov was beside himself with joy. "Where? Where? I'll go at once."

"Don't disturb yourself. Knowing that you were in need of it I brought it along with me. And the strange thing is that the man who has had the most to do with the affair is a rascal of a barber on Voznesensky Avenue, who is now in our custody. I have long suspected him of drunkenness and thieving, and only the day before yesterday he carried off a strip of buttons from one shop. Your nose is exactly as it was." With this the police officer put his hand in his pocket and drew out the nose just as it was.

"That's it!" Kovaliov cried. "That's certainly it. You must have a cup of tea with me this evening."

"I should look upon it as a great pleasure, but I can't possibly manage it: I have to go from here to the penitentiary. . . . How the price of food is going up! . . . At home I have my mother-in-law, that is my wife's mother, and my children, the eldest particularly gives signs of great promise, he is a very intelligent child; but we have absolutely no means for his education . . ."

For some time after the policeman's departure the collegiate assessor remained in a state of bewilderment, and it was only a few minutes later that he was capable of feeling and understanding again: so reduced was he to stupefaction by this unexpected good fortune. He took the recovered nose carefully in his two hands, holding them together like a cup, and once more examined it attentively.

"Yes, that's it, it's certainly it," said Major Kovaliov. "There's the pimple that came out on the left side yesterday." The major almost laughed aloud with joy.

But nothing in this world is of long duration, and so his joy was not so great the next moment; and the moment after, it was still less, and in the end he passed imperceptibly into his ordinary frame of mind, just as a circle on the water caused by a falling stone gradually passes away into the unbroken smoothness of the surface. Kovaliov began to think, and reflected that the business was not finished yet; the nose was found, but it had to be put on, fixed in its proper place.

"And what if it won't stick?" Asking himself this question, the major turned pale.

With a feeling of irrepressible terror he rushed to the table and moved the mirror forward so that he might not put the nose on crooked. His hands trembled. Cautiously and gently he replaced it in its former position. Oh horror, the nose would not stick on! . . .

He put it to his lips, slightly warmed it with his breath, and again applied it to the flat space between his two cheeks; but nothing would make the nose stick.

"Come, come, stick on, you fool!" he said to it; but the nose seemed made of wood and fell on the table with a strange sound as though it were a cork. The major's face twisted convulsively.

"Is it possible that it won't grow on again?" But, however often he applied it to the proper place, the attempt was as unsuccessful as before.

He called Ivan and sent him for a doctor who lived in the best apartment on the first floor of the same house. The doctor was a handsome man; he had magnificent pitch-black whiskers, a fresh and healthy wife, ate fresh apples in the morning, and kept his mouth extraordinarily clean, rinsing it out for nearly three-quarters of an hour every morning and cleaning his teeth with five different sorts of brushes. The doctor appeared immediately. Asking how long ago the trouble had occurred, he took Major Kovaliov by the chin and with his thumb gave him a flip on the spot where the nose had been, making the major jerk back his head so abruptly that he knocked the back of it against the wall. The doctor said that that did not matter, and, advising him to move a little away from the wall, he told him to bend his head around first to the right, and feeling the place where the nose had been, said, "H'm!" Then he told him to turn his head around to the left side and again said "H'm!" And in conclusion he gave him another flip with his thumb, so that Major Kovaliov threw up his head like a horse when his teeth are being looked at. After making this experiment the doctor shook his head and said:

"No, it's impossible. You had better stay as you are, for it may be made much worse. Of course, it might be stuck on; I could stick it on for you at once, if you like; but I assure you it would be worse for you."

"That's a nice thing to say! How can I stay without a nose?" said Kovaliov. "Things can't possibly be worse than now. It's simply beyond everything. Where can I show myself with such a terrible face? I have a good circle of acquaintances. Today, for instance, I ought to be at two evening parties. I know a great many people; Chekhtariova, the wife of a civil councilor, Podtochina, an officer's widow . . . though after the way she has behaved, I'll have nothing more to do with her except through the police. Do me a favor,"

Kovaliov went on in a supplicating voice; "is there no way to stick it on? Even if it were not neatly done, as long as it would stay on; I could even hold it on with my hand at critical moments. I wouldn't dance in any case for fear of a sudden movement upsetting it. As for remuneration for your services, you may be assured that as far as my means allow . . ."

"Believe me," said the doctor, in a voice neither loud nor low but persuasive and magnetic, "that I never work from mercenary motives; that is opposed to my principles and my science. It is true that I accept a fee for my visits, but that is simply to avoid wounding my patients by refusing it. Of course I could replace your nose; but I assure you on my honor, since you do not believe my word, that it will be much worse for you. You had better wait for the action of nature itself. Wash it frequently with cold water, and I assure you that even without a nose you will be just as healthy as with one. And I advise you to put the nose in a bottle, in spirits or, better still, put two tablespoonfuls of sour vodka on it and heated vinegar—and then you might get quite a sum of money for it. I'd even take it myself, if you don't ask too much for it."

"No, no, I wouldn't sell it for anything," Major Kovaliov cried in despair; "I'd rather it were lost than that!"

"Excuse me!" said the doctor, bowing himself out, "I was trying to be of use to you. . . . Well, there is nothing I can do! Anyway, you see that I have done my best." Saying this the doctor walked out of the room with a majestic air. Kovaliov did not notice his face, and, almost unconscious, saw nothing but the cuffs of his immaculate white shirt peeping out from the sleeves of his black tail coat.

Next day he decided, before lodging a complaint with the police, to write to Madame Podtochina to see whether she would consent to return him what she had taken without a struggle. The letter was as follows:

Dear Madam,
     Aleksandra Grigorievna

I cannot understand this strange conduct on your part. You may rest assured that you will gain nothing by what you have done, and you will not get a step nearer forcing me to marry your daughter. Believe me, that business in regard to my nose is no secret, no more than it is that you and no other are the person chiefly responsible. The sudden parting of the same from its natural position, its flight and masquerading, at one time in the form of a government clerk and finally in its own shape, is nothing else than the consequence of the sorceries engaged in by you or by those who are versed in the same honorable arts as you are. For my part I consider it my duty to warn you, if the above-mentioned nose is not in its proper place today, I shall be obliged to resort to the assistance and protection of the law.

I have, however, with complete respect to you, the honor to be
Your respectful servant,
PLATON KOVALIOV

DEAR SIR,
PLATON KUZMICH!

Your letter greatly astonished me. I must frankly confess that I did not expect it, especially in regard to your unjust reproaches. I assure you I have never received the government clerk of whom you speak in my house, neither in masquerade nor in his own attire. It is true that Filipp Ivanovich Potanchikov has been to see me, and although, indeed, he is asking me for my daughter's hand and is a well-conducted, sober man of great learning, I have never encouraged his hopes. You make some reference to your nose also. If you wish me to understand by that that you imagine that I meant to make a long nose at you, that is, to give you a formal refusal, I am surprised that you should speak of such a thing when, as you know perfectly well, I was quite of the opposite way of thinking, and if you are courting my daughter with a view to lawful matrimony I am ready to satisfy you immediately, seeing that has always been the object of my keenest desires, in the hopes of which I remain always ready to be of service to you.

ALEKSANDRA PODTOCHINA

"No," said Kovaliov to himself after reading the letter, "she really is not to blame. It's impossible. The letter is written as it could not be written by anyone guilty of a crime." The collegiate assessor was an expert on this subject, as he had been sent several times to the Caucasus to conduct investigations. "In what way, by what fate, has this happened? Only the devil could understand it!" he said at last, letting his hands fall to his sides.

Meanwhile the rumors of this strange occurrence were spreading all over the town, and of course, not without special additions. Just at that time the minds of all were particularly interested in the marvelous: experiments in the influence of magnetism had been attracting public attention only recently. Moreover, the story of the dancing chair in Koniuchennaya Street was still fresh, and so

there is nothing surprising in the fact that people were soon beginning to say that the nose of a collegiate assessor called Kovaliov was
walking along Nevsky Prospekt at exactly three in the afternoon.
Numbers of inquisitive people flocked there every day. Somebody
said that the nose was in Yunker's shop—and near Yunker's there
was such a crowd and such a crush that the police were actually
obliged to intervene. One speculator, a man of dignified appearance with whiskers, who used to sell all sorts of cakes and tarts
at the doors of the theaters, purposely constructed some very
strong wooden benches, which he offered to the curious to stand
on, for eighty kopeks each. One very worthy colonel left home
earlier on account of it, and with a great deal of trouble made his
way through the crowd; but to his great indignation, instead of
the nose, he saw in the shop windows the usual woolen undershirt
and a lithograph depicting a girl pulling up her stocking while a
foppish young man, with a cutaway waistcoat and a small beard,
peeps at her from behind a tree; a picture which had been hanging
in the same place for more than ten years. As he walked away he
said with vexation: "How can people be led astray by such stupid
and incredible stories!" Then the rumor spread that it was not on
Nevsky Prospekt but in Tavrichersky Park that Major Kovaliov's
nose took its walks; that it had been there for a long time; that,
even when Khozrev-Mirza[2] used to live there, he was greatly surprised at this strange freak of nature. Several students from the
Academy of Surgery made their way to the park. One worthy lady
of high rank wrote a letter to the superintendent of the park asking
him to show her children this rare phenomenon with, if possible, an
explanation that should be edifying and instructive for the young.

All the gentlemen who invariably attend social gatherings and
like to amuse the ladies were extremely thankful for all these
events, for their stock of anecdotes was completely exhausted. A
small group of worthy and well-intentioned persons were greatly
displeased. One gentleman said with indignation that he could not
understand how in the present enlightened age people could spread
abroad these absurd stories, and that he was surprised that the government took no notice of it. This gentleman, as may be seen, belonged to the number of those who would like the government to
meddle in everything, even in their daily quarrels with their wives.

---

[2] Persian prince who arrived in Russia in 1829 to offer an official apology for
the murder of A. S. Griboedov, Russian ambassador to Teheran. (ed.)

After this . . . but here again the whole adventure is lost in fog, and what happened afterward is absolutely unknown.

III

What is utterly absurd happens in the world. Sometimes there is not the slightest semblance of truth to it: all at once that very nose which had been driving about the place in the shape of a civil councilor, and had made such a stir in the town, turned up again as though nothing had happened, in its proper place, that is, precisely between the two cheeks of Major Kovaliov. This took place on the seventh of April. Waking up and casually glancing into the mirror, he sees—his nose! puts up his hands—actually his nose! "Aha!" said Kovaliov, and in his joy he almost danced a jig barefoot about his room; but the entrance of Ivan stopped him. He ordered Ivan to bring him water at once, and as he washed he glanced once more into the mirror—the nose! As he wiped himself with the towel he glanced into the mirror—the nose!

"Look, Ivan, I think I have a pimple on my nose," he said, while he thought: "How horrible it will be if Ivan says, 'No, indeed, sir, there's no pimple and, indeed, there is no nose either!'"

But Ivan said: "There is nothing, there is no pimple: your nose is quite clear!"

"Damn it, that's wonderful!" the major said to himself, and he snapped his fingers.

At that moment Ivan Yakovlevich the barber peeped in at the door, but as timidly as a cat who had just been beaten for stealing the bacon.

"Tell me first: are your hands clean?" Kovaliov shouted to him while he was still some way off.

"Yes."

"You are lying!"

"Upon my word, they are clean, sir."

"Well, be careful."

Kovaliov sat down. Ivan Yakovlevich covered him up with a towel, and in one instant with the aid of his brushes had smothered the whole of his beard and part of his cheek in cream, like that which is served at merchants' name-day parties.

"Look here!" Ivan Yakovlevich said to himself, glancing at the nose and then turning his customer's head on the other side and looking at it sideways. "There it is, sure enough. What can it mean?" He went on pondering, and for a long while he gazed at the nose. At last, lightly, with a cautiousness which may well be imagined, he raised two fingers to take it by the tip. Such was Ivan Yakovlevich's system.

"Now, now, now, careful!" cried Kovaliov. Ivan Yakovlevich let his hands drop, and was flustered and confused as he had never been confused before. At last he began gently tickling him with the razor under his beard, and, although it was difficult and not at all easy for him to shave without holding on to the olfactory portion of the face, yet he did at last somehow, pressing his rough thumb into his cheek and lower jaw, overcome all difficulties, and finish shaving him.

When it was all over, Kovaliov at once made haste to dress, took a cab, and drove to the café. Before he was inside the door he shouted: "Waiter, a cup of chocolate!" and at the same instant peeped at himself in the mirror. The nose was there. He turned around gaily and, with a satirical air, slightly screwing up his eyes, looked at two military men, one of whom had a nose hardly bigger than a vest button. After that he started off for the office of the department, in which he was urging his claims to a post as vice-governor or, failing that, the post of an executive clerk. After crossing the reception room he glanced at the mirror; the nose was there. Then he drove to see another collegiate assessor or major, who was very fond of making fun of people, and to whom he often said in reply to various biting observations: "Ah, you! I know you, you are as sharp as a pin!" On the way he thought: "If the major does not split with laughter when he sees me, then it is a sure sign that everything is in its place." But the sarcastic collegiate assessor said nothing. "Good, good, damn it all!" Kovaliov thought to himself. On the way he met Podtochina, the officer's wife, and her daughter; he was profuse in his bows to them and was greeted with exclamations of delight—so there could be nothing wrong with him, he thought. He conversed with them for a long time and, taking out his snuffbox, purposely put a pinch to each nostril while he said to himself: "So much for you, you foolish petticoats, you hens! but I am not going to marry your daughter anyway. This is only *par amour!*"

And from that time forth Major Kovaliov promenaded about, as though nothing had happened, on Nevsky Prospekt, and at the theaters and everywhere. And the nose, too, as though nothing had happened, sat on his face without even a sign of coming off at the sides. And after this Major Kovaliov was always seen in a good humor, smiling, resolutely pursuing all the pretty ladies, and even on one occasion stopping before a shop in the Gostiny Court[3] and buying the ribbon of some order, I cannot say for what purpose, since he was not himself a cavalier of any order.

So this is the strange event that occurred in the northern capital of our spacious empire! Only now, on thinking it all over, we perceive that there is a great deal that is improbable in it. Apart from the fact that it certainly is strange for a nose supernaturally to leave its place and to appear in various places in the guise of a civil councilor—how was it that Kovaliov did not grasp that he could not advertise about his nose in a newspaper office? I do not mean to say that I should think it too expensive to advertise: that is nonsense, and I am by no means a mercenary person: but it is improper, awkward, not nice! And again: how did the nose get into the loaf, and how about Ivan Yakovlevich himself? . . . no, that I cannot understand, I am absolutely unable to understand it! But what is stranger, what is more incomprehensible than anything is that authors can choose such subjects. I confess that is quite beyond my grasp, it really is . . . No, no! I cannot understand it at all. In the first place, it is absolutely without profit to our country; in the second place . . . but in the second place, too, there is no profit. I really do not know what to say of it. . . .

And yet, in spite of it all, though of course one may admit the first point, the second and the third . . . may even . . . but there, are there not absurd things everywhere?—and yet, when you think it over, there really is something in it. Despite what anyone may say, such things do happen—not often, but they do happen.

---

[3] Large shopping center in St. Petersburg. (ed.)

THE COACH

The little town of B—— has grown much more lively since a cavalry regiment began to be stationed in it. Before then it was incredibly dull. When one drove through it and glanced at the low-pitched, painted houses which looked into the street with a terribly sour expression . . . well, it is impossible to put into words what things were like there: it is as dejecting as though one had lost money at cards, or just said something stupid and inappropriate—in short, it is depressing. The plaster on the houses has peeled off with the rain, and the walls instead of being white are piebald; the roofs are for the most part thatched with reeds, as is usual in our southern towns. The gardens have long ago, by order of the mayor, been cut down to improve the look of the place. There is never a soul to be met in the streets; at most a cock crosses the road, soft as a pillow from the dust that lies on it eight inches thick and at the slightest drop of rain is transformed into mud, and then the streets of the town of B—— are filled with fat animals which the local mayor calls Frenchmen; thrusting out their huge snouts from their baths, they begin grunting so loudly that the traveler can do nothing but urge on his horses. It is not easy, however, to meet a traveler in the town of B——. On rare, very rare occasions, some country gentleman, owning eleven serfs and dressed in a full nankeen coat, jolts over the road in something which is a sort of compromise between a carriage and a cart, and peeps out from behind piled-up sacks of flour, as he lashes his mare beside which runs a colt. Even the market place has rather a melancholy air: the tailor's shop is idiotically located, not facing the street but meeting it sideways; facing it, a brick building with two windows has been under construction for fifteen years; a little further, standing all by itself, there is one of those paling fences once so fashionable, painted gray to match the mud, and erected as a model for other buildings by the mayor in the days of his youth, before he had formed the habit of sleeping immediately after dinner and drinking at night a beverage flavored with dry gooseberries. In other parts the fences are all of wattle. In the middle of the square, there are very tiny shops; in them one may always see a bunch of pretzels, a peasant woman in a red kerchief, forty pounds of soap, a few pounds of bitter almonds, buckshot, some cotton material, and two shopmen who spend all their time playing a sort of quoits near the door.

But as soon as the cavalry regiment was stationed at the little town of B—— everything was changed: the streets were full of life and color, in fact, they assumed quite a different aspect; the low-pitched little houses often saw a graceful, well-built officer with a plume on his head passing by on his way to discuss promotion or the best kind of tobacco with a comrade, or sometimes to play cards for the carriage, which might have been described as regimental because, without ever leaving the regiment, it had already gone the round of all the officers; one day the major rolled up in it, the next day it was to be seen in the lieutenant's stable, and a week later, lo and behold, the major's orderly was greasing its wheels again. The wooden fence between the houses was always studded with soldiers' caps hanging in the sun; a gray military overcoat was always conspicuous on some gate; in the side streets soldiers were to be seen with mustaches as stiff as boot brushes. These mustaches were on view everywhere; if workwomen gathered in the market with their tin mugs, one could always get a glimpse of a mustache behind their shoulders. The officers brought life into the local society which had until then consisted of a judge, who lived in the same house with a deacon's wife, and a mayor, who was a very sagacious person, but slept absolutely the whole day from lunch to supper and from supper to lunch. Society gained even more in numbers and interest when the headquarters of the general of the brigade were transferred to the town. Neighboring landowners, whose existence no one would previously have suspected, began visiting the district town more frequently to see the officers and sometimes to play "bank," a card game of which there was an extremely hazy notion in their brains, busy with thoughts of crops and hares and their wives' commissions.

I am very sorry that I cannot recall what circumstance it was that led the general of the brigade to give a big dinner; preparations for it were made on a vast scale; the clatter of the cooks' knives in the general's kitchen could be heard almost as far as the town gate. The whole market was completely drained for the dinner, so that the judge and his deaconess had nothing to eat but buckwheat cakes. The little courtyard of the general's quarters was packed with chaises and carriages. The company consisted of gentlemen —officers and a few neighboring landowners. Of the latter, the most noteworthy was Pythagoras Pythagorasovich Chertokutsky, one of the leading aristocrats of the district of B——, who made more noise than anyone at the elections and drove to them in a very smart carriage. He had once served in a cavalry regiment and had been one of its most important and conspicuous officers, anyway he had been seen at numerous balls and assemblies, wherever his regiment had been stationed; the young ladies of the Tambov and Simbirsk provinces, however, could tell us most about that. It is very possible that he would have gained a desirable reputation in other provinces, too, if he had not resigned his commission owing to one of those incidents which are usually described as "an un-pleasantness"; either he had given someone a box on the ear in the old days, or was given it; which I don't remember for certain; any-way, the point is that he was asked to resign his commission. He lost nothing of his importance through this, however. He wore a high-waisted dress coat of military cut, spurs on his boots, and a mustache under his nose, since, but for that, the nobility of his province might have supposed that he had served in the infantry, which he always spoke of contemptuously. He visited all the much-frequented fairs, to which those who make up the heart of Russia, that is, the nurses and children, stout landowners and their daugh-ters, flock to enjoy themselves, driving in chaises with hoods, gigs, wagonettes, and carriages such as have never been seen in the wildest dreams. He had a special talent for smelling out where a cavalry regiment was stationed, and always went to interview the officers, very nimbly leaping out of his light carriage in view of them and very quickly making their acquaintance. At the last election he had given the nobility of the provinces an excellent dinner, at which he had declared that, if only he were elected leader, he "would put the gentlemen on the best possible footing." Altogether he lived like a gentleman, as the expression goes in the provinces; he married a rather pretty wife, getting with her a dowry of two hundred serfs and some thousands in cash. The money was at once spent on a team of six really first-rate horses, gilt locks on the doors, a tame monkey, and a French butler for the household. The two hundred serfs, together with two hundred of his own, were mortgaged to the bank for the sake of some commercial operations.

In short, he was a proper sort of landowner, a very decent sort of landowner . . .

Apart from this gentleman, there were a few other landowners at the general's dinner, but there is no need to describe them. The other guests were the officers of the same regiment, besides two staff officers, a colonel, and a fat major. The general himself was a big, fat man, though an excellent commanding officer, so the others said of him. He spoke in a rather thick, important bass. The dinner was remarkable; sturgeon of various sorts, as well as sterlet, bustards, asparagus, quails, partridges, and mushrooms, testified to the fact that the cook had not had a drop of anything strong between his lips since the previous day, and that four soldiers had been at work with knives in their hands all night, helping him with the fricassee and the jelly. A multitude of bottles, tall ones with Lafitte and short ones with Madeira; a lovely summer day, windows wide open, plates of ice on the table, the crumpled shirt fronts of the owners of extremely roomy dress coats, a cross fire of conversation drowned by the general's voice and washed down by champagne—all was in harmony. After dinner they all got up from the table with a pleasant heaviness in their stomachs, and, after lighting pipes, some with long and some with short mouthpieces, went out onto the steps with cups of coffee in their hands.

"You can look at her now," said the general; "if you please, my dear boy," he went on, addressing his adjutant, a rather sprightly young man of agreeable appearance, "tell them to bring the bay mare around! here you shall see for yourself." At this point the general took a pull at his pipe and blew out the smoke: "She is not quite well-groomed; this wretched, damned little town! She is a very"—puff-puff—"decent mare!"

"And have you"—puff-puff—"had her long, your Excellency?" said Chertokutsky.

"Well" . . . puff-puff-puff . . . "not so long; it's only two years since I had her from the stud farm."

"And did you get her broken in, or have you been breaking her in here, your Excellency?"

Puff-puff-pu—ff-puff. "Here." Saying this the general completely disappeared in smoke.

Meanwhile a soldier skipped out of the stables, the thud of hoofs was audible, and at last another soldier with huge black mustaches, wearing a white smock, appeared, leading by the bridle a trembling and frightened mare, who, suddenly flinging up her head, almost lifted the soldier and his mustaches into the air.

"There, there, Agrafena Ivanovna!" he said, leading her up to the steps.

The mare's name was Agrafena Ivanovna. Strong and wild as a beauty of the south, she stamped her hoof upon the wooden steps, then suddenly stopped.

The general, laying down his pipe, began with a satisfied air to look at Agrafena Ivanovna. The colonel himself went down the steps and took Agrafena Ivanovna by the nose, the major patted Agrafena Ivanovna on the leg, the others made a clicking sound with their tongues.

Chertokutsky went down and approached her from behind; the soldier, drawn up to attention and holding the bridle, looked straight into the visitor's eyes as though he wanted to jump into them.

"Very, very fine," said Chertokutsky, "a horse with excellent points! And allow me to ask your Excellency, how does she trot?"

"Her action is very good, only . . . that fool of a doctor's assistant, damn the man, gave her pills of some sort and for the last two days she has done nothing but sneeze."

"Very fine horse, very; and have you a suitable carriage, your Excellency?"

"A carriage? . . . But she is a saddle horse, you know."

"I know that, but I asked your Excellency to find out whether you have a suitable carriage for your other horses."

"Well, I am not very well off for carriages, I must admit; I have long been wanting to get a modern one. I have written to my brother who is in Petersburg just now, but I don't know whether he'll send me one or not."

"I think, your Excellency, there are no better carriages than the Viennese."

"You are quite right there." Puff-puff-puff——

"I have an excellent carriage, your Excellency, of real Vienna make."

"What is it like? Is it the one you came here in?"

"Oh no, that's just for rough work, for my excursions, but the other . . . It is a wonder! light as a feather, and when you are in it, it is simply, if I may say so, as though your nurse were rocking you in the cradle!"

"So it is comfortable?"

"Very comfortable indeed; cushions, springs, like a picture."

"That's nice."

"And so roomy! As a matter of fact, your Excellency, I have never seen one like it. When I was in the service I used to put a dozen bottles of rum and twenty pounds of tobacco in the luggage compartment, and besides that I used to have about six uniforms and underwear and two pipes, the very long ones, your Excellency, while you could put a whole ox in the glove compartment."

"That's nice."

"It cost four thousand, your Excellency."

"At that price it ought to be good; and did you buy it yourself?"

"No, your Excellency, it came to me by chance; it was bought by my friend, the companion of my childhood, a rare man with whom you would have got on perfectly, your Excellency; we were on such terms that what was his was mine, it was all the same. I won it from him at cards. Would you care, your Excellency, to do me the honor to dine with me tomorrow, and you could have a look at the carriage at the same time?"

"I really don't know what to say . . . for me to come alone like that . . . would you allow me to bring the other officers?"

"I beg the other officers to come too. Gentlemen! I shall think it a great pleasure to see you in my house."

The colonel, the major, and the other officers thanked him with a polite bow.

"What I think, your Excellency, is that if one buys a thing it must be good; if it is not good there is no use having it. When you do me the honor of visiting me tomorrow, I will show you a few other practical things I have bought."

The general looked at him and blew smoke out of his mouth. Chertokutsky was highly delighted at having invited the officers: he was inwardly ordering pastries and sauces while he looked very good-humoredly at the gentlemen in question, who for their part, too, seemed to feel twice as amiably disposed to him, as could be discerned from their eyes and the small movements they made, such as half bows. Chertokutsky spoke with more familiarity, and there was a softness in his voice as though it were weighed down with pleasure.

"There, your Excellency, you will make the acquaintance of my wife."

"I shall be delighted," said the general, stroking his mustache.

After that Chertokutsky wanted to set off for home at once so that he might prepare everything for the reception of his guests and the dinner to be offered them; he took his hat, but, strangely enough, it happened that he stayed on for some time. Meanwhile card tables were set up in the room. Soon the whole company was divided into parties of four for whist and sat down in the different corners of the general's room. Candles were brought; for a long time Chertokutsky was uncertain whether to sit down to whist or not, but as the officers began to press him to do so, he felt that it would be a breach of the rules of etiquette to refuse, and he sat down for a little while. By his side there appeared from somewhere a glass of punch which, without noticing it, he drank off instantly. After winning two rubbers Chertokutsky again found a glass of punch at hand and again without observing it emptied the glass, though he did say first: "It's time for me to be getting home, gentlemen, it really is time," but again he sat down to the second game.

Meanwhile conversation assumed an entirely personal character in the different corners of the room. The whist players were rather silent, but those who were not playing sat on sofas at one side and kept up a conversation of their own. In one corner a captain, with a cushion thrust under his back and a pipe between his teeth, was recounting in a free and flowing style his amatory adventures, which completely absorbed the attention of a circle gathered around him. One extremely fat landowner with short hands rather like overgrown potatoes was listening with an extraordinary mawkish air, and only from time to time exerted himself to get his short arm behind his broad back and pull out his snuffbox. In another corner a rather heated discussion sprang up concerning squadron drill, and Chertokutsky, who about that time twice threw down a jack instead of a queen, suddenly intervened in this conversation, which was not addressed to him, and shouted from his corner: "In what year?" or "Which regiment?" without observing that the question had nothing to do with the matter under discussion. Finally, a few minutes before supper, they stopped playing, though the games went on verbally and it seemed as though the heads of all were full of whist. Chertokutsky remembered perfectly that he had won a great deal, but he picked up nothing, and getting up from the tables stood for a long time in the attitude of a man who has found he has no handkerchief. Meanwhile supper was served. It need hardly be said that there was no lack of wines and that Chertokutsky was almost obliged to fill up his own glass at times because there were bottles standing on the right and on the left of him.

A very long conversation dragged on at table, but it was rather oddly conducted. One colonel who had served in the campaign of 1812 described a battle such as had certainly never taken place, and then, I am quite unable to say for what reason, took the stopper out of the decanter and stuck it in the pudding. In short, by the time the party began to break up it was three o'clock, and the coachmen were obliged to carry some of the gentlemen in their arms as though they had been parcels of groceries, and in spite of all his aristocratic breeding Chertokutsky bowed so low and with such a violent lurch of his head, as he got into his carriage, that he brought two burrs home with him on his mustaches.

At home everyone was sound asleep. The coachman had some difficulty in finding a footman, who conducted his master across the drawing room and handed him over to a chambermaid, in whose charge Chertokutsky made his way to his bedroom and got into bed beside his young and pretty wife, who was lying in the most enchanting way in a snow-white nightgown. The jolt made by her husband falling upon the bed awakened her. Stretching, lifting her eyelashes, and three times rapidly blinking her eyes, she opened them with a half-angry smile, but seeing that he absolutely declined on this occasion to show any interest in her, she turned over on the other side in vexation, and laying her fresh little cheek on her arm, soon afterward fell asleep.

It was at an hour which would not in the country be described as early that the young mistress of the house woke up beside her snoring spouse. Remembering that it had been nearly four o'clock in the morning when he came home, she did not like to wake him, and so, putting on her bedroom slippers which her husband had ordered for her from Petersburg, and with a white dressing gown draped about her like a flowing stream, she washed in water as fresh as herself and proceeded to dress for the day. Glancing at herself a couple of times in the mirror, she saw that she was looking very nice that morning. This apparently insignificant circumstance led her to spend two hours extra before the mirror. At last she was very charmingly dressed and went out to take an airing in the garden. As luck would have it, the weather was as lovely as it can only be on a summer day in the South. The sun, directly overhead, was blazing hot; but it was cool walking on the thick, dark paths, and the flowers were three times as fragrant in the warmth of the sun. The pretty young wife quite forgot that it was now twelve o'clock and her husband was still asleep. Already she could hear the after-dinner snores of two coachmen and one groom sleeping in the stable beyond the garden, but she still sat in a shady spot from which there was an open view of the road, and was absent-mindedly watching it, stretching empty and deserted into the distance, when all at once a cloud of dust appearing in that distance attracted her attention. Gazing intently, she soon discovered several carriages. The foremost was a light open carriage with two seats. In it was sitting a general with thick epaulets that gleamed in the sun, and beside him a colonel. It was followed by another carriage with seats for four in which were the major, the general's adjutant, and two officers facing. Then came the regimental chaise, familiar to everyone, at the moment in the possession of the fat major. The chaise was followed by another vehicle known as a *bon-voyage*, in which there were four officers seated and a fifth on their knees; then came three officers on excellent, dark bay dappled horses.

"Then they may be coming to us," thought the lady. "Oh, my goodness, they really are! They have turned at the bridge!" She uttered a shriek, clasped her hands, and ran right over the flower beds straight to her husband's bedroom; he was sleeping like the dead.

"Get up! Get up! Make haste and get up!" she shouted, tugging at his arm.

"What?" murmured Chertokutsky, not opening his eyes.

"Get up, angel! Do you hear, visitors!"

"Visitors? What visitors?" . . . Saying this he uttered a slight grunt such as a calf gives when it is looking for its mother's udder. "Mm . . ." he muttered: "stoop your neck, precious! I'll give you a kiss."

"Darling, get up, for goodness' sake, make haste! The general and the officers! Oh dear, you've got a burr on your mustache!"

"The general! So he is coming already, then? But why the devil did nobody wake me? And the dinner, what about the dinner? Is everything ready that's wanted?"

"What dinner?"

"Why, didn't I order it?"

"You came back at four o'clock in the morning and you did not say one word to me, however much I questioned you. I didn't wake you, precious, because I felt sorry for you, you had had no sleep! . . ."

The last words she uttered in an extremely supplicating and languishing voice.

Chertokutsky lay for a minute in bed with his eyes popping out of his head, as though struck by a thunderbolt. At last he jumped out of bed with nothing but his shirt on, forgetting that this was quite indecent.

"Oh, I am an ass!" he said, slapping himself on the forehead. "I invited them to dinner! What's to be done? Are they far off?"

"I don't know . . . I expect they will be here any minute."

"My love . . . hide yourself . . . Hey, who's there? You wretched girl, come in; what are you afraid of, you fool? The officers will be here in a minute: you say that your master is not at home, say that he won't be home at all, that he went out early in the morning . . . Do you hear? and tell all the servants the same; make haste!" Saying this, he hurriedly snatched up his dressing gown and ran to hide in the carriage house, supposing that there he would be in a position of complete security, but, standing in the corner of the carriage house, he saw that even there he might be seen. "Ah, this will be better," flashed through his mind, and in one minute he flung down the steps of the carriage standing near, jumped in, closed the door after him, for greater security covering himself with the leather apron, and lay perfectly still, curled up in his dressing gown.

Meanwhile the carriages drove up to the front steps. The general stepped out and shook himself; after him the colonel, smoothing the plume of his hat with his hands, then the fat major, holding his saber under his arm, jumped out of the chaise, the slim sublieutenants skipped down from the *bon-voyage* with the lieutenant who had been sitting on the others' knees, and, last of all, the officers who had been elegantly riding on horseback alighted from their saddles.

"The master is not at home," said a footman, coming out onto the steps.

"Not at home? He'll be back at dinner, I suppose?"

"No. His Honor has gone out for the whole day. He won't be back until tomorrow about this time, perhaps."

"Well, I'll be damned!" said the general. "What is the meaning of this?"

"What a joke!" said the colonel, laughing.

"No, really . . . how can he behave like this?" the general went on with displeasure. "Whew! . . . Damn it! . . . why, if he can't receive people, why does he ask them?"

"I can't understand how anyone could do it, your Excellency," a young officer observed.

"What, what?" said the general, who had the habit of always uttering this interrogative monosyllable when he was talking to an officer.

"I said, your Excellency, that it is not the way to behave!"

"Naturally . . . why, if anything has happened, he might let us know at any rate, or else not have asked us."

"Well, your Excellency, there's nothing we can do, we shall have to go back," said the colonel.

"Of course, there is nothing else to do. We can look at the carriage, though, without him; it is not likely he has taken it with him. Hey, you there! Come here, my man!"

"What is your pleasure?"

"Are you the stableboy?"

"Yes, your Excellency."

"Show us the new carriage your master got lately."

"This way, sir; come to the carriage house."

The general went to the carriage house with the officers.

"Shall I push it out a little? It is rather dark in here."

"That's enough, that's enough, that's right!"

The general and the officers stood around the carriage and carefully examined the wheels and the springs.

"Well, there is nothing special about it," said the general. "It is a most ordinary carriage."

"A very ugly one," said the colonel; "there is nothing good about it at all."

"I think, your Excellency, it is not worth four thousand," said the young officer.

"What?"

"I say, your Excellency, that I think it is not worth four thousand."

"Four thousand, indeed! why, it is not worth two, there is nothing in it at all. Perhaps there is something special about the inside . . . Unbutton the apron, my dear fellow, please."

And what met the officers' eyes was Chertokutsky sitting in his dressing gown, curled up in an extraordinary way. "Ah, you are here!" . . . said the astonished general.

Saying this he slammed the carriage door at once, covered Chertokutsky with the leather apron again, and drove away with the officers.

THE PORTRAIT[1]

PART I

Nowhere were so many people standing as before the little picture shop in Shchukin Court.[2] The shop did indeed contain the most varied collection of curiosities: the pictures were for the most part painted in oils, covered with dark green varnish, in dark-yellow gilt frames. A winter scene with white trees, an absolutely red sunset that looked like the glow of a conflagration, a Flemish peasant with a pipe and a broken arm, more like a turkey cock in frills than a human being—such were usually their subjects. To these must be added some engravings: a portrait of Khozrev-Mirza[3] in a sheepskin cap, and portraits of generals with crooked noses in three-cornered hats.

---

[1] This is the final (1842) version of the story. Because Mrs. Garnett translated only the earlier version (which appeared in 1835, as one of the pieces in *Arabesques*), this is an almost completely new translation—only about one hundred lines of the original having survived. The 1842 version is profoundly different from the earlier one; not even the artist's original name (Chertkov) being retained (it becomes Chartkov). The final version, for the most part, is less blatantly fantastic; it is infused with realistic elements (e.g., the portrait no longer simply disappears, but the word "stolen" is added and seriously alters the tone); the emphasis is shifted (from the fantastic and mysterious to the concepts of religion, retribution, and expiation—things with which Gogol was becoming more and more obsessed). Gogol knew of an Indian moneylender who catered to the actors in St. Petersburg, and one of the actors described his "bronze face" and singular eyes. (ed.)

[2] One of the numerous open-air markets in St. Petersburg. (ed.)

[3] A Persian prince (see p. 494, n. 2, for fuller comment). (ed.)

The doors of such shops are usually hung with bundles of pictures[4] which bear witness to the native talent of the Russian. On one of them was the Czarina Miliktrisa Kirbityevna,[5] on another the city of Jerusalem, over the houses and churches of which a flood of red color was flung without stint, covering half the earth, and two Russian peasants in big gloves kneeling in prayer. The purchasers of these creations were commonly few in number, but there was always a crowd looking at them. Some dissipated footman would usually be gaping at them with dishes from the restaurant in his hand for the dinner of his master, whose soup would certainly not be too hot. A soldier in a greatcoat, a cavalier of the flea market, with two penknives to sell, and a peddler woman from Okhta with a box filled with slippers would be sure to be standing before them. Each one would show his enthusiasm in his own way: the peasants usually point with their fingers; the soldiers examine them seriously; the footboys and the apprentices laugh and tease each other over the colored caricatures; old footmen in frieze overcoats stare at them simply because they offer somewhere to stop and gape; and the peddler women, young women from the villages, hasten there by instinct, eager to hear what people are gossiping about and to see what people are looking at.

At this time, Chartkov, a young artist who was passing by, paused involuntarily before the shop. His old overcoat and unfashionable clothes indicated that he was a man who devoted himself to his work with self-denying zeal and had not time to worry himself about clothes, which usually have a mysterious attraction for young people. He stopped before the shop, at first inwardly laughing at the grotesque pictures; at last he sank unconsciously into meditation: he began wondering to whom these productions were of use. That the Russian people should gaze at the Eruslan Lazereviches, at the Gluttons and Imbibers, on Foma and Erioma,[6] did not strike him as surprising: the subjects depicted were well within the grasp and comprehension of the people; but where were the purchasers of these gaudy, dirty oil paintings? Who wanted these Flemish peasants, these red and blue landscapes which bespoke pre-

---

[4] *Lubok*, cheap tricolored work dealing with popular subjects, e.g., a wistful girl, a forlorn soldier, a battle scene, comic figures. (ed.)

[5] Fairy princess of "Bova-Korolevich" ("Prince Bova"), a popular folktale. (ed.)

[6] Comic figures which were often the subject of the *Lubok*. (ed.)

tension to a rather high level of art, though its most profound degradation was displayed in them? If only they had been the works
of a precocious child obeying an unconscious impulse; in that event,
in spite of the intentional caricature of the design, one would have
perceived in them a certain intensity of feeling; but all that could
be found in them was a total lack of talent, the feeble, faltering,
dull incompetence of a born failure that impudently pushes himself among the arts, while his true place is among the lowest crafts,
a failure which is true, nevertheless, to its vocation, and drags its
trade into art. The same colors, the same manner, the same practiced, accustomed hand which seemed to belong to a crudely
fashioned automaton rather than to a man. He stood for a long time
before these grimy pictures without even thinking of them any
more; but meanwhile, the proprietor of the shop, a little drab man
in a frieze overcoat and with a beard which had not been shaved
since Sunday, had been nudging him for some time, bargaining
and discussing prices, without even knowing what pleased him or
what he was likely to buy.

"I'll take a white note[7] for these peasants, and for this little landscape. What art! It almost makes your eyes pop out! I just received
them from the factory; the varnish is not yet quite dry. Or here is
a winter scene—take the winter scene. It's only fifteen rubles!
The frame alone is worth more than that. What a winter scene!"
Here the art merchant tapped the canvas lightly with his finger as
if to demonstrate the fine merits of the winter landscape. "Shall I
tie them all up and take them to your place? Where do you live?
Hey, boy, give me some string!"

"Wait, brother, not so fast!" said the artist, recovering with a jolt
as he saw the enterprising dealer beginning in earnest to tie up the
pictures. He was a little ashamed not to take anything after being
in the shop for so long, and he said, "Wait a minute, I'll see if
there's anything I want here," and bending over, he began picking
up from the floor, from where they had been thrown in a heap,
worn, dusty old paintings, which evidently no longer were considered to be of value. Among these there were old family portraits,
whose descendants, probably, could no longer be found on earth,
totally unknown pictures on torn canvases, frames which had lost
their gilding; in short, all sorts of trash. But the painter began his

---

[7] Colloquial for twenty rubles. (ed.)

search, thinking to himself, "Perhaps I will find something." He had heard stories about pictures of the great masters having been found among the rubbish of popular print shops.

The dealer, perceiving that he was likely to be busy for some time, ceased his importunities, and, assuming his usual attitude and the proper expression which is its concomitant, once more took his position at the door of his shop, hailing the passers-by, and pointing to his store with one hand.

"Come in, friends, look at my pictures. Come in, come in! Just received them from the factory!" He shouted till he was hoarse, and generally in vain, had a long conversation with a rag merchant who was standing opposite him at the door of his shop, and finally, remembering that he had a customer in his shop, he turned his back on the public and again went inside. "Well, friend, have you selected anything?" The artist, however, had been standing motionless for some time before a portrait in a very large and once-magnificent frame, a frame which retained only a trace of its original gilt. The portrait was of an old man with a face of a bronze hue, thin and with high cheekbones; it seemed as if the features of his face were caught in a moment of convulsive agitation, and there was a puissance about the face which bespoke the fact that it was not of the north. The torrid south was imprinted upon the features. About his shoulders a voluminous Asiatic costume was draped. The portrait was dusty and had suffered damage, but Chartkov, after removing the dust which covered the face, could see undeniable evidence of a great artist. The portrait had apparently never been finished, but the strength of the artist's hand was amazing. The eyes were the most singular of all the features; it was apparent that the artist had used the full power of his brush and that all his care had been lavished on them. They seemed to glare, glare out of the portrait, destroying its harmony with their unnatural liveliness. When he carried the portrait to the door, the eyes glared with even more penetration, and the people before the shop were impressed almost the same way. A woman who was standing behind him cried, "He looks at you, he looks!" and she drew back. Chartkov experienced a discomforting feeling, a feeling that was inexplicable, and he put the portrait down on the floor.

"Well? You going to take the portrait?" said the dealer.

"How much?" asked the artist.

"Why quibble about it? I'll take seventy-five kopeks."

"No."

"How much will you give me?"

"Twenty kopeks," said the artist preparing to leave.

"What a price! Why, even the frame couldn't be bought for that! Perhaps you will return and buy it tomorrow. Sir, sir, come back! Add another ten kopeks. All right, take it! Take it for twenty kopeks. The only reason I sell it to you at that price is that, to be honest, you are my first customer today." Then the dealer gestured as if to say, "Ah well, so be it!"

Thus it was that Chartkov quite unexpectedly bought the old portrait, and at once he wondered, "Why did I buy it! Why do I need it?" But there was nothing Chartkov could do about it. He took the twenty-kopek note and gave it to the dealer, and carried home the portrait, under his arm. On the way home, he recalled that the note he had spent for it was his last. He grew depressed. Anger and a certain listlessness took possession of him at the same time. "Damn it! What a miserable world!" he said with the emotion of a man whose affairs have completely collapsed. And he walked toward home almost mechanically, faster than before, totally indifferent to everything. The red glow of sunset still lingered over half the sky; the houses which faced the sunset were faintly illuminated by its warm light, while the cold blue light of the moon grew more powerful. Light, half-transparent shadows were cast by houses and people, fell like long bars on the earth. More and more the artist began to glance at the sky, which was shimmering in a faint, translucent, uncertain light, and almost at the same moment there burst from his mouth the words, "What a delicate tone!" and the words, "Damn it! How upsetting!" He repositioned the portrait which was forever slipping from under his arm, and walked more quickly.

Exhausted, bathed in perspiration, he dragged himself to his home on the fifteenth row of Vasilievsky Island. He climbed the stairs, which were soaked with wash water and decorated with the footprints of dogs and cats. He knocked on the door. There was no answer. There was no one at home. He leaned against the window and determined to wait patiently, until, finally, the steps of a boy in a blue shirt sounded behind him. This was his servant, model, paint grinder, and scrubber of floors, and the one who dirtied the floors with his boots. The boy was called Nikita, and he spent all his free time in the streets. Nikita tried to position the key in the lock for a long time, a task made difficult by the darkness. Finally the door was opened, Chartkov entered his hall which, like the rooms of most artists, was unbearably cold, a circumstance which they hardly ever notice. Without giving his coat to Nikita, he went into his studio, a large, square but low room with frosted windowpanes, filled with all kinds of artistic rubbish: pieces of plaster hands, frames with canvas stretched over them, sketches begun and discarded, draperies thrown over chairs. He was extremely tired. He flung off his coat, absent-mindedly placed the portrait between two other pictures, and threw himself on a narrow sofa, a sofa which could hardly be determined to have been covered with leather, because a row of brass nails which had once fastened the leather to the frame of the sofa had long been standing by themselves, so that Nikita stuffed his dirty socks and shirts and all the dirty linen under it. Having stretched as far as it was possible to stretch on such a narrow sofa, Chartkov finally called for a candle.

"There are no more candles," said Nikita.

"Why not?"

"We didn't have any yesterday either," said Nikita. The artist remembered that there had indeed been no candles yesterday, and he calmed himself and grew silent. He allowed himself to be undressed, and he put on his old and very warm dressing gown.

"The landlord was here again," said Nikita.

"Well, he came because of money," Chartkov said, waving his hand.

"Well, he was not here alone," said Nikita.

"Who was with him?"

"I don't know who. Some policeman, it looked like."

"But why a policeman?"

"I don't know why," he said. "It's because you still haven't paid your rent."

"What will happen?"

"I don't know what will happen. He said, 'He will have to get out of the apartment if he can't pay.' They're both coming again tomorrow."

"Let them come," said Chartkov with mournful indifference, and melancholy gripped him.

Young Chartkov was an artist possessed of talent which augured a bright future; there were instances when his work bespoke his sharp observation, deep understanding, and a powerful inclination to draw closer to nature. "See here, brother," his professor said to him more than once, "you have talent. It would be shameful if you were to waste it, but you have no patience. If you happen to be attracted to something, you become so engrossed in it that everything else becomes meaningless, everything else becomes trivial, you won't even look at it. Be careful that you do not become a fashionable artist. Even now your colors seem to be gaudy and too blatant; your drawing is no longer strong, and many times it is very weak. The lines disappear;·you are already endeavoring to imitate fashionable light effects, because they impress the eye quickly and effectively. Be careful that you do not become merely an imitator of the English school.[8] Take care. The outside world begins to attract you. I have already noticed you sometimes wearing a dandyish scarf or a shiny hat.[9] I know how tempting the prospect is. It is possible to paint portraits for money, to paint fashionable little pictures that sell, but in that event talent is destroyed, not developed. Be patient, devote yourself to every piece of work. Forget about fineries. Let others make money; your own time will not fail to come."

The professor was partially correct. Sometimes our artist wanted to carouse, to show off, in a word, to display in some way the fact that he was still young, but, despite this tendency, he could always control himself. At times, when he took a brush in his hand, he could forget everything, and he could only tear himself away from the brush very reluctantly, as one is reluctant to wake from a beautiful dream. His taste improved perceptibly. He was not yet capable of fathoming all the profundities of Raphael, but he was already attracted to Guido's[10] powerful and swift brush, lingered before the portraits by Titian,[11] was enthralled by the Flemish masters. He was unable to see through the dark veil which hid the works of the old masters, but he already saw something in them, though in his

---

[8] Reference is to those who were led by Sir Joshua Reynolds (1723-92), an eminent portrait painter and first president of the Royal Academy. The works of the English school were especially noted for their dignity and expressiveness, and for the beauty of their coloring. (ed.)

[9] I.e., a new one. (ed.)

[10] Guido Reni (1575-1642), Italian artist famous for the voluptuous sentimentality of his baroque paintings. (ed.)

[11] Tiziano Vecellio (1477-1576), celebrated Venetian painter renowned for his sumptuous, coloristic style. (ed.)

heart he disagreed with the view of his professor that the pinnacle reached by the old masters was unattainable for the modern painter. It seemed to him that the nineteenth century had in many ways already surpassed their accomplishment, that the presentation of nature had somehow become more vivid, clearer, more intimate. In a word, he was reasoning as young people always reason who have already accomplished some understanding and recognize it with conscious pride. He was sometimes angered when he noticed that a foreign artist, a Frenchman or a German, sometimes not even a professional painter but only a skilled dauber, was able to cause a general commotion and to amass a fortune almost immediately. This did not concern him when he was completely absorbed in his work, for on those occasions he quite forgot food and drink and the whole world, but when dire need occurred, when he was devoid of funds with which to buy brushes and paints, and when his relentless landlord came to his apartment ten times a day to demand rent, then it was that the good fortune of wealthy painters appealed to his hungry imagination so strongly; it was then that the thought which so often passes through the mind of a Russian flashed through his: to totally surrender to grief, to devote himself to drink. And now he was almost in such a mood.

"Yes, be patient, be patient!" he repeated angrily. "But even patience has its limits. Be patient! But what am I to use for dinner tomorrow? No one will lend me any money, and even if I were to take all my drawings and sketches to a dealer, he wouldn't give me more than twenty kopeks for the lot of them. They have been of some use to me. I am convinced that not one of them was a waste of time. Each one taught me something. But what use is it? Sketches, drafts. It's an endless process. And without knowing my name who would buy my pictures? Who wants drawings from the antique or from life? Or my unfinished Psyche, or my nature studies, or my portrait of Nikita, though it is, in truth, damned superior to the portraits of the fashionable artists? And what's it all for? Why do I trouble myself and burden myself like a student learning his ABC's when I might be no less famous than the rest of them and make as much money as they do?"

At these words, the artist suddenly shuddered and grew pale; a terribly distorted face stared at him from behind the canvas. Two horrible eyes fixed themselves on him as if getting ready to devour him; a menacing expression was on the lips. Terrified, he wanted to scream and call Nikita who was already loudly snoring in his room. Suddenly, however, he stopped and laughed. The feeling of fear left him in an instant; it was the portrait he had bought and completely forgotten. The light of the moon, illuminating the room, fell upon it and invested it with a singular lifelike quality. He began examining and wiping the portrait. Moistening a sponge with water, he wiped the portrait with it, washing off almost all the accumulated and encrusted dust and dirt, hung it on the wall before him and, more than ever, wondered at the quite remarkable quality of the painting. Almost the whole face seemed to have come alive, and the eyes looked at him in a way that made him shudder, and jumping back, he exclaimed in a voice full of astonishment, "It looks, it looks at you with human eyes!" Suddenly he remembered he had long ago heard from his professor a story of a portrait by Leonardo da Vinci.[12] The great master regarded it as unfinished though he had labored on it for several years, but, despite that, Vasari[13] considered it the most complete and finished example of his art. The most finished thing about it was the eyes, which amazed Leonardo's contemporaries; the most minute, almost invisible veins were not neglected and were committed to the canvas. But here in the portrait now before him there was something strange. This was no longer art. The eyes actually destroyed the harmony of the portrait. They were alive, human! It was as if they had been cut from a living man and inserted in the canvas. Here was none of that sublime feeling of enjoyment which imbued the spirit at the sight of an artist's endeavors, regardless of how terrible the subject he may have put on canvas. There was a painful, joyless sense of anxiety instead. "What's wrong?" the artist had to ask himself. "After all, this is only an imitation of something from life. Where does this strange and discomforting feeling come from? Or is a literal depiction of nature a crime which must affect one like a shrill discordant shriek? Or if you paint objectively and without feeling on some pathetic subject, must it confront you in all its fearful reality, unillumined by the light of some intangible, hidden

---

[12] The reference is very probably to the Mona Lisa. There are also two sketches in which the eyes are singular: his study of the head of St. James (1496), in which the eyes are dominant, and his study of the head of St. Philip (done the same year), a profile, in which both the eyes and the mouth are prominent, but it is unlikely that Gogol knew these. (ed.)

[13] Giorgio Vasari (1511-74), Italian art historian and critic. (ed.)

thought? Will it appear to you with the realism which is displayed when, searching to understand the secrets of the beauty in man, you arm yourself with a scalpel and dissect a man's insides only to discover the man? Why is it that in the work of one artist, simple, lowly nature appears so illumined that there is no sense of degradation? On the contrary! It is very pleasurable for some reason, and later everything flows more quietly and smoothly around you. And yet, in the hands of another artist, the same subject seems low and sordid, though he was true to nature, too. Actually, there is nothing illuminating in it. Something is lacking in it, regardless of how beautiful it is. It is like a landscape in nature; if the sun is not in the sky, regardless of how magnificent it may be, there is something lacking."

He once again approached the portrait to examine those wonderful eyes, and again noticed with horror that they were once more staring at him. This was no imitation of nature. It was a strange kind of life that might have lit up the face of a corpse arisen from the grave. Was it the effect of moonlight which brought with it fantastic thoughts and dreams, transformed everything into strange shapes so different from what they appeared like in absolute daylight? Or was there some other cause? He suddenly became—and he himself didn't know why—fearful of remaining in the room by himself. He walked softly away from the portrait, trying not to look at it, but his effort was wasted; involuntarily his eyes glanced at it furtively. He finally became frightened of walking in the room. He had a strange feeling that someone would be walking up behind him at any moment, and, apprehensively, he kept glancing over his shoulder. He was not a coward, but his imagination and his nerves were sensitive, and he could not have explained to himself of what he was so afraid that evening. He sat down in a corner, but even there he had the feeling that someone would any minute be peering over his shoulder and into his face. Even Nikita's snoring, which resounded from the hall, did not mitigate his fear. Finally he got up timidly, without raising his eyes, went behind the screen, undressed, went to bed. Through the chinks in the screen he could see the illumination of the moon in the room, and he saw the portrait immediately in front of him, hanging on the wall. The eyes were fixed upon him, more terribly and meaningfully than ever, and it seemed as if they would look at nothing but him. Overpowered by a feeling of restlessness, he determined to get up from his bed, seized a sheet and, walking up to the portrait, covered it up completely.

This accomplished, he once more lay down on his bed, and began to think of the poverty and the miserable fate of the artist, of the thorny path that awaits him in this world. Meanwhile his eyes looked involuntarily through the chinks in the screen, at the portrait covered by the sheet. The glow of the moon accented the whiteness of the sheet, and it seemed to Chartkov that the terrible eyes were glaring through the cloth. Terror-stricken, he stared at it as if he wished to convince himself that it was all nonsense. But . . . in fact . . . the sheet had disappeared and . . . the portrait was completely uncovered and, ignoring everything else, it stared straight at him; stared right into his heart . . . His heart grew cold, and suddenly he saw that the old man began moving and, presently, supporting himself on the frame with both arms, he raised himself on his hands and, thrusting out his legs, he leaped out of the frame. . . . Through the chink in the screen only the empty frame was visible. There were footsteps in the room, and they were drawing ever closer to the screen. The poor artist's heart pounded more and more violently. Panting, almost breathless from fear, he awaited the appearance of the old man who would look around the screen at him. Behold! He did indeed look behind the screen, his bronze face no different from before, and his big eyes staring about. Chartkov tried to scream, but his voice failed him; he tried to move, to make some gesture, but his limbs were as if paralyzed. With gaping mouth and failing breath, he gazed at this terrible phantom of great height, wearing some kind of voluminous Asiatic robe, and waited to see what it would do next. The old man sat down almost on his very feet, and pulled something out from between the folds of his wide robe. A bag. The old man untied it, seized it at both ends, and shook it. Heavy rolls of money like large rolls of coins fell on the floor with a dull thud; blue paper was wrapped about each roll, and each was marked: *1,000 gold coins*. The old man stretched forth his long, bony hands from his wide sleeves, and began unwrapping the rolls. The gold glittered, but however great the artist's fear and depression had been, he could not keep from looking greedily at the gold, staring motionless at it as it appeared, gleaming and ringing lightly or dully in the bony hands, and as it was again wrapped up. Then he noticed that one roll had rolled farther than the rest and was near the leg of his bed, near his pillow. He grasped it almost convulsively and, in terror, glanced at the old man to see whether he had seen it. But the old man was too occupied to notice anything. He collected all his rolls, put them back in the bag, and went around the screen without even looking at Chartkov. Chartkov's heart beat wildly as he heard the sound of the retreating footsteps. He clasped the roll more firmly in his hand, every limb quivering, and suddenly he heard the footsteps approaching the screen again. The old man apparently had remembered that one of the rolls was missing. And behold! Again he looked around the screen at him. In despair, the artist grasped the roll in his hand with all his possible strength, exerted all his power to make a movement, shrieked, and . . . he awoke.

He was drenched in cold perspiration. His heart beat as violently as a heart could beat. His chest was constricted as though his last breath was about to leave it. "Was it only a dream?" he said, holding his head with both hands, but the incredibly lifelike appearance of the apparition was not at all like a dream. After he awoke, he saw the old man step inside the frame, and he even saw the skirts of his wide robe, and his hand could still feel that but a moment before there was something heavy in it. Moonlight bathed the room, and from out of the dark corners of the room it illuminated a canvas in one spot, in another the mold of a hand, in another a piece of drapery thrown over a chair, trousers and unclean boots. Then he saw that he was not lying in bed any longer, but that he was standing immediately before the portrait. How he had gotten there he had absolutely no idea, and he was even more surprised to find that the portrait was completely uncovered and the sheet was not to be seen. Frozen with terror, he stared at it and he saw that the human eyes were riveted upon him. Once more a cold sweat broke out on his face. He wanted to run away, but his feet were as if rooted to the earth, and he could see that this was not a dream. The old man's face moved and his lips began to project toward him, as though they wished to suck him in. . . . With a loud shriek of despair, Chartkov jumped back—and woke up.

"Was it a dream?" His heart was beating so that it was about to burst. He groped about him with his hands. Yes, he was lying in bed, and in exactly the same position in which he had fallen asleep. The screen was before him. Moonlight flooded the room. Through the chink of the screen the portrait, covered just as he had covered it, was visible. So this too was a dream? But his clenched fist still felt as though something had been in it. His heart beat violently, terrifyingly. The weight on his chest was unendurable. He set his eyes on the chink and stared steadily at the sheet. Behold! He saw clearly that the sheet began to unfold as though hands were pushing from beneath it and trying to throw it off. "Good God, what is this!" he screamed, crossing himself in despair—and woke up.

Was this also a dream? He sprang from his bed, frantic, half insane, and could not understand what was happening to him: was it the after-effects of a nightmare, or an evil spirit,[14] the raving born of fever, or a real apparition? Attempting to calm himself, to calm his overwrought nerves and the wildly flowing blood which pulsated through his veins, he went to the window and opened the pane. The cool fragrant breeze revived him. Moonlight was on the roofs and on the white walls of the houses, though small clouds passed often across the sky. Everything was quiet. From the distance, he could occasionally hear the sound of a carriage whose driver must have fallen asleep on his box in some obscure alley, lulled to sleep by his lazy nag while he waited for a belated passenger. He put his head out of the window and gazed for a long time. Already the approaching dawn was visible in the sky. At last he felt drowsy, shut the window, went back to his bed, and, like one truly exhausted, he fell into a sound sleep.

He awoke late, with the unpleasant feeling of a man who was stricken with coal-gas poisoning. He had a terrible headache. The room was dim; moisture imbued the air and was coming into the room through the cracks of the windows which were covered up with pictures and primed canvases. Depressed and sullen as a wet rooster, he sat down on his dilapidated sofa without any idea of what to do, what to plan, and finally he remembered his dream. The dream, as he remembered it, became so alarmingly real that he was not sure that it had only been a dream or the result of delirium, and whether there was not indeed something else involved, perhaps an apparition. He removed the sheet and examined the portrait by the light of day. The eyes, truthfully, were peculiarly striking and alive, but there was nothing in them that was singularly terrible, and yet an indescribable feeling of uneasiness persisted.

---

[14] *Domovoi*, either a good or evil spirit that lives in the house. A demon, goblin. (ed.)

He could not be certain that it had all been a dream. He could not keep from feeling that there must have been some terrible fragment of reality within the dream. In the old man's look and in the expression on his face, there was something which bespoke his having been with the artist during the night. Chartkov's hand still felt the weight which had so recently been in it, as if someone had only a minute before snatched it away from him. He had a peculiar sensation that if he had managed to grasp the roll more firmly in his hand it would have remained there even after he awoke.

"Good God, if only I had part of that money!" he said, sighing deeply, and in his imagination he could see all those rolls again, each fascinatingly inscribed: *1,000 gold coins,* pouring out of the bag. The rolls opened up, there was a gleam of gold, and they were wrapped up again. He sat without moving, his eyes staring at nothing, as if he was unable to tear his thoughts away from such a vision, like a child who sits in front of a plate of candy and, with watering mouth, watches other people eating it.

Soon there was a knock on his door which brought him back to reality with unpleasant swiftness. The landlord and a policeman of the district came in, and it is well known that the policeman's appearance is more disturbing to the poor than the presence of a petitioner is to the wealthy. The landlord of the small house in which Chartkov lived resembled the other people who owned houses somewhere in the fifteenth row in Vasilievsky Island, on the Petersburg side, or in some remote corner of Kolomna—people who are very numerous in Russia and whose character is as difficult to describe as the color of a threadbare frock coat. He had been a captain in his youth, and a bully, and a master in the art of flogging. He had served in the civil service. He was stupid and rather foppish, but not without some efficiency; but in his old age he combined all of these different peculiarities of his character into a kind of uniform obtuseness. He was a widower for some time, and he had long been retired. There was no longer anything of the dandy about him, and his temperament was no longer cantankerous. Now he cared only for drinking tea and gossiping as he did so. He walked around his room snuffing the ends of his candles, calling punctually on his tenants for the rent at the end of each month, and he went out into the street, key in hand, to look at the roof of his house, and sometimes he chased the caretaker out of his den where he had hidden himself to take a nap; in brief, he was a retired army officer who after the turmoils and dissoluteness of his life, was left with nothing more than a few trivial habits.

"Please see for yourself, Varukh Kuzmich," the landlord said, gesturing with his hands as he turned to the policeman. "He simply doesn't pay his rent; he does not pay!"

"How do you expect me to pay when I have no money? Be patient and I will pay you."

"I can't wait, my friend," said the landlord angrily, gesturing with the key in his hand. "Lieutenant Colonel Potogonkin has been here seven years; Anna Petrovna Bukhmisterova rents the coach house and stable, except for two stalls, and has three servants. . . . That's the sort of tenants I have. I say to you honestly that this is not a place where I have difficulty collecting rent. Will you please pay your rent immediately or leave."

"Well," said the policeman with a slight shake of the head as he put his finger on one of the buttons of his uniform, "if you've rented the rooms, you have to pay."

"What am I to pay with? That's the question. I haven't got a copper right now."

"Then, in that case, you'd better satisfy the demands of Ivan Ivanovich by giving him some of your pictures," said the policeman. "Maybe he will agree to take the pictures."

"No thank you, my dear fellow, no pictures. If there were some pictures of holy subjects that one could hang on a wall, that wouldn't be so bad, or if there was a picture of a general with a star, or Prince Kutuzov's portrait,[15] but this fellow has painted the peasant, the peasant in a shirt, the peasant who grinds his paint! The idea of painting the portrait of that pig! I'll give it to him! He's been removing all the nails from the bolts, the rogue! Just look at these subjects! Here's a picture of his room. It would not be bad if he had at least chosen a clean and well-furnished room, but he has painted this one with all the filth and rubbish which he has collected. Look at how he has messed up my room! Look! And some of my tenants have been in my house for more than seven years! The Lieutenant Colonel, Anna Petrovna Bukhmisterova. . . . No, I tell you that there is nothing in the world that is a worse tenant than an artist. He lives like a pig!"

---

[15] (1745-1813), Russian field marshal who distinguished himself against the Turks and against Napoleon. (ed.)

And the poor artist had to listen to all of this patiently. The policeman meanwhile amused himself by examining the pictures and the sketches, indicating at once that he was more sensitive than the landlord and that he was not insensible to artistic impressions.

"Aha!" he said, tapping a canvas on which there was a picture of a nude. "This one is—lively. But why does she have that black mark under her nose? Did she use snuff?"

"Shadow," Chartkov said angrily, without looking at him.

"You should have put it in another place. It's too conspicuous under the nose," said the policeman. "And whose portrait is this?" he went on, approaching the portrait of the old man. "It's terrible, too terrible. Was he really so terrifying? Why, he actually sees through you! What a Gromoboy! [16] Who modeled for this?"

"Ah! It is . . ." said Chartkov and did not finish his sentence. He heard a loud crack. The policeman had held the frame too tightly in his policeman's hands, and the molding on the side broke and fell with a loud noise, and with it fell a roll wrapped in blue paper. Chartkov's eyes fastened on the inscription: *1,000 gold coins,* and like a madman he flew to it to pick it up, seized the roll, and clasped it convulsively in his hand, which sank from the weight.

"Wasn't that the sound of money?" the policeman asked, having heard the noise of something falling on the floor, but not being fast enough to see what it was because of the rapidity with which Chartkov had picked it up.

"What concern is it of yours whether I have anything or not?"

"It's my concern because you should pay your landlord the rent you owe him at once. You have money but you won't pay."

"I'll pay him today."

"Why didn't you pay him before? Why do you make all this trouble for your landlord? And why are you bothering the police?"

"I didn't want to touch that money. I'll pay him all I owe this evening and then I'll leave this apartment tomorrow. I will not stay with this kind of a landlord."

"So, Ivan Ivanovich, he will pay you," the policeman said, turning to the landlord. "But if you are not fully satisfied this evening, then I will be very sorry, Mr. Painter." Having said this, he put

---

[16] Hero of a ballad who sold his soul to the devil, by V. A. Zhukovsky (1783-1852). (ed.)

on his three-cornered hat and walked out into the hall followed by the landlord, whose head was bowed as though he were engaged in meditation.

"Thank God the devil has taken him away!" said Chartkov when he heard the hall door shut. He looked out into the hall and, because he wanted to be alone, he sent Nikita off on some errand. Then he locked the door behind him and began, with a wildly beating heart, to unwrap the roll of coins when he got back to his room.

The roll consisted of coins which were all new and glistening like fire. Almost beside himself, he sank down before the pile of gold, asking himself, "Isn't this all a dream?" There were precisely one thousand coins in the roll, which looked exactly as he had seen it in his dream. He turned them over in his hand and looked at them closely for some time without regaining his composure. In his imagination all sorts of tales were conjured up, of hidden treasures, cabinets with secret drawers left by ancestors to their spendthrift descendants in the firm belief that the money would restore their fortune. He began to think that perhaps some grandfather might have wanted to leave a present for his grandchild, and had hidden it in the frame of the family portrait. Filled with such romantic ideas he began to wonder whether this did not have some mysterious connection with his fate. Wasn't the existence of the portrait tied in with his own existence, and wasn't its very acquisition by him due to some kind of predestination? He began to examine the frame with great curiosity. There was a cavity on one side, so skillfully and neatly hidden by a little board that, if the heavy hand of the policeman had not smashed through it, the gold coins might have remained hidden forever. Examining the portrait again, he was once more struck by the remarkable workmanship and the extraordinary treatment of the eyes; they no longer seemed frightening, but each time he looked at them he experienced unpleasant feelings. "No," he said to himself, "regardless of whose grandfather you are, I will put you behind glass and I'll get you a gilt frame." And then he put his hand on the heap of gold piled before him, and his heart raced at the feel of it. "What will I do with them?" he said, staring at the coins. "Now I am free of worry for at least three years. I can shut myself up in my room and work. I have enough money for paints now, for dinner, and for tea, and for rent—no one will trouble me or disturb me now. I'll buy myself an excellent mannequin. I'll order a plaster torso. I'll model feet. I will set up a Venus. I will buy copies of the best pictures. And if I work for three years without hurrying, without being concerned about selling my pictures, I will be better than them all, and I may become a first-rate artist."

That was what he said to himself at the prompting of his good judgment, but within him another voice, growing ever louder, was making itself heard. And when he glanced at the gold again, it was something quite different that was said by his twenty-two years and ardent youth. Everything which he had before looked at with envious eyes was now within his reach. That which he had from afar looked at longingly could now be his. How his heart beat when he merely thought of it! To be able to wear a stylish coat, to be able to eat well after so long a fast, to be able to rent a fine apartment, to be able, at any time, to go to the theater, to the confectioners, or to other places, and seizing his money he suddenly found himself in the street. The very first thing he did was to go to a tailor and clothe himself in fresh attire from head to foot and, like a child, he admired himself incessantly. He bought perfumes and pomades, and then he rented the first elegant apartment, one with mirrors and plate-glass windows, which he came across on Nevsky Prospekt, and without bickering over the price. On an impulse he bought an expensive *lorgnette* and a huge quantity of neckties of every kind, many more than he could possibly need. Then he went to a hairdresser's, and he had his hair waved; he rode twice through the city without any object in mind; he ate an enormous amount of candy at the confectioner's; and he went to a French restaurant in town about which he had heard rumors that were as vague as the rumors concerning the Chinese Empire. And there he dined in majestic style, with his arms akimbo, looking disdainfully at the other diners, and continually fixing his hair in the mirror. He drank a bottle of champagne which had, up to this time, been known to him only through hearsay. The wine went to his head, and he went into the street, alacritous, pugnacious, as though he were the devil's best friend, according to the Russian expression. He strutted along the sidewalk ogling everyone through his *lorgnette*. He caught sight of his old professor on the bridge, and he dashed past him as if he did not see him, leaving the astounded professor quite flabbergasted, rooted to the spot, his face looking like a question mark.

That very same evening everything Chartkov owned—easels, canvas, pictures—was moved to his new elegant apartment. He arranged the best of them in conspicuous places, and threw the worst of them into a corner, and he promenaded up and down the handsome rooms, constantly looking at himself in the mirrors. An inexorable desire to become immediately famous and show the world how great he was took hold of him. He could already hear the shouts. "Chartkov! Chartkov! Have you seen Chartkov's picture? How well he paints! How much talent he has!" He paced the rooms in a state of exaltation, unconscious of where he walked. The next day, taking ten gold coins with him, he went to see the publisher of a popular daily whom he wanted to ask for assistance. The journalist received him with great cordiality, and at once called him "Most respected sir," squeezed both his hands, made careful inquiries as to his name, birthplace, and address, and on the very next day, there appeared in the paper, below a notice of some newly invented tallow candles, an article under the following heading:

CHARTKOV'S ENORMOUS TALENT

We are honored to inform the cultured readers of the capital of a discovery which is highly desirable in every respect. All are agreed that there are very many physiognomies and faces among us, but up till this time there was no way of immortalizing them on canvas. This need has now been satisfied. An artist has been found who combines all desirable qualities. The beauty can now feel assured of being depicted with all the grace of her spiritual charms, bewitchingly as a butterfly fluttering among spring flowers. The respectable father of a family can now behold himself as he is surrounded by all the members of his family. The merchant, the warrior, citizens, statesmen—hurry, hurry from your journey, from your visits to your friends, to your cousins, to the glittering bazaar; hurry to him, to this great artist, from wherever you may be. The magnificent establishment of the artist, Nevsky Prospekt . . . contains portraits from his brush which are worthy of Van Dyck or Titian. One does not know which one to admire most, the reality and likeness to the originals or the extraordinary artistry and freshness of the coloring. Hail to you, my artist, you have drawn a winning number in the lottery. Long live Andrei Petrovich! (The journalist liked familiarity). Glorify yourself and us. We know how to value you, and we are certain that great popularity and wealth—though some of our fellow journalists seem to despise the latter—will be your reward. . . .

The artist read this notice with absolute delight. His face beamed. He was being discussed in print. It was a novelty to him, and he reread the notice several times. He was extremely flattered by the comparison to Van Dyck and Titian, and very pleased by the phrase, "Long live Andrei Petrovich." To be called in print by both his Christian name and patronymic was an honor that he had never known before. He paced up and down the room quickly, running his fingers through his hair, and sat down in a chair for a moment, only to get up and then to seat himself on the sofa, each moment anticipating how he would receive ladies and gentlemen. He walked up to a canvas and swept his brush grandly over it with a graceful movement of his hand.

The next day his doorbell rang and he ran to open the door. A lady, accompanied by a footman in a livery that was fur-lined, entered, and her daughter, a young girl of eighteen, followed her in.

"Are you Monsieur Chartkov?" the lady asked. The artist bowed.

"So much is being written about you. Your portraits are considered to be absolutely wonderful." After these introductory words the lady raised her *lorgnette* to her eyes and glanced quickly over the walls which were bare. "Where are your portraits?"

"I've had them taken away," said the artist, somewhat embarrassed, "I just recently moved into this apartment and that's why it is that they are still on the way . . . they have still not arrived."

"Were you in Italy?" asked the woman, looking at him through the *lorgnette* because there was no other object she could point it at.

"No, I have not been there, but I have always had the desire . . . I have put it off for a while . . . Please, here is an armchair. Aren't you tired?"

"Thank you. I have been sitting in my carriage for some time. Aha, finally I see one of your works," said the woman running to the opposite wall and looking through her glass at his sketches, studies, perspectives, and portraits which were standing on the floor. "*C'est charmant, Lise, venez-ici!*[17] Look, a room in the style of Teniers.[18] Do you see, everything is in disorder! A table, a bust on it, a hand, a palette. Do you see the dust here? Do you see how the dust is painted? *C'est charmant!* And here on the other canvas

---

[17] "That's charming, Lise, come here!" (ed.)
[18] David Teniers (1582-1649), Flemish painter who usually selected homely tavern scenes, rustic games, etc., for subjects. (ed.)

there is a woman who is washing her face. *Quelle jolie figure.*[19] Ah, a little peasant, a muzhik in a Russian shirt! See, a little muzhik! So you don't confine yourself exclusively to portraits?"

"Oh, that is only trash, just experiments, just studies."

"Tell me please, what is your opinion of our contemporary painters? Isn't it really true that there are none like Titian? The strength of colors is lacking, that . . . that . . . I'm sorry that I can't express it in Russian." (The lady was a great admirer of painting, and she had, armed with her *lorgnette*, wandered through all of the Italian galleries.) "But Monsieur Nohl,[20] ah, what a remarkable painter! What extraordinary talent! I find that there is even more expression in his faces than in Titian's. Do you know Monsieur Nohl?"

"Who is this Nohl?" asked the artist.

"Monsieur Nohl? Ah, that is talent! He did my daughter's portrait when she was only twelve years old. You must absolutely come and see it. Lise, you will show him your album. You know, we came here specifically so that you might begin her portrait immediately."

"With pleasure. I am ready right now." He immediately pulled out the easel and a piece of canvas which was already on it, and, his palette in hand, he gazed on the pale little face of the daughter. If he had been an authority on human nature he might at once have seen in it the first traces of a childish passion for balls, the dawning of unhappiness and misery during the long waiting periods before and after dinner, of a desire to promenade new clothes, the heavy traces of uninspired application to various arts which her mother insisted upon so that her soul and her sensitivity could be uplifted. But the only thing the artist saw was this tender face, so alluring a subject for his brush; a body of porcelain transparency, a charming, barely visible languor, a delicate white neck, and an aristocratically slender figure. And he prepared himself beforehand to triumph, to display the brilliance of his brush, because, before this time, he had dealt with only the harsh features of coarse models, the severe lines of classic masters. In his mind he already envisioned how this delicate face would turn out.

"You know," said the lady with a very rapturous expression on

---

[19] "That's a lovely face." (ed.)
[20] Almost certainly intended satirically. The name means "zero" in Russian. (ed.)

her face, "I would like . . . she has on this dress which I don't think is very flattering. I'd like her to be dressed quite simply, and to have her sit under the shade of a tree with fields in the background or just the woods. I don't, you see, want anything in the picture that might indicate that she goes to balls or fashionable parties. Our balls, you know, so murder the spirit, and murder the last trace of feeling. Simplicity, more simplicity!" Alas, it could be clearly seen from the faces of the mother and daughter that they had so exerted themselves dancing at balls that they were now like wax figures.

Chartkov began working. He seated the model, thought a minute, waved his brush through the air, screwed up his eyes a little, stepped back a little, studied the young girl from a distance, and finished the sketching in an hour. Feeling content with his work, he began to paint. The work so fascinated him that he forgot everything else. He even forgot the presence of the aristocratic ladies and began to display some artistic mannerisms, uttering strange sounds, occasionally humming, as is common with an artist who is totally immersed in what he is doing. Without the slightest ceremony, with one movement of his brush, he made the sitter raise her moving head which, because she was fatigued, was beginning to express obvious signs of absolute weariness.

"Enough, that's enough for the first time!" said the lady.

"No, please, just a little more," said the artist, forgetting himself.

"No, it is time to stop! Lise, it is already three o'clock!" said the lady, taking out a watch that hung from her waist on a gold chain. "Ah, how late it is," she said.

"Just a moment," said Chartkov with the innocence and pleading voice of a child. Despite this, the lady did not seem amenable to this proposition. She promised instead to stay for a greater length of time at the next sitting.

"That is irritating," said Chartkov to himself. "My hand had just got involved with it," and he recalled how no one interrupted or stopped him when he worked in his studio on Vasilievsky Island. Nikita used to sit without moving in one spot; you could paint him as long as you desired to. Yes, he even slept in the position which you had him take. Unsatisfied, Chartkov laid his brush and palette on the chair and, in irritation, paused before the portrait.

A compliment which the society woman paid him roused him from his reverie. He ran quickly to the door to show them out. On the stairs he received an invitation to dine with them the next week, and he returned to his room with a happy face. The aristocratic lady had totally charmed him. Before this time he had conceived of such people as being completely unapproachable, as people who were born only to ride in wondrous carriages with footmen dressed in livery and stylish coachmen, and to be disinterested in the poor man with the cheap coat trudging along on foot, and now, suddenly, one of those beings had been in his room, he was painting her portrait, he had received an invitation to dine in an aristocratic house. He was absolutely drunk from happiness, and he rewarded himself with a first-rate dinner and a visit to the theater, and afterwards, for no reason in particular, he rode through the city in a carriage.

During all these days, his ordinary work never occurred to him at all. He prepared only for the next visit, and waited for the moment when the bell would ring. Finally the lady and her pale daughter appeared again. He seated them, pulled the canvas forward with a certain bravado, and began to paint after some show of affectation. The sunny day and the bright light were very helpful. In his dainty sitter he saw a great deal which, if he could capture it and put it on canvas, would make the portrait very valuable. He perceived that he might create something rare if only he could accurately reproduce everything which was now before his eyes. His heart throbbed faster when he anticipated capturing something which others had not yet seen. He was completely engrossed in his work, again totally absorbed in his painting, and once more he forgot that the sitter was an aristocrat. With heaving chest, he saw how he had achieved the presentation of those delicate features and the almost transparent body of the seventeen-year-old girl.[21] He captured every shade, the slight sallowness, the almost imperceptible blueness under the eyes, and he was making ready to paint in a little pimple on her forehead when he suddenly heard the mother's voice.

"Ah, are you going to paint that? It's really unnecessary, and in several spots it's quite yellow, and here there are dark spots." The artist tried to explain that the spots and the yellow brought out the muted and pleasing tones of her face. He was told that they did not bring out the tones at all and that this was merely his impression.

---

[21] Another example of Gogol's not infrequent inconsistency. The girl's age was given as eighteen several pages earlier. (ed.)

"But," said the good-natured artist, "permit me to add a bit of yellow to this spot." But he was not allowed to do this. He was told that Lise was not quite well that day, that she was ordinarily never sallow and that, in fact, her face was always remarkably distinguished for its fresh color. With heavy heart, Chartkov began erasing what he had painted on the canvas. Many almost imperceptible traits disappeared, and with them a part of the resemblance disappeared as well. Apathetically, he added to the canvas that prosaic coloring which is put on mechanically and which gives to a face drawn from life something coldly ideal, something resembling that which is found in paintings in art schools. But the lady was satisfied when the colors she had objected to were removed. She merely expressed surprise that the artist was taking so long, and added that she had been told that he finished a portrait in two sittings. Chartkov could not think of an answer for this. The ladies got up and prepared to leave. Chartkov put his brush aside, walked them to the door, and then, for a long while, stood dejectedly before the portrait.

Chartkov stared stupidly at the portrait, his head full of those soft feminine features, those shades, the ethereal tints which he had copied and which his brush had now destroyed.

Imbued with these thoughts, he put the portrait to one side and searched for the head of Psyche which he had sketched on canvas a long time before. It was a pretty, girlish face, cleverly painted, but entirely idealized, with the cold, prosaic features which belonged to no living being. Because he had nothing to do, he began retouching it, putting into it all that he had observed in his aristocratic sitter. Those features, shadows, and tones which he had noted, appeared on it in the refined form in which they appear when the artist, after closely studying nature, surrenders to her and produces a work of art which is comparable to her own.

Psyche began to come alive, and the faintly dawning idea began gradually to be clothed in a visible form. The type of face of the aristocratic young lady was unconsciously transferred to Psyche, and because she had a unique expression, it could be considered as truly original. He seemed to make use of certain singular features of his sitter and of the total impression that the original suggested to him, and he devoted himself entirely to his own work. It was the only thing that occupied his thoughts for the next few days, and while working on this picture, the ladies surprised him. The picture was still on its easel because he had not had time to remove it. Both ladies uttered a cry of joy and clasped their hands in amazement.

"Lise, Lise, ah, how like you! *Superbe! Superbe!* What a wonderful idea to dress her in a Greek costume. Oh, what a surprise!"

Chartkov did not know how to disillusion the ladies of their pleasant error. Shamefacedly, with drooping head, he muttered, "This is Psyche."

"As Psyche? *C'est charmant!*" The mother said with a smile, and her daughter smiled too. "Admit it, Lise. Doesn't it make you happy to be painted as Psyche rather than in any other way? *Quelle idée délicieuse!* [22] What art! It's a Correggio! [23] I must admit that although I had of course read and heard of you, I never thought you had so much talent. You absolutely have to paint me too." Obviously, the mother also wanted to be painted as some sort of Psyche.

What am I to with them? thought the artist. If they insist that it is so, let it be so. And he said aloud, "Would you mind posing for a few minutes? I'd like to touch it up here and there."

"Ah, I'm afraid you will . . . it is so much like her now!"

But the artist realized that the mother was fearful lest he add yellow tones to the face, and he reassured them by saying that he wished only to add to the brilliance and expression of the eyes. In truth, however, he was quite ashamed, and he wanted to impart a little more likeness to the original so that he might not be accused of barefaced fraud and, indeed, at length the features of the pale young girl did appear more clearly in Psyche's face. "Enough," said the mother, becoming anxious that the resemblance might be too clearly expressed. The artist was paid in every possible way: smiles, money, flattery, gentle pressure of the hands, invitations to dinner—in a word, he was overwhelmed with a thousand flattering words.

The portrait created a sensation in the city. It was exhibited by the lady to all her friends. Everyone admired the ability of the artist to depict the likeness and, at the very same time, to bestow additional beauty on the original. It should be understood, of course, that this latter remark was motivated by a slight tinge of envy. And suddenly Chartkov was overwhelmed with work.

---

[22] "What a delicious idea!" (ed.)
[23] Antonio Allegri da Correggio (1494-1534), great Italian painter of mythological frescoes. (ed.)

It was as if everyone in the city wanted a portrait done by him. The doorbell rang continuously, and from a particular point of view this might even be considered beneficial because it offered him continuous practice with numbers of different faces. Unfortunately, however, they consisted of people who were difficult to please, busy, harassed people, or people who belonged to the world of society and who were consequently more occupied than others and, therefore, extremely impatient. From all quarters of the city the demand arose that the portrait should be done quickly and be done well. Chartkov knew that it was totally impossible to complete his work, that, indeed, it had become necessary to modify his technique so that he could capture only that which was obvious and general and not expend effort painting delicate details. In short, to faithfully represent complete nature was wholly out of the question. It should also be added that most of those who sat for him made many conditions on different points. The ladies insisted that mind and character should be the chief qualities represented in their portraits, and that nothing else was important; that all angles should be rounded and that everything uneven should be smoothed away and, if possible, even completely removed. In a word, they demanded that their face should cause viewers to stare and should provoke admiration, indeed, if not cause them to fall in love with it immediately. Because of this those who sat for him sometimes assumed expressions which completely amazed Chartkov: one made an effort to express melancholy; another, meditation; another desired to make her mouth appear small regardless of the cost, and she so puckered it up that it finally looked like a dot about as large as a pinhead. Despite it all, they demanded that the portraits bear strong resemblance to the original and be completely natural. As for the men, they were no better than the ladies: one insisted upon being painted with an energetic, masculine turn to his head; another on being painted with upturned and inspired eyes; a lieutenant of the guard insisted absolutely that Mars be visible in his eyes; an official in the civil service posed in his full height so that he might express honesty and nobility in his face, and so that his hand might rest on a book in which the following words, plainly printed, stood out: "He always stood for truth." At first, demands such as these threw the artist into cold perspiration: he felt that he had to think it over, to consider it, and yet there was terribly

little time for that. Finally he acquired the knack of it and no
longer concerned himself with such questions. A word was sufficient to indicate to him how someone wanted a portrait painted.
If a man insisted that Mars was to appear in his face, Mars appeared;
those who wanted to look like Lord Byron, he painted in Byronic
pose and attitude. If the ladies wanted to be shown as Corinne,[24]
Undine,[25] Aspasia,[26] he avidly agreed and imaginatively supplied
an adequate measure of good looks, which as everyone knows can
do no harm, and for the sake of which an artist may even be forgiven for any lack of resemblance. Soon he began to amaze himself with the rapidity and verve of his brush, and of course, those
who sat for him were ecstatic, and they proclaimed him a genius.
Chartkov, in every sense of the word, became a fashionable painter.
He dined out, escorted ladies to the art galleries, and even began
to walk and to dress as a fop, and he was heard to express the opinion that an artist must belong to society, that he must uphold the
honor of his profession, that artists usually dress like shoemakers,
that they do not conduct themselves properly, that they lack good
taste, and that they are devoid of sophistication. At home in his
studio everything was exceedingly tidy and clean. He employed
two marvelous footmen, tutored dandyish pupils, changed his costume several times a day, allowed his hair to be waved, concerned
himself greatly with improving his manners, devoted a great deal
of time to adorning his appearance in every possible way so that
he would produce a pleasurable impression on the ladies. In a
word, it would have been quite impossible for anyone to now recognize that this was the once-modest artist who had previously
toiled in obscurity in his squalid quarters in Vasilievsky Island.
He was opinionated about art and artists. He declared that too
much credit had been bestowed upon the old masters and that
all that the artists could paint before Raphael was herrings, not
figures; that the idea that there was anything holy about them
existed only in the imagination of those who viewed them, and
that not even Raphael himself always painted well, and that tradition was responsible for the fame attached to many of his works;

---

[24] Heroine of a novel by Mme Germaine de Staël (1776-1817). *Corinne*,
published in 1807, was eminently successful. (ed.)
[25] Heroine of a popular fairy tale, *Undine*, published in 1811, by Friedrich
de La Motte-Fouqué (1777-1843). (ed.)
[26] The beautiful and learned Greek mistress of Pericles (5th century B.C.)
(ed.)

that Michaelangelo was a braggart because he chose merely to display his knowledge of anatomy, and that there was not any grace about him, and that, in fact, for real brilliance and power of drawing and splendor of colors, you only had to look at the last century. And here, quite naturally, the question involved him personally. "No, I can't understand why other artists slave and work with such difficulty. In my opinion, a man who labors over a picture for months is not an artist at all, he's a hack. He's devoid of talent. Genius works boldly, rapidly." Turning to his visitors he said, "This is a portrait which took me only two days to paint, I did this head in one day, I did this in a few hours, and this only took little more than an hour. No, I confess that I do not recognize as art anything which adds one line to another laboriously. That is hardly art; that is a trade." And in this manner, he lectured those who came to see him, and the visitors marveled at the strength and power of his works, and uttered exclamations of surprise upon hearing how quickly he produced his pictures and said to each other, "That's talent, real talent. Look how he speaks, see how his eyes flash. *Il y a quelque chose d'extraordinaire dans toute sa figure!*" [27]

The artist was flattered to listen to such comments. When the papers contained a notice praising his work he was as delighted as a child, even though his money had bought the praise. Everywhere he went he carried the press clippings with him, showed them to his friends and acquaintances with a practiced air of casualness, and this, in a good-natured, naïve way, pleased him. His words and orders increased as his fame did. He was growing weary of always painting the same portraits over and over again in the same attitudes and poses which he knew quite by heart. Now he painted with no interest in what he was doing, drawing a rough likeness of a head and giving it to his pupils for the finishing touches. In the beginning he had tried to find a new pose for everyone who sat for him, to startle and surprise everyone by the power of his work and the effect achieved. Now even this was devoid of pleasure. His brain was exhausted from planning and thinking. He soon could do it no longer; he did not have the time. The irregular mode of living and society, in which he played the role of a man of the world, estranged him from thought and work.

---

[27] "There is something extraordinary written on his face." (ed.)

His work grew dim and indifferent and, without feeling, he began to paint monotonous, well-defined, exhausted forms. The uniform, lifeless, forever immaculate and, as it were, buttoned-up faces of the government officials, soldiers, and statesmen did not offer his brush adequate scope. The brush forgot how to represent magnificent draperies and strong emotion and passion, and as for composition, dramatic effect and its elevated purpose, there was nothing to be said. The only thing he saw before him was a uniform, a corsage, or a dress coat before which the artist is unmoved, and before which all imagination withers and dies. Even his own peculiar merits vanished from his work; and yet he continued to enjoy fame, this despite the fact that experts and artists merely shrugged their shoulders when they saw his latest paintings. Some who had known Chartkov before could not understand how the talent which was so clearly visible before had now been dissipated, and they tried in vain to solve the enigma of how a man at the peak of his power could suddenly find himself without his gift.

But the intoxicated artist did not hear this criticism. He was already approaching the age of dignity, in mind and in years. He began to grow heavier. He saw adjectives in the papers: "Our honored Andrei Petrovich; our distinguished Andrei Petrovich." And he began to receive offers for important positions in the civil service; he was invited to serve on boards of examiners and on committees. He began, as is usual in maturity, to defend Raphael and the old masters, not really because he had become absolutely convinced of their transcendent merits, but in order to snub the younger artists. He began, as all those who have attained maturity always begin, to indiscriminately accuse all young people of immorality and vicious thoughts, and began to believe that everything in the world is commonplace and simple, that there is no such thing as revelation from on high, and that everything essential can be brought under the stern principles of correctness and uniformity. Already he was reaching that time of life when everything inspired by impulse contracts in a man, when the strains of the mighty violin rouse feebler echoes in the soul and its pure notes no longer thrill the heart, when the touch of beauty no longer turns its virgin forces into fire and flame, but all the burnt-out feelings grow more responsive to the jingle of gold, listen more attentively to its alluring music, and, little by little, imperceptibly permit it to absorb them. Fame cannot satisfy and give pleasure to one who has stolen and not deserved it; it produces a permanent thrill only in those worthy of it. And therefore all his feelings and his impulses turned to gold. Gold became his passion, his ideal, his terror, his pleasure, his goal. Piles of notes grew in his boxes and, like everyone to whom this terrible privilege is vouchsafed, he began to grow tedious, inaccessible to everything, indifferent to everything. It seemed as though he were on the point of being transformed into one of those strange beings, sometimes to be found in the world, at whom a man full of energy and passion looks with horror, seeing in them living corpses. But one circumstance made a violent impression upon him and gave a different turn to his life.

One day he saw on his table a note in which the Academy of Arts invited him as an honored member to come and give his criticism on the work of a Russian painter, who had sent it from Italy where he was studying. This artist was one of his old fellow students, who had from his earliest years cherished a passion for art, had devoted himself to it with the ardent soul of a patient worker, and, tearing himself away from friends, from relations, from cherished habits, had hastened without means to a strange land; he had endured poverty, humiliation, even hunger; but with rare self-sacrifice had remained, regardless of everything, insensible to all but his cherished art.

When Chartkov went into the hall, he found a crowd of visitors already gathered about the picture. A profound silence prevailed such as is rare in a large assembly of critics. He hastened to assume the important air of a connoisseur as he advanced to the picture, but, good heavens! What did he see!

Pure, stainless, lovely as a bride, the painter's work stood before him. There was not the faintest sign of desire to dazzle, of pardonable vanity. No thought of showing off to the crowd could be seen in it! It excelled with modesty. It was simple, innocent, divine as talent, as genius. The amazingly lovely figures were grouped unconstrainedly, freely, as if they were not touching the canvas, and they seemed to be modestly casting down their lovely eyelashes in amazement at so many eyes fixed upon them. The features of these godlike faces seemed to be breathing with the mysteries which the soul has no power, no means, to convey to another: the inexpressible found serene expression in them; and all this was put on to the canvas so lightly, with such modest freedom, that it might have seemed the fruit of a moment's inspiration dawning upon the artist's mind. The whole picture was a moment, but it was a moment for which all human life had been but preparation. Involuntary tears were ready to start to the eyes of the visitors who stood around the picture. It seemed as though all tastes, all sorts of diversities of taste, were blended into a silent hymn of praise. Chartkov stood motionless, open-mouthed before the picture, and as the onlookers and connoisseurs gradually began to break the silence and discuss the qualities of the work and finally turned to him asking for his opinion, he came to himself; he tried to regain his ordinary air of indifference, tried to utter the commonplace vulgar criticisms of blasé artists: to observe that the picture was good and that the artist had talent, but it was to be regretted that the idea was not perfectly carried out in certain details—but the words died on his lips, confused tears and sobs broke from him in response, and he ran out of the hall like one possessed.

For a minute he stood senseless and motionless in the middle of his magnificent studio. His whole being, his whole life had been awakened in one instant, as though his youth had come back to him, as though the smoldering sparks of talent had burst into flame again. Good God! To have ruined so ruthlessly all the best years of his youth, to have destroyed, to have quenched, the spark of fire that glowed perhaps in his breast, that would perhaps by now have developed into greatness and beauty, that would perhaps in the same way have wrung tears of amazement and gratitude from the eyes of beholders! And to have ruined it all, to have ruined it without mercy! It seemed as though at that moment the impulses and strivings that had once been familiar revived in his soul. He snatched up a brush and approached a canvas. The sweat of effort came out on his brow; he was all absorbed in one desire and might be said to be glowing with one thought: he longed to paint a fallen angel. No idea could have been more in harmony with his present frame of mind. But, alas! his figures, his attitudes, his groupings, his thoughts were artificial and disconnected. His painting and his imagination had been too long confined to one pattern; and a feeble impulse to escape from the limits and fetters he had laid upon himself ended in inaccuracy and failure. He had disdained the wearisome, long ladder of steady work and the first fundamental laws of future greatness. In vexation he took out of the room all his fashionable and lifeless pictures, all those portraits of hussars and ladies and state councilors, locked the door, ordered no food, and absorbed himself in his work with the ardor of youth. But alas! at every step he was stopped by ignorance of the most fundamental elements; the humble, insignificant mechanism of his art cooled all his ardor and stood an impassable barrier before his imagination. His brush involuntarily returned to hackneyed forms, his hands went back to his stereotyped manner. The heads dared not take an original attitude, the very folds of the garments insisted on being commonplace and refused to drape and hang on unfamiliar poses of the body. And he felt it, he felt it and saw it himself!

"Did I ever really have any talent?" he finally said. "Didn't I deceive myself?" And having uttered these words he turned to his old paintings which he had once produced so purely and altruistically in his wretched apartment far off in lonely Vasilievsky Island, so far removed from crowds, luxury, and cravings. He turned to them now, and with great care began to examine them all, and all the details of the misery of his former existence came back to him. "Yes," he cried in despair, "I had talent. The traces of it and the signs of it are everywhere. . . ."

He stopped suddenly and trembled all over. His eyes encountered eyes which were staring at him. It was that remarkable portrait he had bought in Shchukin Court. All this time the portrait had been covered up, hidden by other pictures, and he had completely forgotten about it. And now, as if by plan, when all the fashionable portraits and paintings had been taken from the studio, it emerged together with the productions of his youth. As he recalled all of that strange incident, as he remembered that this strange portrait had been responsible for his errors, that, indeed, it was the hoard of money which he so miraculously obtained from it which had awakened in him all those wild desires which had destroyed his talent, he became almost mad. Immediately he ordered that the hateful portrait be removed, but his mental agitation was not mitigated by its removal. His emotions, his entire being, were shaken to their foundation, and he suffered that terrible torture which sometimes appears in nature when a man with feeble talent tries to display it on a scale which is too large for it and fails miserably —the kind of torture which in youth may lead to greatness, but which is converted into unquenchable thirst in a man who should have long ago removed himself from reverie, that horrible torture which renders a man capable of the most terrible things. A horrible envy obsessed him, an envy which bordered upon madness. When he beheld a work which bore the stamp of genius, hatred distorted his features. He ground his teeth and devoured it with the eyes of a basilisk. At last the most hellish design which the heart of man has ever cherished sprang up within him, and with frenzied violence he flew to carry it out. He began buying up all the finest works of art. After buying a picture at a high price he carried it home carefully to his room and with the fury of a tiger he fell upon it, tore it, rent it, cut it up into little scraps, and stamped on it, accompanying this with a horrid laugh of fiendish glee. The enormous wealth which he had amassed enabled him to gratify this fiendish desire. He opened his bags of gold, and he unlocked his chests. No ignorant monster ever destroyed so many marvelous works of art as this raving avenger. Whenever he appeared at an auction everyone despaired of buying any work of art. It was as if a wrathful heaven had sent this terrible scourge into the world specifically to deprive it of its harmony. A horrible color created by this passion suffused his face. On his features were expressed scorn for the world, and blame. It was as if that terrible demon which Pushkin had described[28] had been reincarnated in him. From his tongue, there poured forth nothing but bitter and caustic words. He swooped through the streets like a Harpy, and all his acquaintances, seeing him from a distance, tried to avoid meeting him, noting that it poisoned the whole day for them.

Fortunately for the world and for art, such an overstrained and unnatural life could not last long; its passions were too abnormal and colossal for his feeble strength. Fits of frenzy and madness began to be frequent, and at last it ended in a terrible illness. Acute fever, combined with galloping consumption, took such a violent hold on him that in three days he was only a shadow of his former self. And to this was added all the symptoms of hopeless insanity. Sometimes it needed several men to hold him. He began to be haunted by the long-forgotten, living eyes of the strange portrait, and then his frenzy was terrible. All the people who stood around his bed seemed to him like dreadful portraits. The portrait was

---

[28] In his poem "The Demon." (ed.)

doubled, quadrupled before his eyes, and at last he imagined that all the walls were hung with these awful portraits, all fastening upon him their unmoving, living eyes. Terrible portraits looked at him from the ceiling, from the floor, and to crown it all he saw the room grow larger and extend into space to provide more room for these staring eyes. The doctor who had undertaken to treat him, and who had heard something of his strange story, did all he could to discover the mysterious connection between the hallucinations that haunted him and the incidents of his life, but could not arrive at any conclusion. The patient understood nothing and felt nothing but his sufferings, and in a piercing, indescribable, heart-rending voice screamed incoherently. At last he died in a final paroxysm of speechless agony. His corpse was dreadful to behold. Nor could they find any trace of his vast wealth, but, seeing the torn-up shreds of the great masterpieces of art, the price of which reached millions, they understood the terrible uses to which it had been put.

PART II

Masses of carriages, chaises, and coaches were standing round the entrance of the house in which an auction was taking place. It was a sale of all the belongings of one of those wealthy art connoisseurs who sweetly slumber away their lives plunged in zephyrs and amours, who are naïvely reputed to be Maecenases,[29] and good-naturedly spend on keeping up that reputation the millions accumulated by their businesslike fathers, and often, indeed, by their own earlier labors. As is well known, there are no longer such Maecenases, for the nineteenth century long ago acquired the aspect of a stingy banker who delights himself only with the figures written in ledgers. The long drawing room was filled with the most motley crowd of visitors who had come swooping down like birds of prey on an abandoned body. Here was a regular flotilla of Russian merchants from the bazaar, and even from the old-clothes market, in dark blue coats of German cut. They had here a harder and more free-and-easy air and appearance, and were not marked by the obsequiousness which is so prominent a feature of the Russian merchant. They did not stand on ceremony, in spite of the

---

[29] I.e., patrons of art. Maecenas was the patron of Horace and Vergil. (ed.)

fact that there were in the room many distinguished aristocrats, before whom in any other place they would have been ready to bow down to the ground till they swept away the dust brought in by their own boots. Here they were completely at ease and they fingered books and pictures without ceremony, trying to feel the quality of the goods, and boldly outbid aristocratic connoisseurs. Here were many of those persons who are invariably seen at auctions, who make it a rule to attend one every day as regularly as they have their breakfast; distinguished connoisseurs who look upon it as a duty not to miss a chance of increasing their collections, and have nothing else to do between twelve and one o'clock; and finally there were those excellent gentlemen whose coats and pockets are not well lined but who turn up every day at such functions with no mercenary motives, solely to see how things will go: who would give more and who less, who would outbid whom, and to whom the goods would be sold. Many of the pictures had been flung down here and there without any system; they were mixed up with the furniture and books, which all bore the monogram of their owner, though he probably had not had the laudable curiosity to look into them. Chinese vases, marble tabletops, furniture both modern and antique with curved lines adorned with the paws of griffins, sphinxes, and lions, chandeliers gilt and not gilt, and knick-knacks of all sorts were heaped together, not arranged in order as in shops. It was a chaos of works of art. Generally the impression made by an auction is strange. There is something in it suggestive of a funeral procession. The room in which it takes place is always rather gloomy, the windows are blocked up with furniture and pictures, the light filters in sparingly; there is silent attention on all the faces, and the effect of a funeral procession is enhanced by the voice of the auctioneer, as he taps with his hammer and recites the requiem over the poor works of art so strangely gathered together. All this further accents the singular unpleasantness of the impression.

The auction was at its height. A throng of respectable people were gathered in a group and were excitedly discussing something. From all sides resounded the words, "Rubles, rubles," allowing the auctioneer no opportunity to repeat the last bid which had already mounted to a sum quadruple the original price announced. The surging crowd was bidding for a portrait which could not fail but attract the attention of anyone who had any knowledge of art. The gifted hand of a master was easily discernible in it. Apparently the portrait had been restored and refinished several times, and it showed the dark features of an Asiatic in a wide robe who wore a peculiar expression on his face. But it was the remarkable liveliness of the eyes that struck the buyers most of all. The longer the people looked at them, the more did they seem to bore right into every man's heart. This peculiarity, this mysterious illusion created by the artist, forced the attention of almost all upon it. Many of those who had bid for the picture finally withdrew from the bidding when the price rose to an incredible sum. Only two well-known, art-collecting aristocrats remained, both absolutely determined not to forgo such a purchase. In the heat of excitement they would probably have continued out-bidding each other until the price had finally assumed incredible proportions if one of those in attendance had not suddenly said, "Allow me to interrupt your competition for a while. I, perhaps, have more right to his picture than anyone else." Immediately these words drew the attention of everyone upon him. He was a tall man of thirty-five, with long black hair. His pleasant face, full of a kind of gay nonchalance, showed a soul devoid of all mundane concerns. His clothes made no pretense to be fashionable. Everything about him indicated the artist. In fact, he was the artist B., well known personally to many of those present.

"Regardless of how strange my words may seem to you," he continued, noticing that all attention was focused on him, "you will see, if you agree to listen to a little story, that I was right to speak them. Everything convinces me that this is the portrait for which I have been looking."

A very natural curiosity took hold of nearly everyone, and even the auctioneer, with an open mouth and a raised hammer, paused and prepared to listen. At the beginning of the story many people involuntarily looked at the portrait, but later all attention was fixed on the narrator as what he said grew more and more interesting.

"You all know that part of the city which is called Kolomna," he began. "Everything there is different from any other part of Petersburg. There we have neither capital nor provinces. It seems, indeed, that when you walk through the streets of Kolomna, all the youthful desires and passions are drained from you. There the future never comes; all is still and desolate. Everything suggests withdrawal from the life of the capital. Retired officials move there to live, and widows and poor people who are familiar with the senate and therefore sentence themselves to this district for nearly all of their lives; cooks who have retired and spend the whole day haggling in the market, gossiping with the peasants in the milkshop, buying five kopeks' worth of coffee and four kopeks' worth of sugar every day; and that class of people whom I call ashen, whose clothes and faces and hair all have a dingy appearance like ashes. They are like a gray day when the sun does not dazzle with its brilliance, nor the storm whistle with thunder, rain, and hail, but when the sky is neither one thing nor the other: there is a veil of mist that blurs the outline of every object. And to these must be added retired people who were ushers in the theater, titular councilors, retired disciples of Mars with swollen lips and eyes poked out. These people are quite without passions. Nothing matters to them; they go about without taking the slightest notice of anything, and remain quite silent thinking of nothing at all. In their room they have nothing but a bed and a bottle of pure Russian vodka, which they imbibe with equal regularity every day, without any of the rush of ardor to the head that is provoked by a strong dose, such as the young German artisan, that bully of Meshchansky Street, who has undisputed possession of the pavement after twelve o'clock at night, loves to give himself on Sundays.

"Life in Kolomna is dull: rarely does a carriage rumble through its quiet streets, unless it be one full of actors, which disturbs the general stillness with its bells, its creaking and rattling. Here almost everyone goes on foot. Only at rare intervals a cab crawls along lazily, almost always without a fare, taking a load of hay for its humble nag. An apartment can be rented for five rubles a month, morning coffee included. The widows of government clerks, in receipt of a pension, are the most substantial inhabitants of the quarter. They behave with great propriety, keep their rooms fairly clean, and talk to their female neighbors and friends of the high price of beef and cabbages. They not infrequently have a young daughter, a silent creature who has nothing to say for herself, though sometimes rather nice-looking; they have also a disgusting little dog and an old-fashioned clock with a dismally ticking pendulum. Next to them in precedence come the actors, whose salaries don't allow of their leaving Kolomna. They are rather a free and easy group, like all artists, and live for their own pleasure. Sitting in their dressing gowns they either clean a pistol or glue pieces of cardboard together to make something of use in the house, or play checkers or cards with a friend, and so they spend their mornings; they follow the same pursuits in the evening, mingling them with punch. Below these swells, these aristocrats of Kolomna, come the smaller fry, and it is as hard for the observer to reckon up all the people occupying the different corners and nooks in one room as it is to enumerate all the creatures that breed in stale vinegar. What people does one not meet there! Old women who say their prayers, old women who get drunk, old women who both get drunk and say their prayers; old women who live from hand to mouth by means that pass all understanding, who like ants drag old rags and linen from Kalinkin Bridge to the flea market, to sell them there for fifteen kopeks—in fact all the pitiful and luckless dregs of humanity whose lot not even a benevolent economist could improve. I have listed them so that you will understand how often people like this are driven by need to seek immediate temporary help by borrowing. And among these people a certain kind of moneylender settles, and he lends them small loans on little security and charges exorbitant interest. These petty usurers often are more heartless than the major moneylenders because they live in the midst of poverty among people dressed in rags that the rich usurer who deals only with the carriage trade never sees, and every humane feeling in them is soon extinguished. Among these usurers there was one . . . but I must not forget to mention that the events which I have begun to relate refer to the last century in the reign of our late Empress Catherine II.[30] You will realize that since then the very appearance of Kolomna and its life has altered significantly. Now, among these usurers there was a certain person, a remarkable being in every respect, who had long before settled in that part of the city. He went about in a voluminous Asiatic robe. His dark complexion bespoke his southern origin, but as to his nationality, whether he belonged to India, or Greece, or Persia, no one was certain. He was tall and of enormous height, and had a dark, haggard, scorched face, and in his large

---

[30] Catherine the Great (1729-96) was of German birth, but she became thoroughly Russian and was extremely popular. Greatly influenced by the Enlightenment, she planned vast reforms which were never carried out because of the Pugachev rebellion and the French Revolution. (ed.)

eyes there was the blaze of strange fire, and he had heavy protruding eyebrows which made him so different from all the ash-colored
inhabitants of the capital. Even his house was different from the
other small wooden houses. It was made of stone, of a style which
Genoese merchants had once preferred. It had irregular windows
of various sizes and iron shutters and bars. This usurer was different from other usurers because he was willing to lend anyone any
required amount, from that needed by a penurious beggarwoman
to that required by a profligate courtier. And in front of his house
there were often to be seen splendid carriages, and sometimes, out
of their windows, there would appear the head of an elegant lady
of society. It was rumored, as usual, that his iron chests were
brimming with gold, treasures, diamonds, and all sorts of pledged
articles, but nevertheless, that he was not so enslaved by greed as
other usurers were. He lent money avidly and the terms of payment were fairly stipulated, but by some devious method of figur-
ing, he made the payments amount to an enormous rate of interest.
At least, that's how rumor had it. But what was most striking of all,
and that which could not fail to arouse the attention of many, was
the strange fate of all those who had borrowed money from him:
all came to a miserable end. Whether all this was merely the kind of
thing that people said about him or some superstition-born talk or
reports spread for the purpose of harming him, is not known,
but several things which happened within a short time of each
other, and before everybody's eyes, were remarkable and striking.

"Among the aristocracy of that day there was one young man of
a fine family who quickly attracted the attention of all. While
still young he had distinguished himself in court circles. He was
an ardent admirer of all that was true and noble. He was a patron
of all which art or the mind of man produced, and a man who gave
promise of becoming a Maecenas. Soon, deservedly, he was rewarded by the Empress; she appointed him to an important office
which was exactly what he wished for, and in which he could accomplish much for science and the general good. The youthful
statesman surrounded himself with artists, poets, and men of learning. He desired to give work to everyone, to encourage everyone
and, at his own expense, he undertook very many useful publica-
tions, placed many orders, and offered many prizes to encourage
the different arts. He spent a great deal of money and finally ruined
himself financially. Full of noble impulses, however, he did not

want to stop his work, and he looked for a loan wherever he could find it, and finally he came to the well-known moneylender. After obtaining a loan of considerable size from him, the man changed completely in a short time. He became a persecutor and oppressor of young artists and intellectuals. He saw only the bad side in everything published, and every word he spoke perverted the truth. Unfortunately, at this time, the French Revolution took place, and this supplied him with an excuse for every sort of suspicion.[31] He began discovering a revolutionary tendency in everything; everything hinted of subversion, and he finally became so suspicious that he began even to suspect himself. He began to fabricate terrible and unjust accusations and he made scores of people miserable. Obviously, news of this behavior finally reached the throne of the Empress. The kindhearted Empress, full of the noble spirit which adorns crowned heads, was shocked. She uttered words which, despite their failure to have been preserved, have yet had the memory of their meaning impressed upon many hearts. The Empress observed that it was not under a monarchy that the high and noble impulses of souls were persecuted, not under such a government were the finest achievements of the intellect, of poetry, and of the arts condemned and persecuted; that on the contrary, the monarchs alone were their protectors, and that Shakespeare and Molière flourished under their gracious protection,[32] while Dante could not even find a spot for himself in his republican birthplace,[33] that true geniuses arose at the time when emperors and empires were at the zenith of their brilliance and power, and not at the time of monstrous political unrest and republican terror which had, up to that time, never given the world a single poet;[34] that poets must be marked for favor, for they brought peace and divine contentment, and not excitement and discontent; that learned men and poets and all producers and all those who work in the arts were, indeed, the pearls and diamonds in the imperial

---

[31] During the French Revolution the Czarist regime became more reactionary than ever. (ed.)

[32] Shakespeare flourished under the reign of the brilliant Elizabeth I. Jean Baptiste Molière found Louis XIV a generous patron and a protector against his many enemies. (ed.)

[33] Dante Alighieri went into exile with the White Guelphs (a political faction) in 1302 and died in exile in Ravenna. (ed.)

[34] Gogol's strongly conservative point of view finds clear expression here. (ed.)

crown, for they glorified and immortalized the epic which the great ruler adorned, and made it more brilliant. In short, the Empress, speaking these words, was divinely beautiful for the moment. I recall old men who could not speak of it without tears. Everyone was interested in that affair. It must be noted, to the honor of our national pride, that in the Russian's heart there is always an impulse to aid the persecuted. The statesman who had betrayed his trust was punished in an exemplary manner and degraded from his post. But a much worse punishment could be read in the faces of his countrymen: sharp and universal scorn. Nothing could describe the sufferings of this vainglorious soul: pride, frustrated ambitions, destroyed aspirations, all joined together, and he died in a horrible attack of raving madness.

"Another striking example also occurred in the sight of all. Among the beauties in which our northern capital is decidedly not poor, one completely surpassed all the others. Her beauty was a blend of our northern charm with the charm of the south, a diamond only rarely seen in the world. My father told me that during his whole life he had never seen any woman like her. Everything seemed combined in her—wealth, intelligence, and spiritual charm. Throngs of admirers surrounded her, and the most distinguished of them all was Prince R., the most noble and best of all young men, the handsomest of face, and in chivalrous character, the great ideal of novels and women, a Grandison[35] in every respect. Prince R. was passionately, desperately in love, and his love was returned. But the girl's parents did not approve of the match. The Prince's ancestral estates had long before gone out of his hands and his family was in disfavor. Everyone knew of the sad state of his affairs. The prince suddenly left the capital, leaving the impression that he was bent upon improving his affairs, and he reappeared not long afterward surrounded with luxury and remarkable splendor. Those at court came to know him because of his brilliant balls and parties. The father of the beauty removed his objection, and the town soon witnessed one of the most fashionable weddings. What the real reason was for this change in fortune, and what the source was for this enormous wealth, no one fully knew, but it was whispered that he had made a deal with the mysterious usurer, and that he had borrowed money from him. Be that as it may, the

35 Hero of *Sir Charles Grandison*, third novel of Samuel Richardson (1689-1761), who was designed to portray the perfect gentleman. (ed.)

wedding occupied the whole town, and the bride and the bridegroom were the objects of general envy. Everyone knew of their warm and devoted love, how long they had endured persecution from every quarter, the great virtue of both. Romantic women already spoke of the heavenly happiness which the young couple would enjoy. But it turned out very differently.

"In one year a frightful change took place in the husband. His character, which until that time had been so fine and noble, was poisoned with jealous suspicions, intolerance, and inexorable caprice. He became a tyrant and torturer of his wife, which no one could have foreseen, and he indulged in the most abominable acts, even beating her. In only a year no one recognized the woman who only so recently had been so radiant and who had drawn around her crowds of submissive admirers. Finally, finding it impossible to endure her misery, she suggested a divorce, but at the mere suggestion of such a thing her husband flew into a rage. In the first outpouring of emotion he stormed into her room, and had he not been seized and restrained, he would undoubtedly have murdered her then and there. In a fit of madness and despair he turned the knife against himself, and he ended his life in the most horrible suffering.

"In addition to these two instances which occurred before the eyes of the whole world, there were many stories told of such happenings among the lower classes, nearly all of which ended tragically. An honest, sober man became a drunkard; a shopkeeper's assistant stole from his employer; an honest cabby cut the throat of his passenger for a few kopeks. Naturally such incidents, often told with embellishment, inspired horror in the simple hearts of Kolomna's inhabitants. No one at all doubted that the devil resided in this man. They said that he imposed conditions on a man which made the hair rise on one's head and which the poor wretch never dared to repeat to anyone else; that his money had the power to attract, possessed the power of becoming incandescent, and that it bore strange symbols. In short, there were many fantastic tales which circulated about him. It is worth noting that the entire population of Kolomna, the entire world of poor old women, petty officials, petty artists, and all those insignificant people we earlier mentioned, agreed that they would endure anything and suffer any misery rather than go to the terrible usurer. There were even old women who had died of hunger, prefer-

ring to starve to death rather than lose their souls. Anyone who
met him in the street felt an involuntary fear. Pedestrians were
careful to move away from him as he walked, and for a long time
they gazed at the receding tall figure. Even in his face there was
so much that was strange that they could not help but ascribe to
him supernatural powers. The powerful features, so deeply chis-
eled that they were unlike those in any other man; the glowing
bronze of his complexion; the incredible thickness of his eyebrows; those intolerable, terrible eyes; even the wide folds of his
Asiatic robe—everything seemed to note that all the passions
within other men paled when compared to the passions which
raged within him. Whenever my father met him he stopped short,
and he could not help but say, 'A devil, a real devil!' But I must, as
speedily as possible, introduce you to my father, who is the true
hero of this story.

"In many respects my father was a remarkable man. He was an
artist of unusual ability, a self-taught artist who without teachers
or schools discovered in his own soul the rules and laws of art, and,
for reasons he did not understand, motivated only by his passion
for perfection, he walked on the path which his spirit pointed out
to him. He was one of those natural geniuses whom their contemporaries so often honor with the contemptuous word 'ignorant'
and who are not disheartened by sneers or their own lack of success, who gain fresh strength and are, constantly, in their own
minds, far beyond those works because of which they had earned
the title 'ignorant.' Through some lofty and basic instinct, he perceived the presence of a soul in every object. He grasped, with his
untutored mind, the true significance of the words 'historical
painting.' He understood why a simple head, a simple portrait by
Raphael, Leonardo da Vinci, Titian, or Correggio could be appreciated as an historical painting, while a huge picture of historical
subjects remained, nevertheless, nothing more than a genre picture, despite all the artist's pretensions to historical painting. And
this inherent instinct and personal conviction turned his brush to
Christian subjects, the highest and loftiest degree of the sublime.
He was devoid of vanity and irritability, which are so much a part
of the character of many artists. His character was strong. He was
honorable, frank, even a man with rough manners, covered with a
hard shell, but not lacking in pride, and he always expressed himself about people both gently and scornfully. "What are they look-

ing at?' he usually said. 'I am not working for them. I don't take my pictures to the tavern! He who understands me will thank me. The worldly man cannot be held at fault because he comprehends nothing of painting; he understands cards, and he knows wine and horses—what more need a gentleman know? If he tries one thing and then another, he becomes too much to endure. Let every man concern himself with his own business. So far as I am concerned, I much prefer a man who honestly admits that he does not understand a thing to one who pretends to know something he really does not know and is simply base and intolerable.' He worked for very little pay, that is to say, for just enough with which to keep his family and to buy the tools necessary for his work. Further, under no circumstances did he ever refuse to help anyone or to offer assistance to a destitute artist. He believed with the simple, reverent faith of his ancestors, and, because of that, a lofty expression appeared in all the faces he painted, an expression which even the most brilliant artists could not reproduce. Finally, by dedicated labor and perseverance in the path he had marked out for himself, he began to win the respect of those who had before derided his amateur status and his self-taught talent. They constantly commissioned him to do churches, and he was never without employment. In particular, one of his paintings interested him very strongly. What its precise subject was I can't recall; I know only that he had to represent the Prince of Darkness in it. For a long time, he pondered over what kind of form to present him in because he wanted to represent in that face all that weighs down and oppresses man. And while involved with these thoughts, there suddenly raced through his mind the image of the mysterious moneylender, and he could not help but say, 'That's who ought to be the model for the devil!' Imagine his surprise when, while at work in his studio one day, he heard a knock at the door and immediately the same terrible usurer entered the room. My father could not repress a cold chill which ran through every limb.

" 'Are you an artist?' he asked my father quickly.

" 'I am,' answered my surprised father, wondering what was to come next.

" 'Good. Paint my portrait. It is possible that I may be dead soon. I have no children, and I don't want to die completely. I wish to live. Can you do a portrait that will look as though it were alive?'

"My father thought, 'What could be better? He offers himself as the devil I'm painting in my picture.' So he agreed. They came to terms about time and price, and on the very next day, my father took his palette and his brushes and went to his house. The high walls encircling the courtyard, dogs, iron doors and locks, arched windows, chests draped with strange rugs, and finally, the singular owner himself who was seated motionless before him: all this produced a strange impression upon him. The lower half of the windows were covered so that only from the top of the windows was the light admitted. 'Damn it. How remarkably well his face is lighted up!' he said to himself, and he began to paint feverishly, as though he were afraid that the favorable light would somehow disappear. 'What power!' he said to himself. 'If I even capture half of how he appears now, all my other works will be surpassed. He'll just leap from the canvas even if I capture only a little of his nature. What remarkable features!' he kept repeating to himself, redoubling his energy, and soon he himself began to see how certain traits were already appearing on the canvas. But the closer he approached them the more he became aware of an oppressive uneasiness which was beyond his explanation. Despite this, he began to reproduce them exactly as they were. But he made up his mind, at any price, to discover their most minute characteristics and shades and to penetrate their secret. . . . But as soon as he painted them with redoubled efforts, there arose in him such a terrible revulsion, such a feeling of inexplicable oppression, that he was forced to put aside his brush for a while and then to begin afresh. At last he could endure it no longer. He felt as though those eyes pierced into his very soul and filled it with intolerable alarm. On the second and third days this feeling became stronger. He became frightened. He threw down his brush and bluntly announced that he could paint no longer. You should have seen how the sinister usurer's face changed at these words. He fell at his feet, begged him to finish the portrait, pleading that his fate and his very existence in the world depended on it, that he had already captured his prominent features, and if he would accurately reproduce them his life would be preserved in some supernatural manner in the portrait, and then he would not die completely, for it was necessary for him to remain in the world.

"These words terrified my father; they seemed so strange and so terrible that he discarded his brushes and his palette and dashed out of the room.

"All day and all night he was vexed by what had happened, but on the next morning he received the portrait from the money-lender. It was brought by a woman who was the only human being the usurer employed, and she declared that her master did not want the portrait, that he would not pay for it, and that he had, therefore, sent it back. He learned that the usurer had died on the evening of the very same day, and that preparations were being made for him to be buried according to the rites of his religion. This seemed inexplicably strange, but from that day on there was a decided change in my father's character. An uneasy and restless feeling which he could not explain possessed him and, soon after, he did something which no one would have expected of him. For some time the paintings of one of his pupils had attracted the attention of a small group of connoisseurs and art lovers. My father appreciated his talent and because of that had always been very helpful. Suddenly, however, he became jealous of him. The general interest expressed about his work and the conversations which centered about it became unbearable to my father. Finally, to heighten his annoyance, he learned that a rich church which had recently been rebuilt had commissioned him to do a picture. He was enraged. 'No, this youngster must not be permitted to defeat me!' he said. 'It's too soon for you, my friend, to think of relegating the old men to the gutters. Thank God I am not without strength! We will see who will defeat whom!' And this straightforward and honorable man planned intrigues and schemes which he had hitherto detested. Finally, he succeeded in arranging a competition for the commission so that other artists were offered the opportunity of entering their own works. And then he shut himself up in his room and began painting feverishly. It was as if he wanted to use all his strength for this one occasion, and, indeed, it turned out to be one of his best works. No one doubted that he would win. The pictures were exhibited, and all the others were as night to day compared to his. Then suddenly one of the members present (If I am not mistaken, a person in holy orders) said something which surprised everyone: 'Certainly there is much talent in the picture of this artist,' he said, 'but there is nothing holy in the faces; on the contrary, in fact, there is even something demoniacal in the eyes, as though some evil feeling had guided the artist's hand.' And everyone looked at the picture and could not help admitting that these words were true. My father rushed up to his picture to see for himself whether this offensive remark was justified, and with horror he saw that the usurer's eyes were contained in nearly all the figures. They gazed with such a devastatingly diabolical gaze that he could not help but shudder. The picture was rejected and, to his great vexation, he was forced to hear that his pupil had won the competition. It is impossible to describe the degree of fury in him when he returned home. He almost murdered my mother, he drove all the children away, he smashed his brushes and his easels; and he ripped the usurer's portrait from its place on the wall, demanded a knife, and ordered a fire to be built in the fireplace, intending to slash it to pieces and to burn it. An artist friend caught him in the act upon entering the room. He was a jovial fellow, like my father, who was content, aspired to nothing unobtainable, did anything that came to hand happily, and was especially gay at dinner or at parties.

"'What are you doing? What are you going to burn?' he asked, walking up to the portrait. 'Why, this is one of your best works. It's the usurer who recently died. It's a very fine painting. You didn't cease your efforts until you captured his very eyes. Even in life eyes never look like that.'

"'Well, I'll see how they look in the fire!' said my father, seizing the portrait to fling it into the flames.

"'For God's sake, stop!' shouted his friend, restraining him. 'If it offends you so much, give it to me.' My father began to insist on his way at first, but at length he gave in, and his jovial friend, pleased with his new acquisition, carried the portrait home with him.

"My father was calmer after he had left; it was as if that which oppressed him was removed with the portrait. He was himself surprised at his previous evil feelings, his jealousy, and the apparent change in his character. Reviewing what he had done, he grew sad and, not without inward sorrow, he said, 'It was God who punished me! My picture deserved disgrace. It was intended to ruin a fellow man. A fiendish feeling of envy controlled my brush and the fiendish feeling was reflected in what it produced!' Immediately he went out to find his former pupil, and he embraced him warmly and begged his forgiveness and, as far as possible, he did all he could to assuage the wrongs he had committed. His work continued as undisturbed as it had once been, but his face was more frequently thoughtful. He prayed more often, he became more taciturn, he spoke less negatively about people, and even the coarse exterior of his character was somehow changed. But something soon happened which disturbed him more than ever. For some time he had seen nothing of the friend who had begged him for the portrait. He had been contemplating looking him up when he suddenly appeared in my father's room, and, after the usual words exchanged between friends, he said, 'Well, friend, there was a reason why you wished to burn that portrait. Damn it, there's something strange about it! . . . I don't believe in sorcery, but, and I beg your pardon, there's something evil in it . . .'

" 'What is it?' asked my father.

" 'Well, from the instant I hung it up in my room, I've been so depressed, as if I was thinking of murdering someone. Never before did I know what insomnia was, but now I suffer not only insomnia, but from terrible dreams! . . . I hardly know whether they can be called dreams or something else. It's as if a *domovoi* was strangling me, and the old man appears to me in my sleep. In short, I simply can't describe my state of mind to you. Nothing of the sort ever happened to me before. I have been wandering about in misery all this time—obsessed with fear, expecting something awful. I felt as if I couldn't say a friendly word, a sincere word, to anyone. It's as if a spy were watching over me. And only after I had given that portrait to my nephew who asked for it did I feel as if a stone had been rolled from my shoulders. Immediately I felt as happy as you see me now. Well, brother, you made the devil!'

"My father listened to this story with absolute attention, and he finally asked, 'Does your nephew now have the portrait?'

" 'My nephew, no! He couldn't stand it!' said the jovial fellow. 'Do you know that the soul of that usurer is in that portrait? He leaps out of the frame and walks about the room, and the story my nephew tells of him is beyond comprehension. I would have thought him a lunatic if I myself had not experienced some of it. He sold it to an art collector who couldn't stand it either and who finally got rid of it by getting someone else to take it.'

"The story produced a deep impression on my father, and now he was seriously worried, oppressed with melancholy, and finally he became convinced that his brush had been a tool of the devil and that a part of the usurer's life had somehow or other really passed into the portrait and was now plaguing people, inspiring diabolical ideas, beguiling artists from the righteous path, inflicting the horrible torments of jealousy, and so forth. Three catastrophes which happened afterwards, the sudden deaths of his wife and his daughter and his infant son, he regarded as divine punishment, and he firmly resolved to remove himself from the world. As soon as I reached nine years of age he placed me in an art academy and, paying his debts, he retired to a lonely monastery where he soon took the vows. There he amazed everyone with the austerity of his life and his absolute observance of all the monastic rules. The prior of the monastery ordered him to paint the principal icon in the church after hearing of his skill as an artist, but the humble brother bluntly refused, noting that he was unworthy of touching a brush, that it had been contaminated, that he must first purify his spirit with hard work and great sacrifice before he would deem himself worthy of undertaking such a task. They did not want to force the issue. He increased the rigors of monastic life as much as possible until even this life no longer satisfied him because it did not demand sufficient austerity. With the approval of the prior, he retired into the wilderness so that he could be absolutely alone. And there he built a hut of tree branches, and he ate only uncooked roots, and he dragged a large stone from place to place, and he stood on the same spot with his hands lifted to heaven from the time the sun went up till the time it went down, and, without stop, he recited his prayers. In brief, he experienced, it seems, every possible degree of suffering and pitiless self-abnegation, examples of which can only be found in some Lives of the Saints. In this manner, he long—for several years—exhausted his body and strengthened it at the same time only through fervent prayer. At last, one day he returned to the monastery and firmly said to the prior, 'I am ready now. If God wills, I shall do my task.' And he selected for his subject the birth of Christ. And he worked on it for a whole year without ever leaving his cell, barely sustaining himself with coarse food and praying incessantly. The picture was finished at the end of the year. It was a remarkable achievement. It should be understood that neither the prior nor the monks knew much about painting, but they were all struck by the wonderful holiness of the figures. The expression of divine humility and gentleness on the face of the Holy Mother as she bent over the Child; the profound intelligence in the eyes of the Holy Child, as though they perceived something from afar; the triumphant silence of the Magi, amazed by the Divine Miracle as they prostrated themselves at His feet, and finally, the ineffable tranquillity which pervaded the entire picture—all this was presented with such harmonious strength and great beauty that the impression it created was magical. All of the brethren fell on their knees before the new icon, and the deeply moved prior said, 'No, it is impossible for any artist to produce such a picture solely with the aid of human art alone: your brush was guided by a holy and divine power, and heaven's blessing rested upon your labors!'

"At that time, I had just finished my education at the Academy and had been awarded a gold medal, and with it the joyful hope of going to Italy—the greatest dream of a twenty-year-old artist. I had only to say goodbye to my father whom I had not seen for twelve years. I admit that I had quite forgotten even what he looked like. I had heard some comment about his austerity, and I expected to meet a recluse of rough exterior, a man who had become estranged from everything in the world but his cell and his prayers, a man who was worn out and shriveled from eternal fasting and penance. How great was my surprise when I beheld before me a handsome, almost inspired old man! And on his face there was no trace of exhaustion. It shone with the light of heavenly joy. His beard was white as snow, and his thin, almost transparent hair, of the same silvery hue, fell picturesquely over his breast, and on the folds of his black frock, to the rope which encircled his humble, monastic garb. But still more surprising to me was to hear such words and thoughts about art which, I confess, I will long keep in my mind, and I sincerely wish that all of my friends would do the same.

" 'I awaited you, my son,' he said as I approached him for his blessing. 'The path in which, henceforth, your life is to flow awaits you. It is clear. Do not desert it. You have talent; do not destroy it, for it is the most priceless of God's gifts. Search, study everything you see, master everything, but in everything try to discover the hidden meaning and, above all else, endeavor to attain comprehension of the great mystery of creation. Blessed is he who masters that! For him there is nothing low in nature. A creative artist is as great in lowly things as he is in great ones; in the despicable there is nothing for him to despise, for the glorious spirit of the Creator imbues it, and what is despicable receives glory because it has passed through the purifying fire of His spirit. An intimation of God's heavenly paradise is found in art, and it is for this reason that art is higher than all else. As life spent in triumphant contemplation of God is nobler than a life involved with earthly turmoil, so is the lofty creation of art higher than anything else on earth. As much as the angel is by the purity and innocence of its bright spirit above all invisible powers and the proud passions of Satan, by exactly that much is the great creation of art higher than anything on earth. Sacrifice everything to it and love it with great passion, not with the passion born of earthly lust, but with a gentle and heavenly passion. Without it a man is powerless to raise himself above the earth, and he cannot produce the wonderful sounds which bespeak contentment. For the great creations of art come into the world in order to soothe and reconcile everything. It cannot sow discord in the soul, but it aspires, like a resounding prayer, to God. But there are moments, dark moments . . .' He paused, and I saw a darkness on his face as though some cloud had for a moment passed before him. 'There is one incident in my life,' he said. 'To this very moment, I cannot grasp what that terrible being was whose portrait I painted. It was surely some manifestation of something diabolical. I am aware that the world denies the existence of the devil, and because of that, I will not speak of him. I will only note that it was with revulsion that I painted him. Even at that time I felt no love for my work. I tried to force myself to be true to nature, and I stifled every emotion in me. It was not a work of art, and, therefore, the feelings which are aroused in everyone who looks at it are feelings of revulsion, disturbing feelings, not the feelings of an artist, for an artist puts peace into turmoil. I have been told that this portrait passes from hand to hand and sows dissatisfaction and creates jealousy and black hatred in artists toward their fellow artists, and evil desires to persecute and oppress. May God keep you from such passions. Nothing is more terrible. Better to endure the anguish of the most horrible persecution than to inflict anyone with even a hint of persecution. Keep your mind pure. He who is talented must be purer than all others. Much must be forgiven him. A man who goes forth from his house dressed in brilliant holiday garments has only to be spattered with a single spot of mud from a wheel and people encircle him and point a finger at him and talk of his lack of cleanliness, while the same people do not notice the very many spots on the ordinary garments of other passers-by, for spots on ordinary clothes are never seen.'

"He blessed me and he embraced me. Never in my life was I so deeply moved. I leaned upon his breast reverently rather than with the feeling of a son, and I kissed his flowing silver hair.

"Tears glistened in his eyes. 'Fulfill one request, dear son,' said he at the moment of parting. 'You may one day come across the portrait I have mentioned. You will recognize it at once by its strange eyes and unnatural expression. If you find it, I beg you, destroy it at any cost.'

"You may yourselves judge whether I could refuse to promise to fulfill this request. For fifteen years I have never come across anything which even slightly corresponded to the description of the portrait which my father had given me, until suddenly, at this auction . . ."

The artist did not finish the sentence; he turned his eyes to the wall to look at the portrait once more. And everyone who had listened to him instinctively did the same thing. To their amazement, however, it was no longer on the wall. A soft murmur ran through the crowd, followed suddenly by the word "stolen" which was distinctly heard. Someone had succeeded in taking it away, taking advantage of the fact that the attention of the listeners was distracted by the story. And for a long time those who were present were bewildered, wondering whether they had really seen those remarkable eyes or whether it was merely a dream which had flashed before their eyes, strained from long examination of old pictures.

THE OVERCOAT[1]

In the department of . . . but I had better not mention which department. There is nothing in the world more touchy than a department, a regiment, a government office, and, in fact, any sort of official body. Nowadays every private individual considers all so-

[1] It is usually agreed that the theme of this story was suggested to Gogol by a tale about an indigent clerk who loved to hunt but had no money to buy a gun. After enormous privation, the tale continued, the clerk finally saved enough to buy one. On his first hunting trip, however, he dropped it into the water and it was lost forever. Grief-stricken, the moribund clerk was saved from death by the generosity of his fellow workers, who bought him a new gun. Despite very important differences, there is obviously a strong thematic thread which ties this to *The Overcoat*. Professor Stilman ("Afterword," *The Diary of a Madman and Other Stories* [New York, 1960], pp. 229-32) notes three possible sources. The first, the story of the indigent clerk. The second, "to facts, or anecdotes, recorded in the diary of Pushkin . . ." (and the entry in Pushkin's diary which Professor Stilman quotes notes that strange occurrences had made the streets unsafe—such occurrences consisting mainly of furniture jumping around, thieves very active in the streets). And third, a possible source which was uncovered by F. C. Driessen, a Dutch scholar: namely, a legend of a sixteenth-century saint of the Orthodox Church, Saint Akaky, who died after being abused for nine years by his elder. The elder, the legend continues, was stricken with guilt and, obsessed with the thought that Akaky was still alive, he visited his grave where he heard his voice saying, " 'I am not dead, for a man who lived in obedience may not die.' " We consider this last possible source highly unlikely. Rather, we would suggest, Akaky is "Akaky" (as was his father) because the name is so suggestive, something of which the language-conscious Gogol could not conceivably have been unaware; indeed, to a native Russian who has never read or heard of the story, the name is provocative, the resemblance to *kaka* (defecator) being quite impossible to miss. And Gogol's fondness for the word is evident from a reading of the Russian text. (ed.)

ciety insulted in his person. I have been told that very lately a
complaint was lodged by a police inspector of which town I don't
remember, and that in this complaint he set forth clearly that the
institutions of the State were in danger and that his sacred name
was being taken in vain; and, in proof thereof, he appended to his
complaint an enormously long volume of some romantic work in
which a police inspector appeared on every tenth page, occasionally, indeed, in an intoxicated condition. And so, to avoid any un-
pleasantness, we had better call the department of which we are
speaking "a certain department."

And so, in a *certain department* there was a *certain clerk;* a
clerk of whom it cannot be said that he was very remarkable; he
was short, somewhat pock-marked, with rather reddish hair and
rather dim, bleary eyes, with a small bald patch on the top of his
head, with wrinkles on both sides of his cheeks and the sort of
complexion which is usually described as hemorrhoidal . . . nothing can be done about that, it is the Petersburg climate. As for his
grade in the civil service (for among us a man's rank is what must
be established first) he was what is called a perpetual titular councilor, a class at which, as we all know, various writers who indulge
in the praiseworthy habit of attacking those who cannot defend
themselves jeer and jibe to their hearts' content. This clerk's surname was Bashmachkin. From the very name it is clear that it must
have been derived from a shoe (*bashmak*); but when and under
what circumstances it was derived from a shoe, it is impossible to
say. Both his father and his grandfather and even his brother-in-
law, and all the Bashmachkins without exception wore boots, which
they simply resoled two or three times a year. His name was Akaky
Akakievich. Perhaps it may strike the reader as a rather strange
and contrived name, but I can assure him that it was not contrived
at all, that the circumstances were such that it was quite out of the
question to give him any other name. Akaky Akakievich was born
toward nightfall, if my memory does not deceive me, on the
twenty-third of March. His mother, the wife of a government
clerk, a very good woman, made arrangements in due course to
christen the child. She was still lying in bed, facing the door, while
on her right hand stood the godfather, an excellent man called
Ivan Ivanovich Yeroshkin, one of the head clerks in the Senate, and
the godmother, the wife of a police official and a woman of rare
qualities, Arina Semeonovna Belobriushkova. Three names were

offered to the happy mother for selection—Mokky, Sossy, or the name of the martyr Khozdazat. "No," thought the poor lady, "they are all such names!" To satisfy her, they opened the calendar at another page, and the names which turned up were: Trifily, Dula, Varakhasy. "What an infliction!" said the mother. "What names they all are! I really never heard such names. Varadat or Varukh would be bad enough, but Trifily and Varakhasy!" They turned over another page and the names were: Pavsikakhy and Vakhisy. "Well, I see," said the mother, "it is clear that it is his fate. Since that is how it is, he had better be named after his father; his father is Akaky; let the son be Akaky, too." This was how he came to be Akaky Akakievich. The baby was christened and cried and made sour faces during the ceremony, as though he foresaw that he would be a titular councilor. So that was how it all came to pass. We have reported it here so that the reader may see for himself that it happened quite inevitably and that to give him any other name was out of the question.

No one has been able to remember when and how long ago he entered the department, nor who gave him the job. Regardless of how many directors and higher officials of all sorts came and went, he was always seen in the same place, in the same position, at the very same duty, precisely the same copying clerk, so that they used to declare that he must have been born a copying clerk, uniform, bald patch, and all. No respect at all was shown him in the department. The porters, far from getting up from their seats when he came in, took no more notice of him than if a simple fly had flown across the reception room. His superiors treated him with a sort of despotic aloofness. The head clerk's assistant used to throw papers under his nose without even saying "Copy this" or "Here is an interesting, nice little case" or some agreeable remark of the sort, as is usually done in well-bred offices. And he would take it, gazing only at the paper without looking to see who had put it there and whether he had the right to do so; he would take it and at once begin copying it. The young clerks jeered and made jokes at him to the best of their clerkly wit, and told before his face all sorts of stories of their own invention about him; they would say of his landlady, an old woman of seventy, that she beat him, would ask when the wedding was to take place, and would scatter bits of paper on his head, calling them snow. Akaky Akakievich never answered a word, however, but behaved as though there were no one there. It had no influence on his work; in the midst of all this teasing, he never made a single mistake in his copying. It was only when the jokes became too unbearable, when they jolted his arm, and prevented him from going on with his work, that he would say: "Leave me alone! Why do you insult me?" and there was something touching in the words and in the voice in which they were uttered. There was a note in it of something that aroused compassion, so that one young man, new to the office, who, following the example of the rest, had allowed himself to tease him, suddenly stopped as though cut to the heart, and from that time on, everything was, as it were, changed and appeared in a different light to him. Some unseen force seemed to repel him from the companions with whom he had become acquainted because he thought they were well-bred and decent men. And long afterward, during moments of the greatest gaiety, the figure of the humble little clerk with a bald patch on his head appeared before him with his heart-rending words: "Leave me alone! Why do you insult me?" and within those moving words he heard others: "I am your brother." And the poor young man hid his face in his hands, and many times afterward in his life he shuddered, seeing how much inhumanity there is in man, how much savage brutality lies hidden under refined, cultured politeness, and, my God! even in a man whom the world accepts as a gentleman and a man of honor. . . .

It would be hard to find a man who lived for his work as did Akaky Akakievich. To say that he was zealous in his work is not enough; no, he loved his work. In it, in that copying, he found an interesting and pleasant world of his own. There was a look of enjoyment on his face; certain letters were favorites with him, and when he came to them he was delighted; he chuckled to himself and winked and moved his lips, so that it seemed as though every letter his pen was forming could be read in his face. If rewards had been given according to the measure of zeal in the service, he might to his amazement have even found himself a civil councilor; but all he gained in the service, as the wits, his fellow clerks, expressed it, was a button in his buttonhole[2] and hemorrhoids where he sat. It cannot be said, however, that no notice had ever been taken of him. One director, being a good-natured man and anxious to reward him for his long service, sent him something a little

---

[2] Whereas most clerks of long service wore a medal of achievement. (ed.)

more important than his ordinary copying; he was instructed to make some sort of report from a finished document for another office; the work consisted only of altering the headings and in places changing the first person into the third. This cost him so much effort that he was covered with perspiration: he mopped his brow and said at last, "No, I'd rather copy something."

From that time on they left him to his copying forever. It seemed as though nothing in the world existed for him except his copying. He gave no thought at all to his clothes; his uniform was—well, not green but some sort of rusty, muddy color. His collar was very low and narrow, so that, although his neck was not particularly long, yet, standing out of the collar, it looked as immensely long as those of the dozens of plaster kittens with nodding heads which foreigners carry about on their heads and peddle in Russia. And there were always things sticking to his uniform, either bits of hay or threads; moreover, he had a special knack of passing under a window at the very moment when various garbage was being flung out into the street, and so was continually carrying off bits of melon rind and similar litter on his hat. He had never once in his life noticed what was being done and what was going on in the street, all those things at which, as we all know, his colleagues, the young clerks, always stare, utilizing their keen sight so well that they notice anyone on the other side of the street with a trouser strap hanging loose—an observation which always calls forth a sly grin. Whatever Akaky Akakievich looked at, he saw nothing but his clear, evenly written lines, and it was only perhaps when a horse suddenly appeared from nowhere and placed its head on his shoulder, and with its nostrils blew a real gale upon his cheek, that he would notice that he was not in the middle of his writing, but rather in the middle of the street.

On reaching home, he would sit down at once at the table, hurriedly eat his soup and a piece of beef with an onion; he did not notice the taste at all but ate it all with the flies and anything else that Providence happened to send him. When he felt that his stomach was beginning to be full, he would get up from the table, take out a bottle of ink and begin copying the papers he had brought home with him. When he had none to do, he would make a copy especially for his own pleasure, particularly if the document were remarkable not for the beauty of its style but because it was addressed to some new or distinguished person.

Even at those hours when the gray Petersburg sky is completely overcast and the whole population of clerks have dined and eaten their fill, each as best he can, according to the salary he receives and his personal tastes; when they are all resting after the scratching of pens and bustle of the office, their own necessary work and other people's, and all the tasks that an overzealous man voluntarily sets himself even beyond what is necessary; when the clerks are hastening to devote what is left of their time to pleasure; some more enterprising are flying to the theater, others to the street to spend their leisure staring at women's hats, some to spend the evening paying compliments to some attractive girl, the star of a little official circle, while some—and this is the most frequent of all—go simply to a fellow clerk's apartment on the third or fourth story, two little rooms with a hall or a kitchen, with some pretensions to style, with a lamp or some such article that has cost many sacrifices of dinners and excursions—at the time when all the clerks are scattered about the apartments of their friends, playing a stormy game of whist, sipping tea out of glasses, eating cheap biscuits, sucking in smoke from long pipes, telling, as the cards are dealt, some scandal that has floated down from higher circles, a pleasure which the Russian can never by any possibility deny himself, or, when there is nothing better to talk about, repeating the everlasting anecdote of the commanding officer who was told that the tail had been cut off the horse on the Falconet monument[3]—in short, even when everyone was eagerly seeking entertainment, Akaky Akakievich did not indulge in any amusement. No one could say that they had ever seen him at an evening party. After working to his heart's content, he would go to bed, smiling at the thought of the next day and wondering what God would send him to copy. So flowed on the peaceful life of a man who knew how to be content with his fate on a salary of four hundred rubles,[4] and so perhaps it would have flowed on to extreme old age, had it not been for the various disasters strewn along the road of life, not only of titular, but even of privy, actual court, and all other councilors, even those who neither give counsel to others nor accept it themselves.

There is in Petersburg a mighty foe of all who receive a salary

---

[3] Famous statue of Peter the First. (ed.)
[4] See p. 446, n. 12. (ed.)

of about four hundred rubles. That foe is none other than our northern frost, although it is said to be very good for the health. Between eight and nine in the morning, precisely at the hour when the streets are filled with clerks going to their departments, the frost begins indiscriminately giving such sharp and stinging nips at all their noses that the poor fellows don't know what to do with them. At that time, when even those in the higher grade have a pain in their brows and tears in their eyes from the frost, the poor titular councilors are sometimes almost defenseless. Their only protection lies in running as fast as they can through five or six streets in a wretched, thin little overcoat and then warming their feet thoroughly in the porter's room, till all their faculties and talents for their various duties thaw out again after having been frozen on the way. Akaky Akakievich had for some time been feeling that his back and shoulders were particularly nipped by the cold, although he did try to run the regular distance as fast as he could. He wondered at last whether there were any defects in his overcoat. After examining it thoroughly in the privacy of his home, he discovered that in two or three places, on the back and the shoulders, it had become a regular sieve; the cloth was so worn that you could see through it and the lining was coming out. I must note that Akaky Akakievich's overcoat had also served as a butt for the jokes of the clerks. It had even been deprived of the honorable name of overcoat and had been referred to as the "dressing gown." [5] It was indeed of rather a peculiar make. Its collar had been growing smaller year by year as it served to patch the other parts. The patches were not good specimens of the tailor's art, and they certainly looked clumsy and ugly. On seeing what was wrong, Akaky Akakievich decided that he would have to take the overcoat to Petrovich, a tailor who lived on the fourth floor up a back staircase, and, in spite of having only one eye and being pockmarked all over his face, was rather successful in repairing the trousers and coats of clerks and others—that is, when he was sober, be it understood, and had no other enterprise in his mind. Of this tailor I ought not, of course, say much, but since it is now the rule that the character of every person in a novel must be completely described, well, there's nothing I can do but describe Petrovich too. At first he was called simply Grigory, and was a serf belonging

---

[5] *Kapot*, usually a woman's garment. (ed.)

to some gentleman or other. He began to be called Petrovich[6] from the time that he got his freedom and began to drink rather heavily on every holiday, at first only on the main holidays, but afterward, on all church holidays indiscriminately, wherever there was a cross in the calendar. In this he was true to the customs of his forefathers, and when he quarreled with his wife he used to call her a worldly woman and a German. Since we have now mentioned the wife, it will be necessary to say a few words about her, too, but unfortunately not much is known about her, except indeed that Petrovich had a wife and that she wore a cap and not a kerchief, but apparently she could not boast of beauty; anyway, none but soldiers of the guard peered under her cap when they met her, and they twitched their mustaches and gave vent to a rather peculiar sound.

As he climbed the stairs leading to Petrovich's—which, to do them justice, were all soaked with water and slops and saturated through and through with that smell of ammonia which makes the eyes smart, and is, as we all know, inseparable from the backstairs of Petersburg houses—Akaky Akakievich was already wondering how much Petrovich would ask for the job, and inwardly resolving not to give more than two rubles. The door was open, because Petrovich's wife was frying some fish and had so filled the kitchen with smoke that you could not even see the cockroaches. Akaky Akakievich crossed the kitchen unnoticed by the good woman, and walked at last into a room where he saw Petrovich sitting on a big, wooden, unpainted table with his legs tucked under him like a Turkish pasha. The feet, as is usual with tailors when they sit at work, were bare; and the first object that caught Akaky Akakievich's eye was the big toe, with which he was already familiar, with a misshapen nail as thick and strong as the shell of a tortoise. Around Petrovich's neck hung a skein of silk and another of thread and on his knees was a rag of some sort. He had for the last three minutes been trying to thread his needle, but could not get the thread into the eye and so was very angry with the darkness and indeed with the thread itself, muttering in an undertone: "She won't go in, the savage! You wear me out, you bitch." Akaky Akakievich was unhappy that he had come just at the minute when Petrovich was in a bad humor; he liked to give him an order when

---

[6] Customarily, serfs were addressed by first name only, while free men were addressed either by first name and patronymic or just the patronymic. (ed.)

he was a little "elevated," or, as his wife expressed it, "had fortified himself with vodka, the one-eyed devil." In such circumstances Petrovich was as a rule very ready to give way and agree, and invariably bowed and thanked him. Afterward, it is true, his wife would come wailing that her husband had been drunk and so had asked too little, but adding a single ten-kopek piece would settle that. But on this occasion Petrovich was apparently sober and consequently curt, unwilling to bargain, and the devil knows what price he would be ready to demand. Akaky Akakievich realized this, and was, as the saying is, beating a retreat, but things had gone too far, for Petrovich was screwing up his solitary eye very attentively at him and Akaky Akakievich involuntarily said: "Good day, Petrovich!"

"I wish you a good day, sir," said Petrovich, and squinted at Akaky Akakievich's hands, trying to discover what sort of goods he had brought.

"Here I have come to you, Petrovich, do you see . . . !"

It must be noticed that Akaky Akakievich for the most part explained himself by apologies, vague phrases, and meaningless parts of speech which have absolutely no significance whatever. If the subject were a very difficult one, it was his habit indeed to leave his sentences quite unfinished, so that very often after a sentence had begun with the words, "It really is, don't you know . . ." nothing at all would follow and he himself would be quite oblivious to the fact that he had not finished his thought, supposing he had said all that was necessary.

"What is it?" said Petrovich, and at the same time with his solitary eye he scrutinized his whole uniform from the collar to the sleeves, the back, the skirts, the buttonholes—with all of which he was very familiar since they were all his own work. Such scrutiny is habitual with tailors; it is the first thing they do on meeting one.

"It's like this, Petrovich . . . the overcoat, the cloth . . . you see everywhere else it is quite strong; it's a little dusty and looks as though it were old, but it is new and it is only in one place just a little . . . on the back, and just a little worn on one shoulder and on this shoulder, too, a little . . . do you see? that's all, and it's not much work . . ."

Petrovich took the "dressing gown," first spread it out over the table, examined it for a long time, shook his head, and put his hand out to the window sill for a round snuffbox with a portrait on the lid of some general—which general I can't exactly say, for a finger had been thrust through the spot where a face should have been, and the hole had been pasted over with a square piece of paper. After taking a pinch of snuff, Petrovich held the "dressing gown" up in his hands and looked at it against the light, and again he shook his head; then he turned it with the lining upward and once more shook his head; again he took off the lid with the general pasted up with paper and stuffed a pinch into his nose, shut the box, put it away, and at last said: "No, it can't be repaired; a wretched garment!" Akaky Akakievich's heart sank at those words.

"Why can't it, Petrovich?" he said, almost in the imploring voice of a child. "Why, the only thing is, it is a bit worn on the shoulders; why, you have got some little pieces . . ."

"Yes, the pieces will be found all right," said Petrovich, "but it can't be patched, the stuff is rotten; if you put a needle in it, it would give way."

"Let it give way, but you just put a patch on it."

"There is nothing to put a patch on. There is nothing for it to hold on to; there is a great strain on it; it is not worth calling cloth; it would fly away at a breath of wind."

"Well, then, strengthen it with something—I'm sure, really, this is . . . !"

"No," said Petrovich resolutely, "there is nothing that can be done, the thing is no good at all. You had far better, when the cold winter weather comes, make yourself leg wrappings out of it, for there is no warmth in stockings; the Germans invented them just to make money." (Petrovich enjoyed a dig at the Germans occasionally.) "And as for the overcoat, it is obvious that you will have to have a new one."

At the word "new" there was a mist before Akaky Akakievich's eyes, and everything in the room seemed blurred. He could see nothing clearly but the general with the piece of paper over his face on the lid of Petrovich's snuffbox.

"A new one?" he said, still feeling as though he were in a dream; "why, I haven't the money for it."

"Yes, a new one," Petrovich repeated with barbarous composure.

"Well, and if I did have a new one, how much would it . . . ?"

"You mean what will it cost?"

"Yes."

"Well, at least one hundred and fifty rubles," said Petrovich, and he compressed his lips meaningfully. He was very fond of making an effect; he was fond of suddenly disconcerting a man completely and then squinting sideways to see what sort of a face he made.

"A hundred and fifty rubles for an overcoat!" screamed poor Akaky Akakievich—it was perhaps the first time he had screamed in his life, for he was always distinguished by the softness of his voice.

"Yes," said Petrovich, "and even then it depends on the coat. If I were to put marten on the collar, and add a hood with silk linings, it would come to two hundred."

"Petrovich, please," said Akaky Akakievich in an imploring voice, not hearing and not trying to hear what Petrovich said, and missing all his effects, "repair it somehow, so that it will serve a little longer."

"No, that would be wasting work and spending money for nothing," said Petrovich, and after that Akaky Akakievich went away completely crushed, and when he had gone Petrovich remained standing for a long time with his lips pursed up meaningfully before he began his work again, feeling pleased that he had not demeaned himself or lowered the dignity of the tailor's art.

When he got into the street, Akaky Akakievich felt as though he was in a dream. "So that is how it is," he said to himself. "I really did not think it would be this way . . ." and then after a pause he added, "So that's it! So that's how it is at last! and I really could never have supposed it would be this way. And there . . ." There followed another long silence, after which he said: "So that's it! well, it really is so utterly unexpected . . . who would have thought . . . what a circumstance . . ." Saying this, instead of going home he walked off in quite the opposite direction without suspecting what he was doing. On the way a clumsy chimney sweep brushed the whole of his sooty side against him and blackened his entire shoulder; a whole hatful of plaster scattered upon him from the top of a house that was being built. He noticed nothing of this, and only after he had jostled against a policeman who had set his halberd down beside him and was shaking some snuff out of his horn into his rough fist, he came to himself a little and then only because the policeman said: "Why are you poking yourself right in one's face, haven't you enough room on the street?" This made him look around and turn homeward;

only there he began to collect his thoughts, to see his position in a clear and true light, and began talking to himself no longer incoherently but reasonably and openly as with a sensible friend with whom one can discuss the most intimate and vital matters. "No," said Akaky Akakievich, "it is no use talking to Petrovich now; just now he really is . . . his wife must have been giving it to him. I had better go to him on Sunday morning; after Saturday night he will have a crossed eye and be sleepy, so he'll want a little drink and his wife won't give him a kopek. I'll slip ten kopeks into his hand and then he will be more accommodating and maybe take the overcoat . . ."

So reasoning with himself, Akaky Akakievich cheered up and waited until the next Sunday; then, seeing from a distance Petrovich's wife leaving the house, he went straight in. Petrovich certainly had a crossed eye after Saturday. He could hardly hold his head up and was very drowsy; but, despite all that, as soon as he heard what Akaky Akakievich was speaking about, it seemed as though the devil had nudged him. "I can't," he said, "you must order a new one." Akaky Akakievich at once slipped a ten-kopek piece into his hand. "I thank you, sir, I will have just a drop to your health, but don't trouble yourself about the overcoat; it is no good for anything. I'll make you a fine new coat; you can have faith in me for that."

Akaky Akakievich would have said more about repairs, but Petrovich, without listening, said: "A new one I'll make you without fail; you can rely on that; I'll do my best. It could even be like the fashion that is popular, with the collar to fasten with silver-plated hooks under a flap."

Then Akaky Akakievich saw that there was no escape from a new overcoat and he was utterly depressed. How indeed, for what, with what money could he get it? Of course he could to some extent rely on the bonus for the coming holiday, but that money had long ago been appropriated and its use determined beforehand. It was needed for new trousers and to pay the cobbler an old debt for putting some new tops on some old boots, and he had to order three shirts from a seamstress as well as two items of undergarments which it is indecent to mention in print; in short, all that money absolutely must be spent, and even if the director were to be so gracious as to give him a holiday bonus of forty-five or even fifty, instead of forty rubles, there would be still left a mere trifle, which would be but a drop in the ocean compared to the fortune needed for an overcoat. Though, of course, he knew that Petrovich had a strange craze for suddenly demanding the devil knows what enormous price, so that at times his own wife could not help crying out: "Why, you are out of your wits, you idiot! Another time he'll undertake a job for nothing, and here the devil has bewitched him to ask more than he is worth himself." Though, of course, he knew that Petrovich would undertake to make it for eighty rubles, still where would he get those eighty rubles? He might manage half of that sum; half of it could be found, perhaps even a little more; but where could he get the other half? . . . But, first of all, the reader ought to know where that first half was to be found. Akaky Akakievich had the habit every time he spent a ruble of putting aside two kopeks in a little box which he kept locked, with a slit in the lid for dropping in the money. At the end of every six months he would inspect the pile of coppers there and change them for small silver. He had done this for a long time, and in the course of many years the sum had mounted up to forty rubles and so he had half the money in his hands, but where was he to get the other half; where was he to get another forty rubles? Akaky Akakievich thought and thought and decided at last that he would have to diminish his ordinary expenses, at least for a year; give up burning candles in the evening, and if he had to do any work he must go into the landlady's room and work by her candle; that as he walked along the streets he must walk as lightly and carefully as possible, almost on tiptoe, on the cobbles and flagstones, so that his soles might last a little longer than usual; that he must send his linen to the wash less frequently, and that, to preserve it from being worn, he must take it off every day when he came home and sit in a thin cotton dressing gown, a very ancient garment which Time itself had spared. To tell the truth, he found it at first rather difficult to get used to these privations, but after a while it became a habit and went smoothly enough—he even became quite accustomed to being hungry in the evening; on the other hand, he had spiritual nourishment, for he carried ever in his thoughts the idea of his future overcoat. His whole existence had in a sense become fuller, as though he had married, as though some other person were present with him, as though he were no longer alone but an agreeable companion had consented to walk the path of life hand in hand with him, and that companion was none other than the new overcoat with its thick padding and its strong, durable lining. He became, as it were, more alive, even more strong-willed, like a man who has set before himself a definite goal. Uncertainty, indecision, in fact all the hesitating and vague characteristics, vanished from his face and his manners. At times there was a gleam in his eyes; indeed, the most bold and audacious ideas flashed through his mind. Why not really have marten on the collar? Meditation on the subject always made him absent-minded. On one occasion when he was copying a document, he very nearly made a mistake, so that he almost cried out "ough" aloud and crossed himself. At least once every month he went to Petrovich to talk about the overcoat: where it would be best to buy the cloth, and what color it should be, and what price; and, though he returned home a little anxious, he was always pleased at the thought that at last the time was at hand when everything would be bought and the overcoat would be made. Things moved even faster than he had anticipated. Contrary to all expectations, the director bestowed on Akaky Akakievich a bonus of no less than sixty rubles. Whether it was that he had an inkling that Akaky Akakievich needed a coat, or whether it happened by luck, owing to this he found he had twenty rubles extra. This circumstance hastened the course of affairs. Another two or three months of partial starvation and Akaky Akakievich had actually saved up nearly eighty rubles. His heart, as a rule very tranquil, began to throb.

The very first day he set out with Petrovich for the shops. They bought some very good cloth, and no wonder, since they had been thinking of it for more than six months, and scarcely a month had passed without their going out to the shop to compare prices; now Petrovich himself declared that there was no better cloth to be had. For the lining they chose calico, but of such good quality, that in Petrovich's words it was even better than silk, and actually as strong and handsome to look at. Marten they did not buy, because it was too expensive, but instead they chose cat fur, the best to be found in the shop—cat which in the distance might almost be taken for marten. Petrovich was busy making the coat for two weeks, because there was a great deal of quilting; otherwise it would have been ready sooner. Petrovich charged twelve rubles for the work; less than that it hardly could have been; everything was sewn with silk, with fine double seams, and Petrovich went over every seam afterwards with his own teeth, imprinting various patterns with them. It was . . . it is hard to say precisely on what day, but probably on the most triumphant day in the life of Akaky Akakievich, that Petrovich at last brought the overcoat. He brought it in the morning, just before it was time to set off for the department. The overcoat could not have arrived at a more opportune time, because severe frosts were just beginning and seemed threatening to become even harsher. Petrovich brought the coat himself as a good tailor should. There was an expression of importance on his face, such as Akaky Akakievich had never seen there before. He seemed fully conscious of having completed a work of no little importance and of having shown by his own example the gulf that separates tailors who only put in linings and do repairs from those who make new coats. He took the coat out of the huge handkerchief in which he had brought it (the handkerchief had just come home from the wash); he then folded it up and put it in his pocket for future use. After taking out the overcoat, he looked at it with much pride and holding it in both hands, threw it very deftly over Akaky Akakievich's shoulders, then pulled it down and smoothed it out behind with his hands; then draped it about Akaky Akakievich somewhat jauntily. Akaky Akakievich, a practical man, wanted to try it with his arms in the sleeves. Petrovich helped him to put it on, and it looked splendid with his arms in the sleeves, too. In fact, it turned out that the overcoat was completely and entirely successful. Petrovich did not let slip the occasion for observing that it was only because he lived in a small street and had no signboard, and because he had known Akaky Akakievich so long, that he had done it so cheaply, and that on Nevsky Prospekt they would have asked him seventy-five rubles for the tailoring alone. Akaky Akakievich had no inclination to discuss this with Petrovich; besides he was frightened of the big sums that Petrovich was fond of flinging airily about in conversation. He paid him, thanked him, and went off, with his new overcoat on, to the department. Petrovich followed him out and stopped in the street, staring for a long time at the coat from a distance and then purposely turned off and, taking a short cut through a side street, came back into the street, and got another view of the coat from the other side, that is, from the front.

Meanwhile Akaky Akakievich walked along in a gay holiday mood. Every second he was conscious that he had a new overcoat on his shoulders, and several times he actually laughed from inward satisfaction. Indeed, it had two advantages: one that it was warm and the other that it was good. He did not notice how far he had walked at all and he suddenly found himself in the department; in the porter's room he took off the overcoat, looked it over, and entrusted it to the porter's special care. I cannot tell how it happened, but all at once everyone in the department learned that Akaky Akakievich had a new overcoat and that the "dressing gown" no longer existed. They all ran out at once into the cloakroom to look at Akaky Akakievich's new overcoat; they began welcoming him and congratulating him so that at first he could do nothing but smile and then felt positively embarrassed. When, coming up to him, they all began saying that he must "sprinkle" the new overcoat and that he ought at least to buy them all a supper, Akaky Akakievich lost his head completely and did not know what to do, how to get out of it, nor what to answer. A few minutes later, flushing crimson, he even began assuring them with great simplicity that it was not a new overcoat at all, that it wasn't much, that it was an old overcoat. At last one of the clerks, indeed the assistant of the head clerk of the room, probably in order to show that he wasn't too proud to mingle with those beneath him, said: "So be it, I'll give a party instead of Akaky Akakievich and invite you all to tea with me this evening; as luck would have it, it is my birthday." The clerks naturally congratulated the assistant head clerk and eagerly accepted the invitation. Akaky Akakievich was beginning to make excuses, but they all declared that it was uncivil of him, that it would be simply a shame and a disgrace and that he could not possibly refuse. So, he finally relented, and later felt pleased about it when he remembered that through this he would have the opportunity of going out in the evening, too, in his new overcoat. That whole day was for Akaky Akakievich the most triumphant and festive day in his life. He returned home in the happiest frame of mind, took off the overcoat, and hung it carefully on the wall, admiring the cloth and lining once more, and then pulled out his old "dressing gown," now completely falling apart, and put it next to his new overcoat to compare the two. He glanced at it and laughed: the difference was enormous! And long afterwards he went on laughing at dinner, as the position in which the "dressing gown" was placed recurred to his mind. He dined in excellent spirits and after dinner wrote nothing, no papers at all, but just relaxed for a little while on his bed, till it got dark; then, without putting things off, he dressed, put on his overcoat, and went out into the street. Where precisely the clerk who had invited him lived we regret to say we cannot tell; our memory is beginning to fail sadly, and everything there in Petersburg, all the streets and houses, are so blurred and muddled in our head that it is a very difficult business to put anything in orderly fashion. Regardless of that, there is no doubt that the clerk lived in the better part of the town and consequently a very long distance from Akaky Akakievich. At first Akaky Akakievich had to walk through deserted streets, scantily lighted, but as he approached his destination the streets became more lively, more full of people, and more brightly lighted; passers-by began to be more frequent, ladies began to appear, here and there beautifully dressed, and beaver collars were to be seen on the men. Cabmen with wooden, railed sledges, studded with brass-topped nails, were less frequently seen; on the other hand, jaunty drivers in raspberry-colored velvet caps, with lacquered sledges and bearskin rugs, appeared and carriages with decorated boxes dashed along the streets, their wheels crunching through the snow.

Akaky Akakievich looked at all this as a novelty; for several years he had not gone out into the streets in the evening. He stopped with curiosity before a lighted shop window to look at a picture in which a beautiful woman was represented in the act of taking off her shoe and displaying as she did so the whole of a very shapely leg, while behind her back a gentleman with whiskers and a handsome imperial on his chin was sticking his head in at the door. Akaky Akakievich shook his head and smiled and then went on his way. Why did he smile? Was it because he had come across something quite unfamiliar to him, though every man retains some instinctive feeling on the subject, or was it that he reflected, like many other clerks, as follows: "Well, those Frenchmen! It's beyond anything! If they go in for anything of the sort, it really is . . . !" Though possibly he did not even think that; there is no creeping into a man's soul and finding out all that he thinks. At last he reached the house in which the assistant head clerk lived in fine style; there was a lamp burning on the stairs, and the apartment was on the second floor. As he went into the hall Akaky Akakievich saw rows of galoshes. Among them in the middle of the room stood a hissing samovar puffing clouds of steam. On the walls hung coats and cloaks among which some actually had beaver collars or velvet lapels. From the other side of the wall there came noise and talk, which suddenly became clear and loud when the door opened and the footman came out with a tray full of empty glasses, a jug of cream, and a basket of biscuits. It was evident that the clerks had arrived long before and had already drunk their first glass of tea. Akaky Akakievich, after hanging up his coat with his own hands, went into the room, and at the same moment there flashed before his eyes a vision of candles, clerks, pipes and card tables, together with the confused sounds of conversation rising up on all sides and the noise of moving chairs. He stopped very awkwardly in the middle of the room, looking about and trying to think of what to do, but he was noticed and received with a shout and they all went at once into the hall and again took a look at his overcoat. Though Akaky Akakievich was somewhat embarrassed, yet, being a simplehearted man, he could not help being pleased at seeing how they all admired his coat. Then of course they all abandoned him and his coat, and turned their attention as usual to the tables set for whist. All this—the noise, the talk, and the crowd of people—was strange and wonderful to Akaky Akakievich. He simply did not know how to behave, what to do with his arms and legs and his whole body; at last he sat down beside the players, looked at the cards, stared first at one and then at another of the faces, and in a little while, feeling bored, began to yawn—especially since it was long past the time at which he usually went to bed. He tried to say goodbye to his hosts, but they would not let him go, saying that he absolutely must have a glass of champagne in honor of the new coat. An hour later supper was served, consisting of salad, cold veal, pastry and pies from the bakery, and champagne. They made Akaky Akakievich drink two glasses, after which he felt that things were much more cheerful, though he could not forget that it was twelve o'clock, and that he ought to have been home long ago. That his host might not take it into his head to detain him, he slipped out of the room, hunted in the hall for his coat, which he found, not without regret, lying on the floor, shook it, removed some fluff from it, put it on, and went down the stairs into the street. It was still light in the streets. Some little grocery shops, those perpetual clubs for servants and all sorts of people, were open; others which were closed showed, however, a long streak of light at every crack of the door, proving that they were not yet deserted, and probably maids and menservants were still finishing their conversation and discussion, driving their masters to utter perplexity as to their whereabouts. Akaky Akakievich walked along in a cheerful state of mind; he was even on the point of running, goodness knows why, after a lady of some sort who passed by like lightning with every part of her frame in violent motion. He checked himself at once, however, and again walked along very gently, feeling positively surprised at the inexplicable impulse that had seized him. Soon the deserted streets, which are not particularly cheerful by day and even less so in the evening, stretched before him. Now they were still more dead and deserted; the light of street lamps was scantier, the oil evidently running low; then came wooden houses and fences; not a soul anywhere; only the snow gleamed on the streets and the low-pitched slumbering hovels looked black and gloomy with their closed shutters. He approached the spot where the street was intersected by an endless square, which looked like a fearful desert with its houses scarcely visible on the far side.

In the distance, goodness knows where, there was a gleam of light from some sentry box which seemed to be at the end of the world. Akaky Akakievich's lightheartedness faded. He stepped into the square, not without uneasiness, as though his heart had a premonition of evil. He looked behind him and to both sides—it was as though the sea were all around him. "No, better not look," he thought, and walked on, shutting his eyes, and when he opened them to see whether the end of the square was near, he suddenly saw standing before him, almost under his very nose, some men with mustaches; just what they were like he could not even distinguish. There was a mist before his eyes, and a throbbing in his chest. "Why, that overcoat is mine!" said one of them in a voice like a clap of thunder, seizing him by the collar. Akaky Akakievich was on the point of shouting "Help" when another put a fist the size of a clerk's head against his lips, saying: "You just shout now." Akaky Akakievich felt only that they took the overcoat off, and gave him a kick with their knees, and he fell on his face in the snow and was conscious of nothing more. A few minutes later he recovered consciousness and got up on his feet, but there was no one there. He felt that it was cold on the ground and that he had no overcoat, and began screaming, but it seemed as though his voice would not carry to the end of the square. Overwhelmed with despair and continuing to scream, he ran across the square straight to the sentry box beside which stood a policeman leaning on his halberd and, so it seemed, looking with curiosity to see who the devil the man was who was screaming and running toward him from the distance. As Akaky Akakievich reached him, he began breathlessly shouting that he was asleep and not looking after his duty not to see that a man was being robbed. The policeman answered that he had seen nothing, that he had only seen him stopped in the middle of the square by two men, and supposed that they were his friends, and that, instead of abusing him for nothing, he had better go the next day to the police inspector, who would certainly find out who had taken the overcoat. Akaky Akakievich ran home in a terrible state: his hair, which was still comparatively abundant on his temples and the back of his head, was completely disheveled; his sides and chest and his trousers were all covered with snow. When his old landlady heard a fearful knock at the door, she jumped hurriedly out of bed and, with only one slipper on, ran to open it, modestly holding her chemise over her bosom; but when she opened it she stepped back, seeing in what a state Akaky Akakievich was. When he told her what had happened, she clasped her hands in horror and said that he must go straight to the district commissioner, because the local police inspector would deceive him, make promises and lead him a dance; that it would be best of all to go to the district commissioner, and that she knew him, because Anna, the Finnish girl who was once her cook, was now in service as a nurse at the commissioner's; and that she often saw him himself when he passed by their house, and that he used to be every Sunday at church too, saying his prayers and at the same time looking good-humoredly at everyone, and that therefore by every token he must be a kindhearted man. After listening to this advice, Akaky Akakievich made his way very gloomily to his room, and how he spent that night I leave to the imagination of those who are in the least able to picture the position of others.

Early in the morning he set off to the police commissioner's but was told that he was asleep. He came at ten o'clock, he was told again that he was asleep; he came at eleven and was told that the commissioner was not at home; he came at dinnertime, but the clerks in the anteroom would not let him in, and insisted on knowing what was the matter and what business had brought him and exactly what had happened; so that at last Akaky Akakievich for the first time in his life tried to show the strength of his character and said curtly that he must see the commissioner himself, that they dare not refuse to admit him, that he had come from the department on government business, and that if he made complaint of them they would see. The clerks dared say nothing to this, and one of them went to summon the commissioner. The latter received his story of being robbed of his overcoat in an extremely peculiar manner. Instead of attending to the main point, he began asking Akaky Akakievich questions: why had he been coming home so late? wasn't he going, or hadn't he been, to some bawdy house? so that Akaky Akakievich was overwhelmed with confusion, and went away without knowing whether or not the proper measures would be taken regarding his overcoat. He was absent from the office all that day (the only time that it had happened in his life). Next day he appeared with a pale face, wearing his old "dressing gown" which had become a still more pitiful sight. The news of the theft of the overcoat—though there were clerks who did not let even this chance slip of jeering at Akaky Akakievich—touched many of them. They decided on the spot to get up a collection for him, but collected only a very trifling sum, because the clerks had already spent a good deal contributing to the director's portrait and on the purchase of a book, at the suggestion of the head of their department, who was a friend of the author, and so the total realized was very insignificant. One of the clerks, moved by compassion, ventured at any rate to assist Akaky Akakievich with good advice, telling him not to go to the local police inspector, because, though it might happen that the latter might succeed in finding his overcoat because he wanted to impress his superiors, it would remain in the possession of the police unless he presented legal proofs that it belonged to him; he urged that by far the best thing would be to appeal to a Person of Consequence; that the Person of Consequence, by writing and getting into communication with the proper authorities, could push the matter through more successfully. There was nothing else to do. Akaky Akakievich made up his mind to go to the Person of Consequence. What precisely was the nature of the functions of the Person of Consequence has remained a matter of uncertainty. It must be noted that this Person of Consequence had only lately become a person of consequence, and until recently had been a person of no consequence. Though, indeed, his position even now was not reckoned of consequence in comparison with others of still greater consequence. But there is always to be found a circle of persons to whom a person of little consequence in the eyes of others is a person of consequence. It is true that he did his utmost to increase the consequence of his position in various ways, for instance by insisting that his subordinates should come out onto the stairs to meet him when he arrived at his office; that no one should venture to approach him directly but all proceedings should follow the strictest chain of command; that a collegiate registrar should report the matter to the governmental secretary; and the governmental secretary to the titular councilor or whomsoever it might be, and that business should only reach him through this channel. Everyone in Holy Russia has a craze for imitation; everyone apes and mimics his superiors. I have actually been told that a titular councilor who was put in charge of a small separate office, immediately partitioned off a special room for himself, calling it the head office, and posted lackeys at the door with red collars and gold braid, who took hold of the handle of the door and opened it for everyone who went in, though the "head office" was so tiny that it was with difficulty that an ordinary writing desk could be put into it. The manners and habits of the Person of Consequence were dignified and majestic, but hardly subtle. The chief foundation of his system was strictness; "strictness, strictness, and—strictness!" he used to say, and at the last word he would look very significantly at the person he was addressing, though, indeed, he had no reason to do so, for the dozen clerks who made up the whole administrative mechanism of his office stood in appropriate awe of him; any clerk who saw him in the distance would leave his work and remain standing at attention till his superior had left the room. His conversation with his subordinates was usually marked by severity and almost confined to three phrases: "How dare you? Do you know to whom you are speaking? Do you understand who I am?" He was, however, at heart a good-natured man, pleasant and obliging with his colleagues; but his advancement to a high rank had completely turned his head. When he received it, he was perplexed, thrown off his balance, and quite at a loss as to how to behave. If he chanced to be with his equals, he was still quite a decent man, a very gentlemanly man, in fact, and in many ways even an intelligent man; but as soon as he was in company with men who were even one grade below him, there was simply no doing anything with him: he sat silent and his position excited compassion, the more so as he himself felt that he might have been spending his time to so much more advantage. At times there could be seen in his eyes an intense desire to join in some interesting conversation, but he was restrained by the doubt whether it would not be too much on his part, whether it would not be too great a familiarity and lowering of his dignity, and in consequence of these reflections he remained everlastingly in the same mute condition, only uttering from time to time monosyllabic sounds, and in this way he gained the reputation of being a terrible bore.

So this was the Person of Consequence to whom our friend Akaky Akakievich appealed, and he appealed to him at a most unpropitious moment, very unfortunate for himself, though fortunate, indeed, for the Person of Consequence. The latter happened to be in his study, talking in the very best of spirits with an old friend of his childhood who had only just arrived and whom he had not seen for several years. It was at this moment that he was informed that a man called Bashmachkin was asking to see him. He asked abruptly, "What sort of man is he?" and received the answer, "A government clerk." "Ah! he can wait. I haven't time now," said the Person of Consequence. Here I must observe that this was a complete lie on the part of the Person of Consequence; he had time; his friend and he had long ago said all they had to say to each other and their conversation had begun to be broken by very long pauses during which they merely slapped each other on the knee, saying, "So that's how things are, Ivan Abramovich!" —"So that's it, Stepan Varlamovich!" but, despite that, he told the clerk to wait in order to show his friend, who had left the civil service some years before and was living at home in the country, how long clerks had to wait for him. At last, after they had talked or rather been silent, to their heart's content and had smoked a cigar in very comfortable armchairs with sloping backs, he seemed suddenly to recollect, and said to the secretary, who was standing at the door with papers for his signature: "Oh, by the way, there is a clerk waiting, isn't there? tell him he can come in." When he saw Akaky Akakievich's meek appearance and old uniform, he turned to him at once and said: "What do you want?" in a firm and abrupt voice, which he had purposely rehearsed in his own room in solitude before the mirror for a week before receiving his present post and the grade of a general. Akaky Akakievich, who was overwhelmed with appropriate awe beforehand, was somewhat confused and, as far as his tongue would allow him, explained to the best of his powers, with even more frequent "ers" than usual, that he had had a perfectly new overcoat and now he had been robbed of it in the most inhuman way, and that now he had come to beg him by his intervention either to correspond with his honor, the head police commissioner, or anybody else, and find the overcoat. This mode of proceeding struck the general for some reason as too familiar. "What next, sir?" he went on abruptly. "Don't you know the way to proceed? To whom are you addressing yourself? Don't you know how things are done? You ought first to have handed in a petition to the office; it would have gone to the head clerk of the room, and to the head clerk of the section; then it would have been handed to the secretary and the secretary would have brought it to me . . ."

"But, your Excellency," said Akaky Akakievich, trying to gather the drop of courage he possessed and feeling at the same time that he was perspiring all over, "I ventured, your Excellency, to trouble you because secretaries . . . er . . . are people you can't depend on . . ."

"What? what? what?" said the Person of Consequence, "where did you get hold of that attitude? where did you pick up such ideas? What insubordination is spreading among young men against their superiors and their chiefs!" The Person of Consequence did not apparently observe that Akaky Akakievich was well over fifty, and therefore if he could have been called a young man it would only have been in comparison with a man of seventy. "Do you know to whom you are speaking? Do you understand who I am? Do you understand that, I ask you?" At this point he stamped, and raised his voice to such a powerful note that Akaky Akakievich was not the only one to be terrified. Akaky Akakievich was positively petrified; he staggered, trembling all over, and could not stand; if the porters had not run up to support him, he would have flopped on the floor; he was led out almost unconscious. The Person of Consequence, pleased that the effect had surpassed his expectations and enchanted at the idea that his words could even deprive a man of consciousness, stole a sideway glance

at his friend to see how he was taking it, and perceived not without satisfaction that his friend was feeling very uncertain and even
beginning to be a little terrified himself.

How he got downstairs, how he went out into the street—of
all that Akaky Akakievich remembered nothing; he had no feeling in his arms or his legs. In all his life he had never been so severely reprimanded by a general, and this was by one of another
department, too. He went out into the snowstorm that was whistling through the streets, with his mouth open, and as he went he
stumbled off the pavement; the wind, as its way is in Petersburg,
blew upon him from all points of the compass and from every side
street. In an instant it had blown a quinsy into his throat, and when
he got home he was not able to utter a word; he went to bed
with a swollen face and throat. That's how violent the effects of
an appropriate reprimand can be!

Next day he was in a high fever. Thanks to the gracious assistance of the Petersburg climate, the disease made more rapid
progress than could have been expected, and when the doctor
came, after feeling his pulse he could find nothing to do but pre-
scribe a poultice, and that simply so that the patient might not be
left without the benefit of medical assistance; however, two days
later he informed him that his end was at hand, after which he
turned to Akaky Akakievich's landlady and said: "And you had
better lose no time, my good woman, but order him now a pine
coffin, for an oak one will be too expensive for him." Whether
Akaky Akakievich heard these fateful words or not, whether they
produced a shattering effect upon him, and whether he regretted
his pitiful life, no one can tell, for he was constantly in delirium
and fever. Apparitions, each stranger than the one before, were
continually haunting him: first he saw Petrovich and was ordering
him to make an overcoat trimmed with some sort of traps for
robbers, who were, he believed, continually under the bed, and he
was calling his landlady every minute to pull out a thief who had
even got under the quilt; then he kept asking why his old "dressing
gown" was hanging before him when he had a new overcoat; then
he thought he was standing before the general listening to the
appropriate reprimand and saying, "I am sorry, your Excellency";
then finally he became abusive, uttering the most awful language,
so that his old landlady positively crossed herself, having never

heard anything of the kind from him before, and the more horrified because these dreadful words followed immediately upon the phrase "your Excellency." Later on, his talk was merely a medley of nonsense, so that it was quite unintelligible; all that was evident was that his incoherent words and thoughts were concerned with nothing but the overcoat. At last poor Akaky Akakievich gave up the ghost. No seal was put upon his room nor upon his things, because, in the first place, he had no heirs and, in the second, the property left was very small, to wit, a bundle of quills, a quire of white government paper, three pairs of socks, two or three buttons that had come off his trousers, and the "dressing gown" with which the reader is already familiar. Who came into all this wealth God only knows; even I who tell the tale must admit that I have not bothered to inquire. And Petersburg carried on without Akaky Akakievich, as though, indeed, he had never been in the city. A creature had vanished and departed whose cause no one had championed, who was dear to no one, of interest to no one, who never attracted the attention of a naturalist, though the latter does not disdain to fix a common fly upon a pin and look at him under the microscope—a creature who bore patiently the jeers of the office and for no particular reason went to his grave, though even he at the very end of his life was visited by an exalted guest in the form of an overcoat that for one instant brought color into his poor, drab life—a creature on whom disease fell as it falls upon the heads of the mighty ones of this world . . . !

Several days after his death, a messenger from the department was sent to his lodgings with instructions that he should go at once to the office, for his chief was asking for him; but the messenger was obliged to return without him, explaining that he could not come, and to the inquiry "Why?" he added, "Well, you see, the fact is he is dead; he was buried three days ago." This was how they learned at the office of the death of Akaky Akakievich, and the next day there was sitting in his seat a new clerk who was very much taller and who wrote not in the same straight handwriting but made his letters more slanting and crooked.

But who could have imagined that this was not all there was to tell about Akaky Akakievich, that he was destined for a few days to make his presence felt in the world after his death, as though to make up for his life having been unnoticed by anyone? But so it happened, and our little story unexpectedly finishes with a fantastic ending.

Rumors were suddenly floating about Petersburg that in the neighborhood of the Kalinkin Bridge and for a little distance beyond, a corpse[7] had begun appearing at night in the form of a clerk looking for a stolen overcoat, and stripping from the shoulders of all passers-by, regardless of grade and calling, overcoats of all descriptions—trimmed with cat fur or beaver or padded, lined with raccoon, fox, and bear—made, in fact of all sorts of skin which men have adapted for the covering of their own. One of the clerks of the department saw the corpse with his own eyes and at once recognized it as Akaky Akakievich; but it excited in him such terror that he ran away as fast as his legs could carry him and so could not get a very clear view of him, and only saw him hold up his finger threateningly in the distance.

From all sides complaints were continually coming that backs and shoulders, not of mere titular councilors, but even of upper court councilors, had been exposed to catching cold, as a result of being stripped of their overcoats. Orders were given to the police to catch the corpse regardless of trouble or expense, dead or alive, and to punish him severely, as an example to others, and, indeed, they very nearly succeeded in doing so. The policeman of one district in Kiryushkin Alley snatched a corpse by the collar on the spot of the crime in the very act of attempting to snatch a frieze overcoat from a retired musician, who used, in his day, to play the flute. Having caught him by the collar, he shouted until he had brought two other policemen whom he ordered to hold the corpse while he felt just a minute in his boot to get out a snuffbox in order to revive his nose which had six times in his life been frostbitten, but the snuff was probably so strong that not even a dead man could stand it. The policeman had hardly had time to put his finger over his right nostril and draw up some snuff in the left when the corpse sneezed violently right into the eyes of all three. While they were putting their fists up to wipe their eyes,

---

[7] Mrs. Garnett excepted, this is often translated "ghost," but there is no doubt of Gogol's intention. He uses the word *mertverts* (corpse) and not *prividenye* (ghost). To confuse the two is damaging to Gogol's delight in the fantastic, and seriously alters the tone of the story. (ed.)

the corpse completely vanished, so that they were not even sure whether he had actually been in their hands. From that time forward, the policemen had such a horror of the dead that they were even afraid to seize the living and confined themselves to shouting from the distance: "Hey, you! Move on!" and the clerk's body began to appear even on the other side of the Kalinkin Bridge, terrorizing all timid people.

We have, however, quite neglected the Person of Consequence, who may in reality almost be said to be the cause of the fantastic ending of this perfectly true story. To begin with, my duty requires me to do justice to the Person of Consequence by recording that soon after poor Akaky Akakievich had gone away crushed to powder, he felt something not unlike regret. Sympathy was a feeling not unknown to him; his heart was open to many kindly impulses, although his exalted grade very often prevented them from being shown. As soon as his friend had gone out of his study, he even began brooding over poor Akaky Akakievich, and from that time forward, he was almost every day haunted by the image of the poor clerk who had been unable to survive the official reprimand. The thought of the man so worried him that a week later he actually decided to send a clerk to find out how he was and whether he really could help him in any way. And when they brought him word that Akaky Akakievich had died suddenly in delirium and fever, it made a great impression on him; his conscience reproached him and he was depressed all day. Anxious to distract his mind and to forget the unpleasant incident, he went to spend the evening with one of his friends, where he found respectable company, and what was best of all, almost everyone was of the same grade so that he was able to be quite uninhibited. This had a wonderful effect on his spirits. He let himself go, became affable and genial—in short, spent a very agreeable evening. At supper he drank a couple of glasses of champagne—a proceeding which we all know is not a bad recipe for cheerfulness. The champagne made him inclined to do something unusual, and he decided not to go home yet but to visit a lady of his acquaintance, a certain Karolina Ivanovna—a lady apparently of German extraction, for whom he entertained extremely friendly feelings. It must be noted that the Person of Consequence was a man no longer young. He was an excellent husband, and the respectable father of a family.

He had two sons, one already serving in an office, and a nice-looking daughter of sixteen with a rather turned-up, pretty little nose, who used to come every morning to kiss his hand, saying: *"Bon jour, Papa."* His wife, who was still blooming and decidedly good-looking, indeed, used first to give him her hand to kiss and then turning his hand over would kiss it. But though the Person of Consequence was perfectly satisfied with the pleasant amenities of his domestic life, he thought it proper to have a lady friend in another quarter of the town. This lady friend was not a bit better looking nor younger than his wife, but these puzzling things exist in the world and it is not our business to criticize them. And so the Person of Consequence went downstairs, got into his sledge, and said to his coachman, "To Karolina Ivanovna." While luxuriously wrapped in his warm fur coat he remained in that agreeable frame of mind sweeter to a Russian than anything that could be invented, that is, when one thinks of nothing while thoughts come into the mind by themselves, one pleasanter than the other, without your having to bother following them or looking for them. Full of satisfaction, he recalled all the amusing moments of the evening he had spent, all the phrases that had started the intimate circle of friends laughing; many of them he repeated in an undertone and found them as amusing as before, and so, very naturally, laughed very heartily at them again. From time to time, however, he was disturbed by a gust of wind which, blowing suddenly, God knows why or where from, cut him in the face, pelting him with flakes of snow, puffing out his coat collar like a sail, or suddenly flinging it with unnatural force over his head and giving him endless trouble to extricate himself from it. All at once, the Person of Consequence felt that someone had clutched him very tightly by the collar. Turning around he saw a short man in a shabby old uniform, and not without horror recognized him as Akaky Akakievich. The clerk's face was white as snow and looked like that of a corpse, but the horror of the Person of Consequence was beyond all bounds when he saw the mouth of the corpse distorted into speech, and breathing upon him the chill of the grave, it uttered the following words: "Ah, so here you are at last! At last I've . . . er . . . caught you by the collar. It's your overcoat I want; you refused to help me and abused me into the bargain! So now give me yours!" The poor Person of Consequence very nearly dropped dead. Resolute and determined as he was in his office and before subordinates in general, and though anyone looking at his manly air and figure would have said: "Oh, what a man of character!" yet in this situation he felt, like very many persons of heroic appearance, such terror that not without reason he began to be afraid he would have some sort of fit. He actually flung his overcoat off his shoulders as far as he could and shouted to his coachman in an unnatural voice: "Drive home! Let's get out of here!" The coachman, hearing the tone which he had only heard in critical moments and then accompanied by something even more tangible, hunched his shoulders up to his ears in case of worse following, swung his whip, and flew on like an arrow. In a little over six minutes, the Person of Consequence was at the entrance of his own house. Pale, panic-stricken, and without his overcoat, he arrived home instead of at Karolina Ivanovna's, dragged himself to his own room, and spent the night in great distress, so that next morning his daughter said to him at breakfast, "You look very pale today, Papa"; but her papa remained mute and said not a word to anyone of what had happened to him, where he had been, and where he had been going. The incident made a great impression upon him. Indeed, it happened far more rarely that he said to his subordinates, "How dare you? Do you understand who I am?" and he never uttered those words at all until he had first heard all the facts of the case.

What was even more remarkable is that from that time on the apparition of the dead clerk ceased entirely; apparently the general's overcoat had fitted him perfectly; anyway nothing more was heard of overcoats being snatched from anyone. Many restless and anxious people refused, however, to be pacified, and still maintained that in remote parts of the town the dead clerk went on appearing. One policeman, in Kolomna, for instance, saw with his own eyes an apparition appear from behind a house; but, being by natural constitution somewhat frail—so much so that on one occasion an ordinary grown-up suckling pig, making a sudden dash out of some private building, knocked him off his feet to the great amusement of the cabmen standing around, whom he fined two kopeks each for snuff for such disrespect—he did not dare to stop it, and so followed it in the dark until the apparition suddenly looked around and, stopping, asked him: "What do you want?" displaying a huge fist such as you never see among the living. The policeman said: "Nothing," and turned back on the spot. This apparition, however, was considerably taller and adorned with immense mustaches, and, directing its steps apparently toward Obukhov Bridge, vanished into the darkness of the night.

Plays

The Inspector General

CHARACTERS IN THE PLAY

ANTON ANTONOVICH SKVOZNIK DMUKHANOVSKY	The Mayor
ANNA ANDREEVNA	His wife
MARIA ANTONOVNA	His daughter
LUKA LUKICH KHLOPOV	Superintendent of Schools
HIS WIFE	
AMMOS FIODOROVICH LIAPKIN-TIAPKIN	The Judge
ARTEMY FILIPPOVICH ZEMLIANIKA	Welfare Commissioner
IVAN KUZMICH SHPEKIN	The Postmaster
PIOTR IVANOVICH DOBCHINSKY	} Landowners
PIOTR IVANOVICH BOBCHINSKY	
IVAN ALEKSANDROVICH KHLESTAKOV	A clerk from St. Petersburg
OSIP	His servant
CHRISTIAN IVANOVICH HÜBNER	The District Doctor
FIODOR ANDREEVICH LIULIUKOV	} Retired officials,
IVAN LAZAREVICH RASTAKOVSKY	worthies of
STEPAN IVANOVICH KOROBKIN	the town

STEPAN ILYICH UKHOVERTOV — A police captain

SVISTUNOV

PUGOVITSYN } Policemen

DERZHIMORDA

ABDULIN — A merchant

FEVRONYA PETROVNA POSHLIOPKINA — A locksmith's wife

A SERGEANT'S WIDOW

MISHKA — The Mayor's servant

A WAITER

OTHER POLICEMEN, GUESTS (MALE AND FEMALE), MERCHANTS, CITIZENS, PETITIONERS

THE INSPECTOR GENERAL

CHARACTERS AND COSTUMES

Directions for the Actors

It is no use blaming the mirror if your mug is crooked.

A Proverb

THE MAYOR,[1] an elderly man who has spent his life in the civil
service, very shrewd in his own way. Though he accepts
bribes he is very dignified in deportment; serious and even a
little sententious; he speaks neither loudly nor softly, neither
too little nor too much. Every word he utters is significant.
His features are coarse and heavy, as is always the case with
men who have worked themselves up from the lower ranks in
government service. The transition from fear to joy, from
servility to arrogance is somewhat rapid in him, as is common
in a man of coarse inclinations. He is usually wearing a uniform adorned with frogs and high boots with spurs. His hair
is cut short and streaked with gray.

ANNA ANDREEVNA, his wife, a provincial coquette, not yet middle-
aged, whose life has been spent between novels and albums
and the supervision of household affairs and maids. Very in-

---

[1] *Gorodnichy*, an appointed rather than elected official who served both as
chief authority of a district town and as sheriff. (ed.)

quisitive and given to the display of vanity. Sometimes domi-
neers her husband simply because he doesn't know how to
answer her; but this domineering is confined to trifles, and
manifests itself in scolding and sneering. She wears four different dresses in the course of the play.

KHLESTAKOV, a young man of twenty-three, thin and slender; rather
foolish, what is known as scatterbrained—one of those who in
their office are called featherheads. He speaks and acts without
the slightest thought. He is incapable of concentrating on any
subject. He speaks jerkily and the words dart from his lips
quite unexpectedly. The more candor and simplicity an actor
puts into this part, the more he will succeed in it. He is dressed
in the fashion.

OSIP is a servant like most servants who are getting on in years. He
speaks gravely, is a little condescending sometimes, and likes
to repeat to himself moral reflections intended for his master.
His voice is almost always composed, but when talking to his
master there is a stern, abrupt, and even rather rude tone in it.
He is more intelligent than his master, and so is quicker to
grasp things, but is not fond of saying too much, and is a silent
rascal. He wears a shabby gray or dark blue coat.

BOBCHINSKY and DOBCHINSKY are both short, squat little men; extremely alike and very inquisitive; both have little potbellies;
both speak very rapidly, and eke out their words with em-
phatic gestures. Dobchinsky is a little taller and more serious
than Bobchinsky, but Bobchinsky is livelier and more free and
easy.

LIAPKIN-TIAPKIN, the Judge, is a man who has read five or six
books, and so is something of a freethinker. He is given to
reading meanings into everything, and so attaches weight to
every word he utters. The actor ought to maintain an air of
great importance throughout. He speaks in a bass voice with a
slow drawl, with a wheeze and a hiss like an old-fashioned
clock, which hisses before it strikes.

ZEMLIANIKA, the Welfare Commissioner, is a very fat, slow, clumsy
man, but is, nevertheless, a wily scoundrel. Very officious and
obliging.

THE POSTMASTER is good-natured to the point of simplemindedness.

The other characters do not need special explanation; their proto-
types are continually before us.

The actors must pay special attention to the last scene. The last word should give an electric shock to all present at once. The whole group should change its position instantly. A cry of astonishment should spring from all the women as though from one bosom. Disregard of these instructions may ruin the whole effect.

ACT I

A Room in the Mayor's House

THE MAYOR, THE WELFARE COMMISSIONER, THE SUPERINTENDENT OF SCHOOLS, THE JUDGE, THE POLICE CAPTAIN, THE DOCTOR, TWO POLICEMEN

THE MAYOR. I have called you together, gentlemen, to tell you a most unpleasant piece of news: an Inspector General is coming to visit us.

AMMOS FIODOROVICH. An Inspector General?

ARTEMY FILIPPOVICH. An Inspector General?

THE MAYOR. An Inspector General, from Petersburg, incognito; and with secret orders.

AMMOS FIODOROVICH. That's a pleasant surprise!

ARTEMY FILIPPOVICH. As though we hadn't trouble enough!

LUKA LUKICH. Good God! And with secret orders!

THE MAYOR. I had a sort of premonition of it: all night long I was dreaming of two extraordinary rats. I assure you I never saw rats like them: black and unnaturally large! They came and sniffed about—and went away. Here, I'll read you the letter I've received from Andrei Ivanovich Tchmykhov, whom you know, Artemy Filippovich. This is what he writes: "Dear friend and benefactor!" (*mutters in an undertone, hastily looking through the letter*) "and to inform you" . . . Ah, here it is: "I hasten to inform you, among other things, that an official has arrived with instructions to inspect the whole province, and especially our district (*lifts up his finger significantly*). I have learned this from the most reliable sources, though he passes himself off for a private person. As I know that you have your little failings like everybody else, for you are a sensible man and don't like to let things slip through your fingers" . . . (*pausing*) well, we are all friends here . . . "I advise you to take immediate precautions, for he may arrive any minute, if, indeed, he has not come already and is not living among you incognito. . . . Yesterday I . . ." well, here he goes on to family affairs, "my sister Anna Kirilovna and her husband have come to stay with us; Ivan Kirilovich has grown much fatter, and is always playing the fiddle" . . . and so on and so on. So that's the situation!

AMMOS FIODOROVICH. Yes, it's an extraordinary situation, simply extraordinary. There must be some reason for it.

LUKA LUKICH. What is it for, Anton Antonovich, how do you account for it? Why should an Inspector come here?

THE MAYOR. What for! It seems it was fated to be! (*with a sigh*). Till now, and thank God for it, they have pried into other towns; now our turn has come.

AMMOS FIODOROVICH. I imagine, Anton Antonovich, that there is a subtle and chiefly political reason. I'll tell you what it means: Russia . . . yes . . . is meaning to go to war, and the ministers, you see, have sent an official to find out whether there is any treason here.

THE MAYOR. Pooh, what next! And you a sensible man, too! Treason in a district town! Is it on the frontier? Why, you might gallop for three years and not reach any foreign country.

AMMOS FIODOROVICH. No, I tell you, you are wrong there . . . you are . . . they have all sorts of schemes in Petersburg; they may be far away, but they take stock of everything.

THE MAYOR. They may or they may not; anyway, I have warned you, gentlemen. Mind you, I have taken measures in my own department, and I advise you to do the same. And especially you, Artemy Filippovich! Our visitor is pretty certain to want to inspect the charitable institutions under your supervision first of all, and so make certain that everything is as it should be: see that the nightcaps are clean and that the patients don't look like blacksmiths, as they do on ordinary days.

ARTEMY FILIPPOVICH. Oh, that's not very important. Of course they can put on clean nightcaps.

THE MAYOR. Yes; and over every bed put a sign in Latin or some other language . . . that's for you to decide, Christian Ivanovich . . . the name of each disease, when each patient was taken ill, the day of the week and the month. . . . It's a pity your patients smoke such strong tobacco that it makes one sneeze when one goes in. And it would be better if there were fewer of them: he will suspect at once that there is something wrong with the management, or that the doctor does not know his business.

ARTEMY FILIPPOVICH. Oh, as to doctoring, Christian Ivanovich and I came to the conclusion long ago that the nearer to nature the better—we don't make use of expensive medicines. They are simple people: if they die, they'll die anyhow; if they recover, they recover anyhow. And it would be difficult for Christian Ivanovich to interview the patients; he does not know a word of Russian.

(HÜBNER *emits a sound intermediate between* e *and* a.)

THE MAYOR. I should advise you too, Ammos Fiodorovich, to look after the courthouse. In the hall where the applicants come with complaints and petitions the attendants have begun keeping geese with a lot of young goslings, which are always waddling about under one's feet. Of course poultry keeping is a most laudable pursuit, and why shouldn't the porter keep them? Only it's not the thing, you know, in a public office. . . . I meant to mention it to you before, but I always forgot it somehow.

AMMOS FIODOROVICH. I'll order them all to be taken to my kitchen today. Won't you come to dinner with me?

THE MAYOR. It's a pity, too, that you have all sorts of rubbish hanging up to dry in the court itself, and there's a hunting whip on the top of the case where deeds are kept. I know you are fond of sport, but it would be better to take it away for a time, and when the Inspector has gone you can hang it up again if you like. And as for your assessor . . . of course he is a man who understands his business, but he smells as though he has just come out of a distillery—that's not quite proper either. I meant to speak about it long ago, but my attention was always diverted by something else, I don't know what. Something can be done for it if, as he says, it is his natural smell; he might be advised to try onion or garlic or something. Christian Ivanovich might give him some drug for it.

(HÜBNER *gives vent to the same inarticulate sound.*)

AMMOS FIODOROVICH. No, there is nothing you can do for it: he says his nurse dropped him as a baby and he has smelled a little of vodka ever since.

THE MAYOR. Oh well, I only just mentioned it. As for the way that the business of the court is conducted, and what Andrei Ivanovich in his letter calls "failings," I can say nothing. And indeed, what is there to say? There is no man entirely free from sin. . . . That is ordained by God Himself, and it is no use the Voltairians[2] disputing it.

AMMOS FIODOROVICH. What do you mean by sin, Anton Antonovich? There are sins and sins. I tell everyone openly that I take bribes, but what bribes? Wolfhound puppies. That's a very different matter.

THE MAYOR. Well, puppies or anything else, it's bribes just the same.

AMMOS FIODOROVICH. Oh no, Anton Antonovich. If a man takes a fur coat worth five hundred rubles or a shawl for his wife . . .

THE MAYOR. Well, what of it if the only bribes you take are puppies? You don't believe in God: you never go to church; while I am at least firm in the faith, and I go to church every Sunday. But you . . . oh, I know you: when you begin talking about the creation of the world, it makes my hair stand on end.

AMMOS FIODOROVICH. But I came to my views by myself, by my own thinking.

THE MAYOR. Well, in some cases too much thinking is worse than none at all. I spoke of the district court—but there, to tell the truth it is not likely that anyone will peep into it; it's a spot to be envied indeed; it's under the special protection of Providence. But you, Luka Lukich, as Superintendent of Schools, must be particularly careful about the teachers. Of course they are learned men and have been educated at all sorts of colleges, but they have very strange peculiarities, naturally, inseparable from their vocation. One of them, for instance, the one with a fat face . . . I can't recollect his name, never seems able to go up to his desk without making a grimace like this (*makes a grimace*) and then begins smoothing his beard from under his cravat. Of course, if he makes a face like that at one

---

[2] I.e., freethinkers. Reference is to disciples of Voltaire (1694-1778), French author who was the embodiment of eighteenth-century enlightenment. (ed.)

of the boys it does not matter; it may be necessary, I can't judge; but just think if he does it to a visitor—that might be a dreadful thing: the Inspector or someone else might think it was meant for him. Goodness only knows what it might lead to.

LUKA LUKICH. What am I to do with him? I've spoken to him over and over again. Only the other day, when our marshal of nobility[3] came into the classroom, he made a face worse than anything I've ever seen. He did it with the best intentions, but I got reprimanded for letting radical notions be put into the boys' heads.

THE MAYOR. And I must say a word to you about the history teacher. He is a brainy fellow, one can see, and has a great amount of learning, but he lectures with such fervor that he forgets himself. I heard him once: so long as he was talking about the Assyrians and the Babylonians it was not bad, but when he came to Alexander the Great, I can't describe how he carried on. Damn it! I thought the house was on fire! He jumped out of his desk and smashed a chair on the floor with all his strength. Of course Alexander the Great was a hero, but why smash the chairs? It's destroying government property.

LUKA LUKICH. Yes, he is excitable. I've mentioned it to him several times. He answers: "You may say what you like, but in the cause of learning I am ready to give my life."

THE MAYOR. Yes, such is the mysterious dispensation of Providence: clever men are either drunkards or they make such faces that you don't know where to look.

LUKA LUKICH. I wouldn't wish my worst enemy to serve in the department of education! One is afraid of everyone: everyone interferes, everyone wants to show what a clever person he is.

THE MAYOR. That's nothing. But this damned incognito! He'll look in all of a sudden: "Aha! so you are here, my dear fellows! And who is judge here?" he will say. "Liapkin-Tiapkin." —"Hand him over! And who is Welfare Commissioner?"— "Zemlianika."—"Hand him over!" That's what's so awful!

---

[3] Official elected by landlords of nobility. He had no real power, but would look into administrative matters, concern himself with philanthropic enterprises, etc. (ed.)

(*Enter the* POSTMASTER.)

THE POSTMASTER. Please explain, gentlemen, what's this? What official's coming?

THE MAYOR. Why, haven't you heard?

THE POSTMASTER. I have heard from Piotr Ivanovich Bobchinsky. He was in the post office just now.

THE MAYOR. Well, what do you think about it?

THE POSTMASTER. What do I think? There'll be war with the Turks.

AMMOS FIODOROVICH. My very words! Just what I thought.

THE MAYOR. Yes, you're both way off!

THE POSTMASTER. Indeed, but it's war with the Turks. It's the doing of those stinkers, the French.

THE MAYOR. War with the Turks! It's we who are going to get it, not the Turks. That's certain—I have a letter.

THE POSTMASTER. Oh, in that case, there won't be war with the Turks.

THE MAYOR. Well, what do you say, Ivan Kuzmich?

THE POSTMASTER. What do I matter? How about you, Anton Antonovich?

THE MAYOR. Me? Well, I'm not alarmed—but then, you know . . . The shopkeepers and townspeople make me uneasy. They say I am the plague of their lives; though God is my witness, if I have taken something here and there, it has been with no ill feeling. Indeed, I suspect . . . (*takes him by the arm and leads him aside*) . . . I wonder whether there hasn't been some secret report against me. Why should an Inspector be sent to us? Listen, Ivan Kuzmich, couldn't you, for our common benefit, just unseal and read every letter which reaches your post office, going or coming; just to see whether there is any talebearing or correspondence going on? If not, you can seal it up again; or, indeed, you can deliver it open.

THE POSTMASTER. I know, I know . . . You need not teach me, I do that already, not so much by way of precaution as from curiosity: I do like to know what's going on in the world. I assure you, it makes wonderful reading. It is a pleasure to read some letters—all sorts of incidents are so well described . . . and so instructive . . . better than *The Moscow News!*

THE MAYOR. Well, tell me, haven't you read anything about an official from Petersburg?

THE POSTMASTER.   No, nothing about a Petersburg one, but a lot about those at Saratov and Kostroma.[4] But it is a pity you don't read the letters; there are fine passages in them. For instance, a lieutenant was writing to a friend the other day, and he described a ball in a most amusing way . . . very, very nice it was. "My life, dear friend," he writes, "is passed in Elysium[5]: plenty of young ladies, bands playing, banners flying." . . . It's written with great feeling. I have kept it on purpose. Would you like me to read it?

THE MAYOR.   Oh, it's not the time for that now. Well then, Ivan Kuzmich, do me the favor, if any sort of complaint or report comes into your hands, keep it without hesitation.

THE POSTMASTER.   With great pleasure.

AMMOS FIODOROVICH.   You'd better be careful; you will get into trouble for that one of these days!

THE POSTMASTER.   Goodness gracious!

THE MAYOR.   Nonsense, nonsense. It would be a very different thing if you made public use of it, but this is a private affair.

AMMOS FIODOROVICH.   Yes, there is mischief afoot! And I must tell you, Anton Antonovich, I was coming to offer you a present—a dog, the sister to the hound that you know. You are aware, of course, that Cheptovich is taking proceedings against Varkhovinsky, and now I'm in clover. I hunt hares on the lands of both.

THE MAYOR.   Holy father! I don't care about your hares now: I can't get that damned incognito out of my head. One keeps expecting that the door will open—and in will walk . . .

(BOBCHINSKY *and* DOBCHINSKY *enter, breathless.*)

BOBCHINSKY.   An extraordinary incident!

DOBCHINSKY.   A surprising piece of news!

ALL.   What? What is it?

DOBCHINSKY.   An unforeseen occurrence: we went to the inn . . .

BOBCHINSKY (*interrupting*).   Piotr Ivanovich and I went to the inn.

DOBCHINSKY (*interrupting*).   Oh, allow me, Piotr Ivanovich, I'll tell the story.

---

[4] Provincial capitals on the Volga River, the former in southeastern Russia, the latter in central Russia, northeast of Moscow. (ed.)
[5] I.e., perfect happiness. Elysium is the Greek paradise or residence of the blessed after death. (ed.)

BOBCHINSKY.   Oh no, allow me . . . allow me, allow me . . . you
will never find words to tell it . . .

DOBCHINSKY.   And you will get muddled and forget something.

BOBCHINSKY.   I won't, I swear I won't. Don't interrupt, let me tell
it, don't interrupt! Gentlemen, please tell Piotr Ivanovich not
to interfere.

THE MAYOR.   For goodness' sake, tell us what has happened! My
heart's in my mouth. Sit down, gentlemen! Take a chair, Piotr
Ivanovich, here is a chair. (*They all sit down around the two
PIOTR IVANOVICHES.*) Well, now, what is it?

BOBCHINSKY.   Allow me, I will begin at the beginning. As soon as
I had the pleasure of leaving your company, when you seemed
somewhat perturbed by the letter you had received . . . yes,
I ran then . . . Oh, please don't interrupt, Piotr Ivanovich!
I know it all perfectly well.—So, you see I ran into Korobkin's. And not finding Korobkin at home, I called at Rastakovsky's; and not finding Rastakovsky at home, I went on to see
Ivan Kuzmich here, to tell him the news you had received,
and as I came away I met Piotr Ivanovich . . .

DOBCHINSKY (*interrupting*).   Near the stall where they sell pies.

BOBCHINSKY (*waving him aside*).   Near the stall where they sell
pies. Yes, when I met Piotr Ivanovich I said to him, "Have you
heard the news Anton Antonovich has from a trustworthy
correspondent?" And Piotr Ivanovich had heard of it already
from your housekeeper, Avdotya, who had been sent to Filipp
Antonovich Pochechuev's on some errand, I don't know
what . . .

DOBCHINSKY (*interrupting*).   To get a keg for French vodka.

BOBCHINSKY (*waving him aside*).   To get a keg for French vodka.
So we went, Piotr Ivanovich and I, to Pochechuev's. Please,
Piotr Ivanovich . . . er . . . don't interrupt, please don't interrupt! We were going to Pochechuev's, and on the way
Piotr Ivanovich said, "Let us go into the inn. My stomach
. . . I've had nothing to eat all day, and there is a quaking
in my stomach." Yes, in Piotr Ivanovich's stomach . . . "And
they have just got in a new lot of smoked salmon," he said,
"so let's have lunch." No sooner had we walked into the inn
than a young man . . .

DOBCHINSKY (*interrupting*).   Of pleasant appearance, not wearing
official uniform . . .

BOBCHINSKY. Of pleasant appearance, not wearing official uniform, was walking about the room like this, and in his face such a look of deliberation, so to speak . . . a face . . . gestures, and here (*twirls his hand about his forehead*) a great deal of everything. I had a sort of foreboding and said to Piotr Ivanovich, "There is something behind this." Yes, and Piotr Ivanovich had already beckoned to the innkeeper . . . to Vlas, the innkeeper; his wife gave birth three weeks ago, and a smart little baby too, he will keep an inn like his father. Calling Vlas, Piotr Ivanovich whispers: "Who is that young man?" he says, and Vlas answers: "That," he says . . . Oh, don't interrupt me, Piotr Ivanovich, please don't interrupt me, you can't tell it, you really can't; you lisp, it's one of your teeth, I know, makes you lisp. . . . "That young man," he says, "is an official, yes, and has come from Petersburg, and his name," he says, "is Ivan Aleksandrovich Khlestakov, and he is going," he says, "to the province of Saratov, and he's acting so peculiarly," he says, "he has been here nearly two weeks and never leaves the house, takes everything on credit and won't pay a copper." As he was saying this, an inspiration dawned upon me. "Ah!" I said to Piotr Ivanovich . . .

DOBCHINSKY. No, Piotr Ivanovich, it was I who said "Ah!"

BOBCHINSKY. You said it first, and then I said it. "Ah!" we cried, Piotr Ivanovich and I. "But what is his purpose in staying here when he has to go to Saratov?" Yes. Why, he is that official, not a doubt of it!

THE MAYOR. Who? What official?

BOBCHINSKY. The official that you have had warning of—the Inspector General.

THE MAYOR (*in alarm*). Good God, what are you saying? It can't be!

DOBCHINSKY. It is! He pays no money and he does not go away. Who can it be if not he? And his traveling pass[6] is for Saratov.

BOBCHINSKY. It is he, upon my word it is. So keenly observant: looked into everything. He saw that Piotr Ivanovich and I were eating smoked salmon—chiefly on account of Piotr Ivanovich's stomach—yes; so he peered into our plates. It gave me the shudders.

---

[6] *Podorozhnaya*, an order for relays of posthorses. (ed.)

THE MAYOR. Lord have mercy on us sinners! What room is he in?

DOBCHINSKY. Number five, under the stairs.

BOBCHINSKY. The very room in which the officers who were here last year had a fight.

THE MAYOR. And has he been here long?

DOBCHINSKY. Two weeks already. He came on St. Vasily's Day.[7]

THE MAYOR. A whole two weeks! (*Aside*) Holy saints! Holy martyrs, get me out of this! Within this two weeks the sergeant's widow has been flogged! The prisoners have not had their rations! The streets . . . like a regular alehouse! and the filth! Disgrace! ignominy! (*Clutches his head.*)

ARTEMY FILIPPOVICH. What do you think, Anton Antonovich? Should we all go together to the inn?

AMMOS FIODOROVICH. No, no! Let the provost, the clergy, and the merchants go first; in the book, *The Deeds of John the Mason*,[8] it says . . .

THE MAYOR. No, no; allow me to decide. I have had difficulties before and they have passed off without difficulty, and I have been thanked into the bargain. Maybe God will pull us through this time too. (*Turning to* BOBCHINSKY) You say he is a young man?

---

[7] I.e., February 28. Reckoning by saint's days was a common practice. (ed.)

[8] According to the note supplied in the Academy text (and there is no reason to doubt their disinterestedness in the matter) this refers to "An English Masonic (religious and mystical) work translated in Russia in the 18th century," and in context, this seems wholly correct. The Freemasons, after all, were considered a subversive organization in Russia because of their liberalism, and they were suppressed. Ammos Fiodorovich prides himself on his freethinking, flaunts, whenever possible, his liberal inclinations, is, indeed, treated as a member of the Voltairian camp by the Mayor. His reference to such a book is fully consistent with his attitude and views, and his specific use of the book as an authority in matters of decorum is absolutely funny. In his *Gogol* (New Directions, 1944, p. 39), Vladimir Nabokov misquotes the Garnett translation to suit his ends, takes her to task because of her "reference to one of the five or six books that the Judge had ever read in his life as 'The Book of John the Mason,' which sounds like something biblical, when the text really refers to a book of adventures concerning John Mason (or attributed to him), an English diplomatist of the Sixteenth Century and Fellow of All Souls who was employed on the Continent in collecting information for the Tudor sovereigns." In fact, the Garnett translation refers to "the book of *John the Mason*," not "The Book of John the Mason." It is Nabokov who perverts the text to make it sound "like something biblical." Further, in context, Ammos Fiodorovich's reference to a book of adventures would be inconsistent not only with the tone of the moment, but, indeed, with the particular bent of his psychological make-up. (ed.)

BOBCHINSKY.   Yes, he is—not more than twenty-three or twenty-four.

THE MAYOR.   That's good; it is easier to see through a young man. It is hard work with an old devil, but a young man is all on the surface. You take care of your own departments, gentlemen, while I'll go around myself, alone, or with Piotr Ivanovich here, unofficially, as though taking a walk, to see that visitors to the town are suffering no inconvenience. Hey, Svistunov?

SVISTUNOV.   Yes, sir?

THE MAYOR.   Go immediately to the Police Captain—no, I'll need you. Tell someone to get the Police Captain as quick as he can, and then come here.

(SVISTUNOV *runs off quickly*.)

ARTEMY FILIPPOVICH.   Come along, come along, Ammos Fiodorovich. There really may be trouble.

AMMOS FIODOROVICH.   But what have you to fear? Put clean nightcaps on your patients and nothing improper can be found.

ARTEMY FILIPPOVICH.   Nightcaps! The patients were ordered to have oatmeal soup, and there is such a stink of cabbage in my corridors that you have to hold your nose.

AMMOS FIODOROVICH.   My mind is at rest. When you come to think of it, whoever would look into the district court? And if he does peep into some document, God help him! Here I have been sitting in the Judge's seat for fifteen years, but if ever I look into the statement of a case I throw it away in despair! Solomon himself could not make out the rights and wrongs of it.

(*The* JUDGE, *the* WELFARE COMMISSIONER, *the* SUPERINTENDENT OF SCHOOLS, *and the* POSTMASTER *go out, and in the doorway run into* SVISTUNOV.)

THE MAYOR.   Well, is the chaise there?

SVISTUNOV.   Yes, sir.

THE MAYOR.   Go into the street . . . but no, stay! Go and get . . . But where are the others? Surely you haven't come back alone? I sent word that Prokhorov was to be here. Where is Prokhorov?

SVISTUNOV.   Prokhorov is at the police station, but he can't be put to any use.

THE MAYOR.   How's that?

SVISTUNOV.   Well, he was brought in this morning dead drunk.

They have poured two buckets of water over him, but he hasn't sobered up yet.

THE MAYOR (*clutching his head*). Oh, my God! my God! Quickly, into the street . . . no, run into the other room first and bring me my sword and new hat. Well, Piotr Ivanovich, let's go!

BOBCHINSKY. Me too, me too! Let me go too, Anton Antonovich!

THE MAYOR. No, no, Piotr Ivanovich, you can't! It would be awkward, and besides, there is no room in the chaise.

BOBCHINSKY. Never mind, never mind, I'll manage: I'll hop along after the chaise. If only I can have a peep through the door or something, to see what he will do and all that . . .

THE MAYOR (*taking his sword from* SVISTUNOV). Go at once and get the policemen. Let each one of them take . . . Ah, what scratches there are on the sword! That confounded blackguard Abdulin—sees his Mayor with an old sword and never thinks of sending me a new one from his shop. Ah, deceitful wretches! And I'll bet the rascals are getting up petitions on the sly. Every one of them is to take a street . . . oh, damn it, street! I mean, a broom—and sweep the street leading to the inn, and sweep it clean too. . . . Do you hear? And you mind, now! I know you; you are hand in glove with all sorts of people and slipping silver spoons into your boots—you had better look out; I have a sharp eye! What have you been up to with Chernyev, the merchant, eh? He was giving you two yards of cloth for your uniform and you walked off with the whole piece! You'd better be careful! You take more than is due to your rank. Go along!

(*Enter* UKHOVERTOV, *the Police Captain.*)

THE MAYOR. Ah, Stepan Ilyich! Kindly tell me, where had you vanished to? It's beyond everything.

UKHOVERTOV. I was just here near the gate.

THE MAYOR. Well, listen, Stepan Ilyich! The official from Petersburg has arrived. What arrangements have you made?

UKHOVERTOV. According to your instructions, I have sent Sergeant Pugovitsyn with the policemen to sweep the pavements.

THE MAYOR. And where is Derzhimorda?

UKHOVERTOV. He has gone with the fire engine.

THE MAYOR. And Prokhorov's drunk?

UKHOVERTOV. Yes, sir.

THE MAYOR.   How could you allow it?

UKHOVERTOV.   Goodness only knows. There was a fight just out-side the town yesterday—he went to settle it and came back drunk.

THE MAYOR.   I tell you what, you do this: Sergeant Pugovitsyn . . . he is a tall fellow, so let him stand on the bridge to make a good appearance. And look sharp and pull down the old fence beside the cobbler's and stick in a pole with a wisp of straw tied at the top, as though new streets were being laid out. The more destruction there is everywhere, the more it shows the activity of the town authorities. Ah, I forgot that beside that fence there is a rubbish heap it would take forty wagons to move. What a filthy town it is, to be sure! Wher-ever you put up a monument, or even a plain fence, people dump rubbish there of all sorts—I don't know where they get it from! (*Sighs.*) And if the official asks the police whether they are satisfied, they are all to say, 'Perfectly satisfied, your honor'; and if anybody is dissatisfied, I'll give him something to satisfy him afterwards. . . . Och, och, och! I am to blame, very much to blame. (*Picks up the hatbox instead of the hat.*) God grant it all goes well—and soon too, and I'll put up a candle such as no one has ever put up before: I'll make every damned shopkeeper come across with a hundred and twenty pounds of wax for that candle. Oh, my God, my God! Let us go, Piotr Ivanovich! (*Is putting the cardboard box on his head instead of the hat.*)

UKHOVERTOV.   Anton Antonovich, that's the box and not your hat.

THE MAYOR (*flinging down the box*).   If it's a box, it's a box, damn it! Oh, and if he should ask why the hospital chapel has not been built, though a grant was made for it five years ago, don't forget to say that the building was begun, but it was burned down. I sent in a report about it. Or someone may forget like an idiot and say it was never begun. And tell Der-zhimorda not to be too free with his fists; he keeps order by giving everyone a black eye—innocent and guilty. Come along, Piotr Ivanovich, come along! (*Goes out and comes back.*) And don't let the soldiers go into the street without anything on: those wretched fellows in the garrison put their coats on over their shirts and nothing below.

(*All go out.*)

(ANNA ANDREEVNA *and* MARIA ANTONOVNA *run on the stage*.)

ANNA. Where are they, where are they? Oh my God! (*Opening the door*) Husband! Antosha! Anton! (*Speaking quickly*) And it's all your doing, it's all because of you. You dawdle around, saying, "I want a pin, I want a handkerchief!" (*Runs to the window and calls*) Anton, Anton, where are you off to? Well, has he come? The Inspector? Has he a mustache? What sort of mustache?

THE MAYOR'S VOICE. Presently, presently, my dear!

ANNA. Presently? That's a nice thing! Presently! I don't want it to be presently. . . . One thing you might tell me, what is he —a colonel? Eh? (*Scornfully*) He is gone! I won't let him forget it! And it's all because of her: "Mamma, Mamma, do wait. I'll just pin my handkerchief behind, I won't be a minute!" That is what comes of your minute! Here we have heard nothing! And it's all your confounded vanity: you heard the Postmaster was here, so you had to go preening before the mirror, turning this way and that way. She fancies he is sweet on her, and all the time he is making faces at you behind your back.

MARIA. Well, it can't be helped, Mamma. We shall know all about it in another hour or two.

ANNA. In an hour or two! Thanks very much. A nice answer! I wonder you didn't tell me we shall know better still in a month. (*Leans out of window.*) Hey, Avdotya? Eh? Avdotya, have you heard that somebody has arrived? . . . You haven't? What a stupid girl! He shooed you off? Let him shoo; you should have got it out of him all the same. Couldn't find that out! Her head's full of nonsense, thinks of nothing but young men. What? They went off so quickly! But you should have run after the chaise. Run now, run along! Do you hear, run and ask where they are going: and you'd better find out what kind of gentleman he is, what he is like—do you hear? Look through the door and find out everything, and what color his eyes are, whether they are black—and come back at once, do you hear? Hurry, hurry, hurry, hurry!

(*Goes on shouting till the curtain falls.*)
(*The curtain falls upon them both standing at the window.*)

ACT II

A Little Room at the Inn. A bed, a table, a suitcase, an empty bottle, high boots, a clothesbrush, etc.

OSIP *is lying on his master's bed.*

OSIP. Damn it all! How hungry I am! There's a racket going on in my stomach as though a whole regiment were trumpeting on their trumpets. We don't seem any nearer getting home. What are you supposed to do? It's going on for two months since we left Petersburg! He has frittered away his money on the road, the sweet thing, and now he sits with his tail tucked beneath his legs and doesn't get excited. And there'd have been enough, more than enough, for the journey: but no, he had to show off in every town! (*Mimicking*) "Hey, Osip, go and take a room, the best one, and order a dinner, the best one: I can't eat a bad dinner, I must have the best." It would be fine, in fact, if he was somebody big instead of just a registry clerk! He makes friends on the way and plays cards—so now you've lost all your money! Ugh! I'm sick of this life! Honest, it's better in the country; there's no publicity, but there's less anxiety; you take old bag and spend your time lying on the stove and eating dumplings. Well, who's to argue? Of course, if you come to the truth, living in Petersburg is better than anything. Life there's polite and fine enough, if only you have money: theaters, dogs dance for you, and anything you like. They all speak nice and fine, like the gentry themselves pretty near; if you go to Shchukin,[9] the shopmen call out "Honored sir!"; in the ferryboat you sit next to a government clerk; if you want company you go to the shop: there a soldier will tell you about life in camp and explain what every star in the sky means, so you see it plain as your hand; some old officer's wife will drop in, another time a chambermaid will look in. What a chambermaid! . . . Aie! Aie! Aie! (*Smirks and shakes his head.*) It's all polish and manners, damn it all! You never hear a rude word; everyone calls you "mister." If you're tired of walking you take a cab and sit like a master—and if you

---

[9] A bazaar. (ed.)

don't want to pay him, well, you don't: every house has a gate at the back as well as in front, and you can whisk through, so that no devil can catch you. There's only one bad thing— sometimes you eat your fill gloriously and sometimes you almost drop from hunger, like now, for example. And it's all his fault. What can you do with him? His old man sends money instead of holding on to it, and to where! He goes off on a spree: he drives in cabs, every day I have to get him theater tickets, and then in a week, behold—he sends me to the flea market to sell his new tail coat. Sometimes he carries on until he hasn't a shirt left and walks around in nothing but his jacket and overcoat . . . I swear, it's a fact! And the cloth is so important. English! He gave a hundred and fifty rubles for the coat alone, and he lets it go for twenty; and as for the trousers, there's nothing to talk about, they go for nothing. And why is it? It's all because he doesn't do his work: instead of going to the office he walks up and down the Prospekt [10] or plays cards. Ah, if the old master knew! Little he'd care if you're a government clerk—he'd lift up your shirt and give you such a whipping you'd be rubbing yourself for the next four days. If you've got a job, stick to it. Now, here the innkeeper says he won't give us anything to eat till we've paid for what we've had; but what if we don't pay? (*With a sigh*) Oh, my God, if I only had some cabbage soup! I feel I could eat up the whole world. Somebody is knocking; it's probably him.[11] (*Hastily jumps off the bed.*)

(*Enter* KHLESTAKOV.)

KHLESTAKOV. Here, take these. (*Gives him his cap and cane.*) Ah, you have been loafing on my bed again?

OSIP. Why should I loaf on it? Have I never seen a bed before?

KHLESTAKOV. That's a lie. You've been sprawling on it; you see it's all crumpled.

---

[10] I.e., Nevsky Prospekt. (ed.)

[11] It is quite impossible to effectively reproduce Osip's language in English. Rather than take liberties with the text, it is closely translated. His language is characterized by frequent malapropisms, the use of abstract nouns which are too strong to accurately express what he means, creation of his own words, use of words he simply does not understand, redundancy (an influence of folk literature), a succinctness of expression whereby he sums up a situation with a few apt words, abundance of affective suffixes which express his attitude, etc. (ed.)

OSIP.   What do I want with it? A bed is nothing new to me. I've got legs, I can stand. Why should I lie on your bed?

KHLESTAKOV (*walking up and down the room*).   See whether there is any tobacco in the pouch.

OSIP.   How can there be? You smoked the last four days ago.

KHLESTAKOV (*walks about pursing his lips in different ways; at last speaks in a loud and resolute voice*).   Listen . . . Osip!

OSIP.   Yes, sir?

KHLESTAKOV (*in a loud, but not so resolute voice*).   You go there.

OSIP.   Where?

KHLESTAKOV (*in a voice neither resolute nor loud, but approaching entreaty*).   Downstairs, to the dining room . . . Tell them to . . . send me up some dinner.

OSIP.   Oh no, I don't want to go.

KHLESTAKOV.   How dare you, you blockhead?

OSIP.   Why, nothing will come of it if I do. The landlord says he won't give you any more dinners.

KHLESTAKOV.   How dare he refuse? What nonsense next?

OSIP.   And he says he will go to the Mayor too. "Your master," he says, "has paid nothing for three weeks. You and your master are swindlers," he says, "and your master's a rogue." He says he's seen such scoundrels and cheats before.

KHLESTAKOV.   And, you brute, you enjoy repeating all that to me.

OSIP.   He says, "At that rate anyone might come, live at my expense and not pay, and there would be no getting rid of him. I won't do things by halves," he says. "I'll lodge a complaint and have him taken to the police station and to prison."

KHLESTAKOV.   Come, come, you fool, that's enough! Go along, go along, tell him. What a coarse beast he is!

OSIP.   I'd better tell the landlord to come to you himself.

KHLESTAKOV.   What do I want with the landlord? You go and speak to him.

OSIP.   But really, sir . . .

KHLESTAKOV.   There, run along, damn you! Call the landlord.

(*Osip goes out.*)

(*Alone.*) It's awful how hungry I am! I went for a little walk; I thought my appetite would disappear—no, damn it, it hasn't. Yes, if I hadn't had such a spree at Penza [12] there would have

---

[12] A provincial capital southeast of Moscow, on the road to Saratov. (ed.)

been money enough to get home. That infantry captain gave me the business! How he piled up the tricks! He only sat down for a quarter of an hour, but he cleaned me out. And yet, wouldn't I like another game with him! But there seems no chance of it. What a beastly little town! At the grocer's they won't give you anything on credit. It's really disgusting. (*Begins whistling, first from "Robert le Diable,"* [13] *then "The Red Sarafan,"* [14] *and then nothing in particular.*) There's nobody coming.

(*Enter* OSIP *and the* WAITER.)

WAITER. The master told me to ask you what he can do for you.

KHLESTAKOV. Good day, friend! I hope you are quite well.

WAITER. Yes, thank God!

KHLESTAKOV. Well, how are things in your inn? All going well?

WAITER. Yes, thank God! All is well.

KHLESTAKOV. Many visitors?

WAITER. Yes, a fair number.

KHLESTAKOV. Look here, my good fellow, they haven't brought me my dinner yet, so please tell them to make haste—you see, I have got something I must do directly after dinner.

WAITER. But the master says he won't send you up any more. I think he meant to go to the Mayor today to lodge a complaint.

KHLESTAKOV. What has he got to complain of? Consider for yourself, my good man, what am I to do? I must eat; I shall waste away if I go on like this. I am desperately hungry. I am not joking.

WAITER. No, sir. He said, "I won't give him dinner again till he pays for what he has had." That was his answer.

KHLESTAKOV. But you talk to him, reason with him.

WAITER. But what am I to say to him?

KHLESTAKOV. You point out to him seriously that I must eat. Money is one thing. . . . He thinks that if a peasant like himself can go without food for a day, other people can do the same. That's absurd!

WAITER. Very well, I'll tell him.

(WAITER *and* OSIP *go out.*)

KHLESTAKOV (*alone*). It will be terrible, though, if he won't give

---

[13] *Robert the Devil*, an opera by Jakob Meyerbeer (1791-1864). (ed.)
[14] "The Red Gown," once a popular Russian folksong. (ed.)

me anything at all to eat. I am hungrier than I have ever been in my life. Shall I raise something on my clothes? Sell my trousers? No, I'd rather go hungry than not arrive home in my Petersburg suit. What a pity Yokhim [15] would not let me hire a carriage! It would have been fine, damn it all, to arrive in a carriage; think of driving up like a gentleman to a neighbor's, with lamps lighted and Osip in livery perched up behind! I can imagine what a commotion it would cause! "Who is it? What is it?" And my footman goes up (*drawing himself up and acting as footman*): "Ivan Aleksandrovich Khlestakov from Petersburg; are they at home?" And the bumpkins don't even know what "at home" means. If some goose of a landowner comes to see them, he pushes straight into the drawing room like a bear. You go up to a pretty daughter: "Madam,[16] I am delighted" (*rubs his hands and scrapes with his feet*). Ugh! (*Spits.*) I'm so hungry I'm nauseated.

(*Enter* OSIP *and* WAITER.)

KHLESTAKOV. Well?

OSIP. They are bringing your dinner.

KHLESTAKOV (*claps his hands and gives a little skip on his chair*). Dinner! Dinner! Dinner!

WAITER (*with plates and dinner napkins*). The landlord is sending you dinner for the last time.

KHLESTAKOV. The landlord, the landlord . . . don't give a damn for your landlord! What have you got there?

WAITER. Soup and roast meat.

KHLESTAKOV. What, only two courses?

WAITER. That's all, sir.

KHLESTAKOV. What nonsense! I won't have that. You tell him it's impossible! That's not enough.

WAITER. Well, the landlord says it's too much.

KHLESTAKOV. And why is there no sauce?

WAITER. There is no sauce.

KHLESTAKOV. Why not? I saw them cooking lots of the stuff as I passed by the kitchen. And two little men were eating salmon and all sorts of good things in the dining room this morning.

---

[15] Once the most famous carriage dealer in St. Petersburg. (ed.)
[16] Russians use this term (*sudarinya*) indiscriminately for both married and unmarried women. (ed.)

WAITER.   Well, there is, to be sure, but again there isn't.

KHLESTAKOV.   What do you mean by "there isn't"?

WAITER.   Well, there isn't.

KHLESTAKOV.   And salmon and fish and cutlets?

WAITER.   They are for the better sort, sir.

KHLESTAKOV.   You are a fool!

WAITER.   Yes, sir.

KHLESTAKOV.   You are a nasty pig. . . . What, they are eating it and I'm not? Damn it all, why can't I have it too? Aren't they travelers the same as I am?

WAITER.   Well, we all know they are not the same.

KHLESTAKOV.   What are they, then?

WAITER.   They are the usual sort! They pay for what they have, to be sure.

KHLESTAKOV.   I won't discuss it with a fool like you. (*Helps himself to soup and eats.*) Do you call this soup? You have simply filled the tureen with dishwater: there is no taste in it, though it stinks enough. I won't have this soup, bring me another.

WAITER.   I'll take it away. The boss said, "If he doesn't like it, he needn't have it."

KHLESTAKOV (*protecting the tureen with his hands*).   Come, come, come . . . leave it, you ass! I suppose you are accustomed to treat other people like that, but I am not that sort. I don't advise you to try it with me . . . (*Eats.*) My God, what soup! (*Goes on eating it.*) I don't believe anyone in the world has ever tasted such soup: there are feathers floating in it instead of fat. (*Cuts the fowl.*) Aie, aie, what a hen! Serve the meat. There is a little soup left there, Osip, you can have it. (*Cuts the meat.*) What sort of meat is this? It's not meat.

WAITER.   What is it, then?

KHLESTAKOV.   The devil only knows, but it's not meat. You've roasted the ax instead of the beef. (*Eats it.*) The scoundrels, the dirty beasts! The stuff they give one to eat! Chewing one mouthful makes my jaws ache. (*Picks his teeth with his fingers.*) The sneaks! It's just like the bark of a tree—I can't get it out. My teeth will be black after eating such stuff. Scoundrels! (*Wipes his mouth with his napkin.*) Is there nothing more?

WAITER.   No.

KHLESTAKOV. Dirty beasts! Sneaks! And no sauce or pudding at all. Wretches! Simply fleecing travelers!

(WAITER, *with the help of* OSIP, *clears away the plates and dishes.*)

(*Alone.*) Really, I feel as though I had not eaten anything. I've just had enough to make me hungrier. If I had a copper I'd send to the market and have a bun.

OSIP (*coming in*). The Mayor has come about something; he is making inquiries and asking questions about you.

KHLESTAKOV (*scared*). Good gracious! That beast of a landlord has sent in a complaint already! What if he hauls me off to prison? Well, if I am treated like a gentleman, perhaps . . . no, no, I won't go! There are officers and all sorts of people lounging about in the town, and as ill-luck would have it, I've been flirting and winking at a shopkeeper's pretty daughter. . . . No, I won't go! What is he thinking about? How dare he? What does he take me for? Am I a shopkeeper or a workman? (*Assuming confidence and drawing himself up*) I shall say to him outright: "How dare you? How . . ."

(*The door handle turns;* KHLESTAKOV *grows pale and shrinks. The* MAYOR *comes in with* DOBCHINSKY *and stands still. For some moments he and* KHLESTAKOV *stare at each other in alarm.*)

THE MAYOR (*slightly recovering himself and standing at attention*). I humbly wish you good day.

KHLESTAKOV (*bowing*). I wish you a good day, sir.

THE MAYOR. Excuse me.

KHLESTAKOV. It's all right. . . .

THE MAYOR. It is my duty as the head official of the town to concern myself that visitors and all persons of rank should suffer no inconvenience. . . .

KHLESTAKOV (*at first faltering a little, but speaking more loudly as he goes on*). But what am I to do? It's not my fault. . . . I am really going to pay. . . . They'll send me money from the country.

(BOBCHINSKY *peeps in at the door.*)

He is more to blame: he gives me beef as hard as a board, and as for the soup, goodness only knows what he puts in it. I had to throw it out of the window. He has been starving me for

days . . . the tea is so peculiar, it stinks of fish and not of tea.
Why should I . . . It's a strange thing!

THE MAYOR (*intimidated*).   Forgive me, it is really not my fault.
The beef in the market is always good. It is brought by dealers
from Kholmogory,[17] sober men of exemplary behavior. In fact
I don't know where he could get beef like that. But if anything
is amiss, then allow me to suggest that I should take you to
other apartments.

KHLESTAKOV.   No, I won't go! I know what you mean by other
apartments—prison. But what right have you? How dare
you . . . Why, I . . . I am in the Service in Petersburg.
(*Blustering*) I'll . . . I'll . . . I'll . . .

THE MAYOR (*aside*).   Oh merciful God, what a violent man! He's
found out everything; those damned shopkeepers have told
him everything!

KHLESTAKOV (*bluffing*).   I wouldn't go if you came with a whole
regiment of soldiers. I'll write straight to the Minister!
(*Thumping the table with his fist*). What next? What are you
thinking of?

THE MAYOR (*standing at attention and trembling*).   Have pity on
me, don't ruin me. . . . I have a wife, little children . . . don't
wreck a man's life!

KHLESTAKOV.   No, I won't go! What next? What do I care? Because you have a wife and little children I am to go to prison,
a fine idea!

(BOBCHINSKY *peeps in at the door and vanishes in alarm.*)
No, thank you very much, I won't go!

THE MAYOR (*trembling*).   It was my inexperience, God knows it
was my inexperience, the insufficiency of my income . . .
only consider: my salary is hardly enough for tea and sugar.
If I have taken bribes they are nothing to speak of—something
for the table or cloth for a suit. As for the sergeant's widow
who keeps a shop and the story of my flogging her, that's a
slander; I swear it is. It's an invention of my enemies; they
wouldn't mind killing me.

KHLESTAKOV.   Well, I have nothing to do with them. (*Pondering*)
But I don't know why you are talking about enemies and a
sergeant's widow. . . . A sergeant's wife is a very different

---

17 Kholmogory was renowned for the quality of its beef. (ed.)

matter, but don't you dare flog me; that's too big a job for you. . . . Certainly! Who has ever heard of such a thing! I'll pay, I'll pay the bill, but I haven't the money now. That's why I am staying on here, because I haven't a kopek.

THE MAYOR (*aside*). Oh, the shrewd devil! Oh, where has he cast us! What a fog he has let loose! There's no knowing how to get at him. Well, I'll try my luck, here goes! What will be will be, I'll chance it. (*Aloud*) If you are really in need of money or anything else, I am at your service this very minute. It is my duty to assist visitors to the town.

KHLESTAKOV. Oh yes, do lend me some money! I'll pay the land-lord on the spot. I don't want more than two hundred rubles, even less would do.

THE MAYOR (*offering him notes*). Here are exactly two hundred rubles; don't trouble yourself to count them.

KHLESTAKOV (*taking the money*). I am very much obliged to you. I will send it you back as soon as I am home in the country. . . . I was unexpectedly short of money. . . . I see you are a real gentleman. Now the situation is quite different.

THE MAYOR (*aside*). Well, thank God, he has taken the money. It will all be plain sailing now, it seems, and I managed to slip four hundred into his hand instead of two.

KHLESTAKOV. Hey, Osip!

(OSIP *comes in.*)

Call the waiter! (*To the* MAYOR *and* DOBCHINSKY) But why are you standing? Please sit down. (*To* DOBCHINSKY) Please take a seat.

THE MAYOR. It's quite all right, we can stand.

KHLESTAKOV. Oh, please do sit down. I see now how straight-forward and hospitable you are; I must confess I had thought at first you had come to . . . (*To* DOBCHINSKY) Sit down!

(THE MAYOR *and* DOBCHINSKY *sit down.* BOBCHINSKY *peeps in at the door and listens.*)

THE MAYOR (*aside*). I must be bolder. He wants to be treated incognito. Very good, we'll keep it up; we'll pretend we haven't a notion of who he is. (*Aloud*) We, that is, Piotr Ivanovich Dobchinsky, a landowner of the district, and I, in the discharge of our duties, called at the inn on purpose to ascertain whether visitors to the town are properly treated, for I am not like some mayors who do not care about anything;

apart from my duty, I am prompted by Christian benevolence to desire that every mortal should be well received—and here I am rewarded by the opportunity of making such an agreeable acquaintance.

KHLESTAKOV. I too am delighted. If it had not been for you, I must admit I should have had to stop here a long time: I couldn't think how I was to pay the bill.

THE MAYOR (*aside*). Um, tell that to others! Couldn't think how he was to pay! (*Aloud*) And may I make so bold as to inquire where you are bound for?

KHLESTAKOV. I am going to the Saratov province, to my own estate.

THE MAYOR (*aside, with an ironical expression*). To the Saratov province! Eh? And not a blush! Oh, you have to be pretty sharp for him. (*Aloud*) An excellent undertaking, though in traveling, of course, there is the unpleasantness of not being able to get horses, but, on the other hand, it is a distraction for the mind. You are traveling, I presume, for your own pleasure chiefly?

KHLESTAKOV. No, my father insists on my coming. The old man is upset because so far I have not been promoted in the Service. He fancies that as soon as you arrive in Petersburg they stick a Vladimir ribbon in your buttonhole.[18] I'd like to see him knocking about in the office!

THE MAYOR (*aside*). Just listen! The yarn he is spinning! Dragging in his old father too! (*Aloud*) And shall you stay here long?

KHLESTAKOV. I really don't know. My old father is as stupid and obstinate as a log, the old codger. I shall tell him straight out: I can't live without Petersburg, say what you like. Why on earth should I waste my life among peasants? A man's requirements are different nowadays; my soul thirsts for civilization.

THE MAYOR (*aside*). A wonderful liar! He goes on with one lie after another and never breaks down. And he is nothing much to look at, a puny fellow; you could squash him under your thumbnail. But wait a minute, I'll make you betray yourself! (*Aloud*) That's a perfectly true remark of yours. What can

---

[18] Reference is to a decoration for meritorious service, the St. Vladimir of the Fourth Class. (ed.)

be done in the wilds? Here, for instance: one spends sleepless nights, doing one's utmost for one's country, sparing nothing, but as for recognition there is no knowing when that will come. (*Takes a look around the room.*) This room seems rather damp?

KHLESTAKOV.   It's a horrible room, and the bugs are beyond anything I've ever seen: they bite like dogs.

THE MAYOR.   Just imagine! Such a distinguished visitor, and to suffer from what? From worthless bugs who ought never to have been born into the world! And the room is dark, too, isn't it?

KHLESTAKOV.   Yes, very dark. The landlord has taken to refusing me candles. Sometimes you get a notion to do something: to read, or even, at times, to write, and I cannot—it's dark.

THE MAYOR.   May I venture to beg you . . . but no, I am not worthy of the honor.

KHLESTAKOV.   Why, what?

THE MAYOR.   No, no, I am unworthy!

KHLESTAKOV.   Why, what is it?

THE MAYOR.   I would venture . . . I have an excellent room for you at home, light, quiet . . . But no, I feel that it would be too great an honor. . . . Don't be angry—believe me, it was in the simplicity of my heart that I offered it.

KHLESTAKOV.   On the contrary, by all means, I shall be delighted. I would much rather be in a private house than in a nasty tavern.

THE MAYOR.   And I shall be delighted! And my wife will be overjoyed! It has always been my way from my earliest childhood to put hospitality before everything, especially if the visitor is a man of such distinction. Please don't imagine that this is flattery; no, I am free from that vice; I speak out of the fullness of my heart.

KHLESTAKOV.   Very much obliged to you. I am the same myself— I don't like insincere people. I do like your openheartedness and cordiality, and I must admit I ask nothing but devotion and respect, respect and devotion.

(*Enter the* WAITER, *accompanied by* OSIP. BOBCHINSKY *peeps in at the door.*)

WAITER.   You sent for me, sir?

KHLESTAKOV.   Yes, give me the bill.

WAITER. I gave it to you, for the second time, this morning.

KHLESTAKOV. I don't remember your stupid bills. Tell me, how much is it?

WAITER. You ordered dinner on the first day, and on the second only had some smoked salmon, and after that you had everything put down.

KHLESTAKOV. Idiot! There's no need to go into the items. Tell me what it all comes to.

THE MAYOR. But don't you trouble about it: he can wait. (*To the* WAITER) Away, the bill shall be settled.

KHLESTAKOV. Yes, indeed, that's true. (*Puts the money in his pocket.*)

(*The* WAITER *goes out.* BOBCHINSKY *peeps in at the door.*)

THE MAYOR. Wouldn't you like, perhaps, to look at some institutions of our town, charitable and otherwise?

KHLESTAKOV. Why, what is there to see?

THE MAYOR. Oh well, you might see how things are done with us . . . the management . . .

KHLESTAKOV. Delighted, I am ready.

(BOBCHINSKY *pops his head in at the door.*)

THE MAYOR. And then, if you feel disposed, we might visit the district school and see the methods of instruction in the sciences.

KHLESTAKOV. Certainly, by all means.

THE MAYOR. And then, if you like to visit the prison and the police stations—you can see how criminals are kept in our town.

KHLESTAKOV. But why the police stations? I'd rather look at the charitable institutions.

THE MAYOR. As you prefer. Will you come in your own carriage or in the chaise with me?

KHLESTAKOV. I would rather come with you in the chaise.

THE MAYOR (*to* DOBCHINSKY). Well, Piotr Ivanovich, there will be no room for you now.

DOBCHINSKY. Never mind, I shall be all right.

THE MAYOR (*aside to* DOBCHINSKY). Listen: you run along as fast as your legs can carry you, and take two notes: one to Zemlianika at the hospital and another to my wife. (*To* KHLESTAKOV) May I ask your permission to write in your presence a couple of lines to my wife, to tell her to prepare for our honored guest?

KHLESTAKOV.   Oh, why? . . . Here is the ink, though—but about paper I don't know. Perhaps this bill would do?

THE MAYOR.   I will write on it. (*Writes, and at the same time murmurs to himself*) We shall see how things will go after lunch and a bottle of something good! And we have some local Madeira—not much to look at, but it would knock an elephant off its feet. If only I could find out what he is like and how far I need be afraid of him.

(*After writing the note, he hands it to* DOBCHINSKY, *who goes to the door, but at that moment the door comes off its hinges and* BOBCHINSKY, *who has been listening outside, flies into the room with it. Everyone utters an exclamation.* BOBCHINSKY *gets up.*)

KHLESTAKOV.   I hope you are not hurt?

BOBCHINSKY.   No, no, nothing to speak of, not the slightest derangement, only a little bruise on my nose. I'll run to Christian Ivanovich: he has a plaster that will put it right.

THE MAYOR (*making a reproachful sign to* BOBCHINSKY, *says to* KHLESTAKOV). It's of no consequence. Shall we go now? And I will tell your servant to bring your luggage. (*To* OSIP) My good man, bring everything around to my house, to the Mayor's—anyone will show you the way. After you! (*Shows* KHLESTAKOV *out and follows him, but turning back says, reproachfully, to* BOBCHINSKY) Just like you! Couldn't you find somewhere else to flop? Sprawling there like the devil knows what!

(*Goes out.* BOBCHINSKY *follows him.*)
(*Curtain.*)

ACT III

Scene: *Same as Act I*

ANNA ANDREEVNA *and* MARIA ANTONOVNA *stand at the window in the same position.*

ANNA.   Here we have been waiting a whole hour, and it is all your fault, you and your stupid preening: she was perfectly ready, but no! she must go on fussing . . . I should not have listened to you. How annoying! As though to spite us, not a soul in sight! Everyone might be dead.

MARIA.   But really, Mamma, in another two minutes we shall know all about it. Avdotya must be back soon now. (*Looks out of window and shrieks*) Oh, Mamma! Mamma! somebody's coming, look at the end of the street.

ANNA.   Where? You're always imagining something. Oh yes, there is somebody. Who is it? Rather short . . . dressed like a gentleman. . . . Who is it? Eh? It's annoying! Whoever can it be?

MARIA.   It's Dobchinsky, Mamma!

ANNA.   Dobchinsky! You're always imagining things. . . . It's no more Dobchinsky! . . . (*Waves her handkerchief.*) Hey, you! Come here, make haste!

MARIA.   It really is Dobchinsky, Mamma.

ANNA.   You say that just to contradict me. I tell you it's not Dobchinsky.

MARIA.   What did I say? What did I say, Mamma? Now you see it is Dobchinsky.

ANNA.   To be sure it is Dobchinsky, I see it is now—what do you want to argue about? (*Shouts at the window*) Make haste, make haste! How slow you are! Well, where are they? Eh? Don't wait till you get in, tell me now. What? Very stern? Eh? And my husband, my husband? (*Moving a little away from the window in annoyance.*) What an idiot! Till he gets indoors he won't say a word!

(DOBCHINSKY *comes in.*)

Now, if you please, aren't you ashamed of yourself? I relied upon you as the one man I could trust—all the rest ran off and you went with them! I haven't been able to get a word of sense out of anyone so far. Aren't you ashamed? I stood godmother to your Vanichka and Lizanka, and this is how you treat me!

DOBCHINSKY.   I swear, to show my respect for you I've run till I'm out of breath. How do you do, Maria Antonovna?

MARIA.   Good morning, Piotr Ivanovich.

ANNA.   Well, what happened? Come, tell us! How are things going?

DOBCHINSKY.   Anton Antonovich has sent you a note.

ANNA.   Oh, and what sort of man is he? A general?

DOBCHINSKY.   No, he is not a general, but he is as good as any general: such culture and dignified manners.

ANNA.   Ah! then he is the man they wrote to my husband about.

DOBCHINSKY.   The very one. I was the first to discover it, together with Piotr Ivanovich.

ANNA.   Come, tell us all about it.

DOBCHINSKY.   Well, thank God, everything went off satisfactorily. At first he did give Anton Antonovich rather a curt reception, yes; he was angry, and said that everything was wrong at the inn, and that he wouldn't come and stay with him, and that he did not want to go to prison on his account; but later on, when he found that Anton Antonovich was not to blame and talked a little more to him, he quite changed his mind, and, thank God, everything went off well. They've gone now to inspect the charitable institutions. . . . At first Anton Antonovich really did suspect there had been a secret report sent in against him; I was a little scared myself.

ANNA.   But you have nothing to be afraid of—you are not in the Service.

DOBCHINSKY.   No, but you know you can't help feeling alarmed when a great man speaks.

ANNA.   Oh, well . . . but that's all nonsense. Tell us what he is like? Is he old or young?

DOBCHINSKY.   Young, a young man, about twenty-three, but he speaks quite like an old man. "Certainly," he says, "I am ready to go there, and there too" . . . (*waves his arms*) and all said so nicely. "I am fond of reading and writing," he said, "but it's tiresome that it is rather dark in my room."

ANNA.   And what is he to look at? Dark or fair?

DOBCHINSKY.   No, more of an auburn brown, and his eyes are as quick as squirrels', they make one feel quite uncomfortable.

ANNA.   What has your father written me here? (*Reads*) "I hasten to tell you, my love, that my position was truly dreadful; but trusting in God's mercy two salted cucumbers and half a portion of caviar, one ruble twenty-five kopeks . . ." (*Stops.*) I can't make it out. What have salted cucumbers and caviar to do with it?

DOBCHINSKY.   Anton Antonovich wrote it in haste on an old scrap of paper; it's a bill of some sort.

ANNA.   Oh yes, to be sure. (*Goes on reading*) "But trusting in God's mercy I believe that it will all end well. Make haste and get a room ready for our illustrious guest, the one with the yellow paper; don't trouble to have anything extra for dinner, for we shall have a meal with Artemy Filippovich at the hospital, but have plenty of wine. Tell Abdulin at the shop to send the best he has, or I'll wreck his whole cellar. Kissing your little hand, love, I remain your Anton Skvoznik-Dmukhanovsky." . . . Oh, my goodness! We must make haste! Hey, who is there? Mishka!

DOBCHINSKY (*runs towards the door shouting*). Mishka! Mishka! Mishka!

(*Enter* MISHKA.)

ANNA. Listen: run to Abdulin's shop . . . wait a minute, I'll give you a note. (*Sits down to the table, writes a note, speaking as she writes.*) Give this note to Sidor, the coachman, and tell him to run with it to Abdulin's and bring wine from the shop. And you go and get the room properly ready for a visitor. Put in a bed and a washstand and everything else.

DOBCHINSKY. Well, Anna Andreevna, I'll run along to see how he is conducting the inspection.

ANNA. Run along, run along! I won't keep you.

(DOBCHINSKY *goes out.*)

Well, Mashenka,[19] now we must think of what we are going to wear. He is a Petersburg dandy: God forbid he should laugh at us. The most suitable thing for you is the light blue dress with the little flounces.

MARIA. Oh, Mamma, the blue! I don't like it a bit. The Liapkin-Tiapkin girl is always in blue and Zemlianika's daughter too. No, I'd better put on my bright dress.

ANNA. Your bright dress! . . . Really, you'll say anything to contradict; the blue's much better, for I want to wear my straw-yellow.

MARIA. Oh, Mamma, straw-yellow doesn't suit you!

ANNA. Straw-yellow doesn't suit me?

MARIA. It doesn't . . . I'll bet it doesn't: you should have dark eyes to wear straw-yellow.

ANNA. What next! And haven't I dark eyes? As dark as can be. What nonsense she talks! My eyes not dark, and me always the queen of clubs when I tell my fortune!

MARIA. Oh, Mamma, you ought to be a queen of hearts.

ANNA. Nonsense, absolutely nonsense. I have never been a queen of hearts. (*Goes out quickly with* MARIA ANTONOVNA *and*

---

19 Diminutive of Maria. (ed.)

speaks outside.) What will she think of next! Queen of hearts!
I've never heard of such a thing.

(*A door opens and* MISHKA *sweeps out dust;* OSIP *comes
in at the other door with a suitcase on his head.*)

OSIP.   Which way?

MISHKA.   This way, uncle, this way!

OSIP.   Stop, let me rest. Ah, what a dog's life! Every burden is
heavy when the belly is empty.

MISHKA.   Tell me, uncle, will the general soon be here?

OSIP.   What general?

MISHKA.   Why, your master.

OSIP.   My master? He a general?

MISHKA.   Why, isn't he a general?

OSIP.   Oh, he is a general all right—on the reverse side.

MISHKA.   Why, is that more or less than a real general?

OSIP.   More.

MISHKA.   Well I never! That's why they are kicking up such a
fuss.

OSIP.   Look here, my boy: I see you are a smart fellow; get me
something to eat.

MISHKA.   There's nothing ready for you yet, uncle. You won't
have just anything ordinary, but when your master sits down
to table, they'll give you some of the same.

OSIP.   And what have you got in the ordinary way?

MISHKA.   Cabbage soup, *kasha*, and pies.

OSIP.   Give me that—cabbage soup, *kasha*, and pies. It doesn't
matter, I can eat anything. Come, let us carry the suitcase in.
Is there another way out of the room?

MISHKA.   Yes.

(*The two carry the suitcase into room at side. The* POLICE-
MEN *fling open both halves of the door. Enter* KHLESTA-
KOV, *after him the* MAYOR, *followed at a little distance by*
ARTEMY FILIPPOVICH ZEMLIANIKA, LUKA LUKICH KHLOPOV,
DOBCHINSKY, *and* BOBCHINSKY *with a plaster on his nose.
The* MAYOR *points out to the* POLICEMEN *a piece of paper
on the floor—they run and pick it up, jostling each other
in their haste.*)

KHLESTAKOV.   Excellent institutions! I like the way you show visitors everything in your town. In other towns I was shown
nothing.

THE MAYOR.   In other towns, I venture to assure you, the mayors and other functionaries are more anxious about their own interests, so to speak; while here, I must say, we have no other thought but to deserve the attention of our superiors by our good conduct and vigilance.

KHLESTAKOV.   The lunch was very nice; I've really eaten too much. Do you have lunches like that every day?

THE MAYOR.   On purpose for such a welcome guest.

KHLESTAKOV.   I am fond of good food. That's what life is for—to gather the flowers of pleasure. What was the fish called?

ARTEMY FILIPPOVICH (*running up*).   *Labardan,*[20] sir!

KHLESTAKOV.   Very good. Where was it we had lunch? At the hospital, wasn't it?

ARTEMY FILIPPOVICH.   Exactly, one of our charitable institutions.

KHLESTAKOV.   I remember, I remember; there were many empty beds. And have most of the patients recovered? I don't think there were many there.

ARTEMY FILIPPOVICH.   There are about a dozen left, not more, and the others have all recovered. It's the organization, the management. Ever since I took control there—you may think it incredible—they all get well like flies.[21] No sooner does a patient get into the hospital than he is well, and it is not so much due to the medicines as through conscientiousness and good management.

THE MAYOR.   Ah, how harrowing, I venture to assure you, are the duties of the mayor of a city! So many matters are laid upon him: the cleanliness alone, repairs and reconstruction . . . in fact, the most able man would find himself in difficulties, but, thank God, everything is going well. Another mayor, of course, would be feathering his own nest, but would you believe it, even lying in bed I keep thinking, "Almighty God, how can I contrive to prove my zeal to my superiors and give them satisfaction?" Whether they bestow a reward, of course, that's for them to decide, but anyway my heart will be at rest. When everything in the town is as it should be, the streets are swept, the convicts are well looked after, and not many

---

[20] Salted codfish. (ed.)
[21] Probably an allusion to a popular Russian saying, "The peasants die like flies." (ed.)

drunken people about, then what more do I want? I may say truly I don't care for honors. They, of course, are alluring, but, compared with virtue, all is but dust and vanity.

ARTEMY FILIPPOVICH (*aside*). How the rascal can pour it on! It's a heaven-sent gift!

KHLESTAKOV. That's true. At times I indulge in such reflections myself; sometimes in prose and sometimes I toss off a poem.

BOBCHINSKY (*to* DOBCHINSKY). That's well said, Piotr Ivanovich, very well said! Such observations . . . one can see he has studied learned subjects.

KHLESTAKOV. Tell me, please, have you any entertainments— clubs where one could play cards, for instance?

THE MAYOR (*aside*). Oho, my fine gentleman, I know what you are driving at! (*Aloud*) Heaven forbid! No such clubs have ever been heard of here! I have never held a card in my hand in my life; in fact, I have no notion how you play with them. I could never bear the sight of them; indeed, if I do chance to see a king of diamonds or anything of the kind, it makes me feel perfectly sick. I once happened to build a house with cards to amuse the children, and I was dreaming of the damned things all night afterwards, confound them! How can people waste precious time on them?

LUKA LUKICH (*aside*). And he won a hundred rubles from me last night, the scoundrel!

THE MAYOR. I prefer to devote my time to the welfare of the State.

KHLESTAKOV. Well now, you go too far . . . It all depends on the point of view from which you look at it. If you stop just when you ought to double your stakes . . . then of course . . . No, I don't agree with you; it is very pleasant to have a game sometimes.

(*Enter* ANNA ANDREEVNA *and* MARIA ANTONOVNA.)

THE MAYOR. I venture to introduce my family: my wife and my daughter.

KHLESTAKOV (*bowing*). How happy I am, madam, to have the pleasure, in a sense, of seeing you.

ANNA. It is an even greater pleasure to us to see so distinguished a visitor.

KHLESTAKOV (*gallantly*). Upon my soul, madam, it is quite the opposite: it is a much greater pleasure for me.

ANNA. How can you! You are pleased to say that only for the sake of a compliment. I beg you to be seated.

KHLESTAKOV. To stand beside you is a happiness; but if you particularly wish it, I will sit down. How happy I am to be sitting at last by your side!

ANNA. Indeed, I could never presume to take that as intended for myself. I suppose that after Petersburg your journey must have been very distasteful to you.

KHLESTAKOV. Extremely distasteful. After being used to living, *comprenez-vous*,[22] in the world, to find oneself on the road: dirty inns, in the depths of ignorance . . . But for the chance which, I must admit (*looks meaningly at* ANNA ANDREEVNA *and strikes an attitude*), makes up for everything . . .

ANNA. Indeed, you must find it unpleasant.

KHLESTAKOV. At this moment, madam, I find it very pleasant.

ANNA. How can you! You do me too much honor. I don't deserve it.

KHLESTAKOV. Not deserve it! You do deserve it, madam.

ANNA. I live in the country . . .

KHLESTAKOV. Yes, but the country, too, has its hillsides and brooks . . . though, of course, there is no comparing it with Petersburg! Ah, Petersburg! What a life it is! Perhaps you think I am only a copying clerk; no, the head of my section is on friendly terms with me. He slaps me on the shoulder and says, "Come around to dinner, my boy!" I only look in at the office for two or three minutes, just to say how things must be done. And then the copying clerk, poor rat, goes scratching and scribbling away. They did want to make me a collegiate assessor, but I thought, What's the use? And the porter runs after me up the stairs with a brush in his hand: "Allow me, Ivan Aleksandrovich," he says, "I'll clean your boots." (*To the* MAYOR) Why are you standing, gentlemen, please sit down.

THE MAYOR		In our rank we can very well stand.
ARTEMY FILIPPOVICH	(*speaking together*)	We will stand.
LUKA LUKICH		Please don't trouble on our account.

---

[22] French was the language of sophisticated Russians; Khlestakov uses it to flaunt his worldliness. (ed.)

KHLESTAKOV. Never mind rank. I beg you to sit down! (*The* MAYOR *and all the others sit down.*) I don't like standing on ceremony. On the contrary, I do my utmost, my very utmost, to pass unnoticed. But I never can escape observation, it seems impossible! As soon as I appear anywhere people begin saying, "There's Ivan Aleksandrovich, there he goes!" And once I was actually taken for the Commander-in-Chief: the soldiers all came out of the guardhouse, saluting. And the officer, who is a great friend of mine, said to me afterwards, "Do you know, old friend, we all mistook you for the Commander!"

ANNA. Just imagine!

KHLESTAKOV. I know all the pretty actresses. You see, I have written a few little things for the stage, too. I am often in literary circles . . . on friendly terms with Pushkin. I used often to say to him, "Well, Pushkin, old man, how are things going?" "So-so, old man," he would answer, "only so-so." . . . He is quite a character.

ANNA. So you write too? How delightful it must be to be an author! No doubt you have things in the magazines?

KHLESTAKOV. Yes, I send things to the magazines too. I am the author of lots of works, really: *The Marriage of Figaro, Robert the Devil, Norma.*[23] I can't remember the titles of all of them. And it was all a mere chance—I had no intention of writing, but the Director of Theaters said to me, "Come, old boy, write something for us!" Well, I thought, why not? And on the spot, in one evening I think it was, I wrote the whole thing, to the surprise of everybody. I have a wonderfully ready wit. Everything that has been published under the name of Baron Brambeus,[24] *The Frigate Hope*,[25] and *The Moscow Telegraph*[26] . . . I wrote them all.

ANNA. Just imagine! So you are Brambeus?

---

[23] Famous operas by, respectively, Mozart (1756-91), Jakob Meyerbeer (see n. 13), and Vincenzo Bellini (1801-35). (ed.)

[24] Pseudonym of Osip Ivanovich Senkovsky (1800-58), journalist, critic and humorous writer. (ed.)

[25] Popular novel by Aleksander Aleksandrovich Bestuzhev (1797-1837), a romantic novelist and poet, who also wrote under the pseudonym A. Marlinsky. (ed.)

[26] A journal which published for nine years (1825-1834), encouraged the development of romanticism in Russia. Edited by Nikolai Alekseievich Polevoy (1796-1846). (ed.)

KHLESTAKOV. To be sure, I correct all their articles. Smirdin[27] pays me forty thousand to do it.

ANNA. Then I expect *Yuri Miloslavsky*[28] is your work too?

KHLESTAKOV. Yes, I am the author of it.

ANNA. I guessed it at once.

MARIA. Oh, Mamma, but it says on the book that it is written by Mr. Zagoskin.

ANNA. There, I knew you would want to be arguing even here.

KHLESTAKOV. Oh yes, that's true; that is by Zagoskin, but there is another *Yuri Miloslavsky*, and that is mine.

ANNA. Well, I am sure it was yours that I read. So beautifully written!

KHLESTAKOV. I must confess I live for literature. My house is the finest in Petersburg. Everyone knows it—Ivan Aleksandrovich's house. (*Addressing the whole company*) Please, gentlemen, if you come to Petersburg, I beg that you will all come to see me. I give balls, too.

ANNA. I can imagine the taste and magnificence of the balls you give!

KHLESTAKOV. There's no word for it. On the table, for instance, there'll be a watermelon that cost seven hundred rubles. The soup is brought in a saucepan straight from Paris on a steamer. As soon as you lift the lid there is an aroma—you'd never smell anything like it in nature. I am at a ball every day. We make up a whist party—the Foreign Minister, the French Ambassador, the English Ambassador, the German Ambassador, and I. And I get so tired out with playing that I don't know where I am. I can only run home to my apartment on the fourth floor and say to the cook, "Take my overcoat, Mavrushka." What nonsense I am talking—I forgot that I live on the first floor. My staircase alone is worth . . . you would be interested to see my hall before I am even awake in the morning: there are counts and princes jostling each other and buzzing away there like bumblebees; you can hear nothing but bz-z-z . . . Sometimes, too, the Minister . . .

(*The* MAYOR *and the others, overcome with awe, get up from their seats.*)

---

[27] A. F. Smirdin (1795-1857), a prominent St. Petersburg publisher. (ed.)
[28] Historical novel indebted to Walter Scott, by Mikhail Nikolaievich Zagoskin (1789-1852). (ed.)

My letters actually come addressed "Your Excellency." At one time I was head of a government department. It was a strange business: the Director disappeared—no one knew what had become of him. Well, naturally, there was a lot of talk—what was to be done, and who was to fill his place. Many of the generals were eager and took it on—but as soon as they tackled it they saw it was too much for them. You'd think it would be easy enough, but look into it and it is the very devil of a job! They see there is no avoiding it—they turn to me. And all at once messengers come racing along the street, messengers and more messengers—would you believe it, thirty-five thousand messengers! What do you say to that, I ask you now! "Ivan Aleksandrovich, come and take charge of the department," they say. I must admit I was a bit taken aback. I came out in my dressing gown; I meant to refuse, but there, I thought, it will get to the Czar, and then there is one's official record to think of. . . . "Very well, gentlemen, I accept the post, I accept," I said, "so be it," I said, "only with me, gentlemen, you had better look out! You must mind your P's and Q's. You know what I am." . . . And, as a matter of fact, when I walked through the offices you would have thought there was an earthquake, they were all trembling and shaking. (*The* MAYOR *and the others tremble with alarm;* KHLESTAKOV *grows more excited.*)

Oh, I am not to be trifled with! I gave them all a good scare. Even the Imperial Council is afraid of me. And well they might be! I am like that! No one stands in my way . . . I tell them all, "Don't teach me!" I go everywhere, positively everywhere. I am in and out of the Palace every day. Tomorrow I am to be made a Field Marshal. . . . (*Slips and almost falls on the floor, but the officials support him respectfully.*)

THE MAYOR (*approaches, and tries to speak, trembling all over*). Your—your—your—your . . .

KHLESTAKOV. (*in a sharp, abrupt tone*). What's that?

THE MAYOR. Your—your—your—your . . .

KHLESTAKOV (*in the same tone*). I can make nothing of it. It's all nonsense.

THE MAYOR. Your—your—your . . . cency . . . Excellency, wouldn't you graciously lie down? Here is your room and everything ready for you.

KHLESTAKOV. Nonsense—lie down! By all means, I don't mind lying down. You gave me a good lunch, gentlemen. I am pleased, quite pleased. (*With a theatrical flourish*) *Labardan, labardan!* (*Retires to the room at the side, followed by the* MAYOR.)

BOBCHINSKY (*to* DOBCHINSKY). What a man, Piotr Ivanovich: that's what one means by a man! Never in my life have I been in the presence of a person of so much consequence. I almost died of fright. What do you think, Piotr Ivanovich, what can his rank be?

DOBCHINSKY. I think he must be a general or something like that.

BOBCHINSKY. Why, I think a general would take off his hat to him; and if he is a general he must be the Generalissimo himself. Did you hear how he bullies the Imperial Council? Make haste, let us go and tell Ammos Fiodorovich and Korobkin. Goodbye, Anna Andreevna!

DOBCHINSKY (*to* ANNA ANDREEVNA). Goodbye!

(*Both go out.*)

ARTEMY FILIPPOVICH (*to* LUKA LUKICH). I am terrified, there's no other word for it; but what of I really don't know. And we are actually not in uniform. He will wake up sober, and then what if he sends a report to Petersburg?

(*Exit, plunged in thought, together with the* SUPERINTENDENT OF SCHOOLS, *saying as they go out,* "*Goodbye, madam!*")

ANNA. Ah, what a charming man!

MARIA. Oh, the darling!

ANNA. Just imagine, what refinement! You can see a man of fashion at once. His manners and everything . . . Oh, how delightful! I am awfully fond of young men like that! I am all in a flutter. He seemed very much attracted, though, didn't he? I noticed he kept looking at me!

MARIA. Oh, Mamma, he was looking at me!

ANNA. Keep your silly nonsense to yourself, please! It's quite out of place here.

MARIA. But, Mamma, he was, really!

ANNA. There! God knows, she must always be arguing! Why should he look at you? What should make him look at you?

MARIA. Really, Mamma, he did keep looking at me. When he began talking about literature he glanced at me, and when he told us how he played whist with the ambassadors he gave me a look.

ANNA. Oh well, maybe he did give a glance at you, but that did not mean anything. "Well," he thought, "I may as well give her a look!"

THE MAYOR (*enters on tiptoe*). Sh-sh!

ANNA. Well?

THE MAYOR. I am sorry I made him drunk. What if only one-half of what he said is true! (*Ponders.*) And it must be true. When a man is in liquor he brings it all out; what is in his heart is on his tongue. Of course he did embroider a little; but then, nothing is ever said without a little trimming. He plays cards with the ministers and is in and out of the Palace. . . . Upon my soul, the more one thinks about it . . . the devil only knows . . . my head is in a regular whirl; it's as though I were on the edge of a precipice or just going to be hanged.

ANNA. And I did not feel in the least frightened of him; I saw in him simply a man of the highest society and culture, I don't care about his rank.

THE MAYOR. Ugh! these women! The word covers it all. It's all trumpery to them! You never know what a woman will blurt out. She will get off with a whipping, but her husband will be done for. You behaved as freely with him, my love, as though you had been talking to Dobchinsky.

ANNA. I shouldn't worry about that if I were you. We know a thing or two. (*Looks at her daughter.*)

THE MAYOR (*to himself*). What's the use of talking to them! . . . My God, it is a strange business! It's upset me so, I can't get over it. (*Opens the door and speaks in the doorway*) Mishka! call Officers Svistunov and Derzhimorda, they are not far off, somewhere at the gate. (*After a brief silence*) Things are odd nowadays: you would expect people to be something to look at, anyway, but a thin little whippersnapper like that— who'd guess what he is? In a military uniform a man is presentable, anyway, but put him in a tail coat and he looks like a fly with its wings cut off; but he did keep it up at the inn this morning—he told us such fine tales and allegories that I thought we should never get anything out of him. But he has given in at last. In fact, he said more than he need. You can see he is young.

(Enter OSIP. All run toward him, beckoning.)

ANNA.   Come here, my good man!

THE MAYOR.   Sh! Well? . . . Well, is he asleep?

OSIP.   Not yet, he is yawning and stretching.

ANNA.   I say, what is your name?

OSIP.   Osip, madam.

THE MAYOR (*to his wife and daughter*).   That will do, that will
do. (*To* OSIP) Well, friend, have they given you a good dinner?

OSIP.   Yes, thank you, sir, a very good dinner.

ANNA.   Come, tell me; I suppose a great many counts and princes
come to see your master?

OSIP. (*aside*).   What am I to say? They've given me a good dinner
already, so maybe they will give me a better one. (*Aloud*) Yes,
there are counts too.

MARIA.   You dear Osip, how handsome your master is!

ANNA.   And do tell us, Osip, please, how does he . . .

THE MAYOR.   Hold your tongue! You simply hinder me with your
silly questions. Come, my good man . . .

ANNA.   And what is your master's rank?

OSIP.   Oh, the usual thing.

THE MAYOR.   Oh, my God, how you keep on with your stupid
questions! You won't let one say a word of what matters.
Come, my man, what is your master like? Is he strict? Is he
fond of finding fault?

OSIP.   Yes, he likes things done properly. Everything must be just
so for him.

THE MAYOR.   I like your face, friend. I am sure you are a good
man. Come, tell me . . .

ANNA.   Osip, and does your master wear a uniform at home?

THE MAYOR.   Oh, be quiet, you magpies! This is serious: it's a
question of life and death. . . . (*To* OSIP) Well, friend, I
really like you. An extra glass of tea does not come amiss on a
journey, does it, and it is cold weather too. So here is a couple
of rubles for tea.

OSIP (*taking the money*).   Very much obliged to you, sir! God
give you good health! I am a poor man, you've helped me.

THE MAYOR.   That's all right, pleased to do it. Well, friend, tell
me . . .

ANNA. Tell me, Osip, what sort of eyes does your master like best?

MARIA. You dear Osip, what a charming little nose your master has.

THE MAYOR. Oh, stop, let me speak! (*To* OSIP) Come, friend, what does your master take most notice of—I mean, what does he like best when he is traveling?

OSIP. It's all according to what turns up. What he likes best is being well received, well entertained.

THE MAYOR. Well entertained?

OSIP. Yes, well entertained. Here, I am only a servant, but he sees that I am well entertained too. Yes, indeed. Sometimes when we have been to a place, "Well, Osip," he will say, "have you been well looked after?"—"No sir, very badly!"—"Ah," he'll say, "that's poor hospitality. You remind me when I reach home." Never mind, I think to myself, I am a plain man. (*Waves his hand.*)

THE MAYOR. You are right there, you are right there, you talk sense. I gave you something for tea, so here is something more for buns.

OSIP. You are very kind, sir. (*Puts the money in his pocket.*) I'll drink your honor's health.

ANNA. Come and talk to me, Osip. I'll give you something too.

MARIA. You dear Osip, take your master a kiss!

(KHLESTAKOV *is heard coughing in the next room.*)

THE MAYOR. Hush! (*Walks on tiptoe; the rest of the conversation is in an undertone.*) Don't make a noise, whatever you do! Come, run along, you've talked enough!

ANNA. Come, Mashenka! I'll tell you what I have noticed in our visitor, something we can only talk about by ourselves.

THE MAYOR. Oh, they'll talk, you may be sure! If you had to listen you would soon wish you were deaf! (*Turning to* OSIP) Well, friend . . .

(*Enter* SVISTUNOV *and* DERZHIMORDA.)

THE MAYOR. Sh! You clumsy bears, how you tramp with your boots! They thump like someone dropping half a ton out of a cart! Where the hell have you been?

DERZHIMORDA. Acting on instructions, I went . . .

THE MAYOR. Sh-sh! (*puts his hand over his mouth*). How the

crow caws! (*Imitating him*) Acting on instructions indeed!
Booming like a drum! (*To* OSIP) Go along, friend, and get
everything ready for your master. Ask for anything we have
in the house. (*Exit* OSIP.) And you—stand at the front door
and don't move from the spot! And don't allow any outsider
into the house, especially any of the shopkeepers! If you let a
single one of them in, I'll . . . As soon as you see anyone
coming with a petition, or even without a petition, but looking
like a man who might want to present a petition against me,
throw him out by the scruff of the neck! like this! Give it to
him good! (*indicating a kick with his foot*) Do you hear?
Sh-sh!

> (*Follows the* POLICEMEN *out on tiptoe.*)
> (*Curtain.*)

ACT IV

The Same Room in the Mayor's House

AMMOS FIODOROVICH, ARTEMY FILIPPOVICH, *the* POSTMASTER, LUKA
LUKICH, *all in full dress uniform, together with* DOBCHINSKY *and*
BOBCHINSKY, *enter cautiously, almost on tiptoe. The whole scene is
conducted in an undertone.*

AMMOS FIODOROVICH (*arranging them all in a semicircle*). For
goodness' sake, gentlemen, make haste and form a circle, and
look as correct as you can! Bless the man, he visits at the
Palace and blows up the Imperial Council! Stand in military
order, it must be in military order! You run along over there,
Piotr Ivanovich, and you, Piotr Ivanovich, stand here.

> (*Both the* PIOTR IVANOVICHES *run on tiptoe.*)

ARTEMY FILIPPOVICH.   You may say what you like, Ammos Fiodorovich. You may say what you like, but we ought to take some
steps.

AMMOS FIODOROVICH.   What steps?

ARTEMY FILIPPOVICH.   We all know what.

AMMOS FIODOROVICH.   Slip something into his hand?

ARTEMY FILIPPOVICH.   Well, yes.

AMMOS FIODOROVICH.   It's risky, damn it all! He might make the
devil of a fuss: a great man like that! But maybe in the form of

a subscription from the gentry of the neighborhood for some memorial?

THE POSTMASTER. Or what about money that has reached the post office with no one to claim it?

ARTEMY FILIPPOVICH. You'd better look out that he doesn't pack you off by post somewhere. Listen to me: these things are not done like that in a well-regulated community. Why is there a whole regiment of us here? We ought to pay our respects one by one, and then, *tête-à-tête* . . . you know . . . what's proper—so that no one gets wind of it! That's the way to do things in well-regulated society! It's for you to begin, Ammos Fiodorovich.

AMMOS FIODOROVICH. Oh, better you; our distinguished visitor has broken bread in your establishment.

ARTEMY FILIPPOVICH. It ought to be Luka Lukich, as representing enlightenment and education.

LUKA LUKICH. I can't, I can't, gentlemen! I must confess I have been so brought up that if I am addressed by anyone who is a single grade above me in the Service. I feel more dead than alive and can't open my lips. No, you must let me off, gentlemen, you really must!

ARTEMY FILIPPOVICH. Yes, Ammos Fiodorovich, it must be you and no one else. As soon as you open your mouth it might be Cicero speaking.

AMMOS FIODOROVICH. What next, what next! Cicero! What an idea! If one does get a bit excited at times talking about hounds or retrievers . . .

ALL (*surrounding him*). Oh no, not only about dogs, you can talk about the Tower of Babel too. . . . No, Ammos Fiodorovich, don't fail us, be a father to us! No, Ammos Fiodorovich!

AMMOS FIODOROVICH. Let me alone, gentlemen!

(*At that moment there is a sound of footsteps and a cough in* KHLESTAKOV's *room. All rush headlong to the other door, jostling each other and trying to get out, which they do not accomplish without some of them getting jammed in the doorway. Exclamations in an undertone.*)

VOICE OF BOBCHINSKY. Oh, Piotr Ivanovich, Piotr Ivanovich, you have stepped on my foot!

VOICE OF ARTEMY FILIPPOVICH. You will be the death of me, gentlemen—I am as flat as a pancake!

(*A few cries of "Aie! Aie!" At last they all squeeze their way out and the stage is left empty. Enter* KHLESTAKOV, *looking drowsy.*)

KHLESTAKOV. I think I've had a pretty long snooze. How did they come by such feather beds and pillows? I am in a regular sweat. I think they must have given me something strong at lunch yesterday; there is a drumming in my head still. One might spend one's time very pleasantly here, I perceive. I do like hospitality, and I must admit I like it much better when people try to please me out of pure kindness and not from self-interest. And the Mayor's daughter is not at all bad-looking, and the mamma too might still . . . Well, I don't know, but I do like this sort of life.

(*Enter* AMMOS FIODOROVICH.)

AMMOS FIODOROVICH (*standing still, to himself*). O Lord, O Lord preserve me! My knees are giving way under me. (*Aloud, drawing himself up and putting his hand on his sword*) I have the honor to introduce myself: Liapkin-Tiapkin, collegiate assessor, and judge of the district court.

KHLESTAKOV. Please sit down. So you are the judge here?

AMMOS FIODOROVICH. In 1816 I was elected by the nobility for three years, and I have retained the post ever since.

KHLESTAKOV. It's a profitable job being a judge, isn't it?

AMMOS FIODOROVICH. After nine years of service I was presented with the Order of Vladimir of the Fourth Class with the commendation of my superiors. (*Aside*) The money is in my fist, and my fist feels as though it were on fire.

KHLESTAKOV. Oh, I like the Vladimir. The Anna of the Third Class is not nearly as nice.

AMMOS FIODOROVICH (*gradually advancing his clenched fist. Aside*) Merciful God! I don't know where I am. I feel as though I were sitting on hot coals.

KHLESTAKOV. What have you got in your hand?

AMMOS FIODOROVICH (*disconcerted, drops the notes on the floor*). Oh, nothing.

KHLESTAKOV. Nothing? Why, I see you've dropped some money.

AMMOS FIODOROVICH, (*trembling all over*). Not at all! (*Aside*) O God! Here I am in the dock, and the cart coming to take me to prison!

KHLESTAKOV (*picking it up*). Yes, it is money.

AMMOS FIODOROVICH (*aside*).   Well, it is all over! I am lost; I am done for!

KHLESTAKOV.   I tell you what, do you mind lending it to me?

AMMOS FIODOROVICH (*hurriedly*).   To be sure, to be sure . . . with pleasure. (*Aside*) Courage! Courage! Pull me through, Holy Mother!

KHLESTAKOV.   I got cleaned out on the journey, you know: what with one thing and another. . . . But I will send it to you as soon as I get home.

AMMOS FIODOROVICH.   Oh, not at all, it's an honor. . . . Of course by zeal and devotion to my superiors . . . I will do my poor best to deserve . . . (*Rises from his chair. Drawing himself up, with his hands to his sides*) I will not venture to trouble you further with my presence. Have you any order to give me?

KHLESTAKOV.   What sort of order?

AMMOS FIODOROVICH.   I mean, have you no order to give to the district court?

KHLESTAKOV.   Oh, why? No, I have no need of it at present; no, nothing. Thanks so much.

AMMOS FIODOROVICH (*bowing himself out. Aside*) Well, the town is ours!

KHLESTAKOV (*alone*).   The Judge is a good fellow!

(*Enter the* POSTMASTER *in uniform holding himself erect, with his hand on his sword.*)

THE POSTMASTER.   I have the honor to introduce myself: Shpekin, court councilor, postmaster.

KHLESTAKOV.   Ah, pleased to see you! I am very fond of good company. Please sit down. You always live here, I suppose?

THE POSTMASTER.   Yes, sir.

KHLESTAKOV.   I like this town, you know. Of course it is not a very big town—but what of it? It is not Petersburg or Moscow. It isn't, is it?

THE POSTMASTER.   Perfectly true.

KHLESTAKOV.   Of course it is only in the capital that you get *bon-ton* [29] and no country bumpkins. Don't you agree?

THE POSTMASTER.   Yes, indeed, sir. (*Aside*) He is not a bit proud: asks one about everything.

---

[29] "Good breeding." (ed.)

KHLESTAKOV.   But yet you must admit that one can be happy even in a little town, can't one?

THE POSTMASTER.   Yes, indeed, sir.

KHLESTAKOV.   What does one want? To my mind all one wants is to be genuinely liked and respected—isn't it?

THE POSTMASTER.   Perfectly true.

KHLESTAKOV.   I must say I am glad to find you agree with me. People may think me peculiar, but I am like that. (*Looking into his face, says to himself*) I think I'll ask this postmaster for a loan. (*Aloud*) Such a queer thing happened to me: I got absolutely cleaned out on the journey. Could you perhaps lend me three hundred rubles?

THE POSTMASTER.   Certainly, I shall consider it an honor. Allow me, here. I am truly glad to be of service.

KHLESTAKOV.   Thanks so much. I must confess I hate going short on a journey—there's no point in it, is there?

THE POSTMASTER.   No, indeed, sir. (*Rises. Drawing himself up and holding his sword*) I will not venture to trouble you further with my presence. . . . Have you no observation to make with regard to the post office?

KHLESTAKOV.   No, none.

(*The* POSTMASTER *bows himself out.*)

KHLESTAKOV (*lighting a cigar*).   I think the Postmaster is a very good fellow too; anyway he is obliging. I like such people. (*Enter* LUKA LUKICH, *almost shoved in at the door from behind. A voice is heard almost aloud:* "What are you afraid of?")

LUKA LUKICH (*draws himself up in trepidation, holding his sword*).   I have the honor to introduce myself: Khlopov, superintendent of schools and titular councilor.

KHLESTAKOV.   Am pleased to see you! Sit down, sit down. Won't you have a cigar? (*Offers him a cigar.*)

LUKA LUKICH (*to himself, irresolutely*).   Well I never! That I didn't expect. Should I take it or not?

KHLESTAKOV.   Take it, take it; it's not a bad cigar. Of course it's not like what you get in Petersburg. There, my good sir, I smoked cigars at twenty-five rubles a hundred—you feel like licking your lips when you've smoked one. Here's a candle; light it. (*Holds a candle to him.*)

(LUKA LUKICH *tries to light the cigar, but keeps trembling.*)

KHLESTAKOV.   But that's not the right end!

LUKA LUKICH.   (*In his panic drops the cigar, and with a wave of his hand says to himself in disgust*) The devil take it all! My damned timidity has ruined everything!

KHLESTAKOV.   You are not fond of cigars, I see. Now I must admit they are one of my weaknesses. And the fair sex, too—I can't resist them. And you? Which do you like best, brunettes or blondes?

(LUKA LUKICH *is utterly nonplussed and unable to answer.*)

KHLESTAKOV.   Come, tell me frankly, brunettes or blondes?

LUKA LUKICH.   I can't venture to have an opinion.

KHLESTAKOV.   Come, come, don't turn it off! I really want to know your preference.

LUKA LUKICH.   I venture to lay before you . . . (*Aside*) I don't know what I am saying.

KHLESTAKOV.   Ah! ah! You won't say. I believe you are smitten with some pretty little brunette. Confess, you are?

(LUKA LUKICH *remains dumb.*)

KHLESTAKOV.   Ah! You are blushing! You see, you see! Why won't you say?

LUKA LUKICH.   I am overawed, your hon . . . rev . . . excel . . . (*Aside*) My cursed tongue has betrayed me!

KHLESTAKOV.   Overawed? There really is something in my eye, you know, that inspires awe. Anyway, I know there is not a woman who can hold out against it, is there?

LUKA LUKICH.   Certainly not.

KHLESTAKOV.   A strange thing has happened to me: I've been absolutely cleaned out on the journey here. Couldn't you perhaps lend me three hundred rubles?

LUKA LUKICH (*clutching at his pockets, to himself*).   How awful, if I haven't got it! I have, I have! (*Takes out notes, and gives them, trembling.*)

KHLESTAKOV.   Thanks so much.

LUKA LUKICH (*drawing himself up and holding his sword*).   I will not venture to trouble you longer with my presence.

KHLESTAKOV.   Goodbye.

LUKA LUKICH. (*Darts out almost at a run and says aside*) Thank
God! Maybe he won't look into the schoolroom!
(*Enter* ARTEMY FILIPPOVICH, *drawing himself up and
holding his sword.*)

ARTEMY FILIPPOVICH. I have the honor to introduce myself:
Zemlianika, welfare commissioner and court councilor.

KHLESTAKOV. How do you do? Please sit down.

ARTEMY FILIPPOVICH. I had the honor of accompanying you and
receiving you in person in the charitable institutions committed to my charge.

KHLESTAKOV. Oh yes, I remember. You gave me an excellent
lunch!

ARTEMY FILIPPOVICH. Always glad to do my best for the welfare
of my country.

KHLESTAKOV. I must admit I am fond of good food—it is my
weakness. Do tell me, please, I think you were a little shorter
yesterday than you are today, weren't you?

ARTEMY FILIPPOVICH. Quite possibly. (*After a pause*) I may say
that I spare nothing and zealously perform my duties. (*Draws
his chair up closer and says in a low voice*) Now the Postmaster here does nothing at all: all his work is utterly neglected . . . the despatches are held back. . . . Perhaps you
would look into it yourself? The Judge, too—who was here
just before I came in—does nothing but course hares; he keeps
dogs in the public court, and his conduct, to tell the truth—
and, of course, it is my duty to do so for the good of my
country, although he is a relative and a friend—his conduct
is most reprehensible. There is a landowner here, Dobchinsky,
whom you have seen, and as soon as that Dobchinsky steps
out of his house, the Judge will be sitting with his wife, I am
ready to take my oath on it. . . . And just look at the children: not one of them is like Dobchinsky, but every one of
them, even the little girl, is the very image of the Judge.

KHLESTAKOV. You don't say so! I should never have thought it.

ARTEMY FILIPPOVICH. And the Superintendent of Schools, too.
. . . I cannot think how the authorities came to entrust such
a post to him: he is worse than a Jacobin,[30] and the pernicious

---

[30] No small accomplishment. Jacobins were violent radicals in France during
the Revolution of 1789. (ed.)

principles he instills into the young are beyond words. If you
instruct me to do so, I can put all this into writing.

KHLESTAKOV. Very good, do. I shall be very much pleased. You
know I like something amusing to read when I am bored. . . .
What is your name? I keep forgetting.

ARTEMY FILIPPOVICH. Zemlianika.

KHLESTAKOV. Oh yes, Zemlianika. And tell me, please, have you
any children?

ARTEMY FILIPPOVICH. To be sure. Five, and two are grown up.

KHLESTAKOV. Grown up! You don't say so! And what are . . .
what are they . . .

ARTEMY FILIPPOVICH. You mean, you wish to inquire what are
their names?

KHLESTAKOV. Yes, what are their names?

ARTEMY FILIPPOVICH. Nikolai, Ivan, Elizaveta, Maria, and Pere-
petuya.

KHLESTAKOV. Very nice.

ARTEMY FILIPPOVICH. I will not venture to trouble you with my
presence and rob you of time dedicated to sacred duties. . . .
(*Is bowing himself out.*)

KHLESTAKOV (*accompanying him*). No, it's all right. It's all so
funny what you were telling me. Come and talk to me another
time . . . I like that sort of thing. (*Turns back, and opening
the door calls after him*) Hey, you! What's your name? I keep
forgetting what to call you.

ARTEMY FILIPPOVICH. Artemy Filippovich.

KHLESTAKOV. Do me a favor, Artemy Filippovich; a strange thing
has happened to me: I was completely cleaned out on the way
here. Have you any money you could lend me—four hundred
rubles or so?

ARTEMY FILIPPOVICH. Yes.

KHLESTAKOV. How lucky! Thanks so much.

(*Exit* ARTEMY FILIPPOVICH.)
(*Enter* BOBCHINSKY *and* DOBCHINSKY.)

BOBCHINSKY. I have the honor to introduce myself: Piotr Ivanovich Bobchinsky, a resident of this town.

DOBCHINSKY. Piotr Ivanovich Dobchinsky, landowner.

KHLESTAKOV. Ah, I saw you yesterday. You tumbled in at the
doorway, didn't you? Well, how is your nose?

BOBCHINSKY. Oh, don't trouble; it's healed, thank God, quite healed now.

KHLESTAKOV. That's a good thing. I am glad . . . (*Speaking suddenly and abruptly*) You haven't any money on you?

DOBCHINSKY. Money? Why?

KHLESTAKOV. A thousand rubles to lend me.

BOBCHINSKY. Oh dear, not a sum like that. Haven't you, Piotr Ivanovich?

DOBCHINSKY. I haven't it with me, for my money, if you care to know, has been lodged in the hands of the public trustee.

KHLESTAKOV. Ah well, if you haven't a thousand, let me have a hundred.

BOBCHINSKY (*fumbling in his pockets*). Haven't you a hundred rubles, Piotr Ivanovich? I have only forty in paper notes.

DOBCHINSKY (*looking in his pocket*). Twenty-five rubles is all I have.

BOBCHINSKY. Oh, look a little more thoroughly, Piotr Ivanovich! I know you have a hole in your right-hand pocket; most likely some have slipped through into the lining.

DOBCHINSKY. No, really, there's nothing there.

KHLESTAKOV. Oh, it doesn't matter. I thought I'd just ask. Very good; sixty-five rubles will do. . . . Never mind. (*Takes the money.*)

DOBCHINSKY. I make bold to ask your assistance about a very delicate matter.

KHLESTAKOV. And what is it?

DOBCHINSKY. It is a matter of great delicacy: my eldest son was born, you see, before I was married. . . .

KHLESTAKOV. Oh?

DOBCHINSKY. Though that's only in a manner of speaking; he was born exactly as though in lawful wedlock, and I made it all right and proper afterwards by the bonds of legitimate matrimony. So now you see I want him to become altogether my legitimate son and to bear my name—Dobchinsky.

KHLESTAKOV. Very good; let him bear your name; that's all right.

DOBCHINSKY. I would not have troubled you, but I am sorry, because he is so gifted. The boy . . . is very promising: he can repeat all sorts of poems by heart, and if he can get hold of a knife he makes a little cart as cleverly as a magician. Piotr Ivanovich here can tell you.

BOBCHINSKY.   Yes, he has great talents.

KHLESTAKOV.   Very good, very good! I'll see to that, I'll speak about that. . . . I have no doubt it will all be arranged, yes, yes. . . . (*Turning to* BOBCHINSKY) And haven't you anything to say to me?

BOBCHINSKY.   I have, indeed, a very humble request.

KHLESTAKOV.   Well, what about?

BOBCHINSKY.   I humbly beg you, when you go back to Petersburg, say to all those great gentlemen—senators, admirals, and such, "Do you know, your Excellency or your Highness, in such and such a town there lives a man called Piotr Ivanovich Bobchinsky?" Say that: "There lives a man called Piotr Ivanovich Bobchinsky."

KHLESTAKOV.   Very well.

BOBCHINSKY.   Yes, and if you have a chance of speaking to the Czar, tell the Czar, "Do you know, your Imperial Majesty, in such and such a town lives Piotr Ivanovich Bobchinsky?"

KHLESTAKOV.   Very well.

DOBCHINSKY.   Excuse us for troubling you with our presence.

BOBCHINSKY.   Excuse us for troubling you with our presence.

KHLESTAKOV.   Oh, it's no trouble. It's a pleasure.

(*Sees them out.*)

KHLESTAKOV (*alone*).   There are a lot of officials here. But I think they take me for someone of importance in the government. I must have told them a fine yarn yesterday. What a set of fools! I must write to Petersburg and tell Triapichkin all about it: he is an author, let him write a skit on them. Hey, Osip! bring me ink and paper! (*Osip, looking in at the door, says, "In a minute."*) And if Triapichkin gets his knife into anyone, he'd better watch out: he wouldn't spare his own father to adorn a tale, and he is fond of money too. But they are good-natured fellows, these officials: it speaks very well for them that they have lent me money. I'll just look how much I have got. That's three hundred from the Judge, that's three hundred from the Postmaster, six hundred, seven hundred, eight hundred . . . what a dirty note! Eight hundred, nine hundred . . . Oho, more than a thousand . . . Now you can come on, captain! I am ready for you! We'll see who will get the best of it this time!

(*Enter* OSIP *with ink and paper.*)

KHLESTAKOV. Now you see, you idiot, how they receive me and make much of me? (*Begins writing.*)

OSIP. Yes, thank God. Only do you know what, Ivan Aleksandrovich?

KHLESTAKOV. What is it?

OSIP. You'd better get away from here! It's high time we were off.

KHLESTAKOV (*writing*). What nonsense! Why?

OSIP. Well, you'd better. Bless the people! You've enjoyed yourself here for two days, and that's enough. What's the good of lingering on with them? Have done with them! Our luck may turn, and someone else arrive . . . believe me, Ivan Aleksandrovich! And the horses here are first-rate—how we should race along!

KHLESTAKOV (*writing*). No, I want to stay here a while longer. Tomorrow will do.

OSIP. Tomorrow is no good. Let us be off, Ivan Aleksandrovich, really! It's a great honor for you, of course, but still we'd better make haste and get away; they've mistaken you for somebody else, you know, really. . . . And your papa will be angry with you for dawdling so long on the way. We could race along beautifully! They'd give us wonderful horses here.

KHLESTAKOV (*writing*). Oh, very well. Only take this letter to the post first, and you can get my traveling pass at the same time if you like. But be careful we have good horses now! Tell the drivers I'll pay them a silver ruble each if they'll drive as though I were a special messenger and sing songs! (*Goes on writing.*) I can imagine how Triapichkin will split with laughing. . . .

OSIP. I'll give it to the man here to post, sir; I had better be packing, so as not to lose time.

KHLESTAKOV (*writing*). Very good, only bring a candle.

OSIP. (*Goes out and says behind the scenes*) My boy! Take this letter to the post and tell the postmaster to take it unfranked, and tell them to send round at once the very best *troika*[31]; and say my master doesn't pay the fare, it's at the Crown expense. And tell them to look sharp, or my master will be angry. Stay, the letter is not ready yet.

---

[31] A three-horse carriage. (ed.)

KHLESTAKOV (*goes on writing*).   It would be interesting to know where he is living now—in Pochtamtskaya [32] or Gorokhovaya? [33] He is fond of changing his lodging and not paying his rent. I'll chance Pochtamtskaya. (*Folds up the letter and addresses it.*)

(OSIP *brings a candle.* KHLESTAKOV *seals the letter. At that moment the voice of* DERZHIMORDA *is heard:* "*Where are you shoving to, bushy beard? I tell you, I've orders to admit no one.*")

KHLESTAKOV (*gives the letter to* OSIP).   Here, take it.

VOICES OF SHOPKEEPERS.   Let us in, sir! You can't refuse: we are here on business.

DERZHIMORDA'S VOICE.   Be off, be off! He is not seeing anyone; he is asleep.

(*The uproar grows louder.*)

KHLESTAKOV.   What's going on, Osip? See what the fuss is about.

OSIP (*looks out of window*).   It's some shopkeepers want to come in, and the policeman won't let them. They are waving petitions: most likely they want to see you.

KHLESTAKOV (*going to the window*).   What is it, friends?

VOICES OF SHOPKEEPERS.   We appeal to your Excellency. Command them to admit our petitions, honored sir.

KHLESTAKOV.   Let them in, let them in! Let them come here. Osip, tell them they can come in.

(OSIP *goes out.*)

KHLESTAKOV.   (*Takes petitions through the window, opens one and reads*) "To His Honorable Excellency the Master of Finances, from Abdulin, merchant . . ." What on earth does it mean? There's no such rank!

(*The* SHOPKEEPERS *come in with a basket of wine bottles and loaves of sugar.*)

KHLESTAKOV.   What is it, friends?

SHOPKEEPERS.   We humbly ask your gracious kindness.

KHLESTAKOV.   What do you want?

SHOPKEEPERS.   Do not be our ruin, honored sir! We are suffering cruel wrong.

KHLESTAKOV.   Who is ill-treating you?

ONE OF THE SHOPKEEPERS.   It's all the Mayor here. There has

---

[32] "Post Office" Street, important thoroughfare in St. Petersburg. (ed.)

[33] "Peas" Street, another important thoroughfare in St. Petersburg. (ed.)

never been a mayor like him, sir! There are no words bad enough for the things he does. He has ruined us, billeting soldiers on us and all—we are ready to have the noose put on our heads. His behavior is most unmannerly. He will pull one by the beard and shout, "Ah, you Tartar!" Yes indeed! It isn't enough as though we had shown him any disrespect, we have always done our duty: as for giving something for the dresses of his good lady and his daughter, we have nothing against that. But mind you, that's not enough for him—my word, no! He walks into the shop and takes anything he can lay his hands on. If he sees a piece of cloth, "Hey, my dear man," he will say, "that's a fine bit of cloth; send that round to me." Well, one has to send it—and there may be fifty yards in the piece.

KHLESTAKOV. Is it possible? What a scoundrel!

SHOPKEEPERS. Indeed it is true, sir! No one remembers a mayor like him. One has to hide everything in the shop when one sees him coming. And it isn't only the dainties that he goes for, he takes all manner of rubbish: plums that have been lying seven years in the barrel, my shopmen would not touch them, but he will take a whole handful. St. Anthony's is his name day,[34] and then we take him no end of things, he can't be short of anything; but no, that's not enough for him: he says St. Onufry's is his name day too. There's no help for it: one has to give something for that name day too.

KHLESTAKOV. Why, he is a regular highwayman!

SHOPKEEPERS. Yes indeed! But only try refusing, and he will quarter a whole regiment on you. And if you do anything, he will have the doors locked. "I am not going to flog you or torture you," he says, "that's forbidden by the law," he says, "but you just go on eating red herring, my friend, without a drop to drink."

KHLESTAKOV. Ah, what a scoundrel! Why, he deserves to be sent to Siberia!

SHOPKEEPERS. Wherever your Excellency thinks fit to send him, so long as it's a good way off. Do not despise our humble offerings, honored sir: we beg you to accept some sugar and a basket of wine.

---

[34] An Orthodox Russian formerly celebrated the feast day of his patron saint, after whom he was christened, as his birthday. (ed.)

KHLESTAKOV.   No, don't you think of such a thing. I don't take bribes at all. But if you were to let me have a loan . . . of three hundred rubles, for instance, that would be another thing: I might take a loan.

SHOPKEEPERS.   By all means, honored sir! (*Take out money.*) But what's three hundred—better take five; only help us.

KHLESTAKOV.   Very well, a loan I have nothing against, I'll take it.

SHOPKEEPERS (*offer him money on a silver dish*).   Please accept the tray with it.

KHLESTAKOV.   Well, I might take the tray too.

SHOPKEEPERS (*bowing*).   And you might just as well take the sugar with it.

KHLESTAKOV.   Oh no, I don't take bribes.

OSIP.   Your Excellency, why not accept the sugar? Take it! It will all come in useful on a journey. Hand me over the sugar loaves and the basket. Give it here, it will all come in useful. What have you there? A cord? Give me the cord too—cord comes in handy on a journey too: if the chaise or anything else breaks down you can tie it up.

SHOPKEEPERS.   Pray do us the favor, your Excellency! If you don't help us in our trouble we don't know what we are to do: we are in a desperate situation.

KHLESTAKOV.   Certainly, certainly! I'll do my best.

(*The* SHOPKEEPERS *go out.*)
(*A woman's voice is heard:* "*No, you daren't turn me away! I'll complain of you to the gentleman himself. Don't shove like that, you hurt me!*")

KHLESTAKOV.   Who is there? (*Goes to the window.*) What is it, my good woman?

VOICES OF TWO WOMEN.   We crave your kind help! Grant us a hearing, honored sir!

KHLESTAKOV (*at the window*).   Let her in!

(*Enter the* LOCKSMITH'S WIFE *and the* SERGEANT'S WIDOW.)

THE LOCKSMITH'S WIFE (*bowing down to his feet*).   Graciously help me! . . .

THE SERGEANT'S WIDOW.   Graciously help me!

KHLESTAKOV.   But who are you?

THE SERGEANT'S WIDOW.   Ivanovna, widow of a sergeant.

THE LOCKSMITH'S WIFE.   Fevroyna Petrovna Poshliopkina, wife of a locksmith of the town. . . .

KHLESTAKOV. Stop, speak one at a time. What do you want?

THE LOCKSMITH'S WIFE. Graciously help me, I seek your protection against the Mayor! God send him every evil! May
neither his children nor he, the rascal, nor his uncles nor his
aunts prosper in anything they undertake!

KHLESTAKOV. What has he done?

THE LOCKSMITH'S WIFE. He sent my husband to have his head
shaved to become a soldier, and it was not our turn, the rascal!
and it is against the law, him being a married man. How could
he do it?

KHLESTAKOV. How could he do it?

THE LOCKSMITH'S WIFE. He did it, the villain, he did it, may God
smite him in this world and in the next! May every plague
overtake him, and his aunt too, if he has one, and if his father
is living, may he, the dog, choke or split, the dirty swindler!
It was the tailor's son who ought to have been taken, a drunken
fellow, but his parents gave the Mayor a handsome present.
Then he went after the son of Panteleevna, the merchant's
wife, but she sent his good lady three pieces of linen, so then
he came to me. "What do you want with your husband? He is
no more good to you." Well, I know whether he is any good
or not, it's my business, you scoundrel! "He is a thief," says
he; "though he's stolen nothing yet," says he, "it makes no
difference, he will steal some day, he will be sent as a soldier
next year anyway." But what am I to do without a husband,
you rascal! I am a weak woman, you bastard! May none of
your kindred see the light of day! And if you've a mother-in-
law, I hope she'll . . .

KHLESTAKOV. All right, all right. (*Motions her to the door.*) Well,
and you?

THE LOCKSMITH'S WIFE (*as she goes out*). Do not forget, honored sir! Be merciful!

THE SERGEANT'S WIDOW. It's to complain of the Mayor I've come,
sir.

KHLESTAKOV. Why, what for? Tell me in a few words.

THE SERGEANT'S WIDOW. He flogged me, sir!

KHLESTAKOV. How was that?

THE SERGEANT'S WIDOW. By mistake, sir! Some of our women
were fighting in the market, and the police did not get there

in time, so they took me up and gave me such a drubbing I couldn't sit down for two days.

KHLESTAKOV. What's to be done now?

THE SERGEANT'S WIDOW. Well, there's no help for it now, but make him pay me damages for the mistake. If luck does come one's way, one doesn't want to miss it, and the money would come in wonderfully handy just now.

KHLESTAKOV. Very good, very good! You can go, you can go, I'll see about it. (*Hands holding petitions are thrust in at the window.*) Why, who is there now! (*Goes to the window.*) I don't want them! I don't want them! Take them away! (*Moving away*) I am sick of them, damn it all! Don't let them in, Osip!

OSIP (*Shouts at the window*).   Be off, be off! No time now, come tomorrow!

(*The door opens and a figure appears in a frieze overcoat, with an unshaven chin, a swollen lip, and a bandage around his face; behind him is seen a perspective of other figures.*)

OSIP.   Be off, be off! Where are you shoving to? (*Pushes the foremost figure out, laying both hands on his stomach, and passes with him into the anteroom, slamming the door behind him.*)

(*Enter* MARIA ANTONOVNA.)

MARIA.   Oh!

KHLESTAKOV.   Why are you so alarmed, madam?

MARIA.   No, I am not alarmed.

KHLESTAKOV (*striking an attitude*).   Believe me, madam, it is most agreeable to me that you have taken me for a man who . . . But allow me to ask you, where were you going?

MARIA.   Really, I wasn't going anywhere.

KHLESTAKOV.   And why, may I ask, aren't you going anywhere?

MARIA.   I thought Mamma was here. . . .

KHLESTAKOV.   No, please explain!

MARIA.   I am hindering you. You are engaged in important business.

KHLESTAKOV (*striking an attitude*).   But your eyes are worth more than important business. . . . You cannot hinder me, you cannot possibly; on the contrary, your presence can only be a pleasure.

MARIA.   You talk as they do in smart society.

KHLESTAKOV.   To such a lovely being as you. May I have the

happiness of offering you a chair? But no, you should have not a chair but a throne.

MARIA. Really, I don't know. I ought to be going. (*Sits down.*)

KHLESTAKOV. What a lovely kerchief!

MARIA. You are making fun of me; you only say that to make fun of us provincials.

KHLESTAKOV. How I should like to be that kerchief, madam, to embrace your lily neck.

MARIA. I don't understand what you are talking about . . . a kerchief . . . What peculiar weather it is today!

KHLESTAKOV. Your lips, madam, are better than any weather.

MARIA. You do say such things . . . I should like to ask you to write a few verses in my album. I expect you know ever so many.

KHLESTAKOV. For your sake, madam, I'll do anything you please. Command, what sort of verses would you like?

MARIA. Some sort of . . . you know . . . good ones . . . new.

KHLESTAKOV. What are poems! I know ever so many!

MARIA. Oh, tell me the ones you will write for me.

KHLESTAKOV. But why repeat them? I know them well enough.

MARIA. I am very fond of poetry.

KHLESTAKOV. Oh, I know lots of them of all sorts. Well, if you like, I'll write this one:

>   Oh, man who in thy hour of grief
>   Vainly doth murmur against God.[35]

And there are others . . . I can't think of them at the moment; but it does not matter. Instead of that I had much better offer you my love, which your eyes have . . . (*Draws his chair nearer.*)

MARIA. Love! I don't understand love. . . . I have never known what love means. (*Edges her chair away.*)

KHLESTAKOV. Why do you move your chair away? We are better sitting near each other.

MARIA (*moving her chair farther*). Why nearer? It may just as well be farther.

KHLESTAKOV (*moving nearer*). Why farther? It may just as well be nearer.

MARIA (*moving away*). But why?

---

[35] From a poem by Mikhail V. Lomonosov (1711-65), one of the earliest important Russian poets: *Ode, Adapted from Job*, lines 1 and 2. (ed.)

KHLESTAKOV (*moving nearer*). You only imagine that we are near; you must imagine that we are far apart. How happy I should be, madam, if I might hold you in my embraces!

MARIA (*looking out of window*). What bird was it flew up just now? A magpie, was it?

KHLESTAKOV (*kisses her shoulder and looks out of window*). It's a magpie.

MARIA (*gets up indignantly*). No, that's too much. . . . What impudence!

KHLESTAKOV (*detaining her*). Forgive me, madam: I did it from love, really, from love.

MARIA. You think I am a provincial girl whom you can . . . (*Tries to get away.*)

KHLESTAKOV (*still detains her*). It was love; it really was. I didn't mean any harm; it was only fun: Maria Antonovna, don't be angry! I am ready to beg your pardon on my knees. (*Falls on his knees.*) Forgive me, forgive me! You see, I am on my knees!

(*Enter* ANNA ANDREEVNA.)

ANNA (*seeing* KHLESTAKOV *on his knees*). Oh, what a surprise!

KHLESTAKOV (*getting up*). Oh, damn it all!

ANNA (*to her daughter*). What does this mean, miss? This is nice behavior.

MARIA. Mamma, I . . .

ANNA. Go out of the room, do you hear! Go along! And don't let me set eyes upon you. (MARIA ANTONOVNA *goes out in tears.*) Excuse me, I must confess I am so astounded . . .

KHLESTAKOV (*aside*). She too is very appetizing, she is not at all bad. (*Drops on his knees.*) Madam, you see I am dying with love.

ANNA. What, you are on your knees? Oh, get up, get up! The floor is anything but clean.

KHLESTAKOV. No, on my knees, it must be on my knees. I want to know what awaits me: life or death.

ANNA. Pardon me, I don't quite grasp the meaning of your words. If I understand you correctly, you are declaring your sentiments for my daughter?

KHLESTAKOV. No, I am in love with you. My life is in the balance. If you do not requite my constant love, I am not worthy of earthly existence. With heart aglow I ask your hand.

ANNA. But allow me to observe that I am in a certain sense . . . married.

KHLESTAKOV. That doesn't matter! Love knows naught of such distinctions; as Karamzin said: "Only the laws condemn it." [36] We will flee to some happy dale beside a running brook. . . . Your hand, I ask your hand. . . .

(MARIA ANTONOVNA *runs in suddenly*.)

MARIA. Mamma, Papa says you are to . . . (*Sees* KHLESTAKOV *on his knees.*) Oh, what a surprise!

ANNA. What do you want? What is it? How flighty! She runs in like a scalded cat! What do you think so surprising? What nonsense have you got in your head? Why, you might be a child of three. Nobody, nobody would ever think that you were eighteen. I don't know when you will learn sense, when you will learn to behave like a well-brought-up girl, when you will understand what is meant by good principles and propriety.

MARIA (*in tears*). Really, Mamma, I didn't know . . .

ANNA. Your head is always in a flutter; you model yourself on the Liapkin-Tiapkin girls. Why copy them? There's no need to copy them! There are other examples for you to follow— you have your mother. That's the example you ought to follow!

KHLESTAKOV (*seizes the daughter's hand*). Anna Andreevna, do not oppose our happiness; give your blessing to our constant love!

ANNA (*in amazement*). So then it's her?

KHLESTAKOV. Say, is it to be life or death?

ANNA. There, you see, you fool, you see: for the sake of a worthless girl like you our distinguished visitor was on his knees— and you ran in as though you were crazy. Really, it would serve you right if I refused my consent; you do not deserve such happiness.

MARIA. I won't do it again, Mamma, I'll never do it again.

(*The* MAYOR *comes in breathless.*)

THE MAYOR. Your Excellency, spare me! spare me!

---

[36] Quoted from *Bornholm Island*, a romance, in which it appears in a poem by the Russian historian, poet, journalist, and writer of tales, Nikolai Mikhailovich Karamzin (1766-1826). (ed.)

KHLESTAKOV.　What's the matter?

THE MAYOR.　The shopkeepers have been complaining to your Excellency. I assure you on my honor that not one-half of what they say is true. It's they who cheat and give short measure. The sergeant's widow was lying when she said I had her flogged; it's a lie, indeed it is. She flogged herself.

KHLESTAKOV.　Oh, hang the sergeant's widow—I have something better to think about.

THE MAYOR.　Don't believe it, don't believe it! . . . They are such liars. . . . Why, a babe would not believe them. They are known all over the town for their lying. And as for swindling, I can assure you there have never been such swindlers on this earth.

ANNA.　Do you know the honor that Ivan Aleksandrovich is doing us? He is asking for our daughter's hand.

THE MAYOR.　What next! What next! You are raving! Do not be angry, your Excellency; she is not very strong in the head, her mother was just the same.

KHLESTAKOV.　But I really am making an offer. I am in love.

THE MAYOR.　I cannot believe it, your Excellency!

ANNA.　But when he tells you so!

KHLESTAKOV.　I am speaking seriously. . . . I might go off my head from love.

THE MAYOR.　I dare not believe it; I am unworthy of such an honor.

KHLESTAKOV.　But if you won't consent to give me the hand of Maria Antonovna, God only knows what I may do. . . .

THE MAYOR.　I can't believe it: your Excellency is pleased to jest!

ANNA.　Ah, what a blockhead he is! Why, isn't he telling you so?

THE MAYOR.　I can't believe it.

KHLESTAKOV.　Consent, consent! I am a desperate man; I may do anything: when I shoot myself, you will have to answer for it.

THE MAYOR.　Oh, my God! I assure you I am not to blame, neither in thought nor act! Please do not be angry! Do what your Excellency thinks best. My head at this moment . . . I don't know what's the matter with it. I have become a greater fool than I have ever been.

ANNA.　Well, give them your blessing! (KHLESTAKOV *goes up to him with* MARIA ANTONOVNA.)

THE MAYOR.　May God bless you! It's not my fault! (KHLESTAKOV *kisses* MARIA ANTONOVNA. *The* MAYOR *stares at them*.) What the hell! It's really true! (*Rubs his eyes*.) They are kissing each other! Holy Saints! kissing! They are really engaged. (*With a cry and skip of delight*) Hey, Anton! Hurrah for the Mayor! What a turn things have taken!

(*Enter* OSIP.)

OSIP. The horses are ready.

KHLESTAKOV. Ah, very good . . . I am coming.

THE MAYOR. What? Your Excellency is going?

KHLESTAKOV. Yes.

THE MAYOR. Then, when . . . I mean . . . Your Excellency has deigned yourself to hint at a wedding, I believe?

KHLESTAKOV. Ah, it's only for a moment . . . for one day, to see my uncle, a rich old man; and I shall be back tomorrow.

THE MAYOR. We will not venture to keep you in the hope of your happy return.

KHLESTAKOV. Of course, of course, I won't be long. Farewell, my love . . . no, I cannot express my feelings! Farewell, darling! (*Kisses her hand*.)

THE MAYOR. But don't you need anything for the journey? I believe your Excellency was a little short of money?

KHLESTAKOV. Oh no, why so? (*After a moment's reflection*) Very well, though.

THE MAYOR. How much would you like?

KHLESTAKOV. Oh, well, you lent me two hundred, that is, not two hundred but four hundred—I don't want to take advantage of your mistake—well, perhaps you could let me have the same sum again, to make it a round eight hundred.

THE MAYOR. Certainly. (*Takes notes out of his pocketbook*.) Luckily, I have just got some new notes.

KHLESTAKOV. Ah yes! (*Takes the notes and examines them*.) That is nice. They say it brings good luck to have new notes.

THE MAYOR. Yes, indeed.

KHLESTAKOV. Goodbye, Anton Antonovich. Very much obliged for your hospitality: I say it sincerely: nowhere have I had such a warm reception. Goodbye, Anna Andreevna! Farewell, my darling Maria Antonovna!

(*They go out*.)

KHLESTAKOV'S VOICE (*behind the scenes*). Farewell, angel of my heart, Maria Antonovna!

THE MAYOR'S VOICE.　What, you are going in the ordinary public coach?

KHLESTAKOV'S VOICE.　Yes, that's my habit. Springs make my head ache.

THE DRIVER'S VOICE.　Wo-o-o . . .

THE MAYOR'S VOICE.　Please, anyway, have something to put on the seat. Wouldn't you like me to give you a rug?

KHLESTAKOV'S VOICE.　No, why? It's of no consequence; but perhaps you might let them bring a rug.

THE MAYOR'S VOICE.　Hey, Avdotya! go to the storeroom and fetch a rug, the best, the Persian one with the blue background! Make haste!

THE DRIVER'S VOICE.　Wo-o-o . . .

THE MAYOR'S VOICE.　When are we to expect your Excellency?

KHLESTAKOV'S VOICE.　Tomorrow or the next day.

OSIP'S VOICE.　Oh, is that the rug? Hand it here, put it there! Now put the hay on this side.

THE DRIVER'S VOICE.　Wo-o-o . . .

OSIP'S VOICE.　Here, this side! Here, some more! That's right! That will be fine! (*Slaps his hand on the rug.*) Now, sit down, your Excellency.

KHLESTAKOV'S VOICE.　Goodbye, Anton Antonovich!

THE MAYOR'S VOICE.　Goodbye, your Excellency.

WOMEN'S VOICES.　Goodbye, Ivan Aleksandrovich!

KHLESTAKOV'S VOICE.　Goodbye, *mamenka!* [37]

THE DRIVER'S VOICE.　Giddap, my beauties!

(*Bells ring.*)

(*Curtain.*)

ACT V

The Same Room

The MAYOR, ANNA ANDREEVNA, *and* MARIA ANTONOVNA

THE MAYOR.　Well, Anna Andreevna? Eh? Did you ever expect such a thing? A mighty fine catch, damn it all! Come, confess, in your wildest dreams you never hoped for this—from being just a mayor's wife . . . damn it all! . . . to be related to such a devil of a man!

ANNA.　Not at all; I knew it all along. It seems strange to you be-

---

[37] "Little mother." (ed.)

cause you are just an ordinary man and have never mixed with decent people.

THE MAYOR. I am a decent person myself, my dear. But really though, Anna Andreevna, when one comes to think what high-flying birds we are now, you and I! Eh, Anna Andreevna? Right at the top of the tree, damn it all! You wait a while, I'll make it hot for them—all those talebearers with their complaints! Hey, who's there? (*Enter a* POLICEMAN.) Ah, it's you, Ivan Karpovich! Bring those shopkeepers here, my boy. I'll give them a lesson, the brutes! I'll teach them to complain! Damned bunch of Judases! You wait, my dear fellows! I won't let you off so easily this time! Make a list of all those who came to grumble of me, and above all, those scribblers who polished up their petitions for them. And let them all know what an honor has been bestowed on me by the grace of God —tell them the Mayor is marrying his daughter, not to any ordinary man, but to someone quite special, there is no one like him in the world; he can do anything, anything, anything! Tell them all, let them all know it. Shout it from the housetops, set the bells ringing, damn it all! It's a great day, make the most of it. (*The* POLICEMAN *goes out.*) So that's how it is, Anna Andreevna, eh? How is it going to be, where are we going to live—here or in Petersburg?

ANNA. Naturally, in Petersburg. How could we stay here!

THE MAYOR. Well, if it is to be Petersburg, Petersburg let it be. Though it would be very nice here too. I suppose we'll have finished being a mayor, eh, Anna Andreevna?

ANNA. Naturally; it's not much to be the mayor!

THE MAYOR. What do you think, Anna Andreevna, I might come in for a snug berth in the service now, mightn't I? For, being so thick with all the ministers and in and out of the Czar's palace, he may get me promoted so that I might be a general before long. What do you think, Anna Andreevna, can I hope to be a general?

ANNA. I should think so! Of course.

THE MAYOR. Damn it all, it will be glorious to be a general! With decorations on one's breast! And which ribbon do you like best, Anna Andreevna, the red one or the blue? [38]

---

[38] The red ribbon is for the Order of St. Anne, the blue for the White Eagle —both of equal importance. (ed.)

ANNA. Of course, the blue is the nicest.

THE MAYOR. Eh, so that's what she has set her heart on! The red is not bad either. What makes one want to be a general? Why, if one drives anywhere, couriers and aides gallop ahead everywhere, calling for horses. And they won't give them to anyone else; at the posting stations they all have to wait—the titular councilors, captains, and mayors—but you don't care a damn. You dine at a governor's, and there—a mayor has to stand in your presence! Ha-ha-ha! (*Goes off into a roar of laughter.*) That's what's so alluring, damn it all!

ANNA. Your tastes are so coarse. You must remember that our whole life has to be changed; that your friends will be very different from the Judge who thinks of nothing but dogs and goes hunting hares with you or Artemy Filippovich; quite the contrary: all your friends will be of the most refined manners, counts and people of the highest quality. . . . Though I must say I feel uncomfortable about you: you sometimes blurt out words such as are never heard in good society.

THE MAYOR. What of it? Words do no harm.

ANNA. Yes, that was all very well while you were the Mayor, but there life will be completely different.

THE MAYOR. Yes, they say there are two sorts of fish there, a sea eel and a smelt, which simply make your mouth water.

ANNA. He can think of nothing but fish! I am determined that our house shall be the smartest in Petersburg, and that in my drawing room there shall be such a perfume that there will be no way to get into it—one will simply shut one's eyes like this! (*She shuts her eyes and sniffs.*) Ah, how delicious!

(*Enter* SHOPKEEPERS.)

THE MAYOR. Ah, good morning, fine-feathered friends!

SHOPKEEPERS (*bow*). We wish you good health, little father!

THE MAYOR. Well, my sweethearts, how are you? How is business going? Why, you tea-swilling,[39] piddling hucksters, you bring complaints, do you? You archrogues, you champion swindlers, you sly beasts, you deceitful monsters, bringing complaints? Well, have you gained much by it? So you thought you'd get me clapped into prison? Seven devils and one witch in your teeth!

---

[39] Literally, "*samovarniki*." (ed.)

ANNA. Good gracious, Antosha, what expressions you do use!

THE MAYOR (*with vexation*). It's not a matter of words now. Do you know that that official to whom you brought complaints is going to marry my daughter? Eh? What? What have you to say to that? Now I'll give it to you! . . . You cheat people . . . You take a government contract and pocket a hundred thousand by supplying rotten cloth, and then you bestow twenty yards and expect a reward for it! And if you were caught, you'd be . . . He struts about! He is a shopkeeper, no one must touch him. "We are as good as the gentry," he says. Gentleman indeed! . . . ah, you pig-faces! A gentleman studies the sciences: if he is thrashed at school, it's to some purpose, that he may learn something useful. And what are you? You begin by petty cheating, you're beaten by your master if you don't cheat successfully. When you are a small boy, before you can repeat the Lord's Prayer, you give short measure; and when you've grown a corporation and stuffed your pockets full, you put on airs! Ough, as though you were of consequence! Because you empty sixteen samovars a day, have you anything to be proud of? Spit on your head and on your importance!

SHOPKEEPERS (*bowing*). We are sorry, Anton Antonovich!

THE MAYOR. You want to complain? And who helped you in your tricks when you were building a bridge and charged twenty thousand for wood when you did not use a hundred rubles' worth? I helped you, you goat's beard! Have you forgotten it? If I had informed on you, I might have sent you to Siberia! What do you say, eh?

ONE OF THE SHOPKEEPERS. We are terribly to blame, Anton Antonovich! The devil lured us. We swear we will never complain again. Ask what you like, only don't be angry!

THE MAYOR. Don't be angry! Here you are groveling at my feet. Why? Because I've got the upper hand; but if the luck had been on your side you would have trampled me in the mud, you bastards, and rolled a log on top of me!

SHOPKEEPERS (*bowing down to his feet*). Do not be the ruin of us, Anton Antonovich!

THE MAYOR. Now it's "Do not be the ruin of us!" But what did you say before? I'll . . . (*With a wave of his hand*) But God forgive you! That's enough! I am not vindictive; only now you mind and be careful! I am marrying my daughter not to any stray gentleman; make certain your congratulations are worthy of the occasion . . . you understand? Don't try to get off with a bit of smoked salmon or a loaf of sugar . . . Well, go along. God be with you!

(*The* SHOPKEEPERS *go out. Enter* AMMOS FIODOROVICH *and* ARTEMY FILIPPOVICH.)

AMMOS FIODOROVICH (*in the doorway*). Can it really be true, Anton Antonovich? Have you really come in for this wonderful stroke of luck?

ARTEMY FILIPPOVICH. I have the honor to congratulate you on your great good fortune. I was genuinely delighted when I heard of it. (*Goes to kiss* ANNA ANDREEVNA'S *hand*) Anna Andreevna! (*Goes to kiss* MARIA ANTONOVNA'S *hand*.) Maria Antonovna!

(*Enter* RASTAKOVSKY.)

RASTAKOVSKY. I congratulate you, Anton Antonovich! May God give you long life and the same to the new couple, and crowds of grandchildren and great-grandchildren! Anna Andreevna! (*Goes up to kiss her hand*.) Maria Antonovna! (*Goes up to kiss her hand*.)

(*Enter* KOROBKIN *and his wife and* LIULIUKOV.)

KOROBKIN. I have the honor to congratulate you, Anton Antonovich! Anna Andreevna! (*Goes up to kiss her hand*.) Maria Antonovna! (*Goes up to kiss her hand*.)

KOROBKIN'S WIFE. My warmest congratulations, Anna Andreevna, on your new happiness!

LIULIUKOV. I have the honor to congratulate you, Anna Andreevna! (*Kisses her hand, and then turning to the audience makes a clacking noise with his tongue with an air of swaggering bravado*.) Maria Antonovna, I have the honor to congratulate you! (*Kisses her hand, and turns to the audience with the same swaggering air*.)

(*Numbers of guests in coats and tails enter, say "Anna Andreevna!" and kiss her hand, and "Maria Antonovna!" and kiss her hand.* BOBCHINSKY *and* DOBCHINSKY *push their way to the front*.)

BOBCHINSKY. I have the honor to congratulate you!

DOBCHINSKY. Anton Antonovich, I have the honor to congratulate you!

BOBCHINSKY.   On the propitious event!

DOBCHINSKY.   Anna Andreevna!

BOBCHINSKY.   Anna Andreevna! (*Both approach to kiss her hand at the same moment and knock their heads together.*)

DOBCHINSKY.   Maria Antonovna! (*Kisses her hand.*) I have the honor to congratulate you. You will be very, very happy; you will wear a golden dress and have all sorts of delicate soups and spend your time very divertingly.

BOBCHINSKY (*interrupting.*)   Maria Antonovna, I have the honor to congratulate you! God give you all prosperity and wealth and a baby boy no bigger than this (*shows with his hand*), little enough to sit on your hand. He will cry all the time Oo-ah! oo-ah!

(*Some more Visitors come up to kiss the ladies' hands, with them* LUKA LUKICH *and his wife.*)

LUKA LUKICH.   I have the honor . . .

LUKA LUKICH'S WIFE (*runs forward*).   I congratulate you, Anna Andreevna! (*They kiss.*) I was so delighted. I was told, "Anna Andreevna has made a match for her daughter." Ah, my goodness, I thought, and I was so delighted I said to my husband, "Lukanchik,[40] have you heard of Anna Andreevna's good fortune?" Well, I thought to myself, thank God! And I said to him: "I am so immensely delighted that I am burning with impatience to tell Anna Andreevna herself." . . . Ah, my goodness, I thought to myself, Anna Andreevna always expected a good match for her daughter, and now what a destiny! The very thing she wanted! and I was so overjoyed that I couldn't say a word. I cried and cried, I positively sobbed. Lukanchik said, "What are you crying for, Nastenka?" "Luka, darling, I really don't know," I said, "the tears are simply flowing like a river!"

THE MAYOR.   Please sit down, ladies and gentlemen! Hey, Mishka, bring in some more chairs!

(*Enter the* POLICE CAPTAIN *and the* POLICEMEN.)

THE POLICE CAPTAIN.   I have the honor to congratulate your worship and to wish you long life and prosperity!

THE MAYOR.   Thanks, thanks! Please sit down, gentlemen!

(*The Visitors sit down.*)

---

[40] "Luka dear." Suffixes on given names normally indicate endearment. (ed.)

AMMOS FIODOROVICH. But do tell us, Anton Antonovich, how did all this come about?

THE MAYOR. In a most extraordinary way: his Excellency made the proposal in person.

ANNA. In the most respectful and delicate manner. He expressed himself wonderfully well. "It's entirely out of regard for your virtues, Anna Andreevna," said he. And he is such a delightful, well-bred man, of the highest principles! "Believe me, Anna Andreevna, life is not worth a kopek to me," he said. "I am simply acting from regard for your rare qualities."

MARIA. Oh, Mamma, but he said that to me!

ANNA. Hold your tongue, you know nothing about it, don't interfere! "I am amazed, Anna Andreevna," he said . . . And he said such flattering things. And when I tried to say that we dared not hope for such an honor, he fell on his knees all at once and said in such a refined way: "Anna Andreevna, do not make me the unhappiest of mortals! Consent to reciprocate my feelings, or I will put an end to my life."

MARIA. Really, Mamma, he said that about me . . .

ANNA. Yes, of course . . . it was about you too, I don't deny it.

THE MAYOR. He really frightened us; he said he would shoot himself: "I'll shoot myself, I'll shoot myself!" he said.

MANY OF THE VISITORS. You don't say so!

AMMOS FIODOROVICH. Well, I'll be damned!

LUKA LUKICH. It's the hand of destiny!

ARTEMY FILIPPOVICH. Not destiny, old fellow, destiny has no hands: it's the reward of merit. (*Aside*) These swine come in for all the luck!

AMMOS FIODOROVICH. I'll sell you that puppy you wanted, Anton Antonovich, if you like.

THE MAYOR. No, I've no thoughts for puppies now!

AMMOS FIODOROVICH. If you don't want that one, you might choose another dog.

KOROBKIN'S WIFE. Ah, Anna Andreevna, I am delighted at your good fortune, you can't imagine!

KOROBKIN. And where is our illustrious guest at the moment, may we inquire? I was told he had left you for some reason.

THE MAYOR. Yes, he has left us for one day on very important business.

ANNA. To visit his uncle and ask his blessing.

THE MAYOR. To ask his blessing; but tomorrow he will . . . (*He sneezes: a general hum of* "*God bless you.*") Much obliged! But he will be back tomorrow. . . . (*Sneezes: a chorus of blessings, loudest of all are the voices of*)

THE POLICE CAPTAIN. Good health to your honor!

BOBCHINSKY. May you live a hundred years and have a sack of gold!

DOBCHINSKY. May God lengthen your days for ages and ages!

ARTEMY FILIPPOVICH. A plague on you!

KOROBKIN'S WIFE. The devil take you!

THE MAYOR. I thank you sincerely and wish you the same.

ANNA. We are intending to live in Petersburg now. I must admit that the atmosphere here is . . . so countrified! I must admit it's very distasteful. And my husband too . . . will be made a general there.

THE MAYOR. Yes, my friends, damn it all, I must say that I really want to be a general.

LUKA LUKICH. Please God you will be!

RASTAKOVSKY. For man it is impossible, but with God all things are possible.

AMMOS FIODOROVICH. A big ship sails in deep waters.

ARTEMY FILIPPOVICH. A well-deserved honor.

AMMOS FIODOROVICH (*aside*). It will be a farce if he is made a general! It will suit him like a saddle suits a cow! But there is many a slip 'twixt the cup and the lip. There are better men than you here who are not generals yet.

ARTEMY FILIPPOVICH (*aside*). Damn it all, what next! But then, there's no saying, he may be made a general. He has conceit enough for it, the devil take him. (*Addressing him*) You won't forget us then, Anton Antonovich!

AMMOS FIODOROVICH. And if anything goes wrong—for instance, if we want any assistance in the Service—grant us your protection!

KOROBKIN. Next year I shall be taking my son to Petersburg for the service of the State; be so gracious as to extend your protection to him.

THE MAYOR. I am ready for my part, I am ready to do my best.

ANNA. You are always ready to make promises, Antosha. To begin with, you won't have time to think of it. And besides, how can you, why should you burden yourself with such promises?

THE MAYOR.   Oh, why not, my love? One can sometimes be of use.

ANNA.   Of course, but you can't help all the small fry.

KOROBKIN'S WIFE.   You hear how she speaks of us?

A LADY VISITOR.   Yes, she was always like that; I know her: let her sit down at the table and she'll put her feet on it.[41]

(*The* POSTMASTER *comes in breathless, holding an open letter in his hand.*)

THE POSTMASTER.   An amazing thing, gentlemen! The official we took to be the Inspector General is not the Inspector General at all!

ALL.   Not the Inspector General?

THE POSTMASTER.   Not at all—I've discovered it from a letter.

THE MAYOR.   Good God! From what letter?

THE POSTMASTER.   From his own letter. A letter was brought to me at the post office. I looked at the address—I was flabbergasted —I saw it was addressed to Pochtamtskaya Street. I was flabbergasted. "There," I thought, "no doubt he has found out some irregularities in the Post Office Department and is inform-ing the authorities." I took it and unsealed it.

THE MAYOR.   How could you?

THE POSTMASTER.   I don't know how I could; some supernatural force prompted me. I was on the point of sending for the courier to despatch it by express delivery; but I was overcome by a curiosity such as I have never experienced before. I couldn't let it go, I couldn't, I felt I couldn't. I was simply drawn to open it. I seemed to hear a voice whispering in one ear, "Don't open it, you will be done for!" and in the other an imp seemed to be muttering, "Open it, open it, open it!" And when I touched the sealing wax I felt as though my blood were on fire, and when I opened it an icy shiver ran over me, yes, an icy shiver. My hands trembled and I felt dizzy.

THE MAYOR.   But how dared you open the letter of a personage in such a position of authority?

THE POSTMASTER.   But that's just the point, that he is not a person-age and not in a position of authority!

---

[41] Another popular Russian expression, of which Russians seemingly have an inexhaustible supply. (ed.)

THE MAYOR.   Then what is he, according to you?

THE POSTMASTER.   He is nobody at all; goodness knows what to call him.

THE MAYOR (*angrily*).   What do you mean by nobody? How dare you say that he is nobody, and goodness knows what he is! I'll put you under arrest . . .

THE POSTMASTER.   Who, you?

THE MAYOR.   Yes, I!

THE POSTMASTER.   That's more than you can do.

THE MAYOR.   Do you know that he is going to marry my daughter, that I shall be a great personage myself and can pack you off to Siberia if I like?

THE POSTMASTER.   Oh, Anton Antonovich! Don't talk about Siberia, it's a long way off. I'd better read you the letter. Gentlemen, shall I read it aloud?

ALL.   Read it, read it!

THE POSTMASTER (*reads*).   "My dear Triapichkin, I hasten to tell you of my marvelous adventures. I was cleaned out on the way by an infantry captain, so much so that the innkeeper here meant to send me to prison; when suddenly my Petersburg countenance and get-up induced the whole town to take me for an Inspector General. And I am now staying at the Mayor's, having a gorgeous time, flirting desperately with his wife and daughter; I can't quite make up my mind yet which to begin with—I think I shall start with the mother, for I think she is ready to go to all lengths. Do you remember how hard up we used to be, how we dined by our wits, and how a pastry cook once took me by the collar for telling him to charge our pies to the King of England? Now things have taken quite a different turn. Everyone lends me as much money as I ask for. They are peculiar fishes; you would simply die of laughing. You write sketches, I know; you should put them in. First and foremost the Mayor—as stupid as an old gray horse . . ."

THE MAYOR.   It can't be, it isn't there!

THE POSTMASTER (*shows him the letter*).   Read it yourself!

THE MAYOR (*reads*).   "As an old gray horse." It can't be, you wrote it yourself.

THE POSTMASTER.   How could I have written it?

ARTEMY FILIPPOVICH.   Read!

LUKA LUKICH.   Read!

THE POSTMASTER (*goes on reading*). "The Mayor—as stupid as an old gray horse."

THE MAYOR. Oh, damn it all! You need not repeat it! We all know the words are there.

THE POSTMASTER (*goes on reading*). Hm . . . hm . . . hm . . . "old gray horse. The Postmaster too is a good fellow." . . . (*Pausing*) Well, here he seems to say something improper about me too.

THE MAYOR. No, read it!

THE POSTMASTER. Why?

THE MAYOR. Hang it all, if you are reading it, read it! Read it all!

ARTEMY FILIPPOVICH. Allow me to read it! (*Puts on his spectacles and reads*) "The Postmaster is the very image of our office porter, Mikheyev; I have no doubt the scoundrel is a regular drunkard too."

THE POSTMASTER (*to the audience*). Well, he is a nasty young scamp who needs a whipping, that's all.

ARTEMY FILIPPOVICH (*goes on reading*). "The Welfare Commissioner . . . er . . . er . . ." (*Hesitates.*)

KOROBKIN. Why are you stopping?

ARTEMY FILIPPOVICH. Oh, it's so badly written . . . you can see he is a scoundrel, though.

KOROBKIN. Let me have it! I think my eyes are better. (*Takes hold of the letter.*)

ARTEMY FILIPPOVICH (*not giving him the letter*). No, we can leave that part out; it is more legible farther on.

THE POSTMASTER. No, read it all! Nothing has been left out so far!

ALL. Give it to him, Artemy Filippovich, give it to him! (*To* KOROBKIN) Read it!

ARTEMY FILIPPOVICH. In a minute. (*Gives him the letter.*) Allow me, here . . . (*Puts his finger over the letter.*) Begin here. (*They all surround him.*)

THE POSTMASTER. Read it, read it! Nonsense, read it all!

KOROBKIN (*reading*). "The Welfare Commissioner, Zemlianika, is a regular pig in a skullcap."

ARTEMY FILIPPOVICH (*to the audience*). It is not even witty! A pig in a skullcap! Who has ever seen a pig in a skullcap?

KOROBKIN (*goes on reading*). "The Superintendent of Schools reeks of onions."

LUKA LUKICH (*to the audience*). Upon my soul, I never touch an onion.

AMMOS FIODOROVICH (*aside*). Thank God there is nothing about me.

KOROBKIN (*reading*). "The Judge . . ."

AMMOS FIODOROVICH. There you are! (*Aloud*) Gentlemen, I think the letter is tedious. Damn it, what is the use of reading this rubbish!

LUKA LUKICH. No!

THE POSTMASTER. No, read it all!

ARTEMY FILIPPOVICH. You must read it!

KOROBKIN (*goes on*). "The Judge, Liapkin-Tiapkin, is awfully *mauvais ton* [42] . . ." (*Pauses.*) That must be a French word.

AMMOS FIODOROVICH. Goodness knows what it means! It's all right if it only means a scoundrel, but it may be something worse.

KOROBKIN (*goes on reading*). "But they are a hospitable and good-natured bunch. Goodbye, Triapichkin dear. I want to follow your example and take up literary work. It's dull going on like this, one longs for food for the mind. I see I really should devote myself to some higher calling. Write to me to the province of Saratov, address—the village of Podkatilovka." (*Turns over the letter and reads the address.*) It is addressed to "Ivan Vasilievich Triapichkin, Number ninety-seven, Third Floor Apartment, turning to the right from the entrance by the yard, Pochtamtskaya Street, Saint Petersburg."

ONE OF THE LADIES. What a painful rebuff!

THE MAYOR. It's my death blow! I am killed entirely! I see nothing; nothing but pigs' snouts of faces. . . . Bring him back! Bring him back! (*Waves his arm.*)

THE POSTMASTER. Bring him back indeed! As luck would have it, I told the Superintendent to give him the swiftest horses, and it was the devil's prompting made me send the orders on ahead to the other posting stations.

KOROBKIN'S WIFE. This really is most disconcerting, quite unprecedented!

AMMOS FIODOROVICH. But damn it all, gentlemen, he borrowed three hundred rubles from me!

---

[42] "Ill-bred." (ed.)

ARTEMY FILIPPOVICH. Three hundred rubles from me too!

THE POSTMASTER (*sighs*). Oh! and three hundred rubles from me too.

BOBCHINSKY. And sixty-five rubles in paper money from Piotr Ivanovich and me!

AMMOS FIODOROVICH (*with a gesture expressive of perplexity*). What is the meaning of it, gentlemen? How can we have made such a blunder?

THE MAYOR (*slapping his forehead*). How could I, how could I, old fool that I am? Silly old sheep, I am in my dotage! Thirty years I have been in the Service; not a single merchant, not a contractor could get the better of me; rogues, first-class rogues, I have beaten at their own game; cheats and scoundrels who could have swindled the whole world I've hooked. I've hood-winked three governors! . . . Governors indeed! (*Waves his hand.*) Governors are not much to boast of . . .

ANNA. But this is impossible, Antosha: why, he is engaged to Mashenka . . .

THE MAYOR (*angrily*). Engaged! Pooh! A buttered fig is what the engagement is! (*In a frenzy.*) Come and look, come—all the world, all good Christians, look what a fool the Mayor has been made! Call him a fool, the old bastard! (*Shakes his fist at himself.*) Ah, you fat-nose! To take a suckling, a rag like that, for a man of consequence! His bells are ringing along the highway now! He will spread the tale all over the world. It's not enough to be made a laughingstock—there will come some scribbler, some inkslinger, and will put you in a comedy. That's what's mortifying! He won't spare your rank and your calling, and everyone will grin and clap. (*To the audience*) What are you laughing at? You are laughing at yourselves. . . . You are a fine bunch. . . . (*Stamps on the floor in a fury.*) I'd take care of all those scribblers, the damned liberals and penny-a-liners! The devil's brood! I'd tie you all in a knot, pound you all to a jelly and into the lining of the devil's cap! . . . (*Makes a thrust with his fist and stamps on the floor.*) (*After a brief silence.*) I can't get over it. How true it is— those whom God would punish He first deprives of reason. Why, what was there in the least like an Inspector General in that scatterbrain? Nothing! Not a trace of resemblance—

and yet all at once everyone was crying, "The Inspector General, the Inspector General!" Who was it first started the rumor that he was the Inspector General? Answer!

ARTEMY FILIPPOVICH (*with a gesture of perplexity*). If my life depended on it I could not say how it happened. It's as though our minds were befogged or the devil confounded us.

AMMOS FIODOROVICH. Who started it?—Why, they set it going, these gallant fellows here (*Pointing to* DOBCHINSKY *and* BOBCHINSKY).

BOBCHINSKY. I declare it wasn't me! I never thought of such a thing. . . .

DOBCHINSKY. I had nothing to do with it, absolutely nothing.

ARTEMY FILIPPOVICH. Of course it was your doing . . .

LUKA LUKICH. To be sure it was. They ran here like mad from the inn: "He's come, he's come, he doesn't pay his bill. . . ." A fine bird they picked up!

THE MAYOR. It was certainly you! You're the gossips of the town, you damned liars!

ARTEMY FILIPPOVICH. The devil take you with your tales of an Inspector General.

THE MAYOR. You do nothing but prowl about the town and confuse people's minds, you damned chatterboxes! You scatter gossip, you bobtailed magpies!

AMMOS FIODOROVICH. You damned bunglers!

LUKA LUKICH. You dunces!

ARTEMY FILIPPOVICH. You potbellied shrimps!

(*They all surround them.*)

BOBCHINSKY. I swear it wasn't me, it was Piotr Ivanovich.

DOBCHINSKY. Oh no, Piotr Ivanovich, you were the first to . . .

BOBCHINSKY. Not at all, you were first . . .

(*Enter a* GENDARME.)

GENDARME. The official who has arrived from Petersburg with instructions from the Government summons you to his presence. He is staying at the inn.

(*These words fall like a thunderbolt upon all. An exclamation of astonishment rises simultaneously from the lips of all the ladies; the whole group, changing their attitude, remain petrified. Dumb show—The* MAYOR *stands in the middle like a post, his arms outstretched and his head flung back; on his right hand are his wife and daughter leaning forward toward him; beyond them is the Postmaster, who is transformed into a note of interrogation addressed to the audience; beyond him is* LUKA LUKICH *in a state of innocent bewilderment; beyond him at the farther edge of the stage three Lady Visitors, leaning against each other with the most satirical expression, evidently aimed at the* MAYOR's *family. On the left side of the* MAYOR *stands* ARTEMY FILIPPOVICH, *his head bent a little on one side as though listening to something; beyond him the* JUDGE *with his hands flung up, squatting almost to the ground and making a movement with his lips as though he were going to whistle or say "Here is a nice how-do-you-do!" Beyond him is* KOROBKIN *facing the spectators with a wink and a bitter sneer at the* MAYOR; *beyond him at the farther edge of the stage* DOBCHINSKY *and* BOBCHINSKY, *their hands stretched toward each other, their mouths open, staring at each other with their eyes starting out of their heads. The other Visitors remain standing like posts. For almost a minute and a half the petrified group retains its position.)*

(Curtain.)

Marriage

CHARACTERS IN THE PLAY

AGAFYA TIKHONOVNA	A merchant's daughter, the bride
ARINA PANTELEIMONOVNA	Her aunt
FIOKLA IVANOVNA	A matchmaker
PODKOLIOSIN	A government clerk, of court councilor rank
KOCHKARIOV	His friend
YAICHNITSA	A clerk in a government office
ANUCHKIN	A retired infantry officer
ZHEVAKIN	A naval officer
DUNYASHKA	A young servant girl
STARIKOV	A shopkeeper
STEPAN	Podkoliosin's servant

MARRIAGE

A Quite Incredible Incident

IN TWO ACTS

ACT I

Scene I

A Bachelor's Room

PODKOLIOSIN, *alone, is lying on a sofa smoking a pipe.*

PODKOLIOSIN. Yes, as soon as one has time to begin thinking it over, one sees one must get married. Why, you go on and on living like this till you get sick of it at last! Here I've let the season[1] slip by again, and yet everything is ready and the matchmaker has been coming here for the last three months. So help me, I begin to feel ashamed. Hey, Stepan!

(*Enter* STEPAN.)

PODKOLIOSIN. Has Fiokla Ivanovna been?

STEPAN. No, sir.

PODKOLIOSIN. And have you been to the tailor?

STEPAN. Yes.

PODKOLIOSIN. Well, is he making the tails?

STEPAN. Yes.

PODKOLIOSIN. And how far has he got with it?

---

[1] The period before the seven weeks of Lent. (ed.)

STEPAN. Oh, he has done pretty well; he's started on the button-holes.

PODKOLIOSIN. What do you say?

STEPAN. I say he has begun making the buttonholes already.

PODKOLIOSIN. Did he ask what your master wants tails for?

STEPAN. No, he didn't ask.

PODKOLIOSIN. Perhaps he said: "Is your master thinking of getting married?"

STEPAN. No, he didn't say anything.

PODKOLIOSIN. But you saw some other tails there, didn't you? I suppose he is making them for other people too?

STEPAN. Yes, he has a lot of them hanging up.

PODKOLIOSIN. But I'm certain that the cloth in them is not so good as in mine?

STEPAN. No, yours looks best.

PODKOLIOSIN. What do you say?

STEPAN. I say the cloth in yours looks best.

PODKOLIOSIN. That's right. Well, didn't he ask, "What is your master having tails of such fine cloth for?"

STEPAN. No.

PODKOLIOSIN. Didn't he say anything of your master's wanting maybe to get married?

STEPAN. No, he didn't say a word about that.

PODKOLIOSIN. But you told him my rank and where I am serving?

STEPAN. Yes, I did.

PODKOLIOSIN. What did he say to that?

STEPAN. He said: "I'll do my best."

PODKOLIOSIN. That's right. Now run along.

(STEPAN *goes out.*)

To my thinking now black tails are somehow more dignified. Colored coats are more suitable for secretaries, titular councilors, and such small fry—something of the milksop about them. Persons of higher grade must pay more attention, as they say, to . . . there, I've forgotten the word! And it's a good word, but I can't think of it. Yes, my dear soul; say what you like, a court councilor is as good as a colonel, except perhaps for having no epaulets on his uniform. Hey, Stepan!

(*Enter* STEPAN.)

PODKOLIOSIN. Did you buy the shoe polish?

STEPAN.   Yes.

PODKOLIOSIN.   Where did you buy it? In the shop I told you of on Voznesensky Avenue?

STEPAN.   Yes, sir.

PODKOLIOSIN.   Well, is it good polish?

STEPAN.   Yes.

PODKOLIOSIN.   Have you tried cleaning my boots with it?

STEPAN.   Yes.

PODKOLIOSIN.   Well, does it shine?

STEPAN.   Yes, it shines all right.

PODKOLIOSIN.   And when he gave you the polish, didn't he ask what your master wanted such polish for?

STEPAN.   No.

PODKOLIOSIN.   Didn't he say, perhaps your master is intending to get married, maybe?

STEPAN.   No, he said nothing.

PODKOLIOSIN.   Oh, all right, you can go.

(STEPAN *goes out.*)

PODKOLIOSIN.   You might think boots are a trivial matter, but, you know, if they are badly made and the polish looks rusty,[2] you won't be treated with the same respect in good society. It makes all the difference . . . But there is nothing so nasty as having corns—I'd rather put up with anything than have corns. Hey, Stepan!

(*Enter* STEPAN.)

STEPAN.   What is it, sir?

PODKOLIOSIN.   Did you speak to the shoemaker about not giving me corns?

STEPAN.   Yes.

PODKOLIOSIN.   What does he say?

STEPAN.   He says, "all right."   (STEPAN *goes out.*)

PODKOLIOSIN.   Damn it all, it's a troublesome business getting married! There's this and that and the other. This must be just so and that must be just so. No, damn it all, it's not so easy as they make out. Hey, Stepan!

(*Enter* STEPAN.)

I've something more to say to you. . . .

---

[2] I.e., if it yellows. (ed.)

STEPAN. The old woman is here.

PODKOLIOSIN. Oh, she's come, has she? Show her in.

(STEPAN *goes out.*)

Yes, it is a business . . . there's no denying . . . a difficult business.

(*Enter* FIOKLA.)

Ah, good day, good day, Fiokla Ivanovna! Well, how goes it? Take a chair, sit down and tell me. Come, how goes it? What's her name . . . Melania? . . .

FIOKLA. Agafya Tikhonovna.

PODKOLIOSIN. Yes, yes, Agafya Tikhonovna. And I expect she is an old maid of forty.

FIOKLA. Oh no, what next? Why, when you are married, you'll like her better and better every day and be grateful.

PODKOLIOSIN. But you are telling lies, Fiokla Ivanovna.

FIOKLA. I am too old to do that, my good sir. Dogs tell lies.

PODKOLIOSIN. And the dowry, what about the dowry? Tell me again.

FIOKLA. Well, the dowry is a brick house of two floors in the Moskovsky district, and so profitable that it's a pleasure. The flour dealer alone pays seven hundred for his shop; and the beershop in the basement draws a lot of custom too; two wooden lodges—one made of wood throughout and the other on a brick foundation, and each brings four hundred rubles a year. Then there is a vegetable garden in the Vyborgsky district. A shopkeeper has had it these three years under cabbage, and such a steady man, never takes a drop of anything, and three sons he has: two he has married off already, but the third he says is young yet: "Let him stay a bit in the shop to help with the work a little; I am old," he says, "so let him sit in the shop a bit to help with the work."

PODKOLIOSIN. Well, what is she like?

FIOKLA. Like sugar candy! Pink and white like milk and roses. So sweet that there is no word for it. Why, you will be so perfectly satisfied you'll say to friend and foe, "Ah, it's all thanks to Fiokla Ivanovna."

PODKOLIOSIN. But she's not a lady by birth.

FIOKLA. She is a tradesman's daughter, but she is one that a general might be proud of. She won't hear of a shopkeeper.

"Whatever my husband's like, even if he is nothing to look at," she says, "he must be a gentleman." Yes, she's so genteel. And on a Sunday when she puts on her silk dress, my word, how it rustles! A regular princess!

PODKOLIOSIN. Well, I asked you because you know I am a court councilor . . . you understand? . . .

FIOKLA. Why, of course, I understand well enough. We have had a court councilor along already, but she refused him; didn't like him. He was such a peculiar character; he could never open his mouth without telling a lie, and a fine-looking gentleman he was too. Well, there is nothing we can do about it, God made him so; it's not his fault, he can't help lying. It seems it's God's will.

PODKOLIOSIN. Well, and haven't you any others besides her?

FIOKLA. Why, what more do you want? You couldn't have anyone better.

PODKOLIOSIN. She's the best, is she?

FIOKLA. You might go the world over and not find another like her.

PODKOLIOSIN. We'll think it over, we'll think it over, my good soul. Look in again the day after tomorrow, we'll have another little talk, you know; I'll lie down a bit and you shall tell me . . .

FIOKLA. But upon my word, sir, here I've been coming to you for the last three months and nothing to show for it. Here you sit in your dressing gown and keep smoking your pipe.

PODKOLIOSIN. I'll bet you think that getting married is no more than calling "Hey, Stepan, bring my boots," pulling them on, and going out. One must think it over a little and look about one.

FIOKLA. Well, to be sure, if you want to look, look; the goods are there to be looked at. Bid him bring your coat and drive around now while it's morning.

PODKOLIOSIN. Now! But the weather is a bit uncertain; if I go out it might begin to rain.

FIOKLA. Oh well, it's your loss! Why, your hair's going gray and soon you'll be too old for matrimony. Much good it is your being a court councilor! Why, we'll find plenty of gentlemen better, and we won't so much as look at you.

PODKOLIOSIN. What nonsense are you talking? What possessed you to say that my hair's going gray? Where's the gray hair? (*Feels his hair.*)

FIOKLA. Of course you have gray hair—a man is bound to come to it. You'd better look out! This one's not right for him and that one is not right for him. Why, I've a captain in my eye with a voice like a trumpet—head and shoulders taller than you. He's in the Admiralty.

PODKOLIOSIN. It's a lie. I'll look in the mirror—where did you pick up the notion that I'd gray hair? Hey, Stepan, bring a mirror! No, wait a minute, I'll go myself. What next! God help us, this is worse than smallpox.

> (*Goes off into the next room.*)
> (KOCHKARIOV *runs in.*)

KOCHKARIOV. Where's Podkoliosin? . . . (*Seeing* FIOKLA.) How do you come here? Oh you! . . . I say, why the hell did you find me a wife?

FIOKLA. What's wrong? It's the dispensation of Providence.

KOCHKARIOV. Dispensation, indeed! Much good there is in having a wife! As though I couldn't have done without her!

FIOKLA. Why, you came pestering me yourself: "Find me a wife, granny"; you kept on at it.

KOCHKARIOV. Ah, you old rat . . . and what are you here for? Surely Podkoliosin isn't thinking . . . ?

FIOKLA. Why not? By the grace of God he is.

KOCHKARIOV. You don't mean it? Ah, the rascal, he never said a word to me about it. Isn't he a son of a gun? I swear he is a sly one, eh?

> (*Enter* PODKOLIOSIN *with a mirror in his hands, in which he is looking very attentively.*)

KOCHKARIOV (*stealing up behind him startles him*). Boo!

PODKOLIOSIN (*uttering a shriek and dropping the mirror*). Lunatic! What did you do that for? . . . What idiocy! You startled me so that my heart's in my mouth.

KOCHKARIOV. Come, never mind; it was a joke.

PODKOLIOSIN. Nice jokes you think of! I can't get over the fright you gave me. And see, I've broken the mirror; it's a thing of some value, you know, it was bought at the English shop.

KOCHKARIOV. Come, don't worry. I'll get you another mirror.

PODKOLIOSIN. Oh yes, I'm sure. I know your other mirrors: they make you look ten years older and your face comes out all crooked.

KOCHKARIOV. Well, I've more cause to be cross with you: you hide everything from me, your friend. So you are thinking of getting married?

PODKOLIOSIN. What nonsense! I have never thought of such a thing.

KOCHKARIOV. But here's the proof on the spot. (*Points to* FIOKLA.) Here she stands; we all know what she is here for. Well, that's all right, that's all right. There's nothing wrong in it. It's a Christian duty, essential for the sake of your country, in fact. Allow me, allow me, I'll undertake to manage it all. (*To* FIOKLA) Come, tell me how and who and all about it. Is she of noble family, an official's daughter or one of the merchant gentry, and what's her name?

FIOKLA. Agafya Tikhonovna.

KOCHKARIOV. Agafya Tikhonovna Brandakhlystova?

FIOKLA. Oh no, Kuperdiagina.

KOCHKARIOV. Lives in Shestilavochnaya Street, doesn't she?

FIOKLA. Not at all; it's nearer Peski in Mylny Alley.

KOCHKARIOV. Oh yes, in Mylny Alley, the wooden house just beyond the shop.

FIOKLA. Not beyond the shop, but beyond the beer cellar.

KOCHKARIOV. Next to the beer cellar? Well, I don't know it then.

FIOKLA. Why, as you turn into the alley there's a sentry box facing you, and when you pass the sentry box, turn to the left and it'll be straight before you. That is, there'll be straight before you the wooden house where the dressmaker lives who used to live with the upper secretary of the Senate. You don't go into the dressmaker's, but just beyond her there'll be a second house, a brick house, so that's her house, the one I mean in which she is living, Agafya Tikhonovna, that is, the young lady.

KOCHKARIOV. All right, all right. Now I'll see to it all, and you can clear out: you won't be wanted any more.

FIOKLA. What next? Do you mean to arrange the wedding yourself?

KOCHKARIOV. Yes, yes; only don't you meddle, don't you meddle now.

FIOKLA. Ah, the shameless villain! Why, that's not a man's business; you step aside, sir, upon my word!

KOCHKARIOV. Go along, go along! You know nothing about it, don't you meddle. Mind your own business. Be off!

FIOKLA. He's simply taking the bread out of people's mouths, the godless fellow! Meddling in such a dirty mess. If I'd known I wouldn't have said a word.

(*Goes out in vexation.*)

KOCHKARIOV. Well, old friend, this is a matter that mustn't be put off—let us go.

PODKOLIOSIN. But I've done nothing yet, you know. I've scarcely given it a thought. . . .

KOCHKARIOV. Nonsense, nonsense! Only don't be shy; I'll get you married so that you won't even feel it. We'll go this very minute to the young lady and you'll see how quickly it'll all be done.

PODKOLIOSIN. What next! Go this very minute!

KOCHKARIOV. Why not, why put it off? See what comes of your not being married! Look at your room, what do you see in it? There stands a muddy boot and there's a washbasin. Here's a whole heap of tobacco on the table, and here you lie all day like a sluggard.

PODKOLIOSIN. That's true. I know how untidy it is.

KOCHKARIOV. But when you have a wife you simply won't know yourself or anything else: here you'll have a sofa, a lapdog, a bird of some sort in a cage, needlework. . . . And just imagine: you'll sit on the sofa, and all at once a pretty little woman will sit down beside you and put her little hand . . .

PODKOLIOSIN. Ah, damn it, when you think what little hands there are—as white as milk, old friend.

KOCHKARIOV. I should think so! As though hands were all! . . . Why, old friend . . . But there, there's no word for it; the devil only knows what they haven't got.

PODKOLIOSIN. And you know, to tell you the truth, I do like it when a pretty girl sits beside me.

KOCHKARIOV. There, you see, I needn't tell you. Now we've only to arrange it all. Don't you worry about anything. The wedding breakfast and all the rest of it I'll see to. . . . You can't do with less than a dozen of champagne whatever you say. Half a dozen bottles of Madeira, too, you must have. The bride's sure to have a crowd of aunties and old lady friends, and they don't like to do things by halves. And we don't want Rhine wine, damn it all, do we? And as for the wedding breakfast, I've a caterer in my eye, friend. He feeds one, the dog, so that one can't get up from one's chair.

PODKOLIOSIN. I swear, you throw yourself into it as though the wedding were settled.

KOCHKARIOV. And why not? Why put it off? You've made up your mind, haven't you?

PODKOLIOSIN. I? Well, no . . . I've not quite made up my mind yet.

KOCHKARIOV. Well, I'll be damned! You said just now you wanted it.

PODKOLIOSIN. I only said it wouldn't be a bad thing.

KOCHKARIOV. Well, I'll be . . . Why, we were on the very point of fixing it all up. . . . What is it? Do you dislike the idea of married life, or what?

PODKOLIOSIN. No, I like it.

KOCHKARIOV. Well then, what is it? What's the difficulty?

PODKOLIOSIN. Oh, there's no difficulty. Only it's strange . . .

KOCHKARIOV. What's strange?

PODKOLIOSIN. Of course it's strange. I've always been unmarried. . . . And now all at once to be married.

KOCHKARIOV. Come, come . . . come, aren't you ashamed? Well, I see I must talk to you seriously. I'll talk to you openly, as a father to a son. Just look at yourself attentively—as you are looking now at me, for instance. Why, what are you now? Simply a log, you know, you're of no importance whatever. Why, what are you living for? Come, look in the mirror; what do you see there? A silly face and nothing else: but, just imagine, here beside you will be little ones, not two or three, you know, but maybe a whole half-dozen, and all as like you as two drops of water. Now you are a court councilor, a filing clerk, or some sort of superintendent, God knows what; but then, just imagine, you'll have a whole lot of little forwarding clerks about you, the little rascals, and one little rogue will stretch out his little paws and tug your whiskers while you'll bark at him like a dog: Bow! Bow-wow! Now, is there anything better than that, tell me?

PODKOLIOSIN.   But you know they are awfully mischievous: they'll spoil everything and throw my papers about.

KOCHKARIOV.   What if they are, they'll all be like you—think of that!

PODKOLIOSIN.   It really is pleasant, damn it all. . . . A little dumpling like that, a little puppy, and yet like me.

KOCHKARIOV.   Of course it's pleasant; come, let us go then.

PODKOLIOSIN.   Very well, let us go.

KOCHKARIOV.   Hey, Stepan, make haste and bring your master his things.

(*Enter* STEPAN.)

PODKOLIOSIN (*dressing before the mirror*).   I think, though, I ought to put on a white vest.

KOCHKARIOV.   Nonsense, it doesn't matter.

PODKOLIOSIN (*putting on a collar*).   That confounded laundress has starched the collar so badly nothing will make it stand up. Tell the stupid woman, Stepan, that if she can't iron better than that, I'll engage someone else. I expect she is carrying on with her young man instead of ironing the collars.

KOCHKARIOV.   Come, make haste, old friend! How you do dawdle!

PODKOLIOSIN.   In a minute, in a minute. (*Puts on his coat and sits down.*) You know what, Ilya Fomich, you go alone.

KOCHKARIOV.   Well, what next! Are you mad? Me go! Why, which of us is getting married—you or I?

PODKOLIOSIN.   I don't feel like it, really; we'd better go tomorrow.

KOCHKARIOV.   Come, have you a grain of common sense? Aren't you a moron? You were quite ready—and all of a sudden you don't want to! Kindly tell me, aren't you a swine, aren't you a sneak to go on like that?"

PODKOLIOSIN.   Why are you scolding me, what for, what have I done to you?

KOCHKARIOV.   You are an idiot, a perfect idiot, anyone will tell you so. A fool, simply a fool, although you are a forwarding clerk. What am I doing my best for? Your benefit; someone else will get the goods if you don't look out. There he lies, the confounded bachelor. I swear, what do you look like?—Why, you are trash, a ninny, a booby, I might call you something worse . . . but the word is too improper. You are an old granny, worse than an old granny.

PODKOLIOSIN.   And you are a nice one, I must say. (*In an under-*

tone) Are you crazy? My servant's standing there and you go on scolding me before him in such language; you might have found some other place!

KOCHKARIOV. But how can I help swearing at you, kindly tell me that? Who could help swearing at you? Who could resist swearing at you? Here, like a decent man, you have made up your mind to get married, you listen to the voice of reason, and all at once, from simple idiocy, as though you'd gone crazy, you blockhead . . .

PODKOLIOSIN. Well, that's enough, I am coming. Why do you make such a fuss?

KOCHKARIOV. You're coming; of course, I should think so. (*To* STEPAN) Bring his hat and overcoat.

PODKOLIOSIN (*in the doorway*). What a peculiar fellow he is really! There's no doing anything with him; he starts scolding all at once for no rhyme nor reason, he's no notion how to behave.

KOCHKARIOV. Well, it's all over, I am not scolding you now.

(*They both go out.*)

ACT I

Scene II

A room in AGAFYA TIKHONOVNA's *house.* AGAFYA TIKHONOVNA *is laying out cards for fortunetelling. Her aunt,* ARINA PANTELEIMO-NOVNA, *is looking over from behind.*

AGAFYA. A journey again, Auntie! A king of diamonds is interested . . . tears . . . a love letter; on the left hand a club shows great sympathy, but some wicked woman is an obstacle.

ARINA. And who would you think is the king of clubs?

AGAFYA. I don't know.

ARINA. But I know who it is.

AGAFYA. Who?

ARINA. A good tradesman in the drapery line, Aleksey Dimitrievich Starikov.

AGAFYA. Well, I am sure it's not he. I'll bet you anything it's not.

ARINA. Don't argue, Agafya Tikhonovna, his hair is so dark. No one else could be king of clubs.

AGAFYA. Oh no: the king of clubs means a gentleman here—a shopkeeper couldn't be king of clubs.

ARINA. Oh, Agafya Tikhonovna, you wouldn't talk like that if your poor papa, Tikhon Panteleimonovich, were living. He'd sometimes slap his hand on the table and cry: "I'd spit," he used to say, "on the man who is ashamed to be a shopkeeper: and I'll never give my daughter," he used to say, "to a colonel. Let other people do as they like! And I'll never let my son go into the civil service," he'd say. "Doesn't the merchant," he'd say, "serve his Czar as much as anyone else?" And he'd thump like this on the table with all his five fingers. And he'd a hand as big as a bucket—and what a temper! And to tell the truth, he was the death of your mother; she'd have lived longer, poor dear, but for him.

AGAFYA. There, what if I have an angry husband like that! Oh, I won't marry a shopkeeper for anything!

ARINA. But Aleksey Dimitrievich is not like that.

AGAFYA. I won't have him. I won't! He has a beard; as soon as he begins to eat, everything drops on his beard. No, no, I don't want him!

ARINA. But where are you to find a decent gentleman? You won't pick him up in the streets, you know.

AGAFYA. Fiokla Ivanovna will find him; she promised to find the very best for me.

ARINA. But she's a liar, you know, my love.

(Enter FIOKLA.)

FIOKLA. Oh no, Arina Panteleimonovna, it's too bad of you to slander me for nothing.

AGAFYA. Ah, it's Fiokla Ivanovna! Come, speak, tell me! Have you found him?

FIOKLA. Yes, yes, only let me get my breath—I am worn out! I've been through every house on your business, I've toiled and moiled in offices and departments of barrack rooms. . . . Do you know, my dear, I was all but beaten, upon my word I was: that old woman that married the Aferovs fairly flew at me, calling me all sorts of names: "You are simply taking the bread out of my mouth, keep to your own quarters," she said. "Well," I told her straight out, "for my young lady," I said, "I am ready to give any satisfaction, so don't be angry." But what a bunch of gentlemen I've got for you! As long as the world has stood, and as long as it will stand, there've never been any like them. Some will be here this very day. I ran on ahead on purpose to warn you.

AGAFYA. Today! Fiokla Ivanovna, darling, I'm frightened.

FIOKLA. Don't you be scared, my dear! It's the usual thing. They'll come and have a look, nothing more, and you will have a look at them: if you don't care for them, well, they'll go.

ARINA. Oh, I bet you've enticed a nice bunch.

AGAFYA. And are there many of them—how many?

FIOKLA. Oh, there are six.

AGAFYA. Ough!

FIOKLA. Come, my dear, why are you in such a flutter? It's best to have a choice: if one won't do, another may.

AGAFYA. Are they gentlemen?

FIOKLA. All, every one of them: and such gentlemen as I've never seen before.

AGAFYA. Oh, what are they like, what are they like?

FIOKLA. Wonderful, all such handsome and particular gentlemen. First, Baltazar Baltazarovich Zhevakin, such a nice gentleman; he served in the navy—he's just the one for you. He says he must have a young lady on the plump side, he doesn't like them skinny. But Ivan Pavlovich, who's a managing clerk in the Government Service, is such a grand gentleman that there's no approaching him. Such a fine-looking gentleman, stout: when he shouted at me: "Don't you talk nonsense to me, saying the young lady is this and that; tell me straight out what she's got in real property and what she's got in cash." "So much of this and so much of that, my good sir!"—"You're lying, you daughter of a bitch!" and he rapped out such a word, my dear, but it wouldn't be proper to repeat it to you. I saw in the twinkling of an eye that he must be a gentleman of consequence!

AGAFYA. Well, and who else?

FIOKLA. Then there's Nikanor Ivanovich Anuchkin. He's such a refined man, and his lips, my dear, are raspberries, perfect raspberries—such a nice gentleman. "I want my bride," he said, "to be good-looking and well educated, I want her to be able to speak French." Yes, a man of refined manners, a bit of a German; and he's so refined and delicate, and his legs so thin and slender . . .

AGAFYA. No, these slender men aren't quite . . . I don't know . . . I see nothing in them. . . .

FIOKLA. Well, if you prefer someone more solid, take Ivan Pavlovich. You wouldn't choose anyone better; he now is a gentleman if anyone's a gentleman: he'd hardly get through the doorway, he's such a fine man.

AGAFYA. And how old is he?

FIOKLA. Oh, he's still youngish: about fifty, or maybe not quite fifty.

AGAFYA. And what's his name?

FIOKLA. His name's Ivan Pavlovich Yaichnitsa.[3]

AGAFYA. Is that his surname?

FIOKLA. Yes.

AGAFYA. Oh my goodness, what a surname! Really, Fiokla, dear, if I marry him shall I be called Agafya Tikhonovna Yaichnitsa? Good gracious, what an idea!

FIOKLA. Well, my dear, there are names in Russia so queer you can only spit and cross yourself when you hear them. But there, if you don't like the name, take Baltazar Baltazarovich Zhevakin; he's a nice gentleman.

AGAFYA. And what is his hair like?

FIOKLA. Nice hair.

AGAFYA. And his nose?

FIOKLA. Aie . . . his nose is all right: everything is in its right place, and he's such a nice gentleman. Only you mustn't be perturbed; there's nothing in his apartment but a pipe, nothing else at all—no furniture.

AGAFYA. And who else?

FIOKLA. Akinf Stepanovich Panteleyev, a titular councilor and clerk in the civil service; he stammers a little, but he's such a well-behaved man.

ARINA. Oh, why do you keep on with your clerks? Isn't he fond of drink—that's what you'd better tell us.

FIOKLA. Well, he does drink; I won't deny it, drink he does. There, that can't be helped—you see he's a titular councilor! But he's as smooth as silk.

AGAFYA. Oh no, I don't want my husband to be a drunkard.

FIOKLA. That's as you like, my dear; if you don't like one, take

---

[3] "Omelet." (ed.)

another, though after all, what is there in his taking a drop too much now and again; he's not drunk all week, you know. Some days he's quite sober.

AGAFYA. Well, who else?

FIOKLA. There is only one more, only he's such a . . . God bless the man! the others are a bit better.

AGAFYA. But who is he?

FIOKLA. I didn't mean to speak of him. He's a court councilor to be sure, and wears a ribbon in his buttonhole, but he's got lead in his bottom, there's no getting him out of his house.

AGAFYA. Well, and who else? You've only told us of five, but you said six.

FIOKLA. Well, isn't that enough for you? You are getting greedy; why, a minute ago you were frightened.

ARINA. But what's the use of them, all your gentlemen, though you may have six of them? I'll bet one shopkeeper'll be worth all the lot.

FIOKLA. Oh no, Arina Panteleimonovna, a gentleman is thought much more of.

ARINA. But what's the use of that? Aleksey Dimitrievich, now, in his sable cap driving along in his sledge . . . ?

FIOKLA. But if a gentleman in epaulets meets him, he'll say, "What are you about, you paltry shopkeeper, get out of my way!" or "Show me your best velvet, shopkeeper!" And he'll answer, "With pleasure, sir!"—"And take off your hat, you oaf!" that's what the gentleman will say.

ARINA. And if the shopkeeper likes he won't give him the cloth, and then your gentleman will be left naked and will have nothing to go about in.

FIOKLA. And the gentleman will slash at the shopkeeper with his sword.

ARINA. And the shopkeeper will make a complaint to the police.

FIOKLA. And the gentleman will complain of the shopkeeper to the Senator.

ARINA. And the shopkeeper'll go to the Governor.

FIOKLA. And the gentleman . . .

ARINA. Stuff and nonsense, gentleman indeed! A governor's more than a senator! How she goes on! A gentleman has to knuckle under just the same sometimes . . . (*A ring is heard.*) Surely that's someone at the bell?

FIOKLA.   Goodness, here they are!

ARINA.   Who?

FIOKLA.   They . . . Some of the gentlemen.

AGAFYA.   (*Shrieks*) Ough!   (FIOKLA *goes out.*)

ARINA.   Holy saints, have mercy upon our sins! And the room's not fit to be seen. (*Snatches up everything on the table and runs about the room.*) And the cloth, the cloth on the table absolutely black. Dunyashka, Dunyashka!

(*Enter* DUNYASHKA.)

ARINA.   Quick! a clean cloth! (*Pulls off the cloth and scurries about the room.*)

AGAFYA.   Oh, Auntie, what am I to do, I am almost in my chemise.

ARINA.   Ah, my dear, make haste, run and get dressed! (*Scurries about the room;* DUNYASHKA *brings a cloth; there's a ring at the bell.*) Run and say, "Coming directly."

(DUNYASHKA *shouts into the distance, "Coming directly!"*)

AGAFYA.   Auntie! my dress isn't ironed.

ARINA.   O Lord, have mercy upon us! Put on another.

FIOKLA (*running in*).   Why don't you come, Agafya Tikhonovna? Make haste, my dear. (*A ring is heard.*) My goodness, why, he's waiting still . . .

ARINA.   Dunyashka, show him in and ask him to wait.

(DUNYASHKA *runs into the hall and opens the door. Voices are heard: "At home?"—"Yes, please walk in." All try inquisitively to look through the keyhole.*)

AGAFYA.   (*Shrieks*) Oh, what a fat man!

FIOKLA.   He's coming, he's coming!

(*All run out full speed.*)

(*Enter* IVAN PAVLOVICH YAICHNITSA *and* DUNYASHKA.)

DUNYASHKA.   Please wait here.   (*Goes out.*)

YAICHNITSA.   To be sure, if we must wait we'll wait, if only they're not long; I have only got away from the office for a minute. If the general takes it into his head to ask, "Where's the managing clerk?"—"He's gone to have a look at a young lady with a view to matrimony" . . . he might make me pay dearly for the young lady. I'll have another look at the description anyway. (*Reads*) "A brick house of two floors . . ." (*Raises his eyes upwards and scans the room.*) Yes! (*Goes on reading*) "Two lodges: a lodge on a brick foundation and a wooden lodge." Well, the wooden one is not worth much. "A chaise, a sledge for two horses adorned with carving, with a big rug and a small rug." Maybe they're only fit for firewood, but the old woman declares they're first-class; all right, let's suppose they're first-class. "Two dozen silver spoons"—of course, you must have silver spoons in the house. . . . "Two fox-lined fur coats . . ." H'm! "Four big feather beds and two little ones." (*Purses up his lips significantly.*) "A dozen silk and a dozen cotton dresses, two dressing gowns, two . . ." Come, that's trumpery! House linen, table napkins . . . That's all her affair. Though I'd better make sure of it all perhaps. Now they'll probably promise a house and carriages, but when you're married you'll find nothing but feather beds and pillows. (*A ring at the bell.* DUNYASHKA *runs full speed across the room to open the door. Voices are heard: "At home?"—"Yes." Enter* ANUCHKIN *and* DUNYASHKA.)

DUNYASHKA. Will you wait here. They'll come in. (*She goes out.* ANUCHKIN *and* YAICHNITSA *bow to each other.*)

YAICHNITSA. Good day, sir!

ANUCHKIN. Have I not the honor of addressing the papa of the charming lady of the house?

YAICHNITSA. No indeed, I'm not a papa at all. I've no children yet, as a matter of fact.

ANUCHKIN. Oh, I beg your pardon, I beg your pardon!

YAICHNITSA (*aside*). There's something suspicious about that man's countenance; I shouldn't be surprised if he's come here on the same errand as I. (*Aloud*) No doubt you have some business with the lady of the house?

ANUCHKIN. Well, no . . . No business at all. I was out for a walk and just looked in.

YAICHNITSA (*aside*). That's a lie. Out for a walk indeed! He wants to get married, the scoundrel!

(*A ring is heard.* DUNYASHKA *runs across the room to open the door. Voices in the hall? "At home?"—"Yes." Enter* ZHEVAKIN *with* DUNYASHKA.)

ZHEVAKIN (*to* DUNYASHKA). Please brush me, my dear . . . You know what a terrible lot of dust there is in the street. Take off that bit of fluff, please. (*Turns around.*) That's right! Thank you, my dear, but just look, isn't there a spider crawling there? And isn't there anything behind? Thanks, sweetie! There's something there, I think. (*Strokes the sleeve of his*

coat with his hand and looks at ANUCHKIN *and* YAICHNITSA.)
It's English cloth, you know! How it does wear! I bought it
in '95, when our squadron was in Sicily and I was only a midshipman and had a uniform made of it then; in 1801, in the
reign of Paul I, I was promoted to lieutenant, and the cloth was
perfectly new; in 1814 I made a voyage around the world, and
it was only a little worn at the seams then; then in 1815, when
I left the navy, I had it turned inside out. Now I have been
wearing it for ten years, and it's still almost new! Thanks,
sweetie. H'm . . . h'm, my cutie! (*Kisses his hand to her, and
going up to the mirror slightly ruffles his hair.*)

ANUCHKIN.   And what is Sicily like, allow me to ask . . . you
were pleased to say Sicily; is it a nice country, Sicily?

ZHEVAKIN.   Oh, lovely! We spent thirty-four days there; the view,
I assure you, is enchanting. Such mountains, pomegranate
trees, and everywhere there are Italian girls, such rosebuds
that you want to kiss them.

ANUCHKIN.   And are they well educated?

ZHEVAKIN.   Superbly! Educated as none among us, except count-
esses perhaps. You would go down the street—well, a Russian
lieutenant, naturally, with epaulets here (*points to his shoulders*), with gold lace, and the dark little beauties—you know,
almost every house has little balconies and roofs as flat as this
floor—one looks up, and there's a rosebud sitting . . . well,
naturally, to show what one's made of . . . (*bows and waves
his hand*) . . . while she only does this (*makes a gesture with
his hand*). Naturally she's well dressed—some sort of silk stuff
laced up in front, earrings all over the place . . . a dainty little
morsel, in fact.

ANUCHKIN.   And allow me to put one more question to you, What
language do they use in Sicily?

ZHEVAKIN.   Oh, naturally, they all speak French.

ANUCHKIN.   And do all the young ladies speak French?

ZHEVAKIN.   All, without exception. Perhaps you may not believe
what I'm going to tell you: we stayed thirty-four days, and all
that time I never heard one word of Russian from them.

ANUCHKIN.   Not one word?

ZHEVAKIN.   Not one word. I am not speaking of the noblemen and
other signors—that is, of their officers—but take a simple peas-

ant of those parts who hauls about all sorts of stuff on his back, and try saying to him in Russian, "Give me some bread, brother." He won't understand, upon my word he won't; but say in French, "*Dateci del pane*" or "*Portate vino!*" [4] he'll understand and actually bring it.

YAICHNITSA. That Sicily must be a curious country, I see. Here, you said a peasant; what's the peasant like? Is he exactly the same as the Russian peasant, broad in the shoulders, and does he plow the land or not?

ZHEVAKIN. I cannot tell you: I didn't notice whether they plowed or not; but as for taking snuff, I assure you they don't only sniff it, but even chew it. Transport is very cheap too; it's almost all water there, and everywhere gondolas. . . . Naturally with a little Italian like a rosebud sitting in it wearing a little chemisette, a little kerchief! . . . There were English officers with us too. Well, they're sailors just the same as our fellows . . . and at first certainly it was very strange; there was no understanding each other, but afterwards, as we came to know them better, we began to understand each other easily. You point like this at a bottle or glass—well, one knows at once that means a drink; you put your fist to your mouth and just say with your lips "Puff-puff," and you know it means smoking a pipe. In fact, I can assure you it's quite an easy language —in three or four days the sailors could understand each other perfectly.

YAICHNITSA. Life in foreign lands is very interesting, as I see. I am very glad to make the acquaintance of a man who has seen something of the world. Allow me to ask with whom have I the honor of speaking?

ZHEVAKIN. Zhevakin, retired naval lieutenant. Allow me to ask with whom I have the pleasure of conversing?

YAICHNITSA. I am a managing clerk, Ivan Pavlovich Yaichnitsa.

ZHEVAKIN (*catching only the last word*). Yes, I've had a snack too. I knew I had a good long way to come, and it's a cold day: I had just a herring with a little bread.

YAICHNITSA. No, I think you misunderstand me; that's my surname, Yaichnitsa.

---

[4] Italian for "Give them bread," and "Bring wine!" (ed.)

ZHEVAKIN.   Oh, I beg your pardon, I'm a little hard of hearing. I really thought you were pleased to observe that you'd eaten an omelet.

YAICHNITSA.   Well, what am I to do? I did think of asking the general to be called "Yaichnitsyn," but my people dissuaded me; they said it would be like *sobachiy syn.*[5]

ZHEVAKIN.   It is like that sometimes. In our third squadron all the officers and the sailors too had the very queerest names: "Pomoikin,[6] Yaryzhkin,[7] Lieutenant Perepreev,[8] and there was one midshipman, and a very good midshipman too, whose name was simply Dyrka.[9] And the captain would shout at times, "Hey, you, Dyrka, come here!" and would always be joking at him: "Ah, you little *dyrka,*" he used to say to him . . .
      (*A ring at the bell is heard;* FIOKLA *runs across the room to open the door.*)

YAICHNITSA.   Ah, good day, ma'am.

ZHEVAKIN.   How are you, my dear?

ANUCHKIN.   Good morning, Fiokla Ivanovna!

FIOKLA (*running full speed*).   Very well, very well, thank you, good gentlemen!
      (*She opens the door; voices are heard in the passage: "At home?"—"Yes"; then several words, hardly audible, to which* FIOKLA *answers with annoyance, "You are a man!"*)
      (*Enter* KOCHKARIOV, PODKOLIOSIN, *and* FIOKLA.)

KOCHKARIOV (*to* PODKOLIOSIN).   Remember, just courage, that's all.
      (*Looks about him and bows with some astonishment. To himself*) My, what a crowd! What does it mean? Surely they are not all after her! (*Nudges* FIOKLA *and says to her, aside*) Where have you picked up all these crows?

FIOKLA (*in a low voice*).   There are no crows here, they are all honest gentlemen.

KOCHKARIOV (*to her*).   Threadbare guests drop in uninvited.

FIOKLA.   Look at home and you'll find nothing to boast of; your cap cost a ruble, but you don't have a pot to cook in.

KOCHKARIOV.   I'll bet yours are a fine lot with holes in their pock-

---

5 "Son of a bitch." (ed.)
6 "Slop pail." (ed.)
7 "Drunkard." (ed.)
8 "Overripe." (ed.)
9 "Hole." (ed.)

ets. (*Aloud*) But what is she about? I suppose this is the door to her bedroom? (*Goes up to the door.*)

FIOKLA. For shame! I tell you she has not finished dressing.

KOCHKARIOV. Much harm in that! What does it matter? I'll just have a look and nothing more. (*Looks through the keyhole.*)

ZHEVAKIN. Allow me to be curious also.

YAICHNITSA. Allow me just one little peep.

KOCHKARIOV (*still looking*). But nothing can be seen, gentlemen! And there's no making out what that white thing is—a woman or a pillow. (*All surround the door, however, and try to get a glimpse.*) Sh . . . someone is coming! (*All skip away from the door.*)

(*Enter* ARINA PANTELEIMONOVNA *and* AGAFYA TIKHO-NOVNA. *All exchange bows with them.*)

ARINA. And to what are we indebted for the pleasure of your visit?

YAICHNITSA. I learned from the newspapers that you want to enter into a contract regarding the sale of timber and firewood, and so, as I am a managing clerk in a government office, I've come to inquire what kind of timber, the quantity of the wood, and the date when you can furnish it.

ARINA. Though we are not taking any contracts, we are glad to see you. And what is your name?

YAICHNITSA. Ivan Pavlovich Yaichnitsa, collegiate assessor.

ARINA. Please be seated. (*Turns to* ZHEVAKIN *and looks at him.*) Allow me to inquire . . .

ZHEVAKIN. I too saw an announcement of something in the newspaper. I thought I might as well come around; the weather seemed pleasant, and grass everywhere along the road.

ARINA. And what is your name?

ZHEVAKIN. I am a lieutenant in the naval reserve, my name's Baltazar Baltazarovich Zhevakin the second. There was another Zhevakin among us, but he left the navy before I did; he was wounded, ma'am, under the knee, and the bullet took such a peculiar turn that it didn't touch the knee itself but caught a sinew—threaded it like a needle, so when one stood next to him it seemed as though he were trying to hit you with his knee.

ARINA. Please sit down. (*Turning to* ANUCHKIN) Allow me to inquire to what we are indebted?

ANUCHKIN.   To my being a neighbor. Finding myself a rather near
neighbor . . .

ARINA.   Aren't you living in widow Tulubov's house just opposite?

ANUCHKIN.   I am living for the time in Peski, but I'm intending
later to move into this neighborhood.

ARINA.   Please sit down. (*Turning to* KOCHKARIOV) Allow me to
inquire . . . ?

KOCHKRIOV.   Do you mean to say you don't know me? (*Addressing* AGAFYA TIKHONOVNA) And don't you either, miss?

AGAFYA.   I don't think I've ever seen you before.

KOCHKARIOV.   Oh, think again: you must have seen me somewhere.

AGAFYA.   Really, I don't know. It wasn't at the Biriushkins', was it?

KOCHKARIOV.   Yes, at the Biriushkins'.

AGAFYA.   Oh, you don't know; something dreadful's happened to
her!

KOCHKARIOV.   To be sure, she's married.

AGAFYA.   No, that would be a good thing, but she's broken her
leg.

ARINA.   And broken it very badly too. She was coming home
rather late in the chaise, and the coachman was drunk and upset her.

KOCHKARIOV.   Ah yes, to be sure, I remember there was something
—either she got married or broke her leg.

ARINA.   And what is your name?

KOCHKARIOV.   Why, Ilya Fomich Kochkariov; you know we're
related: my wife is continually talking about it. . . . Allow
me, allow me (*takes* PODKOLIOSIN *by the hand, leads him up*),
my friend Podkoliosin, Ivan Kuzmich, a court councilor; he
is a forwarding clerk in the service, does all the business himself and has brought his department into perfect working
order.

ARINA.   What is his name?

KOCHKARIOV.   Podkoliosin, Ivan Kuzmich Podkoliosin. There is a
director in charge of the department just for show, but he,
Ivan Kuzmich Podkoliosin, does all the work.

ARINA.   Oh indeed! pray sit down.

(*Enter* STARIKOV. *He bows briskly and rapidly like a shopkeeper, slightly holding his sides.*)

STARIKOV. Good day, Arina Panteleimonovna, ma'am! The boys in the bazaar told me that you've wood to sell, ma'am.

AGAFYA (*turning away disdainfully, in a low voice, but so that he hears*). This is not a shop.

STARIKOV. Phew! Have we come at the wrong time? Or has someone else got the order?

ARINA. Please come in, please come in, Aleksey Dmitrievich; though, we've no wood to sell, we are glad to see you. Please sit down.

(*All are seated. Silence.*)

YAICHNITSA. It's strange weather today: in the morning it looked quite like rain, but now it seems to have passed over.

AGAFYA. Yes, this weather is beyond anything; sometimes fine and at other times quite wet. It's very disagreeable.

ZHEVAKIN. Now, we were in Sicily with the squadron, ma'am, in the springtime—if you'll reckon it out it was our February: if you went out the sun would be shining, and then it would look like rain—and in a minute the rain would come on.

YAICHNITSA. What is most disagreeable is sitting alone in this weather. For a married man it's quite another matter, he's not bored; but if one's in solitude, then it's simply . . .

ZHEVAKIN. Oh, deadly, perfectly deadly . . .

ANUCHKIN. Yes, one may say that . . .

KOCHKARIOV. Oh, it's torture! One wishes one was dead! God preserve us from such a situation.

YAICHNITSA. And, miss, what would you say if you had to choose an object of your affections? Allow me to inquire your taste. Pardon me for coming so straight to the point. In what branch of the Service do you think it's more fitting for a husband to be?

ZHEVAKIN. Would you, miss, care to have for a husband a man who has experienced the tempests of the ocean?

KOCHKARIOV. No, no! To my thinking the best husband is a man who manages a whole department almost alone.

ANUCHKIN. Why be prejudiced? Why disdain a man who, though he has indeed served in the infantry, can appreciate the manners of the best society?

YAICHNITSA. Miss, it's for you to decide.

(AGAFYA TIKHONOVNA *remains mute.*)

FIOKLA. Do answer, my dear, say something to them.

YAICHNITSA. What do you say to me?

KOCHKARIOV. What is your opinion, Agafya Tikhonovna?

FIOKLA (*aside to her*). Say something, say "Thank you," say "I am delighted"; it's not nice to sit like that.

AGAFYA (*in a low voice*). I am ashamed, I am really ashamed, I'm going, I'm really going, Auntie, you stay instead of me.

FIOKLA. Oh, don't do that, don't go away, you'll disgrace yourself. There's no knowing what they will think.

AGAFYA (*in a low voice*). No, I can't stay, I can't, I really can't!
(*Runs off.*)

(FIOKLA *and* ARINA PANTELEIMONOVNA *go out after her.*)

YAICHNITSA. Well I never, they've all gone; what does that mean?

KOCHKARIOV. Something must have happened.

ZHEVAKIN. Something to do with the lady's dress . . . to fix something . . . to pin up the lady's chemisette or something.
(*Enter* FIOKLA. *All go to meet her with questions: "What is it? What's the matter?"*)

KOCHKARIOV. Something happened, I suppose?

FIOKLA. How could anything happen? Dear me, nothing's happened.

KOCHKARIOV. Why did she go away then?

FIOKLA. Oh, you made her feel bashful, that's why she went away; you put her into such confusion that she couldn't sit in her place. She begs you to excuse her and that you'll all come and drink a cup of tea in the evening.   (*Goes out.*)

YAICHNITSA (*aside*). Ough, I know their cup of tea! That's why I don't like matchmaking, it leads to such a fuss. Nothing doing today, but come tomorrow, and then again to tea the day after tomorrow, and then they must think it over. And yet it's a nonsensical business, nothing to rack the brains over! Hang it all, I'm a busy man, I've no time to waste.

KOCHKARIOV (*to* PODKOLIOSIN). The young lady is nice-looking, though, isn't she?

PODKOLIOSIN. Yes, she's nice-looking.

ZHEVAKIN. The little lady is pretty, though, isn't she?

KOCHKARIOV (*aside*). Damn it! This fool's in love with her. He'll get in the way maybe. (*Aloud*) Not at all pretty, not at all.

YAICHNITSA. Her nose is too big.

ZHEVAKIN. Oh no, I didn't notice her nose, she's such a little rosebud.

ANUCHKIN. I agree with you there. But no, she's not quite it, not it at all . . . I doubt whether she is conversant with the deportment of the best society. And does she know French?

ZHEVAKIN. But why, I make bold to ask, didn't you try her, why didn't you speak French to her? Perhaps she does know it.

ANUCHKIN. Do you imagine I speak French? No, I've not been so fortunate as to have the advantage of such an education. My father was a scoundrel, a brute. He never even thought of teaching me French. When I was still a child I could easily have learned; they need only have thrashed me well and I should have known French, I should certainly have known it!

ZHEVAKIN. Well, but as it is, since you don't know it, what would you gain by her knowing it . . . ?

ANUCHKIN. No, no, a woman is quite a different matter, she must know French; without it she'll be . . . (*gesticulates*) it will never be the proper thing.

YAICHNITSA (*aside*). Well, anyone else may trouble his head about that. I'll go and have a look around at the house and lodges from outside; if everything is as it should be, I'll settle it up this very evening. I've nothing to fear from these fellows—a wishy-washy lot. Young ladies aren't fond of men like that.
(*Goes out.*)

ZHEVAKIN. I'll go and have a pipe. And aren't we going the same way? Where, allow me to ask, do you live?

ANUCHKIN. In Peski, Petrovsky Lane.

ZHEVAKIN. Yes, it will be out of my way. I live in Eighteenth Row, on the Island; still, I'll go with you.
(*He goes out with* ANUCHKIN.)

STARIKOV. Yes, this is all too high and mighty for me. Aie, Agafya Tikhonovna, you'll think of me yet! A very good day to you, gentlemen! (*Bows and goes out.*)

PODKOLIOSIN. What are we waiting for?

KOCHKARIOV. But the girl is sweet, isn't she?

PODKOLIOSIN. Why, I must confess she doesn't attract me.

KOCHKARIOV. Well I never! What's this? Why, you agreed yourself that she was pretty.

PODKOLIOSIN. Oh well, I don't know: her nose is too long and she doesn't speak French.

KOCHKARIOV. What next! What do you want French for?

PODKOLIOSIN. A young lady ought to know French anyway.

KOCHKARIOV. Why?

PODKOLIOSIN. Why, because . . . I really don't know why, but is it not the proper thing?

KOCHKARIOV. There! One fool has just said it and he's picked it up. She's a beauty, she's a regular beauty; you won't find a girl like that anywhere.

PODKOLIOSIN. Well, at first she did take my fancy too, but afterwards, when they began saying, her nose is too long, her nose is too long—well, I thought again and saw myself that her nose was too long.

KOCHKARIOV. Oh you, you won't see through a stone wall in a hurry, you feebleminded creature! They said that on purpose to put you off; I didn't praise her either—that's how things are done. What a girl, my boy! Just look at her eyes: only the devil knows such eyes; they're speaking, they're breathing. And her nose? I don't know what to call her nose! The whiteness of alabaster! And indeed alabaster cannot always be compared with it. You look at it carefully yourself.

PODKOLIOSIN (*smiling*). Yes, now I do see again that she may be called pretty.

KOCHKARIOV. Of course she's pretty. Now that they've all gone, let's go in to see her, talk it over, and settle it.

PODKOLIOSIN. Oh, I can't do that!

KOCHKARIOV. Why not?

PODKOLIOSIN. Why, such impertinence! There are a lot of us; let her choose herself.

KOCHKARIOV. But why need you think about them? Are you afraid of rivals or what? If you like, I'll get rid of all of them in a minute.

PODKOLIOSIN. Why, how will you do that?

KOCHKARIOV. Oh, that's my business; only give me your word that you won't beg off afterwards.

PODKOLIOSIN. Certainly I'll give it; I am not opposing you, I want to get married.

KOCHARIOV. Your hand on it!

PODKOLIOSIN (*giving his hand*). Take it!

KOCHKARIOV. Well, that's all I want.

(*Both go out.*)

(*Curtain.*)

ACT II

The Same Room in the House of AGAFYA TIKHONOVNA.

AGAFYA TIKHONOVNA *alone.*

AGAFYA. Ah, how difficult it is to choose! If there were only one or two gentlemen, but there are four—take which you like. Nikanor Ivanovich isn't bad-looking, though of course he's rather thin. Ivan Kuzmich isn't bad-looking either. But to tell the truth Ivan Pavlovich too is a very presentable man, though he is fat. Now what am I to do? Now, Baltazar Baltazarovich again is a man of fine qualities. How difficult it is to decide! There's no telling how difficult! If only Nikanor Ivanovich's lips could be fitted to Ivan Kuzmich's nose, and if one could take some of Baltazar Baltazarovich's easy manners and add perhaps Ivan Pavlovich's sturdiness—then I could decide at once. But, as it is, it's hopeless! My head's begun to ache. I believe it would be best to cast lots. Rely on God's will in everything. Whichever is drawn shall be my husband. I'll write them all down on bits of paper, twist them into little screws, and then let be what is to be. (*Goes up to a little table and takes out of a drawer a pair of scissors and a piece of paper, cuts it up into slips, writes on them, and rolls them up, still talking.*) What an unhappy position a girl is in, particularly when she's in love. No man enters into her feelings, and indeed, they simply refuse to understand it. Here, they're all ready! I have only to put them in my purse, close my eyes, and then let be what is to be. (*Puts the slips of paper in her purse and shakes them together with her hand.*) How dreadful! . . . Ah God grant I pick out Nikanor Ivanovich! No, why him? Better Ivan Kuzmich. Why Ivan Kuzmich? In what way are the others worse? . . . No, no, I won't. . . . Whichever I pick out, that one it shall be. (*Fumbles in the purse and instead of one picks out all.*) Ough! All! They've all come out! And my heart's beating like a hammer! No, one, one, it must be one! (*Puts the slips back in the purse and mixes them.*)

(*At that moment* KOCHKARIOV *enters stealthily and stands behind her.*)

Ah, if I could draw out Baltazar . . . What am I saying!

I meant Nikanor Ivanovich . . . No, I won't, I won't! Let fate decide.

KOCHKARIOV.   Take Ivan Kuzmich; he's the best of them all.

AGAFYA.   Ah! (*Utters a shriek and hides her face in both hands, afraid to look behind her.*)

KOCHKARIOV.   But why are you so scared? Don't be frightened. It's me. Yes, take Ivan Kuzmich.

AGAFYA.   Oh, I am ashamed, you overheard.

KOCHKARIOV.   Never mind, never mind! Why, I am one of yourselves, a relation, you needn't mind my hearing; do uncover your pretty face.

AGAFYA (*half uncovering her face*).   I am really ashamed.

KOCHKARIOV.   Come, do take Ivan Kuzmich.

AGAFYA.   Oh! (*Gives a shriek and puts her hands over her face again.*)

KOCHKARIOV.   Really, he's a splendid man, he has done wonders in his office, simply a marvelous man!

AGAFYA (*uncovering her face a little*).   And the others? Nikanor Ivanovich—he's a nice man too, you know.

KOCHKARIOV.   I swear he's good for nothing beside Ivan Kuzmich.

AGAFYA.   Why so?

KOCHKARIOV.   The reason's clear. Ivan Kuzmich is a man . . . well, simply a man . . . a man such as you don't find every day.

AGAFYA.   Well, but Ivan Pavlovich?

KOCHKARIOV.   Ivan Pavlovich is good for nothing either. They are all good for nothing.

AGAFYA.   Do you mean all?

KOCHKARIOV.   Why, you've only to compare. Judge for yourself; anyway, he's—Ivan Kuzmich! While the others are just anything, Ivan Pavloviches, Nikanor Ivanoviches . . . pooh!

AGAFYA.   But you know they're very . . . well-behaved, really.

KOCHKARIOV.   Well-behaved! Bullies, a most cantankerous bunch. Of course, if you want to be beaten the day after your wedding . . .

AGAFYA.   Oh my goodness! That really would be a misfortune, nothing could be worse.

KOCHKARIOV.   No indeed! Nothing worse could be imagined.

AGAFYA.   So you advise me that it's best to take Ivan Kuzmich.

KOCHKARIOV.   Ivan Kuzmich: naturally Ivan Kuzmich. (*Aside*)

I believe it's working. Podkoliosin is sitting in a candy shop. I must run and get him.

AGAFYA. So you think Ivan Kuzmich?

KOCHKARIOV. It must be Ivan Kuzmich.

AGAFYA. And the others . . . must I refuse them?

KOCHKARIOV. Of course, refuse them.

AGAFYA. But how's that to be done? I should feel ashamed to do it.

KOCHKARIOV. Why? Tell them you are too young and don't want to be married.

AGAFYA. But they won't believe it, you know. They'll begin asking why and how's that.

KOCHKARIOV. Oh well, if you want to make an end of it once for all, say simply, "Go along with you, you fools!"

AGAFYA. I couldn't say such a thing.

KOCHKARIOV. Oh well, you just try. I assure you that after that they'll all get lost.

AGAFYA. Wouldn't that be rather rude?

KOCHKARIOV. But you'll never see them again, you know, so what does it matter?

AGAFYA. Well, it's not very nice somehow. They'll be angry.

KOCHKARIOV. What does it matter if they are angry? If any harm would come of it, then it's a different thing, but the most that could happen in this case would be one of them spitting in your face—that's all.

AGAFYA. There, you see!

KOCHKARIOV. But what harm is there in that? Why, good gracious, some people have had that experience more than once! I know one, too: a very handsome man with rosy cheeks; he went on nagging and worrying his chief for an increase of salary, till his chief couldn't bear it at last and spat right in his face. Yes, that he did! "There's your increase for you," he said. "Get away, Satan!" But he did raise his salary, though. So what does it matter if they do spit? It would be different if there were no handkerchief near, but there it is in your pocket. (*A ring at the bell.*) There's a knock: one of them, I expect. I would rather not meet them just now. Haven't you another way out?

AGAFYA. Oh yes, by the back stairs. But really I am all in a tremble.

KOCHKARIOV. It's all right. Only have presence of mind. Goodbye! (*Aside*) I'll make haste and bring Podkoliosin.

(*Exit* KOCHKARIOV.)

(*Enter* YAICHNITSA.)

YAICHNITSA. I have purposely come a little earlier to have a word with you alone. Well, madam, as for my position in the Service, I imagine that is known to you. I am a collegiate assessor, a favorite with my superiors and obeyed by my subordinates. There's only one thing I lack—a partner to share my life.

AGAFYA. Yes, sir.

YAICHNITSA. Now I've found such a partner. That partner's you. Tell me straight out—yes or no? (*Stares at her shoulder. Aside*) Oh, she's very different from some of these thin little Germans—there's something to her.

AGAFYA. I am still very young . . . I am not disposed to marry yet.

YAICHNITSA. Upon my soul! I'll be damned! Then why is the matchmaker busy with you? But perhaps you mean to say something else—explain yourself. . . . (*The bell rings.*) Damn it all! They never will let one attend to business.

(*Enter* ZHEVAKIN.)

ZHEVAKIN. Excuse me, madam, for being perhaps too early. (*Turns and sees* YAICHNITSA.) Ah, someone already . . . My respects to Ivan Pavlovich!

YAICHNITSA (*aside*). Confound you with your respects! (*Aloud*) So how is to be, madam? Say but one word—yes or no? . . . (*The bell rings.* YAICHNITSA *curses with anger.*) The bell again!

(*Enter* ANUCHKIN.)

ANUCHKIN. Perhaps, madam, I may be a little earlier than the rules of propriety would dictate . . . (*Seeing the others, utters an exclamation and bows.*) My respects!

YAICHNITSA (*aside*). Keep your respects to yourself!! It's an ill wind that's brought you: I wish your thin legs would shatter! (*Aloud*) So how's it to be, madam—I am a busy man, I haven't much time to spare. Yes or no?

AGAFYA (*in confusion*) . . . You needn't . . . (*Aside*) I don't know what I'm saying.

YAICHNITSA. Needn't what?

AGAFYA. Never mind, sir, nothing . . . I didn't mean that . . .

(*Pulling herself together.*) Go along with you! . . . (*Aside, flinging up her hands in despair*) Oh my goodness, what have I said?

YAICHNITSA.   "Go along with you." What does that mean? "Go along with you!" Allow me to inquire what you mean me to understand by that? (*Putting his arms akimbo, he goes up to her with a menacing air.*)

AGAFYA (*glances into his face, utters a shriek*).   Ough, he'll beat me, he'll beat me!   (*Runs out.*)
YAICHNITSA *stands open-mouthed. At* AGAFYA's *shriek* ARINA PANTELEIMONOVNA *runs in, and after a look at his face she too screams: "Ough, he will beat us!" Runs out.*)

YAICHNITSA.   Well, I'll be damned! What a strange business!
(*A ring at the bell and voices are heard in the passage.*)

VOICE OF KOCHKARIOV.   Come, go in, go in, what are you stopping for?

VOICE OF PODKOLIOSIN.   You go in first. I'll come in a minute; my trouser strap [10] has come unbuttoned, I must fasten it.

VOICE OF KOCHKARIOV.   Oh, you'll slip off again.

VOICE OF PODKOLIOSIN.   I won't, really I won't!
(*Enter* KOCHKARIOV.)

KOCHKARIOV.   Damn his strap!

YAICHNITSA (*turning to him*).   Tell me, please, is the young lady crazy or what?

KOCHKARIOV.   Why, has anything happened?

YAICHNITSA.   Yes, inexplicable behavior: she ran away and began screaming, "He'll beat me, he'll beat me!" What the devil does it mean?

KOCHKARIOV.   Oh well, it does happen to her at times: she's not too bright.

YAICHNITSA.   You are a relation of hers, aren't you?

KOCHKARIOV.   Oh yes.

YAICHNITSA.   And what sort of relation, allow me to inquire?

KOCHKARIOV.   I really don't know. My mother's aunt is something or other to her father, or her father is something or other to my aunt; my wife knows—it's their affair.

YAICHNITSA.   And has she had these attacks long?

KOCHKARIOV.   Oh, she's been the same from childhood.

---

[10] Reference is not to a belt, but rather to the strap placed across the sole to keep trouser legs taut, as in riding breeches. (ed.)

YAICHNITSA.   Well, of course it would have been better if she had more sense; though, even if she is not too bright, it's not so bad if the items listed in the dowry are in good order.

KOCHKARIOV.   But she's got nothing, you know.

YAICHNITSA.   Nothing! How about a brick house?

KOCHKARIOV.   Well, that's just talk. If only you knew how it's built! The walls are only faced with one thickness of brick, and inside all manner of litter, rubble, chips, and shavings.

YAICHNITSA.   You don't mean it?

KOCHKARIOV.   Of course. Don't you know how houses are built nowadays? Anything will do so long as they are good enough to mortgage.

YAICHNITSA.   But the house isn't mortgaged?

KOCHKARIOV.   Why, who told you so? It's not only mortgaged, but no interest's been paid for the last two years. Besides, there's a brother in the senate who's got an eye on the house too—a more grasping, quarrelsome fellow you never saw! He'd rob his own mother of her last petticoat, the godless wretch.

YAICHNITSA.   Then how was it the old matchmaker . . . Ah, the old beast, the monster in human form . . . (*Aside*) But perhaps he's lying. I'll put the old woman to the strictest examination! And if it's true . . . well . . . I'll make her sing on the wrong side of her mouth.

ANUCHKIN.   Allow me also to trouble you with an inquiry. I confess, not knowing French, it's excessively difficult to judge for oneself whether a woman speaks French or not. Does the young lady know French?

KOCHKARIOV.   Not a blessed syllable!

ANUCHKIN.   Do you mean it?

KOCHKARIOV.   To be sure, I know it for a fact. She was at the same boarding school as my wife and was famed for her laziness, she was always in the dunce's cap. And the French teachers simply beat her with a stick.

ANUCHKIN.   Just imagine, from the very moment I set eyes on her I had a sort of presentiment that she did not know French.

YAICHNITSA.   Oh, damn French! But how that confounded matchmaker . . . ah, the beast, the witch! If only you knew how she laid it on; a picture, a regular picture she painted! "A house, a lodge on a brick foundation," she says, "silver spoons, a sledge—you've only to get in it and drive about!" In fact, you wouldn't often come on such a description in a novel. Ah, you old hag! you wait till I come across you . . .

(*Enter* FIOKLA. *All on seeing her turn to her with the following words:*)

YAICHNITSA. Ah, here she is! You just come here, you old sinner! Just come here!

ANUCHKIN. So this is how you've deceived me, Fiokla Ivanovna!

KOCHKARIOV. Come and answer for your sins, you wicked woman!

FIOKLA. I can't make out a word: you quite deafen me.

YAICHNITSA. The walls are only of one brick, you old slut, and you boasted that it had extra rooms and the devil knows what.

FIOKLA. I don't know, I didn't build it. Maybe it had to be built with one-brick walls and that's why they built it so.

YAICHNITSA. And mortgaged into the bargain! May the devils devour you, you damned witch! (*Stamping.*)

FIOKLA. My word, what a man! And scolding too. Anyone else would be thanking me for the pleasure of troubling about him.

ANUCHKIN. But, Fiokla Ivanovna, here you told me, too, that she knew French.

FIOKLA. She does, my dear, she knows it all, and German too, and all the rest; whatever accomplishments you like, she knows them all.

ANUCHKIN. Oh no; it appears she speaks nothing but Russian. . . .

FIOKLA. What's amiss in that? Russian's easier to understand, and that's why she speaks Russian. But if she could speak any heathen tongue it would be none the better for you, and you wouldn't understand a word of it. There, I needn't tell you what Russian is—we all know what a language it is; the saints all spoke Russian.

YAICHNITSA. You come here, you confounded woman! Let me get at you!

FIOKLA (*staggering nearer to the door*). I won't come, I know you; you're an ill-tempered man, you'll beat a person for nothing at all.

YAICHNITSA. Well, you can look out, my good woman, you won't get off so easily; wait till I take you to the police, I'll teach you how to cheat honest people. You shall see! And tell the young lady she's a scoundrel! Do you hear, mind you tell her.

(*Goes out.*)

FIOKLA.   My word, what a man, what a rage he's in! Because he's fat he thinks no one's a match for him. I say you're a scoundrel yourself, so there!

ANUCHKIN.   I must confess, my good woman, I never imagined that you were going to deceive me like this. Had I known that the young lady was of such an education, well, I . . . well, I should never have set my foot in here. So that's how it is!

(Goes out.)

FIOKLA.   They are all crazy or they've had a drop too much. What a bunch for picking and choosing! They've gone mad from thinking too much.

(KOCHKARIOV laughs aloud, looking at FIOKLA and pointing his finger at her.)

FIOKLA *(annoyed)*.   What are you hysterical about?

(KOCHKARIOV goes on laughing.)

He is having a fit.

KOCHKARIOV.   Oh, the matchmaker! Oh, the matchmaker! she's a fine hand at making marriages, she knows how to manage things! *(Goes on laughing.)*

FIOKLA.   Ough, how he's running from the mouth! Your mother must have been crazy when she brought you into the world!

(Goes out angrily.)

KOCHKARIOV *(goes on laughing)*.   Oh I can't! I really can't! I shall die, I feel I shall split with laughter. *(Goes on laughing. ZHE-VAKIN, looking at him, begins laughing too.)*

KOCHKARIOV *(sinks on a chair exhausted)*. Oh, I am worn out, I really am! I feel I shall burst if I laugh any more.

ZHEVAKIN.   I like the mirthfulness of your disposition. In Captain Boldyrev's squadron we had a midshipman, Anton Ivanovich Pyetukhov; he too was of a merry disposition. Sometimes it was enough for him if you just shook a finger at him—he'd go off laughing and laugh all day. And looking at him one would sometimes be amused oneself, and at last one would begin laughing too.

KOCHKARIOV *(recovering his breath)*.   O Lord, have mercy on us sinners! Why, what was the stupid woman thinking of, how could she make a match? As though she could make a match! Now, if I make a match, I do the job!

ZHEVAKIN.   Really? So you really can arrange a marriage?

KOCHKARIOV. I should think so! Anyone you like to anyone you like.

ZHEVAKIN. If that's so, marry me to the young lady here..

KOCHKARIOV. You? But why do you want to get married?

ZHEVAKIN. Why? Well, allow me to observe that's rather a strange question; we all know why.

KOCHKARIOV. But you've just heard she has no dowry.

ZHEVAKIN. Of course that's a pity, but with such a very charming young lady, with her attractions, one might manage without a dowry. A little room (*indicates size with his hands*), with here a little lobby, a little screen or something like this partition . . .

KOCHKARIOV. But what is it you like so much about her?

ZHEVAKIN. Well, to tell you the truth, I like her because she's a plump woman. I am a great lover of plumpness in women.

KOCHKARIOV (*with a sidelong look at him, says aside*). Well, he's not much to look at himself; he's like a pouch with the tobacco shaken out of it. (*Aloud*) No, you ought not to get married at all.

ZHEVAKIN. How's that?

KOCHKARIOV. Well, confidentially, you are not a very handsome figure. Like a chicken's leg . . .

ZHEVAKIN. A chicken's?

KOCHKARIOV. Of course. What do you look like?

ZHEVAKIN. How do you mean—a chicken's leg?

KOCHKARIOV. Why, simply—a chicken's.

ZHEVAKIN. But it seems to me that's a personal remark . . .

KOCHKARIOV. Well, I tell you so because I know you're a sensible man; I shouldn't say it to anyone else. By all means I'll marry you, only to another lady.

ZHEVAKIN. No, I will beg you not to marry me to another lady. Do me the favor to let it be this one.

KOCHKARIOV. Very well, I'll marry you, but only on one condition; you mustn't interfere in anything or even let the young lady see you—I'll manage it all without you.

ZHEVAKIN. But how can it all be without me? I shall at least have to show myself.

KOCHKARIOV. Not in the least necessary. Go home and wait: everything shall be done this very evening.

ZHEVAKIN (*rubs his hands*). Well, that will be nice! But don't you need my certificate, my record of service? The young lady may want to make inquiries. I'll run and fetch them in a minute.

KOCHKARIOV. Nothing will be needed, you only go home and wait; I'll let you know this very day. (*Accompanies him to the door.*) Yes, indeed, you may wait!   (*Exit* ZHEVAKIN.) Say! How is it Podkoliosin doesn't come? It's strange. Can he be fastening his trouser strap all this time? Perhaps I'd better run and find him.

(*Enter* AGAFYA TIKHONOVNA.)

AGAFYA (*looking about her*). Well, have they gone? No one here?

KOCHKARIOV. They've gone, they've gone, there's no one here.

AGAFYA. Ah, if you only knew how I trembled all over! I've never felt anything like it. But what a dreadful man that Yaichnitsa is, what a bully he will be to his wife. I keep imagining he'll come back in a minute.

KOCHKARIOV. Oh, nothing will ever bring him back. I'll stake my head that neither of those two puts his nose in here again.

AGAFYA. And the third?

KOCHKARIOV. What third?

(ZHEVAKIN *pops his head in at the door.*)

ZHEVAKIN. I should very much like to know how she'll speak of me with her pretty little mouth . . . the rosebud.

AGAFYA. Baltazar Baltazarovich?

ZHEVAKIN. Ah, here it comes, here it comes! (*Rubs his hands.*)

KOCHKARIOV. Ough, plague take him! I couldn't think of whom you were speaking. Why, he is simply out of the question, a regular ninny.

ZHEVAKIN. What's the meaning of that? I must confess I can't make it out.

AGAFYA. Yet to look at him he seemed a very nice man.

KOCHKARIOV. He drinks!

ZHEVAKIN. I swear, I can't make it out!

AGAFYA. You don't say he's a drunkard too?

KOCHKARIOV. Believe me, he's an out and out scoundrel.

ZHEVAKIN (*aloud*). No, excuse me, that I did not ask you to say. To say a word in my favor, to praise me, would be a different thing. But if you want to go on in that way, to speak like that, please choose somebody else—no indeed, much obliged.

KOCHKARIOV (*aside*). What possessed him to turn up? (*To* AGAFYA TIKHONOVNA *in a low voice*) Look, look, he can't stand on his legs. He zigzags every way; kick him out and make an end of it! (*Aside*) And Podkoliosin not here, not here. The scoundrel! Won't I pay him back in! (*Goes out.*)

ZHEVAKIN (*aside*). He promised to speak for me, and instead of that he's been abusing me! Very peculiar person! (*Aloud*) Don't you believe, miss . . .

AGAFYA. Excuse me, I don't feel well . . . my head aches.

ZHEVAKIN. But perhaps there's something about me you don't like? (*Pointing to his head*) You mustn't mind my having a little bald patch here: it's nothing; it came from a fever; the hair will grow soon.

AGAFYA. It's all the same to me what you have there.

ZHEVAKIN. My complexion looks much nicer, miss, when I put on a black coat.

AGAFYA. So much the better for you. Goodbye! (*Goes out.*)

ZHEVAKIN (*speaking to her as she goes*). Allow me, miss, do tell me the reason why, what for, is there some fundamental defect in me or what? . . . She's gone! Very strange thing! Here it's the seventeenth time it's happened to me, and every time in almost the same way: everything seems going well at first, but when it comes to the point—they go and refuse me. (*Walks about the room, pondering.*) Yes . . . this really will be the seventeenth young lady! And after all, what does she want? What could she expect, for instance . . . on what grounds . . . ? (*Thinking a little*) It's strange, extremely strange. I could understand if I were ugly in some way. (*Looks himself over.*) I think no one could say that; everything is as it should be, thank God, nature's not been unkind to me. There's no understanding it! Hadn't I better go home perhaps and rummage in my box? I had a poem there which no woman could resist . . . I swear, it's beyond all comprehension! At first I seemed to be getting along beautifully. . . . So I've to steer another course it seems, but I am sorry, really sorry.

(*Goes out.*)

(PODKOLIOSIN *and* KOCHKARIOV *come in and both look behind them.*)

KOCHKARIOV. He didn't notice us. Did you see how disappointed he looked?

PODKOLIOSIN. Do you mean to say he's been refused too, like the others?

KOCHKARIOV. Point-blank.

PODKOLIOSIN (*with a self-satisfied smile*). How embarrassing it must be, though, to be refused!

KOCHKARIOV. I should think so!

PODKOLIOSIN. Still, I can hardly believe that she told you straight out that she prefers me to all the others.

KOCHKARIOV. Prefers, you say! She's simply wild over you. So much in love! The endearing names she has bestowed upon you, such passion—she's simply boiling.

PODKOLIOSIN (*with a self-satisfied smirk*). Well, what words won't a woman utter when the fancy takes her! We should never think of them: my sweet little snouty, my sweet little roachy, my sweet little blacky . . .

KOCHKARIOV. Oh, that's nothing. Wait till you're married, you'll see what pet names come in the first two months. Why, old friend, you'll melt like butter.

PODKOLIOSIN (*with a chuckle*). Really?

KOCHKARIOV. As I am an honest man! But look now, we must make haste and get to work; have it out with her, open your heart to her this very minute and ask for her hand.

PODKOLIOSIN. This very minute? What are you talking about?

KOCHKARIOV. It must be this very minute. . . . And here she is.

(*Enter* AGAFYA TIKHONOVNA.)

KOCHKARIOV. I have brought you, miss, the mortal whom you see. Never has man been so in love, indeed I wouldn't wish my worst enemy . . .

PODKOLIOSIN (*nudging him under his arm, softly*). Come, old friend, you're going too far, I think.

KOCHKARIOV (*to him*). It's all right, it's all right! (*To her softly*) Be a little bolder, he's very modest, try to be as free and easy as you can. Give a twitch of your eyebrow, or look down and then suddenly raise your eyes and destroy him, the villain, or thrust out your shoulder and let him have a look at it, the bastard!—It's a pity you didn't put on your dress with the short sleeves; though that's nice too. (*Aloud*) Well, I'll leave you in pleasant company! I'll just peep for a brief minute into your dining room and your kitchen; I must see to things, the grocer from whom I ordered the supper will be here soon; perhaps the wines have been brought. . . . Goodbye for the present! (*To* PODKOLIOSIN) Be bold! be bold!

(*Goes out.*)

AGAFYA. Please sit down.

(*They sit down and remain silent.*)

PODKOLIOSIN. Are you fond of rowing, miss?

AGAFYA. Rowing?

PODKOLIOSIN. It's very pleasant rowing in a boat in the summer.

AGAFYA. Yes, we sometimes go on a trip with friends.

PODKOLIOSIN. There's no knowing what the summer will be like.

AGAFYA. It's much to be hoped that it will be fine.

(*Both are silent.*)

PODKOLIOSIN. What flower do you like best, miss?

AGAFYA. That one that has a strong scent, a carnation.

PODKOLIOSIN. Flowers are just right for ladies.

AGAFYA. Yes, a delightful occupation. (*Silence.*) What church did you go to last Sunday?

PODKOLIOSIN. The Church of the Ascension, but the week before I was at the Kazansky Cathedral. But one can pray just the same whatever church one is in. Only the decorations are finer in the cathedral. (*They are silent.* PODKOLIOSIN *drums with his fingers on the table.*) The promenade at Ekaterinhofsky will be here soon.

AGAFYA. Yes, in another month, I think.

PODKOLIOSIN. Not so long as a month.

AGAFYA. I expect it will be an agreeable festival.

PODKOLIOSIN. Today's the eighth (*counts on his fingers*), ninth, tenth, eleventh . . . in twenty-two days.

AGAFYA. Think, how soon!

PODKOLIOSIN. I don't count today. (*Silence.*) How brave the Russian people are!

AGAFYA. How do you mean?

PODKOLIOSIN. The working men. They stand on the very top . . . I passed by a house and a plasterer was at work and not a bit afraid.

AGAFYA. Yes. And where was that?

PODKOLIOSIN. On the way by which I go every day to my office. You know I go every morning to the department. (*Silence.*

PODKOLIOSIN *again begins drumming with his fingers; at last he picks up his hat and begins bowing.)*

AGAFYA. Why, are you going already . . . ?

PODKOLIOSIN. Yes, forgive me, perhaps I've been boring you.

AGAFYA. How can you! On the contrary, I must thank you for passing the time so pleasantly.

PODKOLIOSIN (*smiling*). But really I think I've been boring you.

AGAFYA. Oh no, really!

PODKOLIOSIN. Well, if not, then allow me some other time, one evening. . . .

AGAFYA. I shall be delighted.

(*They take leave of each other bowing.* PODKOLIOSIN *goes out.*)

AGAFYA. What an excellent man! Only now I've come to know him thoroughly; no one could help liking him; he's both well behaved and sensible. Yes, his friend spoke the truth just now: it's only a pity that he's gone away so soon. I should have liked to listen to him a little longer. How delightful to talk to him! And what's so nice is that he's not a chatterbox. I wanted to say two or three things to him too, but I must admit I am shy, my heart began beating so violently . . . What a splendid man! I'll go and tell Auntie.

(*Goes out.*)

(PODKOLIOSIN *and* KOCHKARIOV *enter.*)

KOCHKARIOV. But what are you going home for? What nonsense! What are you going home for?

PODKOLIOSIN. Why, what am I to stay here for? I've said everything I should already.

KOCHKARIOV. Then you've opened your heart to her?

PODKOLIOSIN. No, that's the only thing perhaps. I haven't opened my heart yet.

KOCHKARIOV. That's a nice thing! Why haven't you?

PODKOLIOSIN. Oh well, would you have me before speaking of anything else blurt out all at once: "Let me marry you, miss!"

KOCHKARIOV. Well then, what on earth, what nonsense have you been talking about for a good half-hour?

PODKOLIOSIN. Well, we talked of all sorts of things, and I confess I was very much pleased. I spent the time very pleasantly.

KOCHKARIOV. But, just think: when shall we have time to get through it all? Why, in another hour you have to go to church for the wedding!

PODKOLIOSIN. Goodness, are you mad? The wedding today! . . .

KOCHKARIOV. Why not?

PODKOLIOSIN. The wedding today?

KOCHKARIOV. But you gave me your word yourself; you said as soon as the others were kicked out you were ready to marry her at once.

PODKOLIOSIN. Well, I don't go back from my word now, only it can't be this minute. You must let me have a month's respite at least.

KOCHKARIOV. A month?

PODKOLIOSIN. Yes, of course.

KOCHKARIOV. Are you mad?

PODKOLIOSIN. It can't be less than a month.

KOCHKARIOV. But I've ordered the supper from the caterer, you blockhead! Come, I say, Ivan Kuzmich darling, don't be obstinate, get married now.

PODKOLIOSIN. Upon my word, what are you saying, how can it be now?

KOCHKARIOV. Ivan Kuzmich! Come, I entreat you. If you won't do it for your own sake, do it for mine anyway.

PODKOLIOSIN. But I really can't.

KOCHKARIOV. You can, darling, you can do anything; oh, please don't be a bore, sweetheart.

PODKOLIOSIN. But I really can't, it would be awkward, quite awkward.

KOCHKARIOV. But what's awkward? Who told you so? You judge for yourself, you are a sensible man, you know; I tell you this not to flatter you, not because you're a forwarding clerk, I simply say so from affection. . . . Come, surrender, make up your mind, look at it with the eye of a rational man.

PODKOLIOSIN. Well, if it were possible, then I'd . . .

KOCHKARIOV. Ivan Kuzmich! my pet, my angel, would you like me to go down on my knees to you?

PODKOLIOSIN. Why, what for? . . .

KOCHKARIOV (*going down on his knees*). Well, here I am on my knees! Come, you see I'm entreating you; I will never forget your kindness; don't be obstinate, darling!

PODKOLIOSIN. Oh, I can't, old friend, I really can't.

KOCHKARIOV (*getting up angrily*). Pig!

PODKOLIOSIN. Very well, scold away.

KOCHKARIOV. Stupid fellow! There never has been anyone so stupid.

PODKOLIOSIN. Scold away, scold away.

KOCHKARIOV. For whom have I done my best? Why have I taken all this trouble! It's all been for your benefit, you idiot. Why, what is it to me? I give you up on the spot, what is it to do with me?

PODKOLIOSIN. Whoever asked you to take trouble? By all means give it up.

KOCHKARIOV. But you'll be lost without me, you know, you'll do nothing without me. If we don't get you married, you'll stay a fool all your life.

PODKOLIOSIN. What's that to do with you?

KOCHKARIOV. It's for your sake I'm exerting myself, blockhead.

PODKOLIOSIN. I don't want your exertions.

KOCHKARIOV. Well then, go to hell!

PODKOLIOSIN. Well, I will go.

KOCHKARIOV. And a good journey to you!

PODKOLIOSIN. All right, I will go.

KOCHKARIOV. Do, do. And I hope you'll break your leg there directly. From the bottom of my heart I hope that a drunken cabman will drive his shaft into your throat! You're a rag, not a government clerk! Here I swear it's all over between us now, and don't let me ever set eyes on you again!

PODKOLIOSIN. I won't!

(*Goes out.*)

KOCHKARIOV. Go to the devil, to your old friend! (*Opening the door shouts after him*) Idiot! (*Walks up and down the room in great agitation.*) Oh, has such a man ever been seen? What an idiot! Though, to tell the truth, I'm a nice one too. Come, tell me, please, I ask you all, am I not an idiot, a noodle, am I not an ass? Why have I been working hard, shouting till my throat is dry? What is he to me? a relation or what? And what am I to him, a nurse, an aunt, a godmother, or what? Why, why the devil am I worrying about him and upsetting myself? The evil one take him entirely! Goodness only knows what for! You may well ask a man sometimes what he does a thing for! The scoundrel! What a nasty revolting face! I could take you, you stupid beast, and flip you on the nose, the mouth, the ears, the teeth, and everywhere! (*In his anger makes several flips in the air.*) What's so annoying is that he has walked off, he doesn't care, it's all like water off a duck's back with him: that's what's insufferable! He'll go home to his lodging, lie down and smoke his pipe. What a nasty creature! There are nasty faces of all sorts, but you'll never invent one like his: you couldn't think of a nastier face, I swear you couldn't! But no, I'll go. I'll make a point of bringing him back, the wretch! I won't let him sneak out of it. I'll go and fetch the rascal!

(*Runs off.*)

(*Soon after,* AGAFYA *enters.*)

AGAFYA. My heart's throbbing: there are no words for it. Everywhere, wherever I turn, Ivan Kuzmich seems standing before me. How true it is there's no escaping one's destiny. I've just been trying my utmost to think of something else, but whatever I take up—I tried winding wool, and embroidering the purse—but Ivan Kuzmich seems always to spring out upon me. (*A pause.*) And so at last I am to change my maiden state! They will take me, lead me to church, then leave me alone with a man—ough! It makes me shudder. Farewell to my girlhood. (*Weeps.*) How many years I've spent in peace . . . here I've gone on living and now I have to be married. All sorts of troubles before me. Children, little boys, such quarrelsome creatures, and there'll be little girls: they'll grow up and will have to be married. And one must be thankful if they marry good men; but what if they marry drunkards or men who are ready to gamble away everything they have on! (*Begins by degrees sobbing again.*) I have not managed to enjoy my maiden state and have not even been single for twenty-seven years. (*Changing her voice*) But why is Ivan Kuzmich away so long?

(*Enter* PODKOLIOSIN, *thrust onto the stage from the door by* KOCHKARIOV.)

PODKOLIOSIN (*stammering*). I've come to you, miss, to explain one little point . . . only I should first like to know whether you'll not think it strange?

AGAFYA (*dropping her eyes*). What is it?

PODKOLIOSIN. No, miss, do tell me first, will you not think it strange?

AGAFYA (*still looking down*).   I can't tell what it is.

PODKOLIOSIN.   But confess, you will most likely think what I am saying to you is strange.

AGAFYA.   Oh dear, how could I think it strange; it's pleasant to hear anything from you.

PODKOLIOSIN.   But you've never heard this yet. (AGAFYA *drops her eyes more than ever; at this moment* KOCHKARIOV *enters stealthily and stands behind* PODKOLIOSIN's *shoulders.*) The point is this . . . but perhaps I'd better tell you some other time.

AGAFYA.   But what is it?

PODKOLIOSIN.   Why . . . I confess I was meaning to tell you now, but I cannot help hesitating still.

KOCHKARIOV (*to himself, folding his arms*).   Good Lord, what a man! He's simply an old woman's slipper, not a man: a mockery of a man, a satire on a man.

AGAFYA.   Why do you hesitate?

PODKOLIOSIN.   Well, I am overcome by doubt somehow.

KOCHKARIOV (*aloud*).   How stupid it is, how stupid it is! Why, you see, miss, he's asking for your hand. He wants to declare he can't live without you: can't exist. He's only asking whether you consent to make him happy.

PODKOLIOSIN (*almost panic-stricken, nudges him, saying quickly*).   Upon my soul, what are you doing?

KOCHKARIOV.   So what do you say, miss? Do you consent to make this mortal happy?

AGAFYA.   I do not dare to suppose that I could make him happy . . . however, I consent.

KOCHKARIOV.   Naturally, naturally; so you should long ago! Give me your hands.

PODKOLIOSIN.   Presently. (*Tries to whisper something in his ear.* KOCHKARIOV *shakes his fist at him and frowns. He gives his hand.*)

KOCHKARIOV (*joining their hands*).   Well, God bless you!! I give my consent and approval to your union. Marriage is a thing . . . it's not like calling a cab and taking a drive: it's a duty of a very different kind: it's a duty . . . I haven't the time now, but afterwards I'll tell you what a duty it is. Come, Ivan Kuzmich, kiss your bride. You may do that now; you should do that now. (AGAFYA *looks down*.) Never mind, never mind, miss. That's as it should be! Let him kiss you!

PODKOLIOSIN. No, miss, allow me, allow me now. (*Kisses her and takes her hand*.) What a lovely little hand! Why have you such a lovely little hand, miss? . . . And allow me, miss, I should like the wedding to be at once, at once.

AGAFYA. At once! Isn't that perhaps too soon?

PODKOLIOSIN. I won't hear it! I should like it to be sooner. I should like the wedding to be this minute.

KOCHKARIOV. Bravo! Excellent! Good man! I confess I always expected great things of you in the future. You'd better make haste now and get dressed, miss. As a matter of fact, I've sent for a carriage already, and have invited the wedding guests. They've all gone straight to the church. You've got your wedding dress ready, I know.

AGAFYA. Oh yes, I've had it a long time. I'll be ready in a minute.
(*Goes out*.)

PODKOLIOSIN. Oh, thank you, old friend! Now I see all you've done for me. My own father would not have done what you have. I see that you've acted from affection. Thank you. I shall remember your kindness all my life. (*Moved*) Next spring I shall certainly visit your father's grave.

KOCHKARIOV. It's all right, my boy. I am delighted too. Come, I'll kiss you. (*Kisses him on one cheek and then on the other*.) God grant that you live happily. (*They kiss each other*.) In abundance and prosperity. I hope you'll have a crowd of children . . .

PODKOLIOSIN. Thank you, old friend! Indeed, only now at last I have grasped what life means. A quite new world is opening before me now. Now I see that it is all moving, living, feeling, that it is somehow effervescing; somehow or other one doesn't know oneself what's happening. Until now I saw nothing of this and did not understand it—that is, I was simply a man deprived of all understanding. I didn't reflect, didn't go into things, but just went on living, as every other man lives.

KOCHKARIOV. I am delighted, delighted! Now I'm going just to have a look how the table's been laid. I'll be back in a minute. (*Aside*) But still, it might be better to hide his hat in any case. (*Pick up the hat and goes out, taking it with him*.)

PODKOLIOSIN. What have I been till now, in reality? Did I understand the significance of life? I didn't. I understood nothing. What, what has my bachelor life been like? What was I good for? What did I do? I went on from day to day, did my work, went to the office, ate my dinner, and went to sleep—in fact, I've been the most frivolous and ordinary man in the world. Only now one sees how stupid everyone is who doesn't get married; yet if you come to think of it, what numbers of men go on living in blindness. If I were a king, I would order everyone to be married: absolutely everyone, so that there shouldn't be one bachelor in my kingdom. When one thinks, you know, in a few minutes one will be married! All at once, one will taste bliss such as is only to be found in fairy tales, which there's no expressing, nor finding words to express. (*After a brief pause*) But, say what you will, it is positively alarming when one thinks it over. To bind oneself for all one's life, for all one's days, come what may, and no getting out of it afterwards, no retracting it, nothing, nothing—everything over, everything settled. Why, even now it's impossible to turn back; in another minute I shall be in church: it's quite impossible to get away—there's the carriage there already and everything prepared. But is it really impossible to get away? Why, naturally it's impossible. There are people standing there, and at the door and everywhere. Why, they'll ask what for? I cannot. No! But here's the window open. What about the window? No, I can't; why, to be sure, it's undignified; besides, it's a long way from the ground . . . (*Goes up to the window.*) Oh well, it's not so high: there's only the one floor, and that's a low one. Oh no, how could I: I haven't even a cap. How can I go without a hat? So awkward! Though, after all, can't I go without a hat? What if I were to try, eh? Shall I try? (*Stands on the window, and saying, "Lord help me!" jumps into the street; is heard moaning and groaning below.*) Oh, it was a long way, though. Hi, cabman!

CABMAN'S VOICE. Where to, sir?

PODKOLIOSIN'S VOICE. Kanavka, near Semenovsky Bridge.

CABMAN'S VOICE. Ten kopeks.

PODKOLIOSIN'S VOICE. Settled! off! off! (*There is the rattle of a chaise driving away.*)

(AGAFYA, *in her wedding dress, enters timidly, her head hanging.*)

AGAFYA. I don't know what's the matter with me! Again I feel shy and am trembling all over. Oh! if only just for a minute he were not in the room; if only he'd gone to fetch something! (*Looks around timidly.*) But where is he? There's no one here. Where has he gone? (*Opens the door into the passage and says*) Fiokla, where is Ivan Kuzmich gone?

FIOKLA'S VOICE. Why, he's there.

AGAFYA. But where is "there"?

(FIOKLA *comes in.*)

FIOKLA. Why, he was sitting here in the room.

AGAFYA. But he isn't here, you see.

FIOKLA. Well, he didn't come out of the room either: I was sitting in the passage.

AGAFYA. But where is he, then?

FIOKLA. I can't say; did he go the other way out, by the back stairs, or is he in Arina Panteleimonovna's room?

AGAFYA. Auntie! Auntie!

(*Enter* ARINA *dressed in her best.*)

ARINA. What is it?

AGAFYA. Is Ivan Kuzmich with you?

ARINA. No, he must be here; he hasn't been to see me.

FIOKLA. Well, he hasn't been in the passage either. I was sitting there, you know.

AGAFYA. Well, he's not here either, you see.

(*Enter* KOCHKARIOV.)

KOCHKARIOV. What's the matter?

AGAFYA. Why, Ivan Kuzmich isn't here.

KOCHKARIOV. Not here? Has he gone away?

AGAFYA. No, he hasn't gone away either.

KOCHKARIOV. How's that? Not here and not gone away?

FIOKLA. I can't think wherever he can have got to. I've been sitting in the passage all the time and never left my seat.

ARINA. Well, he couldn't have gone out by the back stairs.

KOCHKARIOV. Well, hang it all! he can't have got lost without leaving the room; can he be in hiding? Ivan Kuzmich, where are you? Stop now, don't play the fool! Come now, surrender. It's time you were in church! (*Looks behind the cupboard, even casts a sidelong glance under the chairs.*) It's incomprehensible! No, he couldn't have gone away, he couldn't possibly! he's here; why, his hat's in the next room. I put it there on purpose.

ARINA.   Shall we ask the girl whether she knows anything? She was standing in the street all the time. . . . Dunyashka! Dunyashka!

(*Enter* DUNYASHKA.)

ARINA.   Where is Ivan Kuzmich? Haven't you seen him?

DUNYASHKA.   Why, the gentleman jumped out of the window.

(AGAFYA *utters a shriek, clasping her hands.*)

ALL THREE.   Out of the window?

DUNYASHKA.   Yes, and then took a cab and drove away.

ARINA.   Are you speaking the truth?

KOCHKARIOV.   You're telling a lie. It can't be!

DUNYASHKA.   Oh yes, he did jump out! The man at the grocery shop saw him too. He took a cab for ten kopeks and drove away.

ARINA (*stepping up to* KOCHKARIOV).   How's this, my good man, to make fun of us? Did you think to have a laugh at our expense? Are we here to be made fools of? Why, I am sixty and never have seen such a disgrace. If you are a respectable man, I'll spit in your face for doing such a thing. If you are a respectable man, you are acting like a scoundrel. To put a girl to shame before all the world! Why, I'm not a lady, but I wouldn't do such a thing, and you're a gentleman! You're gentleman enough to be a scoundrel and a rogue, it seems!

(*Goes out in a rage and leads out* AGAFYA.)

(KOCHKARIOV *stands as though overwhelmed.*)

FIOKLA.   Well, so this is the man who knows how to do the job! He can arrange a marriage without a matchmaker! I may have gentlemen on my list who are a motley crew and all sorts, but I haven't any who'd jump out of a window. No, thank you.

KOCHKARIOV.   It's nonsense, it can't be so! I'll run. I'll bring him back.

(*Goes out.*)

FIOKLA.   Yes, you go and bring him back! You don't know much about the business of getting married! If he'd run out of the door it would be another matter. But if a bridegroom jumps out of the window—the game is up!

(*Curtain.*)

The Gamblers

CHARACTERS IN THE PLAY

Ikharev	
Gavriushka	His servant
Aleksey	A waiter
Krugel	
Shvokhnev	
Uteshitelny	
Glov, Mikhail Aleksandrovich	An elderly man
Glov, Aleksander Mikhailovich	His son
Zamukhryshkin	A government clerk

THE GAMBLERS

A Room in a Provincial Inn

IKHAREV *comes in, accompanied by* ALEKSEY *and* GAVRIUSHKA.

ALEKSEY. Please walk in! Here is a nice little room! It's very quiet, there is no noise here at all.

IKHAREV. No noise, but I bet there are plenty of mounted cavalry, hoppers?

ALEKSEY. Your honor means fleas? Set your mind at rest. If a flea or a bug bites you, we take the responsibility; we make a point of that.

IKHAREV (*to* GAVRIUSHKA). Go and bring the things from the carriage. (GAVRIUSHKA *goes out. To* ALEKSEY) What's your name?

ALEKSEY. Aleksey, sir.

IKHAREV (*significantly*). Tell me, who is staying here?

ALEKSEY. Oh, a lot of people. Almost all the rooms are full.

IKHAREV. And who are they?

ALEKSEY. Piotr Petrovich Shvokhnev, Colonel Krugel, Stepan Ivanovich Uteshitelny.

IKHAREV. Do they gamble?

ALEKSEY. Why, they have been playing cards for six nights on end.

IKHAREV. Here is a couple of rubles! (*Thrusts them into his hand.*)

ALEKSEY (*bowing*).   Much obliged, sir.

IKHAREV.   There will be more for you later.

ALEKSEY.   Much obliged, sir.

IKHAREV.   Do they play together?

ALEKSEY.   No; lately they played with Lieutenant Artunovsky till he lost all his money; they won thirty-six thousand from Prince Shenkin.

IKHAREV.   Here's another ten rubles for you. And if you serve me faithfully you'll have more. Tell me, did you buy the cards?

ALEKSEY.   No, they bought them together.

IKHAREV.   From whom?

ALEKSEY.   From the shop here, Vakhrameykin's.

IKHAREV.   That's a lie, that's a lie, you rogue!

ALEKSEY.   They really did!

IKHAREV.   Very good. I shall have a word with you again. (GAVRIUSHKA *brings in a box*.) Bring it here! Now go and bring me things for washing and shaving.

(*Servants go out*.)

IKHAREV (*opens the box, which is entirely filled with packs of cards*[1]).   A lovely sight, hey! Every pack is worth its weight in gold. Each has been won by the sweat of my brow. I may say, my eyes are still dizzy with the damned marks on their backs. But then, they are a solid investment that I might leave to my children. Here, this pack is a pearl beyond price. And that's why I have given it a name—it is Adelaida Ivanovna. You do your duty by me, darling, as well as your sister did it; you win me another eighty thousand, and when I get home I'll erect a marble monument to you—I'll order one in Moscow. (*Hearing a sound, hurriedly closes the box*.)

(ALEKSEY *and* GAVRIUSHKA *come in, bringing a basin, a jug of water, and a towel*.)

IKHAREV.   Where are these gentlemen now? Are they in?

ALEKSEY.   Yes, they are in the lobby.

IKHAREV.   I'll go and see what sort of people they are.

(*Goes out*.)

ALEKSEY.   Do you come from far?

GAVRIUSHKA.   From Ryazan.

---

[1] Each box contained twelve decks of cards, the numerous decks being essential for serious games of *shtoss* which required the banker to use a fresh deck for each hand. (See p. 732, n. 3. (ed.)

ALEKSEY.   And are you from that province?

GAVRIUSHKA.   No, we come from Smolensk.

ALEKSEY.   I see. So your master lives in the Smolenski province?

GAVRIUSHKA.   No, he doesn't. We have a hundred souls[2] in Smolensk, and we have eighty in Kaluzhski province.

ALEKSEY.   I understand. He has property in two provinces then?

GAVRIUSHKA.   Yes, in two provinces. In the house alone we have Ignaty the butler, Pavlushka who used to travel about with the master, Gerasim the footman, Ivan another footman, Ivan the huntsman, another Ivan who plays in the band, then the cook Grigory, then the cook Semion, Varukh the gardener, Dementy the coachman—we have all those!

(KRUGEL *and* SHVOKHNEV *enter cautiously.*)

KRUGEL.   I am afraid he will find us.

SHVOKHNEV.   Nonsense, Stepan Ivanovich will keep him. (*To* ALEKSEY) Run along, my boy, they are calling you! (*Exit* ALEKSEY. SHVOKHNEV *goes rapidly up to* GAVRIUSHKA.) Where does your master come from?

GAVRIUSHKA.   Why, he comes now from Ryazan.

SHVOKHNEV.   Is he a landowner?

GAVRIUSHKA.   Yes, sir.

SHOVKHNEV.   Does he gamble?

GAVRIUSHKA.   Yes, sir.

SHOVKHNEV.   Here is a little something for you. (*Gives him paper money.*) Tell us all about him!

GAVRIUSHKA.   You won't tell my master?

BOTH.   No, no, never fear!

SHVOKHNEV.   Tell us, how is he doing now, has he been winning?

GAVRIUSHKA.   Why, do you know Colonel Chebotariov?

SHVOKHNEV.   No, why?

GAVRIUSHKA.   Three weeks ago we cleaned him out of eighty thousand rubles as well as a Warsaw carriage, and a box, and a rug, and gold epaulets . . . the gold in them alone worth six hundred rubles.

SHVOKHNEV (*looks significantly at* KRUGEL). Eh? Eighty thousand? (KRUGEL *shakes his head.*) Not quite above-board, you think? We shall find that out in a minute. (*To* GAVRIUSHKA) Tell me, when your master stays at home what does he do?

---

[2] Male serfs. (ed.)

GAVRIUSHKA. What does he do? Why, to be sure, he is a gentleman and he behaves like one—he does nothing.

SHVOKHNEV. That's a lie. I bet you he is never without a card in his hands.

GAVRIUSHKA. I can't say. I have been only two weeks with the master; Pavlushka always used to go with him on his travels. We've Gerasim a footman too, and Ivan, another footman, and Ivan the huntsman, and another Ivan who plays in the band, Dementy the coachman, and the other day another one was brought from the village.

SHVOKHNEV (*to* KRUGEL). Do you think he is a cardsharp?

KRUGEL. Very likely.

SHVOKHNEV. We might give it a try, anyway.

(*Both run off.*)

GAVRIUSHKA (*alone*). They are shrewd gentlemen! But I am glad to have the money. That will be a cap for Matriona and some goodies for the little rascals. Eh, I like traveling! One is always picking up something; master sends you out to buy something, and out of every ruble you can put some coppers into your pocket. What a fine life the gentry lead, when you think of it! Drive about wherever you like! He is tired of Smolensk, so he goes to Ryazan; if he doesn't care for Ryazan, then there's Kazan; if he doesn't care for Kazan, he can go to Yaroslav. I can't make up my mind which town is superior—Ryazan or Kazan? Kazan may be superior because in Kazan . . .

(*Enter* IKHAREV.)

IKHAREV. There is nothing special about them, I think. And yet . . . Ah, I'd like to clean them out! My God, how I'd like to! It makes my heart beat to think of it. (*Takes a brush and soap, sits down before the mirror, and begins to shave.*) My hand is shaking, I can't shave properly.

ALEKSEY (*enters*). Shall I bring your honor something to eat?

IKHAREV. Certainly, bring lunch for four—caviar, salmon, and four bottles of wine. And feed him. (*Points to* GAVRIUSHKA.)

ALEKSEY (*to* GAVRIUSHKA). Come into the kitchen, everything is ready for you there.

(*Exit* GAVRIUSHKA.)

IKHAREV (*goes on shaving*). Did they give you much?

ALEKSEY. Who, sir?

IKHAREV. Come, don't wriggle out of it, tell me!

ALEKSEY.   Yes, they gave me something for my service.

IKHAREV.   How much? Fifty rubles?

ALEKSEY.   Yes, sir, fifty rubles.

IKHAREV.   And from me you will get not fifty rubles, but you see there is a hundred rubles lying on the table: take it. What are you afraid of? It won't bite you! Nothing is asked of you except honesty—do you understand? Whether the cards come from Vakharmeykin or any other shop is not my business, but here is another dozen. (*Gives him a sealed packet.*) Do you understand?

ALEKSEY.   Of course I do. Your honor may rely on me, I'll see to it.

IKHAREV.   And put those cards out of sight in case you are seen or searched. (*Puts down the brush and soap and rubs his face with the towel. ALEKSEY goes out.*) It would be fine, awfully fine! How I'd love swindling them!

(SHVOKHNEV, KRUGEL *and* STEPAN IVANOVICH *enter, bowing.*)

IKHAREV (*goes to meet them, bowing*).   You must please excuse me: the room is not much to boast of—four chairs, that's all.

UTESHITELNY.   Warm welcome from one's host is better than any luxury.

SHVOKHNEV.   It's not the room that matters but the company.

UTESHITELNY.   That's very true. I can't exist without company. (*To* KRUGEL) Do you remember, my good sir, how I came here all alone? Just imagine—no one I knew! The landlady is an old woman. On the stairs a chambermaid, a perfect monster; I see an infantry man dangling after her, obviously thankful for what he can get, poor fellow. . . . Deadly dull, in fact. All at once fate brought this gentleman along and chance threw us together. . . . Wasn't I pleased! I can't spend an hour, not an hour, without pleasant company. I always want to open my heart to everyone I meet.

KRUGEL.   That's a vice in you, my friend, not a virtue. All excess is bad. I expect you've been taken in more than once.

UTESHITELNY.   Yes, I have, I have been and I always shall be. And yet I can't help being sincere.

KRUGEL.   Well, I must admit that's beyond me—to be candid with everyone. Friends are a different matter.

UTESHITELNY.   Yes, but a man belongs to society.

KRUGEL. But not the whole of him!

UTESHITELNY. Yes, the whole of him.

KRUGEL. No, not the whole of him.

UTESHITELNY. Yes, the whole of him.

KRUGEL. No, not the whole of him.

UTESHITELNY. Yes, the whole of him.

SHOVKHNEV (*to* UTESHITELNY). Don't argue, dear friend, you are wrong.

UTESHITELNY (*hotly*). No, I'll prove it. It's a moral obligation. It's a . . . it's a . . . it's a . . . it's a duty! It's a . . . it's a . . . it's a . . .

SHVOKHNEV. Come, now he's off! It's amazing how hot he gets: one can make sense of the first two or three words he says, but after that there's no making head or tail of it.

UTESHITELNY. I can't help it, I can't! If it's a question of principle or duty, I don't know what I am saying. I usually warn people beforehand: "Gentlemen, if anything of the sort is discussed, you must excuse me, but I shall be absolutely carried away, absolutely." It's a regular intoxication, and my blood simply boils.

IKHAREV (*to himself*). Oh no, my friend. We know the sort of people who grow hot and are carried away at the word "duty." I dare say your blood does boil, but it's not on that account. (*Aloud*) Well, gentlemen, while we are discussing our sacred duties, how would it be to sit down to a game of *shtoss*?

(*During their conversation breakfast is served.*)

UTESHITELNY. By all means, if it is not for high stakes.

KRUGEL. I am never averse to an innocent pastime.

IKHAREV. And what about cards, I suppose we can get them here?

SHVOKHNEV. Oh, you have only to ask for them!

IKHAREV. Cards! (ALEKSEY *arranges the card table.*) And meanwhile, gentlemen, may I offer you . . . ? (*points to the table and comes up to it*). The smoked salmon I think is not much, but the caviar isn't so bad.

SHVOKHNEV (*putting a piece of salmon in his mouth*). No, the salmon is not bad either.

KRUGEL (*eating*). And the cheese is good. The caviar isn't bad either.

SHVOKHNEV (*to* KRUGEL). Do you remember the splendid cheese we had two weeks ago?

KRUGEL. No, I shall never forget the cheese I had at Piotr Aleksandrovich Aleksandrov's.

UTESHITELNY. But do you know when cheese is good, my friends? It's when you have to eat one dinner on the top of another—that's its true use. It's just like a good quartermaster who says, "Welcome, gentlemen, there's still room."

IKHAREV. Welcome, gentlemen, the cards are on the table.

UTESHITELNY (*going up to the card table*). Ah, this is like old times! Look, Shvokhnev, cards, eh? How many years . . .

IKHAREV (*aside*). Enough of your deception!

UTESHITELNY. Would you like to hold the bank? [3]

IKHAREV. By all means: a small one, five hundred rubles. Will you cut? (*Deals. The game begins. Exclamations.*)

SHVOKHNEV. Four, an ace—ten on each.

UTESHITELNY. Give me your pack, brother, I will pick a card for myself in the name of our marshall's wife. May she bring me luck!

KRUGEL. Allow me to add a nine.

UTESHITELNY. Shvokhnev, give me the chalk. I'll put the stakes down and figure them out.

SHVOKHNEV. Damn it, double!

UTESHITELNY. I go another five rubles!

KRUGEL. *Attendez!* [4] Let me have a look. I think there must be two threes left in the pack.

UTESHITELNY (*jumping up from his place, aside*). Damn it, there's something wrong here. These are different cards, that's obvious.

(*The game goes on.*)

IKHAREV (*to* KRUGEL). May I ask, are both going?

KRUGEL. Yes, both.

---

[3] The only game played throughout this work is a German variation of faro, *shtoss* in Russian. The player selected a card from his deck, placed it on the gaming table, established the amount he wished to stake on the card. The dealer (banker) broke the seal on a fresh deck and began to deal cards face up, one by one, placing the first card to his right, the second to his left, the third to his right, etc., until all the cards were dealt. When a card equal in points to the card on which the player had bet came up on the dealer's right hand, the dealer won, but he lost when it came up on the left. When two similar cards turned up in the same stroke (a doublet), the player lost all he had bet. (ed.)

[4] "Wait a minute." A call for a halt of play for reckoning of money or points. (ed.)

IKHAREV. You won't raise your stake?

KRUGEL. No.

IKHAREV (*to* SHVOKHNEV). And you, aren't you staking?

SHVOKHNEV. Let me sit out this round. (*Gets up from his chair, goes hurriedly up to* UTESHITELNY *and says rapidly*) Hell, old friend! He is cheating like anything! He is a first-rate card-sharp!

UTESHITELNY (*disturbed*). We can't give up the eighty thousand, can we?

SHVOKHNEV. Of course we shall have to, if we can't get it.

UTESHITELNY. Well, that's still the question, and meanwhile we must have it out with him.

SHVOKHNEV. How?

UTESHITELNY. Make a clean breast of it.

SHVOKHNEV. What for?

UTESHITELNY. I'll tell you later on. Come along. (*Both go up to* IKHAREV *and slap him on either shoulder*.)

UTESHITELNY. It's no use your going on firing blank shots!

IKHAREV (*starting*). How so?

UTESHITELNY. What's the good of talking? A man always spots his own sort.

IKHAREV (*courteously*). Allow me to ask in what sense I am to understand . . .

UTESHITELNY. Oh, simply, without wasting words or standing on ceremony. We see your skill and, believe me, we can do justice to your accomplishments. And so in the name of my comrades I suggest a friendly alliance. By combining our wits and our capital we may be much more successful than by acting separately.

IKHAREV. How far may I credit your words?

UTESHITELNY. I'll tell you how far: we meet frankness with frankness. We'll confess to you openly that we had agreed to swindle you, for we took you for an ordinary person. But now we see that you are familiar with the higher mysteries. And so, will you accept our friendship?

IKHAREV. I cannot refuse such a kind offer.

UTESHITELNY. And so let us all shake hands. (*All in turn shake* IKHAREV's *hand.*) Henceforth all is in common; all pretense and ceremony laid aside! Allow me to ask how long have you studied the secrets of the science?

IKHAREV. I must admit that I have had an inclination that way from my earliest youth. When I was at school, during lectures I used to hold a bank for my schoolmates under my desk.

UTESHITELNY. I thought so. Such skill cannot be acquired without practice in the years of supple youth. Do you remember that wonderful child, Shvokhnev?

IKHAREV. What child?

UTESHITELNY. Tell him.

SHVOKHNEV. I shall never forget a case like that. His brother-in-law (*pointing to* UTESHITELNY) said to me, "Shvokhnev, would you like to see a prodigy? A boy of eleven, the son of Ivan Mikhailovich Kubyshev can play tricks with cards better than any cardsharp. Go to Tetushevsky county and see for yourself." I went off there at once. I asked for Ivan Mikhailovich Kubyshev's country house and went straight to see him. I sent in my name. A middle-aged man met me. I introduced myself and said, "Excuse me, I hear that God has blessed you with a son of rare parts."—"Yes, I must confess it is so," he said (and I was pleased, you know, by the absence of affectation and pretense in him). "Though I am his father, and it is not for me to sing the praises of my own son, he really is a prodigy in a way. Mishka!" he said, "come here, show our visitor what you can do." The boy was only a child, not as high as my shoulder, and nothing special to look at. But he began to deal the cards, and I was positively aghast. It baffles description.

IKHAREV. Couldn't you see how he did it?

SHVOKHNEV. Not at all, not the faintest trace. I simply stared.

IKHAREV. That is extraordinary!

UTESHITELNY. A phenomenon, a natural phenomenon!

IKHAREV. And when I come to think what skill it needs, combined with keenness of sight and prolonged study of the marks on the cards . . .

UTESHITELNY. That has all been made so much easier now. Marking of cards is out of fashion now. People try to study the key now.

IKHAREV. You mean, the key of the pattern?

UTESHITELNY. Yes, the key of the pattern on the back. In a town which I won't mention by name there is a worthy individual who does nothing else at all. Every year he gets several hundred packs of cards from Moscow—from whom, is a question wrapped in obscurity—his whole duty consists in analyzing the marking of each card and sending out the key. Observe how the pattern on the two is arranged and how it differs on another. For that alone he gets five thousand a year in cash.

IKHAREV. It's a very important duty, though.

UTESHITELNY. It's bound to be done like that. It's what is called in economics division of labor. Take a carriage builder—he does not build the whole of the carriage himself; he hands over the job partly to the blacksmith, partly to the upholsterer. Life would not be long enough without it.

IKHAREV. Allow me to put one question to you: what methods have you adopted so far for getting your packs used? One can't always bribe a servant.

UTESHITELNY. God forbid! Besides, it's risky. It sometimes means mortgaging yourself. We do things differently. This is how we set to work on one occasion. Our agent arrived at the fair and put up at the town inn, passing himself off for a trader; he hadn't time to take a shop, he had all his boxes and parcels at the inn. He stayed at the inn, eating and drinking, ran up a bill, and suddenly disappeared without paying. The innkeeper ransacked his room and saw only one parcel left; he undid it and found a hundred dozen packs of cards. These were naturally at once sold by auction; they were sold a ruble under the regular price; the shopkeepers instantly stocked their shops with them; and in four days the whole town was lamenting its losses at cards.

IKHAREV. That was very neat.

SHVOKHNEV. And then with that fellow, that country gentleman?

IKHAREV. What about him?

UTESHITELNY. That wasn't badly managed either. I don't know whether you know him, Arkady Andreievich Dergunov, a very wealthy man. He is a first-rate player, of exemplary honesty; there is no way of getting at him: he looks into everything himself, his servants are refined people, perfect gentlemen, his house is a regular palace, his estate, his parks are all in the English style; in fact he is a Russian gentleman in the fullest sense of the word. How were we to set to work? There seemed simply no possibility. At last we thought of a plan. One morning a cart dashed by the very yard with a lot of young fellows. They were all as drunk as could be, bawling songs and driving at full speed. All the servants turned out to look at such a sight, as they always do, gaping and laughing. Then they noticed that something had dropped out of the cart, ran up and found a bag. They waved and shouted "Stop!" but no chance of that, no one heeded; they had raced off, leaving nothing but dust on the road. They undid the bag, found linen, clothes of some sort, two hundred rubles, and forty dozen packs of cards. Well, naturally they didn't throw away the money, the cards found their way to the master's tables, and next evening the master of the house and his visitors were left without a kopek in their pockets when the game was over.

IKHAREV.   Very clever! Why, that would be called roguery and all sorts of names, but you know it's subtle intelligence, a refinement of culture.

UTESHITELNY.   People don't understand gambling. It is no respecter of persons. It takes nothing into consideration. If my own father were to sit down to cards with me, I would cheat my father: he shouldn't risk it! All men are equal at cards.

IKHAREV.   What they don't understand is that a gambler may be the best of men. I know one who is fond of juggling with cards and all such tricks, but he would give his last kopek to a beggar. And yet nothing would make him refuse to join forces with two others and win for certain from a fourth. Well, gentlemen, since we are being so frank, I will show you a wonderful trick. Do you know what is meant by a composite or made-up pack in which one could guess any card a good way off?

UTESHITELNY.   Yes, but perhaps it's a different sort.

IKHAREV.   I believe I can boast that you would not find another like it. It meant nearly six months' work. I could not stand the sunlight for two weeks afterwards. The doctor thought I had inflammation of the eyes. (*Takes a pack out of the box.*) Here it is! You may think it foolish, but it has a name like a human being.

UTESHITELNY.   A name?

IKHAREV.   Yes, a name: Adelaida Ivanovna.

UTESHITELNY (*laughing*).   Do you hear, Shvokhnev, that's a new idea—calling a pack of cards Adelaida Ivanovna. I think that's really witty.

SHVOKHNEV. Excellent! Adelaida Ivanovna. Very good.

UTESHITELNY. Adelaida Ivanovna! A German girl. Krugel, that's the wife for you.

KRUGEL. Me a German! My grandfather was a German, it's true, but even he could not speak the language.

UTESHITELNY (*examining the cards*). This is certainly a treasure. Why, there are no signs on it at all. But can you really identify any card at any distance?

IKHAREV. Try me. I will stand five paces away from you and I'll name every card from here. I'll hand over two thousand if I fail.

UTESHITELNY. Well, what card is this?

IKHAREV. A seven.

UTESHITELNY. Right. And this one?

IKHAREV. A jack.

UTESHITELNY. Damn it, yes! And this one?

IKHAREV. A three.

UTESHITELNY. It's incredible!

KRUGEL (*shrugging his shoulders*). Incredible!

SHVOKHNEV. Incredible!

UTESHITELNY. Let me have another look at it. (*Examines the pack.*) It's marvelous! It deserves a name. But allow me to observe, it is difficult to make use of it except with very inexperienced players; you would have to slip it onto the table yourself.

IKHAREV. But, of course, it is only done in the very heat of the game, when the stakes are so high that the most experienced player is a little agitated; and if a man is only a little off his guard you can do anything with him. You know that even the best players at times play themselves silly, as it's called. When a man has been playing for two days and two nights on end without a wink of sleep—well, he's played himself out. In the heat of the game I can always manage to change the cards. I assure you it all lies in being cool when the other man is excited. And there are thousands of ways of distracting people's attention. Suddenly accuse one of the players, say that his score is put down wrong. The eyes of all will turn upon him, and meantime the cards are changed.

UTESHITELNY. Well, I see that in addition to your skill you possess the gift of coolness—that's a very important thing. Association with you will be all the more valuable to us. Let us drop ceremony, lay aside unnecessary etiquette, and speak to each other as comrades.

IKHAREV. It is about time we did.

UTESHITELNY. Waiter, champagne! To our friendly cooperation!

IKHAREV. Yes, that's worth a drink.

SHVOKHNEV. Well, here we are gathered for heroic deeds, our weapons are in our hands, our forces are ready, only one thing is lacking . . .

IKHAREV. That's so, that's so, a fortress for us to attack, that's the trouble!

UTESHITELNY. What's to be done? There's no foe in sight so far. (*Looking intently at* SHVOKHNEV) Well? Your face seems to say that you know of one.

SHVOKHNEV. Yes, I do. . . . (*Pauses.*)

UTESHITELNY. I know at whom you are hinting.

IKHAREV (*eagerly*). Whom? Whom? Who is it?

UTESHITELNY. Oh, it's nonsense, all nonsense. There's nothing in it. You see, a country gentleman is staying here, Mikhail Aleksandrovich Glov. But what's the good of talking of him since he doesn't play at all? We have had a try at him already. . . . I have been at him for a month; I have gained his affection and his confidence, but I have had no luck.

IKHAREV. But couldn't I see him? Perhaps . . . you never can tell.

UTESHITELNY. Well, I can tell you beforehand that it is trouble thrown away.

IKHAREV. But let us try, let us try him once more.

SHVOKHNEV. Well, bring him in, anyway. If we don't succeed, we'll simply have a talk. Why not try?

UTESHITELNY. By all means, I don't mind, I'll get him.

IKHAREV. Please bring him now!

UTESHITELNY. Very well, very well.

(*Goes out.*)

IKHAREV. Yes, indeed, you can never tell. Sometimes a thing seems quite out of the question . . .

SHVOKHNEV. I am of the same opinion myself. It is not God you have to deal with, but a man, and a man is always but a man. He may say "no" today and "no" tomorrow and "no" the day after tomorrow, but on the fourth day, if you attack him properly, he will say "yes." A man will make a pretense, you

know, of being unapproachable, but, as you get to know him
better, you will see there was no need for any anxiety.

KRUGEL. This man is not like that, though.

IKHAREV. Oh, if only he were! You can't imagine how eager I
feel now to set to work. You must know that I won eighty
thousand from Colonel Chebotariov last month. Since then
I have had no practice. You can't imagine how bored I have
felt all this time! Bored to death!

SHVOKHNEV. I understand your condition. It is just like a general
—what he must feel when there is no war! . . . It's simply
a deadly interval, my dear fellow, I know by myself. It's no
joking matter.

IKHAREV. Would you believe it, it comes to such a pitch that if
anyone were to start a game for five rubles I would be ready
to sit down and play.

SHVOKHNEV. A natural thing. That's how the most skillful players
come to grief sometimes: they are so bored, they have no
work, and they are driven by desperation to play with some
beggarly rat—and then they lose money for nothing!

IKHAREV. Is this Glov rich?

KRUGEL. Oh, he has money. I believe about a thousand souls.

IKHAREV. Ech! Damn it! Shall we make him drunk? Send for
some champagne?

SHVOKHNEV. He never touches a drop.

IKHAREV. What are we to do with him? How can we tackle him?
But yet I keep thinking . . . gambling is a tempting thing. I
believe if he would only sit down beside players he couldn't
resist.

SHVOKHNEV. Well, we'll try it. Krugel and I will have a game for
very low stakes here, to one side. But you mustn't pay too
much attention to him; old men are suspicious.

(*They sit down at one side with cards.* UTESHITELNY *and*
MIKHAIL ALEKSANDROVICH GLOV, *an elderly man, come
in.*)

UTESHITELNY. Here, Ikharev, let me introduce—Mikhail Aleksandrovich Glov.

IKHAREV. I have long been desirous of the honor . . . staying
in the same inn . . .

GLOV. I am very much pleased to make your acquaintance too.
I only regret that it is just as I am leaving.

IKHAREV (*handing him a chair*). Please sit down. . . . Have you been staying in this town long?

(UTESHITELNY, SHVOKHNEV, *and* KRUGEL *whisper together.*)

GLOV. Ah, my good sir, how sick I am of the town! I shall be thankful, body and soul, to get out of it as quickly as possible.

IKHAREV. You are detained by business, then?

GLOV. Business? Yes. Such troublesome business too.

IKHAREV. A lawsuit, I presume?

GLOV. No, thank God, there is no litigation, but all the same the circumstances are complicated. I am marrying my daughter, sir, a girl of eighteen—do you understand a father's position? I've come to make various purchases, but the principal task is to raise a mortgage on my estate. It would all have been finished, but the Treasury hasn't paid the money so far. I am staying here for nothing at all.

IKHAREV. And allow me to ask for what sum are you mortgaging your estate?

GLOV. For two hundred thousand. They should pay it any day, but it keeps dragging on, and I am so sick of being here. I left everything at home, you know, expecting to be back very soon. My daughter is engaged to be married. Everything is being delayed . . . I have made up my mind not to wait any longer, but to leave it all.

IKHAREV. Why? Won't you wait to receive the money?

GLOV. What am I to do, sir? Consider my position: it is a month now since I have seen my wife and children. I don't even get any letters; God knows what is happening there. I am leaving the business to my son, who will stay here. I am sick of the whole thing. (*Turning to* SHVOKHNEV *and* KRUGEL) What are you doing, gentlemen? I believe I am interrupting you: you were engaged in something?

KRUGEL. Oh no. It's of no consequence. We began playing to pass away the time.

GLOV. Something like a game of *shtoss*, I believe?

SHVOKHNEV. Oh well! *Shtoss* for a kopek, just to pass the time.

GLOV. Ah, my friends, listen to an old man. You are young people. Of course there is no harm in it, it's just for diversion and you can't lose much over kopek stakes, it's true; but yet . . .

ah, gentlemen, I've played myself and I know from experience, everything in the world begins in a small way, but small stakes quickly lead to big ones.

SHVOKHNEV (*to* IKHAREV). Well, the old man is off now! (*To* GLOV) You always make a lot of every trifle. That's the usual thing with all elderly people.

GLOV. Oh, I am not so old. I judge from experience.

SHVOKHNEV. I am not speaking of you; but it is the way with old people in general: if, for instance, they have burned their fingers over anything, they are firmly convinced that everyone else is bound to do the same. If they've gone down some road and stumbled on a slippery place, they set up an outcry and make it a rule that no one must go down that way, because there is a slippery place there and everyone is sure to slip down on it, without considering that other people may be more careful and not have slippery boots on. No, they never think of that. If a man has been bitten by a dog in the street, all dogs bite, and so no one must go down the street.

GLOV. That's true, sir, it is so. On the one hand, there is that failing; but on the other, look at young people! They really are too reckless: they may break their necks any minute!

SHVOKHNEV. It is quite true that one never finds a happy medium. When a man is young he is so wild that he is insufferable, when he is old he plays the saint so that he is insufferable again.

GLOV. Have you such a bad opinion of old people?

SHVOKHNEV. No, why a bad opinion? It's the truth and nothing more.

IKHAREV. Excuse my saying that it is rather a harsh view . . .

UTESHITELNY. As for cards, I fully agree with Mikhail Aleksandrovich. I used to play myself, play a lot: but I am thankful to say I have given it up forever—not because I lost money or thought luck was against me; I assure you, that's of no consequence. The loss of money is not so important as losing one's peace of mind. The mere agitation experienced during gambling, people may say what they like, but it obviously shortens one's life.

GLOV. That is so, sir, indeed! That's a very wise observation! Allow me to ask you an indiscreet question: though I have had the honor of your acquaintance for some time, so far . . .

UTESHITELNY.   What question?

GLOV.   Allow me to ask, though it's a delicate subject, how old are you?

UTESHITELNY.   Thirty-nine.

GLOV.   Imagine! What's thirty-nine? Still a young man—oh, if only we had more men in Russia so wise in their judgments! Good heavens, the difference it would make! It would simply mean the golden age! Upon my word, how thankful I am to have made your acquaintance!

IKHAREV.   I can assure you I think as he does. I would never allow boys to touch a card. But why shouldn't persons of discretion amuse themselves? Elderly people, for instance, who can't dance?

GLOV.   Yes, that's quite true; but I assure you there are so many pleasures, so many duties, sacred duties I may say, in our lives. Ah, gentlemen, listen to an old man! There is no better vocation for a man than family life and the domestic circle. Everything that is surrounding you, young men, is nothing but excitement, but you haven't tasted true bliss yet, while I—you will hardly believe it—am longing for the minute when I shall see my dear ones again! I imagine how my daughter will fling herself on my neck: "Papa, my dear papa!" My son is home again from high school, I haven't seen him for six months. . . . I have no words to describe it, no indeed. Well, after that, one doesn't care to look at cards.

IKHAREV.   But why do paternal feelings interfere with cards? Paternal feelings are one thing and cards are another . . .

(*Enter* ALEKSEY.)

ALEKSEY. (*to* GLOV).   Your servant is asking about the trunks. Shall he carry them out? The horses are ready.

GLOV.   I am coming! Excuse me, gentlemen, I will leave you for a brief moment.

(*Goes out with* ALEKSEY.)

IKHAREV.   Well, there is no hope at all!

UTESHITELNY.   I said so before. I don't understand how you fellows can fail to see what a man is made of. You have only to look at a man to see that he is not disposed to play.

IKHAREV.   Oh well, we ought to have tackled him thoroughly, though. Why did you back him up?

UTESHITELNY. That's the only way of doing it. With people like that you have to be subtle, or they guess at once that you want to fleece them.

IKHAREV. Well, but what has it led to? Here he is going away all the same.

UTESHITELNY. Well, wait, it is not all over yet!

(*Enter* GLOV.)

GLOV. I thank you most sincerely for your pleasant acquaintance; I am only sorry that I did not meet you earlier, but maybe God will bring us together again somewhere.

SHVOKHNEV. Oh, very likely. The world is a small place, and one always comes across people again; it's all a matter of luck.

GLOV. Yes, indeed, that's perfectly true! It may chance that we shall meet tomorrow. It's perfectly true. Goodbye, gentlemen. Thank you most sincerely. And to you, Stepan Ivanovich, I am truly grateful, you have really relieved my solitude!

UTESHITELNY. Please, there is no need. I did what I could.

GLOV. Well, since you are so kind, will you do me one more favor? May I ask it of you?

UTESHITELNY. What is it. Tell me! I am ready to do anything you like.

GLOV. Set my mind at rest—you know an old father's anxiety.

UTESHITELNY. How?

GLOV. I am leaving here my Sasha. He is a splendid fellow with a good heart, but one can't rely upon him entirely. He is twenty-two, well, what's that? Almost a child. He has finished his studies and he will hear of nothing now but the Hussars. I say to him: "It's still early, Sasha, wait a while and have a look round first. What do you see in the Hussars? How do you know, maybe you are better fitted for the civil service. You've scarcely seen anything of the world yet. You have plenty of time before you!" Well, you know what the young are! What dazzles him in the Hussars, you know, is the gold braid, the gorgeous uniform. What's one to do? You can't restrain their inclinations . . . so will you be so generous, my good Stepan Ivanovich! He will be left alone now; I have entrusted him with some little matters of business. He is a young man; anything may happen; I only hope the Treasury clerks won't cheat him. . . . I shouldn't wonder. So will you take him under your protection? Keep an eye on him and guard him from harm; will you be so kind, my good sir? (*Takes* UTESHITELNY *by the hands.*)

UTESHITELNY.   Certainly, certainly. Anything a father can do for his own son I will do for him.

GLOV.   Ah, my good friend! (*They embrace and kiss each other.*) One can always see when a man has a good heart! God will reward you for it! Goodbye, gentlemen, I sincerely wish you good luck.

IKHAREV.   Goodbye, a good journey to you!

SHVOKHNEV.   I trust you may find all well at home.

GLOV.   I thank you, gentlemen.

UTESHITELNY.   I'll see you off and help you into your carriage.

GLOV.   Ah, how kind you are!

(*Goes off with* UTESHITELNY.)

IKHAREV.   The bird has flown!

SHVOKHNEV.   And he would have been worth plucking!

IKHAREV.   I must confess, when he said two hundred thousand, it sent a thrill to my heart.

KRUGEL.   It is pleasant even to think of a sum like that.

IKHAREV.   And when you think how much money is wasted without the slightest benefit to anyone! Why, what's the good of his having two hundred thousand? It will all go on buying rags and frippery.

SHVOKHNEV.   And it's all worthless trash!

IKHAREV.   And how much of it is wasted without being put into circulation! How many dead fortunes there are which lie like corpses in the banks! It's positively piteous. I have no desire to have more money than what is lying idle at the Board of Trustees.

SHVOKHNEV.   I should be resigned to take half.

KRUGEL.   I should be satisfied with a quarter.

SHVOKHNEV.   Come, don't tell lies, German. You want more.

KRUGEL.   As I am an honest man . . .

SHVOKHNEV.   You will cheat us.

(UTESHITELNY *comes in hurriedly, looking pleased.*)

UTESHITELNY.   It's all right, gentlemen, it's all right! He has gone, damn him, so much the better! The son is left. The father has given him an authorization and the right to receive the money from the Treasury, and has commissioned me to look after everything. The son is a fine fellow, he is dying to be a Hussar. We shall reap a harvest! I will go and bring him to you this minute.

(*Runs out.*)

IKHAREV. Hurrah for Uteshitelny!

SHVOKHNEV. Bravo! Things have taken a fine turn!

(*All rub their hands in delight.*)

IKHAREV. Uteshitelny is a fine fellow! Now I see why he made up to the father and backed him up. And how smart it all was! How subtle!

SHVOKHNEV. Oh, he has a remarkable talent for that sort of thing.

KRUGEL. Extraordinary abilities!

IKHAREV. I must admit, when the father said he was leaving his son here, the idea flashed upon me too, but only for a moment, while he at once . . . How clever!

SHVOKHNEV. Oh, you don't know him yet.

(*Enter* UTESHITELNY *with* ALEKSANDER MIKHAILOVICH GLOV, *a young man.*)

UTESHITELNY. Gentlemen, let me introduce Aleksander Mikhailovich Glov—he is the best of company. Make a friend of him as of me.

SHVOKHNEV. Delighted! (*Shakes hands.*)

IKHAREV. Your acquaintance is . . .

KRUGEL. We'll receive you with open arms.

GLOV. Gentlemen, I . . .

UTESHITELNY. No ceremony, no ceremony. . . . Equality is the first thing. Glov, here you see all are comrades, and to hell with etiquette.

SHVOKHNEV. Yes!

GLOV. Oh yes! (*Shakes hands with all of them.*)

UTESHITELNY. That's right, bravo! Waiter, champagne! Do you notice, gentlemen, that one can see something of the Hussar about him already? Yes, your father—no offense meant—is a brute. Excuse me (we are comrades, you know), how could he think of putting this gallant young man into the ink-slinging service? Well, my boy, when is your sister's wedding to be?

GLOV. The devil take her with her wedding! It annoys me that my father is keeping me three months in the country on her account.

UTESHITELNY. But is she good-looking, your sister?

GLOV. Too good-looking. . . . If she weren't my sister I wouldn't have let her go.

UTESHITELNY. Bravo, bravo, Hussar! One can see the Hussar at once! Would you help me if I wanted to carry her off?

GLOV. Why not? I would.

UTESHITELNY. Bravo, Hussar! That's what's meant by a true Hussar, damn it all! Waiter, champagne! That's just what I like; I love such frank people. Stay, dear boy, let me embrace you!

SHVOKHNEV. Let me embrace him too. (*Embraces him.*)

IKHAREV. Allow me to embrace him! (*Embraces him.*)

KRUGEL. Well, if that's how it is, I'll embrace him too! (*Embraces him.*)

(ALEKSEY *brings in a bottle with his finger on the cork, which goes off with a pop and flies to the ceiling; he fills their glasses.*)

UTESHITELNY. Gentlemen, to the health of the future Ensign of Hussars! May he be the greatest swordsman, the greatest flirt, the greatest drunkard . . . in fact, may he be all that he wishes . . .

ALL. May he be all that he wishes! (*They drink.*)

GLOV. To the health of all Hussars! (*Raises his glass.*)

ALL. To the health of all Hussars! (*They drink.*)

UTESHITELNY. Gentlemen, we must initiate him now into all the traditions of the Hussars! He drinks passably well, we can see, but that's a trifle. Then he must be a desperate card player! Do you play *shtoss?*

GLOV. I would play, I'd like to very much, but I have no money.

UTESHITELNY. What nonsense, no money! You need only have enough to begin with and then you will have money: you will win it.

GLOV. But I have nothing to begin with.

UTESHITELNY. Oh, we will trust you. Why, you have an authorization for the receipt of the money from the Treasury. We can wait; and when they give it to you you can pay us; till then you can give us an I.O.U. But what am I talking about? As though you were destined to lose! You may win several thousand on the spot.

GLOV. But if I lose?

UTESHITELNY. For shame! Nice sort of Hussar you are! Naturally it's one of two things—either you win or you lose. But that's the very point, the chief zest lies in the risk. Where there is no risk, anyone is brave; if the result is certain, any paltry scribbler is bold and a Jew will scale a fortress.

GLOV (*with a wave of his hand*). Damn it all! If that's how it is, I'll play! Why should I listen to my father?

UTESHITELNY. Bravo, Ensign! Waiter, cards! (*Pours him out a glass.*) The greatest thing in life is boldness, dash, spirit. . . . So be it, gentlemen. I'll hold a bank of twenty-five thousand for you. (*Deals to right and to left.*) Well, Hussar . . . What is your stake, Shvokhnev? (*Deals.*) What a strange sequence of cards! It's a mathematical curiosity! The jack's beaten and the nine takes. What's there, what have you got? And the four takes, too! And the Hussar, the Hussar, what a Hussar! Did you notice, Shvokhnev, the masterly way he is raising his stakes? And the ace not out yet. Why don't you fill his glass, Shvokhnev? Here, here, here is the ace! There, Krugel has swept it all up. Germans always have luck! The four takes, the three takes. Bravo, bravo, Hussar! Do you hear, Shvokhnev? The Hussar has won nearly five thousand already.

GLOV (*bends a card*). Damn it all, double my stake! And there is a nine on the table, I'll put another five hundred rubles on it!

UTESHITELNY (*goes on turning up the cards*). Ah, bravo, Hussar! The seven is beaten. . . . Ah, no, *plie*,[5] damn it all, *plie!* Ah, the Hussar has lost. Well, it can't be helped, my boy. We can't all be the lucky man. Krugel, don't go on weighing the chances! Stake on the one you pulled out. Bravo, the Hussar has won! Why don't you congratulate him? (*All drink and congratulate him, clinking their glasses.*) They say the queen of spades always lets you down, but I shouldn't say so. . . . Do you remember your little brunette, Shvokhnev, whom you used to call the queen of spades? Where is she now, poor dear? I expect she has gone to the dogs. Krugel, your card is beaten! (*To* IKHAREV) Yours is beaten too! Shvokhnev, yours is beaten too; the Hussar has lost too.

GLOV. Damn it all, *va, banque!* [6]

---

[5] "Fold." Term signifying a bent or folded card indicating one's stake on a given card. (ed.)
[6] "Go to the bank." Term signifying a stake which is equal to the total sum of money in the bank. (ed.)

UTESHITELNY.   Bravo, Hussar! That's the true Hussar spirit at last! Do you see, Shvokhnev, how the real feeling always comes out? Hitherto we could only see that he would make a Hussar, but now it is clear that he is a Hussar already. You see how a man's nature shows itself. . . . The Hussar's beaten.

GLOV.   *Va, banque!*

UTESHITELNY.   Bravo, Hussar! The whole fifty thousand? That's what I call doing it handsomely! You don't find many people who are capable of it. There's something heroic in it. The Hussar's come down again.

GLOV.   *Va, banque,* damn it all, *va, banque!*

UTESHITELNY.   Oho, Hussar, a hundred thousand! What a fellow, isn't he? And look at his eyes! Do you see how his eyes are glowing, Shvokhnev? He is a second Barclay-de-Tolly! [7] Here's heroism for you! And the king still not out. There is a queen of diamonds for you, Shvokhnev! Here, German, here's a seven for you. Failure, nothing but trash! And there seems to be no king in the pack. . . . Ah, here he is, here he is. . . . The Hussar's beaten again!

GLOV (*getting excited*).   *Va, banque,* damn it all, *va, banque!*

UTESHITELNY.   No, my boy, stop! You've lost two hundred thousand already. You must pay that first, you can't begin a new game until then; we can't trust you for so much.

GLOV.   But where am I to get the money? I haven't got it.

UTESHITELNY.   Give us an I.O.U.; here, write it.

GLOV.   Very well, I am willing. (*Takes a pen.*)

UTESHITELNY.   And give us the authorization for receiving the money too.

GLOV.   Here is the authorization too.

UTESHITELNY.   Now sign this and then this. (*Gives him papers to sign.*)

GLOV.   Very well, I am ready to do anything. There, I've signed it. Now let us play again.

UTESHITELNY.   No, my boy, wait a minute, show us the money first.

GLOV.   But I shall pay you, you may count on that.

UTESHITELNY.   No, my boy, money on the table!

GLOV.   But what's this? It's an ugly trick.

---

7 (1761-1818), Russian field marshal of Scottish descent. Commanded Russian forces against Napoleon in 1812. (ed.)

IKHAREV. No, it's quite a different matter; the chances are not equal.

SHVOKHNEV. You might begin in order to win from us. We all know that if a man sits down to play without money he means to win for certain.

GLOV. Well, what do you want? Fix any interest you like, I am ready for anything, I'll pay you twice over.

UTESHITELNY. What do we want with your interest? We too are ready to pay you any interest you like if you give us a loan.

GLOV (*resolutely and despairingly*). Well, 'say the last word, then: won't you play?

SHVOKHNEV. Bring the money and we will play at once.

GLOV (*taking a pistol out of his pocket*). Then goodbye, gentlemen! You will not meet me again in this world.

(*Runs out with a pistol.*)

UTESHITELNY (*in alarm*). What are you about? He's gone mad! Run after him! What if he really shoots himself! (*Runs out.*)

IKHAREV. There will be a scandal if that devil of a fellow goes and shoots himself.

SHVOKHNEV. Oh, damn him, let him shoot himself, as long as it is not now; the money is not in our hands yet! That's the trouble!

KRUGEL. I am anxious, anyway. It's so possible . . .

(*Enter* UTESHITELNY *holding* GLOV *by the hand with a pistol in it.*)

UTESHITELNY. What are you thinking about, my boy? Are you crazy? Do you hear, gentlemen, he was thrusting the pistol in his mouth? For shame!

ALL (*pressing around him*). How could you? How could you? What next?

SHVOKHNEV. An intelligent man too! To think of shooting himself for such nonsense.

IKHAREV. All Russia might shoot itself at that rate: everybody has either lost at cards or is going to lose, and if it weren't so— judge for yourself—how could anybody win?

UTESHITELNY. You are simply a fool, allow me to tell you. You don't see your own luck. Don't you feel what you have gained by losing?

GLOV (*with vexation*). Do you think I am such a fool as all that? What gain is there in losing two hundred thousand, damn it!

UTESHITELNY. Ah, you simpleton! Don't you see what glory you will gain in the regiment by it? It's not a trifling matter! Before you are even an ensign you've lost two hundred thousand. Why, the Hussars will carry you on their shoulders.

GLOV (*growing more cheerful*). Do you imagine that I haven't the spirit to damn it all if it comes to that? The devil take it! Hurrah for the Hussars!

UTESHITELNY. Hurrah for the Hussars! Tra-la-la! Champagne!
                (WAITER *brings a bottle.*)

GLOV (*glass in hand*). Hurrah for the Hussars!

IKHAREV. Hurrah for the Hussars, damn it all!

SHVOKHNEV. Tra-la-la! Hurrah for the Hussars!

GLOV. I don't care a rap if it comes to that! (*Puts his glass on the table.*) The only trouble is, how am I going home? My father, my father! (*Clutches his head.*)

UTESHITELNY. But why should you go to your father? There's no need.

GLOV (*staring at him*). What?

UTESHITELNY. You go straight from here into the regiment! We'll give you the money for your equipment. We must give him two hundred rubles now, Shvokhnev, let the Ensign have some fun! I've noticed he has got his eye on a . . . that black-eyed girl, eh?

GLOV. Hang it all, I'll go straight to her, I'll take her by storm!

UTESHITELNY. A regular Hussar, isn't he? Shvokhnev, haven't you got two hundred rubles?

IKHAREV. Here, I'll give him that, let him have a jolly good time!

GLOV (*takes the note and waves it in the air*). Champagne!

ALL. Champagne!
                (WAITER *brings bottles.*)

GLOV. Hurrah for the Hussars!

UTESHITELNY. Hurrah! . . . Shvokhnev, I have an idea! Let us give him a tossing, as we used to in the regiment! Come, pick him up! (*All go up to him, seize him by the arms and legs, and toss him, singing to the well-known tune*)

ALL. He's a jolly good fellow!

GLOV (*raising his glass*). Hurrah!

ALL. Hurrah! (*They put him down on the ground. He smashes his glass on the ground; all smash their glasses, some on the ground, some on their boots.*)

GLOV. I go straight to her!

UTESHITELNY. And may we not follow you?

GLOV. No, not one of you! And if anyone goes near her . . . the sword shall decide!

UTESHITELNY. Ah, what a swashbuckler! Jealous and defiant as the devil! He will be a regular desperado, a gay Lothario, a daredevil.

GLOV. Goodbye.

SHVOKHNEV. But come and tell us all about it afterwards.

(GLOV *goes out.*)

UTESHITELNY. We must treat him kindly till we get hold of the cash, and then to the devil with him!

SHVOKHNEV. The only thing I am afraid of is the Treasury may delay in paying the money.

UTESHITELNY. Yes, that would be bad . . . but there are ways of hurrying them, you know. After all, one has to come to oiling the palm if business is to be done.

(ZAMUKHRYSHKIN, *a clerk, wearing a rather shabby coat, puts his head in at the door.*)

ZAMUKHRYSHKIN. Allow me to ask, is Aleksander Mikhailovich Glov here?

SHVOKHNEV. No, he has just gone out. What do you want with him?

ZAMUKHRYSHKIN. I've come about his business, about the payment of some money.

UTESHITELNY. And who are you?

ZAMUKHRYSHKIN. I am a clerk from the Treasury.

UTESHITELNY. Ah, do come in! Please sit down! We all take a warm interest in the business, especially as we have had some friendly transactions with Aleksander Mikhailovich. And so you may readily understand that you will earn the substantial gratitude of this gentleman and this gentleman and this gentleman (*pointing to each in turn*). The vital thing is to get the money out of the Treasury as quickly as possible.

ZAMUKHRYSHKIN. Well, in any case it can't be paid in less than two weeks.

UTESHITELNY. Oh, that's far too long. You forget the gratitude to come from us.

ZAMUKHRYSHKIN. Oh, that's a matter of course. That's all taken for granted. How could I forget it? That's why I say "two weeks," or you might be hanging around for three months. We will not get the money for another ten days, we haven't a kopek at the Treasury at the moment. Last week we received a hundred and fifty thousand, but we paid it all out— three landowners are still waiting who mortgaged their estates in February.

UTESHITELNY.   Oh, well, that may be so for others, but you will treat us as friends. . . . We must become better acquainted. . . . But there! We are all friends here! What's your name, eh? Fentefley Perpentich, isn't it?

ZAMUKHRYSHKIN.   Psoy Stakhich.

UTESHITELNY.   Well, that's almost the same thing. Come then, Psoy Stakhich! We will all be like old friends. Tell us, how are you getting on? How is business? How is your service?

ZAMUKHRYSHKIN.   Service? Oh, just as usual.

UTESHITELNY.   Well, there are different ways of making money in the Service. Do you get much?

ZAMUKHRYSHKIN.   As you know, of course one must live.

UTESHITELNY.   Tell us openly, are they all sharks in the Treasury?

ZAMUKHRYSHKIN.   What next! I see you are joking. Ah, gentlemen . . . The gentlemen who write stories are always making jokes about people taking bribes, but when you look closer, our superiors take bribes too. Why, you too, gentlemen, though perhaps you give it a finer name, subscribing to this or that or God knows what; but in reality it comes to the same thing. The man is the same if the coat is different.

UTESHITELNY.   Here Psoy Stakhich has taken offense, I see. That comes of wounding a man's sense of honor.

ZAMUKHRYSHKIN.   Well, honor, you know, is a delicate point. But there is nothing to take offense about. I have seen something of life, sir.

UTESHITELNY.   That's enough. Let us have a friendly talk, Psoy Stakhich. Tell us how things are going on with you, how you are getting on, how is the world treating you? Have you a wife and children?

ZAMUKHRYSHKIN.   Thank God, the Lord has been bountiful. I have two sons attending the district school and two others, smaller, one running about in a smock and the other crawling on all fours.

UTESHITELNY. But I bet they all know how to use their little hands. (*Makes a grabbing gesture.*)

ZAMUKHRYSHKIN. Well, you will have your joke, gentlemen! Here you are beginning again.

UTESHITELNY. Never mind, never mind, Psoy Stakhich, I spoke as a friend. Why, there's nothing in it. We are all friends. Hey, bring a glass of champagne for Psoy Stakich; make haste! We must get to know each other better. We'll come and pay you a visit.

ZAMUKHRYSHKIN (*taking a glass*). You will be very welcome, gentlemen. I tell you plainly that you will get a better glass of tea with me than you would at the governor's.

UTESHITELNY. A free gift, I bet, from the tea merchant?

ZAMUKHRYSHKIN. Yes, straight from Kiakhta.

UTESHITELNY. You don't say so, Psoy Stakhich? Why, you don't have to deal with merchants?

ZAMUKHRYSHKIN (*emptying his glass, leaning his fists on his knees*). It was like this. A merchant here had to pay up pretty heavily, chiefly through his own stupidity. A landowner called Frakasov was mortgaging his estate; it was all arranged, and he had only to receive the money next day. He was starting a factory of some sort in partnership with the merchant. Well, you understand it is not for us to know whether the money is wanted for a factory or anything else, or with whom he is in partnership. That's not our business, but the merchant in his foolishness went spreading it all over the town that he was in partnership with him and was expecting money from hour to hour. We sent word to him that if he forwarded to us two thousand the money should be paid at once, or else he would have to wait! And the boilers and all sorts of tackle had already arrived for the factory, and the dealers were only waiting for the deposit money. The merchant saw there was nothing for it, he paid us two thousand as well as three pounds of tea each. People will call it a bribe, but it was only fair: he needn't have been so stupid. It was his own doing—why couldn't he hold his tongue?

UTESHITELNY. Psoy Stakhich, about this little business, please. We'll give you something, but you do what's right with your superiors. Only, for God's sake, Psoy Stakhich, make haste!

ZAMUKHRYSHKIN.   We'll do our best. (*Getting up.*) But I tell you frankly, we can't do it as soon as you want it: as God's above, we haven't a kopek in the Treasury, but we'll do our best.

UTESHITELNY.   And how are we to inquire for you there?

ZAMUKHRYSHKIN.   Ask for Psoy Zamukhryshkin. Goodbye, gentlemen.

(*Goes toward the door.*)

SHVOKHNEV.   Psoy Stakhich! (*Looks about him.*) Do your best!

UTESHITELNY.   Psoy Stakhich, make haste, let us have it!

ZAMUKHRYSHKIN (*going out*).   I've told you already, I'll do my best!

UTESHITELNY.   Damn it all, how slow it is! (*Slaps himself on the forehead.*) Yes, I'll run after him, perhaps I may do something. I won't spare money. The devil take the man! I'll give him three thousand out of my own pocket.

(*Runs off.*)

IKHAREV.   Of course it would be better to get it as soon as possible.

SHVOKHNEV.   We do so need it! We do so need it!

KRUGEL.   Oh, if he could only get round him somehow!

IKHAREV.   Why, are you in such a . . .

(UTESHITELNY *enters.*)

UTESHITELNY (*despairingly*).   Damn it all! He can't possibly do it in less than four days. I feel like banging my head against the wall!

IKHAREV.   But why are you in such a hurry? Can't you wait four days?

SHVOKHNEV.   The fact is, it is very important for us.

UTESHITELNY.   Wait! But do you know that we are expected in Nizhny at the Fair from hour to hour? We haven't told him yet, but four days ago we had a message to hasten there as quickly as possible, bringing with us at all costs a sum of money. A dealer has brought six hundred thousand worth of iron. He will dispose of it finally on Tuesday and will receive the money in cash. And yesterday a man arrived with a half-million's worth of hemp.

IKHAREV.   Well, what of it?

UTESHITELNY.   What of it? Why, the old men have stayed at home and sent their sons instead.

IKHAREV.   But is it certain that the sons will play?

UTESHITELNY. Why, where have you been living? In China? Don't you know what merchants' sons are? Why, a merchant brings up his son either to know nothing or to know only what is suitable for a nobleman and not for a merchant. Naturally all he cares about is walking arm-in-arm with officers and drinking. They are the most profitable people to us. They don't know, the fools, that for every ruble they get out of us they pay us back in thousands. But that's our luck. The merchant thinks of nothing but marrying his daughter to a general or getting a grade for his son.[8]

IKHAREV. And is the job perfectly safe?

UTESHITELNY. Safe! They wouldn't have let us know if it hadn't been. The money is almost in our hands, every minute is precious now.

IKHAREV. Ah, damn it all! Why are we sitting here? We agreed to act together, friends!

UTESHITELNY. Yes, that's to our mutual advantage. Let me tell you the idea that has occurred to me. You have no reason to hurry off for a moment: you have money—eighty thousand—give it to us and take Glov's I.O.U. You will receive a hundred and fifty thousand for certain, namely nearly twice the amount, and, indeed, you will be obliging us too, for we so need the money now that we shall be delighted to pay you three times over.

IKHAREV. Certainly; why not? To prove to you that ties of friendship . . . (*Goes to his box and takes out a roll of notes.*) Here is the eighty thousand!

UTESHITELNY. And here is the I.O.U. Now I'll run at once and fetch Glov, I must bring him and arrange it all in due form. Krugel, take the money to my room, here is the key of my strong box. (KRUGEL *goes out.*) Oh, if only we could manage to get away by evening!

(*Goes out.*)

IKHAREV. Naturally, naturally, better not waste a minute here.

SHVOKHNEV. And I advise you too not to linger on. As soon as you get the money, come and join us. With two hundred thousand, you know, one could do anything and buy up the

---

[8] In the civil service. (ed.)

whole market. . . . Oh, I'd forgotten to speak to Krugel about something very important. Wait a minute, I shall be back directly.

(*Runs hurriedly off.*)

IKHAREV (*alone*). How strangely things have turned out! In the morning I had only eighty thousand and before evening I have two hundred! For some men that means a lifetime of service, of effort, endless perseverance, privation, ill health—and here in a few hours, in a few minutes I am a ruling prince! It's no joke —two hundred thousand! Where could you get two hundred thousand nowadays! What estate, what factory would bring you two hundred thousand? I can imagine what I should be like if I were to stay in the country and potter about looking after peasants and village elders, making some three thousand a year. Yes, education is not to be despised. You get crusted up with ignorance in the country and can't scrape it off with a knife afterwards. And what would one waste one's time over? Discussions with the village elder, with the peasants. But I prefer . . . talking to an educated man! Now I am independent, now my time is my own! I can devote myself to improving my mind. If I want to go to Petersburg, I can go to Petersburg. I will see the theaters and the Mint, and will walk by the Palace, along the English embankment in the Summer Garden. I'll go to Moscow, I'll dine at Yar's. I can dress in the fashion, I can be on an equality with others and perform the duties of a man of culture. And what is the origin of it all? To what am I indebted for it? To what is called cheating. And that's nonsense, it's not cheating at all! A man may become a cheat in one minute, but this has needed practice, study. Well, granting it is cheating. . . . But you see it's inevitable; what can one do without it? In a sense it is mere precaution. If I, for instance, didn't know all the tricks, if I hadn't mastered it all, they would have cheated me at once. They meant to cheat me, of course, but they saw it was not an ordinary man they had to do with, and they had recourse to my help. No, sense is a great asset, cunning is needed in the world. I look at life from quite a different point of view. To live as a fool lives is easy enough, but to live with subtlety, with art, to cheat everyone and not be cheated oneself, that's really a task and an object!

(GLOV *runs in hurriedly.*)

GLOV. Where are they? I've just been in their room, it's empty.

IKHAREV. They were here just now; they have only gone out for a minute.

GLOV. Gone out already? And have they taken the money from you?

IKHAREV. Yes, I have come to an arrangement with them, I am only waiting on your account.

(*Enter* ALEKSEY.)

ALEKSEY (*addressing* GLOV). Your honor asked for the gentlemen.

GLOV. Yes.

ALEKSEY. But they've gone.

GLOV. Gone?

ALEKSEY. Oh yes. They have had a chaise and horses standing ready for the last half-hour.

GLOV (*wringing his hands*). Oh, we are both done!

IKHAREV. What nonsense! I can't understand a word you are saying. Uteshitelny was to be back here in a minute. You know that all your debt is to be paid to me now, they have transferred it to me.

GLOV. A debt! The devil you'll get! Don't you feel you've been made a fool of like a blockhead?

IKHAREV. What nonsense you are talking! One can see you are still a bit fuddled.

GLOV. It seems we both are. You'd better wake up! Do you think I am Glov? I am about as much Glov as you are the Emperor of China.

IKHAREV (*uneasily*). Good gracious, what are you saying? What nonsense! And your father . . . and . . .

GLOV. The old man? To begin with, he is not my father, and a devil of a child he is likely to have. And secondly, his name is not Glov either, but Krynitsyn, and he is not Mikhail Aleksandrovich, but Ivan Klimych, one of their gang.

IKHAREV. Listen, tell the truth! This is not a joking matter.

GLOV. A joking matter! I've had a hand in it and I am cheated too. They promised me three thousand for my trouble!

IKHAREV (*going up to him, emphatically*). Now, no trifling, I tell you! Do you suppose I am such a fool! . . . And the authorization? And the Treasury? And there was a clerk here just

now from the Treasury, Psoy Stakhich Zamukhryshkin. Do
you suppose I can't send for him this minute?

GLOV. To begin with, he is not a Treasury clerk but a retired
lieutenant, one of their gang; and his name is not Stakhich
Zamukhryshkin but Murzafeikin, and not Psoy Stakhich but
Flor Semionovich.

IKHAREV (*in despair*). But who are you? Are you a devil? Tell me,
who are you?

GLOV. Who am I? I was an honorable man, but I have been driven
to be a rogue: they stripped me to my last rag, they did not
leave me a shirt. What was I to do? I couldn't starve! For
three thousand I undertook to play my part, to trick you and
deceive you. I tell you this frankly: you see I am acting honorably.

IKHAREV (*seizes him by the collar in a fury*). You swindler!

ALEKSEY (*aside*). Well, it's coming to blows, it seems. I'd better
clear out.

(*Goes out.*)

IKHAREV (*dragging* GLOV *along*). Come along, come along!

GLOV. Where? Where?

IKHAREV (*in a frenzy*). Where? To the police!

GLOV. But you have no case at all.

IKHAREV. I've no case? To cheat, to rob me of money in the middle of the day in this scandalous fashion? I have no case? To
use such underhand means! I have no case? When I've got you
in prison in Nerchinsk,[9] you can tell me I have no case. You
wait a while, they'll catch your whole damned crew. I'll teach
you to take advantage of the trustfulness and honesty of good-
hearted people. The law! I'll have the law on you! (*Drags him
along.*)

GLOV. Yes, you might appeal to the law if you hadn't acted il-
legally yourself. But just think—why, you joined with them
to deceive and fleece me, and the packs of cards were of your
own manufacture. No, my friend, that's the point, that you
have no right to complain.

IKHAREV (*slapping himself on the forehead in despair*). Damn it
all, that's true! (*Sinks helplessly on a chair; meanwhile* GLOV
runs out.) But what a diabolical trick!

---

9 Siberian town where criminals were sent for penal servitude. (ed.)

GLOV (*peeping in at the door*). Don't give way to despair! You have something to comfort you: you have Adelaida Ivanovna!
(*Disappears.*)

IKHAREV (*furiously*). The devil take Adelaida Ivanovna! (*Snatches up the pack and flings it at the door. The cards fly to the floor.*) To think that there should exist such scoundrels to the shame and disgrace of mankind! I feel as though I should go mad—how devilishly it was all acted! How cunningly! The father and the son and the clerk Zamukhryshkin. And all trace is lost! And I can't even complain! (*Jumps up from his chair and walks about in excitement.*) What's the good of being cunning! What's the use of being clever! Of discovering and inventing means! Damnation take it! It's a waste of splendid zeal and effort! In a minute a rogue will steal up and outwit you! a scoundrel who at one stroke will destroy the edifice you've been working at for years! (*With a gesture of vexation*) Damn it, what a deceitful country it is! Luck is only thrust on stupid blockheads who understand nothing, think of nothing, do nothing, and only play boston for kopek stakes with battered old cards!

(*Curtain.*)

CHRONOLOGICAL LIST
OF GOGOL'S WORKS

1824-28   Done while Gogol was at school in Nyezhin, some of these pieces appeared in the school magazine to which he was an avid contributor: "The Brothers Tverdoslavich" (a story on an historical theme—the first piece burned by Gogol); "Something about Nyezhin, or a Fool Is His Own Law" (a satire); "Two Little Fishes" (a ballad); "The Robbers" (a tragedy in verse); "Russia under the Yoke of the Tartar" (a poem in the epic style).

1829   *Hans Küchelgarten* (published anonymously, at Gogol's expense, as *Hanz* [*sic*] *Küchelgarten*); his only published poem. He burned all the copies he could get his hands on after its disastrous reception.

1830   *Woman* (an essay important for understanding Gogol's highly romanticized "alabaster-breasted" women); *St. John's Eve* (printed anonymously in *Annals of the Fatherland*).

1831   *Hetman* (a chapter from an historical novel, never completed, which Gogol signed OOOO); *The Teacher* and *The Successful Mission* (both stories from the never-completed *The Terrible Boar*). *Hetman* appeared in *Northern Flowers*, an almanac, the other two in *The Literary Journal*.

Evenings on a Farm near Dikanka (*Vechera na Khutore Bliz Dikanki*), Volume I, which consists of: *The Fair at Sorochintsy*, *St. John's Eve*, *A May Night*, *or The Drowned Maiden*, *The Lost Letter*.

1832   *Evenings on a Farm near Dikanka*, Volume II, which consists of *Christmas Eve*, *A Terrible Vengeance*, *Ivan Fiodorovich Shponka and His Aunt*, *A Bewitched Place*.

Completed a play, *The Order of Vladimir of the Third Class*, of which only four scenes survive; the first, "An Official's

Morning," was published in Pushkin's magazine, *The Contemporary*, in 1836. The other three scenes, published in the 1842 edition of Gogol's collected works, are "A Lawsuit," "The Servant's Hall," "A Fragment." Completed *The Suitor* (to become *The Marriage* in 1842).

1834 *On Ukrainian Folksongs* (first published by the Ministry of Public Education, in April. Republished in the second part of *Arabesques*).

1835 *Arabesques*, a collection of essays and stories in two parts. The first part consists of *The Portrait; A Chapter from an Historical Novel* (both fiction); *Sculpture; Painting and Music; About the Middle Ages; On the Teaching of World History; A Peek at the Composition of the Ukraine; A Few Words on Pushkin; On Modern Architecture; Al Mamun* (an historical portrait). The second part consists of *Nevsky Prospekt, The Prisoner* (a fragment), *Diary of a Madman* (all three fiction); *Life; Schlözer, Müller, and Herder; On Ukrainian Folksongs; Thoughts on Geography* (for children); *The Last Days of Pompeii* (a painting by Briulov); *On the Migrations of Peoples at the End of the Fifth Century.*

King Alfred (fragment of an historical play).

Mirgorod, which consists of two parts, the first containing *Old-World Landowners* and *Taras Bulba* (which is seriously revised for the 1842 edition of his works), and the second containing *Viy* and *The Tale of How Ivan Ivanovich Quarreled with Ivan Nikiforovich.*

1836 *The Nose; The Coach* (both published in *The Contemporary*); *The Inspector General* (performed for the first time on the first of May); *Development of our Journalistic Literature in 1834, 1835.*

1837 *Petersburg Notes for 1836* (published in *The Contemporary*).

1842 *The Portrait* (totally revised, published in *The Contemporary*).

Dead Souls (the first part only, on the second of June).

Late in the year, the first collection of Gogol's works appeared in four volumes, and included *Evenings on a Farm near Dikanka; Mirgorod* (with the revised version of *Taras Bulba*); *The Portrait* (the revised version); *Nevsky Prospekt; Diary of a Madman; Rome* (a long fragment containing interesting impressions); *The Nose; The Coach; The Overcoat; The Marriage; The Gamblers; The Inspector General* (partially revised); *A Lawsuit, The Servant's Hall, A Fragment* (the three dramatic fragments begun in 1832, in revised form); *Home-going from the Theater.*

1846   *The Dénouement of The Inspector General.*

1847   *Addition to The Dénouement of The Inspector General.*
        Selected Passages from Correspondence with Friends.

——   The second part of *Dead Souls* (he burned almost all of it), *An Author's Confession* (invaluable psychological material), *Meditations on the Divine Liturgy* (the voice from above), and several less important pieces which were published posthumously.

SELECTED BIBLIOGRAPHY
of Essays and Books Partially or Wholly Concerned with Gogol

IN ENGLISH

Baring, Maurice. *An Outline of Russian Literature*. New York, 1914.
———. *Landmarks in Russian Literature*. London, 1910.
Belinsky, Vissarion. "Letter to N. V. Gogol," *Belinsky, Chernyshevsky, and Dobrolyubuv*, ed. Ralph E. Matlaw. New York, 1962.
Besoushko, Volodymyr. "Nicholas Gogol and Ukrainian Literature," *Ukrainian Quarterly*, XVI, 3 (1960), 263-68.
Birkhead, A. "Russian Pickwick," *Living Age*, CCLXXXVII (1915), 312-15.
Bowen, C. M. "*Dead Souls* and *Pickwick Papers*," *Living Age*, CCLXXX (1916), 369-73.
Bowman, N. E. "The Nose," *Slavonic and Eastern European Review*, XXXI, 76 (1952), 204-11.
Brasol, Boris L. *The Mighty Three: Poushkin, Gogol, Dostoevski*. New York, 1934.
Brückner, A. *A Literary History of Russia*. London, 1908. [A translation of his *Geschichte der russischen Literatur*. Leipzig, 1905.]
Bryner, C. "Gogol's *The Overcoat* in World Literature," *Slavonic and Eastern European Review*, XXXII, 79 (1954), 499-509.
Čiževsky, Dmitry. "Gogol: Artist and Thinker," *Annals of the Ukrainian Academy of Arts and Sciences in the U.S.*, IV (1952), 261-78.
———. "The Unknown Gogol," *Slavonic and Eastern European Review*. XXX (1952), 476-93.
———, and Hofre, P. "An Illustrated Manuscript of Gogol," *Harvard Library Bulletin*, VI (1952), 397-400.
"The Cloak," *Lippincott's Monthly Magazine*, XCII (1913), 249-62.

Cook, A. S. "Reflexive Attitudes: Sterne, Gogol, Gide," *Criticism*, II (1960), 164-74.

Dupuy, Ernest. *The Great Masters of Russian Literature*. New York, 1886. [A translation of his *Les grands maîtres de la littérature russe au XIXe siècle*. Paris, 1885.]

Erlich, Victor. "Gogol and Kafka: a Note on 'Realism' and 'Surrealism,'" *For Roman Jakobson*. The Hague, 1956, 100-108.

———. *Russian Formalism*. New York, 1955.

Futrell, M. "Dickens and Three Russian Novelists: Gogol, Dostoevsky, Tolstoy." School of Slavonic and East European Studies, London, 1954 (Dissertation).

———. "Gogol and Dickens," *Slavonic and East European Review*, XXXIV (1956), 443-59.

Gassner, J. W. "Chekhov and the Russian Realists," *Masters of the Drama*. New York, 1954.

Guerney, Bernard G. "Introduction," *The Portable Russian Reader*. New York, 1947.

Hare, Richard. *Russian Literature*. London, 1947.

Harkins, William E. "Gogol," *Dictionary of Russian Literature*. New York, 1956.

Hasenclever, Nora. "Gogol and Dostoyevsky." Bennington College, 1951 (Dissertation).

Kaun, A. "Poe and Gogol: A Comparison," *Slavonic Review*, XV (1937), 389-99.

Kropotkin, P. *Russian Literature*. London, 1945.

Landry, Hilton. "Gogol's *The Overcoat*," *Explicator*, XIX (1961).

Lavrin, Janko. *Gogol*. New York, 1926.

———. "Introduction," *Studies from St. Petersburg*. London, 1945.

———. "Introduction," *Tales from Gogol*. London, 1945.

———. *Introduction to the Russian Novel*. London, 1942.

———. *Nikolai Gogol (1809-1852). A Centenary Survey*. London, 1951.

Littell, R. "Gogol," *The New Republic*, XLVIII (1926), 218-19.

Magarshack, David. "Introduction," *Tales of Good and Evil*. New York, 1957.

———. *Gogol*. New York, 1957.

Martin, Mildred A. "The Last Shall Be First: A Study of Three Russian Short Stories," *Bucknell Review*, VI, i (1956), 13-23.

Masson, E. "Russia's Gogol: A Centenary," *Pacific Spectator*, VII, 3 (1953), 322-31.

McLean, H. "Gogol's Retreat from Love: Towards an Interpretation of *Mirgorod*," *American Contributions to the Fourth International Congress of Slavicists: Moscow, September, 1958. Slavic Printings and Reprintings*, XXI (1958), 225-43.

Miliukov, Paul. *Literature in Russia*. New York, 1943.

Mirsky, D. S. *A History of Russian Literature*, ed. F. J. Whitfield. New York, 1959. [This volume contains almost all of the next entry.]

——. *The History of Russian Literature from Earliest Times to the Death of Dostoevsky*. London, 1927.

Muchnic, Helen. *An Introduction to Russian Literature*. New York, 1947.

Nabokov, Vladimir. *Gogol*. Norfolk, Connecticut, 1944.

Noyes, G. R. "Gogol, a precursor of modern realists in Russia," *The Nation*, CI (1915), 592-94.

Perry, Idris. "Kafka, Gogol and Nathanael West," *Kafka*, ed. Ronald Gray. Englewood Cliffs, New Jersey, 1962.

Phelps, William L. *Essays on Russian Novelists*. New York, 1911.

Selig, Karl. "Concerning Gogol's *Dead Souls* and *Lazarillo de Tormes*," *Symposium*, VIII (1954), 34-40.

Simmons, E. J. "Gogol and English Literature," *Modern Language Review*, XXVI (1931), 445-50.

Slonim, Mark. *An Outline of Russian Literature*. New York, 1958.

——. *The Epic of Russian Literature: From its Origins through Tolstoy*. New York, 1950.

Spector, Ivar. *The Golden Age of Russian Literature*. Idaho, 1943.

Stilman, Leon. "Afterward," *The Diary of a Madman and Other Stories*. New York, 1961.

——. "Gogol's *Overcoat*—Thematic Pattern and Origins," *American Slavic and Eastern European Review*, XI (1952), 138-48.

Strakhovsky, L. I. "Historianism of Gogol," *American Slavic and Eastern European Review*, XII, 3 (1953), 360-70.

Tilley, A. "Gogol, the father of Russian realism," *Living Age*, CCII (1894), 489-97.

Turner, Charles E. *Studies in Russian Literature*. London, 1882.

deVogüé, E. M. *The Russian Novelists*. New York, 1900. [A translation of his *Le roman russe*. Paris, 1886.]

Waliszewski, K. *A History of Russian Literature*. New York, 1900.

Weathers, Winston. "Gogol's *Dead Souls*: The Degrees of Reality,' *College English*, XVII (1956), 159-64.

Wellek, René. "Introduction," *Dead Souls*, trans. B. G. Guerney. New York, 1948.

Wilson, Edmund. "Gogol: the demon in the overgrown garden," *The Nation*, CLXXV (1952), 520-24.

——. "Nikolai Gogol," *The New Yorker*, XX (1944), 72-73.

Yurieff, Zoya. "Gogol and the Russian Symbolists." Harvard University, 1954 (Dissertation).

IN GERMAN

Adams, V. "Gogols Erstlingswerk 'Hans Küchelgarten' im Lichte seines Natur- und Welterlebens," *Zeitschrift für slavische Philologie*, VII (1931), 323-68.

Anderson, W. "Gogols *Porträt* als Posener Volkssage," *Zeitschrift für slavische Philologie*, XX (1950), 234-36.

Berdjajew, Nikolai. "Gogol in der russischen Revolution," *Wort und Wahrheit*, XV (1960), 611-16.

Braun, M. "Gogol als Satiriker," *Die Welt der Slaven*, IV (1959), 129-147.

Emmer, H. "Neuere Gogol-Literatur," *Wiener slawistisches Jahrbuch*, III (1953), 79-114.

Emmer, Karl. "Vergleichende Studien zu Gogols *Porträt*." Vienna, 1948 (Dissertation).

Gorlin, M. *N. V. Gogol und E. Th. A. Hoffmann*. Leipzig, 1935.

Harder, Johannes. *Der Mensch im russischen Roman. Deutungen: Gogol, Dostojewski, Leskov, Tolstoi*. Wuppertal-Barmen, 1961.

Kasack, Wolfgang. *Die Technik der Personendarstellung bei Nikolaj Vasilevič Gogol*. Wiesbaden, 1957.

Kassner, R. "Stil u. Gesicht: Swift, Gogol, Kafka," *Merkur*, VII, 8 (1955), 737-52.

Kraus, Otto. *Der Fall Gogol*. Munich, 1912.

Leiste, H. W. *Gogol und Molière*. Nurnberg, 1958.

Luther, A. *Geschichte der russischen Literatur*. Leipzig, 1924.

Nilsson, Nils Åke. "Zur Entstehungsgeschichte des Gogolschen *Mantels*," *Scando-Slavica*, II (1956), 116-33.

Pollok, Karl-Heinz. "Zur dramatischen Form von Gogols 'Spielern,'" *Die Welt der Slaven*, IV (1959), 169-80.

Pypin, A. "Die Bedeutung Gogols für die heutige internationale Stellung der russischen Literatur," *Archiv für slavische Philologie*, XV (1903).

Setschkareff, V. *N. V. Gogol. Leben und Schaffen*. Berlin, 1953.

——. "Zur Interpretation von Gogols *Nase*," *Zeitschrift für slavische Philologie*, XXI (1952), 118-21.

Stender-Petersen, A. "Der groteske Stil Gogols," *Welt und Wort*, XV (1960), 71-73.

——. *Geschichte der russischen Literatur*. Munich, 1957.

——. "Gogol und die deutsche Romantik," *Euphorion*, XXIV (1922).

——. "Gogol und Kotzebue. Zur thematischen Entstehung Gogols 'Revizor,'" *Zeitschrift für slavische Philologie*, XII (1935), 16-35.

——. "Johann Heinrich Voss und der junge Gogol," *Edda*, XV (1921).

Thiess, F. *Gogol und seine Bühnenwerke*. Berlin, 1922.

Triomphe, Robert. "Gogol und die russische Kritik über den *Revisor*," *Vorträge* (1957), 140-61.

Tschizewskij, D. "Zur Komposition von Gogols 'Mantel,' " *Zeitschrift für slavische Philologie*, XIV (1937).

Wissemann, Heinz. "Struktur und Ideengehalt von Gogols 'Mantel,' " *Stil- und Formprobleme in der Literatur*. Heidelberg, 1959, 389-96.

Zabel, E. *Russische Literaturbilder*. Berlin, 1899.

IN FRENCH

Charrière, Ernest. "Preface" to his translation of *Dead Souls*. Paris, 1859.

Eng, J. van der. "Le personage de Basmackin: Un assemblage d'éléments comiques, grotesques, tragi-comiques et tragiques," *Dutch Contributions to the Fourth International Congress of Slavicists: Moscow, September, 1958. Slavic Printings and Reprintings*, XX (1959), 37-101.

Gourfinkel, Nina. *Nicolas Gogol dramaturge*. Paris, 1956.

Hofman, M. *Gogol. Sa vie, son oeuvre*. Paris, 1946.

Landolfi, Tommaso. "La femme de Gogol," *Nouvelle Nouvelle Revue Française* (1957), 673-88.

Leger, Louis. *Nicolas Gogol*. Paris, 1914.

Lourié, Osip. *La psychologie des romanciers russes du XIXe siècle*. Paris, 1905.

Marthe, Robert. "L'imitation souveraine," *Temps Modernes*, XVI (1961), 1124-49.

Merejkovsky, D. S. *Gogol et le diable*. Paris, 1939.

Mérimée, Prosper. "La littérature en Russie," *Revue des Deux Mondes*, November, 1851.

Mongault, H. "Gogol et Mérimée," *Revue de Littérature Comparée* (1930).

Nilsson, Nils Åke. *Gogol et St. Petersbourg. Recherches sur les antécédents des contes Petersbourgeois*. Stockholm, 1954.

Radoyce, Lubomir. "La conception du 'Poète national' chez Gogol," *Langue et littérature* (1962), 343-44.

Rudnyčki, Jaroslav. "Gogol et Chevtchenko: deux hommes—deux symboles," *Etudes slaves et est-européennes* (1956), 158-63.

Schloezer, Boris, F. *Gogol*. Paris, 1932.

Smirnova, O. N. *Etudes et Souvenirs* in *La Nouvelle Revue*. Paris, 1885.

Troyat, Henri. *Sainte Russie. Souvenirs et reflexions*. Paris, 1956.

deVogüé, E. M., and Leger, Louis. *Inauguration du monument élévé à la mémoire de Nicolas Gogol à Moscou le neuf mai 1909*. Paris, 1909.

Webber, Jean-Paul. "Les transpositions du nez dans l'oeuvre de Gogol," *Nouvelle Nouvelle Revue Française* (1959), 108-20.

NIKOLAI GOGOL was born in the province of Poltava, in southern Russia, on April 1, 1809. He was educated at the gymnasium at Niezhin, where he began writing as an adolescent. In 1828 he went to St. Petersburg, where he made an unsuccessful attempt at a career on the stage. In 1830 he published the first of the stories which subsequently appeared under the title of *Evenings on a Farm near Dikanka*. This work immediately obtained a great success. Gogol was appointed to a professorship in the University of St. Petersburg, where he taught history with no distinction and for a very short time. In 1835 he resigned and subsequently traveled to Western Europe, where he resided, especially in Rome, while working on essays, stories, and novellas. The first part of his novel *Dead Souls* appeared in 1842. In 1848 he made a pilgrimage to Jerusalem, and on his return, settled at Moscow, where he died on March 4, 1852. (See the critical-biographical introduction to this volume by Leonard J. Kent.)

ABOUT THE EDITOR

LEONARD J. KENT was born in Brooklyn, New York, in 1927. He received a Bachelor's degree from Long Island University, a Master's degree from New York University, and a Doctorate in Comparative Literature from Yale University. He has taught on all levels in public and private institutions, and is now Chairman of the Department of English at Quinnipiac College.

MODERN LIBRARY GIANTS

A series of sturdily bound and handsomely printed, full-sized library editions of books formerly available only in expensive sets. These volumes contain from 600 to 1,400 pages each.

THE MODERN LIBRARY GIANTS REPRESENT A
SELECTION OF THE WORLD'S GREATEST BOOKS

THE COLLECTED TALES AND PLAYS OF

NIKOLAI GOGOL

Edited by Leonard J. Kent

"It is good to have a complete collection of Gogol's tales and plays under one cover... Only *Dead Souls*, easily available elsewhere, is excluded. Here is God's plenty: the early Ukrainian folk tales, the Cossack epic *Taras Bulba,* and all the incomparable humorous and grotesque stories: *Old-World Landowners, The Tale of How Ivan Ivanovich Quarreled with Ivan Nikiforovich, Nevsky Prospekt, Diary of a Madman, The Nose,* and, of course, *The Overcoat.* Here is even *The Portrait* in its final version...and here are all three plays, *The Inspector General, The Marriage,* and *The Gamblers.*

"Mr. Kent has thoroughly revised the translation of Mrs. Garnett, which has long been out of print and difficult to find. Mrs. Garnett is now often disparaged as a translator, but she is always conscientious and skillful. Mr. Kent has eliminated the Victorianisms of her style, has corrected mistakes and pruderies of diction, and has made the whole translation sound much more contemporary and alive. But he has avoided the whimsicality and 'curliness' in which some recent translators indulged, and he has not changed or suppressed anything